Gavin was brought up in Belfast and Bournemouth. Since 1988, he has lived in London. He is married with two children.

After university, Gavin got a job with the Bank of England and worked in financial regulation through to 2016. He competed for Great Britain in rowing at the Seoul and Barcelona Olympics. He began writing *Walk the Line* in 2004.

Dedication

To Annie, Robert and Laura

Gavin Stewart

WALK THE LINE

AUSTIN MACAULEY PUBLISHERS™

LONDON • CAMBRIDGE • NEW YORK • SHARJAH

A CIP catalogue record for this title is available from the British Library.

ISBN 9781788782197 (Paperback)
ISBN 9781788782203 (Hardback)
ISBN 9781788782210 (E-Book)

www.austinmacauley.com

First Published (2018)
Austin Macauley Publishers Ltd
25 Canada Square
Canary Wharf
London
E14 5LQ

Table of Contents

Part 1: London, July 2005

Chapter 1
Saturday 2nd

Despite much thinking and worrying, Sam had failed to say anything meaningful, or even particularly sincere. As the train carrying his daughter moved off, he watched it shrinking into the distance, squeezed by the perspective, losing its identity. As he walked away, he reached for Mary's hand.

His final goodbye to Ruth had been perfunctory and awkward, Mary's affectionate and measured. He had hugged and kissed her on one cheek but hesitated uncertainly before kissing the other, and lost the moment as she turned away. He had also tried to give her a look intended to be full of varied meaning – of a loving parent stepping back – but knew he had failed. Unlike his friends, he had little faith in either his ability to convey what he wanted or in others' ability to understand him. Perhaps everyone else was kidding themselves. Mary offered to drive and soon their car was turning out into the Marylebone Road, back to the house that would inevitably seem larger than the one they had left an hour before.

What he was sure of was that the real answer would elude him. He suspected it could only really be discerned by someone who seeks wisdom with such obsessiveness that they reach a point where, through neglect, they lose their ability to convey any truth they ultimately discover. And so it would dissolve with them, like the train vanishing in the distance and leaving only a memory to untangle. Mary's face also sometimes disappeared in this way, and each time he had to force himself to re-configure it. He lapsed into internal silence and began chatting to Mary, who was relieved his brooding hadn't lasted. By the time they got home, he had found a way to move on to thinking about the evening ahead.

Ed was on the TV news again, reporting from Baghdad – shame he wasn't able to get back to London in time to see his god-daughter off as planned. It often seemed that most of his friendships existed in some form of ether, strangely preserved, despite an almost complete absence of nurturing. They survived because mutual expectations had evolved to the point where even the slightest effort was taken as a re-dedication of bonds forged many years before. Another suicide bomber had blown himself up, a car bomb this time, and at least 26 had been killed, almost all children. Ed was attempting, again, to strike a balance between explaining the consequences for the US and British forces in Iraq on the one hand, and on the other the damage the corrosive and bloody insurgency was doing to the prospects for a peaceable co-existence between Sunni and Shi'ite Muslims. But Ed was failing, Sam thought. The links were too complex and his rational explanations were overwhelmed by the visual horror of the subject matter.

Mary came in with a cup of tea. He sat for another five minutes, then took it up to the bath, where he lay in the hottest water he could bear and stretched his limbs, enjoying his skin tingling, the weariness receding. He skimmed the sports pages, then turned back to the news. He was looking forward to escaping on holiday.

Getting out, Sam dried himself and wrapped the towel around his waist. He grabbed a small towel to rub his hair, and as he wandered out of the bathroom badly stubbed his left toe, the little one, hard on the door stop. He yelled silently and hobbled to the nearest chair, where he collapsed, dropping the smaller towel and grasping the now throbbing digit with both hands. At first he thought it must be broken, but no, it still wiggled around without the pain increasing. Squeezing his toe like this never made any difference and today was no exception; after a minute, he got up and limped, still swearing, across to his bedroom, where he struggled into his clothes. Gradually, the pain did begin to go away, not that he noticed. Blood began to re-circulate, and he became distracted in trying to decide which shirt to wear. None of them were right, but he settled on one, which he thought looked okay, grabbed a jacket and hobbled downstairs. Later that night, the toe, already swollen, turned a dark shade of blue and would continue to mutate its colour over the next week into an unhealthy looking shade of mustard yellow before gradually returning to its normal appearance. But after a couple of days, it mostly stopped aching.

Downstairs, he made a second pot of tea, but then grabbed a beer from the fridge instead. Mary was getting ready, and he wandered out into the garden with the paper, flicking past the sports section into the finance pages. Nothing there for him today, so he went on to the obituaries. Until a few years ago, he had never even glanced at this part of the paper, but since his father's death, he had become increasingly drawn to these short crafted summaries of people's lives, attempts to describe events and ascribe significance to their existence. They had taken on a new meaning for him as he tried, fascinated and frustrated, to unravel the meaning of the lives they aimed to encapsulate. As for his parents, thinking of their lives had proved a largely barren exercise. He could get only so far in working out what they were about, what made them tick. The rest was impenetrable.

One caught his eye – 'Soul star Vandross dies at 54' – Luther Vandross had died peacefully two years after having a stroke. A bachelor, who had sold, apparently, nearly 25m records, won Grammys first for his production work and then for his own records, and collaborated with, it seemed, almost everyone from David Bowie to Aretha Franklin; there seemed to be nothing but praise for the great man. And yet there was a gaping hole in the middle of the obituary, marked 'his life' as opposed to 'his works'. Even by the standards of obituaries, there was almost nothing about the man himself, aside from his love of food and the fact that he had never married.

How did Luther Vandross see himself, Sam wondered, particularly in the years since his stroke, when it must have been apparent that his time was limited? Imagine having worked with Bowie as a soul musician. It appeared he didn't drink or smoke drugs and yet he'd been at the absolute centre of US musical culture for the last quarter of the 20th century. The article said he'd died with family and friends but who were they – parents, siblings, partner? The impression given was that Luther was pretty much at home with himself. It had taken a while for him to reach the mainstream with his own music – 1989, when he would have been 38 – but his own record sales were more than impressive. He was clearly respected by his peers and seemed like a New York kid made good, who gave everything to the music he cared about so much. Was there something about this love of music that had all but excluded everything that cut across that commitment? Were the friends who were with him at the end those who had accepted that music (and perhaps food) always came first with Luther and had been willing to take him on these terms? Were there others who had fallen by the wayside over the years, who had grown tired of always being second best to Luther's art? Or was this just too simplistic an interpretation of an artist's life? Which did he care for more, people or music? Did he feel the need to choose?

Sam heard the doorbell and looked at his watch. It was later than he thought but the taxi was a couple of minutes early. He picked up the paper and the almost empty bottle of beer; he drained it and walked in through the kitchen and into the hall, dropping off the bottle on the way. He called up that the taxi had arrived, and Mary shouted back that it was ten minutes early and could he ask it to wait? He thought about pointing out that the taxi was only marginally early but decided it would be pedantic. So he asked the taxi driver to hang on for a couple of minutes, making a mental note to up the tip a little. He walked back towards the kitchen, spun the paper into the living room, where it landed on the sofa and then slid onto the floor, grabbed a couple of bottles of wine, white from the fridge and red from the cupboard, shoved them in a bag, and grabbed his jacket off the stair post on the way back to the door as she swept past. She smiled and flicked a v-sign.

Earlier, Mary was finishing getting ready. This stuff didn't take her long any more. Her mind went back to the train station. She hadn't been surprised at Sam getting so emotional. He cared so much about things, too much, she sometimes thought, and Ruth leaving home, no matter that she would be back in October, was always going to be a tipping point for him. She had realised this some time ago, which was why she had arranged this evening; the last thing Sam needed today was a quiet night at home. His silence on the walk back to the car showed she was right, and since getting home, she had tried to keep his mind occupied, making him tea, putting the television on at a time of day when she would normally have resisted it. She had heard the thud upstairs, but since he had said nothing when he came downstairs neither had she, though she surmised from the slight limp that he had either stubbed his toe or banged his knee against something; neither was unusual. She went up to the shower; it was going to be a long evening, after an already long day, and she wanted to be in the right mood. As she put her shoes on, she heard the doorbell and a few moments later, Sam's voice. "Taxi's here!" he shouted.

"Just coming…can you ask him to wait? He's ten minutes early," she replied, having glanced at her watch.

"Okay…and I'll get some drinks to take." She heard some mumbled words as Sam spoke to the taxi driver, then some clunks and clinks as he got the wine bottles and put them into a carrier bag. They were only going three miles, so it should stay cold. Two minutes later, they were in the car and on their way. They chatted sporadically in the taxi, finding it slightly awkward having a two-way conversation when there was a third person in the car. Mary preferred a black cab, with the separation from the driver, where an intercom or the sliding back of the window was needed to bridge the communication gap. But today she wondered whether, in fact, it was better for Sam to have to talk in the hearing of the driver. Although it took away the privacy of their conversation, it forced them to think about how what they were saying would be heard, and subconsciously to edit.

As she talked about seeing Michelle and Philip – it had been a couple of months – Mary thought again about Ruth. Although she knew there would be other, future calls on her as a mother, her parenting role was now essentially complete. Over the last few weeks, she had been organising her photos of Ruth in chronological albums and the memories in her mind. She had been surprised at the extent to which the act of thinking had itself unlocked long-forgotten layers of memory and emotion. All the way through, since before Ruth had been born, people had been telling her it would go so quickly, and it mostly had; but at the same time, the experience of re-finding memories of experiences and events had made it seem an almost unbelievably long and densely populated time. Rather than perceiving them as a single amorphous collective, Mary had gradually distinguished each of the mainly minor arguments she and Ruth had had over the years, maybe about tidying her room or about which pair of new shoes to buy, so that they became distinct from each other. She also remembered that, while the first few of these had quite wound her up, thereafter she had learned not to be over-serious in how she approached them.

Sam was asking if Mary knew who else would be there this evening. She had told him already but, without the slightest sign of impatience, she repeated that Linda and John would also be there. Mary observed calmly that she hadn't really seen Linda since New Year.

"No, you don't see her as much as you used to," remarked Sam. "There was a time, years ago, when you saw each other pretty much every week."

"Yes, but that was when Ruth had just gone off to secondary school, and all of a sudden we both seemed to have a lot more time on our hands, and, in my case certainly, a yearning for adult female company. Ruth was just entering her 'adults are rubbish' phase."

Mary thought she had probably overdone the justification a bit, but Sam didn't seem to notice and let it pass. "I know what you mean," he said, "or rather, I remember it well. I think I started going out a bit more as well at about the same time, though probably more with people I worked with. All of a sudden, Ruth wanted to be self-sufficient, to the point of not letting you anywhere near her. Probably that was the worst bit of her teenagerhood; the rest was pretty harmless and actually quite nice at times."

"Linda was still with Tim then, that was the other thing. Because it was starting to go wrong, she really liked having me around I think, to talk to about it. It's funny, I don't think she ever stopped loving him, but it was like its time just began running out."

"Having sex with someone else probably didn't help," Sam observed.

"Presumably not," laughed Mary, "but you know what, I'd almost forgotten about Tim's misbehaviour. Linda didn't really talk about it much; not that it didn't matter to her but I think she was already growing away from him somehow, so it wasn't as big a deal to her as it would have been otherwise."

Mary realised the taxi driver had heard everything they had been saying. She had forgotten what she had only just been thinking to herself. "Anyway," she said, "it'll be really good to see her again, and John, who I really like, with all his youthful radicalism."

"Yes, I like him too," said Sam, "though some of it does grate now and then, not least since he's now a servant to Mammon, aka Barclay's."

Mary thought Sam still seemed immune to the fly-on-the-wall presence of the taxi driver and was actually being more strident than normal. She wondered whether he was still really saying goodbye to Ruth. She hoped this evening would be good and knew she could rely on Michelle to understand his mood and adjust accordingly.

Suddenly, she shot forward against her seatbelt. The driver had slammed the brakes on just before they were hit by another car. The impact, though not hard, had been against the door of the driver's passenger seat. The driver swore but Mary could tell he was relieved at the same time. She looked at Sam, who seemed calm – he usually was. She looked across at the other car. The driver, a man in his 30s she thought, had his head in his hands. She could also see a baby in a booster seat in the back, and immediately she felt for him. The baby was crying, but it was clear no one had been hurt and that the damage to both cars had been minimal.

Their taxi had been virtually stationary, about to turn right into a side road. The other car, turning right onto the main, had simply run into them. There was no doubt about who was at fault, and once it became clear the other driver was fully accepting the blame, even the initially irate taxi driver mellowed. The baby's father, Greg, had begun fairly distraught at the thought of what could have happened to his daughter if the cars had been going quicker, but gradually calmed down, adjusting to the mood of the other three adults. Mary asked if she could hold the infant and within a minute the baby, Louise, was calm again. Maybe it was the sun, or perhaps he was thinking about something else, but Greg had simply not seen them. Everyone agreed it was an awkward blind junction, not because it was but to make the event more explicable, Greg less culpable. Addresses and insurance details were exchanged, and 15 minutes later, they were on their way again.

"Do you remember that accident we nearly had in Dorset when Ruth was about three?" Sam asked as they moved off.

"No," replied Mary, who couldn't remember anything that would qualify as a 'near-accident'. Sam was exaggerating some minor event again.

"Never mind, maybe I'm thinking of something different," said Sam. "I felt sorry for the father, Greg. I can't imagine what he felt like when he realised they were going to crash into us. Good job we were both barely moving."

Even if Mary didn't, he did remember Dorset. He had been driving, and they had been swooping through the countryside around Corfe Castle. Mary had been in the back with Ruth. She had grown out of the car seat and had never taken to a booster, so she just had a normal seatbelt on. Because both his passengers had been in the back, some of Sam's attention had been directed there. He didn't think, but could not be sure, that he had ever looked around; he thought he had kept his eyes on the road ahead. But, however it happened, suddenly he was coming quite fast around a wide corner, doing maybe 50mph, when he saw a stop sign perhaps 75 yards ahead, a T-junction. He had hit the brakes hard, then harder. There had been a screech and a skid, but he had managed to keep the car under control and stop it about six feet before the line.

"What the fuck!" Mary had exclaimed. She had sworn more back then, he thought, smiling.

"Sorry about that," he had replied, failing to stop his voice trembling, "just practising my Steve McQueen impression."

And that had been it. Clearly, Mary simply did not recall, or had blanked it from her mind. He still remembered though, how he had instantly broken out in a cold sweat the moment the car stopped, just how gingerly he had moved off when the road ahead was completely clear, and how he had barely touched 30mph and stayed long periods in third gear on the way back to the hotel. Unlike Greg, he had not hit anything; but if he had done, the consequences would have been dire. Although he had never said as much, Sam had mostly avoided driving since then, covering himself with a variety of excuses: feeling tired, wanting to sit with Ruth in the back, not being able to remember the way. Gradually, Mary and others had accepted that Sam didn't really like driving, and it had ceased to be an issue. He had never spoken about it.

"It's not done my door any good," interjected the taxi driver. "Mind you, could have been worse."

They turned into the street where Philip and Michelle lived. "It's just on the right here, number seven," said Sam, slightly absent-mindedly.

They weren't late despite their mini adventure, but John and Linda had already arrived and had gone out into the garden with drinks. This was large for that part of London, with a patio backing onto the house and a small pond. There was a small tree back right and a compost heap behind it, next to a tiny shed. It was drenched in warm evening sunshine, and John and Linda were sitting at a small table on the patio.

She had met them at the door, smiling and with a gin in her hand. "Hi there, everyone's arriving really early this evening, or maybe I just started cooking late." Michelle admired Mary's outfit and, as Mary duly returned the compliment, looked slightly askance at Sam's shirt. "Come on through," she said. "Linda and John are out the back. How was the traffic? What can I get you to drink?"

Sam went into the kitchen to help Michelle make the drinks and explain about their near accident while Mary went straight out onto the patio to say hello. By the time the other two had appeared with drinks, Mary was herself well into the re-telling of their minor accident.

"The poor man!" exclaimed Linda, "How sweet to be so upset at the mere thought of what might have happened."

"But it was his and nobody else's fault," said John. "Anyway, he was probably absconding with the baby, running away to some secret hide-out in North Wales. It's the mother we should be worrying about." He held out his arms as the others stared at him, then shrugged his shoulders and reached for the Pimm's.

"I thought the taxi driver was going to go off on one for a minute," said Sam. "I don't think I've ever been in a proper accident before, just on a bus once that bumped into a car that was trying to squeeze in front of it, but I don't think that counts."

"The baby girl, Louise was her name, was very sweet, calmed down really fast and was as good as gold. I remember so well when Ruth was that age."

"You saw her off on the train today, didn't you?" asked Michelle.

"Yes, she got off smoothly enough. What about Richard?" asked Sam, turning to Linda.

"He's just moved down from Birmingham, renting a flat with some friends in Clapham, and theoretically, earning some money to pay off his student loan, though

I think, as far as I can tell, he's still piling up the debts. Sooner he starts work in September the better."

"He's doing fine," said John. "He worked really hard that last year, managed to get a fantastic degree from nowhere, and a decent job into the bargain. I don't blame him for letting his hair down a bit. Reality will hit again soon enough when he starts work proper. You know you're really proud of him."

"I know, I know," replied Linda, "but I do wish he owed less money."

"Taking after his mother, if you ask me," said Mary smiling. "I remember us scraping together money to get into that night club off Tottenham Court Road, and you admitted you had an overdraft of about two thousand, which was a fortune back then."

Linda laughed. "Okay, you've got me. He's obviously a wonderful lad who can do no wrong, a credit to his errant mother. Can I have some more Pimm's please, John?"

"How's work?" Sam asked.

"Fine," replied John, "couldn't be better really. I can't think of a time when business has been better. There's so much demand, the mortgage market is just easy money at the moment." John was conscious Sam worked for the government and believed, wrongly, that everything he said would somehow feed its way into Civil Service thinking. "The thing at the moment is that the UK market's so mature – not much new going on really, pretty boring in fact – that it's getting hard to make decent margins at home, so we're having to diversify a bit more internationally. Of course, everyone's waiting for China to open up properly, but there's good money to be made elsewhere, particularly in the US, where the margins are a bit better."

"That's pretty close to what they were saying back in the mid-80s," replied Sam. "But then there was the '87 stock market crash, the Lawson boom and Black Wednesday. If history does repeat itself, then I suspect there are some interesting times around the corner."

"Perhaps, but we've got people now who are so good at calculating risk that the sort of silly lending that went on back then simply wouldn't get beyond first base now. And everything's so much more global, so that any problems won't be nearly as concentrated as they were."

"Not for now, John," replied Sam, "but sometime could you talk me through all that?" He wanted John to see the request as a sign that he liked him and saw him as a good friend, someone he was prepared to ask favours from.

"No problem, just give me a ring next week, and we can arrange lunch sometime." John was flattered by the idea of Sam, the senior civil servant, asking his advice on how the global financial system worked. He might let it slip out when someone asked him what he was doing for lunch on a given day.

Michelle had been surreptitiously popping in and out of the kitchen. Now she paused in the doorway and people-watched her guests, assessing what she would think if she turned up not knowing any of them, as she knew Carol was about to do.

John, she observed, had begun to look fairly prosperous. She remembered when Linda had first started seeing him, how wiry he had looked. But after ten years of living the high life with Linda, his stomach needed a belt to rein it in. But he was a long way from fat, and probably his career, which she knew had been going particularly well, had played its part. All in all, she thought dispassionately, interesting but not exciting.

Linda herself looked tanned and healthy; perhaps they had been away somewhere, maybe golf again. Having only taken up the game, together with tennis, when she had begun living with John, Michelle wondered at how good she was now at both sports. She also marvelled at Linda's figure, no discernible difference now from 20 odd years ago, when they had first met. Linda was being the life and soul of the evening so far, she nearly always was, full of energy, quick-witted and funny. Impossible to dislike, and yet Michelle had never fully taken to Mary's best friend. She believed Linda was slightly more calculating and cynical than was decent, and had never quite trusted her but had worked hard over the years to disguise this view.

Mary was looking at her quizzically, in the way that always made Michelle feel slightly guilty, as though the other knew she was up to something. Was she? Maybe, maybe not, but it was one of several games the two women played with each other, sometimes subconsciously. Michelle smiled back. "Just going to check on the oven."

Sam asked Linda if they'd been somewhere to play golf. He was only mildly interested in the answer but thought Linda would want to talk about her latest trip. It transpired they had been for a weekend break in the Algarve, with work friends of John's, and Sam wondered wryly what magnetic attraction golf held for middle-age professional prosperity. It had never done much for him, and he thought the fact he was no good at it – three games of pitch & put on holiday in his teens had been all the evidence he needed – was only a small part of the reason.

"We played 18 holes every morning we were there," Linda was saying, "then lay on the beach in the afternoon, or in my case in the shade by the pool, which happened to be next to the bar. Then we'd hit the town in the evening; there were some fabulous new restaurants."

"It was a grand time," continued John, "though I eventually ran out of steam on the last night and came back a couple of hours before the others. Linda's golf swing is pretty hot these days. She won a good £100 from the other wives, which didn't hurt the drinks kitty."

"How many of you were there?" asked Mary.

"Six," replied Linda. "Bob and Diane, who you met at ours at New Year, and Andy and Rachel, who I don't think you know. Bob joined the bank the same time as John, and Andy and Rachel both work there too, though Rachel's thinking of leaving. They're a bit younger than the rest of us. Andy worked with John in the US in the late 90s."

Michelle began to re-fill everyone's glass. "What's keeping Philip?" asked Mary.

"He's gone to collect our extra guest, an old American journalist friend called Carol, who I haven't met, only spoken to on the phone. She's just flown in from New York; rang at lunchtime, so Phil asked her over. She and Phil go way back, spent years working together at Sports Illustrated in the 70s and have kept in touch, though they only ever seem to meet up for weekends in somewhere like Hong Kong or Bangkok, very dodgy, if you ask me." She arched an eyebrow. "Ugly as hell, apparently!"

Of those present, only Sam was completely at home with Michelle's humour. Mary was pretty much used to it, but Linda and John looked sideways at each other, slightly uncomfortable. "Only kidding," laughed Michelle, "Hope you don't mind her joining us? She and Phil are pretty close, been through a lot together." Again, she let the phrase hang momentarily.

"Not at all," replied Mary, "I'll enjoy quizzing her about Phil's dubious past. What's she, sorry Carol, in town for anyway?"

"She's stopping off on the way to Singapore for the IOC vote on 2012. Phil says Carol's covered every Olympics since Mexico in '68."

"I'm glad we're not going to get the damn thing," said John. "It'd cost a fortune and we'd win nothing. Anyway, the IOC's pretty much as corrupt as any organisation you'll find. That Samaranch bloke used to work for Franco for God's sake!"

"I'm not sure I agree," said Sam but without the merest hint of confrontation in his voice, "I actually think we'd put on a pretty good show, but I do agree that we're not going to get them, so everything else is academic. Anyway, Phil's friend sounds interesting; I've always thought sports writing fascinating, though I can't imagine doing it for what, nearly 40 years."

"Mind you, Sam, you've been in the Civil Service for more than 25 years, and I've been in universities for even longer." Mary was reflective.

"Well, I've pretty much always been in advertising," Linda observed, "but I worked for about eight different agencies, a couple of them twice."

"Let's face it," said Sam, "there's quite a lot of variety in most professional jobs these days. I mean, from my point of view, I've had several different jobs in different departments. Maybe not very different from Linda's working in advertising. Mind you, I still don't quite get the sports thing. After a while it must all get a bit repetitive. Still," he mused, "there seems to be a lot going on at the Olympics – boycotts in '76, '80, '84, and the Munich massacre in '72."

"You're just showing off now," said John, "no one who finds sport boring knows that much useless information about it."

"I only said I found it repetitive, not that I didn't read anything about it. And besides, you can't spend two decades around Philip and not pick up some of his geeky sports trivia."

"We saw Ed on the TV this evening," said Mary, "before we came out. Baghdad looks like a hell-hole."

"It makes me ashamed to be British that we're there," exclaimed Linda. "All the things that came out last summer; I was lied to, and I don't think I'll ever trust a politician again. I really wish I'd gone on the 'Stop the War' march, but I was stupid enough to believe in all that WMD rubbish."

John shifted his weight imperceptibly backwards, away from his wife, subconsciously distancing himself. He knew that 20 years ago he would have been on that march, but at work he was now involved in financing infrastructure projects in Iraq. In his own mind, he had rationalised these shifts; Thatcher was gone, Saddam was evil and using global finance to rebuild Iraq was a positive thing. But he did not want to expose these arguments tonight.

Michelle was talking. "Whatever the rights and wrongs, and as far as I can tell there are certainly more of the second, we're in there now and have some responsibility to help sort it out. I wish we weren't there but I can't pretend I think

Saddam was a good man. It's hard to argue that he wasn't one of the worst dictators around, which isn't to say we should have taken it on ourselves to get rid of him."

"That's a bit of what Ed was trying to get at in his report this evening," agreed Sam, "but although it seems fairly straightforward standing here in a lovely North London garden drinking gin, watching him on TV, I have to say the argument just seemed irrelevant against a background of daily suicide bombings."

"How do you know Ed originally?" asked Linda, who had mostly calmed down.

"He was my best mate when we were at Manchester. We shared digs one year and basically hung around together most of the time. He's from Derby and I'm from Nottingham, so we had Brian Clough in common." He put his hands up as if in surrender.

Mary knew this was Sam's standard spiel, and she was surprised that Linda hadn't heard it before. Maybe she had forgotten. She herself always thought of Ed as Sam's older brother, there to help him pick up the pieces on the rare occasions when Sam had somehow got himself into trouble. She wished he had been around when Sam's father had died. "All I know," she said, "is they're a nightmare when they get together, especially after not seeing each other for a while. I normally can't get any sense out of Sam for a week. It's like they lapse into some special '70s 'boy-language' they developed when they were about 20."

"I was more into punk," said John. "The Ramones and Johnny Rotten made a lot of sense to me. I was pretty angry as a teenager, used to love going to the concerts."

Michelle briefly visualised John the corporate banker standing at the front of the pit at some Damned gig, pogo-ing up and down with a Mohican, covered in spittle and screaming obscenity. She kept the vision to herself and drifted back into the kitchen to check the food, wondering what was taking Phil so long. The phone call that lunchtime had come totally out of the blue. Phil hadn't seen Carol since she had passed through briefly the summer before on the way to the Athens Olympics, and hadn't heard from her since a phone call in February apologising for not getting in touch at Christmas. She was intrigued to meet Carol. All she knew after all these years were the photos and the stories, and the odd chat on the phone.

When she returned to the patio, the others had begun talking about Live 8, which was taking place that day. Mary, Sam and Linda were all pretty positive about it. John, however, who was the only one of them who had been to Live Aid back in 1985, was (inevitably, Michelle had begun to think) pretty damning of the whole idea.

"We tried it that way 20 years ago and it didn't work then. The only reason Geldof and Bono are doing it now is for their own egos, and so they can have something to talk about over cocktails with Bush and Blair."

"Anything that brings Pink Floyd back together can't be all bad," said Mary. "If it hadn't been for Ruth going away today, and us coming here, I'd be there in Hyde Park with the best of them!"

"I had no idea you liked Pink Floyd!" exclaimed Sam, laughing.

"It was part of my Prog Rock period, somewhere between my Simon & Garfunkel fixation and my Fleetwood Mac musical middle age. But Floyd were always the thing for me. I even had a poster of them, and you know how much the very idea of that goes against the grain of my character."

"If only I'd known!" exclaimed Sam in mock horror. "Linda, did you know this? Why did nobody tell me?"

"Friendship before honour every time. Anyway, as for me, I'm happy to take Saint Bob at his word on this one. After all, it's not as if Damon Albarn and co would have been doing anything if Live 8 wasn't happening. I didn't go to Live Aid like John did, but I do think it helped change the way we saw the world. I think it changed the way people thought about Africa and Africans and was part of that shift that led to the South African boycott and the end of Apartheid."

"Who knows," added Mary, conscious of supporting her friend, "today may have the same kind of effect; five years from now, African debt might have been effectively wiped out and action against global warming might have become the first example of real global cooperation. After getting Pink Floyd to speak to each other, let alone do a set, anything is possible."

"Well, I still think it's all delusion, a massive con trick," persisted John, who was starting to feel outnumbered. "I just don't think rock music and politics work together. Geldof and Bono should be criticising politicians – that's part of what they're for – not sitting on committees with them and nodding away at press conferences."

"I know what you mean," said Sam. "It just doesn't really work, does it? I don't think the Beatles or the Stones would have been caught dead in some of the situations Geldof and Bono seem happy enough to walk into."

"Maybe, but I don't think they were necessarily faced with the same sorts of issues," said Michelle. "The world seemed much more diffuse back then. Like John I'm pretty much in the sceptical camp, but there must at least be a chance, given the billions of people it's now possible to reach at the same time."

Michelle heard Philip's key in the door. "Hi, we're back... Sorry we've been so long... The traffic was dire!" He came through on to the patio. "It's Carol's fault for staying at the Dorchester; expense accounts have obviously become a lot bigger since I left. The traffic around Marble Arch was virtually gridlocked by Live 8. Anyway, here she is!" Philip did the introductions.

Carol said hello and made various appropriate comments. As she explained how her trip to the IOC vote in Singapore had been arranged at very short notice – she hadn't been scheduled to do it originally, but Tom had twisted his ankle coaching his son at Little League baseball only a few hours before the flight, which was why she hadn't been able to call Phil earlier – Carol took her bearings

Michelle was prettier than Phil, always big on understatement, had described her. Her black hair fell persistently across her left eye, and she only bothered to brush it away once in a while. Her eyes were clear and green, and looked at her, at everyone Carol suspected, very directly but with an edge of amusement. She knew Michelle had worked in hospitals for years and could imagine her in charge of a ward.

She continued looking around. Sam was about 6'3", with just the hint of a stoop in his shoulders. His hair was maybe three parts grey and just starting to thin around the crown. He had large hands and wiry forearms but otherwise looked as though he did little exercise. He had a friendly smile and a warm voice but a slightly pre-occupied look in his eyes. He had made contact with hers when they had been introduced but hadn't quite engaged. She sipped her drink as Phil was enthusiastically explaining the detours and short-cuts he'd taken to prevent them being even later. Mary, Sam's wife, looked to be a combination of vulnerability and hardness. Her slightest comment seemed laced with meaning but her eyes were soft. Linda, conversely, was as lively as hell and almost professionally flirtatious. Carol half turned so she could reply to Mary, who was asking about her flight, and while she did so took a half-glance at John.

Meanwhile, Michelle had disappeared into the kitchen. Now she shouted that the meal was ready. It was 8.50 in London, mid-afternoon in New York, almost dawn in Singapore.

Only Sam hadn't been slightly shocked when Carol had walked out of the French doors, blinking in the evening sunshine. She was taller than average, maybe 5'10", with square shoulders, short black hair and even features. Only the lines at the side of her eyes suggested she was in her 50s. She introduced herself, clearly picking up on Linda's vanity and flattering her slightly, and working out that John was a football fan. She then spent the next ten minutes chatting easily about English football and speculating whether Abramovitch had changed the game.

As they sat down to eat, the conversation moved on, and Sam mentioned again that he'd seen Ed's report from Baghdad on TV earlier. There was a slight pause this time, as they wondered how offended Carol would be by what they said. The group was self-consciously anti-war, yet everyone knew it was a subject that could lead to heated argument. The issue had eaten into Labour's majority at the May election. Carol was an American though, and Michelle in particular was wary, more than half expecting some push back, if for no other reason than to justify the mounting death toll of US soldiers. Instead, Carol said she thought the motive for the invasion was wrong, probably falsified in part, but that doing nothing about countries like Iraq wasn't really a moral option for the UN, or else there would be another Rwanda sooner or later; Darfur was a warning of what was possible. In countries like Iraq, sanctions didn't really work, they hurt the people but not the rulers. She agreed the absence of WMDs and the use of flawed intelligence had fatally weakened the arguments in favour of the invasion but believed Saddam would sooner or later have sparked another crisis anyway.

The others were, to varying degrees, all uncomfortable with Carol's arguments, and Mary talked passionately about the loss of Iraqi life and the largely indiscriminate attack on Fallujah. Carol seemed to agree with the substance of their arguments at every turn, while drawing a subtly different set of conclusions. Michelle found this frustrating, but no one else seemed to notice.

Michelle and Philip got up to serve the salmon, and after everyone had admired the food, conversation turned back to Live 8. John recalled the original Live Aid happily, if hazily, having woken up on a bench in Regent's Park the following morning. It had been a defining moment of his youth.

The dining room opened through French windows onto the garden, and these had been left open to let the warm summer breeze circulate through the room. By this stage, the wine was beginning to take effect, and the conversation was beginning to flow more easily. Taking another drink of wine and refilling his glass, Sam sat back slightly and surveyed the table. He quite liked the people but, apart from Mary and Michelle, they meant very little to him at the end of the day. Philip he liked but didn't really know, even now. In some ways, he found Carol as appealing as any of the others. He wondered whether he should be disappointed by this, or at least surprised, and concluded neither. John, for example, was a decent enough bloke but could really be anyone this evening. He was Linda's husband, and he doubted a banker would have been attracted to this particular circle other than through the bedroom.

Then Sam realised what a misanthrope he was being and instantly regretted his thoughts. They were all good in their different ways, and he made a mental note that this sounded more of a qualified statement than he intended. 'Good' for a human being was probably as much as any of us could hope for.

Chapter 2
Monday 4th

It was another scorching day and Philip was feeling the heat. He'd got drunk with Carol and Michelle the night before, and after what he used to call a weekend double header, he was feeling not a little dehydrated, wondering why he was trekking down to St James' for lunch. But it was what he did, even if it was harder than it used to be to shrug off hangovers.

He was meeting a US investor who was potentially interested in funding a TV drama he was trying to make, about the double crisis of 1956 around Hungary and the Suez Canal. It was the most ambitious project he had ever tried to put together, and he couldn't help being excited about it despite the money not being in place. And that was where his lunch date came in. Jan Bachman was that rare creature, someone who'd made a fortune in the Dotcom boom and got out at the top of the market. His idea had been to provide households and small companies with the ability to look at their financial position, across all their accounts, in an integrated way, and the firm had gone out of business in early 2003, when the three US banks who had signed up to fund it pulled out. Bachman still believed in the scheme, but in any case the idea had been good enough for him to make something in excess of $300mn out of the sale.

And now he was keen to invest in television and cinema. Hollywood was his ultimate goal, but Bachman knew his current wealth wouldn't go far in that world and so he had backed a couple of independent film makers in California and was looking also at high-end television. What had intrigued Philip was that his grandparents had been Hungarian Jews, and that was part of what had attracted him to the script of 1956. Bachman's grandparents had presumably been persecuted in Hungary, but Suez was probably one of the least successful episodes in Israel's short history. All in all, the attraction wasn't overwhelmingly obvious to Philip but there was no reason not to explore the potential. Bachman had sounded okay on the phone, and Philip could uncover no horror stories about him, and his money could ensure 1956 got made.

Bachman was already there when Philip arrived, a huge sprawl of a man, about 6'3" and 22 stones, he guessed. But the smile seemed genuine enough to dispel the slight aura of physical threat that hung around him, and his handshake, while firm, didn't try to intimidate.

Once they had sat down and ordered, Bachman was predictably direct. "I'm really attracted to your script, but I'm still going to need some convincing I can make a decent return on my investment."

"Well," Philip began, "1956 has always fascinated me as the time when a lot of what we've seen in the world over the last 50 years really began."

"How do you mean?"

"Well, it's the first time it really becomes clear that Communism didn't work and that the people of the countries behind the Iron Curtain were being suppressed by the Soviets. Of course, there had been all the trials after the war, when Stalin had purged the non-Communists and so on, but Hungary didn't happen until after Stalin was dead. And then of course, the Soviet tanks rolling into Budapest happened at exactly the same time as Nasser seizing the Suez Canal; and the British, French and Israelis trying to get it back. So for me, it's always seemed like an irresistible context for a drama."

"There's certainly a lot going on there," agreed Bachman, "but what I don't see is how you create a story involving real people that actually has relevance to what's going on in the outside world. I mean I see the significance of the world events you describe, but from what I understood from our call and what you sent me, there's no Nasser or Eisenhower or Khrushchev or MacMillan in your series. And to be honest, it might be pretty tired if there was. So you need to give me a feel for how it would work dramatically and how the characters will be made credible."

"I think," replied Philip, who hadn't expected the question but was delighted it had been asked, "there's been too much focus in TV on the major political protagonists as the only way to do programmes about great historical events. Sure, it's important to do television about Churchill and JFK, but it's also incredibly hard to get right. Why? Two reasons: you need an amazing performance from the actor playing the role, because they'll need to own and redefine the already strong images most viewers will have of those people, and also because if you succeed and you get that great performance, then the series almost inevitably becomes about that performance, and the event itself, which you're trying to make the focus of the whole thing, gets drowned out.

"So the idea with 1956 is to concentrate on a group of people only one or two of who are involved directly in what's happening, and then only peripherally, two or three steps removed. And these are people who are politically aware and interested but not obsessed. So it's part of their conversation but doesn't dominate it."

"And what do they do the rest of the time?" asked Bachman.

"They carry on their lives as normal. Part of the point for me is that there are always other things going on, so that the events of Budapest and Suez are always seen against a broader landscape and are not quite as all-consuming as they would be in a normal, set-piece historical drama. There's an ebb and flow to the action rather than the assumption that nothing else happens in the characters' lives beyond the odd predictable affair. And because the majority of the characters have no direct relationship with the great world events that are occurring, it's possible to have other independent story lines that add to the richness of the overall series."

"Won't that detract from the narrative of the global diplomacy and the events on the ground? To me it sounds like you'll have trouble nailing the importance of the central story, particularly if most of the characters involved know virtually nothing about what's going on. After all, news and media were slow enough in the 1950s that most people found out what was happening a couple of days after it occurred."

"But part of the challenge – and this is why the project is better suited to a six-part TV series than cinema – is to convey that sense of dislocation of time and distance to a modern audience, used to 24/7 news and live satellite links. The criticality of the telephone and the difficulty of validating information are aspects of the story that would build the tension of the narrative, not dilute it. And because all the characters wouldn't have access to the same information at the same time, there's more space to debate motive and for arguing about who's doing what and scope to speculate how and why different players will react as events unfold."

"So…oh by the way, you can call me Jan from now on, is that okay with you?" Bachman was clearly enjoying the conversation. "I think I now understand what you're trying to do, but I'm still going to need some convincing that all this cleverness is going to make me some money."

"Well, we obviously need a strong cast but I think we're going to get that because there are at least half a dozen parts that have real substance to them. And I think that's what'll give it the dramatic drive that'll make it a commercial success."

"Go on…"

"Well, I just think it gives you the chance to introduce the sort of strong stories you don't often see in historically set dramas. Usually, as I said, you get relatively two-dimensional characters who are slaves to the plot line, apart from the odd affair they might have to add a bit of colour, or maybe give them some implied motivation for a maverick act that then masquerades as a clever twist in the narrative."

"You're not a big fan of sex on television then?"

"On the contrary," laughed Philip, "I even produced an adaptation of John Updike's 'Couples' about 15 years ago. I just think that for something like 1956, the sex would be part of the characters' lives rather than an integral element of the narrative. So you do see the characters leading their lives, that's a really key part of the story, and you do occasionally see them having sex, but I think it's really important not to confuse that with what motivates them. So when the rest of the time they're arguing about whether the British and French are right to be sending troops into Suez, they're not taking sides on the basis of who just got laid with who."

"Okay, I get it, Phil, and I think I like what I'm hearing, though it would be a hell of a thing if we really pulled it off. But before I get ahead of myself here, I need to hear a bit more about your own motivation and passion to make this series. Why do you want to make this?"

"That's a pretty direct question but a fair one." The two men nodded. "The idea for this began way back in 1968, when I was what you might call a cub reporter for the Guardian newspaper covering the US presidential election, very much supporting Alistair Cooke, usually from a long way back. I won't go into much detail but in essence, I spent nine months being completely immersed in what was going on without being anywhere near the action, except on one or two occasions when I was close by almost by chance. And all the while I was an 18-year-old let loose in America with not a lot of money but with a reasonable expense account. And so I had a professional and a personal life running in parallel, but to all intents and purposes, not interfering with each other beyond the odd hangover. Like most people, I kept the two largely separate – part luck, part judgement – and I see the characters in 1956 as a bit analogous to my own situation, or at least for the two of them who have a direct connection to the events we're talking about. So I think the closest I got was being in the same San Francisco hotel, but a long way from the scene, when Sirhan Sirhan shot Bobby Kennedy. It was probably the most vivid, and at the same time the most surreal, experience of my life. Even the swirl of rumours as the news started to drip out felt like some kind of slow, lingering water torture, even though it only lasted a few minutes."

"So, without going into details," Philip realised Bachman was probing, "what do you think the kind of example you've just described could add to a drama like 1956?"

"Simply, it allows you to position the narrative and action in that wonderfully ambiguous and rich space between fact and perception."

"Sorry," said Bachman, "but I'm going to need to ask you again what that means. You need to give me some kind of example."

"No problem," replied Philip, marginally flustered. "I don't mean to speak in jargon, but I'm conscious some does occasionally creep in to the way I describe things." Inwardly he was thinking that either Bachman wasn't as clever as he'd first thought – you can only make things that are inherently complex sound simple up to a point, beyond which it becomes misleading – or else the American was playing some kind of game with him.

"So," he continued, "what I mean is that there is enough fact and first-hand experience available to this group of people that they aren't wholly reliant on hearsay and received truth. But at the same time they are a long way from being caught up in the immediacy of the crisis and the decision-making around it; they have no special axe to grind and so can have a relatively independent take on events. The modern world is very caught up in 24/7 news, and I believe it would be really interesting to see people from a previous generation, where they feel less overwhelmed by news and events."

"But if we think for a moment about 1956," Bachman said, "the events we're talking about – in Hungary and Egypt – were a long way geographically and every other way from the lives of your characters. And when you add in the time delay and the absence of much film of most of what was actually happening on the ground, and then you're talking just now about people not being overwhelmed by great events… Well frankly, I'm not sure they'd be very bothered by them at all."

Philip was starting to worry. From the phone call they'd had and this invite to lunch, he had convinced himself that Bachman was hot and had begun to take it for granted that he was sitting in front of a future investor. The discussion too had been going well, at least up until five minutes ago, but now the tone had become cooler and Bachman seemed to be more doubtful. He tried again.

"Mr Bachman, if you'll pardon me a moment, for this group of people the events of 1956 could scarcely have been more significant without, as I said, overwhelming them. For a start, two of them have direct links with what's going on: one because he has relatives in Budapest, the other because she's a desk officer at the Foreign Office. But secondly, they're from a small but growing segment of the British population that's interested in and is even passionate about international affairs, both in the sense of what Britain's role would be when the Empire was gone and also in the emerging shape of the Cold War."

"But come on!" argued Bachman, "We can't keep making programmes about this professional elite who know everything about politics, art and so on. That obsession with class went out with the millennium."

29

"Maybe it did but if so, it was wrong to do so. We're no more classless now than we ever were, and neither is the US for that matter. Besides, 1956 is about a time when class unambiguously did matter. And as for a professional elite, well, I wouldn't personally put it like that but there were people then – and still are today – who are interested in knowledge and understanding right across the board, no matter what class they are." Philip could feel himself becoming frustrated. He kept going. "One of the ideas behind 1956 is to convey to the audience the power of information, where ignorance of certain key facts, at the highest levels of government as well as among ordinary people, could often lead to terrible and costly misjudgements."

But Bachman was speaking again. "I understand what you're saying, but I'm just not convinced how interesting it would be or what audience it would get."

So that was it, thought Philip, another ratings contest. He believed Bachman was underselling the audience, but it was clear he was now going to be hard to shift. He tried once more… "Can I call you Jan?" He carried on without waiting for an answer. "I really believe, Jan, that there's an important place for complex ideas in TV drama. It needs to be wrapped up in a strong narrative, and very well-written, presenting its themes simply but without patronising the viewer. But then you could say that about most TV programmes, certainly drama. Television is much better than cinema at capturing an audience with this sort of material; there's more time available, and you can bring an audience with you over a number of episodes and weeks. And the small screen, of course, focuses the viewer much more on close-ups and dialogue; in some ways, it's just a much less obsessively visual medium than cinema. Come on, Jan, you know how important a story this is and how much it deserves to be told. Give me the opportunity to do it properly."

"I'm sorry, Philip," said Bachman, suddenly signalling for the bill. "Everything you say makes sense to me logically, and I can see how passionate you are about it. I also know from your previous work what a talented producer you are, and if anyone could pull this off, I believe it would probably be you. But I'm afraid it just doesn't do it for me. I am interested in the subject, you're right about that – my family left Hungary in 1956 and came to America as refugees, while I am, of course, Jewish and so have an interest in that side of the story too. But at the end of the day, I'm a businessman, and before I invest a cent of my money, I need to be convinced the project is going to make me a decent return."

"So given what you've just said, why don't you believe this project will meet your tests? You've seen our projections for worldwide sales; they're very much on the conservative side but the numbers really do stack up. I accept your decision – reluctantly, because I was looking forward to working with you and I think it's your loss – but I'd like to be sure I know the real reason before approaching another potential investor."

Philip sat back and sipped his water, working to remain composed and not show any weakness. If Bachman wasn't going to invest, he at least wanted to make credible his statement that he believed it was the American's loss. Bachman too sat back in his chair and took a drink, looking every inch the prosperous American entrepreneur, also resolved not to show any trace of doubt. He had been in this position many times before, it was in the nature of what he did, and he was happy making the other man wait. Although the decision had been made and Bachman would leave Philip still looking for funding, there was suddenly an element of competition between the two men, something wholly missing from their earlier conversation.

"I think," said Bachman at last, "that you're probably too passionate about this project and, if it hasn't already, your passion will cloud your judgement at some stage. And that's a risk I'm not prepared to take. And secondly, I want to invest in projects that have clearly delineated, vivid colours. Your 1956 is too messy and blurred for me. It doesn't have enough reality about it."

"Thank you for being frank," Philip responded. "You treat passion and judgement as if they're mutually exclusive but nothing changes for good in this world without a combination of both. Yes, I do care enormously about this project, as I do about all the work I've done. Money's important and none of my projects have ever not made a decent profit but that's not why I made them, and if it was, I believe the programmes would have ended up a good deal less profitable. The mistake you're making is to stereotype and patronise the audience."

"Oh come on, Philip!" complained Bachman, visibly irritated for the first time. "Don't accuse me of patronising the audience, I work out what they want and make it for them. You and your kind, you're the ones who are patronising people by imagining they're all like you, with your so-called sophisticated middle-class attitudes to everything, and your misplaced liberal assumptions about the power of government and society to change fundamental aspects of human nature. I mean, how arrogant is that?"

Philip was pleased by the vehemence of this outburst from a man who was his potential investor until a few minutes ago, elated that he had gotten under the American's skin and made him lose his cool. He thought quickly about how to respond and decided to laugh it off. "If that's what you think, Jan, then you haven't been paying attention and it's better that we don't work together. I don't believe the way to make truly successful television programmes is either to assume you have any of the answers or to give the audience what you believe they want. Both can work, but neither is really the way forward. Most of what I do is for myself. I'm not blind to the commercial side, far from it, but I believe the best way to do that is create as good a piece of art as I can. So far that approach has made my investors and me a good deal of money, and I don't believe 1956 is going to be any different."

"I can see we're not going to have a long or beautiful relationship," Bachman laughed, conscious he still held the upper hand by virtue of the money he wasn't going to be spending. "This isn't about the idea of a drama about 1956, don't forget; it's about the particular drama you want to make, which I don't believe will be accessible to the people I want to be watching the films and television programmes I finance."

"So where exactly is the barrier that makes my project so inaccessible?"

"Well, Phil," Bachman began, relaxed now and deliberately using the short version of Philip's name, "I reckon the whole idea of a bunch of people sitting round a dinner table having the sort of discussion about geopolitics you would be lucky to see on your BBC's Question Time... For Christ's sake, how many people watch Question Time? It sure as hell is a lot fewer than I want to be watching my programmes."

"And what would you have instead?"

"Action, pace!" said Bachman with complete certainty. "You need to be on the streets of Budapest, in the Canal Zone itself, inside the Kremlin and the White House. If you want people to understand what's happening, you need to show it to them. I mean, it's not rocket science, is it?"

"I'm sorry, Jan, but you don't get it." Philip had decided the conversation was approaching its end and it was time to stop listening. By this stage he even meant what he had said about being glad Bachman was not investing. "It's simply wrong to parrot that if you want people to understand something, you simply show it to them."

"And why's that?" jeered Bachman.

"Because you're not showing them what happened, you're showing them what you think happened, or, even worse, what you want them to think happened. The set of uncontested facts about a period of crisis like 1956 is seriously small, and their relative significance is even more ambiguous. What you're doing is serving up a Janet and John view of the world, with good guys and bad guys and everything happening in a neat linear sequencing, each event caused by the one preceding it and in turn leading on to the one that follows. You're lying to your audience because your version of what happened isn't true, and you're patronising them because you're denying them any right to make up their own minds, the right even to be intrigued by the hint there might be an alternative narrative out there. And you aren't even being that commercial! Soon the audience will work out they're not being given the chance to do any of their own thinking and stop watching. Sooner or later, the viewers always catch up with you, and yes, you might make a lot of money out of something formulaic but eventually, the type of programmes you're talking about become recognised as a cheap, off-the shelf-commodity, no matter how much they cost. And don't get me wrong, there's nothing inherently bad about formulaic commodity TV; the issues only arise when you pretend it's something it isn't. That's when people feel cheated, and not just the middle-class viewers you claim to despise but everyone. You're trying to sell these programmes as full of historical insight but in fact, they have less insight and content than your average B Movie Western."

"Right," said Bachman, "I think we're finished then. He stood up and signalled again for the bill. "If you'll excuse me?" He spoke brusquely, the question pronounced as if it was an order, then turned towards the waiter and picked up his coat. It wasn't hard for Philip to understand he had been dismissed. However, he was far from ready to leave and so took his time finishing his wine and then putting on his jacket. The relationship with Bachman was clearly fractured beyond repair. He offered his hand. Bachman looked for a moment as if he would ignore it but then thought better, and the two men shook hands quickly and carefully, Philip looking up into the taller man's eyes, determined not to break eye contact early. He knew this was all macho ridiculousness but it still mattered to him. "Thanks for lunch," he said, before turning and walking, deliberately but not too slowly, out of the door.

Once out of sight, Philip paused and breathed deeply. It was funny how a conversation that had begun so well could turn toxic so quickly. He was convinced Bachman would have been the wrong investor but somewhere along the line, he had also clearly sold it badly. Perhaps he had simply gotten too close to it, as Bachman had inferred. He spotted a free table at a wine bar and decided on the spot to sit down and have a drink, think it through properly. A couple of minutes later he was settled, with his notebook out and a large glass of Sancerre in front of him. He wanted to come up with a Plan B before he got back to the office, and even more so before he got home, where Michelle would be ferocious in urging him to work out his next steps.

When he'd been out last night with Michelle and Carol, he had been intensely aware how lucky he was to have these two women so pivotal in his life. Seeing how well they got on, he felt the circle was complete, and he could now move on, free to embark on fresh journeys. However, all that had been with the implicit belief that today's lunch with Bachman would produce the desired result. But that wasn't how it had turned out, and the financial viability of 1956 was now very much in doubt. Philip was still convinced it would happen, but he knew it wouldn't do so by accident.

He took a sip of wine and began, methodically, to make a list of possible investors, rating them out of four by both their likely interest in the project and their practical ability to finance it. It didn't look over-promising but at least there were a couple of possibilities. He thought again about Bachman's allegation that he was too close to it and that this would cloud his judgement if it hadn't already done so. He conceded there was some truth in it. Philip still looked back at that 1968 period as his reference point. He had pitched up as a young reporter, sent to provide research and draft material for the great Alistair Cooke, and within the year he had left the Guardian and become a freelance sports writer. All he had done since, he was certain, could be traced back to those months.

Bachman was right; he was very close to it. But not too close; he knew he had been harder edged in his professional judgement with 1956 than with anything else he had worked on. The idea had first come into Philip's mind in 1990, after the Berlin Wall had come down, when the countries of the Soviet Bloc, one by one, did away with the stultifying regimes that had ruled them for the last 40 years. Born in 1950, he had to that point spent his whole life with the Iron Curtain firmly in place and, not least with the failure of Nagy's and Dubcek's attempts to give their countries greater independence, Philip had assumed it would still be in place long after he died. But now it was possible to see 1956 and 1968 not as hopes crushed, footnotes to history, but as symptoms of a building pressure that would ultimately become unstoppable.

It was the Velvet Revolution, when Czechoslovakia shook itself suddenly and peacefully free of its chains that had triggered the idea. Vaclav Havel, the writer who had been there behind the scenes as a young man in 1968 and had been one of the founder signatories of Charter 77, found himself suddenly president of the newly independent state. Havel's story set off in Philip's mind a whole swathe of memories; of Russian tanks rolling into the streets of Prague in August 1968 at the same time as the Civil Rights movement was starting to unravel. But 1990 had changed all that. It had relit his faith in politics and the power of people to change things. The reality of the project had then taken ten years to emerge, and then a further five to get to its present state, where Philip believed it was ready to go. But there was no escaping the fact that it needed investment and that Bachman had looked far and away his best option. It wasn't quite back to the drawing board, but it was close.

"Excuse me?"

Philip turned around to face a dark-haired woman in her mid-40s, who was sitting at the table behind him drinking espresso with some water on the side. Her sunglasses hid her eyes. "I was wondering if by any chance you knew where the Hazlitt Hotel is; I think it's in Soho somewhere."

"Yes, it is," he replied. "It's in Frith Street I think, about ten minutes' walk from here."

"Good, I thought it was close." Her accent was American, probably Midwest somewhere. There was a time when Philip could have told a US accent to within two or three states, but not anymore.

"Would you like me to draw you a map?"

"Yes please, thank you! I just got in from Boston this morning and had to go straight to a meeting, so I haven't had a chance to check in yet." She gestured to a small wheelie suitcase on the ground next to her. "What about yourself?" she asked quizzically. Do you usually drink wine by yourself on a Monday afternoon?"

Philip laughed. "There was a time, but not anymore, today's an exception. No, I've just had a meeting over lunch that more or less bombed, so I'm working out what my next steps are, and partly drowning my sorrows I guess, or at least anaesthetising my frustration. How did your meeting go?"

"Well, at least a bit better than yours I suspect, but they're thinking about it still. They've invited me back tomorrow to hear the verdict. I'm sorry yours bombed. For what it's worth, my experience of that sort of meeting is that it's usually for the best. In any event, I always tell myself, and them as well usually, that it's their loss."

Philip grinned. "Funnily enough, that's exactly what I told him." He half stood up to go, then paused. "Do you mind if I join you for a few minutes? My name's Philip, Philip Coulter." He held out his hand.

The woman took it, briefly, in both of hers. "Yes, of course. I'm never quite sure what the protocol is over here, or I'd have asked you already. I'm Alison Parker. You've been really helpful drawing me this map by the way, thank you so much."

"It's my pleasure. By the way, would you like a drink?"

Alison raised her sunglasses briefly and made eye contact. "Thanks, I'll have the same as you."

She was a lawyer, working for a company in environmental energy, selling wind farm technology. Philip had ordered a bottle and chatted happily.

"I thought there was some American in your accent," said Alison, "but I couldn't quite place it; now it makes sense though. What made you come back to Britain?"

"A bunch of things really; a bit of me felt it was time to come home, but there were some other factors, like I didn't really have much time for Reagan."

"Oh really, why was that?"

"I sort of took against him the first time I saw him, which was at the Miami Convention in 1968. He just came across to me as too smooth and too conservative. Of course, he then reinvented himself a bit, and by the time he got elected he sort of came across as everyone's favourite uncle. So I started looking for opportunities back here in London and eventually, one came up."

"So does this current project of yours kind of bring you full circle? I mean you began as a news journalist in 1968 and now you're looking to make television about being a news journalist in 1968? It sounds like you're being pretty autobiographical."

Philip laughed, "You have a point there, it's not meant to be autobiography though. Don't forget I haven't done any of the writing, and I think Fred's just used a journalist as a technique for getting a bit closer to the action than normal people would ever be able to."

"I can't believe you were so close to all those things back in '68."

"It was just how it was back then. I really understood not very much of what was happening, not at the time anyway. How long are you in London for?"

"I fly back on Thursday, but after tomorrow, I'm pretty free till then." She looked at Philip again, then down at her drink. "I'm pretty free now actually."

Philip felt himself go red and almost smiled at the absurdity of it. It had been a very long time since a woman had tried to pick him up. But he stopped himself from smiling. It would be wrong to give any impression, however inadvertent, that might look as though he didn't take her seriously. In fact, Philip was flattered. Alison was smart and good looking, over in London on business, and there was a part of him that wanted to say yes, to go back to her hotel. It had also been a long time since he had done anything adventurous, anything that felt dangerous in any way, or that created the pangs of guilt that when younger he had even relished. It was even longer since he had had a sexual adventure. In the more than 20 years he had been with Michelle, sleeping with another woman had hardly crossed his mind in that time.

But now it had, and he was starting to find the idea beguiling. And Alison's offer had come out of the blue, almost as if it had been meant. Philip also knew he had no other meetings that afternoon, and his partner, Jack, wasn't particularly expecting him back after his lunch with Bachman. There would be no real need for him to lie to cover anything up. As far as he could tell, there was no sign either of Alison wanting the relationship to last beyond this single summer afternoon.

In the couple of seconds it took for him to think, Alison had taken a sip of her wine and had calmly turned to watch the Londoners hurrying past in the sunshine. "It's funny," she said, "how people in big Western cities never really slow down to connect with each other."

"Slowing down's a good thing to do once in a while," said Philip. "I've got nothing pressing on, so I've certainly got time to show you where your hotel is. And my map drawing's never been any good anyway. Just say when you're ready."

Without a word they both stood up. Philip took a last sip of his wine, then signalled for the bill, which he swiftly paid. He offered to pull Alison's case, but she declined, and he didn't try to insist. Slowly, they made their way up Haymarket to Piccadilly, then turned right into Shaftesbury Avenue. The street was bustling even though it was 3pm on an oven-hot Monday afternoon, and it was impossible for them to walk side by side, let alone talk to each other. When they got to Wardour Street, Philip steered Alison up into Soho, where the pavements were clearer and it was possible to chat, and soon they were turning right into Old Compton Street.

"How well do you know London?" Philip asked.

"Reasonably. I've been here maybe six or eight times over the years but I don't really know Soho at all. I thought it would make a nice change staying in a new part of town; the hotel was recommended and it's closer to where my meetings are; I normally stay farther west, nearer to Heathrow."

Philip wondered how Soho would seem to a professional American woman, seeing it for the first time, with its sex shops and quirky bars and restaurants. He loved its sense of self and its openness to the panorama of humanity, but he wondered how Alison would view it. As far as he was aware, Boston, let alone the Midwest, had nothing like it. To her, this could well seem like Sodom and Gomorrah territory. She was looking around with evident curiosity, but with no obvious sign of her brows furrowing with horror.

However, he was starting to feel concerned about the prospect of spending the rest of the afternoon with Alison in her hotel. The idea itself was no less appealing, but it now seemed a long way removed from the act without consequence he had found so appealing only a few minutes before. It wasn't either that he had any greater fear of being found out, if anything it was the opposite. For all Philip knew, Michelle might not even care less, but oddly, at this particular moment, that seemed to put the onus on him.

"Listen," he said, just as they reached the corner of Frith Street, "I've just remembered something I need to get back to the office for." He knew it was lame and that Alison would know he had made it up.

"That's okay," Alison said, turning to look at him, "I wasn't at all sure it was going to be right, but I liked you, still do, and thought it was worth a try. It's not my usual style, and afternoon sex in a hotel with someone you've known only a couple of hours didn't seem to be your style either, or not any more anyway."

"You've got me there, on both counts. Back when, I think I would feel differently. But I'm not that person anymore."

"That's good," said Alison, "I'll take it as a compliment you thought about it for so long. I think on these occasions it's customary to say words to the effect that she's a lucky woman, but in this case, I'll say that you're a lucky man."

"Thanks, I am."

Alison continued. "But it is time to say goodbye, or else we run the risk of starting to re-think the whole thing, which would be a bad idea." She gave Philip a hug and kissed him swiftly on both cheeks. "There's the hotel, I can see it from here. Hope you find your investor, Philip. Everything else I think you've got already. Goodbye."

"I wish it was true but thanks for the thought!" he called. "Goodbye, Alison, and take care…"

Chapter 3
Tuesday 5th

It was another glorious day, and Mary had decided to go into work early, before the Tube got busy and before it became uncomfortably hot. She had one doctoral student to see and some administration that needed doing to tidy up the loose ends of the year. She arrived at her office just after 7.30am, the first one there.

Her room was one of four off a small central area. This could accommodate small discussion groups but the main seminar room was on the floor below, together with two smaller offices for research fellows and the admin office. There was also a small kitchen off to the side, with a kettle and a microwave.

When she got inside, Mary, as she always did, went upstairs to her room, where she left her bag and quickly assessed what needed to be done, composing a mental picture and getting out the latest submission by her favourite post grad, Ingrid, who was coming in to see her at 11am. Then she went downstairs past the cartoons of Peel, Disraeli, Palmerston and Gladstone, juxtaposed with other more flattering portraits of George Eliot, Elizabeth Gaskell, and Charlotte and Emily Brontë.

Mary herself had a soft spot for Vanity Fair but Thackeray had been sacrificed in the cause of gender balance. She hoped, maybe in another five or ten years, when it was possible to claim perspective on the 20th century, to replicate the juxtaposition of the most recent completed century, but in a more balanced way. Perhaps Lloyd George, Churchill, Attlee and Thatcher on one side, and Lawrence, Woolf, Orwell and Murdoch on the other. But really it was far too soon to work out what the 20th century meant. One key difference, of course, was the decline of Britain's overall power and influence. The impact of all that on the politicians who presided over the change and the writers who chronicled it, or at least wrote against its background, was still unclear.

Mary wondered what character and set of circumstances conspired to produce this sort of impact. She remembered having been introduced to Tony Blair in the late 1970s, when he was a young lawyer and thinking he was bright but nothing more, quite enthusiastic and puppy-like. She could have imagined him becoming a backbench Labour MP, but political success beyond that would have seemed totally ridiculous to her. Even looking back over 25 years, she remained confident in her judgement that she knew several people who had been cleverer and more impressive than Blair at the same age, including, of course, herself. Mary had never been shy at estimating her own ability, and few along the way had disagreed with her assessment. She believed implicitly not only in her intellectual ability but in her practical skills in making things happen. Mary could still recall the odd sinking feeling when she heard that Blair had become Shadow Home Secretary. What did that tell you when you weren't yet a professor?

That Gore Vidal phrase, equally true and wicked, that for him to succeed others must fail, drifted across her mind like a shadow. Of course what she did was quite different to being a politician; the latter were no more intelligent or able than academics, notably less so in many cases. But usually, and certainly with Blair, they had more power. Mary had always been intrigued by power and wondered, again, how it had so easily passed her by. She had held various administrative posts within UCL, posts whose titles should be associated with power and influence but somehow had never felt that way. As a result, Mary had, on each occasion, quickly decided she preferred teaching and research. She remembered a point back in the autumn of 1993, soon after John Smith had died and Blair had just become leader of the Labour Party. She had been encouraged to apply for a Professorship at Yale and had flirted with the idea for a couple of months. But the flirting was never serious; she knew lots of academics who taught and had homes thousands of miles from their partners, but almost always the partner was an academic too and seldom were children involved. Mary could never quite see it working in her own situation; Ruth was nine, happily settled in school, while Sam, working for the Civil Service, might have had trouble finding an equivalent job in New Haven.

Mary looked back on this as a turning point, though it was far from certain she would have got the job. She had been having more 'what if' moments lately. Maybe it was Ruth finishing university and now leaving home, or maybe it was a reflective extension of her worrying about Sam. But she knew how difficult it is to establish causation; the significance of a past event was hard to assess, and while the perspective of time allowed you to see the bigger picture, the distance also meant you lost touch with the contemporary details which necessarily contribute to the accuracy of any judgement. Anyway, making these sorts of judgements about her own life seemed unhealthy somehow, like she was deciding nothing important would happen to her from now on.

Logical as all this was, it felt like a cop out. Mary had begun to feel this quite strongly at dinner on Saturday, when she had been struck by Carol's rational view of her life and how she had responded to challenges she had faced. Just because it would have to be reassessed in the future, Mary reasoned, was nowhere near enough justification for not having a view of the choices you made. After all, if you had no view of your decisions, then it was hard to claim you were learning from experience, which was one of the things humanity was meant to be about.

And aside from Carol, on Saturday, Mary had also found herself making judgements about Michelle and Linda and John and Philip. Or, to be precise, she became newly aware of the judgements she had already formed and, in some cases, of judgements they had made about each other. And there was no credible line she could draw that would allow her to escape admitting to herself the judgements she had made about her own life, her own decisions. She couldn't on the one hand hold that Linda should never have married John, and on the other not admit to having a view of the wisdom of her own marriage to Sam.

For the truth was she had always wondered if that had been the true turning point of her life and career. Before, she had been a star at everything she touched, straight A's and a 1st in her degree, Head Girl, Debating Club president and so on. But after she married Sam, the early promise never quite materialised in the way she had dreamed. As a teenager, Mary had kept a secret bottle of Pernod in her bedroom, hidden under the mattress. Late at night, as she read by candlelight, the 16-year-old Mary would sip her Pernod and imagine herself in fin de siècle Paris, like a young Gertrude Stein, mixing with the Impressionists, with Picasso, meeting Zola, the young Proust, understanding what they were trying to achieve, and being appreciated for her perception, for wisdom beyond her years. And she had plotted how she would write books that would reveal complex issues to huge new audiences, while also writing op-ed columns for the Sunday Times.

Mary knew even then that teenage dreaming hardly ever translates precisely, but at the time, and for a decade after, she really believed that she would somehow be at the heart of public life. But none of this had happened, and she was at a loss to explain why, and the problem, her nagging fear, was that, for all the joy it had brought her otherwise, the wrong turning she had taken was when she married Sam.

At the time, she had been attracted physically, despite his only average good looks. But it was his lack of phoniness that had really made Sam stand out from the other men she knew. Nearly all of them had more money, better jobs, more expensive suits and faster cars. Mary smiled as she remembered Sam's tragic taste and lack of interest in clothes, together with his rather clapped out Ford Escort. Against this kind of competition, it would have been virtually impossible for any of the other men she knew at the time to appear other than sophisticated and flash. But somehow Sam's plainness, his occasional gaucheness, had worked for her. Where others would grate on her sensibility with their unrelenting self-promotion, Sam was guilelessly self-denigrating, talking about what he had been doing with a natural modesty that never tipped over into falseness. Where others bought her presents and expensive meals when they took her out, Sam recorded a cassette of music he thought she might like and took Mary to his local pub. And while her own background was at the wealthy end of middle class, Mary, as a young woman trying to make her way in academia, had begun to acquire less expensive tastes – cinema rather than theatre, walking rather than tennis – tastes that subliminally pulled her towards a greater appreciation of Sam's simpler lifestyle. But she feared this had come with its own hefty price tag.

When she had met him in her mid-20s, Mary had been quietly but ferociously driven, while still enjoying the party life of a young woman in London. Far from wealthy and in a not very well paid academic job, she did, however, have some family money to support her and a range of much wealthier friends who, by her standards, earned a fortune, largely in law or in the City. Mostly though, she worked long hours to push on with her research, so she could publish articles in the right journals and maintain momentum on the book which was meant to establish her reputation. Articles had been published and the book too. Focused on the role of women in the early trades union movement, it had hit a chord and, though too densely written and slightly too self-satisfied with its own scholarship to become quite the success she had envisaged, it had earned her respect and a reputation that had begun to open doors to guest lectures and garner invitations to review books for the Sunday papers. Although more slowly than she would have wanted, Mary was steadily becoming a public figure.

And it was just before she finished the book in early 1979 that she had met Sam. It had been at a friend's drinks party at the end of January, one of those organised at a week's notice in an attempt to break out of the cycle of short gloomy winter days that can depress even normally optimistic young people. Penny was an old school friend who was now a solicitor at Linklaters. They had stayed lazily in touch during their university years – Penny had gone to Durham while Mary stayed in London – and reunited when Penny moved back to the capital to take her law exams and start her Articles. Together they had shopped in the West End, joined a poetry class and gone to fringe theatre. It had been while drinking coffee on Mary's sofa in Earl's Court the previous Saturday afternoon that the decision had been made.

"God, it's miserable outside," Penny said. "It's barely 4 o'clock and it's already dark."

"Another couple of weeks and it'll start to still be light at this time," replied Mary, "but you're right, it is miserable. I've felt cold all winter for some reason. I need the sun on my back every so often, and I've barely seen it at all since October. And all the strikes don't help; the news is even more depressing than normal."

"I got soaked yesterday on the way to work, did I tell you?" continued Penny. "I'd just got out of the Tube and was about 200 yards from work, when this van went by and drove straight through this huge puddle. I was drenched from head to foot. The air turned blue I can tell you, but the bastard just kept going. Anyway, luckily for me, Beth was already at her desk and had brought her gym kit in; you know I told you she goes jogging at lunchtimes. Anyway, she lent me her towel and ran out to get me a whole new dry set of clothes. So within 45 minutes, I was dried off and warm in a whole new outfit. I don't know what I would have done if she hadn't been there."

"She sounds lovely."

"She is, you must meet her soon. I know, I'll have a drinks party. What are you doing next Saturday?"

"Well, nothing at the moment," Mary replied, amused by Penny's stream of consciousness that had taken her from being splashed by a puddle to organising a drinks party in a few short sentences. How this woman had become a lawyer, she wondered, not for the first time.

"Right, let's do it. Okay if I use your phone?" Penny asked, while searching for her address book in the bottom of her bag.

"Yes, of course," Mary replied. Within ten minutes, Penny had spoken to five people and left messages for a further eight.

"Right, we're on," she announced, "next Saturday at my flat. Joel's bringing a bunch of his friends from Birmingham who are staying with him. We should have 30 odd people to start with and a good few more once word gets round."

"How is Joel?" asked Mary. "It seems like I haven't seen him in ages."

"He's fine. Strangely, he seems to quite enjoy the Civil Service. I'd have thought it was a bit of a cloning machine, even the alleged fast track, but he says not. Mind you, he's at the Treasury, which I guess must be a busy place these days; certainly, he seems to work long hours. I've even worried Fiona might ditch him because he's never around."

"I hope not," said Mary. "They're so sweet together, and he's only trying to establish his career. I'm sure he feels at least as bad about having to come home late as she does."

"Well, let's just say the last time I spoke to her she intimated she was becoming a little frustrated."

Mary was silent while Penny cheerfully ignored her friend's embarrassment, just enough to make a little space between them. After a moment, Penny continued, "Joel also said he'd try and bring a couple of friends from work, the non-Oxbridge crowd, he called them; someone called Steve from Bristol and a guy called Sam from Nottingham who went to Manchester. He's a bit square but Joel swears he's really interesting."

And that had been the first time Mary had heard his name. In the intervening years, it had stayed with her, viewed from different angles depending on situation and mood, always being mined for fresh meaning. Mary didn't know what had prompted Penny to describe Sam as 'square but interesting'. Was that what Joel had said or was it Penny's interpretation? Sam could never recall having met Joel's sister before the party and didn't object massively to the phrase, thought it fairly accurate, a concession that irritated Mary hugely.

Penny had asked Mary if she would arrive early to help set up, while Joel had asked Sam to help him carry drinks up to the flat from his car. Penny lived on the second floor, and Sam had pitched up in Joel's second-hand BMW half an hour before the advertised start time. And so Mary's first glance at her future husband, and this she recalled with absolute clarity, and in this case accuracy, was of a tousled mop of brown hair, with the beginnings of a bald patch at the crown, protruding over the top of a crate of Hofmeister from a nearby off-licence.

"Hi," she had said, feeling slightly overwhelmed given he did not know she was there and they had never met, "it's left at the top of this flight and straight through to the kitchen."

"Thanks," Sam had grunted, then, after a couple more grunts, "Hi, I'm Sam, a friend of Joel's." The carrying was obviously taking up plenty of effort, more than Mary would have expected, but there was no doubting his determination, whatever you might think of his strength. Finally, Sam had found space to put down the box on the kitchen table and turned around. Despite the cold temperature outside, he was glistening. "Hello, I'm Sam," he repeated, this time staring straight at Mary.

"You're Joel's friend," she stated rather than asked.

"Yes," he replied, "we were in the same intake and both ended up at the Treasury."

"You should give more money to Higher Education," she immediately responded.

"And you're presumably an academic?"

"Indeed, I am," Mary replied, and caught herself smiling as she did so.

Now, sitting in the seminar room with her mug of tea, Mary could remember that first meeting as vividly as if it had just happened. And this wasn't a memory that had suddenly surfaced; it had been a constant companion across the years, fresh and eternally young. Mary shook her head slowly and grinned girlishly as the visceral force of the familiar recall drenched her in re-accumulated emotion. She had been with Sam for a quarter of a century and now, with Ruth gone, they were entering a new stage. Mary was confident they would adjust, though she knew the wrench of living in an empty nest would be much greater for Sam. And Ruth would not be far away, she would still come and visit, and they could go and see her. Although there would be an initial gulf, there was a strong bridge connecting them and a comforting absence of barriers. All would be fine.

With this thought still fresh, Mary's mind turned again to her lost dreams and thwarted ambition that now seemed a little less galling. Where were the choices she would have made differently? There was no sense in which Sam had done anything but encourage her to succeed in whatever she wanted. Equally, she had always wanted and expected to have children, and in those same dreams there were always more than one of them. What she hadn't realised back then was the all-consuming nature of even a single child. The only realistic alternative would have been to spend less time with Ruth when she was very young, and Mary knew she would never have countenanced that even if the career implications had been much worse.

The decision not to go for the Yale job had been a part of the equation and all hers. But wasn't it also true that Sam, while ambitious in his own right, was far from the driven individual Mary saw herself as being? There was little about him that could be described as ruthless or self-serving. Was it not therefore reasonable to suppose his whole approach to life might have taken the edge off her own ambition?

Again, Mary's mind drifted back to that first evening in the winter of 1979. Her memory of later in the evening was more influenced by alcohol, and therefore less definite and factually accurate, but also more layered and coloured by emotional truth. One incident still brought mixed emotions as she smiled and winced at the memory. At one point, Mary saw Sam from across the room. Surrounded by a small group, Sam's arms gesticulated as he spoke. Unaware of what Sam was saying, Mary watched as Joel, standing behind Sam, began to wave his arms about in mock impersonation of his friend. Sam's audience dissolved into laughter, and he went red and looked over his shoulder. He stood there until the laughing subsided and he could carry on making his point, this time with his elbows glued to his side, exuding a strange combination of pride and humility.

Mary had felt part sorry for Sam, but also a little in awe of what she saw as enormous self-assurance, despite his obvious vulnerability. The men she knew, almost without exception, were more confident than Sam, but their confidence tended to be built from the outside in, like a shell, toughened by exposure to the outside world. Inside, and she loved them for it, they always seemed sensitive, fragile even. Sam, though, was different; he had little external shell as far as she could see, and it was hard to credit someone had reached their mid-20s without any real defence mechanism. What existed closer to the surface was vulnerable and fragile, but it also repaired quickly when it was damaged, leaving no visible scars.

Looking back, Mary marvelled at how quickly the bond between them had been forged, so soon after they first met. So much water had flowed since then that it was almost impossible to disentangle cause and effect. Unusually for her, Mary became almost misty-eyed as she felt again the surge of excitement that had bubbled through her veins and arteries that first evening. However, the passage of time had enhanced the experience, and the result was a richer sensation, although it would be wrong to dismiss this as in any sense false. Rather, it was a better version of the original, an oil painting to the original pencil sketch. From the first, she had discerned Sam's true self, and it was this which had propelled her into an unlikely attraction.

Later that first evening, Mary also recalled becoming suddenly aware there were only the two of them in the kitchen. She had wandered in looking for some water and had edged past a group of people to reach the sink. While she had her back turned waiting for the tap to run cold, the group had left and when she turned back round, the only other person in the kitchen was Sam, peering inquisitively into the fridge.

"Oh, hi," he said, with a slightly distracted air, "I was just looking to see if there was any more white wine."

"I wanted to say, I think you dealt with that whole thing with Joel really well," Mary found herself blurting.

To her surprise, Sam laughed. "Joel's okay really," he said, "He doesn't mean anything bad and doesn't have a genuinely malicious bone in his body."

"Well, it certainly didn't look that way." Mary was surprised at her own vehemence, "And it wasn't as if you were some random gatecrasher, you're one of his best friends and had helped carry the drink upstairs."

"Yes, there's a certain irony in there some place. By the way, you can defend me in court any day,"

"How long have you known Joel?"

"We both started at the Civil Service on the same intake, October '77, so almost a year and a half. Funny, it seems longer."

"Is that comment on Joel or life in general?"

"Mostly the job, with a bit of getting used to living in London, neither of them in a bad way."

"London's all right, but then I've always lived here so I've got used to it. It must be different coming here for the first time. How do you find it now? Have you settled in?" Mary was conscious that a note of solicitude had crept into her voice, but she observed it rather than felt it, as though this unfamiliar emotion was being experienced by someone else. She didn't consider its implications or wonder if Sam noticed.

He looked at her thoughtfully, "It's been okay, but I'll be glad when the days start to get longer in the next couple of weeks. It'll be easier to get out a bit and find my way around properly again. At the moment I feel I only really know Clapham, Whitehall and Waterloo Station. Do you want some wine to go with your water?"

"Yes, okay, thanks," Mary said automatically.

Sam filled a plastic cup with deliberate care and handed it to her before doing the same for himself and replacing the bottle in the fridge. As he did so, a group of four people wandered into the kitchen, singing along to the Sister Sledge song playing next door. Without exchanging a word or glance, Mary and Sam both slipped out of the door and gravitated to the foot of the stairs, where there was space to stand in the hallway far enough from the music to hear each other talk.

"And how is work?" Mary continued once they had settled. "From what I hear, you must all be working really long hours."

"That bit's okay," replied Sam. "I mean, it's hard work, but it's sort of what you're there for, and it needs doing. Making sure the essential stuff keeps going as far as possible is a big job for the whole Civil Service. So, to answer your first question, yes, I think I have settled in reasonably well now. I feel a bit lost sometimes, and there seems to be quite a lot of process and hierarchy, even compared to what I expected. But I'll get used to it over time."

"Do you think you'll stay in the Civil Service? Will you still be there in five or ten years' time?" Again Mary was aware she hadn't asked this question casually.

"I think so," Sam had replied.

"Me too," she had heard herself saying. "I mean, I think I'll stay in academia, provided I get a permanent job."

"If Joel's any judge, then I'm sure you will. According to him, you're absolutely brilliant."

Mary had been struck by the natural ease with which Sam stressed Joel's compliment. Given how Sam had just been treated by Joel, most people would not have put Joel in such a positive light.

"I'll tell you what," she had said, "next week it'll be February and the days will be starting to lengthen. Why don't we meet up for tea somewhere, and I'll show you around North London, maybe Camden, or Hampstead Heath; let's see what the weather's like."

And that was how it had begun. Mary could still recall the conversation verbatim. Today was the first time in a couple of years she had traced back over that evening but there had been periods in the last 25 years when the memory had visited her almost weekly. Unlike the layers of her perception, however, this memory was resistant to revision, and as a result, the freshness and innocence of the conversation had endured.

At the time, Mary had been seeing someone called Daniel Greenway. He wasn't at Penny's party, being in the US with work. Good-looking, intelligent and well-heeled, Daniel had a lot going for him and by extension was fancied by most, if not all, the women Mary knew. Predictably, he knew this and it did little for his humility; there was always a bit too much checking himself out in the nearest mirror, and the unspoken assumption that all would go well, a confidence in his own Midas touch. To be fair, only small signs of his sense of self-worth surfaced in his personal relationship with Mary. Instead, the fact that she didn't pretend to faint in his presence was part of her attraction for him. They had been seeing each other since the previous summer, maybe a couple of times a week, depending on their different schedules. The idea of moving in together hadn't been discussed, although both knew it was looming.

Mary liked Daniel and was aware many of her friends, Penny included, considered him something of a trophy boyfriend. She wasn't displeased by this idea, or by the fact others might envy her. What she did resent was the idea there was an element of her being lucky.

Sam wasn't as good-looking as Daniel, or as successful, but Mary had still proposed what amounted to a date the following Saturday and had kept it, in the process turning down an invitation to spend the weekend at Daniel's parents. Even now, more than 25 years later, and having been married to Sam for more than twenty of those, Mary didn't really understand the motivation behind her decisions at the time.

It had been ten days after the party before she eventually met Daniel for a drink, having made excuses not to see him twice, not to mention the weekend. A general malaise consumed her desire to go out, or to see anyone. On the other hand, she had really enjoyed seeing Sam on the previous Saturday. They had been deeply self-consciousness, despite their conversation barely going beyond the routine, and Mary had been back in her flat, alone, by 6.30 pm. So when Daniel had suggested she was behaving oddly, had asked if she was seeing anyone else, and had mentioned that his mate, Craig, had seen her being chatted up at Penny's party, Mary couldn't think of an honest answer that would have taken less than ten minutes to explain.

Shorn, for once, of a fluent reply, Mary had sat silently at the table in the pub, sullenly as it appeared to Daniel, playing meaninglessly with her half-drunk vodka and orange. She always recalled the jukebox had been playing 'Ever Fallen in Love?' by the Buzzcocks, one of those soundtracks of our lives' moments that always seem to come around more often than we expect.

"No, I'm not," she eventually said after what seemed like an age, "but I've thought about it, and I don't want to be anything but honest with you, so I think we should stop seeing each other." She spoke slowly and quite deliberately, without inflection. The words hung in the air as the Buzzcocks hurtled along in the background. She remembered Daniel, staring into his pint, as he seemed to search for the right words.

"What's gone wrong, Mary? What happened to you while I was away? What wasn't I doing? I never treated you badly. There is someone else, isn't there? I can't believe we're having this conversation, let alone that we're having it in an ordinary pub the weekend after you were due to come down and meet my parents."

"There isn't anyone else, Daniel, and this isn't about you – you've always behaved impeccably towards me." Mary found herself feeling coldly detached even as she sought to sooth her, now ex, boyfriend's ego and feelings. She made these efforts genuinely but without emotional engagement. Aware of her sudden objectivity, Mary wondered idly if this meant she hadn't ever really cared for Daniel, but she already had the sense that her own world had shifted, and the relationship had already receded into the distance. She had cut the noose, but she was happy, consciously, to bend the truth slightly to salve Daniel's ego and to preserve the narrative of her reputation.

"I'm sorry, Daniel. Looking back, I've been drifting away for a while, but I didn't realise it until you were away. I just think, I mean I've decided, I'm not ready for a relationship, a serious one, a commitment right now. I want to establish myself at the university and think about what I want to do with my life." As she spoke, Mary knew her words were a concoction of truth, semi-truth and inaccuracy.

"But, Mary, we're all the same, getting started in careers, finding our feet. I don't understand, and I really don't know where this has come from. I thought we were really good together. That Saturday before I went away... Look," he said, "it's terrible we're having this conversation in a public place; come back to mine and we can talk it all through properly."

"No," said Mary quietly. "I'm sorry, Daniel, but I'm not going back with you."

"You really mean it, don't you?" Daniel sagged visibly as he spoke.

"I'm afraid so," Mary spoke quietly, her voice wavering but only slightly. "I really think it's the best thing." She got up, put on her coat and pecked Daniel on his head, gently pushing his arms away. "Goodbye," she said, then turned on her heels and walked out, consciously neither quickening nor slowing her pace compared to normal.

She resurfaced. For a few moments she had submerged herself in the past, where she was young and attractive and sought after, and had felt again that exquisite sense of power and control that comes with ditching someone. Two months later she'd started going out with Sam, and she had never really doubted they would stay together. The idea of ditching him had never crossed her mind.

And so here they were, with a grown-up daughter and two successful but far from stellar careers between them, looking at another 30 plus years of life together. In her mind's eye, all those years ago, Mary would have become by now a kind of female version of Alan Taylor, appearing on Question Time, writing bestseller history books and fronting her own TV series. Meanwhile, Sam would have left the Civil Service and be running a think tank, or have become a key official at the UN or something. Meanwhile, of course, Daniel was a multi-millionaire, his family wealth bolstered and multiplied by a successful business career, and had now become a renowned altruist, canvassing government, even appearing on Question Time. When occasionally they met at parties, they acknowledged each other and chatted politely, if a little stiffly. Few knew, and fewer remembered, they had once been a couple, even Sam was ignorant of their previous connection.

Mary wondered why she was thinking about all this, remembering so much, and then she realised this was another turning point for her. Sam had been the lodestar on whom she had depended, but Mary was no longer sure that dependence was healthy. Especially since Ruth had gone to university, she had felt confined. She felt she ought to be able to start travelling to the international conferences, accepting the invitations to lecture she had denied herself since Ruth had been born. But she had continued to turn them down, constrained by what she saw as Sam's expectation. They had had the conversation maybe half a dozen times, and on every occasion Sam had been clear he wanted her to travel as much as she wanted to, that he would be absolutely fine. But Mary didn't believe him. Too often, she had seen him retreat into his inner shell, feeling isolated and deprived of support and friendship. Once that support was present, he was as strong and reliable as you could imagine, but she also knew she was the only person who could supply it consistently, and in a dark recess of her soul, had begun to resent it.

Chapter 4
Singapore, Wednesday 6th

"London…"

Jacques Rogge's words set loose a storm of noise, both in Singapore and London, while the Paris delegation and the crowd gathered back in the Parisian sunshine looked as though they wanted to shrink down to miniature size, where their identities became indistinguishable.

The IOC had delivered another upset, different in nature but equivalent in size to 1993, when Sydney had squeezed past Beijing. That had been a case of human rights concerns, post-Tiananmen Square, trumping financial and sponsorship considerations. The mechanics of that upset were opaque but the engine behind it was clear; in this case, both engine and mechanism were shrouded by the cloaked preferences and loyalties of the IOC membership.

Carol had been in the convention centre in 1993 but had chosen to watch this announcement in her hotel bar with two journalist friends. Doug was Australian and had been a marathon runner, the ascetic lifestyle of the long-distance runner translating with surprising ease into the peripatetic one of a sports journalist. He specialised in writing witty one-liners and consuming margaritas. Sergei was much more of a technical writer, schooled in the history of each event and prone to lengthy erudite comparisons between the athletes of different areas. Carol had begun covering the Olympics at Mexico City in 1968, but Sergei was the veteran, having started in Melbourne in 1956. Doug was the relative newcomer, selected to compete in Moscow 1980, but stymied by the US-led boycott over Afghanistan. Los Angeles, four years later, had been his debut.

The three had held a small wager on the outcomes, with Carol and Doug going for Paris and only Sergei choosing London. "I still don't see why you were so certain," said Doug, scratching his head.

"It was obvious from the 1st round of voting. The moment London showed it was genuinely in the running, the calculations of the vote altered completely."

"I still don't get it," said Doug. "Paris was miles ahead, even last night. Sure the gap had closed, but I still had the French winning outright on the 2nd or 3rd round, not losing in the 4th."

"But that is exactly it, my friend. After Round 1 it was clear, with the strength of London, as well as Madrid, which was expected, that there would be a 4th round. These contests are like diplomacy, like politics, like war, and their nature has never changed."

"Come on, Sergei," said Carol, "you're just being an old Cossack on us."

"No, not at all. It is not an accident that people still read Sun-Tsu, still read Clausewitz, still read Machiavelli. And not just scholars but generals and politicians. When and where to attack and defend, how and in which situations to make alliances, who to trust and why; these truths are as old as human kind, they affect all the ways in which we deal with each other and do business. And they do not change, these things. From the outside it seems clear that Paris forgot these great truths and that London acted on them."

"Okay, so why was London's 1st round vote so important?" asked Doug.

"Because it meant that London's votes were needed to win; needed by Madrid and, just as important, by Paris. Now, whether Paris made its mistake long ago by being too arrogant, or too preoccupied, to build good relationships with the other cities; or whether they chose, after that round, to go it alone does not matter; in either event, it was *folie*."

"And London and Madrid both realised they could win with the help of the other's votes."

"Of course. It is as Machiavelli says, the wise prince only makes alliances with those who pose no threat to him. This means he can trust them because, unless they are stupid, they will see there is no advantage in betraying him."

Veils were beginning to drop from Carol's eyes but Doug remained stubborn. "So why," he asked, "didn't Paris do a deal with Madrid or London?"

"For the same reasons, my friends. Paris had nothing to offer Madrid or London, who were both there to win. With the other cities, they were present not to win the 2012 Games but for other reasons – to set themselves up for a future bid, to gain prestige, or possibly to gain favour from the winner. I do not know if Paris had talked to these cities in advance. Either it did so and then chose not to go firm on its side of the bargain, or it did not talk to them at all. In either event, as I say, it was *folie*."

"But Madrid and London, because they were both in the game but trailing Paris, could not hurt each other. But their combined votes would be enough to win, so they did a deal where whoever went out in the 3rd round pledged their votes to the other."

"Of course, Carol, now you understand."

"But how do the votes transfer as a block?" Doug was still trying to be conventionally rational. "I mean, I understand how small groups might stick together, but we aren't talking about political parties here, are we? And it's a secret ballot, so no one knows for sure who voted for which city."

"Come on, Doug, this is the IOC. Everyone knows everything about everyone else. It's an enormous dysfunctional family; it's like the, I don't know…"

"It is like the Medici court, where Machiavelli lived and about which he wrote," interjected Sergei. "You should both read 'The Prince', or better still, 'The Discourses'. They are the key to understanding international sport and international politics also. But Carol," continued the Russian, "Doug is right in many respects. There are no political parties. There are, however, certain commonalities of interest that come together at moments like this. The most obvious, that everyone now understands, is about rotating continents. Satellite television has made this possible. There was no live satellite back to Europe or North America or Australia or Russia when the Olympics were in Tokyo. But four years later, in Mexico City, suddenly it was different. Carol, that was your first time – believe me, it was very different

48

before – and your brave Black athletes, Tommy Smith and John Carlos, sent a signal to the world.

"But I – how do you say? – digress. There are other commonalities of interest. As well as the continental groupings, there are the summer and winter sports, and then there is language and culture and history. For example, it would make sense for the English-speaking members to have natural affinity and to vote for London this time. This would include the IOC members who voted for New York. The US will have another city building for 2016, probably Chicago from what I hear. Similarly, there will be a South Americancity – probably Rio – also bidding, and much will depend on how the balance of economic power is changing by 2009."

"Okay, Sergei," said Carol, "I understand all that. Most of it I knew, but, as always, you have a knack, a skill, of adding to my knowledge. But, if we accept your analysis, it still leaves the question of how London got so may votes in the 1st round, having earlier been so far behind."

"Ah, my two friends, as usual you have quickly got to the heart of the question. This I do not know, and it must have been a feat of great skill because for a long time the London bid was very poor. But I can make some guesses. One is that Paris thought it had the bid won and began to be less responsive, less approachable, to the IOC voters; another is that it is often better to finish fastest than to start fastest – we all know that from watching sport; a third is that when London became professional, it became very good indeed – you see that from the serious people they have hired, and from things like their wonderful promotional video, with David Beckham and James Bond.

"Finally, though, you ask me why London got so many votes in the 1st round. My most important reason, which only really appeared to me this morning, is that London was the only bid to really understand, maybe even more than the IOC members understood, their great fear that the Olympic Games will prove to be a phenomenon of the 20th century and will have less importance in the 21st. You have seen the latest analysis of the age of people who watch the Olympics on television? It is getting much older! Football and computer games are the choice of the world's youth. Sydney was really the last Olympics of the 20th century, and Athens was a debt repaid to the home of the Ancient Games, although I suspect the debt will finally belong to Greece. Beijing will be Games of the 21st century, but for the corporations, not for the youth. London has said it will focus on youth, and the faces it put up this morning were a demonstration of that. The demographic of Paris is as young and multi-cultured as London, but you would not know that from the people it brought up on stage this morning. Craig Reedie gave the IOC confidence that the Games would be in safe hands, then Sebastian Coe gave the promise and commitment that London would be for the youth of the world. And we all, quite simply, believed them both. It was a truly wonderful combination."

"So is that cold-blooded commercial calculation about London's greater ability to access the younger audience, or is it a romantic surge for some ideal?" Doug was still left feeling there was somehow a gap.

"It is both, my friend," Sergei replied. "The beauty of the presentation was that it provided the rhetorical rationale for the cold-blooded commercial calculation, as you put it. Where would the French Revolution have been without Voltaire, Rousseau and Diderot to provide the justification for overthrowing the monarchy

49

and aristocracy?" Sergei was now in full flow. "These principles never change; today has proved it."

Carol and Doug glanced at each other. At different speeds, they had both travelled from incredulity at Sergei's certainty, through phases of growing understanding and respect, back to a slight exasperation at his sweeping statements. The pattern was not unfamiliar – Sergei was older, and Beijing would be his last Olympics. They knew each other well, but the two younger journalists still underestimated his difficultly in speaking English. This was the root of his overblown phrases, which in Sergei's own mind were as subtly nuanced as they would have been in his native Russian.

"A while back," said Carol, "you said these principles applied equally well to international politics. What did you mean?"

"The best examples, the most obvious, are those where politics and sport met during the Cold War. In 1956, there was no American boycott when the Soviet Union invaded Hungary. Neither was there one in 1968, when we invaded Czechoslovakia and there were Soviet tanks rolling into Prague on every television in America. Neither did we boycott the Olympics in Tokyo, Mexico City or Munich because of Vietnam. These wars and invasions were all much more significant, much greater offences than Afghanistan was in 1980 and yet there was a boycott, and there was even less excuse for a boycott in 1984. Why where there boycotts in these years and not in previous ones? It is because, in each case the country that led the boycott, the USA or the USSR, was feeling weak and insecure.

"In 1980, your President Carter was weak and was about to be defeated by the actor Reagan, the US diplomats in the Embassy in Tehran had been captured by the Iranians, and the two OPEC oil crises in the 1970s had exposed your Achilles heel. In 1984, it was the same. Of course, the West had interpreted our invasion of Afghanistan as an aggressive move, when in fact, it was a sign of our own weakness. Some of the 'old' Europeans, as you call them, understood that we had much more reason to have fear of the Islamic fundamentalism that Khomeini had let loose. By 1984, our economy was very bad, and the greater technology of American weapons would have overwhelmed us if the Cold War had ever become hot. Also, the days when we could subsidise Africa were over. Conclusion: boycotting the Olympic Games is not a weapon you use unless you feel it is your only weapon."

"So how does all that fit with your eternal principles?" asked Carol.

"It is the same as the idea that you only make alliances with those who cannot threaten you," replied Sergei. "From that it follows when you are weak, you make gestures to try and appear strong to those who you fear."

"So how do these principles apply to the Middle East?"

"Ah, the Middle East is both interesting and difficult, because everyone feels forced into bad alliances that then make it hard to find a solution."

"How do you mean?"

"Well, take the Americans, your country. Many of its alliances in the Middle East are disastrous. To start with Israel, this alliance does nothing but harm to the US. The Israelis are not reliable; this was obvious from the Suez crisis in 1956. That was when the Soviet Union stopped being Israel's ally, because we realised they could not be trusted. In truth, they trust no one but themselves, and who can blame them given their history. But in the end, it does them no good because it means no one trusts them, and so their only real friend is the US, and that is of little long term benefit to either of them.

"Why not?"

"Because everyone knows the US is Israel's ally, and yet has no control over its conduct. Because of this the US cannot be the peacemaker. To us, it makes no sense; you support Israel's economy, sell it weapons cheaply, and yet you have no influence. Why would the Arabs trust you if you cannot bring Israel's honesty to the table? And because Israel too knows this, there is no control on its behaviour, which means other countries both fear its military power and distrust its word."

"So who should the Americans make their alliances with?"

"Egypt, Jordan and Syria, of course," Sergei continued "You can see the Americans sense this because of how close you try to be to Cairo and Amman, and how you have always worked hard not to demonise Damascus in the way you are happy to do with Baghdad and Tehran."

"Why those three?" asked Doug.

"Because, again, like the voting today, these are allies who do not threaten each other but can offer benefits. In this case, the benefits are that they are major opinion leaders in the Arab world, that they have strategic control of Lebanon and the Suez Canal. They cannot hurt the Americans because they do not produce significant amounts of oil, but they can deliver peace to Israel because together they control Israel's border and so can police and avert the steady flow of weapons to Hamas. But instead, the US makes alliances with the countries that can damage its interest – Israel, by its unpredictability, and the oil producers around the Gulf. Both know they have the Americans over a barrel, so to speak." Sergei laughed at his own joke.

"But what's so bad about having alliances with the oil producers?" asked Carol. "After all, if we need oil, aren't they the people we should be talking to?"

"Talk to them by all means but don't be their allies. It tells them how weak you are, which gives them the freedom to ignore you, because you'll always come back no matter how much they offend you. By making them your allies you demonstrate how much you need them, and in return deny them any sense of how much they need you."

"So how should we deal with Saudi Arabia and Iran and Iraq?" asked Carol. "It's too easy to say we should do business with these countries without being their allies."

"I admit that is hard while your love affair with oil continues, but that is, after all, the great strategic weakness you refuse to acknowledge. Until you do, and then act to reduce your reliance, you will always be at risk to the great oil producers."

"So where did the Soviet Union fit in your complex Middle East jigsaw, and where does Russia sit now?" Carol was direct.

"Well, from the outside, it looked as though we played the game well with the cards we had, but, in the end, the US could offer Egypt much more without the risk to itself than we could. And so now we do business with Syria, and also with Iran. Iran can damage us in some ways less than they can damage you, because we too are now significant net producers of the black gold – that is one thing that has changed much since the USSR broke up – but of course, Iran can still damage us much in other ways."

"How come?" asked Doug.

"Because the fundamentalist Islam that triggered the Iranian Revolution and destroyed the Soviet Union now threatens to sweep across what we still see as our southern provinces. So you see, it is not only America that makes alliances from a position of weakness. The only difference is that we work hard to camouflage our weakness and in Chechnya we fight it, whereas the Americans still pretend their dependence on oil doesn't matter."

"You said something earlier," Carol remembered, "about the Soviet invasion of Afghanistan being a defensive move; is this what you meant, to defend your southern provinces, to act as a buffer against Islamic fundamentalism?"

"But of course, it was terrible! Afghanistan for us was a disaster, both military and economic, and psychologically. It is an incorrigible country as your Americans are beginning to discover. I do not know why the British are there still, they should know better. I do not know if it was a big mistake for the Soviets in 1979 but if not, then the evil we were avoiding must have been very great."

"Obviously, you lost, but why such a disaster?"

"In so many ways, my friend. Before Afghanistan, everyone was afraid of the Red Army – after all, we had defeated Hitler, and we ruled over the Warsaw Pact as the Hungarians and Czechs discovered; but, long before the end in Afghanistan, no one feared us, and the morale of our Red Army had died. Economically, also it showed our poverty. If we could not send our army to defeat Afghan guerrillas, what did it say about our ability to match the Americans in the Cold War, or to feed our people? It was our Vietnam, but it was on our doorstep and still we could do nothing about it. The only sweet irony, and it is a small one, is that the Afghan fighters the Americans funded and armed to fight us are now the Americans' terrorists and Taliban. And yes, Afghanistan for us was wholly defensive, perhaps desperate, and it signalled the end of the Soviet era. The wonder for us was that it took the West almost ten years to begin to understand this."

Sergei sat back, and Doug and Carol looked at each other before both turned towards their slightly pompous but never dull Russian friend. "So why," asked Carol, "do we never hear politicians or journalists or commentators talking about these things?"

"Some of them are too stupid to understand, or worse, they have not done the required reading; some think the people are too stupid to understand and that it would simply confuse them; and some, the clever ones, never like to fully reveal their own thinking, because it gives the enemy greater certainty over their future actions. And, I almost forgot, there is a fourth group that wishes the people to believe foreign policy is about executing some higher moral purpose."

Carol tried again, "But isn't foreign policy about trying to make the world safer, more prosperous?"

"Yes, but for who, Carol? Countries that try to operate beyond their own interests often do more harm than good. Look at Iraq and Afghanistan! The Americans and British have gone from liberators to occupiers in the time it took for them to decide they did not only want to overthrow Saddam and the Taliban but also to introduce Western democracy. What folly and arrogance! In each case, the first aim was clear and most people could agree about it. But the moment you begin to behave as an invading army, entitled to its spoils, as the Americans so quickly did in Iraq, then you have outstayed your welcome."

"So, when the Americans boycotted the Moscow Games back in 1980 and other countries like Australia followed them, that was a wasted gesture?"

"For me, my friend, it was, though even then I thought we might do the same – how do you say it, reciprocate – in 1984. I saw a good deal of the West, and I knew how much richer and more free your society was. Much of the Soviet criticism of your decadence was true, but it is never good when you have to build a wall to keep your people in. But the American boycott of Moscow was the only period when I believed it might be possible for us to win the Cold War. Although I feared our invasion of Afghanistan would have terrible consequences, these had not yet begun to transpire, and it was still possible to delude oneself that all would be well."

Sergei turned to Doug, "My friend," he said, "because of our own stupid boycott, we did not meet until after Los Angeles, but I have always worried about talking to you about 1980. It is a terrible thing when politicians use sport in such a way to hide their own weakness and cowardice. The purest athletes, those who value the competition above the winning, are always the ones who suffer the most, and so it was with you and your comrades."

Doug nodded, just perceptibly, "It was a terrible thing at the time all right. I remember arguing and being angry, and questioning all kinds of stuff. Don't know what I think about what you said, about it effectively being worse than a waste of time – the boycott – but then, that's what I always thought it was myself, though obviously for different reasons. I didn't really think much about politics back then, not that I do a lot now, but back then I was a young athlete who just ran and ran; that was all I cared about. I never believed I would go to the Olympics until I was selected, and then, only a few weeks later, just when I was starting to get used to the idea, we pulled out, and it was gone."

"It was the same for our athletes in 1984," said Sergei. "Of course, they weren't permitted to show their disappointment and anger as you were, but because I was close to some of them, I know how they felt. They were devastated, and it also meant the taking of illegal drugs went to new levels. I'm sure in Seoul, if Ben Johnson hadn't tested positive…"

"But that, my friend is for another time," said Carol, suddenly tired of talking to Sergei and wanting to stretch her legs. "I have a story to write and some parties to attend. A pleasure as always!" She got up and the others rose with her. She kissed them both on each cheek, then gave Sergei what had become the requisite bear hug. "My flight's tomorrow morning, so I doubt I'll see you but let's arrange to meet in Helsinki before the Worlds next month."

She wandered across to another hotel, where she knew she would find members of the respective bid teams. Carol felt slightly worn out by Sergei's various rants, no matter how perceptive they might or might not be. Her own world was more grey, and she thought direct links between sport and politics were only made to appear so strong by a certain laziness of thought. Despite this, Carol did think it was worth it to dig around for evidence of a pact between London and Madrid.

It wasn't hard to find people from the London bid, who were transparently shocked as well as delighted; only a few of them were at all disposed to try and rationalise what had contributed to their victory, but she found them good company with little sign of obvious triumphalism; she decided they were too relieved, having lived for so long on the edge of humiliation, let alone defeat.

She got into conversation with an earnest young woman, who worked for the bid. Her name was Angela. "We didn't really think it was going to happen until we got into the 4th Round, although there had been a growing sense that it was somehow possible since Craig and Seb spoke this morning. It's really just been a remarkable day." She smiled, "What's it been like covering it?"

"Fascinating, to be honest," replied Carol, "and engrossing. My name's Carol; sorry, I should have introduced myself earlier."

"That's okay, I'm glad you didn't really. So many journalists, and some athletes, are very keen to tell you their name but then just pause, expecting you to say how wonderful it is to meet them."

"And I take it you don't indulge them?"

"Not at all. There are some people you're genuinely impressed by but they're not the people who do that. So many of those out here – Denise Lewis, Steve Redgrave, even David Beckham – just weren't like that."

"Do you think that's one of the reasons the bid came together?"

"It's hard to say, isn't it, but I do think it's important that it's been quite an open process, where we've tried to bring in people who had the ability to contribute and then given them the space to do that. I don't know anything about the Paris bid, and it's obviously excellent, but from the outside it looks a bit more formal."

"Well, I'm certainly struck by the fact you're on first name terms with Sebastian Coe and Craig Reedie."

"It's not just me, everyone is. That's the way they are too. And after all, it's sport, isn't it? It's not about what you've done before, it's about what you can do now."

"If you don't mind, that sounds a bit clichéd."

"Yes, I know, I'm sorry – Carol, isn't it? It's so easy to fall into that trap; any phrase worth using quickly gets exploited these days, all the goodness squeezed out of them."

"No need to apologise; if I said sorry for every cliché I put in my articles, I'd not have time for anything else. But I think you're maybe right about the London bid being good at pulling in and using talent. That often doesn't make the difference between winning and losing though, does it? I mean everyone thought London's bid was technically at least as good, but a week ago that wasn't making any difference."

"Yes, I know, annoying, isn't it?" Angela's joy was unconfused and simple, and Carol was starting to find it infectious.

"So what do you think changed?" she persisted.

"Like I said, it's far too soon to be rational about it but it certainly felt like David Beckham and Tony Blair both gave it a big boost."

"I'd heard that. I only got in yesterday from London; what sort of boost was it?"

"Well, it's odd really. I'm not a fan of either of them but seeing the impact they both have on people who weren't British, well, it is just completely weird."

"What's Beckham like? I'm American, so I don't quite understand your obsession with soccer – sorry, football – but I get that he's a star."

"Let me see, where to start? Well, the first thing is he's a really good footballer – not like Pelé or Maradona, or Zidane, but really good – but the amazing thing about him is that he's become some kind of global symbol that crosses over differing sports, different cultures, even different sexuality."

"He sounds a bit like Michael Jordan was but not quite the same."

"I know what you mean, but Jordan was mostly to do with sport whereas with Beckham sport's just one piece in the jigsaw. It might be the biggest, but the way he looks and dresses, even his hair for God's sake, all have reams of articles written about them. And as for the photographs, he's all over the place, not just in Britain – just look at the paparazzi here in Singapore! And the crowds around him are just mind-blowing, but they don't seem to faze him at all."

"And what about Blair, your prime minister?"

"Well, in some ways, that's been even stranger. I kind of knew about Beckham before – like I said, you only have to read the papers to get some kind of idea of how popular he is out here. But Blair's been a real shock. I mean, Labour just won the election, but Blair's on his way out; he only really won the election because Brown, who's the Chancellor and his rival – they used to be friends, but now they hate each other – got involved in the campaign, and he's been really unpopular since the Iraq War; he's been like George Bush's poodle for the last five years, since 9/11. So when we heard he was likely to come out to Singapore, I was really depressed about it because we've always been worried about losing votes because of Iraq; but instead, it seems to have worked brilliantly for us. Blair's somehow suddenly become an international statesman, leading the way on world poverty and climate change. So suddenly, his coming out here, in the middle of final preparation for the Gleneagles Summit, made the London bid seem really important; and then to see him work the room at one of these receptions, and to see the faces of IOC members as they enter and leave their bilateral meetings with them; let's just say it's obvious that he's really good at this stuff."

"Do you think he's been more effective than Chirac?" Carol tried to probe.

"Pass, but Chirac would have needed to be brilliant to be as good, and I don't think he was here long enough for that."

Angela casually sidestepped the journalistic bait while still managing to make the point. Carol was impressed; by this stage most people would either have loosened up and let out some revealing fact or opinion, or their conversation would have shrivelled up into boring platitudes.

"What is it you do for London?"

"Just admin really, making sure the wheels turn when they're meant to. I've only been involved in the last six months; my contract runs out on Saturday."

"What will you do then?"

"I don't know really. There's a chance to apply for a job with LOCOG, sounds great, doesn't it? But there's seven years to go till the Games, so it would be a big decision to commit for that long. I'll be 31 in 2012," she mused, talking half to herself.

Carol tried to remember what it was like being 24. She had a quick vision of herself back in 1972 – making a late deadline, going for a beer with Phil down on the Lower East Side; grabbing some Chinese food and watching her friend, inevitably, chatting up a beautiful blonde and disappearing off into the night while she went home; packing her life, with only sleep seeming to suffer. She laughed inwardly at the absurdity of trying to live like that now, before deciding it would be boring if she still lived that lifestyle.

Since saying goodbye to Sergei, Carol had been feeling unusually wistful for her youth, and for a time when she would have dismissed the Russian's cynical explanation of events. A big part of her wanted to believe London had won because the majority of IOC members had decided it was the city that would host the best Olympics. However, her own experience now told her there was likely to be a fair amount of truth in Sergei's theory, and nothing Angela had said contradicted it. If anything, what she had told her tended to support the idea that London had found enough impetus in the last week to become a contender but not enough to break through and win. For that, some extra ingredient was needed. She decided to try and find some Spaniards.

"It's been great meeting you," Carol said, focusing again on Angela, who was still smiling. "There aren't many sports' administrators I talk to who are as thoughtful and lucid as you are, particularly at the start of what looks like being a long, old party."

"Thank you, that's the most praise I've had in the last six months."

"If that's so, then maybe the London bid isn't quite as good as I was starting to think. But I'm serious, if you decide to stay in sports' administration, you should go a long way."

"Well, thank you again," said Angela, "and I hope we meet up again sometime." Slightly impetuously, she leaned forward and pecked the middle-aged journalist on both cheeks.

"Me too," Carol said warmly and turned away. She headed for the hotel where the Madrid bid team was staying. They too were having a party, though the mood was inevitably more sombre. After about ten minutes, Carol got chatting to a young Spaniard called Jaime who, like Angela, turned out to be a relatively junior member of the bid operation. He was disappointed but sanguine.

"Maybe it was just too soon after Barcelona," he mused. "Only the US has held the Games less than 20 years apart, with Los Angeles and Atlanta, and that was a mistake, yes? So it was always hard for us."

"I know what you mean," said Carol, "though in retrospect, it's hard to criticise the IOC for not giving the Games to Athens on the centenary."

"Did you not like the Athens Games?"

"Yes, I did, actually, though many of my journalist colleagues were not complimentary. What I meant was that Greece found the timetable for delivering the Olympics very tight."

"And what did you think of Atlanta?"

"I agree it was a disappointment but it was far from as bad as, again, many of my colleagues have argued. The Olympics must provide a story and some defining judgement is always made."

"Why do you think they thought Atlanta was so poor then?" Oddly, Carol felt as though she was the one being probed.

"The combination of pro-Athens sentiment and the easy identification of Atlanta with corporate America, most obviously with its being the HQ of Coca Cola, meant that it started behind; then it got all the media pissed when the media centre systems crashed on Day 1 and served up more than the normal quota of Olympic mistakes – bus drivers who got lost etc."

"You seem to be saying that managing the media is part of shaping the legacy of the Olympic Games; is that also true of the bid? This is important to me as I am looking for ways in which we in Spain can do this contest better for the future."

"Well, the media matters now much more than it did when I started out. Partly everything builds up so much quicker – stories used to take way longer to develop before rolling news channels and the internet. So if you don't have a good communication strategy, with good people and the ability to react quickly when negative stories crop up, then you're really kind of handicapping yourself."

"When do you think it began to change for the Olympic movement? Was it Munich?"

Carol thought for a moment. "No, I think it started with Mexico City in '68."

"How do you mean?"

"Oh, it would take too long to go into now and I'm already starting to sound like an old woman."

"No, please!" Then Jaime smiled, "Trust me, señora, I promise to tell you immediately if you sound boring."

"All right, but you did ask for it," Carol filled her glass and clinked it with her new young Spanish friend; what was it about this generation of bid teams? Why had it suddenly become cool?

"Well, a lot of what happened in 1968 and a good deal of the way news and sport, and media generally, has worked since goes back to the invention of satellite television. It's why most of us remember Mexico. It's the first TV Olympics, the first to be seen around the world live."

Jaime nodded, "You don't just mean Bob Beaman and Dick Fosbury, do you? You mean Tommy Smith and John…"

"Carlos," Carol completed. "Good. It's a relief to me to know these names mean something to younger generations."

"Of course."

"And the reason you know about it is because of satellite. It took their salute on the podium into households around the world."

"But they got stripped of their medals and sent home, didn't they?"

"Yes," Carol shook her head. "I blame myself – though I was young then, I should still have done much more – and my journalist colleagues; we should all have made much more of it. No one really confronted Brundage – the means didn't really exist back then."

"Was he the IOC president?"

"Yes, he was, and I pretty much disagreed with everything he did and said."

"Did you write about it?"

"Yes, when I thought I could, but the world was different then."

"How do you mean?"

"Well, it was also harder to attack establishment figures then. And Brundage was definitely that."

"Would it be different today?"

"Yes, I think the Salt Lake City scandal showed that; although, thanks to maverick journalists like Andrew Jennings, that story more or less fell into our collective laps."

"So do you believe it is a good thing, this obsessive media focus on the Olympic Games and the bidding process?"

"Yes, I do, because otherwise, without the media, there would be almost no pressure for bids and the process around them to be transparent or accountable. I'd admit we don't always exert that pressure for the right reasons, but the pressure itself is a good thing. Without it, the whole thing would be much more opaque and potentially corrupt."

"But you just said that the Salt Lake story fell into the hands of the media."

"That is true," said Carol.

"So what then, senora," challenged Jaime, "does the media truly add to the Olympics if the biggest story after the last 50 years as you put it fell into the media's arms?"

"A whole lot!" Carol suddenly felt affronted and for no clearly rational reason reacted to the challenge. She immediately caught herself and switched back into her usual demeanour. "What I mean," she continued, pouring another glass for them both to cover the slip, "is that it's been a gradual opening up. The IOC remains a secretive organisation but a whole lot less than it was."

"And what then did you think of President Samaranch? Many of your Anglo-American colleagues are very critical of him."

"I was never a fan of President Samaranch," Carol admitted, "but I do think he saved the Olympic Games, both politically and financially, and that he is not given sufficient enough credit for doing so."

"Why then are you not a fan?" asked Jaime.

"Several reasons, one of which," Carol laughed, "is that he never gave me an interesting interview. But also, I think he let the drug problem develop for too long, and he was partly responsible for the culture that led to Salt Lake."

"Those are reasonable points," said Jaime. "I respect you for making them, the bad as well as good." And the Spaniard shook Carol's hand, then turned away.

Walking back to her hotel, Carol reflected that she was really none the wiser about how London had won, but also realised nothing she had heard was inconsistent with Sergei's theory. That was the trouble with conspiracy theories, they were so damned hard to disprove. Both Angela and Jaime had been bright and intelligent, but they were both quite junior and so she was probably imagining that they could have told him anything meaningful in the first place.

Her mind wandered back to when she had been 24, Angela's age, and she started calculating how many hours till her flight in the morning. And with that she stopped, shook her head at the ridiculousness of it and, turning around, began walking back towards the hotel where the London bid were having their party.

Chapter 5
Wednesday 6th

Ed had flown into London on Monday, still pissed off he hadn't been able to catch Ruth in London – there had been just too many loose ends to tie up. Today he had wandered down to Trafalgar Square for the Olympic announcement out of sheer curiosity. It was a shimmering hot July day, the sort that happens quite often in London but was rarely predictable. However, this was one of those spells where day after day, the weather surprised by remaining the same. Ed had never been anywhere near anything to do with the Olympics before, except on television, and even then they had only periodically made a real impression, usually for the wrong reasons – terrorist attack, boycotts, drug scandals. But Trafalgar Square was less than ten minutes' walk from his hotel and the prospect, with a live feed from the IOC in Singapore, seemed too good to miss.

He had lain in and enjoyed a leisurely breakfast at a Covent Garden café, where he took renewed pleasure in watching people stroll past and imagining the back story and their relationship to those around them. Then his mind meandered, savouring his coffee and croissant in the sunshine, feeling his muscles and nerves relax as they always did the first couple of days back in Britain. Finally, looking at his watch, he had paid and strolled along past St Martin's and down into Trafalgar Square. He had called Sam to see if he was free for lunch later and left a message – "Hi, it's Ed, just wandering down to Trafalgar Square to watch the Olympic stuff from Singapore. Bound to be miserable when we lose but who knows, and it'll be professionally interesting whatever. Anyway, wondered if you were around for lunch? Could probably get over to your office about 1.30, so would be a late one. Give me a call."

As he emerged into the Square, Ed was surprised by how big the crowd was. He had expected 4–500 at most but there seemed to be about three or four times that. He was struck by how beautiful it all was, with the National Gallery as a backdrop, itself framed against a cloudless sky. Ed recalled coming here as a child with his parents on a day trip. It must have been winter and he had been too hot, wrapped up for Derby weather, in duffel coat and scarf, feeling like he was about to suffocate on a totally unfamiliar and quite scary Underground journey. He'd bought some bread to feed the birds and had marvelled at the height of Nelson's Column, far taller and more evocative of travel and the idea of a wider world than anything he had seen before. The lions guarding it seemed equally massive but less daunting, more amenable to conquest by clambering children.

Now, more than 40 years on, Ed found himself trying to superimpose his adult self on the child he had been. He felt again the shivers of excitement as he raced around, alternately feeding the birds and chasing them. He stood, taking in the oddly idiosyncratic and expectant scene in front of him, and considered whether the eight-year-old would recognise himself now. But, nervous of indulging in too much self-analysis – an act his student self would have judged close to criminal – he sought to concentrate instead on how Steve Cram and Kelly Holmes would deal with the inevitable disappointment and the deflated expectations of the crowd. Frankly, he had no idea and assumed it would be a muddled mess.

His phone rang, Sam calling back. "Hi," he said, "did you get my message?"

"Yes," said Sam, "I think I can probably make it if you get here by 1.30. I've got a 2.30 but I can tell them I'll be a little late."

"Deal."

"What are you doing in Trafalgar Square anyway? I didn't know you had any interest in Olympic stuff, and besides, we're going to lose anyway."

"Call it professional curiosity. I'm very unlikely ever to get so close to an Olympic bid city ever again – Cairo's probably my best bet! – and it seems a good idea to take a look and see what happens when you lose."

"What's it like there now?"

"Busier than I thought, and of course it's a gorgeous day, almost too hot, something I rarely say in Britain."

"That's global warming for you. What have you been up to this morning?" Sam asked.

"Not much, got up late, hung around Covent Garden for a bit, had breakfast, and wandered down here."

"That hardworking journalist lifestyle."

"You bet!"

"Well listen, see you later, but make sure you're on time."

"No worries, I'll be there. The announcement's due 12.30, so shouldn't be a problem."

Ed put his phone away and looked up towards the stage and the screens beaming in pictures from Singapore. It still seemed amazing to him that this was happening in real time. They had just finished the second round of voting, and London was still in, alongside Paris and Madrid. Much more remarkably, it was doing well and if you didn't know, you would think it still had a decent chance of winning.

Ed had heard part of the speech Coe had given to the IOC while he had been showering and getting dressed earlier and had been surprised how good he'd been, both measured and passionate, deliberate and inspirational. Almost all public speakers, no matter how experienced, ended up coming down one side or the other of this rhetorical seesaw, while those who tried to play it both ways inevitably sounded mawkish and false. On this occasion, however, Coe had somehow managed to pull off the balancing act. Days, weeks of practice must have gone into it.

Almost better, however, had been Craig Reedie, whom Ed had never heard of. He had spoken ahead of Coe, a British IOC member who had previously run the BOA. He spoke with a Glasgow burr and wore his expertise lightly, speaking effortlessly in diplomatic code and, Ed suspected, doing much to reassure the voters in this strange election that London represented safe hands. The nature of this opaque world of international sport was intriguing, not least due to the contrived but still heightened sense of theatre around the vote itself. Having read the papers at breakfast, and now listening to the BBC feed, he was starting to understand the different, overlapping blocks of potential votes. Navigating your way through this world would be hazardous.

And now the third, penultimate round of voting was complete. As the result was announced, the crowd gasped, then cheered wildly. Madrid was out and London was through to the final vote against Paris, remarkably ahead by 39 to 33, with Madrid edged out on 31, apparently having gained the bulk of New York's 16 votes.

And then there was the glamour of the occasion. Ed had been surprised Blair had taken two days out of his schedule in the week of hosting the G8 to fly to Singapore and, despite the deep and lingering resentment over Iraq, there was undoubted impact from his visit. Even more surprising had been the dismay that greeted Chirac's late show. This status that was so clearly attached to the IOC, both by itself and others, seemed somehow obscene to Ed. He wasn't against sport or the Olympics but the palpable sense of entitlement jarred uncomfortably with the essentially trivial nature of what was at stake, which amounted to no more than a struggle for the right to host an incredibly expensive party. Ed couldn't get much beyond vanity and hubris as the main motivation. Despite his disgust, however, he was finding it impossible not to be caught up in the drama and, oddly, the excitement of what was unfolding some 6,000 miles away.

Ed remembered the time and looked at his watch. It was gone 12.45 and he knew he wasn't leaving until Jacques Rogge announced the winner. He rang Sam, who answered immediately. "It's okay, mate," he said, "I'm watching too; so is everyone who's still in the office, and all the rest are probably watching in the pub."

"Hi," interrupted Ed, "I was just going to say I don't think I'm going to be able to tear myself away."

"I guessed as much, but listen, it doesn't matter 'cos my 2.30's been cancelled, not unconnected I suspect, so to be honest I'm pretty clear the whole afternoon. You're flying out tomorrow, aren't you?"

"Yes, bright and early, I've even got a taxi picking me up."

"I thought so; listen, I've just booked the afternoon off. It's a beautiful day, and I don't get to see you nearly enough, so let's just find somewhere to sit and shoot the breeze, whether we win the Olympics or not. We won't run short of stuff to talk about."

"That's a great idea," replied Ed, "are you sure you've got the time?"

"Absolutely, just turn up when you're able to get over here, and we can take it from there. Hey, it looks like Rogge's coming back on stage; this might be it. Listen, call me again when you're on your way."

Ed put his phone away and looked up again. Rogge was fumbling slightly with his papers. Then he spoke. "And the winner is," he paused briefly, "London."

The Square seemed to become momentarily silent, as though not recognising what it had heard. Then it erupted in ecstatic chaos. Holmes and Cram were bouncing up and down like school kids, and the noise levels had become deafening. Over in Singapore, with the satellite delay, the London delegation seemed to be responding to what was happening back home. Denise Lewis and Matthew Pinsent, and Redgrave and Beckham all seemed likewise transported back to their own childhoods, to the days before they had learned how to conduct themselves in public. Standing to the back and slightly outside the main body of the crowd, Ed still found himself losing his natural detachment and became conscious he too was bouncing up and down inanely. The journalist in him could anticipate some of what lay ahead but for now he found himself being hugged by total strangers, and hugging and kissing them back.

When he eventually got away, some 20 minutes later, the Trafalgar Square party was still in full swing, and as he walked down Whitehall, his own sense of euphoria was still high, as it was in those he passed. The pubs had filled up, and it was obvious only limited work would be done that afternoon. The sky was cloudless and, for that moment, there wasn't much that seemed wrong with the world. Past Downing Street he walked and then right at Parliament Square, turning away from Big Ben and past Westminster Abbey. Passing Palmerston and Canning's statues, he wondered what the gunboat diplomats who had defined the British Empire's foreign policy would have made of global institutions like the UN and the IOC. Nothing if not pragmatists, Ed suspected Canning and the others would have adapted. However, they might have struggled more with the reality that so few of the solutions to Britain's problems lay within its own gift, and he was convinced they would have blanched at our submissive relationship with Washington.

Once in Victoria Street, Ed rang Sam, and by the time he reached his office, his friend was waiting outside. "That was quick!"

"The place is like a morgue up there," said Sam. "Pretty much everyone's cleared out for the afternoon. There's a couple of people covering the phones but aside from that everyone's just booked off-the-cuff leave, or in some cases simply not come back from lunch."

"I'm impressed, I didn't know the Civil Service was capable of such spontaneity."

"Even we have our moments. Come, there's a pub I know just round the back of the cathedral. It's a bit off the beaten track but it does good beer and we should get a seat with a bit of luck."

By the time they got there, however, even this back street pub was full and they had to stand outside, no great hardship.

"It really is one of the great joys of coming home," agreed Ed, "not having to drink lager the whole time."

"What about the wine?" Sam asked, "I thought Lebanese wine was meant to be excellent."

"Oh it is, but it's not cheap. Israeli wine's okay too, a benefit of its occupying the Golan Heights for the last 40 years. But after that it goes downhill fast; Jordanian wine's sort of okay but Egyptian wine is terrible, at least the stuff I've had is. By the way, thanks for taking the afternoon off to see me, I really appreciate it. Cos I know I'm not around that much, so it's really quite special when my oldest friend puts himself out to spend time."

"Now don't go and get sentimental on me," cautioned Sam, "much more of this and I'm out of here. It doesn't become you."

"All right, I'll revert to hard-bitten, cynical mode. But it's not easy when less than an hour ago I was cavorting around Trafalgar Square with a bunch of total strangers. I mean, what was that all about? How the hell did we win and why does it seem to matter so much?"

"It's weird, isn't it?" agreed Sam, "I guess it's partly the sheer fact of having won from nowhere that helps create the feel-good thing. I mean, we haven't had any time yet to become cynical. I'm sure the cynicism will arrive soon enough, but for the moment it's kind of a surprise and some sort of obscure joy that we're just not used to."

"I always used to think of Britain as an old, quite wizened country; you know, normal stuff, post Imperial, looking for our role in the world, quietly decaying. But then, having worked for so long in the Middle East, a lot of our problems seem very modern. That doesn't at all invalidate the first judgement by the way, it just means we're a bit schizophrenic."

"And the point is?" asked Sam.

"Well, it's not a big deal, but today in Trafalgar Square it felt like Britain was a young country, perhaps the first time in my life I've felt that. It was strange but, despite being next to Nelson's Column, I was somehow in a 21st century city."

"What do you think caused it?"

"Maybe it was seeing the London people in Singapore – young, dressed in tracksuits, multi-ethnic. I'm sure they'll have thought hard about it all, but Paris looked nothing like that."

"But the IOC must have seen all this before?"

"Oh yes, I'm sure they do, but equally, it must give them a degree of assurance that a bid is being run professionally and that it has a good idea of the sorts of boxes it will have to tick to execute the Games successfully."

"That's more like you!" Sam sounded relieved. "For a moment, I thought you were saying everyone fell for all that rubbish about legacy and the youth of the world."

"It's strange for you to be more cynical than me, usually I win that one by a street."

"Yes, maybe," said Sam, sounding for a moment as though he was drifting off. "It's been a strange week, with Ruth going off and then with all the Live 8 and G8 stuff going on. I guess I'm running a bit low on goodwill."

"Of course," apologised Ed, "For a moment I'd forgotten Ruth was heading off again. How's it been?"

"Odd really, I'm not sure it's really kicked in yet. The house feels a bit emptier, I guess…"

"It must be very strange. I'm sure Mary and you will cope admirably, but I can see how it would be disconcerting. You're quite close to my god-daughter, aren't you?"

"I guess so, though I've always been wary of these father-daughter things. But I have been thinking about it a bit over the last month or so, and particularly since Saturday."

"And?"

"Well, I reckon I've been an okay parent on the whole, and I also think I'm maybe a little more similar to Ruth in terms of character than Mary is; she's much more straight down the line, literal even, than either of us. But then on the other side, there were huge swathes of Ruth's growing up where I was completely irrelevant."

Ed laughed, "I'd forgotten how depressingly rational you are about this sort of thing. It's only you and Ruth we're talking about here, not some Greek tragedy."

"Okay, you got me," said Sam, relaxing again. "But you know what I mean."

"You are uptight about something," said Ed. "I don't know what it is; you seem pretty relaxed but then suddenly you say something that makes it sound like you're quite wound up."

"Who knows?" Sam replied, "It might not really feel like it but I'm okay, honest!"

"How's Mary about Ruth going back up to Manchester?" asked Ed.

"Oh, she's fine… Already she's planning our next extension or whatever. She misses her though. Mary used to talk and argue with Ruth more in a day than I would in a week, so already I'm having to work some to fill the gap."

"That must be easy for you!"

"Thanks for the support," smiled Sam, pretending to be grim, "I'm getting better at thinking of stuff to say but trying to fit it in when Mary's already talking at full throttle is easier said than done. I suspect she's over-compensating herself, but it's only been four days, so it's hardly surprising."

"Do you think you'll end up going out more now that you both have more time on your hands?"

"Hard to say, but probably."

"You don't sound too sure?"

"Sorry," Sam corrected himself, slightly distractedly, "I'm sure we will, but Mary and I have never exactly lived in each other's pockets, and we haven't wanted to."

"But won't the two of you just find a way to, I don't know, recalibrate your lives?"

"You're right and I'm sure we will. All I'm saying is that it's only been a few days, far too soon to tell, and consequently, I'm still a little worried about it."

Ed decided to let it lie. But he did wonder about Sam and Mary's relationship, and how much of his own worry Sam had shared. He wanted to ask but consciously bottled it. He did not see Sam often enough to be confident about how to pitch such a question.

"How are Michelle and Philip?" he asked

"Pretty good, I think," Sam replied, "Hard to think we've known each other for about 20 years and yet there are still times when I feel I scarcely know him at all."

"I think it's to do with what stage in your life you're at when you meet people. If you think about the two of us and all the stuff we know about each other, a hell of a lot of it goes back to university. But when you met Philip, it was a couple of years after you and Mary had got married and just after Ruth was born. So it's hardly a surprise that you know him less well, or at least feel you do."

"I get all that," said Sam, "but it's still been 20 years. And there are plenty of friends from university I've lost touch with completely." He paused, "But yes, they're both fine and still happy as far as I can tell."

"I assume Michelle's still being a lady of leisure?"

"Pretty much, though leisure's not really the right word for it. She does it all very quietly, but a lot of the time it seems like she's almost back in full-time education. She properly studies stuff, mostly around art, taking classes and so on."

"Is there much purpose to it at all?" Ed asked.

"When you ask her about it, she denies there's any purpose, but I'm not sure. It's typical Michelle."

"What do you think it is?"

"Haven't a clue," admitted Sam, "but I find it hard to believe Michelle's spending all that time and energy on a whim, or for the pure joy of knowledge. I'm only guessing but I wouldn't be surprised if she didn't start to do a bit of buying and selling."

"Are you sure," asked Ed, "I'm not sure I can see Michelle wheeling and dealing in the art world but you know her a lot better than me. You know, I still can't remember meeting Michelle at your wedding, even though she swears blind that she introduced herself."

"Well, she looks very different from she did back then; her hair's longer and more 'expensive', same with her clothes, so in a way I'm not that surprised."

"You make it sound like she's completely reinvented herself."

"Well, in a way she has, but a great deal of it is that she simply has more money. I'm pretty sure Philip earns some multiple of what you or I do."

"Remind me again, why did she go straight into nursing at 18 rather than to university?" asked Ed. "Did she screw up her A Levels or something?"

"Not at all," laughed Sam, "she got really good grades but just decided to get a job instead."

"Was it a vocational thing?"

"Not really, or at least not mainly, but I think the major reason was a simple class one. We were working-class kids from the East Midlands, same as you, and whereas my parents, yours too I suppose, supported and encouraged us to go to university, Michelle's didn't really. And there was also quite a big thing about earning cash straight from school."

"I remember what it was like but it seems like quite a big call 30 years on."

"Well yes," replied Sam, "but there's a lot of people we went to school with who would have walked into a university today. We didn't see ourselves as a knowledge economy in the early 70s, and the security of a salary was a big deal to most of the families I knew."

"Sorry," said Ed, "I didn't mean it was a wrong decision at the time, only that it's shaped the course of her life since."

"Maybe," replied Sam, "but I think I envy Michelle's life more than she does mine."

"What do you mean?"

"Well, if I think about it, all Michelle's years in nursing – what was it, a decade? – All those years she was doing something directly worthwhile, the sort of thing we wanted to do, but we ended up frustrated by the sheer impossibility of knowing whether anything we've done has had any positive impact. Michelle doesn't have any of that doubt, and I don't think she regrets a moment of that time. And then of course, along comes Philip to whisk her away to a life of ease and luxury, where she can develop in an entirely different way with virtually no restrictions."

"Your round?" Ed suggested, "I need a couple of minutes to digest the profound meaning of all that."

When Sam returned, Ed was looking concerned, "So why all this melancholy, my friend? There was me thinking you had the most sorted life of anyone I know, and I'm not going to detail its finer points unless you force me. And yet here you are making all these unfavourable comparisons, and even drawing my own unblemished existence into the equation." He spoke with a deliberate lightness. "Don't get me wrong, I bow to no one in my unalloyed adoration of Saint Michelle, though I doubt her own narrative would be quite such hagiography, but you're right that her inspiring tale does lend itself well to such treatment. And indeed your approach, through its beguiling humility and self-denigration, does add to your own, already burnished, lustre."

"Oh come on, Ed! You're sounding like some smartarse English undergraduate."

"Well, you've always brought out the juvenile in me; it's one of my most endearing qualities. But seriously, my guess would be that Michelle wouldn't recognise your analysis of her. As for me, it's exactly those frustrations and minor humiliations that I value most. They're the unpredictable things that make my life uniquely mine."

"But it's just that unpredictability I'm still looking for," Sam smiled, but only in a small way. "I've tried and tried to inject some of it into my life, but it's stubbornly refused to reveal itself, and my life and career seem set to continue on the same, narrow, preordained lines they began on nearly 30 years ago. I've got a decent job, lovely wife, beautiful daughter, great friends, coupled of course with a good deal of prosperity and financial security. You could have written a script for my life back in 1978, and I've barely deviated from its plumb-line straight path."

"Whew!" exclaimed Ed, "You don't half know how to make someone feel good."

"Sorry, rant over," apologised Sam, speaking in what he thought was a cheerful tone. "I was just playing around. When's your plane tomorrow?"

"Early, remember."

"You could still come round tonight if you're free. We don't have anything on, either of us, and it'd be great to rustle something up for the three of us, just like in that old social life we once had."

"Thanks, but I've got some things I need to do back at the hotel. Normally, I'd love to but it doesn't quite work this evening."

"No problem, that's fine." He looked at his watch. "I don't have to get back for a while though. I rang Mary before I came out, and she's not expecting me home until after I ring her. Do you want to stay here or go somewhere else?"

"How about one more here while we think about it?"

Chapter 6
Thursday 7th

He couldn't see her face. The lines were blurred, contorted by the multitude of memories and expressions. He saw her now emotionally rather than visually. The layers of shared time could no longer be peeled back, and there was no photographic version of her remaining. He tried hard again to focus the image, but the harder he tried, the less precise became the picture.

Giving up, he opened his eyes, looked at the clock – it was 5.12am – gave a deep sigh, pulled back the duvet and went down to put the kettle on. Sam reached for his briefcase and began work. Just before 7am, he went into the bathroom to shave and put on the radio. The news was full of London having won the Olympics and the impact made by Blair's flying visit, taking time out just before Gleneagles, particularly in contrast to Chirac's clumsy off-hand comments about Finnish cooking and the like.

If nothing else, the bid's success was a supreme triumph of British marketing – for perhaps the first time, London had portrayed itself as a confident 21st century city, no longer reliant on heritage for its identity. Thinking back to the atmosphere yesterday, even to Ed's surprising enthusiasm, he thought this could end up as the Games' biggest legacy.

Mary was awake now but still curled up, blinking at the sunshine streaming through the small gap between the curtains. "When did you get up?" she asked.

"Just after five. It didn't seem worth it trying to go back to sleep – and you know I had those policy papers to read for this afternoon. The news is all about 2012, who'd have thought it?"

"It's that Beckham/Blair thing. The rest of the world still falls for them every time. They'll find out soon enough when nothing's ready."

Mary was an instinctive sceptic about politics and politicians in general. Sam thought this was in part because he worked in the Civil Service, intended as a subtle corrective to any tendency he might have had to parade his political connections a little too proudly. He had long accepted this implicit warning. He knew too many colleagues who were too free with their political name-dropping, people who had once been intelligently eclectic in their conversation but had become monotonously boring.

He was now half-dressed, and Mary had got to the point where she was sitting on the side of the bed with her head in her hands. "Why did I ever marry an office worker?" she mock-moaned. "Part of the whole point of staying in universities was to avoid all this early morning crap." Sam slipped a second arm into his shirt, walked round the bed, bent down and kissed the top of her head. She looked up, smiling this time. She showered quickly, so that by the time he had checked that all the right things were in each pocket of his jacket, she had gone downstairs to re-boil the kettle.

They chatted lightly over breakfast, about the Olympic success, Ed's flying visit and Mary's day. She was seeing her prospective editor about a book she was writing on the intellectual and cultural foundations underpinning the revolutions of 1848. They were due to meet for lunch at a little Italian restaurant near the Post Office Tower. Mary had never been there, but Sam had eaten there a couple of years before for a work do, someone's birthday. He remembered the food as being good, and that the people who owned it were from right down in the heel of Italy and so the walls were covered with posters of some quite obscure Serie A football team, Lecce, he thought.

Sam went up to clean his teeth and put on his shoes while Mary tidied away the breakfast things and put the kettle on again. She could hear Sam skipping down the stairs. He came back into the kitchen for a final kiss. "What time are you home tonight?" she asked.

"Hopefully, about 7.30," he replied. "I've got a couple of things to finish up before tomorrow, and I said I'd try and go for a swift drink with Rachel."

"You'll probably be home before me. I can't see myself getting away before about then. I won't bother buying anything for tonight. There's the smoked salmon we got at the weekend, or we can get a takeaway."

"Fine, let's see how tired we are."

It was a beautiful and clean early summer's morning, devoid of that clinginess that sometimes hits big cities in July and August. School terms were still on but the school run hadn't yet started and the urban air was still unclogged. There was already a slight shimmer as he looked along the street, and it was clearly going to be another scorcher. He'd put his jacket on to make it easier to fill his pockets. But he took it off as he walked out of the door and the heat hit him, swinging it over his shoulder.

The newsagent's, Khan's, was about five minutes' walk. Because of the heat, the door was already propped open, and Sam nipped in and picked up the Financial Times as usual, gave the right money and smiled at Mrs Khan.

The Underground was up the spout, so he decided to jump out at Maida Vale. He was near the front of the crowd exiting the station and headed down towards the Euston Road. When he got there, a bus had just stopped and the queue, bolstered and swollen by a large group of ex-Underground passengers, was bustling to get on. Up ahead though, he could see another bus, a No30, stuck at the next set of lights, far enough back that he thought it would take two changes for it to get through. Ideally, it would get him to King's Cross but in any event, it would take him further into town. He began to jog towards it, conscious of his quietly aching toe, without much expectation because there was a junction in between that he would have to cross to give himself any chance, and the lights at this first junction were against him even as those further on were in his favour, still holding up the bus.

Then both sets of lights changed. The cars ahead of the bus began to roll forward and the green man light came on ahead of him. He wasn't ready. He should have run to those lights and got there before they changed. That would have given him a real chance. By jogging the first bit, however, he now had only a slim chance of making it. This flashed through his mind as he began to run and then to sprint. He was about 20m away when the green man began to flash. There were still people on the crossing, so the cars had not yet started to move but the engines had begun to rev. Only 5m to go but now the cars on his side of the road moved forward. There were still people on the crossing but they were all now on the far side of the road and the drivers were taking advantage.

As he pulled up, he noticed that the bus was now at the lights ahead. It would get through as soon as the lights changed again. Although it was only just after 9am, his sprint had left his shirt dripping. He undid his top button and stood for a moment, feeling awkward, while he thought about what to do. His diary was clear until 10.30 and his chances of getting into work quickly were small to non-existent. The bus queues were huge and the taxis full. The lights changed again, allowing him to cross the road. He wandered on another 20m, still thinking, and then noticed a café. He walked in and ordered tea and toast. He rang work and left a message explaining the situation and that he would be in by about 10.15. If there was any further problem, he would ring again.

Sam gave himself a rueful smile, sat down just inside and took out the paper. A stroll into work would do him the world of good. He reckoned it would take him just under an hour, which meant he had 30 minutes here to relax. Maybe the transport would have eased up by then. While he didn't fancy getting back on the Tube this morning, the buses might be okay. In any event, the walk would be good.

The café radio was talking about a power surge, and it became clear there was something major wrong with parts of the Tube system. Only a day late, he thought – imagine if this had happened 48 hours ago – no way would we be getting the Olympics!

Then the radio penetrated his thinking again; there had been a bomb somewhere – Aldwych he thought he'd heard but it couldn't be; it must be Aldgate. Then, only a couple of minutes later it seemed, the radio was reporting a second bomb, this time at Edgeware Road. Five minutes later and there were reports of a third, somewhere near King's Cross. He was initially sceptical they could all be genuine, having been aware in other situations of how the media can become carried away with its own stories. There was something going on though. Gradually, over the next ten minutes, it became clearer that, yes, there were three bombs – the last at King's Cross – but no one knew much in the way of detail, although people were beginning to emerge from the tunnel at Aldgate.

Sam's mind went back to that period in the mid-70s when the IRA was causing havoc in London. He remembered too the bomb scares on the Tube in the early 90s and the way in which people had responded to the Harrods' bomb and the others. Whoever was responsible for these bombs wouldn't win either, of that he was sure. He looked at the clock. It was 8.35, time for him to make a move.

He paid and walked out into the street. It was clearer now, and he began to walk briskly down towards Warren Street. Just past Madame Tussauds, he heard the explosion. For the first time, his phlegmatic nature was shaken. It was clearly another bomb. That meant four had gone off in the last hour or so. The others had been on Tube trains, but this one sounded as if it was on the street, and sure enough he could now see a thin plume of smoke rising. He rang into work again, cursing himself that he had not done so before. Rachel answered, sounding calm as ever. The fourth bomb seemed to have been detonated on a bus, somewhere near Russell Square.

There were clearly casualties and some deaths from the three other bombs, though it sounded as though the death toll might be lower than he was fearing. It would clearly rise though and there might be more bombs. Rachel said about half the office had made it in, and that a couple of others had called, saying they had been thrown off trains and were looking for other ways in. They tried to work out whether anyone could have been caught up in any of the explosions but decided it was unlikely. There was an emergency meeting called for 11am.

Sam cut down a couple of back streets where the pavements were close to deserted. Great Portland Street was very busy, and he could hear the constant sound of the emergency services. He paused outside a shop where News 24 was on. There had still been four bombs, news of casualties and deaths was very sketchy still. Blair had obviously been informed up in Gleneagles, and Cobra was about to meet, chaired by Charles Clark. The fourth bomb had been on a bus, and the entire top deck seemed to have been blown off, though there were no pictures yet.

As he walked, Sam switched into work and tried to think ahead to the next few weeks. If you assumed that the bombings were somehow linked to Al Qaeda, then there would be a political battle over the extent to which the bombings were the result of Britain's support of the US in Afghanistan, and particularly Iraq. It seemed, however, that the number of deaths was unlikely to be much above 100. Thankfully, this was no World Trade Center, or even Madrid, and if the number of deaths stayed below say 70, then he thought any immediate political fall-out would be overshadowed by the search for the bombers. He became conscious of the callousness of his calculations and momentarily bit his lip.

Then he began, almost immediately, to think ahead again and to analyse the potential implications. That was his over-riding concern, it had to be. He did not think the Tories would seriously attack the government at this moment. They were still licking their wounds and Michael Howard had just resigned, signalling the start of a leadership contest. The Liberal Democrats might conceivably make such a case, but despite Charles Kennedy's consistent opposition to the Iraq War that would matter much less.

He had no real doubts as to how people on the street would respond. 'There was something in their DNA', he thought, 'that just hated the idea someone was trying to bully them'. People would simply get back to business as usual as soon as they could. Even if there was another set of attacks, or a third and fourth, he thought this would be the case. Presumably, there was a breaking point, yet the more the attacks were turned on the UK, the more he thought the public would start to accept the Blair thesis that the real war was against global terror, with Iraq only its most immediate theatre. He was more doubtful about what would happen to ethnic relationships within the UK's increasingly diverse society. Events since 9/11 had focused increasingly on the Muslim community, despite the weight of evidence for their essential non-violence. Unfortunately, however, together with events overseas, this was creating fertile ground for the tiny number who wanted to radicalise.

He was now halfway down Tottenham Court Road and the streets were still full. It was approaching 10am but he knew that, as soon as he got to Oxford Street, he could zigzag down through Soho and Piccadilly. He reckoned he'd probably make in by about 10.40. He turned to wondering who could have set off the bombs. His assumption was that they were Al Qaeda-linked, and likely to be Muslim. The obvious assumption was that the bombers were not British but originated from overseas. The UK's borders seemed to leak like a sieve, no matter what his Home Office colleagues might argue, and it wouldn't be hard for such people to enter the country. There did exist, however, the small but real possibility, perhaps a one in five chance he thought, that the bombers might have been born and grown up in Britain. That really would set the cat among the pigeons. Sam could not begin to imagine the repercussions should the bombers turn out to be young British Muslims who'd grown up in British cities, gone to British schools and held down normal jobs.

Having reached the unsatisfactory end of this thread of argument, he mentally filed it away until another time. He was now on Lower Regent Street, about to cross Carlton House Terrace. He had made good time under the circumstance, he thought, and would be at his desk with a cup of coffee in his hand by twenty-five to. But it refused to stay filed, and its incessant whispering continued and grew through the day, worming its way into the most mundane of his thoughts.

Part 2: Perspectives (I)

Chapter 7
Nottingham, Saturday, 22 February 2003

Sam was travelling up to see his parents for a short weekend, planning to arrive for afternoon tea on the Saturday and leave after lunch on Sunday. Ruth was in Leeds, and Mary was at an academic conference, and he hadn't been up to Nottingham since Christmas.

The train was peaceful and he had more time to read the Guardian than usual. It looked increasingly inevitable that the US would invade Iraq, probably with the UK's help and no one else's. The political argument was still swirling around with various theories on the strength of the evidence for Iraq having weapons of mass destruction, or WMD as they were now universally known, focused on whether Saddam had chemical and biological weapons, and on the extent of Iraq's long-range missile capability – could they hit Israel as they had in 1991? – and its alleged nuclear capability.

Sam's views on all this had long been mixed, and there was little substantial in the news or analysis to shift them. Since he'd already used them back in the 80s, Sam thought it was pretty obvious Saddam had chemical weapons. He had felt strongly about it back then, and it now seemed all the more ironic that the West had done so little at the time and indeed had armed Iraq during its war with Iran. Only the invasion of Kuwait had triggered the Iraq War. Before then, the combination of oil interests and US antipathy toward Iran had led to a reprehensible alliance between Saddam and Reagan's America. As a consequence, there had been only muted Western condemnation and no action when Baghdad had used chemical weapons on its Kurdish minority, mustard gas against Iran. Given the history, Sam also found it easy to imagine Iraq would have biological weapons; by all accounts, they were easy enough to produce and he had little doubt Saddam had the appetite. Long-range missiles and a nuclear capability seemed less likely.

There was no solid evidence Iraq had made any real progress – yes, they had probably tried, but the technology was much more advanced, and despite the break-up of the Soviet Union, raw nuclear material was still hard to come by. Iraq had obviously not played ball with the UN weapons inspectors, but even so the failure to find anything of note remained telling. Neither was any of the intelligence information produced by the US and UK governments particularly convincing. He also thought that Bush and his Neocon allies had decided a long time before to invade Iraq, irrespective of the evidence. Bush's identification of Iraq shortly after 9/11 as part of his 'axis of evil' had been a ridiculous piece of rhetoric but carried an unmistakeable purpose. By contrast, Sam did have some sympathy for Blair's increasingly contorted gymnastics, unedifying though they had become, as he tried to keep any US action within the envelope of UN resolutions.

While all this could be argued about endlessly, Sam had no doubt that Saddam himself was as vile as any ruler around, having tyrannised large swathes of his own population, arguably attempted genocide on the Kurds and attempted to invade two of his neighbours with bloody consequences. What alarmed Sam most was the number of Neocons, starting with Rumsfeld, who'd been intimately involved in the US's support for Iraq in the 80s. Those pictures of Rumsfeld shaking Saddam's hand looked even more mortifying now than they had at the time; US foreign policy had been drastically wrong then, so why, with the same crowd directing it, was there any good reason to believe it was any better now?

Sam had always found this sense of American invincibility, which lay behind so many of its current foreign policy assumptions, hard to justify. He still remembered watching the humiliating pictures of the last US helicopters evacuating Saigon. Subsequently, and despite the huge military investment of the Reagan years, there had been a string of disasters, from the failed attempt to rescue Tehran Embassy staff to the Black Hawk Down incident in Mogadishu, long enough to raise severe doubts over the ability of the US to execute any kind of military operation on foreign soil. Not least, the White House's desire to limit US casualties as far as possible would always limit severely the situations in which it would intervene. The corollary, now obscenely referred to as collateral damage, was the increased willingness to conduct warfare at arm's length, with far greater reliance on technology, and the consequent surge in civilian deaths. This was nothing new of course, but there was something worse about more advanced technology and the consequent fact that those pressing the button were effectively insulated against any personal risk.

There was also the argument, sometimes heard, that another invasion of Iraq would effectively be completing unfinished business from 1991 when, in accordance with the terms of the broadly-based alliance formed to fight the war, the chance to oust Saddam wasn't taken. Sam had more sympathy with this view and was among those who believed oil interests were the main drivers of US policy in the region.

Whatever the exact mix, it had left Blair with a weak hand. Even so, he'd played it poorly, hardly trying at all to establish himself as independent of the US, not even when his stock in America was sky high after 9/11. As a result, virtually everyone else distrusted him, including otherwise supportive swathes of UK voters and much of his own party. It was hard to avoid the conclusion that his inability to separate himself from Bush over Iraq in any meaningful way had effectively broken him as a politician. Sam could see nothing ahead but a bloody and protracted war, probably involving the use of chemical and even biological weapons. The Revolutionary Guards would certainly be outgunned in the end, but it seemed premature to be sure about the easy superiority of US military might, and he suspected the reality of conflict might again expose weaknesses in strategy and hardware. The invasion of Afghanistan had seemed rapid and painless, but Sam thought Iraq would be different.

As he skimmed the pages of news and analysis, it struck him for the umpteenth time that by far the most ridiculous strand of the so-called 'case for war' was the argument that Saddam was somehow an ally of the Taliban. All the available evidence pointed towards a deep antipathy between them, and as far as he could tell, the only thing they had in common was being on Bush's blacklist.

76

But there was also something that bothered him deeply about the argument of those who, often viscerally, opposed an invasion. The Biafran disaster of the 1960s had affected him deeply. He had been entering his teens and hadn't understood why no one had been able to stop the hundreds of thousands of people being starved to death. More than a decade later, the revelations about the killing fields of Cambodia had jolted him again, as had Rwanda. In a globalised world, there needed to be some mechanism by which the international community would be able to intervene before acts of genocide were committed. He was disdainful that some the people opposed to an invasion of Iraq were the same who wrung their hands repeatedly about the inability of the UN to act.

He had hoped reading the paper would have relaxed him but instead the arguments continued to fester in Sam's mind as he got off at Nottingham station and got a taxi to his parents. Although he loved them both dearly, Sam had stopped looking forward to these visits a few years ago. He had hoped he would become closer to them as he himself got older but the combination of their increasing age and the distance, both physical and cultural, between London and Nottingham had widened the gap, so that his mum and dad now confined themselves to asking only the most general of questions about his life. He was sure they liked Mary, while being convinced she was too clever and sophisticated for them, and adored Ruth, but believed she was too young to want to spend any real time with her grandparents. And now Sam was in his late 40s, they were finding it harder to treat him as their son. All relationships, he decided, are continually blurred.

Sam's dad had been a butcher and his mum a primary school teacher, and as a family they had quietly prospered through the 1960s when Sam was growing up, but without ever losing that edge of vulnerability common to those who'd lived through the Depression, WW2 and the poverty that followed. During the war, Dad had worked in a munitions factory, his myopic eyesight ruling him out of military service, while Mum had still been at school. Sam was their only child and, without him ever feeling pushed, they had consistently nurtured his intelligence and ambition to the point where, unlike many of his contemporaries, university always seemed a natural step, but one that inexorably pulled him away from his roots.

Jim and Pam still lived in the semi-detached house they'd bought back in 1961, moving from the post-war prefab that had been their only other home. The carpet, and most other things, in what had been Sam's room were the same as when he had last properly occupied it 30 years before. There was no sense it had been deliberately preserved, but there had never seemed to be a good reason to change it, and even his old homework desk, a secondhand piece of office furniture, was still there. He quickly opened his overnight bag and distributed the contents between a couple of drawers before going back downstairs for coffee.

Pam was opening a new jar of Gold Blend, and as he entered the kitchen, began to stir the granules into the milk already in the cups. When done, she loaded the tray with an assortment of cake and biscuits. Sam then carried it into the sitting room and placed it carefully on the coffee table. These were time-honoured rituals, worn into easy grooves by comfortable repetition. Jim was in his normal chair by the window and reached across to get his cup before placing it on the beer mat that sat on the sill. He asked about Sam's journey up, and Pam asked about Mary and Ruth, and they chatted amiably about Sam's family and work while they drank the coffee, and Sam ate what felt like a month's intake of sugar.

"Tell us about our favourite granddaughter," Pam said, "how's she getting along with her studies?" To Sam's parents, hard work was almost everything. Sam assured them she was studying hard, and then reassured them she hadn't fallen in with the wrong crowd or gotten involved with drugs. He calmed these fears as he always did; he'd met most of her friends, some of whom had been to stay, and thought they were all lovely kids. Pam asked if Ruth had thought yet about what she wanted to do as a career; she'd read an article last time she was in the hairdresser's about how hard graduates were finding it to get a job. He said again that Ruth was working hard and was certainly getting good grades; he was sure the graduate job market would have improved by the time she finished.

He asked about their neighbours and friends. Mrs Allison didn't go out much anymore but her eldest daughter Melanie only lived a couple of miles away and came around every day to see her and check she was okay. Len and Susan Graham were still in the same house, but their son Gary had recently lost his job, and so it was hard for him and Frances as their two sons were still living at home. Michelle's parents, David and Kate, were both fine, though David now needed a stick for walking and Kate didn't get out in the garden as much as she used to. Lately, his parents had begun giving him pieces of news they had told him already on the phone, or during his last visit, as if it was the first time. But deep down he sensed it was all part of how they now related to each other, and it was counter-productive for him to get frustrated or irritated. After coffee, Pam went back into the kitchen to start preparing the evening meal, while Jim had his customary nap and Sam, as he always did in these situations, switched on the television and watched Final Score.

They had dinner in the kitchen, pork chops with new potatoes and cabbage, followed by ice cream. Despite his expectations, Sam was enjoying the comfort of talking to his parents; Iraq and London seemed a long way away. When he came up to stay, Pam always treated herself and her son to a dry sherry and Jim would open a can of Stella. His parents seemed well enough in themselves, though it was obvious they were slowing down and didn't get out as much either. He was struck by how little he knew about them beyond the outline of their lives and what he could remember from his childhood.

As he lifted his glass of sherry, Sam listened to his dad talking away in his familiar semi-monologue tones about how worried the local shopkeepers were by the planned new superstore. Jim rasped a cough and Sam took another sip. As he did so, he noticed Pam staring at her husband, and turning around, saw Jim removing a hanky from his mouth. The carefully ironed white linen had come away glistening red.

"Jim, look!" she said.

"I can see it, dear. Just now, I don't feel so good either. Could you ring the doctor for us?"

"Of course... I'll make it 999 just to be on the safe side."

Sam didn't know what to do. His heart was beating fast as he tried to take in and make sense of what was going on. Something very bad was clearly happening to his dad, but he didn't know what it was and couldn't understand why both his parents were behaving so calmly. He overheard Mum on the phone in the hall explaining what had occurred, and it sounded like an ambulance was on its way. Meanwhile, Jim had coughed again and brought up more blood, so that the once pristine handkerchief was now a dripping scarlet rag.

"Don't worry your head about me, Sam," he said, too deliberately, "this happens once in a while. The old body's starting to creak on me a bit. It's probably a touch of pneumonia again; they'll do some tests and then give me the antibiotics to sort it out."

So many thoughts flashed through Sam's mind at this point that he didn't know which of them to articulate; instead he just blurted out something like, "You mean this has happened before?"

"Only a couple of times," Jim replied. "Pam's as calm as anything now. Sorry we never told you, but you've got your own life to lead, and we neither of us ever wanted to bother you." Pam bustled into the kitchen carrying a small bag.

"I've got your pyjamas and your toothbrush and toothpaste and your book in here; the ambulance should be here in about five minutes." She bent down and squeezed his hand, seeking out eye contact. "You'll be okay now, won't you?" She tried to phrase it as an instruction, an assertion of fact, but it refused to come out as anything other than an imploring plea.

"I'll be fine dear, I've told Sam not to worry. They'll look after me well in the hospital."

No one said anything for the next three minutes, 25 seconds. Each of them had turned wordlessly inwards. Then they heard what could only be the ambulance pull up outside. Still without any of them speaking, Sam went to open the door then came back to help his dad, while Pam helped her husband up and then followed with the bag.

"Hello, Mr Jackson," said one of the paramedics, "I'm Pat and this is Jessica. We got here as quickly as we could. We're going to take you to hospital but, before we do, we just need to do some tests in the back of the ambulance here, and you can tell us how you feel and what's been happening. Then we can phone ahead and make sure they're properly ready for you when we arrive."

Pat helped Jim into the back of the ambulance, and Jessica took the bag of overnight stuff from Sam's mum. She quickly checked the contents before putting it in the ambulance and then asking if they wouldn't mind waiting inside; she'd come and let them know before they left.

"Is it okay if I just wait here?" Sam asked.

"Yes, of course," replied Jessica.

"I'll just go inside and tidy up a bit," said Pam, nodding to her son. Sam for his part felt marginally less surplus to events than he had but, with only a shirt on, the February wind was soon cutting through, impelling him to stamp his feet, and hug and hit himself vigorously, to try and keep his circulation moving. Then it started to rain, the weather almost comical in its nastiness. He wondered if he should nip inside and grab a jacket but didn't want to risk not being there when the ambulance doors opened. He checked he had his mobile and moved onto the footpath from standing in the roadway behind the ambulance, trying to seek some shelter under a small tree. He wondered what tests they were doing and again felt impotent. How many times had this happened, he wondered, but couldn't really bring himself to even pretend surprise that his parents hadn't told him. It was how they were, a simple extension of their self-sufficient approach to life. He thought of his mum determinedly tidying up after dinner, trying to keep her mind straight. He thought she would also be calling her sister Maureen and ask if she'd come over to keep her a bit of company. He thought of his dad's calmness but also how much Jim had needed to lean on him as they'd walked to the door.

He heard Pat's urgent but muffled voice from within the ambulance, then the vehicle started to sway, slowly but with some violence, and there followed a series of grunts and clinking metal. Sam's mind was jumping around without pattern. Telling Mum wasn't an option, it would just confuse things, while he knew he could be no use inside the ambulance. So he just carried on standing, mute and limp by the ambulance, inside which two paramedics were fighting to save his dad's life.

Then the back doors flew open and Pat jumped out. "We have to get your dad to hospital right now," he said quickly. "Can you follow us in your car?"

"No," replied Sam. His voice sounded disembodied. "I came up by train from London today."

"Okay, I guess you should jump in. Will your mum be okay? Can you ring her as we go? Come on, quick as you can please!" Then, as he scrambled up into the ambulance, Pat caught his arm, "I'm sorry, Mr Jackson."

As the engine came alive and he heard the gears being slammed, Sam reached for his phone; it was engaged and he cursed quietly. The other paramedic, Jessica, was bent over Jim and glancing unflinchingly at his heart rate. This looked okay to Sam but was plainly less than satisfactory, and Jessica anticipated the acceleration of the ambulance as the siren went on, and the vehicle cornered hard right. Sam nearly fell onto the floor and only saved himself at the cost of a nasty crack to his left shin. There was an oxygen mask over Dad's face, but he seemed conscious even though he looked pale and week. Sam reached out and took his father's hand, rewarded by only the slightest of squeezes. He tried to make eye contact but his dad only stared up towards the ceiling of the ambulance without seeming to focus on it.

Within five minutes they had reached the hospital, but four minutes later Jim Jackson was pronounced dead from coronary thrombosis; it seemed a bit longer at the time but that was what the record would say.

Only afterwards was Sam able to get through to his mum, who had only just got off the phone from her sister. Sam never felt he could reliably recall what he thought or said during these nine minutes. His impression was that he had been oddly preoccupied with how he would tell Mum if Dad did die, but he couldn't be sure how long this lasted, five minutes or five seconds. He also remembered wondering what he should do, whether to ask if he could help, when he had started to cry.

One thing he didn't remember was his flashback memories of his dad: in the Lake District back in the early 1960s; teaching him to drive through gritted teeth but with infinite patience, finishing his cup of tea each morning before putting on his coat and hat to go to work. Sam's mind denied him access to these memories, perhaps because of the grief they caused him at the time as he stared at the still form of his father lying on the ambulance bed. Maybe too, their sheer brevity in elapsed time made them too easy to discard in the flurry of activity and myriad of emotions that engulfed him over the next few hours. These too were dominated by grief but of a more thoughtful, duller sort, that ached rather than seared. The shards of memory that had assailed him, and then departed with equal speed during the final handful of minutes, had shaken him in a way he couldn't cope with, and so he wiped his memory of them. This left a gap, both in his recall of that specific time and in his understanding of how he had reacted, and with that came a small but gnawing guilt that he had somehow not responded in the right way during those final minutes, that he had failed.

He'd thought about telling his mum in person rather than by phone but decided it would be difficult enough for her. The call itself was predictably a non-event, with Pam taking the news stoically, as if he had rung to say he would be a bit late home. Both his parents had always internalised everything that mattered. It was okay to give someone a hard time for not tucking their shirt in, but if they had genuinely insulted you, then you would keep it to yourself, avoiding giving any satisfaction or sign of weakness, and waiting for comeuppance, as they would have put it. She had realised from the tone of his voice the moment he started to speak, and Sam had picked up, because he was attuned for it, his mum's small gasp at the other end of the phone, and imagined for himself the tiny rivulets of tears making their way relentlessly down the laughter lines of her cheeks.

Chapter 8
Nottingham, Friday, 28 February 2003

Through the days that followed, leading up to Jim's funeral, Sam found himself leaning on Pam for support. He had expected to be supporting her, had assumed he would be the core of strength for the family, the shoulder on which others would cry, but the reality turned out to be different. Sam had very few conceits but this one had slipped through and quickly proved empty. His mum knew what to do and where everything was, and immediately ended up making all the arrangements and contacting family and friends herself, throwing her soul into the logistics, where it could rattle around and become inured to the pain.

Ruth had seen her father cry only once before but couldn't recall when. The days leading up to Granddad's funeral altered that, with Sam crying more than daily, and Ruth had been left wondering if she really understood her father. She had grown up associating him with emotional strength and stoicism, but these assumptions became fragile, and at times he hadn't seemed in control of himself, still less of the events she'd imagined him dictating. By the day itself, this had left her confused and questioning. She had relied on the solidity of her father's character, but this was now exposed as uncertain, dithering, and she was at a loss who to turn to about it.

By the time she entered the church, she was feeling as scared as she could recall, and sitting in the front row made it worse. When the service began, she mumbled through the hymns and the liturgy, and agonised through the prayers. The readings, one of them by her father, meant little. The funeral was meant to have been small but in the end the church was full. Ruth had liked her granddad without feeling particularly close to him but found herself weeping freely throughout. She had always seen him as a rather private, self-contained man, and was overcome by the number of people who had showed up, whose lives he had presumably touched. Ruth had been to church only rarely, and never to this sort of unadorned Congregationalist church, housed in an unremarkable 1960s building. She thought the vicar looked slightly wild for someone in his mid-50s but he had a down-to-earth manner, devoid of the patronising pomposity she disliked so much. Even so, she was surprised when, towards the end, she found herself listening.

"Many of you here aren't familiar faces in this church, quite possibly in any church. Equally, many of you probably won't know each other. In some ways, that is as it should be. One of the important functions of the church in any age, but perhaps especially in quite secular times such as the one we live in, is to be a place where human beings can congregate at important moments; important times in their own lives, in the lives of others and in the life of their community. Each of us will have our own reasons for being here today. Many of you may not believe in God, Christian or otherwise, or in life after death, but perhaps some of you do, while others are not sure. But, in some way, we are all here because of Jim Jackson, perhaps because we believed in him and how he led his life.

"I know Pamela won't mind me saying that Jim and she weren't regular worshippers here, but they did darken the doors from time to time, for midnight carols on Christmas Eve, for Easter, for others' weddings, baptisms and, yes, funerals; and, very occasionally, just because they decided to come. I can't claim to know what Jim thought about God, but from talking to him, and from observing him and talking to others, I believe he very much sought to live his life according to the simple commandments Jesus laid down – to love others as yourself, and to behave toward them as you wanted them to behave towards you. This is simple to say – try it, it rolls off the tongue – but extraordinarily difficult to live your own life by, to act out day by day. Seeing so many of you here is an indication of Jim's success in adhering to that one simple phrase.

"Pamela, Sam, Mary and Ruth want me to thank all of you. They said Jim would be both shocked and honoured to know you had turned up to see him off, having travelled from near and far at very short notice, taking the time to pay your respects and participate in this formal goodbye..." The service ended with 'Jerusalem' because of Jim's love of William Blake.

As they emerged, the drizzle fell steadily from an unsmiling grey sky. Ruth was feeling a little bolstered by the vicar's address, which had been inclusive and loving in a way she hadn't expected. But the burial itself, in a nearby cemetery, did nothing to lighten her mood and everything, her own life included, was suddenly a thankless slog with nothing at the end of it. She was surrounded by largely unknown faces of people who had almost certainly known Granddad better than she had. But then she didn't really believe she knew anyone anymore, not even her own dad. It would be impossible and wrong for her to slip away now but was still trying to think how she might do so. And then she saw Michelle making her way towards her through the crowd.

The older woman gave her an unexpectedly firm hug. "I'm ever so sorry," she said, "but we only just made the service. The traffic was terrible. I only managed to see Sam a moment ago. He asked me just to check you were all right. He's caught up talking to some of Jim's old friends. But of course, you're not all right!" Michelle said suddenly. "The whole of the last few days must have been dreadfully disorientating for you. Listen, come to the hotel with Phil and me. He's just over there by the car."

Michelle took Ruth's had and steered her through the crowd towards where Philip was leaning casually against the bonnet of their Mercedes. "Quit looking so laconic, Phil. Bring that umbrella over, we're giving Ruth a lift to the hotel." Philip met them with the opened umbrella and escorted them back towards the car, where he opened the door and bowed low as they got into the back seat together. "You must forgive my husband," Michelle confided mercilessly, "his manner comes across much more flippantly than he means it to; it's all those years he's spent working with heartless, cynical media types. It's left him devoid of normal human sensitivity."

"I heard that, dearest," said Philip as he opened his door. "Don't believe a word she says. My work colleagues are only driven to heartlessness by the content of the stories they have to deal with." He paused. "More seriously though, Michelle's right to apologise for me. I've seen too much over the years, and it means I've developed this shell that I retreat into far too often. I only really met Jim the once, at your parents' a few years back, when Sam had persuaded his mum and dad to come down to London for a rare weekend. He struck me as a very genuine human being, and I'm deeply sorry he's passed on, especially as suddenly as he did."

"Thank you, Philip, I really appreciate the thought."

Michelle sat back, silently pleased. As the car move off, she half-whispered, "Ruth, why don't we have a quiet cup of coffee when we get there, and you can tell me what the last week's been like."

"Thanks, I'd like that. It has been strange, and I think you're just about the only person I could talk to about it." As Ruth said this, she turned towards the front of the car, effectively addressing Philip, suddenly confident he would realise she was talking to him.

"Of course," he replied, "I'll go and see if I can help Sam or Mary at all."

They arrived early, and so Ruth and Michelle were able to procure coffee and a quiet corner of the lounge bar before the main block of guests arrived. It took Ruth about ten minutes to lay out the doubts that had swollen over the last week. Michelle listened intently, her brows uncharacteristically knitted.

"Phew, you've had a lot to deal with!" she said finally. "The first and most important thing to say is that I don't really think you need my help. From what you've told me, it sounds like you've had a quite sharp and fairly brutal introduction to some of the darker corners of adult life. I don't know any complete answers to your questions, all of which make total sense – probably there aren't any – but I reckon you've made a pretty good start at working them out for yourself. But there are a couple of specific things I might be able to help you out with.

"The first is about your dad. I think you're right to say that he has great emotional strength, and that he can sometimes come across as too stoical. I don't think you inevitably need to view that as inconsistent with the struggles you've witnessed him going through over the past few days. Sam's always felt things deeply; I think he cried more often than any boy I knew at school, often over seemingly small events – a dead animal on the road, something he'd seen on the news that no one else thought significant. As he grew up, he learned how to cry less; I suppose kids gave boys who cried a much harder time back then. Sam did acquire a tougher shell, but mainly I think he just learned to hide it better. I suspect he still feels the impact of events as deeply, and what you've seen is simply the excess of that, overwhelming his ability to disguise it.

"When I was a young nurse, I was on a geriatric ward for a while and, almost on a daily basis, I witnessed the enormous depths of grief experienced by the family and close friends of patients who died. This happened even when they knew the end was near, even to the day or almost the hour. Don't forget Jim's death was pretty sudden, a complete shock really, certainly to Sam if not to his mum; and that Sam was right there, when Jim had the first heart attack, and then right by his side when he passed away, before they could get him into theatre. Given all that, I'm not surprised it's been so hard for him, and I don't think you should read too much into it. Once today's out of the way, Sam will work out a way to deal with his dad's death quite quickly – they were pretty close, you know, in that silly, understated way men are – and get back to being the father you know.

"The other thing that might help isn't anything I can really claim credit for. I heard it from a rather odd man I met once quite a long time ago, late 80s I think, just got chatting over a drink, never saw him again. I've always thought he was probably the most humble, but at the same time the most ambitious, man I've met; but the main thing about him that's relevant to your situation is that he said his main aim was just to deal with people honestly, as he found them, to discharge his responsibilities to those who depended on him and to help other people when he could. It sounds simple put like that but, when you break it down and think about the obligations it would impose on you in practice, I reckon it's about as daunting and difficult a mission as you could imagine.

"The reason I remember this, not having thought about it in years, is what the vicar said about Jim's approach to life, which sounded pretty similar, and it's mostly how I'd describe Sam as well. Anyway, the only advice I can really offer is that you deal with your dad just as you find him. If he's different this week from how he was last, then that's fine, and he'll probably be back to normal next week. You have some responsibilities towards him as he has to you but mostly I suspect you can just be here; there'll be time for other things later."

"I think you're right," said Ruth. "It's partly being here in Nottingham and imagining Dad as a boy with his parents. But, you're right, I should just deal with everyone, especially Dad, as I find them."

"Times have changed quite a lot since we – your parents, Phil and me – were growing up and I'm sure it's hard to draw parallels with your own life. You're lucky that your parents don't really have financial worries. I'm sure Jim and Pam did when they were bringing up Sam; my mum and dad certainly did, and it does matter. I know Sam values the freedom of not having to worry about the costs of things you need for everyday life. Phil feels it even more acutely, which I think is why he sometimes throws money around too freely; it's a reaction, I guess, against the poverty he grew up with. He's a real baby boomer.

"Anyway, the point I wanted to make was that your dad hasn't really changed much from when he was growing up. In fact, I'm pretty sure he still misses not having the same sense of local community a smaller place like Nottingham gives you. People did use you look out for each other, say hello and chat when they passed each other in the street. I've got a friend who tells me bits of the East End are still like that but it's not been true of anywhere I've lived in London. And maybe part of his sense of loss these last few days is connected with the sense that, with his dad's dying, a big part of his route back to those values has passed away."

"It's funny, odd, I mean," said Ruth. "I mean, seeing Dad here and talking about him like this. I mean, we've always lived in quite posh parts of London. Not Chelsea or anywhere like that, but I realised when I was about 12 that we had a lot more money that nearly all of my friends at school. And when we went on holiday, we'd stay in what must have been quite expensive hotels. But then hearing you talk about Dad just now made complete sense. And it's all him, completely him; I've just never thought about the different things I know about Dad all at the same time before."

"Well, there aren't too many people like him. Back in the 70s, and for a while before I guess, there was a generation of real working-class kids who were suddenly able to go to university – a lot of them were the first in their family to have higher education. Anyway, this generation has always had to find a way to square the circle between the relative poverty of their background and the wealth that their access to university opened up for them."

Ruth nodded, though she was just starting to feel slightly bored. She realised Michelle was trying to help her understand her dad, but her concentration was beginning to drift. In fact, Michelle had reached the stage where she was talking mainly for her own benefit, though not in a self-conscious way. Michelle was just realising this and wondering how to explain it to Ruth, when a flurry of other mourners began congregating at their end of the room, ending their solitude.

The mood changed. The sun blinked an appearance, only briefly but long enough to lift the weight of dealing with Jim's death. Alcohol helped too, as people swapped stories and remembered memories. Sam realised he was more relaxed. There was a burden of responsibility he had been assuming gradually for the last 20 years or so, since, aged 29, he had noticed he was more than half his dad's age; suddenly, it was gone. At the same time, his own mortality had become starker – he was next – but that, for now at least, was a feeling of lightness rather than weight.

Standing with his uncle, half listening to stories of Jim's, actually quite mild, escapades in France just after the war, he contentedly watched Mary and Michelle chatting away and Ruth listening to Phil, who was looking rather more serious than usual. He glanced across at his mum sitting with Maureen and decided she too was looking relieved it was all over. He wondered how Ruth would feel when he or Mary died, whether women felt the passing of the baton between generations in the same way.

Chapter 9
London, Saturday, 30 April 1978

Ed was walking along somewhere in the middle of a long and winding march, en route from Trafalgar Square to Victoria Park, somewhere in East London. The march had been organised by Rock against Racism, or RAR, and it was only the fourth demonstration he had ever been on. He'd been working for the BBC about six months and although he was barely 22, there was a part of him that felt he was already too old for this sort of thing. When his friends in Manchester had gone on student demos, about Vietnam, Ireland or whatever, he'd mostly stayed home. Even Sam had been on more marches than him.

This was different, however; the cause was free of grey areas, or that was how he justified it to himself. Some years before, he'd concluded, sadly, that his parents were quietly racist. Not in the way the National Front was, nothing like that, nor were they anything like Alf Garnett. But they had a set of assumptions that began with a sense that being British meant being both White and different from other cultures and races, and then moved seamlessly to a belief that there was a natural hierarchy of races, the British at the top, with all that implied. He vividly recalled them listening to Enoch Powell's 'Rivers of Blood' speech; hard to believe that was a decade ago. They'd not been aroused by it at all but they'd listened carefully and talked about it afterwards. At the time, Powell was a serious mainstream politician, and they'd begun worrying a lot more about the implications of immigration. But there was little malice or prejudice in their characters, and he sometimes wondered if he was being unfair to them.

Part of it was generational, the uncertainty of living in a country that, for all its outward continuity, was subject to continuous, sometimes withering, change. End of Empire and increased immigration had visibly cracked the surface of social confidence. His parents were ordinary, hardworking people, born at the start of the Depression, and when they had married in 1951, still saw Britain as a major world power. That was what they'd been taught at school and, despite Indian independence, it wasn't until Suez that they had begun to understand that the Empire they'd grown up taking for granted was coming to an end.

But there was a personal side too, and what had happened with his sister Diane had created a barrier between them. A couple of years older than Ed, Diane had left school after A Levels and got a job at a local solicitors'. Shortly after, she started going out with a bloke at work called Alex. But Alex's parents had been born in Jamaica and he was Black. He was sharp and funny, and as far as Ed could see, nothing but good for Diane. But she was worried about introducing him to their parents, so worried she used every possible excuse to avoid it happening. She didn't talk about Alex at all and ended up lying to them in more and more ridiculous ways, sometimes even dragging him into the deception. After about eight months, it all came to a head in the run up to Christmas when Alex, who had been amazingly tolerant of his non-existent status, began to argue, quite reasonably, that he wanted to be able to come around and pick Diane up from her house. Diane's response had been to break off the relationship, simply ditching Alex in the pub one night before going home to cry herself to sleep. She had stayed in her room for three days, pretending to be ill.

Throughout, Ed had tried and tried but failed to get his sister to talk about it. As far as he could work it out, the cause was Mum and Dad's attitude to race, that they believed mixed marriages were doomed to fail, the odds too stacked against them. Related to this was the sense of foreboding Diane had every time she went out with Alex in public. Occasionally, someone had thrown an insult at them and, though it hadn't gone further, she worried about physical attack in a way she hadn't ever done before. Their parents couldn't have made this risk disappear, but it made it much harder that she couldn't confide in them. And because Alex never came around to her house, they ended up being out in public more often.

What worried Ed most was that his sister internalised the whole thing, and he could see it was doing her no good. Within three months of the break up, Alex had given up his job and left Derby, supposedly for Birmingham. Ed found it hard not to lay the ultimate responsibility at his parents' door. Diane had recovered, though he didn't think she smiled as much, and had been seeing someone, White of course, steadily for a couple of years. He hadn't heard of Alex since, but still thought about him, hoped he was okay.

When Ed had gone to Manchester the following year, he'd found himself in a more cosmopolitan city, with a large Asian community as well as a Caribbean one. He'd found their accent hard to understand to start with, and their culture more obviously different from the West Indian one he had known in Derby. It seemed obvious to him that British society was changing, especially in its cities. However, he also felt in a different place himself, and where in Derby he had felt part of the community, here he was a student.

Not that the student experience was constricting; he met openly gay and lesbian people for the first time and even his first Conservatives. These people had simply not been visible where he'd grown up, and suddenly he found himself arguing over coffee or beer about issues he'd previously only come into contact with via TV, newspapers or books. Looking back, he was shocked by how quickly the feeling of novelty had worn off; abortion and homosexuality, Vietnam and Palestine, Friedman and Keynes all became the subject of small talk.

In the process, Ed's views on racism had also hardened. He now saw each person as an individual human being; intolerance of that difference now seemed impossible not to condemn. Prejudice was prejudice. And then, just as he was doing his Finals, and getting ready to move to the capital to work for the BBC, the National Front did particularly well in London local elections. And this had sharpened his anti-racism, so that he felt the need to show his face publicly rather than just argue the toss individually with people who mostly agreed with him.

All of which had brought him to this march, which was due to be followed by a rock concert in Victoria Park. The thought occurred to him that, aside from voting, this might be his first overtly political act; ironic that it was taking place after he'd begun working for the BBC. He wondered distractedly if his participation might be in contravention of some small print in his contract but dismissed the idea, comfortable in the anonymity conferred by a large crowd.

About five yards to his left, Patricia was marching with him. He'd known her in Manchester and, while never close friends, they'd ended up swapping phone numbers after Finals. Patricia had done a good deal of work for Third World First, and he knew she was in London so, once he'd decided he wanted to march, he'd traced her via that original number to get more information. Unsurprisingly, she had every detail at her fingertips, and she'd invited him to meet her in the pub where she and her crowd were gathering before the rally.

Patricia had been typically bolshie with him on the phone. "You really haven't been paying attention, have you?" she'd said. "RAR started after Clapton had his rant against foreigners in the Birmingham venue where Enoch Powell made his Rivers of Blood speech. A lot of the organising's been done by the SWP, though they've kept their profile low, and there'll be people there from all over."

"And I heard The Clash were playing; what's that about?"

She laughed, "Lots of punk bands get racist groups following them, but they're a long way from being racist themselves, and one of the cool things RAR do is book them on the same gigs as Reggae bands. They've got X Ray Specs and Jimmy Pursey playing, as well as Aswad. It's gonna be neat."

Patricia seemed to be at a demo almost every week when she was a student, and when he met up with her and her friends in the Tom Cribb, she'd looked little different; baggy black jeans and a CND T-shirt, her hair even spikier.

"And what about The Clash?" he asked.

"Like what?" she replied.

"Like why them?"

"Well, they play a lot more reggae than your typical punk band, and I guess they're more conventionally political than the Sex Pistols."

"But isn't everyone?"

"Okay, but you know what I mean. The Pistols are dead political in their own way but I can't see them saying anything coherent about something like racism. The Clash know where a lot of their music has its roots."

"So the fact they're playing today is quite a big deal?"

"You bet!" said Patricia, "It's an explicit 'up yours' to the NF and Clapton. They're going to politicise our generation, and the one after us."

"I can't tell if you're being angry or passionate or ironic."

Patricia looked at him sharply, "Definitely angry, always passionate, hardly ever ironic – how about you?"

Ed took a sip of his beer, "Not really the first two but I'm often ironic, I guess." "Why?"

"Because I want to be as rational as possible and think about what I say and do. And as for the irony, well, there's a hell of a lot to be ironic about."

"But that's the whole thing," argued Patricia, "what you've just said, it just drains the emotion out of life. Why can't you just believe in something sometimes, or even just someone, and just go with it?"

"Maybe I've just not found my cause yet, or maybe I just think this is my role in life."

"That's just a cop out!"

"Maybe it sounds like that but it's not meant to; I could just as easily argue that you don't ever really analyse anything, you simply react to it." Ed spoke normally, but there was an edge to his voice which both decided not to acknowledge. He was embarrassed and annoyed that Patricia had got under his skin.

When Patricia thought about Ed, her view had never really shifted from her first impression, that he was a decent enough bloke from Derby who probably thought too little and read too much. Her friend Siobhan had quite fancied him, and they'd gone out for a term before she ditched him; Siobhan said there'd been nothing terrible, in fact he'd been quite sweet, but that she'd just found him a bit boring and square after a while. Beyond that, she and Ed had knocked around in the same general group of friends for the three years they'd been students without ever getting to know each other. That's how it had been – you met a lot of people but got to know very few.

When Ed had rung her a couple of weeks before, she couldn't even recall having given him her number. They hadn't seen each other since leaving university, and she hadn't recognised his voice, but once she'd worked out who she was talking to she'd been happy enough to pass on the details. She'd even found herself suggesting they meet up before in this pub. Patricia had spotted Ed as soon as he'd walked in the pub door – he hadn't changed much, but she found the rhythm of talking to him surprisingly easy, even when they disagreed. Patricia had been spending her time with people who either agreed with her on pretty much everything or who disagreed on everything. Ed was in neither camp; he often appeared to be sitting on the fence. Once, she recalled, Siobhan had said he'd an opinion about everything but a conviction about almost nothing.

"What do you mean when you say you care?" Patricia asked after a moment.

"That's an odd question," he responded. "What I mean is something that moves me emotionally as well as rationally."

"You really do analyse things to death, don't you? Don't you ever just go with the emotion?"

"Only with people."

Patricia found herself blushing. "I'm sorry, Ed, I didn't mean to suggest anything; I mean Siobhan never said a word or told me anything about when the two of you were seeing each other."

Ed smiled. "It's okay, I knew what you meant, although I'd be surprised if Siobhan was quite as uncommunicative as you're saying. For a start, she used to tell me what your reaction was to my many and varied misdemeanours."

Patricia blushed again. "Okay, you've got me! For what it's worth, I think you were really good for her."

Ed glanced down at his drink. "Thanks for that. I think she was good for me too, but neither of us was ready for it to last longer than it did."

"Probably not, but that's the way most of us were."

"When should we go to the rally?"

They were too late to get close to the front and so Ed, whose hearing had never been great, spent half the time asking Patricia what various speakers had just said.

He felt a bit useless and she thought the same. But when the march began, he began to feel more comfortable and started chatting amiably to the people around him. Denise from Kentish Town, with spiky red hair, pierced jewellery and leather to match, was first and last a Clash fan; while Brian was an archetypal academic kid from Solihull, all round glasses and Fred Perry T-shirt; and Andrew from Glasgow – Celtic shirt and DMs – was gay but hadn't come out at home.

Ed loved the atmosphere. There was something about RAR that simplified the arguments for him and, for once, made it easy to take sides. He understood the feelings of insecurity that provided fertile ground for the racists but that didn't change the fact they were wrong, evilly wrong. Growing up in a post Holocaust, post Empire world, anti-racism had become an article of faith for Ed, and so he felt at home walking alongside Patricia, somewhere in the middle of this huge snake of humanity weaving its way towards East London. They were walking down Cheapside, through the City, where men in suits and bowler hats, almost all male and White, would be plying their business during the week; he smiled to himself at the contrast and wondered how many City workers were marching. But then he wondered how many BBC types or civil servants were.

Ed had been genuinely shocked by the National Front's rhetoric but not really by the speed and extent of its impact, the way it had resonated with swathes of the British population. Until his own lifetime, Britain had largely been a homogenous island nation and had characterised itself as an exporter rather than importer of people. This had been a shock, not least to his parents' generation, and left segments of the population ripe to be exploited by a racist party.

And so here he was, experiencing a strange sense of togetherness with a crowd of people he'd never met before. This was new for someone who was more comfortable in small groups of people he knew well and who sometimes sought solitude. Even standing on the terraces of the Baseball Ground felt different from this. For the first time, he had a proper sense of what it might be like to be part of a big political movement.

He became conscious of Patricia walking purposefully beside him, totally in her element as far as he could tell. "Are most marches like this?" he asked, "It seems like a really good atmosphere."

"No, they're not all like this, or not so much at any rate. Maybe it's because there's lots of people like you instead of everyone being like me," she smiled, "or maybe there's just a load of Clash fans."

"But that doesn't necessarily mean they're just along for the ride."

"Maybe not, but I still worry how many of them'll stick it out, stand up to racists in their communities where they live and work. But you're right; for today, everyone gets the benefit of the doubt, even you!"

When they got there, Victoria Park was a sea of colour and the vast stretch of grass between them and the stage was heaving. "This is way bigger than anyone thought it would be!" Patricia whistled.

Ed too was exhilarated by the experience, being part of such a big public statement. "Do you think rock music's ever been so openly political before? This could really become the catalyst for social change."

"Don't get carried away," warned Patricia, "the anti-racism could be completely forgotten after today."

"Come on, Patricia, you don't really believe that! I mean, just look around you, you said yourself this was an unusual crowd. I mean you've got Led Zep fans here, even Prog Rockers, just look at the T-shirts." Patricia began laughing. She'd just noticed they were standing behind a couple of Yes fans, who were chatting away to a woman wearing a Damned T-shirt.

The Clash came on, for some reason halfway through the concert. They were standing about three quarters of the way back and could see the chords being played and the lyrics sung what seemed like a good second before it reached them. The section of the park they were in was beautifully landscaped to create its own space, with its own identity and, it almost seemed, acoustics as well. As they pogo'd to the music, each lyric was captured by this space and held there for several seconds before being broken down into particles to be collectively absorbed by the crowd.

For Ed, the energy of the performance was addictive. Although he'd read about the Pistols and the Clash, and so had been expecting the event to be adrenalin-fuelled, the fury of it still hit him. The anger in the lyrics and the Reggae-inspired rhythms made it into something new, a manifesto of sedition, a bonfire of manners. It wouldn't bring down the government but it might change something. Certainly, he sensed for the first time some solidarity with his own generation, no matter their class or skin colour. They'd been betrayed, the whole country had, by the institutions and the politicians, as well as by those like the National Front, who falsely claimed to represent them. The NF weren't going to be defeated by the politicians, most of whom had denounced them in code at best. Only events like today could realistically stop it.

He looked around with a faint sense of awe. He knew in his head that this was a moment in time, the energy and idealism would inevitably wither, but he was still proud of his generation for rejecting notions of compromise and the mantra that British society was tied to a set of bigoted traditions. Instead, they were declaring that racism was wrong, end of story, and using their Rock music to do so. Many were probably people the NF would have identified as potential recruits but here they were rejecting all the NF stood for. Ed muttered a little prayer of thanks that he was here too, and promised himself never to undervalue direct action. On TV, demonstrations and marches often appeared tired and contrived but this wasn't, or at least being on a march was different from watching it on a small screen in your living room.

The Clash ended their set, and he expected the day to start winding down but then Tom Robinson came on and the noise roared again. 2-4-6-8 and Glad to be Gay exploded around the Park. A crowd that had come together in the cause of anti-racism turned out to be anti-homophobic as well. Before he'd gone to university, Ed hadn't met anyone who was out, and even in Manchester it was quite rare. Yet here he was in the middle of the most profound musical crossover he could have imagined. It was as if a gang of Hell's Angels had suddenly discovered the excitement of needlework. He looked across at Patricia, who was as captivated as he was.

When it was over, they decided to walk back rather than head for the nearest Tube. Crossing into the smaller side of the Park, they passed a beautiful lake and fountain and a pair of stone-carved Alsatians – the Dogs of Alcibiades – before turning south and filtering their way through Bethnal Green towards the City again. This was the area of London the Kray twins had dominated back in the 60s, but now it was beginning to look quite Asian, with headscarves and saris being worn and sold. As they walked, they chatted away, the hesitant tone of earlier in the day washed away by the thrill of the afternoon. Patricia thought the generation born since 1945 was naturally more immune to the NF but Ed was less sure, recalling the casual racism of his school playground and the already-ingrained attitudes of so many of his contemporaries. Anti-racism was obvious to him, but he wasn't convinced it was anywhere near so simple for lots of others. For one thing, the insults, chanting and banana skins on the pitch at football matches told a different story, and he was more inclined to see RAR as a beacon in the fog than the inevitable shape of things to come.

They decided to stop near Liverpool Street for a final drink. "We can change this, Ed," she implored as they sat down. "We can, our generation; you saw what it was like today, how it brought together people who normally hate each other."

"But that's the whole point," he replied. "Today was astonishing but nothing you've said persuades me it's going to be repeated anytime soon. Yes, it was special, but I don't think it was properly representative of our generation. Look, it was an incredible day and an amazing crowd, but those people were self-selecting just by virtue of having chosen to be there in the first place. Sure, they more or less both love music and hate racism – but mostly the two are separate rather than causal."

"But people's lives do get changed by days like this," she persisted. "You've changed for starters, and you're not going to tell me that many of those punks didn't leave affected somehow by finding themselves dancing next to a bunch of gay men who'd come to see Tom Robinson."

"Okay, but all I'm saying is that the people there today were at least some of the way along that road already. I'm not saying it hasn't changed them, and, yes, I'll look at stuff differently myself. But I'll bet you there's quite a core of punks who wouldn't be seen dead at anything involving RAR; they're happy enough wearing swastikas and beating the shit out of anybody they don't like, or who just happened to be in the wrong place. And I'm not saying all those punks are racist, but neither do I believe they'd have been comfortable in the Park this afternoon."

"But Ed, your whole theory completely ignores the possibility of change and kind of just accepts the status quo will go on as it is. And we both know that isn't how history works. People do have their minds changed and their eyes opened. The suffragettes are just an obvious example of how an idea can sweep society and turn assumptions upside down."

"And you think anti-racism is like votes for women?"

"Yes, I absolutely do, after today I absolutely do! The world's getting more crowded, and we've got to learn how to live with and love people from other races."

Suddenly tired of argument, Ed decided to agree, and so let the conversation drift.

Chapter 10
Manchester, Thursday, 12 June 1975

Ed got to the pub first, bought himself a pint of Guinness and sat down at a corner table with the newspaper. The bar was functional, with big-patterned, furry, flowery wallpaper and a port-red carpet. It was a gloomy place most of the year, but Andy the landlord was a good sort and they sometimes had lock-ins. Usually these were on Fridays or Saturdays, and traditional Irish instruments – Ed didn't know what they we're called – would appear from behind the bar for use by some of the regulars. The pub also had decent darts and football teams, the latter of which Ed had turned out for a couple of times, with no distinction, and in the second, his team had only passed to him twice. This was his local, The Bridge Inn; he only lived a street away and he liked to come here and read, to soak up some of the atmosphere.

He was waiting for Sam, who was cycling over from his house. They hadn't properly been for a drink together in a couple of weeks, and it was almost the end of summer term. Thursday was a good night to go out – there weren't usually any parties, and because of the way their lectures and essay schedules worked, they could sleep off any hangover on the Friday morning. It had just gone 7.30 and he had already eaten, as would have Sam. Ed had also bought a bottle of Bell's at lunchtime in case they decided to go back to his house after closing time. There was no regularity to this arrangement; the two saw each other daily anyway and had kind of wanted to live together, but Sam had been offered a room in another house before they'd managed to find somewhere.

The Bay City Rollers were playing on the jukebox, following on from Tammy Wynette – someone had been putting a seven-song selection in when he was ordering, and Ed had made a mental note to play DJ himself for the next set. It had been a long term and he was looking forward to going home, and now he'd handed in his last essay. Tonight was just for relaxing, then there would be end of term parties…

The news was still full of the Common Market referendum. Some of the coverage annoyed him but mostly he found it interesting. He had enjoyed the TV programmes and debates during the campaign, though he couldn't quite understand why politicians were so very excited by the issue, nor why the electorate was so very unexcited by it. His own favourite moments, perversely because they bore little particular relevance to the debate, were of Peter Shore, repeatedly removing and then replacing his glasses while talking, a clever rhetorical device that had presumably grown from a real physical need. These were closely followed by the bizarre sight of so many Left-wingers, such as Shore, arguing so passionately about the need to maintain and strengthen trade links with the former colonies of the Commonwealth.

The argument seemed to be more about the politician's emotional disposition towards the Common Market than any rational analysis. To Ed, it seemed obvious that the countries of the former British Empire would in time move away from their current trade relationship with the old colonial power. To that end, joining the Common Market was the only rational move – the Commonwealth simply wasn't an option even in the medium term.

Sam wandered in and briefly scanned the room before clocking Ed in the corner. He nodded, noting the almost empty glass and went to the bar to order a couple more pints of Guinness. Ed nodded back and returned to the paper; neither of them had yet spoken. The previous December they had started a game of trying to guess what the other meant without asking, and drinks' orders were one of its simplest manifestations; harder challenges included asking the other to rescue them from someone else's boring conversation at a party. It had been Ed's idea after reading a book about people who were able to communicate subconsciously and wondering if it was possible to create a similar link on purpose. Most of the signs they'd worked out so far were relatively simple but their vocabulary had begun to extend to the more subtle; for example, Sam wrinkling his forehead and then using his thumb and forefinger to smooth it out meant Ed should finish the sentence because Sam wanted to go to the toilet. While Ed had spent what seemed like hours practicing various signals, Sam was much the more intuitive.

"Here you go," Sam said as he sat down. "What's in the paper? Haven't properly read one all week, not since Sunday." Sam folded himself awkwardly onto his chair, choosing to hitch one foot up so the heel was resting on the seat of the chair, by definition the most uncomfortable position possible, leaving him with his chin perched precariously on his bony left knee. Ed observed that his friend's hair was even more of a wreck than normal; no comb or brush would have been near it since Christmas.

"Still loads of Common Market stuff," Ed replied. "They reckon Wilson's going to ditch Benn in the cabinet reshuffle."

"I doubt it," responded Sam, "I don't think he's strong enough, and anyway, he'd rather have his enemy close. People like my dad, the party members who would agree with a lot of Benn's actual views, really don't like what they see as the disloyalty he shows."

"He's not the only one, what about Foot?"

"He never comes across as so abrasive or strident. I don't know, perhaps he's just playing a longer game. Dad has a lot more time for him. It probably helps that he wasn't ever in the House of Lords."

"What've you been up to this afternoon anyway?" asked Ed.

"Just pottering about really; I wrote a couple of letters, went shopping but only to the Co-op, popped into the SU but there wasn't anyone around, so I just went home and watched some tele. What about you?"

"I went to bed!" Ed laughed. "You know I was up till six this morning writing that essay; well, after that I was knackered, obviously, so I crashed. Just lay down on top of the bed and was gone. Did you see Sue at all?"

"No, I think she's lying low."

"I don't blame her. After what she's always said about him, he's the last person I'd have expected her to get off with. You know he's been telling people about it."

"Gross, the thought of it!" said Sam, sagely shaking his head. "There's no accounting for taste when sex is involved. But in a week or so, everyone will be off home and it will be mostly forgotten by the time we're all back in September. What're you up to in the summer?"

"Still planning to go Inter-railing – booked last week. Hoping to get down to the south of Spain, not so much the beaches as the cities – Valencia, Madrid, Barcelona, Seville. I want to see what Franco's Spain is like before it changes. Sorry you can't make it."

"Me too," replied Sam, "but I just couldn't quite afford it. There'll be other times though. I'll try and get some work, sign on if or when I can't, and hope the weather is half decent. Oh, and the World Rowing Championships are in Nottingham."

"Yippee!" responded Ed. "Right, it's my round, and I also need to do some serious damage to that jukebox."

As Ed got up, Sam began flicking through the newspaper. He was disappointed not to be able to go round Europe with Ed, but he didn't want to go overdrawn. Also, he thought Ed had asked him a little late and suspected that his friend, at least initially, had preferred to go alone.

Ed returned and put down Sam's pint. "Give me a minute," he said, "the jukebox is calling and I need to save the world from the Bay City Rollers."

"You haven't put on an album's worth of Neil Young again, have you?" Sam asked when he came back some five minutes later.

"No, I've gone Disco for this evening! – 'Fame', 'Jive Talkin', something called 'Lady Marmalade' and the rest I can't remember."

"I've never really got into Bowie," said Sam, "somehow he's passed me by."

"That's cos you never bother about how you look," Ed replied.

"If Bowie's caring about how you look, then I plead guilty," Sam replied. "Remember, I'm just a poor working-class lad from Nottingham!"

"Yea, but he's different."

"I know, but my mum and dad would freak, seriously, if they thought I liked Bowie. They'd think I was queer or something. Sure, I wasn't even allowed to watch Top of the Pops until I was 16!"

"That's cos you're from Nottingham!"

"My dad just has these standards that he thinks won't ever change. I sometimes feel like everything's accelerating. When I talk to my dad, life seems to have moved a hell of a lot slower when he was our age."

"I'm sure lots of things were happening – it was the 1930s, remember – it's just that he didn't know about it. And TV's changed everything. We can see things happening the other side of the world pretty much live, and I think that will just intensify from here on."

"But if you take that to its logical conclusion," Sam argued, "it massively increases the pressure on decision-making compared to what, say Churchill, experienced during the war. You'll end up having to respond as much to TV as to what's actually happening, and that would just be ridiculous!"

"Perhaps, but do you remember that last US helicopter taking off from the roof of the US Embassy in Saigon? With all those people hanging onto it? It must be one of the most dramatic pieces of live TV there's ever been, and we all saw it actually happen!"

"Going back to Bowie for a minute, I was thinking just now that a lot of his appeal is visual as much as anything else. It must have mattered a lot less to Bing Crosby, who my dad loves, because you only saw him in the flesh or in a film; the rest of the time, you just heard his voice, or saw him on an album cover. Dad always talks about a guy called Al Bowley, who was a British band singer about the same time."

"What do you reckon to Disco anyway?" asked Ed.

"You've got me, I'm afraid, I'm rubbish at pop music; which track is this you've put on?"

"'Lady Marmalade' by Labelle I think. I like Disco, it's way better than all that 'Seasons in the Sun' stuff and the Osmonds! I don't like all of it, Kool & the Gang for instance, but Barry White's totally cool and this stuff's not bad, though I'm not sure how the French got in there; it could well be a classic!"

"You're hilarious," said Sam, "I'm not sure there's anyone has more opinions than you…mostly rubbish, of course!"

"Hey, it's music, the culture of the streets. Love it or hate it. And virtually everything comes from America. Look at Thatcher and Milton Friedman. If she ever becomes prime minister and goes through with it, God will there be chaos!"

Sam was laughing. "I've no idea how we got from Barry White to Maggie."

"Seriously though," Ed took a drink, "she might be the most extreme politician to lead a major political party in Britain since I don't know, Charles James Fox maybe."

"What about Lloyd George or Gladstone?" asked Sam.

"Not when they were PM," Ed was precise. "I don't trust people who don't seem to have any doubt; the world just isn't made that way."

"But I think she's onto something when she talks about everyone having middle-class values, wanting to own their own home and all that. I know loads of people back home, friends of my mum and dad's, and parents of my friends, who live in council houses and absolutely would want to own their own place and be middle-class. All those people whose fathers worked in the steel works and down the mines, but themselves work in offices and own cars and colour TVs. They think they're middle-class now and Thatcher's agreeing with them, while Labour can sound like it's trying to keep them down. I wouldn't be surprised if the Tories won the next election. You're probably right about her being extreme but most people just see her as a grocer's daughter from Grantham made good."

"You'd get murdered if you said that in an SU meeting," observed Ed.

"As you know, that's why I don't get involved with student politics; in fact, I'd run a mile given the chance. Look, you know I disagree with the Tories on most things, but I can't see any value demonising a party so much of the electorate votes for. Dad's a bit of a union man, been a member since he was 14, but I can see why lots of ordinary people would vote Tory to prevent the country being run by Arthur Scargill, and others being turned off by all those dodgy votes at mass meetings, and the beer and sandwiches at Downing Street."

"Well, I hope you're wrong," sighed Ed, "Thatcher's hardly going to fix all the inequality in Britain, she'll just make it worse. There's part of me that really hates the British Establishment, but at the end of the day, I'm not a revolutionary. Maybe that's the real British disease, not enough revolutions?"

Sam ignored the question. "What's this you've put on? Bowie again?"

"Not bad for you." As he drummed out the beat of Diamond Dogs, Ed wondered why Sam didn't get involved in more things; he pretty much seemed to keep to himself and as a consequence, had a mixed reputation. Ed took another drink and glanced up into the mirror. Sam was nonchalantly but carefully checking his parting and pushing back his hair so it was just behind his ears. In fact, Sam had a small but significant female following. Partly, this was because they wanted to mother him. "So much of success in politics is about timing anyway," he observed neutrally.

"How do you mean?" Sam asked.

"Well, if you take Ford," Ed continued, "he must be the most unlucky US president ever! Think about it, you take over from Nixon after Watergate, and then you're burdened with losing the Vietnam War your predecessors have screwed up for you. The poor sod! I reckon all he wanted to do as vice president was play a little golf and go to a few dinners, but there he is evacuating Saigon. You're the historian – is Vietnam the first war America has officially lost?"

"Basically yes," Sam replied. "I couldn't believe it when the South Vietnamese collapsed the minute the Yanks pulled out I remember getting really angry when those students got shot at Kent State and trying to start an anti-war petition in school; it didn't get very far."

"Such a radical!"

"The only other petition, I remember, was one to allow 6th Formers to wear moustaches. I think that was the most seditious thing that ever happened at our school. It was a long way from 'If', let's say."

Ed smiled, "My only school petition experience was that one about Bloody Sunday I told you about. As befits a student approaching the world of work, I've now turned my mind to subverting the Establishment from within. It's much more effective, and lucrative, that way."

"So young and yet so cynical."

"Stop being so bloody sensible all the time! I don't think I've ever seen you angry about anything Sometimes, it gets really frustrating talking to you because you never seem to lose your temper."

"Really?" asked Sam, rather defensively, I think I just say what I think, more or less whatever comes into my head. I think that's just the way I am."

"I guess I know that, and sorry, that wasn't fair of me." Ed visibly lightened, "Have you always been so damned mature about every subject under the sun? Or was the immaturity brutally beaten out of you at some stage?"

Now it was Sam's turn to smile, still a little warily. "I don't know, to be honest, I think I became less angry when I became a teenager, which I know is the opposite of what happens to everyone else."

When he thought about it later, the fact Sam had chosen to answer this question literally struck Ed as possibly the most remarkable aspect of the evening. At the time though, he was too much in the flow of the conversation to clock it. He laughed instead. "How the hell did that happen?" Then he took another sip of his beer and tried to remember how many of his selected tracks were left.

"Not sure really," responded Sam after a moment, "I think I just realised that almost nobody actually means to hurt you, or to act like they're an idiot, apart from a few complete bastards. I don't believe people want to fail, and they sure don't want to be hated. In the same way, they don't have bad taste and tell rubbish jokes or screw things up on purpose; they're just not so good at doing these things well. Take somewhere like Northern Ireland – Protestants and Catholics would probably agree about 90% of stuff." He stopped and laughed. "Though I guess it doesn't work if they're killing each other over the 10."

"I was about to mention that one, but seriously, are you telling me you decided all this when you were 13?"

"Well, yes," replied Sam, almost apologetically.

"No, it's fine, a bit weird, but absolutely fine. You do realise though that it makes you sound like some kind of Western shaman or something."

"No it doesn't," Sam protested, "don't be stupid."

"No, I mean it, not in a bad way or anything. In fact, I think it's fantastic. For a start, I believe you, which is a compliment in itself. Not that I agree with you or anything, no chance of that! You're far too trusting; not nearly cynical enough about human nature. But it's a beautiful and spiritual approach to life, and I love you for it."

"No, it's not, it's none of those things," said Sam, reddening. "It's just what I think; there's no philosophy or system or spirituality about it. You know I'm not like that. I don't even know what a shaman is for Christ's sake,"

"I didn't mean to imply anything different. One day miles in the future, if we still know each other, we'll laugh about it."

"You're on, I'll look forward to it!" Sam got to his feet, "Just going to the loo; while I'm gone, you can think about articulating your philosophy of life, 'cos I'll be asking you about it when I get back!"

When Sam returned, he looked quizzically across the table, "Well?"

"Okay, here goes," began Ed, "the short answer is that I haven't found one yet, still looking. I sort of got religion, Church of England sort, when I was about 12, but it only lasted a couple of years and I ended up thinking that the people who went to church, who called themselves Christians, were no better on average as human beings than a group of non-believers, just a bit more self-satisfied, or too many of them were for my liking."

"How do you mean?"

"Well, a lot of my friends and I went to the church youth club, and that was quite cool and fun. We used to meet after Evensong on Sundays and then we'd stand around outside afterwards and just chat. They were some of my best friends at the time, and we used to go on organised day trips together in the school holidays; a couple of times we even went away youth hostelling in the summer."

"So what happened?" asked Sam.

"Well, the religious stuff was sort of fine, I mean I've never really had a problem with what's in the Bible, certainly Jesus and the Gospels, but the other stuff around it started to grate more. I guess I was getting more conscious as I got older that a lot of people had other faiths, or were atheist or agnostic, and what I was hearing made no reference to any of that, except occasionally to say that they were lost souls who needed rescuing and converting. But as far as I could tell, the other faiths weren't all that different from Christianity. If the Jews worshipped the same God and called him Yahweh, and if Islam came from the same Old Testament root, then I just couldn't accept that every non-Christian was second class or worse. The final straw came at a midweek discussion group at someone's house, designed to encourage us to think more 'seriously' about stuff. Anyway, we were asked who we would save first from a burning house – a Christian, a Buddhist, a Muslim, a Hindu or a dog. I'm not kidding here, there was an element of poor stand-up about it. Anyway, apparently, the Christian was the right answer. I tried to introduce other considerations beside the nature of the person's faith – I know, but I was 14 – their age, ability to save themselves, who you found first etc., but they were all waved away, and all the time everyone else was looking at me like I'd gone mad or had committed some heinous crime or something."

"Did you have a massive row about it?" asked Sam.

"Not really, I kept thinking I must've missed something, that this guy called Richard, who was leading the group, wouldn't have made it sound as if the answer was meant to be so easy unless there was something I'd missed. So I kind of just went quiet for the rest of the evening and then didn't go again, which just meant I gradually drifted away from that group of friends."

"So much for the 'love thy neighbour as thyself' bit," laughed Sam.

Ed continued, "It made me think Christians were often just people like the rest of us, who liked the comfort belonging to the church gave them, and perhaps even the feeling of being chosen in some way."

Sam sat for a moment, "You've certainly thought it through more than I have."

Ed shook his head, stood up and banged the table. "But enough! We've been talking about far too much heavy stuff for this early in the evening, and on what could charitably be described as a small amount of beer."

Some six hours later, Sam was cycling home. It was a beautifully warm summer's night and the darkness was just starting to fade. He was drunk but happy, ecstatic even, within the strange contentedness in which alcohol acts as both anaesthetic and stimulant, the one dampening the pain of self-awareness while the other boosts self-belief and pushes us beyond the boundaries of normal perception. Life seemed suddenly straightforward, with all problems soluble and his daily dilemmas swept away by a wave of confidence that all his hopes were possible. As they had talked through the night, drinking Bell's and listening to music, Sam could see the path ahead of him with crystal clarity. There was a strangeness to this given the heaviness of much of what they had been talking and arguing about. But perhaps, having discussed them, he was temporarily free of their weight.

Cycling along, a random mix of memories flitted through his mind, drifted around and then, one by one, departed as whimsically as they'd arrived. He greeted each with a small, loose introverted smile. He thought that a good deal of how we think of ourselves is bound up in a particular time. Only through a longer lens could a single picture be built up, but that would be too time-consuming. And the chance of assigning certain memories an importance they didn't deserve seemed too great.

One of Sam's most vivid memories was of lying in bed as a child, trying to go to sleep and systematically praying for his parents, family and friends. But in those moments before sleep, all he could see of them in his mind's eye was an indistinct face, its lack of definition almost in inverse relation to how well he knew them, their features overlaid so that delicate lines became broad strokes of crayon, with all character and expression lost in the tangle that surrounded them. Some nights he had cried himself to sleep in frustration at how far he was from even those to whom he was closest

Chapter 11
London, Tuesday, 20 November 1979

"Hi Ed, what can I get you?" Sam was matter of fact. For once it was he who'd arrived at the pub on time and Ed who was late.

"Guinness please," Ed replied. "Sorry I'm late, I only got in at lunchtime, and there's quite a lot on, so it took me a while to get away from the office."

"You must be exhausted, I've no idea how you manage it."

"It's like anything, after a while it gets to be a habit, either in a good or a bad way."

"Maybe, but I've always seen you as the jet-set type," quipped Sam, "all those French films and all that surrealist art."

"If only it were even close to reality! I've never been worried about BO until I started this job, and I've never had to survive on so little sleep. Calling it work doesn't even begin to do it justice."

"But you love it, right?"

"Pretty much, I'm not bored at any rate."

"That sounds a bit like damning with faint praise," Sam observed. Speaking for myself, I'm far too bored. Anyway, given what's going on in the Middle East, boredom must be the least of your problems."

"Perhaps, but most of the time I'm struggling just to understand the basics; the political systems and different demographics of each country – whether the Muslim majority is Shia or Sunni, that sort of thing."

"I'm just writing papers and briefing notes that disappear into the ether. And now the ministers have just changed, all hell is breaking loose."

"Well, at least you won't be bored!"

"Ha, ha! Let's just say I feel a damn sight further from the front line than you are!"

"Okay," said Ed, "I get your point, and we should talk about work because I'm really interested in the change of government and all that. But what I really want to know first is where Mary fits in these days?"

Sam had expected Ed to ask, but not like this, so his half-prepared answer was suddenly useless. "Well, we're still going out...and, we're looking for somewhere to rent together." He trailed off.

"Really!" exclaimed Ed, "That's great news!" Personally indifferent, except to Sam's happiness, he mustered a bit more enthusiasm than what he considered was the minimum demanded by such an announcement. "What's brought this on?"

Sam was sheepish, "I don't know really, I'm not really very good at this kind of thing. We've just kind of ended up seeing each other quite a lot, and we live quite a long way apart – Mary's in Kentish Town, I'm in Earl's Court – so it just seemed to make sense to find somewhere together."

"You really are the last of the great Romantics!" Ed shook his head ostentatiously, smiling broadly. "Here we are in the late 1970s, and you're talking about the most intimate relationship of your life as if it's some cost-saving efficiency drive. Come on, Sam, this is about sex and love, and finding someone you want to wake up next to and have breakfast with every morning. It's sure as hell not about saving a few Tube fares and not having to buy a second toothbrush."

"Okay, you win!" laughed Sam. "You've always been much more of a poet than me, but perhaps that's why you're a journalist and I'm a civil servant."

"Well, at least that's progress of a sort," Ed replied, "though your self-effacement is going to get you into trouble one of these days. But I suppose I should at least be grateful you've told me the news without me having to drag it out of you."

Sam attempted to be sardonic, "Not quite the ringing endorsement I've come to expect from my best friend."

"So have you met Mary's parents yet?"

"You are being inquisitive today," said Sam, visibly relaxing. "I have to say it's the biggest house I've ever been in; not quite National Trust size but not far off. Seriously, I've never seen such a big garden or been in such a big house. But her mum and dad were fine, really genuine and nice. They even seemed to understand my accent! They live in Surrey, and Mary and I were on our way down to Brighton, so we dropped in."

"So did her dad offer you a cigar, check on our prospects and ask when you were going to make an honest woman of his daughter?"

"No, he didn't, but he did – let me see, explore is probably the right word – he did explore my career prospects rather pointedly."

"Excuse me, mate," laughed Ed, "but this seems much more a matter of when than if to me."

Sam reverted to caginess. "Well, to be honest – I've told no one else this – we have talked about getting married some time, no date or anything." Ed deliberately raised his eyebrows, while Sam started staring at the table. "It was when we were talking about living together. And we thought if that worked, then after a year or two we'd probably want to get married."

"Wow!" Ed consciously gasped, "That's a bit more like it, if still somewhat lacking in romantic rhetoric. I'd never have put money on that, I was only taking the piss really."

"Well, at least I can still surprise you occasionally, even if it's only in the context of you thinking I'm rubbish at something and me being just slightly better than that."

"Let's just say that I'm pleasantly impressed that the somewhat practical approach the two of you seem to have taken to human relationships at least appears to have a long-term strategic element to it. And from the one time I've met Mary, she didn't seem the type of woman who falls head over heels in love very often."

Sam was cagey, "Well, you'd have to ask her, but I suspect that would be right."

"So where's the magic spark?" Ed probed. "I mean, when I saw you in February, the two of you had just started going out but there was no sign it was going to become this serious, let alone so quickly."

"It was strange really," said Sam, "we were seeing each other two or three times a week. And that meant that either we didn't have time to see anyone else, or that we saw them together. And once you start doing that, then everyone you know automatically assumes you're a couple and you start getting joint invitations to parties and dinner and stuff."

Ed was thoughtful for a moment, "You still have this knack of describing it as if it's something that happened to the two of you rather than something you both did. Plus, you haven't answered my question, I mean what does she see in you?"

"Glad you haven't lost your natural Derby charm."

"Anyway, how is work really? You didn't sound that excited about it earlier."

"I haven't told anyone else this, not even Mary really, but it's a bit of a slog, to be honest."

"It sounds like you're playing a different game from everyone else and getting left behind as a result."

"Go on."

"Well," Ed continued, "from what I've seen, the unfailingly successful way to get on in any career is to score more points than other people."

"What happened to just doing your job well?"

"Doesn't cut it anymore, if in fact it ever did. But like it or not, getting on in any job is about impressing your boss, making him look good and, just as important, never making him look bad. It all matters in terms of scoring points, and if you don't score more points than the next person, then they'll be the one who gets promoted and not you."

"But what you're describing sounds like some kind of follow-my-leader game."

Ed was emollient, "I don't necessarily disagree. It is the reality though, and once you accept that you can start trying to make it work in your favour."

"Before we go any further," asked Sam, "how the hell did we get here from talking about why Mary might hypothetically fancy me?"

"Just natural genius, and by the way, you're just trying to dodge the issue the way you normally do. And I moved on, for goodness sake, because I realised I wasn't going to get you to say anything meaningful about the most important relationship you've ever had. And I moved on – don't stop me now, I'm on a roll – to a subject, your career, that's now even more important than it was before, because you're trying to buy a house with someone.

"And also, frankly, you should just be doing better. Look, I've met Julian and Stephen and all the others who you call friends. But actually, first of all, they're taking you for a ride – it's all take and no give with them; and secondly, they're busy playing the angles and scoring points with your boss. And that's the fatal flaw in your argument because unless you acknowledge that there's a game that needs to be won, you're leaving the field clear for people like them to go in and clean up. So you have to find a way to get into the race. Because if you don't, the rest of us will be on the receiving end of bad government, and you'll go to your grave feeling virtuous but having copped out. But I still love you like a brother and always will. Here endeth the rant!"

"You've been waiting a while to get that off your chest," Sam said at last.

"And you've always brought out the worst in me. Sorry though, I shouldn't have gone on. It's your life and you're a better judge than me about pretty much

104

everything. Let's talk about something else... It's good to be back in London. Recently, I've been flitting back and forth between Tel Aviv and Amman, which is interesting enough but isn't where the real action is."

With an effort, Sam made the mental shift as well. "I'm sure your time will come. Sooner or later, you'll find yourself right in the middle of it and this period will seem like a blessed oasis of calm. After all, I can't see anyone solving the Middle East's problems any time soon. What do you think of the Iranian Revolution, the Ayatollah and all that?"

"It's just too early to tell," Ed replied. "I'm still pretty reliant on the received wisdom of my more experienced colleagues, but the popularity of the whole thing is a good indication the Shah wasn't greatly loved, let's say." He paused, "I also think it's quite a profound challenge to the other regimes in the region, particularly those who have close links with the West."

"How do you mean? I mean Saudi Arabia could scarcely be more hard-line Islamic than it is already."

"Maybe, but it's bought that freedom from Western criticism by its generally moderating influence in OPEC and its hosting of US bases."

Sam understood, "So that means it's susceptible to criticism for being friends with the Great Satan who propped up the Shah for so many years, who supports Israel and so on."

"Exactly!" replied Ed. "We don't really get an accurate view in Britain of the way the US, and ourselves, are intimately involved and implicated in the Middle East. The news we get tends to concentrate on the here and now, with not very much time devoted to the wider context, but it becomes much worse when the local population looks at events almost exclusively through the opposite end of the lens."

"Sounds like normal end of Empire stuff," ventured Sam.

"Well, it would be serious enough if that was all there was to it – after all, you can only get away with the post-colonial bit for so long. But the whole oil thing makes the problem several quantums worse. BP and Shell mean we're inextricably caught up in Middle East politics for the foreseeable future, and that inevitably puts us on the opposite side from ordinary Arabs. And sooner or later that's going to be a dangerous place to be. At the minute it feels as though I'm just kicking my heels. But I do think I'll get my chance."

Sam was wry, "You mean the same way you think I'm sitting back and waiting for things to happen instead of making them happen?"

"Something like that." Ed smiled and raised his glass in acknowledgement. "You know it's all genuinely meant, but I do let myself go a bit sometimes, and it's always easier to come up with the simple solution when looking in from the outside."

"I know, but it doesn't mean you're necessarily wrong either, and I'll think about what you've said. I do have quite a big thing though about not playing the game as you describe it, so I'm not sure how far I can compromise."

Ed was thoughtful again, "Even if it meant you had more influence as well as money and status? There's a moral issue involved in not wasting your talent as well."

"Perhaps, but if everyone just conforms and plays the same old game all the time, then nothing changes. And please don't talk to me about changing things from the inside; I had enough of that sort of debate at uni. Besides, I reckon I'm already conforming enough just by being in the Civil Service at all. There are loads of our friends who think I've sold out already."

"Okay, you're right probably," admitted Ed, "I can just see Patricia arguing for the overthrow of the State, so the idea of working for it would be complete anathema to her."

"Tricia went off to work for Third World First, didn't she?" asked Sam. "I actually thought she was okay; sorry, I didn't mean 'actually', it's just that sometimes she made it hard to have a sensible conversation with her. Everything was so absolute, with no middle ground."

"I think she's still there, but I've lost touch a bit since last Christmas. You know we had a bit of a fling about a year ago?" Ed looked guilty, and Sam shook his head slowly in mock disappointment.

"Well, strangely enough," he said, after an over-theatrical pause, "I've been ignorant of that one up until now."

Ed smiled. "Sorry, but it didn't last long. Three or four meals, quite a lot of alcohol and some sex, all of which was fine and fun, but there wasn't much else. Patricia never quite said she thought I'd sold out, but it was obvious I was a bit of a disappointment to her."

"I thought you said the sex was fine."

Ed opened his mouth, then shut it again more slowly. "Okay, you've got me. I had it coming. Listen, it's good to see you."

"Come on, Plummer, stop spouting that crap!" laughed Sam, "You'll need to do better than that when the roof falls in on the Middle East and you're our man in Cairo or wherever."

"We've been here almost an hour and not talked yet about Thatcher and the election," remarked Ed when he returned with the pints. "And I haven't seen you since before May; it was still the Winter of Discontent when I was last here. Whoever thought that one up anyway?"

Sam smiled, "I don't know, to be honest, all of the sudden it just became what everyone called it. In the end, I think it did for Labour though. There seemed to be just a general feeling that Callaghan had lost control. Not that I think there's any real understanding of what actually happened, or much confidence the Tories would have dealt with it any better at the time. But it was bad enough to create one of those 'time for a change' feelings."

"What's she like? I remember I always used to loathe her when we were students."

"Too soon to tell really; from what I can work out, she's got extraordinarily clear views on just about everything, which is arguably good because we keep saying we want conviction politicians, but bad because I don't think they're often based on very much evidence. I'm told that if you properly argue with her, she does respond to evidence, at least up to a point, but I suspect her manner massively discourages any dissent."

Ed was faintly incredulous. "But isn't that what cabinet ministers and senior civil servants are there for?"

"Oh come on, Ed, you sound like you were born yesterday, or at least as if you're still stuck in some 1st Year Politics class. It's all part of that balance you were half lecturing me about earlier. I don't want to care too much about my career so that I don't do a good job. There are already too many people I know who'll only ask a question of a senior person if they already know what the answer is. I try to ask important questions, but it's not always that well received. From what people say, Thatcher's bright, but nowhere near bright enough to justify her level of self-belief; by all accounts, we're talking Papal infallibility."

Ed was thoughtful. "That sounds dangerous but I can't think of the last time Britain had a PM so sure of themselves, possibly Churchill in wartime. Isn't Mrs Thatcher a fan of his?"

"She's certainly meant to be," replied Sam, "joined the Young Conservatives when she was at Oxford."

"Old undergrad habits die hard," admitted Ed wryly.

"And what does that mean?" asked Sam.

"Well, I think it means she'll either be around a very long time, or she'll be gone within a couple of years."

Sam laughed, "This is all very precise of you. I don't remember you ever being so sure before."

"I'm not really, just playing around. But she does sound like more of a populist president-type."

"I've not thought about it that way but I can see what you're getting at. As I said before, there's definitely a feeling already of them and us, even within the cabinet from what I hear."

"That sounds bad, especially as they're only six months in. Going back to Patricia for a moment, there's an argument from the Left, at least as much as there was from the Right a few years back, that democratic governments aren't really the best people to be running the country. Scargill and co clearly think parliament isn't really legit unless they agree with it, or rather it agrees with them."

"You could argue that," said Sam, "not least after last winter, and it may well end up with some kind of face-off between government and unions. But, to be honest, I think it's unlikely. The 70s have been a really hard decade for working people, and I think it's remarkable there's been as little unrest as there has, but that means it's unlikely to be repeated, particularly given North Sea oil."

"How do you mean?" asked Ed.

"Well, when we were growing up in the 60s, there was quite a lot of talk about different ways of organising society, making it more democratic and less about established power structures. The world was becoming a global village if you remember, and that was part of what made Vietnam so abominable, it seemed a relic of a colonial world we wanted rid of. But then the reverse happened, and we've ended up in a world of entrenched power structures. And in parallel with that, in countries like ours, traditional working-class manufacturing jobs are disappearing at a rate of knots, often overseas."

"Okay," said Ed, "I get most of that but I'm less sure how much most ordinary people are aware of any of it. A lot of the stuff in the 60s was surely only about a very small slice of society, certainly the more revolutionary end of it you're talking about, though obviously a lot of the more general social changes went much wider. And as far as the 70s are concerned, doesn't it in practice get subsumed by the various oil crises and jumps in inflation? But as far as most people are concerned, I think they're more worried about Arthur Scargill running the country and everyone being on strike."

Ed was interested in how Sam had changed. In the mainstream press, the strikes which had caused the collapse of the Labour government's pay policy had been predictably massacred. He was intrigued to find Sam taking what was essentially a contrarian view. "So, are you pushing this line of argument at work?" he asked.

Sam laughed, "Not exactly, or at least not so explicitly. But you're right to the extent that it's not exactly hard to work out that I don't exactly fit the mould. But I suspect that comes from my silence in certain discussions rather than from anything I actually do say."

"Okay, I get that, but I don't remember you talking about class and globalisation in the same sentence before; that take on things must have come from somewhere."

"Well, to be honest," Sam replied, "it's been less what's actually been happening out there," he gestured vaguely at the window, "than seeing Mary's friends... Let's just say they're as much a product of their class and background as I am of mine."

Ed nodded, "Yes, I can just see you, even you, bristling in those sorts of discussions. What's Mary's attitude?"

"Mainlyshe thinks it's hilarious."

"Mary seems good for you."

"I think so," Sam replied. "I reckon I'm fairly independent in a lot of ways, but it's undeniably special when someone else seems to love you every bit as much as you love them."

"Wow!" gasped Ed, "You've suddenly gone all confessional and romantic on me, but in a good way. Listen, mate, I'm more pleased for you, for both of you, than I can say. Seriously, it's great to see you so happy."

"Thanks. And what about yourself? Is there not a good woman lurking somewhere that you haven't told me about? Tricia was a bit of a bolt from the blue by the way; that must've been pretty intense while it lasted."

"You could say that, but to tell you the truth, she was really lovely with me and thoughtful in little ways that I wouldn't have imagined. Like she would sense immediately whether I needed a cup of tea or a drink. It's funny but, although it didn't work out, Patricia was completely different in lots of ways from how I'd thought. It makes me think none of us ever really knows anyone else properly; maybe we don't even know ourselves that well."

Sam was puzzled, "Why do you think that? After all, you and I pretty much know each other."

"I think that's only true up to a point. Now you and I spent a hell of a lot of time together when we were at Manchester, but we do completely different things now that might surprise the other. Have you been watching Alec Guinness in Le Carré thing by the way, 'Tinker, Tailor...'?

"Yes, mostly, but not every week. Everyone seems to think it's wonderful, but I haven't really managed to get into it. I don't know, maybe I'm just not clever enough; why do you ask?"

"It's just that it's really a story about the complexity of the human character, and how impossible it is for one person to really know another. There's all these little things, the ones we don't even know about ourselves until a specific set of circumstances throws them into relief. Say you're in a corporate environment and

I'm in a war zone; well, we neither of us really knew how we'd react to these environments until we ended up in them. For instance, I'm dead scared by gunfire, even when it's miles away, to an extent I wouldn't have believed possible, while I'm also often physically sick at the mere sight of blood. And even just knowing about those two small things probably slightly alters your view of me. But this new picture you'll now have will only be a little more complete."

"Jesus," said Sam, "you've got my head spinning with that one."

"Maybe, but it's only the tip of the iceberg. I've seen so much of people under pressure, even in the last six months, that it's made me question every assumption I've ever held about anyone. People I thought would be brave sometimes haven't been and vice versa. Not just correspondents by any means but the ordinary people you just come across."

"Okay," reasoned Sam, "but it sounds like you're talking about how people react in extreme situations. I'm sure that's true, but it's quite different to extrapolate from that to general statements about their characters."

"Fair point, but you could just as easily argue that the way people behave under pressure is more revealing because it strips away all the artifice."

Sam tried to be playful. "So does that apply also to countries or societies? That you only really understand what they're like when you see them under pressure?"

"Well, I've always been a bit sceptical about whether it's valid to talk about national character at all; it's too easy to fall into stereotypes. I think it can make sense to talk about a collective consciousness in a period of crisis. And countries do react differently in these situations. The Second World War is an obvious example in terms of how different populations responded differently to German occupation and then, post war, to the challenges of rebuilding. And you see it again now in the Middle East."

"But that collective consciousness, as you call it, is in reality created by a small number of people, who then articulate it and become a catalyst?"

"Yes, but then you quickly get into a chicken and egg argument."

"How do you mean?"

"Well, if you take a country like Egypt, one of the world's great ancient civilisations, it has a history of being a repressed colony, subject to a series of empires – Ottoman, French, British, whatever. It's now an independent country but only as a result of, effectively, the military coup that brought Nasser to power; and so it's now been subject to a military dictatorship for a quarter of a century or whatever it is. That's not really anything to do with the Egyptian people as such So then you get down to Nasser, and whether he represents progress for his people or a new version of the same old thing."

"But," argued Sam, "Nasser and people like him – Saddam, Gaddafi and so on – they all come from somewhere, they're products of their society."

"Except," Ed was persistent, "their success is still dependent on specific circumstances and whether they're able to overcome or exploit them. And some of that must be down to the individual."

"So what about Khomeini?"

"To be honest, I think Khomeini has been the author of his own success. I think the Shah was time limited, whatever, but the focus and nature of the Iranian

Revolution would have been completely different if it had been led by someone else."

"Go on."

"Well, there was the whole thing about his being in Paris – the way he gave all those 'exclusive' interviews to various influential journalists, which I'm sure he knew would have a positive impact on Western opinion and thereby filter back to Iran in a way that could only add legitimacy to his claims and the role of national liberator he was trying to carve out for himself. And then there was the superb choreography of his return flight to Tehran, packed out, of course, with those same influential journalists, it was fascinating to watch it all unfold."

"But you said the Shah was time expired anyway."

"Well yes, but I don't think there was necessarily anything inevitable about the timing of his fall, not to the extent we now assume. The tendency to post-rationalise these things is almost irresistible. We need it to be that way to keep us sane, give us some sense the world can be predicted or understood."

"You really have become quite the philosopher these days," laughed Sam.

"Maybe, but a phoney, self-deluding one!"

"Now you're just being boring. I remember one time we stayed up late, one of those Glenfiddich evenings when we solved the problems of the world while listening to everything from the Beatles to Van Morrison to Genesis, but then couldn't remember a word of our wonderfully elegant solutions in the morning. Anyway, I vaguely recall you explaining, totally persuasively, how the Domino Theory had been planted at the core of US foreign policy by Soviet spies, to persuade Washington the Commies were much richer and more influential than they really were, and to induce the Yanks to get into bed with a whole host of unsavoury dictators; which would then give the Russians automatically more influence within all those countries, and with protest groups within NATO countries. It was truly brilliant!"

"That's obviously why I became a journalist."

"Anyway, I put the argument in a paper I wrote for the minister the other day, unattributed, I'm afraid!"

"You're joking?"

Chapter 12
Tel Aviv, Monday, 20 September 1982

Ed got into Tel Aviv just after lunch and had been sat in his hotel bar since about 30 minutes later, having forced himself to have a shower. It was now just after 6pm, and he was exhausted in every way possible, but despite his best efforts still only slightly drunk. He had spent the day before filing his copy on Sabra and Shatila but still didn't feel as though he had told anybody anything. Despite having slept dreadfully the night before, he also still felt wide awake. Finally, he went to the hotel phone and called Yuri, an Israeli academic friend, and arranged to meet him in the hotel for a drink at 7pm. Yuri he could talk to, shout and rant at, and he would still understand.

Ed knew, or believed he knew, that he'd become a decent, objective journalist who reported fairly on what he saw in front of him. He paid attention to the evidence and was confident he didn't just jump to the obvious conclusion, or simply agree with the consensus view. He also believed he had a deserved reputation for understanding Israel's position, its intractable dilemma. But, here and now, he was finding it impossible not to believe the Jewish state had just been complicit in a war crime. The evidence of slaughter he'd just witnessed in the two Palestinian camps was way beyond anything he'd come across.

All day, throughout the drive south and during the afternoon, he'd been trying to rationalise what he'd just seen. This must be what the Thirty Years War had been like, perhaps the Crusades as well, probably other wars he couldn't recall just now. But it felt, as much as anything, like what he imagined a pogrom must have been like; the methodical slaughter of the unarmed men, women and kids, motivated by a cocktail of fear, revenge and religious hatred. If the Israeli Army was involved, even if its crime was to stand aside and let others do the killing, the ironies were too obvious.

He signalled to the waiter and ordered a gin and tonic, deciding it was time to switch to something other than beer. He wanted something he could legitimately sip, contemplate with some emotion other than thirst or despair. There had to be a bigger picture that would offer some shape and causation to what he'd just witnessed.

Somehow, Lebanon and the refugee camps on its southern border had become the landscape against which a series of confrontations between forces much greater than the people caught on the ground was being played out. The Iranian Revolution and Russia's invasion of Afghanistan seemed to be having a ripple impact across the region. Elsewhere, Sadat had been assassinated and many of the oil kingdoms were beginning to look more vulnerable. Only now was Ed properly starting to come to terms with the way the faith of a country's ruler didn't necessarily match that of the majority of the population.

Saddam, for example, was a Sunni ruler of Iraq, a majority Shiite country, but with large Sunni and Kurdish minorities. Meanwhile, its large neighbour, Iran, was pretty much a Shiite country from top to bottom. This fact alone meant relations between the two were complicated at best. As part of the same cocktail, Saudi Arabia's Sunni leadership tacitly supported Saddam as a bulwark against Iran's Shiite theocracy. The US, meanwhile, had been dragged ever deeper into this unfamiliar quagmire by the fall of the Shah. Iran's seizure of the US Embassy and the abortive attempt to rescue the hostages had fatally holed Jimmy Carter's re-election campaign. And Reagan had taken note, so the US was working to make itself less dependent on Iran, building closer connections with Riyadh and Baghdad. That was the problem with the Middle East, there were simply no win-wins; everything had a price, usually a high one.

All this had made it harder for the moderates in Israel to maintain negotiations on any kind of overall settlement for the West Bank and Jerusalem. Ed was more and more drawn to the idea that only the hardliners had the clout to make a lasting peace; only they carried the credibility to sell it to their own, and by implication, only they could persuade the other side that what was on offer could be delivered.

It was all a mess and it was hard to see how it could get better. If anything, America's involvement sometimes made things harder, both because its influence was limited by its sensible unwillingness to commit its military, and because the resulting gap was filled by rhetoric, making it the only game in town and absolving everyone else of responsibility. The final irony, of course, was that US oil dependency on the Middle East was growing just at the point where its influence there was on the wane. Oil was the key and always had been, but where it had once been about empire and corporate profit, now it was about surging demand in the West's economies. This was pretty much the first lesson he had learnt, and it was arguably still the most important.

Against this landscape, Israel, seen through a Washington lens, could do no wrong. As the sole democracy in the region, with by far the most effective military, bankrolled by the US Treasury, Ed well understood the real politik of the situation. But his own view was that Israel, certainly its post 1973 incarnation, with control of Sinai and the Golan Heights secure, was in fact a destabilising force. During the Six Day and Yom Kippur wars, it had proved itself so militarily superior to its Arab neighbours that they had turned to the Soviet Union for military support at the expense of economic development. That relationship had since cooled but the fact of it was still significant.

Ed simply couldn't see any way in the present situation that the US would be trusted as an honest broker. Its history of supporting Israel was too consistent, while its wider national interest in the region was too narrowly confined to oil. Ed felt about 50 years old, his body tired and aching, his brain whirring but in slow motion, thoughts succeeding each other as in his mind he zigzagged across the various jigsaw pieces. He knew they were an unlikely mix of fact and interpretation but it was all he had. He sat back, slumping in the chair, eyes shut.

"Hey, amigo!" Yuri's voice, rasping from too many fags, penetrated his fog. "How goes it?"

Ed opened his eyes and smiled wanly. "Surviving," he volunteered, "it feels like he's only just surviving at the moment, but I suspect the patient will pull through. How goes it with you?"

"Not so bad," Yuri replied. He was 58, overweight by about 20 kilos, with a craggy face that told of too little care and sleep, and unkempt hair but alert eyes that followed you around. "You look terrible," he observed, "let me get you, and me, a drink." He beckoned to a waiter and ordered. "Where've you been?"

"Sabra and Shatila."

"Ah, that would explain it – it's war Jim, but not as we know it!" Yuri took a long drag on his beer, Ed did the same on his gin. "I can only begin to imagine what you saw, what you must feel like, my friend." Yuri looked at the beer and shouted to the waiter for a bottle of white wine, an ice bucket and two glasses. "I can see this beer won't last long but white wine's the strongest thing I can drink these days; it keeps me hydrated."

Ed continued as if Yuri hadn't spoken. "It's been the longest week of my life, Yuri. I know you're trying to distract me but I need to talk to you about it."

"Don't worry, that's what I'm here for," the other replied, "and I'll stay here for as long as you want me to. Reporting on our lovely, fragrant region of the world must be the hardest jobs in journalism, and I have the utmost respect for the way you approach it, my friend. In the right way also, you are a friend to Israel, even if some of my colleagues and many of our politicians would not agree. I especially like it that you do not dislike us even when we are rude to you, which is often. But what is rude in other cultures is simply being honest for us. But tell me, when are you going home? You should have some rest."

"In a couple of days."

"It will be well-earned. You must rest properly this time, and then I hope you will return."

Ed sighed. "I will."

"Good!" Yuri was definite. "And now you must tell me what sort of country you think Israel is."

Ed sighed again. "I really don't want to play a game with you, Yuri. I'm just not up for it this evening."

"I know, Ed, trust me, I'm not into games tonight either." He examined Ed carefully, reached across the table and grasped his wrist lightly, then released it.

"Okay then," Ed relented. "Israel! So, first of all, I'm far from an expert. I've been in and out of Tel Aviv and Jerusalem for nearly five years now but that hardly qualifies me, nowhere near. And while I know you fairly well, and maybe a few others, my dealings with Israelis have on the whole been brief and business-like, sometimes pleasant, sometimes not. But it won't surprise you that these limitations to my knowledge don't prevent me drawing conclusions."

He looked down, took another long drink and paused for a long five seconds. "You're quite a schizophrenic country, which would be unusual for such a young nation until you recall the history, and of course, the history is never far away. But I don't just mean your recent history, the Holocaust and since, but your older history, going back to Biblical times and the diaspora of the Jewish people. And only against that background is it really possible to form an objective view of Israel's creation – thinking always only about the Holocaust distorts everything too much. The creation of Israel was itself such a sudden event, almost like the eruption of that volcanic island – I always forget its name – off the coast of Iceland in the early 60s. And then you've had to defend its existence ever since, so it's not surprising you haven't decided what sort of a nation you want to be. My sense is that the idealism of those early decades, the Kibbutz Movement and so on, has faded a little, but that might just be a jaded European talking. But even over the last five years, I'm not conscious of people talking about the future now the way they did even back in '77. Now that might be me, but I think there's something about the wars and stress of the last 15 years having slowly taken the edge off what this country was about."

Yuri interrupted gently. "If that's the case, why do you think it's happened? And is there any other better response you could reasonably have expected from us?"

"I'm not sure I know the answer to either of those questions, but it looks to me as though you've become quite a militarised society, beyond the National Service thing, to the point where the military is, for many people, almost synonymous with the state of Israel. And their experiences in the army and the relationships they formed there are for many people the most important shaping influences in their lives. And I think that might come from the fact that, when the army isn't actually in action, the state of readiness is still so high – far higher than the US and Russia. And I think that comes from being surrounded by Arab states, even Egypt and Jordan, that don't really want you to exist, so that even when they're not actually at war with you, you're convinced they're watching carefully for any sign of weakness. And because at the end of the day you're a tiny country with a small population, that engenders a huge and inevitable paranoia all its own. And that makes what would otherwise be normal, rational decisions seem ridiculously risky. So I guess I'm saying that Israel is extremely paranoid but for darkly understandable reasons, and that given the precarious nature of your existence since 1948, that's probably okay."

"Fine," said Yuri quietly, "so tell me about Sabra and Shatila."

"I don't know if I should love you or hate you for this. But I can't forget, and you should never underestimate, how horrific it was. And having said I needed to talk to someone about it, I now don't know if I'm physically able to. Sorry, the last thing I want is to make a melodrama out of this but it was awful and I don't think…"

Ed paused again, looked down then up at the ceiling. "You see, there's a back story to all this. I grew up very much with my parents' memories of the war. It was all still so fresh in their minds, rationing had only ended a couple of years before and National Service was probably still going. My dad had taken part in the D Day landings and the subsequent advance through northern Germany. He was only in his early 20s, and even now he has vivid memories of what he saw and experienced, but it's plain he still only talks to me about some of them. He's told me about meeting some Russian soldiers and getting hammered with them on some carrot vodka they were carrying. But most of all he remembers helping groups of Jews who had survived the concentration camps. For a while, he was stationed at a bizarre kind of rehab camp where those who'd survived were able to get themselves together and begin to decide what they were gonna do, where they were gonna go. And, of course, he was appalled by the physical state they were in, but also unbelievably impressed by their bravery and their lack of bitterness for what had been done to them and their families and their people. That's what still brings tears to his eyes rather than how weak and vulnerable they were. And so I got from him an incredible respect for the Jewish people, their resilience but even more their humanity, despite everything.

"But the other thing he taught me, probably above everything else, was that human beings, nations, peoples, need to find better ways of living together in peace, that nothing like what had happened in the war, and especially the Holocaust, could be allowed to happen ever again. Dad obviously wasn't alone in wanting that, and it was in many ways a hopeless wish. But it's what millions of people around the world wanted and believed in after 1945, about the Holocaust especially.

"But since then, other terrible events have happened, maybe not as terrible but still terrible in their own right, most obviously the attempted genocide in Cambodia. I'm sorry…" Ed sat back, "I've lost my train of thought, and can't even recall what the original question was."

Yuri winced but managed a small smile. "It's okay, you're tired, and I know only too well myself how much that messes with your thought processes." He made himself laugh, "I have to tell you that it's also what I've begun to call 'age-related', and so it will happen more frequently as the years pass by. But what I suspect you were going on to say, and I suspect this on the basis of the extensive studies I've made of how your mind works, is that what you've just seen in Sabra and Shatila came uncomfortably close to what you imagine genocide would be like; entirely purposeful slaughter of children, women and men for no other reason beyond their ethnicity. And that you feel all the more uncomfortable because this slaughter seems to have been condoned, connived at even, by the Israeli Army. And given the recency of the Holocaust, still within many people's lifetimes, you're struggling to come to terms with the implications."

Ed sat back, the tension draining from his features, leaving only a relaxed exhaustion. "Yuri, you're a god. I can't tell you how glad I am you were in tonight and willing to spend some time to come down here and talk to me. You've just captured what I'm feeling and what I would never have been able to articulate properly. So yes, there's a kind of despair in me that humanity isn't capable of learning, even the people who've suffered most directly and terribly. And I don't think I'm particularly naïve or innocent. But it was the helplessness of the victims that made me gasp. I was even physically sick, which I've never been close to in my life before."

Yuri looked calm, as though he had expected this, or something like it. "Right, would you like me to explain to you at least part of the other side of the coin, give you a view of how at least some Israelis might view the Sabra and Shatila massacres, why it does have a kind of connection with the Holocaust but not, I suspect, in the way you imagine."

"Yes, of course," said Ed, sounding slightly apprehensive.

"So," began Yuri, "first, let's start with history; for someone Jewish, certainly someone of my generation or older, the most remarkable thing about the Holocaust was not that it happened when it did but that it, or something similar, didn't happen earlier. The half century before was punctuated by pogroms across Russia and Eastern Europe, while in England and France anti-Semitism was a fashionable belief to hold, its references dropped casually into much of the literature of the period. It was an age of increasing nationalism; and the otherness of Jews, our cosmopolitanism and the international networks we constructed, were common objects of suspicion and often of outright hostility. So too were our financial and intellectual successes, which could have been celebrated and embraced, but instead were reviled as evidence of conspiracy and political treason."

Yuri paused. Not for the last time, he made a point of seeking eye contact. "As a consequence, relatively few in Europe saw much unusual about Hitler's early purges, his confiscation of Jewish businesses and property, much of which, completely illegally, still remains in the hands of the German state, or in some Swiss bank vault, to this day. And similarly, while there had been nothing like the Holocaust in terms of scale, the state planning involved and the systematic execution," he laughed dryly and briefly, "to many Jews of my and my parents' generation, there has always been a fear that the next time the pogrom would be bigger and better organised; you need to understand that my parents had no doubt there would be other pogroms; it was a matter of where, when and how big, not if. That was why they emigrated to America in 1920, and why my American passport, my insurance against the prejudices of that old Europe people now like to reminisce about as a cultural golden age, is my most precious possession."

Now it was Ed's turn to take a drink, conscious that a well of emotion was being released opposite him. Again, Yuri sought eye contact before continuing, "So after the war, there was never really any question of Jewish people wanting to go back to the Europe of before 1939. To be fair, few Europeans wanted to return to that world either. But on the other hand, particularly in Russia and what became the Soviet bloc, the fact of no longer having a significant Jewish population was part of the attractiveness of the post-war world. The property of the Jews who'd been taken to the camps had mostly been sold or reallocated, and the new owners weren't exactly queuing up to return it. And while Nazism was gone, a more general anti-Semitism returned to the Eastern bloc not long after 1945. So there wasn't, and still isn't, much enthusiasm among Jews for the modern version of old Europe. For sure, many Jews still live in these countries, but they're typically not those who had a free choice without strings or attachments; these people headed for the United States or Palestine."

Ed wondered where the conversation was heading and failed to see how it could bear any relation to Sabra and Shatila. But he liked Yuri and trusted him; so instead of interrupting to ask, he simply took another sip and sat back, still in an ostentatious listening mode, head raised slightly and turn to one side, brow furrowed, waiting for the other to continue. Although Ed thought he'd disguised it, Yuri had observed his audience's impatience with a mix of amusement and irritation. No wonder Israelis tended to be sharp and direct when Europeans were so poor at listening, particularly, he thought, when they were being asked to listen to something involving their own somewhat murky past. For a moment, Yuri wondered if Ed was going to interrupt, and considered how abrupt he would be with the Englishman if he did, but then he noted, with no little relief, that Ed was still listening.

Carefully concealing his approval of this, Yuri continued. "Ever since Israel came into being, it has deeply distrusted all other nations, especially the old European powers – Britain and France – who have always had an undisguised affinity for the Arabs. Germany, meanwhile, tries to forget, while the Soviet Union is, at root, no less anti-Semitic than was its Russian Imperial predecessor. Even the United States only really uses us for its own purposes. It was only at the last minute,

I am told, that Nixon finally agreed to help us during Yom Kippur and, although we are quite numerous and live in important electoral states, the votes of Jewish Americans are not always sufficient to ensure the presidents keep their promises to us. Because of that, malign though they clearly are in other ways, the Iranian Revolution and the Soviet invasion of Afghanistan both have their uses in reminding Washington of the value of Israel's friendship. But I digress, my friend, even if only a little.

"What I'm seeking to convey is that the consequences of Israel's birth and history have, with good reason, left us with an acute sense of our own vulnerabilities and the absolute necessity of self-reliance. The world is a hostile and unforgiving place to be Jewish, not least for those of us living in Israel, but at least here we have a greater measure of control of our own destiny and some ability to protect and defend ourselves. Our neighbours all want to destroy us; I understand that because we have taken land they believe is theirs, taken it from them. But it's our land also and our need is greater.

"And this is our struggle for survival as a nation. All of us living in Israel, and many Jews living in other countries, are involved in this and no quarter has ever been asked for or offered since 1948. What happened in Sabra and Shatila is another part of this story, neither more nor less. No doubt it is a tragedy, but it is only one among many and its roots go back many generations; back through Israel's history as a nation state, back through the Holocaust, back through France's colonial involvement in Lebanon, back through the Ottoman Empire and beyond. If we and others have been somewhat brutalised by that history, and if the massacres at Sabra and Shatila are a result of that, then that is something the Israeli people will have to live with. Most of us know we carry some guilt from the deaths Israel has caused or has allowed to happen, but for us that guilt has always been part of the price of survival, and we are willing to pay it. It is a much smaller burden than the alternative, which would be the extinction of the first Jewish state to have existed in two millennia. That is something we cannot allow to happen, but it is a burden we carry alone."

Ed sat back. He was aghast at what he'd just heard. While he could recognise Israel's sense of vulnerability, the idea this could translate seamlessly to a straightforward justification for Israel's conduct was anathema to him. Choices had been made and crimes had been committed; it was as simple as that and everything else was secondary. But, even if the views Yuri had just expressed were narrowly held, they opened a new window on the Israeli psyche. He had never really understood the profound sense of paranoia shared by so many Jews, but now he realised how little he'd appreciated the continuing relevance of European anti-Semitism. But none of this in any way abnegated the responsibility for the massacres allowed by Sharon and the officers close to him. To accept Yuri's argument was to accept that two wrongs can make a right, as well as a complex guilt-transfer system across peoples and generations. But Ed also realised that, psychologically, this idea of needing to rewind the clock of history to get to the real culpability provided Israel with a fool proof get-out-of-jail card. Given the centuries of persecution, there was an almost inexhaustible reservoir of causation and justification on which to draw.

He wondered what to say. The explanation was clearly a heartfelt one, intended to provoke a response, and Ed knew he'd have to think quickly. The merest slip in language or tone, and that might well be it. Ed badly wanted to challenge the older man, to try and get him to recognise that guilt for crimes committed could not be avoided, passed back down the chain in the way Yuri had described, but he also knew this wasn't the right time. Yuri had stayed calm all the way through, but Ed supposed the sheer emotional energy Yuri had invested already meant the fuse would be short if he felt his argument was being undervalued or challenged unfairly.

It had been only a few seconds but Ed felt he needed to say something. He tried to think quickly but his mind was still slow and blurred – from the scenes he'd witnessed, from the long drive south and now from the alcohol. "I knew I'd called the right person to talk to this evening," he said at last. "I was really confused and didn't know what to make of what I'd just seen. It was really terrible there, and I needed someone to talk to about it. You're right, I couldn't comprehend how the Israeli army's role could be reconciled with the terrible persecution of the Jewish people."

Ed paused and carefully made eye contact with the other man, just as he had noted Yuri had done. "I have to say, I've never heard any of that explained before. Look, I know the five years I've spent in the region is only the briefest of moments in its history, but I've never understood before the connections between the Holocaust and the earlier pogroms, and the cumulative impact they've had on Israel's attitude to old Europe, as you called it, and even to the United States." He paused again, and took a long sip of wine, partly to buy himself a couple more seconds of preparation. "I confess I hadn't fully appreciated the context of the isolation Israel feels at the lack of support it believes it receives from the rest of the world, and the real depth of that feeling."

Yuri spoke, slightly faster than before, "I'm glad. I wanted you to understand, as a friend and someone I have respect for."

"Well, I'm not sure I understand it yet," Ed replied frankly, "but I certainly have a much better idea than before."

"Good, I'm pleased."

As far as it went, Ed was being entirely truthful. He was doubtful how many Israelis would have taken the time to explain the context, and Yuri had given him a new lens. Ed wanted to express his appreciation of Yuri's efforts. And Yuri was also a valuable contact and a potential conduit to other influential Israelis.

"What do you think happens now?" Ed asked. "Enough other journalists saw what happened and this will probably be all over the press tomorrow, if it isn't already."

Yuri sighed, "I don't know, I agree it looks terrible but sins of omission are rarely looked upon as being as culpable as when the blood is on your own hands. My guess therefore is that, after a period of handwringing, views of Israel will settle back into their normal spectrum, with those who usually support us continuing to do so and those who would obliterate us being newly confirmed in their opinions. This process will be assisted by the Israeli media, which is skilled at ensuring our side of the story receives a hearing, and by Jewish communities in other countries, who will write into their press and politicians; and probably also by the Arabs and Palestinians, who are not so skilled in communications and who, at some point, probably soon, will most likely commit another atrocity of their own, which will give the world's media the chance to move on to a new story."

"What makes you think the media wants an opportunity like that?"

Yuri sat back, "I think it is because they are all in love still with Israel's story and do not want it to end. We are a brave little country, born out of the ashes of the Holocaust, surrounded by hostile neighbours but able so far to defend ourselves, the sole regional nursery for some Western liberal values, and the only democracy in a region dominated by authoritarian dictators and extreme conservative theocracies."

Despite himself, Ed laughed out loud. "You put it very well; I recognise every part of that narrative, including in my own reporting. One of my lecturers at university once told me that political and historical judgements are always relative, never absolute. Who you are compared to matters just as much, perhaps more, than who you are."

Now it was Yuri who laughed, "It is true, my friend, humanity's view of right and wrong is rooted in time and context. There is the famous saying, I think by Chou En Lai, that it is still too soon to judge the significance of the French Revolution. I think we can caveat that by saying it is inevitable we will make judgements but that we need to recognise none of these judgements are likely to be final or definitive. No reputation, good or evil, is ever secure, and revisionism is the fashion of every age."

"If you don't mind my saying, you're sounding a little definitive yourself?" observed Ed drily.

Both were conscious their conversation had moved on, satisfied they had made the points that needed making at this time and place. The impact of each's comments on the other had been rather less than either imagined.

Yuri had taken some time to contemplate Ed's last question. "Before this century, warfare was essentially man to man, hand to hand. Of course, there were rifles and cannon, and before that muskets, and before that arrows, and always cavalry of some kind, but the science of warfare remained close combat. The two World Wars of the last 70 years have changed that, and the growing list of ever more sophisticated killing machines being supplied to the military continues to grow, almost exponentially it seems. From the tank to the nuclear bomb to the cruise missile and ICBM, the ability to kill the enemy at distance has multiplied decade by decade. And this pace of change, probably the fastest in history, and the increasing distance between mankind and the consequences of our actions, has demolished our sense that there is any order or hierarchy in the universe."

"That's interesting," Ed replied. "For me, the Berlin Wall and so on are sterile but stable realities, almost boring in some ways. I've grown up with them and can't really imagine what it was like before. World War 2 already seems ages ago. So when you start talking about these cataclysms that forever shifted people's assumptions, I struggle to really understand what you mean. For my generation, I think it still seems like the 60s was the decade when everything changed, not the 40s."

"Okay," replied Yuri, "but you can't properly understand what happened in the 60s until you recognise it as a reaction to the war and its aftermath. The sheer exhaustion of Europe and the sudden, exuberant dominance of the US – economic, cultural, whatever – set the scene for the '60s. And what were the '60s anyway when you start to analyse them? There's the Rebellion of Youth – attempted and failed; the Prague Spring – attempted and failed; a war to prevent the spread of Communism

119

in South East Asia – attempted and failed; the Civil Rights movement in the States – let's be generous here – attempted and partially successful. I could go on, but apart from the crossover of Blues into White pop music, the Space Race, and a lot of sex for quite a small number of people, it's hard to see what really altered that made a difference."

"Now you're just being provocative," laughed Ed. "Okay, the things you mentioned might have technically failed or whatever, but those so-called failures still changed the world, our attitudes and assumptions." Ed was cheerful but challenging. He'd begun the evening feeling very much in Yuri's thrall, less knowledgeable as well as knackered and depressed, but something in the dynamics of the last hour had shifted the balance.

"All right, so I was being provocative," Yuri conceded, "but I do get tired of people going on about the '60s as though they were somehow completely disconnected from the '50s and the '70s. There's nothing in history that isn't somehow prefigured by what went before and isn't part of the causation of what follows. Sometimes you have to look hard for the evidence but not in this case. It's staring you in the face, from Rosa Parks, to Hungary in '56 to Yuri Gagarin and Telstar."

"And how do you see this decade?" asked Ed, "What do you think the '80s will look like in retrospect?"

"That's an excellent question, my friend," Yuri replied, raising his glass, "but not really one for a historian like me. However, there are a few predictions I might make. The Middle East will become yet more unstable, partly because of the Ayatollahs but also due to the chronic instability of Lebanon and the weakness of our other neighbours, which means we have no one reliable to talk to about our security. And the importance of oil will continue to grow; it will become more vital to Western economies even as they try to diversify away from it."

Ed sat back. "Once again, you've gifted me a wealth of ideas. Nothing surprises me in what you've just said, but I'd have struggled to frame it the way you've just done. Where do you think Afghanistan fits in?"

"Fair question," Yuri replied. "It's only a hunch but I worry for the Russians. The Soviet army is far from equipped for guerrilla warfare, which is what Afghanistan is all about."

Ed looked sceptical, "Then why the huge NATO reaction?"

"Hard to say," Yuri replied, unfazed, "but I think it's the Cold War mentality that your enemy is always strong and aggressive. It's hard to get out of that mind-set." Yuri shrugged. "And now it's time we both got to bed. It's been a long day for you, my friend, and a long evening for me. What are you doing next?"

"Flying back to London the day after tomorrow. I was due back anyway at the end of next week, and it was easy enough to bring it forward. After everything, I'm just going to find a quiet place in the country to hang out for a few days."

Yuri was sensitive now, "Whatever you think best, my friend, but be careful of relying solely on your own company. Our real friends are there for times such as this."

The two men stood up and said their goodbyes, accompanied by a slightly hesitant hug. On his way up in the lift, Ed thought again about how much he owed the sharp academic who'd taken him under his wing. A flicker of suspicion drifted across his mind, the thought that his relationship with Yuri might have been subtlety engineered. But just as quickly he dismissed the idea; Yuri was a demonstrably independent academic who'd had easily his share of run-ins with the Israeli authorities. He shook his head at the depths of paranoia he was plumbing. The temptation was to assume nothing was as it seemed, when the reality, he'd learned, was that much of what you experienced was exactly what it seemed.

Twenty minutes later he was asleep, head buried in the pillow, reading light still on, book lying open on the floor next to the bed, face down with its pages crumpled. But it wasn't the deep sleep Ed needed, for he dreamed vividly of Sabra and Shatila. The men, the fighters, had departed and at the time he had been confused at first, not understanding what he was seeing. But in the dream he knew at once what had happened, knew that around the next corner he would come across a pile of corpses against a wall daubed with blood in the shape of a cross. The light was artificial, as if he was moving in a spotlight that followed him as he drove through the silent streets. He could barely hear his jeep's engine, which seemed muffled by the fog even though there was no fog. The sight he lingered on the longest was of a mother slumped against a brick wall with her arms spread wide, protecting her two daughters, who seemed to be about five and three. All of them had been shot in the head, executed at short range, and the mother's stomach had been sliced open.

Ed turned over restlessly in his sleep, and under normal circumstances would probably have woken in a cold sweat. But so tired was he that he continued to sleep. For maybe two hours, his slumber was disturbed, the same images recurring, refusing to leave him be. Finally, they subsided, and he settled peacefully, curled up in the same foetal position as the older of the two daughters.

Chapter 13
New York, Monday, 29 January 1968

Philip stepped out of his taxi opposite the dive hotel in Greenwich Village, where he had booked in for his first three nights in New York. It was his first time outside Britain, and his heart pumped hard as he adopted the casual, matter-of-fact manner he had seen in films. He paid the taxi driver, having counted the cash out in the back of the cab on the way down 5th Avenue. He had only brought a single medium-sized suitcase and a rather worn, soft brown briefcase that he'd bought second-hand. He figured he'd buy clothes as he needed them.

'It was just after 3pm, 8pm in London,' he thought. He hadn't slept on the flight but was looking forward to jetlag in the way a boy looks forward to a new experience that, while not especially pleasant, signalled that he was growing up and moving forward in the adult world. He knew only one other person who had flown to the USA, his uncle Patrick, who sold US-imported women's underwear, but Philip already 'knew' both that he would spend a major part of his life in America and that everyone his age would fly a lot more and a lot further than his parents' generation had done.

Although only just 19, he certainly 'knew' a lot. He knew that satellites in space were about to begin beaming live events around the world, that 1968 was the year when the US would finally win the Vietnam War, that Johnson would be re-elected president, and that Martin Luther King and the Civil Rights movement would change America completely, that men would almost certainly walk on the Moon sometime in the next couple of years, that Britain was no longer 'Great', and that at some point the Cold War would get hot – Philip had already decided he wanted to be in Tahiti, like Gauguin and that character in the Somerset Maugham novel, when the balloon went up.

All of this Philip looked forward to with relish. He wanted to report on it, tell the story of what he saw. He would be the British Capote, a Sean Connery version, telling it like it really was, in Technicolor. And on the way, he would travel by jet, visit new continents, sample new cities and have sex with beautiful women. New York was the perfect place to start, and he wanted the new experiences it would bring. Whatever life threw at him, he would find a way to succeed.

He had bought the New York Times at the airport but had barely glanced at it, mesmerised by the strange TV-familiarity of the approaching Manhattan skyline. He'd also quickly discovered that, travelling by cab, the driver invariably provided a blow-by-blow version of the main stories – front page as well as back, always with added commentary and insight. The lowdown on a couple of the most salacious stories was often also there on tap. He had always assumed the portrayal of New

York taxi drivers was caricature but so far it had turned out to be an understatement – the truth, but only in black and white. Peter, he had soon learned, was a Polish-American Jew whose grandmother had arrived on Ellis Island with her parents in 1902 – "It was the most lost she'd ever felt in her life," he said, "but also the safest. For all the bad people on the Lower East Side back then, she said it was the first time she wasn't scared to tell people her name."

Peter had been just like those the taxi drivers Philip had seen on TV, just more extrovert, opinionated and confessional. Standing on the sidewalk, as he would now learn to call it, he decided to revise his jaundiced view of American TV and Hollywood films. He'd not really been able to envisage a culture so different from provincial England, or even London, certainly not in a country that spoke the same language. And yet, he thought, apart from the language and the fact that they were both democracies – though of very different sorts – what exactly was it that was so similar? He felt as though someone had just turned the pole on a set of venetian blinds, opening them enough to let into his mind a series of narrow, unconnected horizontal slivers of light; looking out, he could see some unfamiliar sights but not how they fitted together. He wanted someone to rotate the pole further, let in more light, let him see more.

He checked in, dumped his stuff at reception and went straight out to find some coffee, determined – with the help of a nap – to make it through to at least midnight. As he sat down in the coffee bar 20 minutes later, his mind was still teeming. If first impressions proved right, then the US was spectacularly different from England. Maybe the people had once been more alike than unalike, from the same ethnic stock. But how to factor in the bravery, determination and recklessness that had led the early British-born immigrants to take the risk of sailing across the Atlantic to set up a new life? And there had since been millions of other immigrants, from entirely different places, seeking economic opportunity or fleeing poverty and persecution. And then there were the native American Indians and... another twist of the pole... African Americans, descendants of slaves...

Coming from Bristol, he was far from shocked by the presence of non-white faces. But New York was still different and the Blacks he saw seemed more confident, sure they had a "I won't change place here", even if they didn't necessarily like where it was. And then Philip made another link, an obvious one really; Bristol, like Liverpool but unlike say Newcastle, had thrived on the slave trade.

Philip's vision of his coming American experience was gaining more texture by the moment but he needed to be practical for a while. He ordered more coffee, went to the toilet and tried to force himself to concentrate on the matter in hand. When he returned, he got out the briefing papers he had been given in London and began to read through them again, checking what he thought against the comments he had written in the margin. If he was going to make this work, he needed to start by focusing on the bread and butter. After that, he could begin to get clever. But first off, he had to persuade Mr Cooke he could do a good job. If that didn't happen, he'd be on a plane home.

Back at the hotel, he rang Mr Cooke's office to confirm his safe arrival and sent the telegram he had promised to his mother. The Guardian newspaper had sent him over to help Cooke, its long-time US correspondent, who also did a weekly broadcast for the BBC. The year 1968 already promised to be tumultuous – student riots, anti-

Vietnam and Civil Rights demonstrations all seemed inevitable. There was also a presidential election, and, in a broader sense, continuation of the social revolution that had begun properly the previous year. Finally, Philip nursed a distant hope to get down to Mexico City in the autumn for the Olympic Games, to see in real life what he had faithfully recorded in scrap books ever since the Melbourne Games 12 years before.

All this, Philip had written in his notebook on the flight over. Each element had been racing around in his head since he had been given the job the week before Christmas, so there was no practical need to write them down. But in a strategic sense it was valuable to work through the timing of likely events and how they might affect each other. And Philip was nothing if not strategic. He thought, for example, that LBJ's election was not as likely as many assumed because of the potential confluence of Civil Rights and anti-Vietnam anger – particularly if US troops had not won by that stage – that could easily be reached at the height of the Democratic primaries, though it was hard to see who else the Democrats would nominate. At any rate, the paper, at minimal expense he thought, had decided to give Cooke an extra pair of legs to cover events "as they unfolded" – Philip remembered the line with relish.

Philip got undressed, set his alarm for two hours later, lay down and, despite the coffee, was asleep immediately. When the alarm went off, he felt like death but forced himself out of bed and into a cold shower, as Bond always seemed to, which shocked him awake with a vengeance, time-warping him into US Eastern Time. He shaved, then dressed in Levi's, brown turtleneck sweater, beige corduroy jacket and suede shoes. He brushed his hair, deciding he would grow it longer, reassured himself in the mirror, tried unsuccessfully to raise his right eyebrow independently of the left, smiled self-consciously and grabbed his duffel coat from the back of the door.

It was early evening, bitterly cold, and he decided to find a nice warm bar as soon as he could, get himself a beer and read up on what was going on; he anticipated a grilling from Alistair Cooke in the morning. He planned to eat later, then find a livelier bar or club for a couple of hours before turning in. After wandering for about ten minutes, passing a couple of more or less empty bars, he found one that was half full and went inside to order a beer.

When it arrived, he pulled up a stool, took off his coat and jacket, rolled up his sleeves and retrieved the thickish folded envelope from the side pocket of his duffel. He'd already been through the papers twice on the plane, as well as over coffee earlier. They were divided into four sections – the 1967 riots, the Civil Rights movement, Vietnam, and the election. The riots had shaken US society and there was a sense the decade was turning darker, with speculation of a growing gap between generations. Differing attitudes to Vietnam and the Civil Rights movement were clearly factors: Vietnam because it was the young who were having to fight and who were now dying in increasing numbers, and Civil Rights because social changes and the charisma of Martin Luther King meant racial equality was far more popular with the younger generation – outside of the South – than with many of their parents. The divide was further widened by the increasing doubts in parts of the Black community, that Dr King's strategy of non-violence would bring change quickly enough. Young people, particularly in the context of Vietnam, shared some of this growing impatience and anger; their parents, who had lived through an era of growing prosperity, but had grown up in the Depression, often struggled to appreciate their children's lack of respect for institutions.

The really strange thing for Philip was that none of this seemed to be having any effect on the assumptions that LBJ would be elected in November. If nominated, Philip could see that his chances of election would be high. But would the Democratic Party, much of which was sympathetic to the anti-war and Civil Rights movements, nominate a candidate who was opposed to one and sometimes ambivalent towards the other? Vietnam, he thought, must be the key. In the unlikely event the continual news of South Vietnamese and US victories did not translate into real military gains by the spring then, with casualties mounting, Johnson would come under real pressure. He couldn't conceive how a similar set of factors in the UK – particularly an unpopular, increasingly bloody and attritional war – would not translate into massive unpopularity for any prime minister.

He wondered again what Cooke made of it. The way Philip's job had been explained to him, it was a combination of research and tracking stories as they developed. From his own reading, Philip wanted to discover more about the SDS, which seemed to be a growing influence in the anti-war movement and one of the main ways White students got involved in the Civil Rights struggle. The Guardian notes were silent on the SDS. Cooke, he was sure, would have heard of them but unless he mentioned them himself, Philip decided that he would say nothing, preferring to do his own digging. He finished his reading. There was a TV above the bar, and its noise began to penetrate his internal conversation as he replaced the papers in the envelope, folded it and put it back in his pocket. Something about a ceasefire in Vietnam for the Tet national holiday; at least there would be a pause in the killing.

"Want another beer, man?"

Philip looked up. The barman was gesturing at his empty glass. "Yea, I'll have the same again, thanks."

"You from England?"

"Yes, got here this afternoon; here till November."

"What you doin' with all that time?"

"I'm covering the election for a British newspaper." Philip consciously exaggerated his role, partly from self-importance, but also, he reasoned later, to give the barman some encouragement to open up a bit. Whether or not Philip's explanation was a premeditated invitation, the barman, Alex, did begin to talk to the young English reporter.

"Who do people over in England reckon will win?"

"Mostly, they think Johnson, but I'm not so sure myself. What do you think?"

"Aw man, it's all a game for White folks really. The only things that really matter in this country are the Vietnam War and Civil Rights, and as far as I've been able to make out, they're the only two things none of the candidates wants to talk about. Well, maybe McCarthy a little, but he ain't goin' to get elected anyway."

"Why is that? I mean, why aren't any of the candidates talking about the War or Civil Rights?"

"Cos it ain't what any of their voters want to hear." He looked at Philip for a moment, as if trying to decide if it was worth going on. "The people fighting the war,

125

the soldiers out in Asia somewhere, are either Negroes or poor White folks, and we don't tend to vote much. So none of the politicians care about us much, unless, of course, we start losing, or dying a lot; then it starts to get embarrassing."

Philip wondered if he should take notes, decided not to, then changed his mind. "Do you mind if I write some of this down? It's very interesting to someone like me who is just learning about the United States."

"No problem, man. Just make sure you get my name right in that English paper of yours – Alex Jones it is – I wouldn't want you plagiarising me!"

Philip looked up, smiled. "Of course, I'll get your name right, and I always quote my sources."

Alex looked back at him, then extended his arm. "No worries, man, ask me anything you want."

"Okay, you said none of the candidates would say much about Civil Rights, except maybe McCarthy. What about Dr King? I would have thought he'd pretty much forced it onto the agenda of all the candidates?"

Another customer was indicating his empty glass at the other end of the bar.

"Maybe that was true a few years back," Alex went on when he returned, "but then they passed them laws back in '65 and since then we just been waitin'. Don't get me wrong, Dr King is a good man, but we're starting to get old waitin'. And meanwhile, lots of the brothers are dying in some Vietnam jungle. How can we just keep talkin' about non-violence when lots of our young men are dying? How does that work?"

Alex was speaking with a twinkle in his eye. He knew he wasn't talking to an American, and he liked the young Englishman who had looked him straight in the eye without aggression. He poured himself and Philip another drink; Philip smiled and paid. He hadn't heard anyone speak like this in the UK, and he wondered how White Americans could ever kid themselves Blacks were stupid.

"Do you think you'll win in Vietnam?"

"Don't bother me much. Don't see as how them Vietcong are goin' to do me much harm, or the South Vietnamese much good."

"What about communism?"

"If they're over in Asia, they can be what they want as far as I care. From what I know of it, I don't much like communism, but it still don't seem like any kind of good reason to send thousands of our young people to the other side of the world to kill and be killed."

"Who would you vote for if the presidential election was tomorrow?"

"If none of the candidates were going to get us out of Vietnam, then I wouldn't vote for any of them."

"What do you think about Dr King's planned march on Washington?"

Alex paused, sighed, "Dr King's a good man and a brave man. He's done a lot of good, and I'll always respect him for it. But I just don't see how he's gonna change things any more than he has already, which ain't a whole lot, not in my lifetime anyway."

Philip scribbled down every answer, carrying on asking questions until he'd finished his beer. The bar was starting to fill up now, and Alex was increasingly getting called away to serve other customers. When he had drained the last mouthful, he got up and put on his jacket, ready to go.

"Thanks," said Philip, extending his hand, "I really appreciate your time and your thoughts. I understand a hell of a lot more than when I walked in here. If this ever gets published, I'll make sure a copy of the Guardian gets sent to this bar with your name on it. And I'll make sure you're quoted by name. You have my word on it." Alex nodded and the two shook hands for the last time. Alex watched as the young English reporter pushed open the door and walked into the cold night, pulling his coat tight against the wind, then went back to work.

Later, Philip sat at the bar of a small nightclub in the Village trying to put the story together in his head. Was it a story? Well, not exactly, but it gave him a different lens through which to see things. Although looking back, it had been a bit of a rant, Philip was sure Alex hadn't been faking it. Were there any real consequences? Well, it depended on Vietnam. If the war went badly, he was convinced Johnson was a lot more vulnerable than many seemed to think.

He'd grabbed a pizza nearby and eaten it quickly while tidying up his notes. Now, he was drinking bourbon for the first time, leaning against the bar, smoking a cigarette, imitating – subtly, he hoped – the various detectives and spies he had seen on film and television. He hoped he didn't look as nervous as he felt, confident he couldn't. The music was mostly West Coast stuff, he thought, but he had so far only recognised one thing, an Animals track he had heard his sister's boyfriend play. The area immediately around the bar was quite dark but the dance floor – small, maybe five yards in diameter – was being periodically illuminated by simple coloured strobe lamps. The club was quite warm, and he took off his jacket, rolled up his sleeves, conscious he was a bit over-dressed. Over in the corners on the other side of the dance floor were half a dozen small, round tables with couples in various stages of embrace. Philip, as casually as he could, reached up and tousled his hair.

He signalled for another drink. As he did so, two women came up to the bar and ordered martinis. They got served before him, and when they got their drinks, they stayed at the bar, turning and leaning backwards, arching their backs against it, the closer one only a couple of inches from his left shoulder. So far, neither had even glanced at him, which he reasoned was a good sign as it probably meant they'd watched him before they came over. When Philip's drink came, he deliberately exaggerated his accent while he was paying.

"Are you British?" the taller asked. She had long, slightly frizzy brown hair and was wearing a green embroidered kaftan and knee-length tan leather boots. Philip replied he was from London, and she began asking him questions about England, mostly about music and fashion. Philip did his best to answer without saying anything stupid.

The shorter of the two women had blonde hair, slightly shorter and curlier, half hanging over the outside corner of her left eye, more swept back on the right. She was wearing jeans and an orange-dyed smock, and mostly listened. Both, he noted, were bra-less. Philip wondered if he'd looked so out of place that they'd decided he must be British, and that was why they'd come over. Then he decided it didn't really matter much. The two women chatted to him for maybe 20 minutes, mostly asking him questions, listening to his answers. By this stage, he'd finished his drink and, as they – Jennifer and Linda – were coming to the end of theirs, he asked if he could buy. They declined politely; they had to go, and soon after they did.

Later, lying in bed reading a John Updike book he'd picked up at the airport, Philip wondered what he could have done differently to persuade the two women to stay with him, maybe persuade one of them to have sex with him. He decided he had been too passive, answering too many questions, asking too few, and that he should flirt more openly. What he had taken to be his signals of availability, gleaned almost exclusively from the movies, had been too subtle. Celluloid, he concluded, magnifies the significance of every gesture.

Philip wasn't due to see Alistair Cooke until 11am. Jetlag, however, kicked in and he awoke at 6.15, with the inner certainty that further sleep was not possible. Still, he lay determinedly in bed for a further hour before accepting the inevitable. Then, after another cold shower, he dressed – the light grey suit he had bought specially for the trip, blue shirt, yellow tie – and wandered outside. Pausing at the exit, he decided to head down to Wall Street. The morning was crisp, and Philip felt similarly alert, ready for pretty much anything.

He found a breakfast bar, Italian-owned, ordered coffee and toast, and sat in the window watching the bankers and financiers scurry briskly towards their offices. Without their work faces on, they looked pretty much like ordinary people, features relaxed, or sagging with worry or lack of sleep. If yesterday had been about the differences between the US and Britain, this morning, at least so far, had been about the likeness. He finished his second coffee and wandered through the back streets for a bit, then up Broadway, all the way to Central Park, along and then back down 5th Avenue. Philip tried to take in as much as he could, the children going to school, cleaners clearing away the detritus from the previous night, shops opening, people rushing up the steps out of subway stations, taxis, horns, shouting. If he knew nothing about the US, what conclusions would be reach? No answer came, so he banked the question along with what he could of the sensations and atmosphere.

Suddenly, the screech of brakes and the blare of a taxi horn followed by the shouts of the driver halted him. He had stepped off the sidewalk against the lights. Philip put up his hand in acknowledgement and stepped backwards up onto the sidewalk again, bumping into a woman behind him and stepping on a man's foot; both had walked right up to the edge, oblivious to the fact that Philip would have to retreat. He apologised and edged along and around to the back of what was now a group of maybe ten people waiting for the lights to change. Standing there, he felt, for just a moment, young and isolated in a city of seven million people on a different continent. He remembered the time, aged eight, he had got lost on a school trip to Bath and had cried at the thought he might never find his way home.

At 11am, he was standing outside Alistair Cooke's office. "Come in," said the familiar voice. As he opened the door, Cooke got up from his desk and came over to shake his hand. Philip recognised the slicked back hair and the bold Roman nose. Cooke was a couple of inches taller than he was and just beginning to have a slight stoop. "Hello, Mr Coulter, did you have a good flight over? What time did you get in?"

Shortly after, Philip was sat down by the fire, opposing Cooke, both sitting in high-backed but comfortable armchairs. Coffee had been brought, and Cooke had opened a notebook whose pages were covered in tidy writing. Pictures adorned the walls of the office – Chaplin, Roosevelt, Adlai Stevenson, Bette Davis, JFK – he was comfortable with celebrity, and with his visitors knowing it.

128

"The people in London tell me you write well and have an eye for a story. These seem simple things but are harder than they appear." Philip nodded, deciding to let Cooke's monologue run its course. He half glanced out of the windows; they were closed but did not prevent the sounds of the street permeating the room. "New York and London are similar in many ways but New York is indisputably the noisier," Cooke observed. "Tell me what your briefing said about what's going on over here. I'm always intrigued to know how America looks from the Guardian offices and what discrepancies I need to correct," his eyes twinkled in mock-conspiracy, "and which to allow to persist."

Philip ran through a summary of his papers, pretty much verbatim but trying here and there to hint that he had his own independent view, slightly at odds with the line he had been given. He mentioned nothing of the SDS, nor of what he had learned from Alex the night before, but implied that he thought Johnson's re-election far from the certainty his briefing papers indicated.

"I sense," said Cooke at the end, "that you doubt LBJ and Lady Bird will be occupying the White House a year from now." Philip nodded. "Why do you think that? After all, he controls his party machine, Robert Kennedy isn't standing and McCarthy is unelectable. Meanwhile, the Republicans are in disarray."

"It's Vietnam, sir," despite his antipathy to deference, Philip found himself addressing Cooke respectfully, awed at his ability to encapsulate complex analysis in a few pithy phrases. He had heard the famous broadcasts were painstakingly put together but, whatever the truth of that, the man spoke naturally in short phrases, meaningful and elegant. He tried to mirror the style. "The war's gone on too long. There are lots of victories, apparently, but very little success, and casualties are mounting. I just can't see how, in an election year, that situation can continue without affecting Johnson's chances of re-election."

Cooke looked at him. "Not bad," he said, topping up his coffee, "I admire your analysis and share much of it. My own hunch, for what it's worth is that, unless there is clear progress in Vietnam and Johnson does well in the New Hampshire primary in March, Kennedy will enter the race. The sense of destiny runs very deep in the Kennedy family psyche and, if there are any encouraging signs, in the tea leaves as it were," Cooke paused and sipped his coffee, "then I don't think Bobby will be able to resist."

"That would change the whole context of the Democratic convention, wouldn't it?"

"It would, although it will be hard for Bobby to get enough delegates unless he can find a way to appeal to the McCarthy wing of the party. Even then, he would struggle to beat the Democratic machine, but he does have a chance. The Kennedy name still carries lustre, and Bobby's a good politician if he decides to give rein to his ambition."

"What do you want me to work on first?" asked Philip.

"There are a couple of things I have in mind. First of all, you should spend some time here in New York. Soak it up, feel the pace and rhythm of the place. Do you like jazz? Then spend some evenings up in Harlem, go to some clubs. But remember, New York is very different from the American heartland. Most of what you hear in Manhattan simply doesn't hold true anywhere else, except maybe California – the two are much more alike than they want to believe, Sodom and Gomorrah and all that. Then, I'd like you to catch up with McCarthy's campaign and follow it through to the New Hampshire primary on 12 March. The result there will provide the first real indication of whether the Democratic race is on for real. If it is, then you should stick with it. If not, then there's a Republican called Reagan; he used to be an actor, not a bad one as it happens, and you'll recognise him from his films. He's Governor of California – quite conservative, not a big supporter of the counter-culture; he's made some fairly extreme speeches. Something is going on in the GOP that I don't yet fathom.

"Send me a written weekly report every Monday; phone me in between if anything more interesting happens. Does that suit you?"

"It does, sir," Philip was baffled but pleased. He had not expected to learn so much, or for Cooke to be so open. He was also satisfied that he had taken the initiative sufficiently, distinguishing himself from the received wisdom of London. "About Harlem," Philip turned back as he was opening the door, "are there any clubs in particular you would suggest I begin my research?"

Cooke laughed, turned back to his desk and scribbled down a couple of addresses. "Try these for starters; they should further your American education. I haven't been there in a while myself but I doubt they've changed much."

Chapter 14
Kinshasa, Friday, 1 November 1974

"I still can't believe what happened, they'll remember this fight for as long as there's boxing." Philip was sitting by the side of his hotel pool a couple of days after Ali had defeated George Foreman, the overwhelming favourite, in the 20th May stadium. "Ali is just unreal; I can't believe he could take so much punishment for so long, and then have the strength to come off the ropes and nail Foreman." George, a fellow reporter from a rival paper, much more of a pure boxing man, was lying on a lounger sipping a long cocktail. "And the weird thing is, I'm sure Ali's not half as quick as before he was stripped of the title. You can even see he's slower and heavier, but to do that to Foreman after Foreman had taken Frazier apart? Well, it beats me! I still can't believe I'm paying you out over this."

George was sanguine. "Well, sometimes you just gotta believe, as Yogi Berra once said. I don't know, I just had a strange feeling that with this fight being in Africa, Muhammad would be able to dig very deep, turn any fear he had into a strength. I don't know, maybe if they had this fight ten times, Foreman would've won the other nine. I don't necessarily think that's the case, but the beauty is that we'll never find out. I'll tell you one thing, I think you're right about him being afraid of Foreman; after all, Muhammad is far too intelligent not to be. Did you see Foreman hitting the heavy bag? It's one of the most frightening things I've ever seen; the size of the dents he was leaving in it! Mailer thought it was amazing too, you know what he's like, he couldn't take his eyes off it, just staring at George hitting the heavy bag. It became kinda funny in the end."

"I've never really got on with him," sighed Philip, "but he's a hell of a writer. The book he wrote about the '68 Conventions was complete genius. I was there and I can't imagine anyone else capturing them better."

"Well, he's certainly had his share of controversy," admitted George, "most of which he adores. We get on because he's hardly ever boring. He's totally loved it out here, you know, the magical, the mythical and the mesmeric all in one."

Philip smiled, "You're the one getting carried away now. I'm starting to think you're as much of a romantic as I am. We all know it's a damned cliché but at times like this I feel as though we have the best job in the world. I haven't seen the figures but just think what the global TV audience must have been for that fight! And there we were, pretty much sitting at ringside. I mean, it could have been bigger than the Olympics or the World Cup. I loathe Don King, but it was genius getting Ali and Forman to come here to fight, not to mention James Brown and all the rest of them; nobody's gonna be forgetting this in a hurry."

"I don't know though," said George, looking down at his feet. "There's a bit of me that can see your idea of a string of global sporting events being beamed around the world, but mostly I reckon people know what they like and like what they know. I just can't see Americans altering their lifestyles and viewing patterns other than for something exceptional like this."

Philip was pensive. "I agree with every word, but there's just something about the last few days that means sport won't ever be the same again. Just the idea that you can watch, live, something taking place thousands of miles away has to change something. Look, when I first came into sports reporting, I was told it had taken the industry a while to understand even a little of what slow motion could be used for. And now look where we are! I accept satellite is a solution in search of a problem, but I still believe that one day we'll simply take it for granted."

"Maybe, but I reckon I'll be long dead before it happens. I've no real idea what King made from this fight, but from what he's given the boxers, it must've been a huge money spinner."

"Why do you think Ali's quite such a magnet for attention?" Philip wondered aloud. "I mean I know how good a boxer and fighter he is, and a smart publicist with it. And there's obviously the whole Vietnam thing, but still…"

"I've been asking myself the same question. I do reckon television has a lot to do with it. The extent it's permeated and defined American life since Clay first beat Liston in 1963 is totally remarkable. And I think that's where his being so smart comes into it; it makes him uniquely placed to exploit the media. But you've also got to remember how big boxing's been in the past; Dempsey v Tunney and Louis v Schmelling were huge national events, attracting almost unimaginably vast crowds and huge radio audiences. But I think you're right that he is different. I thought I'd seen it all but nothing really prepared me for the instant rapport he struck up with the people of Zaire. Somehow he's transcended his sport on a scale that's totally unique. How? Do you have a clue?"

"Not really," admitted Philip, "but part of it, I think, is that the rest of the world doesn't really see him as American, they see him as one of them."

"Do you really think that? Is that about his refusal to be drafted and his Vietcong quote?"

"Well, yes, but it's not only that; it's also becoming a Muslim, changing his name, joining the Nation of Islam. And there's his whole thing about the way he treats us all, not seeming to take anything or anyone at all seriously. All of that's very un-American. Ali's not really a part of any of that; he resigned when he threw his Olympic Gold Medal into the Mississippi, he resigned again when he refused to be drafted and a third time when he took the piss out of Howard Cosell's wig! All that makes him problematic back home, but it also opens him up and makes him accessible and attractive to the rest of the world in a way that Pete Rose, or Mark Spitz, or OJ will never be."

"Oh, come on, Phil, I don't really buy that," complained George.

"Trust me, I'm being polite. A load of people start off thinking I'm American and, almost without exception, they're all perfectly nice to me. But if I then explain I'm really British, but have an accent because I live in the States, you can see them relax and loosen up. They don't exactly dislike me when they think I'm a Yank, but neither are they really my friend; and I suspect it would be better again if they found out I was Irish, or Canadian, or Brazilian. Maybe it's because we don't have an Empire anymore, in which case there's hope for you yet."

"But we don't have an Empire, quite the opposite."

"Sorry, but I don't think that's how the rest of the world see it. Even though many would genuinely thank you for protecting them against the Soviets, they're still afraid of you."

"How do you mean? I don't really get what you're on about. Why are they afraid of us when we're all about liberty and democracy?"

"Maybe they do... God, do I need another drink!" Philip caught the waiter's attention and indicated another round. "However, even if they don't often articulate it, they prefer to get there in their own messy, idiosyncratic way."

"How do you mean?"

"I think it's just that when the White House goes on about freedom and democracy, the meaning of these values automatically changes. For a start, it also becomes somehow inextricably merged with market capitalism and free trade, so no restrictions on US imports and the freedom for US corporations to buy your best companies. Now don't get me wrong, everyone has an agenda, always, and everyone else knows it, if only because they see it in themselves. Bad old Europe and the Third World both know that well. The difference with the US, apart from the fear, is that you're way more shameless about pretending otherwise, claiming to be selfless and that you're doing it for us rather than yourselves."

"Okay, so we have a tendency to preach a little," he admitted, pausing between words, "but in reality we do also help other countries, not least Europe with the Marshall Plan after the war."

"Okay, I'll give you that," Philip replied, eager not to appear too critical, "and my parents still talk about it, but memories are short and I'm sure there was some self interest in there, no matter how enlightened."

"Yes, there was," replied George, "but it still deserves to be remembered much more than it seems to be. It's interesting, you know, because I'm that little bit older than you, but I completely see that younger generations like yours might not see it the same way. After all, it was a huge success but an almost silent one, not a big bang. I haven't thought about it for a while but I doubt there are many Americans who remember the Marshall Plan."

"You're right about the fading of that memory – I was only born in 1950, so I'm dependent on my parents for it. Almost anything American was by definition good; it was glamorous, wealthy, successful, all the things Europe wasn't but wanted to be. And then there were events like the Berlin Airlift, that just made your reputation even better."

"So when did that all change?"

"No idea really," said Philip, "and I'm not even sure I'm in a good position to have a view. Living in the States for the last six years means I'm not really able to judge like with like."

"Maybe, but then I don't know who would be. And I'd still like to know what you think."

Philip was silent for a few moments. "Okay, so I think there's something about the scale of the US, and the cultural and political extremes within it, that Europeans and others find it really hard to get their heads around; like you could basically fit the whole of the UK into New York State. And then there are Native Americans and Black Americans, both of which seem bigger moral issues to the rest of the world than they do to many Americans. This issue of scale is important because it makes America seem almost like another world at times. And I think this means you get judged by different, bigger standards. And when, up close, your behaviour ultimately turns out to be as depressingly grubby as everyone else's, the let-down is all the greater."

"Okay," said George, "I think I get that. It's bred into us to believe in our destiny and reality is always going to be something of a disappointment in those circumstances. What else?"

"Well, then there's the Tocqueville thing about all power corrupting, and frankly, the US has had increasing amounts of power all the way through this century, especially since 1945. And because of that, I suspect you're just not as nice, not as pure and disinterested as you were. Of course, these things are always deeply relative, but in Latin America for example, there's quite a distinction between the Monroe Doctrine, which basically warned Europe off intervening in the American hemisphere, and the situation now where the CIA gets rid of democratically elected governments which either do things it or US corporations don't like."

"Well, maybe we've changed, maybe we haven't," George argued, "but the world has changed, that's for sure. We believe in our country and in our way of life. I don't think we should apologise for that, or for wanting to share it with people from other countries who live in poverty under oppressive systems of government. You British were like that once. And Communism represents a challenge to all of us. It's insidious and dangerous, and yes, it has forced us into doing some things that under normal circumstances would be reprehensible. But we're bearing our responsibility, and without us doing that, there wouldn't be a free world any more.

"The Soviets would control Europe and Red China would rule the roost in Asia. Between them, they'd probably also have divided Africa up and be fighting over its gold, diamonds, copper, whatever. Britain's too weak and small to be able to stop them, France probably wouldn't try and neither would Germany or Japan. There is only us, you see, and if we've made a few mistakes along the way, getting our hands dirty in the process, well, at least we did it with our eyes open. Remember, the Founding Fathers knew Europe would corrupt us if we got involved there. It does still grate a little that we're so freely criticised by the same Europeans who are quite happy being protected by us from the Soviet Union, who would more than happily roll their tanks across West Germany if we let them."

Philip smiled. "I know all that, George, I really do. You know I love the States; I'm British but it's very much my second home. And I agree we Europeans can be more than a touch two-faced about you guys. I was just trying to explain why there isn't a little more gratitude out there towards you."

"Okay, friend, I get you." George shook his head. "Sorry for being so touchy about it but it's hard not to be when you travel as much as I do, and hear all the shit, have to just sit there and take it from people who, frankly, owe us their right to free speech."

This time Philip burst straight out laughing. "You know there's a superb irony in there. Part of what you offer people is the right of dissent, the right to say what they want, and then, as often as not, they go and use it to give you shit. Where's the gratitude in that, or the self-awareness for that matter? And I don't remotely blame you for getting riled at it sometimes. All I'm saying, I guess, is that being able to make your own mistakes is part of what freedom and democracy are about."

"All right, enough already," laughed George this time, relaxing back into his lounger. "I'm not sure we're ever going to quite agree on this, but I don't think we're really arguing about much either."

Philip nodded. He half-wanted George to move a bit further and acknowledge the US had fallen short. But he didn't want to push it anymore, not today.

"What about Civil Rights?" George's question surprised him.

"Okay," he replied, "but just so long as you know I'm really trying hard not to get you pissed at me here, so don't go getting upset on me."

"I promise," George replied, "so long as you don't accuse me of being a closet Klansman!"

"Deal!" said Philip, "I wasn't sure we were going to get to this but I do think it's a big part of the story. So, first off, anyone who thinks about this for any length of time can't not conclude how hard it is. Not only were you bequeathed slavery by us British, but you then had to go through a bloody civil war to get rid of it. I know very well how divisive all of that history still is, how toxic, but, looking from the outside, it's just terrible to see some of what still happens in the Deep South. And the projects and ghettos in Northern cities aren't much better. Now don't get me wrong; I'm well aware Europeans can get pretty hypocritical about this. But there's still the fact that we naturally look to you for a lead, to set the standard and show us the way. And yet the more other countries understand America, the less this seems to be the case."

"Sorry, but I'm not sure I get it," George said at last. "Are you saying that we're racist and that, on the one hand that's okay because everyone else is too, but on the other it's not, because we owe it to the world to be better than anyone else? Or have I missed something?"

"Let me try and put it a bit better," replied Philip, trying to smile, "What I mean is that other countries hold the US to a higher standard partly because you yourselves do and partly because most of the rest of us see in you – certainly want to – a younger, better version of their own country. After all, the immigrants you took in, or almost all of them, while they may have been poor and destitute, were also young, strong, intelligent, many of them literate, ambitious, inventive, and so we see some of the better part of ourselves in the US. Look, pretty much every people in the world wishes it was they who had the Declaration of Independence and the US Constitution. All I'm saying is don't ever give up on trying to live up to them."

"Wow!" said George, "I was all prepared to get mad at you but instead I'm lying here trying to blink back the tears. I always thought you liked America, not the way most Brits do – because it's big and shiny and new, and has Hollywood – but because of the freedom to try to be who you want to be. But I didn't get until just now how much the place has got under your skin. I apologise."

"Not a problem at all… After all, when it comes down to it, I am still a Brit and always will be. And someday I'll probably go home."

"You're killing me, Phil!" George almost shouted. "Britain's a basket case; only North Sea oil can save you and you'll probably piss that away. You got through the '60s with the Beatles and James Bond but even they've run their course. I mean, don't get me wrong, I love the place, but it's a museum. It's run by the unions, you've just lost your Empire, you're probably committing all sorts of crimes in Ireland and you've just joined the Common Market – a club you don't even want to be part of!"

Philip had always found this line of argument difficult and it was, more or less, how he'd felt himself when he'd gone to the US first. But looking back across the Atlantic, it now appeared better than that. But now wasn't the time to have this discussion. Having somehow found himself pointing out America's deficiencies and just about managing to bring George with him, the last thing Philip wanted was to become all defensive when the positions were reversed. "I don't disagree with any of that," he said at last, "right down to your assumption that we'll probably piss the oil away. But even the US needs allies sometimes, and I doubt you'll find anyone more reliable."

"Okay, but seriously," pleaded the American, "you can't go back there. I mean, how can you swap LA for London in February?"

Philip didn't want to get into this. "What are you up to this evening?" he asked.

"Hanging around the hotel really," replied George. "I've still got some copy to file, and then just relaxing. What about you?"

"Much the same really, except Virginia's coming over."

"Even to an old middle-aged hack like me she's hot, I wish you luck. Do you know her at all from Stateside?"

"A little bit, but we never got it together until we met out here."

"You're quite into her, aren't you? Maybe it's time you settled down a bit?"

"Perhaps but I don't like to rush these things. I'm still only 25. Neither of us have any expectations and it works out pretty well. I'm not sure it would be as good if we were getting heavy about it all. What about you? You're what, mid 40s? You've never settled down, as far as I know anyway, and you don't seem any the worse for it."

"Well, it sort of works for me, I guess. But it hasn't exactly been a smooth road, and I'm sure as hell not the guy to give advice to anyone on anything to do with women – I've crashed and burned far too often for that."

Philip was suddenly sorry he'd ever mentioned Virginia. At the time it had seemed like an obvious thing to say, but looking back it had the taint of a gratuitous boast. He kicked himself realising how little he knew about his friend. The talk petered out and both lay back on their loungers, contemplating the slightly edgy conversation they'd just had, but each also thinking about the image of Ali standing poised over Foreman's crumpled figure, already frozen in time.

Although Philip was still struggling to unpick its meaning, the significance of the fight and everything that went with it was already beyond doubt. He knew from the telephone conversations he'd had, and from the news coming down the wires, that the fight was probably the biggest global television sports event, or maybe event full stop. Because it was boxing, and because it was Ali, it had transcended both its natural boxing audience and that slightly geeky community of international sports fans brought together by ABC's Wide World of Sports. Critically, the fight itself had delivered; and in winning as he did, Ali had added to his own irresistible narrative. Already, Philip was conscious that his own written report of the fight had been widely syndicated and was by far the most profitable article he'd penned.

A few minutes later, George got up to go and do an hour or so of work before lunch, and they agreed to meet for a drink with Virginia before dinner. When George had gone, Philip wondered about their conversation and whether he'd been too openly critical of the US. Maybe it was Watergate that had first breached his deference towards his adopted home. Thinking back, he also recognised his own loss of innocence.

Philip was part-amused and part-shocked, thinking back to what he was like when he'd first arrived in the US. But when he looked back now on that 18-year-old, what he saw was barely recognisable. He hadn't only grown up more quickly but had altered direction. Where before he had been fundamentally trusting, now cynicism was his default option. In the same counter-intuitive way, he had become personally more trustworthy. At 18 he had been quite sly and manipulative, always looking for an angle to exploit and not often fussy about who was hurt along the way. For all that he'd changed for the better; however, Philip found it impossible to disown his 19-year-old self. He'd always been up for whatever adventure came his way. Things hadn't turned out how he'd expected but he had no inclination to feel disappointed.

By the time Philip and Virginia met up with George, they'd already had sex, and Philip, as he ordered drinks, could still feel the brush of her skin and the tangle of their limbs. It was easy for George to surmise much of this and he envied them. Virginia had long auburn hair and longer legs. Like the others, she'd been in Zaire almost three months but, unlike them, she'd made a determined effort to get out into the city and surrounding countryside rather than stay close to the hotel and its pool. She'd been largely indifferent to the fight itself, neither entranced by the magic of Ali nor repulsed by the violence of the combat. For her the job was a vehicle to enable her to travel and meet interesting and different people. Philip qualified on both counts, and she'd enjoyed every moment of their coupling, while knowing they would go their separate ways once they set foot back on American soil.

This wasn't particularly a matter of regret to Virginia, it was just the way life worked, and part of Philip's attraction was that she knew he would feel the same. She liked the way he lived in the moment, observing and valuing small details while realising that many things of beauty and value were temporary; they either died or they changed and it was naïve to imagine otherwise. All American life was like this, in constant search of the next thing. Africa was different, however, mostly in obvious ways but no less striking for that. The river and the jungle were ancient presences, more immediate and oppressive than anything Virginia had come across. The people, on the other hand, were young and optimistic despite the palpable terror that oppressed them.

Virginia thought George a bit boring, but much less annoying that many of his generation of reporters, who were mostly sexist bastards she would happily have kicked in the testicles. She felt a little sorry for him; perhaps it would be better if he had a darker past or a few rough edges to help define him. As it was, he felt too easygoing, able to fit into whatever space or corner he was offered. She knew there was some hypocrisy in this but, at 27, she was happy to see this contradiction as his problem, not hers. Phil was a different case altogether.

She'd first come across him a couple of years before at a press conference before a routine Mets game in mid-season. Sitting halfway back, he'd seemed bored for much of the time before, near the end, asking a couple of odd questions about left-handed pitching in the bullpen. He was young and good-looking and so, even though she was seeing someone at the time, she'd contrived to get herself introduced to him. Why had he been looking so bored, she had asked, and why had he asked those questions?

"Well," he'd responded evenly, "it doesn't always do to look too interested, especially if you are. Coach was talking about areas where the Mets roster is thin, which usually means he's got talent in the AAA franchise that the staff feel is ready to step up to the Majors. On the other hand, I've heard a couple of rumours about chronic injuries in the bullpen, particularly with the long relievers, and I was trying to draw him out a little. My suspicion is he's trying to line up a trade, quite a big one, and he's trying to divert attention to avoid pushing the price up."

A couple of other reporters had turned up, and their conversation changed tack. Philip had written an article that had acknowledged but then ignored the coach's messaging while inferring his suspicions, and a fortnight later the Mets had duly acquired a left-handed long reliever in a complex trade. Virginia had since spent a lot more time trying to work out what coaches were trying to avoid talking about and why, and also trying to spot when a reporter succeeded in getting them to answer questions on a previously off limits subject where they didn't seem comfortable. Within weeks, it seemed such an obvious strategy and yet she hadn't thought of it; and neither, as far as she could tell, had any of the other reporters.

After this, Virginia had begun to follow Philip's columns and was relieved to discover that his writing was okay to good, no better. He wrote well but the words he put together were a long way from great journalism; he didn't seem able to convey the immediacy of the event, and sometimes fell into the trap of confusing his readers with too much complexity. But this Englishman obviously understood baseball, as well as a good deal about the underbelly of sports generally. And in her mind, when she found out they were both heading to Zaire for Ali–Foreman, it seemed inevitable they'd get together.

But Philip had turned out to be a more complicated character than she'd expected. Outwardly confident, he'd turned out to be quite insecure and introverted. She liked him but he was too often serious. Virginia wasn't into long relationships anyway, but this would have been enough by itself, and going home seemed the obvious opportunity to draw the line. When she broke the news later, as they were getting into bed, Philip hadn't looked shocked but had simply shrugged. "It's a shame," he'd responded, quite dryly, "but if that's what you want, no hard feelings."

"I don't want you to be upset," she said.

"Of course not," he said, "but I'm not easy to be with for long, I know that. And it's been okay, hasn't it?"

It hadn't even been a proper question but somehow Virginia found herself staring back at him. There wasn't a trace of self-pity in his voice.

Chapter 15
Nottingham, Friday, 25 March 1977

The A&E shift had been quiet but Michelle was tired. She'd been on call and it had been one of those nights where she hadn't got more than about 45 minutes' sleep at a stretch. Michelle had gone into nursing straight from school two and a half years earlier, and in that time it had gone from a job she liked the idea of into the job for her. The NHS, and the politics around it, had become her passion.

The year previously, she had joined the Labour Party and was already becoming caught up in its struggle to continue as a viable government. She would have described herself as 'soft Left' but a big part of Labour's worth, in her eyes, was its function as a 'broad church' – she used the phrase often – that brought together people who believed in a fairer society. It, therefore, angered her when members behaved as though the real enemies were inside the Labour rather than the Tory Party. This crime was all the greater now that the Tories were led by a woman who so often seemed to favour those who stood for prejudice and intolerance.

Michelle hadn't been interested in politics at all when she was at school. She had worked hard but mechanically at her subjects and her 'O' Levels had been good – eight of them (2As, 3Bs, 3Cs) – as had her A Levels (B in English, Cs in Biology and Chemistry). She'd read the text books thoroughly, listened in class and tried to do the work and the homework well. But the teachers hadn't encouraged her to make connections and so she had seen the world in compartments, with no doors between them.

The partial exception had been English, in which she was a late developer. The trigger had been coming across a compendium of Steinbeck novels in her dad's bookcase one rainy morning in the holidays. Her mum and dad had been at work and Jimmy Young was on the radio.

From then on, Michelle's appetite for reading became all-encompassing, though this didn't translate into better results. Her taste was too modern, and she was drawn to Willa Cather and Sylvia Plath rather than Shakespeare and Chaucer, to Zola and Dostoyevsky in translation rather than Dickens and Austen. Neither did she take to Mr Bates, her English teacher, or the essays he set; they bored her, and she routinely switched off. Only right at the end, in her final two terms of Sixth Form, had her aptitude for the subject begun to feed through into her school work and in the end everyone, including Michelle, was pleasantly surprised by her result.

Although she could have gone to university, Michelle's expectations had been set early, and she'd never really considered doing anything other than getting a job. It was 1974 when she finished school, and Britain was between the two elections of that year, with a minority Labour government, still recovering from the oil crisis and the Three Day Week. Slowly, she had become politicised. Gradually too, she began to oppose South African apartheid, and to support CND and the Palestinians. Michelle joined the Nottingham Labour Party in January 1976.

All her family, including her grandparents, were proudly working-class Conservatives, who believed implicitly in nuclear families and hard work, grammar schools and Empire. Fortunately for her, they were more Butler than Powell, but they still found the idea their daughter had become a Socialist difficult to stomach.

Party politics in the mid-70s had suddenly become more aggressive. And yet it was also evident that Britain was falling behind.

Michelle instinctively understood this scorpion dance between capital and labour, and felt the senselessness of a pay bargaining process that often resembled Russian roulette. She marvelled at the ridiculousness of strike ballots decided by a show of hands, judged by shop stewards who had a stake in the result, matched only by the routine condescension of patently out-of-touch management. By this time, Harold Wilson had been replaced by Jim Callaghan, whom she much preferred. In many ways, except his politics, Callaghan seemed quite like her father. But personalities were not really the point for Michelle, compared to modernising the British economy so that it would deliver full employment and good public services. And for all the flaws of some of their leaders, who seemed way too fond of themselves, she knew the British working class was a world away from the work-shy bunch often depicted by the bosses and the Tories. By stepping over that line time and again, the political right alienated her in a way Scargill could never quite do.

In March 1977, Michelle had just started living in a shared flat in West Bridgford, on the outskirts of Nottingham, which she had bought with money inherited from a distant aunt serving as the deposit. She paid the mortgage with help from her flatmate Jennifer, who was from Loughborough and made her laugh. Their housewarming party had been the signal for Jenny to get drunk and be sick, first in the toilet and then again all over a bloke who was trying to snog her, and since then they had become inseparable.

"Are you ready yet?" Michelle shouted up the stairs.

"Just in the loo, won't be a minute," piped back the voice.

"We're just going around the corner, aren't we? Otherwise I'll change my blouse."

"Yea, but change it anyway!" shouted back Jennifer, "It's Friday night, you owe it to yourself."

"Okay, I'll just be a minute," and she rushed up stairs past the ajar toilet door.

Not long after, Jennifer and Michelle were standing in the Lounge Bar of the Swan, ordering halves of lager and Guinness, with a packet of salt 'n shake to share. There were about a dozen other customers spread around in small groups and 'Where Do You Go to My Lovely' was playing on the jukebox.

They went and sat in the corner. Michelle had been going to pubs since she was 17, but only in the last year had she started going with a girlfriend rather than with a boy or as part of a larger group. Her mum had never set foot in a pub without her dad until she was over 50. Jennifer, however, was either oblivious to the looks or blithely ignored them.

Michelle had been awed by Jennifer's willingness to ask boys out rather than wait for them to ask her, to have sex when she wanted, and for arguing with men, including doctors, if she felt they were patronising her.

"So what exactly did he say?" asked Michelle.

"Well," Jennifer laughed, "he asked if I'd burned my bra, and I told him it was none of his business. Then he said there were only three reasons why women burned their bras: they didn't need them in the first place, they wanted to pull or they were lesbians. So I told him to fuck off."

"How did it start?"

"Well, we were having a cup of coffee and were both just reading the paper – he had the Mirror and I had the Sun, and we were just reading out the headlines to each other, the way you do. And there was some article about the difference between men's and women's pay – I can't even remember what the headline was – and Richard just went off on some rant about raving feminists."

Michelle had been trying to stifle her laughter, but now the dam burst and she spluttered her drink halfway across the table. Finally, she recovered, "Well, I doubt it had much to do with you, Jen. Something else must have happened to start him off, but I don't blame you for swearing at him."

"You should've seen his face!"

"I'm not sure I need to. I'm not sure any woman's ever told him to fuck off before, certainly not a nurse. Did anyone hear, anyone else, I mean?"

"I think so, well, I did say it pretty loud and Jill, Denise, Josh and that were at the next table."

Michelle roared this time, giving up on any pretence she didn't find the whole thing hilarious. "Well, I guess that's all over the hospital then."

"Well, I have noticed a couple of rooms go a bit quiet when I've walked in," Jennifer conceded.

"It's called celebrity, Jen, and I reckon you've got a natural talent for it. I wouldn't worry about it though. I mean, I don't naturally think of him as a chauvinist pig – there are far worse examples around – but I doubt anyone will think for a minute that you swore at him without him having made an arse of himself. Tomorrow night, Brenda Matheson will probably sleep with some junior doctor and everyone will have something new to talk about."

"No, they won't," groaned Jennifer, "Jill and Denise will go on about it for ages."

"Well, if they do, everyone will pretty soon find it boring. Look, the main thing is that Richard won't take it any further. He's too smart not to know he'll come out of it worse, and in any case, he's off to St Thomas in a couple of months. Trust me, it'll be fine."

"Thanks, I'm not near as sure as you are but it helps to be talking to someone about it. I know I can be loud and all, but I don't usually lose my temper like that. By the way, how are you? I've barely seen you all week... How's Tony?"

"Well, we broke up Monday, so I don't really know." She looked up.

"Oh no, why? Why didn't you tell me? How are you?"

"Don't worry, I'm fine," Michelle replied steadily. "We weren't really getting on, hadn't been for a while really. He's the opposite of all those blokes who run a mile at the first mention of commitment. He wanted me to go and meet his parents for goodness sake, all the way to Bury! He's a lovely bloke and all, but not like that. I don't want to spend the rest of my life with him or anything."

"Okay, but why didn't you tell me?"

"Well, we haven't really had time for a good chat this week, not till now anyway, and I sort of think it's a bit presumptuous to assume people'll be interested, even you."

"Don't be ridiculous, Michelle, of course I'm bloody interested. I'm your flatmate, your friend, it's my job to be interested!" Jennifer leant across and took hold of Michelle's hand in her own. "Are you sure you're okay now? Tell me about it. Where did it happen?"

"Yes, really I'm fine," said Michelle, meaning it. "I was around at Tony's and he suggested looking at diaries; he wanted us to plan ahead when we would see each other, when we would go away for a weekend, that sort of thing. And then suddenly – I say suddenly but it'd been building up for a while – suddenly, it just didn't feel right to me. I mean I like him and all, and could see us staying together quite happily, but I didn't feel like we should be assuming we would definitely be staying together. I didn't feel comfortable. It's hard to explain but there's a real difference for me once you start planning things. I mean, once you go forward a month or so, you begin making some pretty big assumptions about your relationship, what the other person thinks of you and what you think of them. And then it becomes about meeting the other person's expectations. But that's not why I went out with Tony at all, or would go out with any other bloke for that matter. I go out with them to be surprised, to get to do things I wouldn't have done otherwise, couldn't have expected! Quite the reverse, in other words."

"So what did you say?"

"Well, I asked why we needed to plan so much, why we couldn't just go on as we were, each of us just arranging to see each other in the slots available. That was how it had worked perfectly well up till now, and I didn't see the need to change it. And Tony said we'd been seeing each other for six months, and he wanted the relationship to be going somewhere, and he was worried that if we didn't start planning ahead, then we would start growing apart. Jen, I almost laughed, it sounded so very sensible and mature. I couldn't fault or criticise him, and he probably deserves better than me, or at least better than to fall for the one woman in a hundred who's not really interested in commitment.

"Stop sniggering," she laughed, "you know what I mean. But the thing is, in order to do that, I need to have a recognisable social life outside of seeing Tony. He's great, I mean it, but it's setting him on some ridiculous pedestal or something to pretend he's the only person, even the only man I know, who I want to spend time with. And I also just want to live my life now. God knows nursing provides enough of a structure and routine to satisfy anyone, and the last thing I want is for my love life to be full of structure and routine as well. Part of the reason I never wanted to go to university was because work offered freedom and independence. I want to have some choice about how I spend my time and money, and trips to Lancashire to see Tony's parents come pretty low on that list." Michelle sat back and drained her glass.

"So did you tell him all that?"

"More or less; come on, let's get another drink."

142

When they'd sat down again, Jennifer began, "Well, as a friend I think you're mad. Tony's just great, and we all thought..."

"I know, but that's the whole point. I don't really want people thinking about me that way. It's not a problem, Jen, I mean I'm not at all angry or anything, but it's just not right for me at the moment. Anyway, that's pretty much what I told Tony."

"And what did he say? How did he take it?"

"Well, not great I guess, but he was mostly okay as far as I could tell. I've not seen him since, so it's hard to tell for certain. He seemed disappointed but he didn't shout or cry or anything, and like I say, we haven't spoken since. I don't know, maybe Tony subconsciously expected it, maybe he could tell I just wasn't the commitment type, and was sort of pushing that side of it as a test of our relationship. But I'm just guessing really."

"You're just a weird girl, you know," sighed Jennifer. "He is gorgeous, , and as for all that stuff about commitment, well it sounds like you've either been reading too much, or you're waiting for some kind of knight in shining armour on a white horse or something. And men just aren't like that. But anyway, here's to freedom and singledom!"

"And another thing," Jennifer continued after they'd drunk some beer, "are you happy with how the flat's working out?"

"Yes, Jen, of course I am, why are you asking?"

"Just checking, you know how it is. We talk about loads of stuff, everything but how we're actually getting on, and, well, you know, it seems to be going all right, it sure is for me, and, well, I just wanted to ask."

"Phew, I was worried there for a minute," said Michelle, "I thought maybe I'd said something, or not said something, that had upset you. And I couldn't think what it was. No, I mean, I think the flat is fine. I've barely thought about it, which I think must be good. Seriously, it's been really lovely sharing a flat with you, don't know why we didn't do it before."

Jennifer laughed, "That's cos we hardly knew each other until about a month before."

"Seriously though, Jen, it's been great. I feel like an adult for the first time. Don't laugh at me, it's just one of those things, a rite of passage or something, where I feel like us having our own space rather than being in a nurse's block means I'm independent in a way I've never been before."

"But Michelle, you're one of the most grown up people I know."

"Ha, ha, ha!" Michelle mocked, "You say the nicest things; that's why I love you so much."

"But I mean it!"

"Okay, I believe you, maybe. But I've always felt terribly shy and immature and young when I'm with people who are older or more intelligent."

"But what about all those junior doctors? Of all of us, you're the only one who'll challenge them when they start talking crap. I know they're not that old but they're doctors!"

"But they don't really know what they're talking about, it's all show with most of them."

"So what would you call intelligent then?" Jennifer was faintly incredulous. "You must be judging them against something."

143

"I don't know really… I had a friend at school who was really bright, much more than any of the doctors we know. Anyway, he went to Manchester University – he was the only person from my school to go to any university that year, though a couple went to Poly."

Jennifer ostentatiously raised her eyebrows. "That's the first I've heard of him, what's his name?"

Michelle laughed, "Like I said, he's a friend, his name's Sam. I've certainly never fancied him – he's not my type anyway, and it would be like incest or something."

Jennifer giggled, "You're so funny, you're so proper most of the time, and then once in a while you come out with something smutty like that. But what were you saying?"

"Just that I went to see Sam in Manchester for a weekend and I felt totally out of my depth. Even Sam was cleverer than I remembered him, and he had a couple of friends who were at least as brainy. It's not even as though I could hate them for being pretentious or arrogant or up themselves, there was none of that."

"What was it then?"

"Well, they were just normal really, like you and me, except they were able to talk about really difficult stuff in a way that made sense to me."

At this point, one of the group of lads down the other end of the pub started shouting "smegma" quite loudly. "Smeg ma," he shouted, "you mustn't forget the ma."

"Come on, Jen, I'll buy a drink, you put something on the jukebox."

Michelle did feel different since she started living with Jen, like a wave of sustainable independence had gradually enveloped her so that an entire universe of previously untouched responsibility had suddenly floated within her reach. From relatively simple things like sorting out gas and electricity for the flat, to making a will and understanding her pension.

"Same again please," she said when she got to the bar.

"Just be a sec, Michelle, got to change the barrel," Paul replied, opening the door to the cellar and disappearing.

She sat on a bar stool and drummed her fingers aimlessly on a beermat, then stacked five mats and manoeuvred them until they were half overhanging the edge of the bar and flipped them expertly into a somersault before snatching them cleanly out of the air with the same hand. She then repeated the same trick just as neatly a couple of times more.

Satisfied, she glanced around the bar at the increasingly familiar photos, mostly of the pub's own football team but also of the Cup-winning Forest team from 1959, when Dwight and Adams had scored the goals that beat Luton 2–1, and the team had finished with nine fit men after Dwight had broken his leg and Bill Whare was reduced to hobbling around with cramp. She smiled at the stories from her dad, who had gone down to Wembley, and the faint memories of watching the match herself on Grandstand. Under Brian Clough, they looked like they might just scrape back to the First Division, but that '59 team would never be surpassed.

This bar almost felt like an alternative front room to her, friendly and cosy, undecorated in a decade, with a slightly decrepit carpet whose red floral design had faded badly. There was a small raised stage in the back left corner, where local bands occasionally played. Jen was standing by the pillar at the corner of the stage, restlessly flicking through the albums on the jukebox. "Hey look!" she shouted, "they've got the Bay City Rollers on here, whadda you think?"

"No!"

"Emerson, Lake and Palmer?"

"No!!!"

"Abba?"

"Better!"

Paul came back up from the cellar. "Sorry about that, it was a bit stiff."

"That's okay, there's no rush."

"Not working this weekend?"

"Nope, the first free Friday I've had this month…"

"Doing anything special?"

"Not really, we're just tired, to be honest. Maybe tomorrow after we've had a lie in."

"Here you go." Paul handed her the change.

"Thanks," said Michelle; and took the drinks back to the table where Jen was just sitting down.

"Thank God for Bob Marley and the Stones," said Jennifer as the opening bars of Satisfaction sounded out. "I love this song!"

"Yea, me too," said Michelle, "but Mick Jagger's not really my type."

"Yea, and you've got all them Joni Mitchell and Van Morrison records, ain't you?"

"And I sometimes break out and buy the odd Neil Young album."

"Listen to this line," said Jen as she sang along. "I've never understood it."

"Well, the Stones are all Art School types," retorted Michelle, "which isn't to say it does mean something clever, just that they almost certainly think it does."

"Oh Michelle!" laughed Jen, "You say the oddest things sometimes. It could just be a clever bit of song writing but you're never prepared to just leave it at that."

"I'm sorry," replied Michelle, "I didn't mean to be awkward or anything."

"That's okay, it's just that most of the time, when we're getting on really well, I almost sort of know what you're thinking, but then every once in a while you say something that makes me wonder."

"Don't worry," laughed Michelle, "I'm not that complicated, just a bit mad sometimes. Just tell me to stop if I begin going off again. By the way, was there anything on the news? Only I was in the bath and missed it."

"Just more about the Liberals agreeing to support the government."

"It's all a bit of a mess, isn't it?"

"I don't really follow politics but I guess it must be."

"I know what you mean. I mean, if you just listen to the news and read the papers, it sounds like the country's falling apart. But it's hard to see how it affects the way we actually live."

"Yea, it's all pretty much just London stuff as far as I can see."

"I kind of agree with you, but that loan from the IMF last year means we're having to cut public spending. And then we might end up with another Tory government."

"But then at least you'd have a woman prime minister," argued Jen, "you should be pleased about that."

"Mm," said Michelle, "I'm not sure Margaret Thatcher's really the sort of woman I'd want to see as PM. She just seems so cold and so driven. But you're right, she is a woman and it's high time we had a female leader, even if I disagree with her on almost everything."

"Do you reckon she's really that right-wing?"

"I don't really know," Michelle replied, "but she's more right-wing than Heath was, and she also seems, I don't know, too certain of herself or something."

"Isn't she from near here?"

"Yes, Grantham, just down the A1. I think, though, she's an MP for somewhere in North London." Michelle paused for a moment, sipped her drink, "You got any holidays planned?"

"You must be a mind-reader, I was just going to ask you about that. I was thinking of picking up a package to Majorca and was wondering if you'd like to come with me; we could go together."

"Why that'd be great! I'd love to, I've never been abroad before, Mum and Dad could never afford it."

"Mind you," said Jen, "I'm not having you going off and being mad about stuff!"

"I promise, I'll be on best behaviour."

"That's settled then, we can get some brochures tomorrow and go through them together on Sunday."

"I can probably only afford to go for a week you know, is that okay?"

"Me too."

The two women smiled and clinked their glasses. Jen's holiday invite had been a shock, and momentarily, Michelle had thought of passing on it. She had no other plans but inside her head was the kernel of an idea to go on a walking holiday to the Lake District or Scotland, perhaps as part of an organised group to maybe meet some new people. But Jen's invitation had been so transparently generous, and her momentary hesitation went completely unnoticed by the other woman, who saw and heard only an immediate acceptance.

"So you really like all that US West Coast Hippie stuff?" she asked.

"Well yea!" Michelle replied, "I like Bowie, Roxy Music and stuff as well, so I guess I do the Art School scene too. But yea, I like the late 60s," she laughed, "I've even got a Crosby, Stills and Nash album, but I generally keep it quiet, Buffalo Springfield as well!"

"Who are they?"

Michelle laughed again, "Don't worry about it, I promised to be on best behaviour and so I won't go mad on you. And it's not important anyway."

"What about Punk, the Sex Pistols and all that? I mean, they're quite funny sometimes, and I quite like the way they want to tear everything up, but, I don't know, maybe me and Jonny Rotten is a bit like you and Mick Jagger?"

"It's hard to say. I started off getting put off by all the swastika stuff, but people tell me that it's an ironic piss-take and not anything racist. Which I kinda get, but there's still a lot about it I don't understand. I think I get where the anger comes from, but the Mohican haircuts, the skinhead bit, all kind of leave me cold. I don't really know anyone like that. I mean I thought the swearing on TV and stuff was

146

okay, particularly as I thought the guy interviewing them had it coming. But I don't really get how Punk fits in with anything else that's happening."

"What sort of things?" Jennifer was only half interested but she was happy talking to Michelle for the sake of it.

"Oh, I don't know," Michelle was saying, "unemployment, racism and the NF, the Cold War, there are lots of things really."

Jennifer thought it over for a minute. "But surely," she said at last, "if Punk's about young people, then surely, these days, that's about unemployment and sex and race and so on?"

"Yea, I guess you're right."

"Cos losing your job, or not having one to start with, is a really big deal for loads of people our age and younger," said Jennifer. "We're really just so lucky the two of us, me anyway."

"You're no luckier than me," replied Michelle. "Over half my year left school at 16, and some of them – I know cos they live quite close to where my mum and dad are – have basically been in and out of jobs ever since. Most of us have ended up in jobs but some of my friends have found it really hard."

"I know what you mean. My school was the same."

"My friend Sam, the one who went to Manchester, always said that he thought everyone would have benefitted from the right kind of education up till 18, but it all needed the right teachers, the right courses, the right funding."

"That sounds a long way off," said Jen.

"Oh he knew that, but he thought it was worth aiming for because otherwise you were wasting too much talent."

"What's he doing now?"

"Still at Manchester but he finishes this summer."

"What's he gonna do then? He sounds nice."

"He is, I think he's going to try and get into the Civil Service. I've lost touch a bit though; he might even have taken the exams already."

"When did you last see him?"

"Not since last summer; we missed each other at Christmas."

"Do you miss him at all? You used to be quite close from what you said."

"I do a bit, but we all grow up and apart, and it's not as if we ever fancied each other or anything."

"Are you sure?"

"Yes," replied Michelle, relaxed, "I thought about it a lot for a while, and Sam's lovely, but not my type, even if he fancied me, which I'm sure he doesn't. I'm sort of looking for someone who's a bit more spontaneous, surprises me sometimes; Sam never surprises me."

"What does he look like? I could do with a man who doesn't surprise me too much."

"He's okay looking, a bit gangly and clumsy and skinny, but okay I guess. Light brown hair, glasses, cute nose, lovely smile, nothing to go mad about but you could do worse. Although if you think I talk a bit weird, he's totally off the scale. Always reading, and trying to explain things you've never heard of."

"Does sound a bit out there, but still sort of fun."

"He is, but Sam's also a bit too much into himself, if you know what I mean. No, not like that, not like he fancies himself or anything, more the opposite really. It's more like he worries about himself too much."

"Is he still a virgin?" asked Jen.

Michelle blushed slightly but Jen didn't notice. "I don't know, but maybe. He's never talked to me about anyone but then, like I said, I've not seen him since last summer, and I'm not sure he'd tell me about that stuff anyway. Just too polite and well brought up, if you know what I mean."

"So why do you like him so much? Is it just because you grew up together?"

"I suppose so. But he's also a bit embarrassing sometimes. And he's also much cleverer than me, so it's sometimes hard to have a chat to him about normal stuff."

"Yes, I can see how that would be a problem," said Jen. "I used to know boys like that, who I quite liked but were just useless at talking to you."

"So," continued Michelle, "we just drifted apart naturally once he went to university. Manchester's a world away; I went up there once, like I said, in his first term, and everyone was really nice to me and everything, but it was obvious I didn't fit in. And it was expensive, and my training here took up a lot of time."

"Yea, it's hard getting away at weekends; even getting back home to my mum's is hard. And I reckon I've seen more, grown up more in the last three years, well, sort of…" Jen laughed. "Oh, I can hardly wait till we go on holiday in the summer, I'm looking forward to it already; beers, night clubs, what's that drink called? Sangria? Sunshine, suntans, it'll be great!"

"I've never been abroad, you know, never mind to Spain or Majorca. It'll be funny, people speaking a different language and all."

"Don't worry," laughed Jen again, "I've never been to Spain either, but I think they speak English in places like Majorca anyway."

"Phew!" Michelle shook her head, "The furthest I've ever been on holiday was to Blackpool, nine or ten years ago, with my parents and grandparents. We all stayed in this same B&B, with musty sofas and a traditional battle-axe landlady, and it rained about every day. I remember going on a donkey a couple of times but I was too old really. And I'd not taken hardly any warm clothes – Mum let me pack myself – and I remember being cold almost the whole time we were there."

"Well," Jen hadn't stopped laughing, "I think I can guarantee Majorca'll be better than that. Mind you, knowing my luck, the first time I ever go abroad for some sun it'll be another boiling hot summer here. Though it couldn't be hotter than last year."

"That was amazing, wasn't it, all those weeks without rain?"

"This summer is the Queen's Jubilee, isn't it?"

"Yes," said Michelle.

"Do you think there'll be street parties and stuff?"

"Probably, something came through the door a couple of weeks ago. I think it is a street party but I haven't read it properly."

"That'll be fun!" Jen enthused. "My mum still talks about the street parties they had after the war."

"How old would your mum have been then?"

Jen paused. "Let's see, she's 47 now, so she'd have been 22 in 1952 and 15 at the end of the war. Wow! I've never really thought about it like that. Hard to imagine her as a teenager; I wonder if she was as horrible as I was?"

"Impossible! Come on, let's go, we've got some food to eat and maybe a party to go to." As the two of them walked back to the house, Michelle felt happier than she had for ages. She smiled at the idea she'd briefly consider saying she couldn't go on holiday. Now she shivered slightly in anticipation.

She thought for a moment about Jen's mum being only 15 when the war ended. Her own mum had been 17, and had already left school to go work in a factory. And the summer after, when she was 18, her mum had hitchhiked across Europe with a friend, Hilda, mostly in France but also in Switzerland, Holland and Belgium. After that her mother had never done anything like it again; instead she'd settled down, got married and had children.

Chapter 16
Nottingham, Saturday, 20 June 1981

Michelle had forced herself out of bed and down to the kitchen just after 9.30am. Her head was sore and she suspected she should have stayed in bed but there were things she needed to do today. Just normal things but still important. She boiled the kettle for tea, then put some cereal out and sliced a banana on top.

The kitchen was quite small, with a Formica topped table over at the side to create space to walk around easily. When they had people around to dinner, maybe once a month or so, she and Jen would pull it out into the centre of the kitchen; positioned like this, it would sit six comfortably. Jen would cover it with the kitchen table cloth her mother had given her, and they would stock the fridge with beer and wine. Today, however, the fridge was empty, and Michelle remembered they'd not done this normal Thursday night supermarket run because Jen had needed to go home to Loughborough because her mum was in hospital.

In Jen's absence, Michelle had ended up going out to the Trent Bridge Inn last night and was now feeling the effects; though not, she smiled ruefully, as badly as she deserved. She thought she had got home at around 2am, and had woken up with a half-eaten cheeseburger beside her bed. With this now safely disposed of and her bedroom windows flung open, Michelle, now sipping her tea, was starting to feel semi-normal again.

Strong sweet tea always made her feel better. She wondered if she was now getting too old for Friday night drinking. But 28 wasn't that old, and if all the girls drinking with her last night had been younger, more junior nurses, then that was simply a function of that particular group. Michelle knew her mum would be horrified at the thought of her daughter drinking unaccompanied and drinking so much, but she had long ago left behind that part of her values. Feeling better, she switched on Radio 1, where they were playing 'Bette Davis Eyes', and poured another cup of tea. She had only been nibbling at her cereal until now but her appetite was starting to return; after all, the cheeseburger had only been half-eaten.

Michelle heard the post drop on the mat as she went back upstairs for a shower. This was the glory of their flat, she thought, with a nozzle that squirted water that blasted your skin into submission. Jen and she sometimes joked that the owner, a forty-something property developer with several other flats he rented around Nottingham, had seen too many American porn movies.

Refreshed, she pulled on her jeans, Ché t-shirt and Docs, dragged a comb through her hair and put 'One Hundred Years of Solitude' in her shoulder bag. On her way out, she picked up the post and then walked to the end of the road, bought the Guardian and a Kit-Kat at the newsagent, then another 50 yards to the bus stop.

A bus turned up within a couple of minutes, with her barely having time to glance at the headlines – more job losses.

Once in town, she visited Boots and M&S, window shopped for about 20 minutes and then found a tea shop where she ordered herself a pot of tea and a scone. She was looking forward to the paper but decided to go through the post first. There was a utility bill and a postcard from her Aunt Ethel, who was on holiday in Spain. And then there was what looked and felt like an invitation. Michelle immediately thought it must be a wedding invite – what else would she be invited to so formally, but then she didn't know anyone who was even close to getting hitched. There was a little gold sticker on the back saying if not delivered, please return to somewhere in Surrey. She hadn't heard of the place and didn't think she knew anyone in Surrey.

Michelle shrugged her shoulders, took a bit of scone and tore open the envelope. There were some pieces of folded paper inside the card, sure enough, an embossed card inviting her to the marriage of Louise Mary Carter and Samuel Harold Jackson. So it was Sam. She quickly looked at the date, the first Saturday in September, far enough ahead that she could make sure she was free. Well, well, she had heard from Sam no more than half a dozen times in the last six years and not at all since they'd had that drink, when was it? Two, maybe three years back. The drink had been a bit weird, not awkward exactly but definitely a world away from the easy banter they had shared growing up. It had left her sad, but accepting. Inwardly, she'd wished him well, not resenting his successful career, better lifestyle, escape from Nottingham. She had assumed she wouldn't see him again, or if she did it would be on relatively distant terms. And then this! Who was Mary? What was she like? It looked from the invite as if she was well off. Michelle had imagined Sam a potential lifelong bachelor, so the idea of him getting married seemed, in a funny sort of way, mildly shocking.

She was worried she would stick out like a sore thumb. But she was also curious and pleased, and if Sam had taken the trouble and thought to invite her, then she would go. She got out her diary and put in the date, mentally began to think about what she could wear. For a moment, she wondered if she should buy something new but dismissed it immediately, she couldn't afford it, particularly as the weekend away, with a B&B, would cost her a fortune.

Ordering more tea, she settled back to read the paper. But her concentration was repeatedly broken by pictures intruding, all of Sam at various stages of growing up. She herself was sort of present in each of them but only as a shadowy figure almost lurking in the margins.

The first was of Sam at school, aged about eight, wearing blue shorts and a grey pullover. It was a crisp, sunny day in winter, and she smiled to herself at the idea of school kids wearing shorts all year round. If Sam was eight, that meant it was around 1964, which was when the Beatles took the US by storm. Did they know about the Beatles? An older boy, maybe two years above, had a boy from Sam's class in the corner of the playground. Michelle thought the older boy was called Simon something, the younger one Tim Alderton. Simon didn't have hold of the younger boy but he was leaning against the wall with an arm either side, preventing him from escaping. Michelle couldn't hear what Simon was saying despite the fact he was talking quite loudly. Sam was playing football on the far side of the playground, he was a rubbish player but ran around a lot.

He looked up and caught sight of Simon and Tim, who were probably 30 yards away. She saw him gulping, and then start to walk across the playground towards them. As he got nearer, Tim looked over Simon's shoulder, he was clearly scared. Simon turned round. His face wasn't red as bullies tend to be depicted, it simply looked cold, lacking emotion. Michelle couldn't make out what he said but he was obviously telling Sam to get lost and mind his own business.

For some reason, Michelle could hear what Sam said. "What are you talking to him about?" he asked. "What are you trying to get him to do?" Again, Simon told him to get lost and mind his own business, adding that Sam would get hurt too if he didn't. "I'm going to stand here to make sure you don't hurt him," said Sam, who was clearly petrified and whose face was much redder than Simon's. Simon turned back to Tim and started talking to him earnestly again but in a menacing whisper now rather than the suppressed snarl he had used earlier. Nevertheless, Sam, who was standing only about six feet away, could obviously hear what was said. "Don't do what he says, Tim. It will get you into trouble. If he doesn't leave you alone, I'll tell Mr Jones."

At this, Simon turned around towards Sam, letting Tim go in the process. Now his face was red as he put it right up close to Sam, who was probably six inches shorter. Again, Michelle couldn't hear what he said but after about ten seconds, he gave Sam a shove on his right shoulder, turned around and left. After a couple more seconds, Sam turned away too and walked in the opposite direction, with tears beginning to run down his cheeks. Michelle saw how scared Sam had been. Inside, she thought he was probably one of the most naturally scared people she had met. Michelle didn't know why he was so scared, or how he had managed to suppress them.

Michelle smiled guiltily. One of the reasons she was most curious about going to Sam's and Mary's wedding would be to see how he coped. There would be the actual service, all the 'I do' stuff; then there would be all the meeting and greeting, how he dealt with Mary's family and friends; there would also be the speech and toast – usually horrible in Michelle's experience – and finally all the dancing stuff. None of this, she thought, Sam was naturally cut out for.

The second image was of Sam at secondary school. Each year there was a cross-country race that Michelle remembered as being something like four miles long. She thought of Sam at around 14 or 15, when he had just grown and was maybe 6'2", much taller than most of his contemporaries, and Michelle remembered him quite gangly and self-conscious. This had caused him to be hesitant in his movements, so that he would often stand with one forearm horizontal across his body, the hand gripping the other elbow as if to prevent it lurching outwards by mistake into some passer-by. Every couple of minutes he would swap which hand was holding which elbow. As part of this, the way he gesticulated to demonstrate something had become smaller than his body. His hands nearly always remained within the bounds of his shoulders, elbows clamped solidly to his side.

Meanwhile, it was almost as if Sam's emotions had similarly shrunk to be smaller than himself. Where he had once been quite effusive, he was now reserved; where he had been chatty, he was now taciturn; where he had been gregarious, he was now, if not a loner, then a boy who had mostly closed himself off to all but a few friends. He was still popular at school but in a far more passive way, nodding at others rather than engaging with them. Michelle saw him as a lovable but slightly embarrassing brother.

Everyone ran in the cross-country race, no matter how bad a runner you were, and there was a separate girls' race around half the length of the boys'. Because of this, Michelle, who was a good runner and had come 6th, had finished and was watching the boys. It was a lovely day and the sun was shining, quite pleasant really for March. However, it had rained heavily the previous few days, so the ground was really wet and had cut up badly. The end of the boys' race involved running out of a small copse on the edge of the playing field, then turning right to run alongside rather than across the 1st XI football pitch before turning left at the corner flag for the final 100 yards or so to the finish, just in front of the changing rooms.

Michelle had put on a sweatshirt and her school v-neck and thrown the rest of her school uniform into her duffel bag. She was standing on the small wall in front of the changing rooms, looking up towards the woods. Her friends Wendy and Caroline were sitting beside her on the wall, also looking towards the gap in the fence through which the runners were emerging. The race had been won, as last year by Martin Beck, a tiny boy who floated over the ground and seemed to use up no energy. Just behind him had been Bill McBride, a much bigger boy, whose effort was much more palpable but who had somehow managed to get within about five yards of Martin – the year before he had only come 8th, Michelle remembered, but the year after he had won.

Michelle thought about half the boys had finished when Sam emerged from the woods. He looked ungainly and exhausted but was still trying to catch the boy ahead. Try as she might, Michelle couldn't remember his name but he was only about ten yards ahead and was slowing slightly as they ran along the side of the football pitch. She felt she was seeing these events more forensically than she had at the time; the colour was sharper, and her appreciation of distance more precise, even as the action itself was moving in slower motion.

If the gap to the next boy had been ten yards when he came out of the woods, it was probably seven yards when he got to level with the 18-yard box and maybe four yards by the time they reached the corner flag. Michelle felt proud at the effort exuded by Sam's every stride, buoyed by the expectation he would overtake the boy in front on the final run to the finish. But it was not to be. As Sam rounded the corner flag, his right foot planted itself at 45° to his line of running; but he had got carried away and not slowed down; so when his plimsoll, instead of gripping the grass, started slipping on the muddy ground, cut up by the dozens of runners who had already passed, he had no time to recover. His right arm went out and up, his left out down to the side to cushion his fall. Sam tried to bring his left foot down to stabilise himself but his sliding right foot was a long way from his centre of gravity, and it had barely touched the ground before his arm did. Watching, Michelle saw first Sam's elbow and then his left thigh and hip hit the ground. He was still sliding and, as he did so, rolled over onto his front. A blast of laughter blew out from the children grouped around the Finish.

By the time he had got to his feet, the boy in front was some 30 yards clear. Sam's white PE shirt was streaked with mud a foot wide and his left leg was similarly caked, as was his forearm. What's more, the grip had entirely gone on his right plimsoll and before he got to the finish, embarrassed and also wary of slipping over again, two more boys had overtaken him.

Mr Beech was the PE teacher at the finish and pretty sadistic at the best of times – his swimming periods usually ended up with half a dozen children retching on the side of the pool, and he had been known to throw plimsolls at children who he decided weren't paying attention or trying hard enough. He did not spare Sam's feelings. "You looked like a dying giraffe going around that corner up there Jackson; I've seen collapsing towers of Lego that looked more co-ordinated." It wasn't funny but because he was a teacher, and because most of the children were scared of him, they laughed as Sam turned redder.

"Sorry, sir, I slipped," was all he could say as he looked for the changing room door across the heads of the other children. Michelle heard his voice wobble slightly, but he managed to keep himself together until he had disappeared from sight, the last ripples of the slightly forced laughter following him through the swing doors. She bit her lip and imagined him sat on a bench in the corner, his head bent low to his knees as he clumsily undid his laces.

Michelle couldn't work out whether this incident had any real long-term effect. In one sense, it was not so different from the other countless small knockbacks that every human receives. But she had always seen this particular humiliation as a defining moment in the way Sam viewed the outside world. All the way through their childhood, he had been an open, relaxed character, if not quite an extrovert. It was true that his sudden growth spurt and the clumsiness that came with it had made the teenage Sam more wary, sensitive to what others thought and how they reacted to him. Yet she felt the cross-country race was a tipping point. The symptoms had only appeared gradually, as he put up his hand to answer question in class less often, played less sport, read more and studied harder. Socially, she thought he laughed more at other people's jokes, told fewer of its own. Interestingly, this meant Sam again became more comfortable in large groups. He never really became a follower and always, ultimately, did what he himself thought was right; but equally, he never became the leader she had once thought of him as being. As a result, there had since that time always been a little part of her that was disappointed in him.

The final image was of a party he had taken her to when she had gone up to see him in Manchester that first term he was at university. It had been, she now realised, a typical student party, lots of alcohol, some drugs, heavy overtones of sex and even, possibly, sex happening in one of the bedrooms while the party was going on. Sam was wearing a turtleneck pullover and a pair of jeans. They didn't really match, and the pullover was bright orange and clung too tightly to his body, accentuating his lack of any obvious muscle. Michelle thought Sam's mum or aunt had got it for him the previous Christmas. Despite this fashion crime, Sam seemed hugely more popular than he had ever been at school. He was the centre of attention, more relaxed than he'd been in years. Nobody seemed to think he was gauche or clumsy, and when he made a joke, everyone laughed.

Part of it, she realised, was that no one here had seen him fall over at the end of that cross-country race. And no one had been around when his height had suddenly shot up. Sam himself seemed just the same to her but these people he'd only just met, these new friends, simply didn't have the history. And somehow this had led to them reaching different conclusions. They evidently thought he was cool, thought he was funny; far more so than his friends back home in Nottingham would recognise, more even than she would have said.

Michelle had seen this at the time but it was only looking back on it now that she really saw the magnitude of the shift. And at the time she had not really thought about what this must have meant for Sam. Now she could see that it must have been both a surprise and a liberation. Simply by moving, by going somewhere different, and being forced to talk to new people who were forced to talk to him, he had become more popular, better liked. Michelle found this worrying because it implied that these people who knew him less well actually knew him better. It was as if all these years of knowing Sam, all the shared experience, had obscured rather than revealed him. For while they seemed to think him cooler and more funny than even she did, standing there and listening, watching him interact with these people, Michelle decided they were more right than she was. What was it about knowing someone well that meant you stopped really seeing them? At the time, Michelle had been more confused than anything, not understanding what was happening.

A tall, good-looking dark-haired girl wearing a kaftan was standing talking to Sam, swaying gently to the music, with her right foot crossed in front of her left. Michelle remembered she was called Siobhan. Next to her was a man with slightly boyish face and sandy hair. He was slim and normal height, so about as tall as Siobhan was. Michelle thought he was called Ed and he was looking slightly quizzically at Sam as Siobhan was talking to him, his right eyebrow expertly raised from time to time. Pink Floyd was playing and there was a strobe light whirring slightly amateurishly in the next room. Sam and Ed were drinking beer, Siobhan looked like she was drinking white wine, all from paper cups.

"What do you think will happen with the demo tomorrow?" Siobhan asked. There was a student protest scheduled for Saturday afternoon about British Army brutality in Northern Ireland.

"I'm not sure really." Sam replied. "It's important we protest, but I hope it doesn't turn into a 'bash the troops' event. Some of my mates from school joined the army at 16 and they're all okay blokes." This was the sort of stuff Sam had come out with for years, and Michelle just took it for granted. However, it seemed to blow Siobhan away.

"I can't believe you can see both sides. It's like everyone's a victim."

"I'm not sure it's that simple," interrupted Ed. "There needs to be conversation somewhere. The Marxist view would be that the British were focusing economic power in the hands of the Protestants and then using the army to suppress the Republican community. Yes, the soldiers may be victims of a sort but they're also being used as pawns to subdue fellow workers."

"Is that what you think?" Sam asked.

"Of course not. But it's a starting point for understanding the difference between cause and symptom." He took a gulp of beer. "But I do get what you're saying about the British Army."

"So who is to blame?" asked Siobhan. "Is it the British government? Labour have only just got into government, but I'm not confident they're going to do anything very different."

"I know," replied Sam, "all I'm saying is that British troops are human beings as well. Jim's brother over there is in the army, and it's hard to believe he's a monster."

"Okay, you're right on that," said Siobhan, "but it's still important to show we don't support the brutal things that are happening in Belfast and Derry."

"Setting aside who's to blame for a moment, I still don't really see what the cause is. Nothing I've read has ever really traced it back and explained why it's like it is," Ed was persistent, "I mean until you know, really know, what caused something, you don't have much chance of sorting it out."

"But basically isn't it still a colonial war, a freedom struggle against the British Empire?" said Siobhan.

"Yes," said Sam, "but it's more complicated when the majority want to remain in the UK. I know that's all about the partitioning of Ireland and all that but it still makes the whole thing harder. Anyway, tomorrow sounds like a good event."

"And probably fun as well," said Ed. "And a good demo is usually followed by a good party."

"You're full of shit," laughed Siobhan. "Stop pretending you only turn up to try and get laid. Come on, let's get a drink. Do you want a top up, Sam? What about you, Michelle?" They both said yes, and Siobhan disappeared with Ed towards the packed kitchen.

"I like your friends," Michelle had said, thinking inside how she never met anyone remotely like them; in fact, anyone their age who ever admitted they were interested in politics. Equally, she was pretty shocked to see Sam talking easily with these people about these things.

"Yeah, they're all right I think, though I sometimes miss you and the rest of the crowd." Sam replied, "Ed's a really good mate I think, or will be, and Siobhan's one of the cleverest people I've met here, and just good fun with it."

"She's really pretty as well," Michelle had said. Looking back through the lens of her memory, she cursed at herself for being so simultaneously gauche and gushing. At the time, she had simply been wide-eyed, visually and intellectually gasping at the new people and what seemed to be rarefied conversations. She did like these people and was oddly proud that they so obviously thought Sam was a good guy. But she also felt that, in the act of going to Manchester, Sam had left their Nottingham estate and could never come back even if he wanted to.

"You're probably a better judge than me," Sam had replied, "She's certainly not short of potential boyfriends."

The unanswered question remained so. Sam had realised too late the gap he had left and his complexion reddened and burned, not because of reality – he liked Siobhan but didn't fancy her – but because he knew he had said too much and at the same time not enough, and also that he couldn't undo it. Michelle had thought Sam was shy, afraid of saying that he fancied someone else.

Ed and Siobhan came back with drinks. "It's a jungle in there," Siobhan said. "Ed needed to clear space for me to get through, pushing the various would-be gropers out of the way."

"Surely not," exclaimed Sam in mock horror, recovering from his previous embarrassment.

"Oh yes," laughed Ed. "All the usual prats with trailing arms and protruding bottoms looking for that passing, but oh so significant, sensual contact. But I jest, it's all just Siobhan's feminist self-regard."

"Careful," said Siobhan.

Taken together, the three memories simply confused Michelle. Although she had known Sam the best of all her childhood friends, they now seemed like three different people, none of whom were recognisable as Sam when she thought about him generally.

The last time they had tried to get together, about three years ago, had been a disaster. They had been due to meet in Central London, near Leicester Square. Michelle had thought they had agreed on a pub and so had sat by herself for some two hours in The Coach and Horses while Sam, it later transpired, had been standing outside Leicester Square Tube, which was where he had thought they had agreed to meet. Bizarrely, it seemed now, neither had thought to look elsewhere. She had simply assumed Sam had been held up and saw herself as showing faith in him by remaining where she was. Eventually, Michelle had to leave to catch the last train back to Nottingham. At the station, she had called and left a message with Sam's flatmate, who had only been able to say that as far as he knew Sam had been intending to meet up.

When, the following day, they had managed to speak to each other and realised what had happened, both had admitted that they would probably have done the same thing as the other. Yet Michelle had somehow felt emotionally aggrieved enough to not make an effort to go to London for a while after. And when she did, in April the following year, she had allowed the trip to be arranged so as to make it impossible to meet up with Sam. This had, in turn, been influenced by knowing Sam had been home for Christmas and not got in touch.

And yet here she was, four years later, sitting with his wedding invitation in her hand. She had no clue why she had been invited. He had slipped from her mind, and she had barely thought about him at all for the last year. Maybe he had very few friends? But, remembering the party in Manchester, she thought this was unlikely. Perhaps it was a huge wedding? This was possible – the reception sounded as though it was at a huge hotel – but she had also been asked to the service itself, which looked to be in a small village church. Most likely, Sam was just going through his life and inviting people who had been important to him along the way even if he had not seen them in ages.

Satisfied, Michelle begun to read the paper. The fallout from Israel's bombing of Iran's nuclear reactor was continuing, the Irish General Election looked like it was going to turf out Charles Haughey, and the build up to the first Ashes Test was in full flow. She felt funny about the idea of going to the wedding. The invitation contained a note asking her to contact Sam and Mary if there was someone she wanted to come with. This emphasised how little Sam knew about her but also how much her presence was valued; Michelle had been to several weddings and had never been offered to bring a boyfriend with her.

Of course, there had never really been a boyfriend. A few short-lived relationships and a small selection of one-night-stands was all she had to show for her 25 years. The idea of a proper long-term relationship, let alone living with someone, or getting married and potentially having children, seemed in a different

157

place entirely from her life. The longest had been with Richard, a policeman she had met at a party. It was mostly a hospital party but his sister was a nurse and she had brought him along. He'd been fun but he had wanted them to live together. She hadn't been ready for that and felt deep down that sooner or later they would run out of things to talk about. Maybe if he'd been more patient, it might have developed into something more, or at any rate lasted longer. The end had come at another party; this time they arrived together and left separately after Richard objected to her talking to other people.

"The two of us are together, I want to be with you this evening," he had complained.

"Yes, but we can be together after," Michelle had replied. "We're at a party now, and there are other people here, my friends, your friends, our friends. I want to talk to them, and I want you to be confident enough not to worry about that. And I'd like you to feel comfortable doing the same."

"But," he argued, "we don't see anywhere near enough of each other, not with all the shift work and everything we both do."

"I know that, and we need to work that out, but we both knew it when we started going out. We both love our work and I think that's great, it's part of why we're with each other."

"So what does that mean?" Richard's voice rose. They had started the conversation in the kitchen but had now edged out into the hall, yielding to various people sliding past them. This meant they were closer to the music – 'Being with You' – playing out of the sitting room where the furniture had been pushed back against the walls. As their proximity to the music increased, their voices had risen naturally and Richard's had now soured. "Are you saying you're going out with me because of my fucking job?" Michelle tingled as she remembered the row.

"No, but I just think we have a lot in common." After a short paused, she added, "Or at least I thought we did… I'm sorry, Richard, I do really like you, maybe even love you, but I don't think this is going anywhere." With that, she bit her lip, then shrugged her shoulders and walked past him out the door. She was halfway home before she realised she had forgotten her coat, but kept walking.

Sitting in the café, with the invite to Sam and Mary's wedding in front of her, nibbling her scone and sipping her tea, the memory of that night, some six months before, was vivid. She found herself blinking away a tear, shed not for Richard but for her lost opportunities and misunderstood moments, for all the unjustly harsh words she had spoken and received, and for the ultimately unknowable and unknowing space at the core of each of us.

When, shopping done, Michelle returned to the flat, Jen had arrived back early. Her mum had improved slightly and been discharged. Later, they decided to go out, but before doing so shared half a dozen tequila slammers. They went to a club and danced and drank a lot. Michelle flirted more than usual and with an unusual edge. By 11pm, she had pulled a bloke called Martin and for the remainder of the evening they danced in a clinch, semi-groping each other as if starved of sensation. Later, Michelle went back to his flat and stayed the night. Early on the Sunday morning she went home, making no arrangements to call.

Chapter 17
Surrey, Saturday, 12 September 1981

Ed turned up ten minutes before the service, unfortunate as he was doing one of the readings. Slightly bizarrely, he thought, it was from Song of Solomon – Sam told him he'd had to argue to get it included. But he re-focused his thoughts on the practical as he parked his rental car in front of the Black Horse Inn and walked calmly across to the gateway – what was the proper name for it? – To the churchyard. The church looked Norman but again he put the thought out of his mind.

His flight from Amman had been delayed three hours and so had only landed a few minutes before midnight. Consequently, by the time he'd collected his car and got to his hotel – thank God he'd opted to stay near Heathrow – it was almost 1.30am. Jetlag and the impact of rushing around meant he had laid in bed for ages, trying to get to sleep, until finally dropping off about 4.30am. He'd dozed initially, but then slept through his alarm and not woken till almost 11am. Fine, he'd thought, the wedding's not till 2pm and it's only an hour's drive; so he left a message to say he would be there by 1pm instead of 12 noon as originally planned. But he had forgotten to allow for getting stuck behind caravans and tractors on quiet English roads.

At least he was already wearing a suit, having almost unconsciously decided against changing when he got there. Ed smiled at the recognition that, even though he had assumed no delays, part of him had not quite believed. He was also thankful for the fourth cup of coffee he had drunk, so removing the chance of jetlag-induced sleep during the service. A side-effect, however, was that he felt as though he was flying at 30,000 feet, and operating in that semi-detached way caffeine can induce. Ed knew this feeling, the insouciance that came with it, could get him into trouble and revelled in the prospect. He looked around as he strolled up to the church porch, confident he could wing it.

When he walked in, nodding to ushers he didn't know, he muttered groom and found a seat some three quarters of the way back but beside the aisle. The church was full, with upwards of 120 people, including children. He took his time sitting down, looking around as much as he could for familiar faces or, more likely, backs of heads. He found none. There were a few that might have been friends from Manchester but then they would turn their heads slightly to confirm they were someone else. He sat down next to a lady of about 65, wearing a pink jacket and big hat, who turned out to be Sam's Aunt Miriam.

He noticed too that almost everyone, with the exception of himself, was in a couple. Perhaps that was how it was. His last few visits to England, he had noticed fewer people had been able to meet up with him, and if they did they were much more likely to arrange to meet him for a drink than to invite him around for dinner.

His assumption was that most of his contemporaries now had partners, and so dinner parties only happened in even numbers. Sam of course had been different, always cancelling other commitments, and when he began sharing a flat with Mary, had immediately invited Ed round. There had, too, been dinner parties, often thrown together at short notice and usually with comfortingly odd numbers, often involving some other people who were single.

As the organ jumped into action and Mary walked in on her father's arm, he reflected that despite meeting her maybe a dozen times over the last two years, he didn't really know her. That said, he was certain in his own mind that within the slightly diffident exterior, she loved Sam deeply. This took her a long way in his book but, despite that, always seemed a bit too flawless for him to genuinely warm to; beautiful, intelligent, always stylishly dressed, with nothing out of place. Ed tended to love human beings partly for their failings and, unable to detect any in Mary, knew he was withholding some affection and friendship.

After the second hymn, it was his reading. He strode up to the front, holding in his left hand the sheet of paper he'd been sent. It was soiled and lop-eared from having been carried around in his jacket for the last two months. He smoothed it out on top of the enormous Bible that sat on the lectern and began. Except he wasn't reading but knew it from heart, having learnt it during his wait at Amman airport. His words filled the church in an authoritative but conversational tone. Ed had learnt how to speak, had found his voice, and was able to use his hard-won craft to reveal meaning in the words and phrases. He looked down at Sam briefly as he approached the closing lines and then back up at the guests as the rhythms of the ancient phrases washed over the congregation.

"And lo, the winter is past, the rain is over and gone. The flowers appear on the earth. The time of the singing of birds is come. And the voice of the Turtle is heard in our land." He pursed his lips, bowed his head slightly and walked slowly back to his seat.

During the vows, Mary's voice was strong and piercing, Sam's slightly wobbly. Ed loved him for it. As they walked out at the end, he drifted to the back corner to get a glimpse of their faces just before they turned right to exit into what had become a slightly blustery September afternoon, with clouds scudding across the sky. They both glowed with the typical happiness of newlyweds, but Ed could see Sam was also relieved. His face, while radiant, was drained of energy, but only for a moment before a slight grimace brought him back into control.

Ed waited until the church was almost empty before joining the line. He wanted to see if he recognised anyone; he didn't. It seemed he was the only person from Manchester. Had they not been invited, or had they cried off? He couldn't imagine the former while the latter, though hard to believe, seemed more plausible. Those who were there seemed wealthier, more confident somehow, than Sam's uni friends, more like the Oxbridge public-school types he came across at the BBC. He smiled at the internal rhetoric of the generalisation and acknowledged it might not stand up to the evidence test he would impose before uttering such views even in private company. But it was hard not to think in terms of social class and privilege; British society simply did not allow it.

He knew that, later on, when he had a couple of drinks, he would find most of them quite likeable. First impressions were often right in his experience, but they rarely offered the whole picture and usually lacked context. In this case, he could tell most of the men's suits were quite new and rarely worn, some of them looked made to measure, the odd one probably tailored. An old reporter at the BBC had taught him the trick of making this distinction. The things to look for were tiny creases at the backs of the knees; slight fraying at the bottom of the trouser leg – he knew his were terribly frayed from continual rubbing against his shoes; whether the sleeves rode up the wrist as their arms swung; and the extent to which there was a gap or overlap in the breasts of the jacket when they were hanging loose. As for the women, it was harder to judge given the propensity to buy new outfits for weddings, and Ed knew he was a poor judge of fashion at the best of times. So he tended to focus on hair, where he could sometimes tell when an excess of cash had been sploshed.

Overall, he imagined a mix of lawyers (solicitor as well as barristers), accountants, merchant bankers and high-flying civil servants. Some of the first two groups would already be partners, he suspected, while all were probably buoyed by a measure of family money and influence. He knew well how cynical his view would sound. But this was how he had experienced and observed the world. The closer you got to the top of British society, the more prominent and vivid these strata became. From university, career choice seemed in the eye of the beholder but the barriers to entry for some careers were in fact vastly higher depending on your educational background and family wealth and connections. Ed wasn't particularly bitter about this. It did mean, however, that he started from a perspective where there were few unbiased questions and few genuinely open job adverts. Everything had a context and the context often dictated the result.

As he left the church, the wedding photos were already well under way. Someone – he suspected Mary – had decided the receiving line should happen at the reception and that the photos should take place straight after the service. Fortunately, the sun was out, briefly, and so it was pleasant standing in the church grounds surrounded by ancient, moss-marked gravestones and the slightly sunken stone paths wending between them. There was an ancient oak in one corner, probably as old as the church, which would make it 800 plus years, and the whole scene had an attraction Ed struggled to describe in language that wasn't trite and superficial. He had no one to talk to so he stood for a couple of minutes, just looking round, drinking it in. He thought it stemmed from the unstated, overlaying washes of history and culture. The church was seeped in the generations of clergy who had served there, and of the births, marriages and deaths commemorated. And now, approaching the end of the second millennium AD, here they all were, in an increasingly post-industrial and secular world, taking part in an ancient ritual performed in an ancient rural setting. And yet, it felt perfectly comfortable, somehow utterly appropriate and suitable. Ed knew this phenomenon was not unique to the UK. But he did think nowhere he had seen captured quite the same mix of ancient and modern; in other cultures, there was usually more of an explicit acknowledgment of the past.

He could tell the photos were coming to an end and briefly thought he had escaped when the final call came from Sam and Mary's 'friends'. Still not recognising anyone else, Ed strolled across the grass, hands deep in pockets. He went up to Sam.

"Hi, sorry I cut it so fine. My driving turned out to be more responsible than I'd expected."

"Not a problem," said Sam, characteristically phlegmatic. "We just think it was wonderful you were able to fly back, not least with that French ambassador just having been shot. And thanks for the reading – I knew you would do it justice."

Spontaneously, Ed hugged him, then moved on to Mary, apologising again and muttering something appropriate about how beautiful she looked, before kissing her on each cheek. A few seconds later, he was standing at the left end of the back row trying to summon up his best 'camera' face for the photo.

When the crowd broke up, he headed straight for his car. He wanted to check in and at least vaguely unpack before going down for the reception; because he was flying in from Jordan, Sam had offered to book him one of the handful of rooms in the hotel where the reception was. When he got there, he was pleasantly impressed with the character of the place. It was an old coaching house in the high street and, although a bit musty, had been reasonably well-preserved. His room had a low doorway that he just scraped under without ducking, then opened into quite a large corner space, albeit in the back of the hotel. It had no view to speak of but plenty of natural light. The bathroom, however, looked old and ropey – when would the British learn to put in decent showers? The bed looked inviting, but that was for later. He quickly freshened up and changed his shirt, and was downstairs relaxing, perched on a bar stool with a large gin and tonic, before anyone else arrived.

He thought about how strange it was to be here for Sam's wedding when he himself was light years from finding anyone he would want to marry, let alone who would marry him. His life was just too peripatetic, and he was just too obsessive. And yet he knew colleagues who seemed to be making their marriages work. He ordered another gin just as the first guests trickled in. Viewed here, in a different setting, they seemed altogether less homogeneous. He began chatting to people as they drifted up to the bar, using his craft to discover how they knew Sam and Mary, what work they did and so on. In terms of careers and social background, they were pretty much as he had surmised, but within those groups they turned out to be quite varied.

There was Alex, who worked for Morgan Grenfell and had played rugby for Oxford's 2nd XV, the Greyhounds, in the Varsity Match against Cambridge, having been to Ampleforth before. He was huge, about 6'4" and 17 stone and had an irreverent sense of humour that Ed immediately liked. He knew Mary through her sister, his girlfriend, and, when he found out what Ed did, and how long he'd known Sam, immediately asked what skeletons there were in Sam's cupboard, and went into a mock rant about how inconceivable he found it that weddings in Islamic countries didn't involve any alcohol.

Alex also had his own theory about how people got off with each other, based on thresholds of attractions between sexes. So, for example, the average man would, under the right circumstances and usually involving alcohol, happily have sex with at least half the women at a party. The equivalent for a heterosexual woman was lower but still about a third. He claimed to have drawn various Venn diagrams demonstrating the theory. All this was explained briskly, with a wry but inoffensive omniscience. Ed decided Alex was simply a natural comic, just plain funny, incongruously so in such a large frame. He was still in full flow when Ed saw a woman with long, flowing black hair falling over her shoulders making a beeline for him. She came up behind him and wrapped her arms around his waist.

"Come on you," she said, "we're waiting for our round next door."

Alex shrugged in mock disappointment, "Excuse me," he said, bowing, "duty calls. By the way, Linda, this is Ed, who was at university with Sam."

"Hello," she said, "I believe we're sitting on the same table. But until then I must drag this useless bloke into the next room. But you need to be prepared to tell us all about Sam's scandalous youth."

"I'm bound by a vow of omertà," Ed replied, "but I'm always bribeable."

"Really!" she turned again to Alex, "Come on you, the natives are revolting next door."

***

Michelle had struggled with the service and felt completely out of place. She had stayed the Friday night with Rachel in Elephant & Castle and they had gone out for a curry. Rachel wanted Tom, her boyfriend, to move in with her but he was resisting, and Rachel had decided this meant he didn't love her. They had been together two years and Michelle had felt quite sad as she sat on the train out of Waterloo.

The small Surrey station where she got off was almost deserted, and quite ugly and run down. Its only impressive aspect was the size of the car park. The invite had come with a list of local places to stay, and Michelle had chosen the cheapest. It was a homely B&B about ten minutes' walk from the station, and the same distance from the hotel where the reception would be. She had resigned herself to getting a taxi to the church, hoping to be able to scrounge a lift back. However, when she arrived at the B&B, the first thing Mrs James, the archetypal landlady, said to her was to ask if she knew Tim and Karen, her other guests, who were also going to the wedding. Michelle said she didn't but would like to meet them before if possible. Mrs Adams duly offered to introduce her, and five minutes later Michelle had secured a lift both ways.

Tim was a lawyer and Karen worked for the Home Office. Both had been to Durham University and looked like they could have been on magazine covers. Karen was about five months pregnant with their first child – they had been married the year before and lived in North London. Karen had been to school with Mary and they would have stayed with her parents, but her father had died in 1978 and her mother soon after. The jealousy Michelle had felt earlier was more than cancelled out. She found most of this out in the first two minutes, before she had even had a chance to put her stuff in her room, and the rest during the car journey to the church. Karen drove so that Tim would be able to drink.

When they got to the pub, there was about an hour to go before the wedding began. Michelle was beginning to feel as out of place as she had suspected she might. She didn't dislike Karen or Tim but felt little in common with them. She saw ahead an evening of awkward, polite conversation and was just starting to dread it when they walked into the pub and she saw Sam, who looked up and came straight across to them. He said hello to Karen and Tim but hugged Michelle first, telling her with an honesty beyond doubt how glad he and Mary were that she'd been able to make it. He made room for them at the table where he had been sitting with the best man, Mary's brother, and the two ushers. For the next half hour, Sam scarcely talked to her but a couple of times would look over and smile hello; at other times, he would try and bring her into the conversation.

Mostly, Michelle mumbled something relatively bland, but when the talk turned to the newly formed SDLP, she said she thought they were cowards who should have stayed in the Labour Party and fought for what they believed. There was a hesitant silence and then Tim began talking about Europe being one of the biggest fault lines in British politics, gradually taking the conversation away from the apparently toxic subject. Rather than embarrassed, Michelle felt suddenly energised. She liked argument and the fact that these people, so well-educated, didn't want to argue on such an important subject stripped away a lot of the awkwardness and slightly inferiority she had been feeling till then. Sam was quite plainly relaxed about the fact she had just brought the conversation to a shuddering halt. If anything, he looked slightly amused by the whole thing.

At 1.30pm, Sam, the best man and the ushers rose to go, while Tim insisted on buying another round for those who remained. Michelle asked for another half of bitter and made a mental note to go to the toilet before walking across the road to the church. She tried to focus and pay attention during the service but kept finding her mind drifting, and not even to important things but to everyday ones, like what time she would get back to Nottingham tomorrow and what she would have for tea. Her family had never been churchgoers and Michelle had only really been in churches for a handful of weddings, apart from a school trip to Lincoln Cathedral when she was 14. Beside her, Tim was singing lustily and Karen was crying with happiness. Michelle passed her a hanky. After the service, there were some quick-fire photos in the church grounds. The last one was Sam's friends, none of whom she knew. There was no one from Nottingham apart from herself and, as far as she could tell, only one from Manchester University, someone called Ed, whose name Michelle recognised and whose face seemed dimly familiar. The confidence from the period in the pub lingered, but the rest of the day looked like a tale of tedium stretching out ahead of her.

But gradually she cheered up. Karen was babbling all the way to the hotel, even if she drove too fast for Michelle to be entirely relaxed and kept half turning her head to make a particular point to her in the back seat. But she was so obviously enraptured by the service, by Mary's dress, by the vows, by the readings; all of these had totally passed Michelle by, but she found Karen's enthusiasm for the detail infectious, and by the time they reached the reception, Michelle was starting to enjoy the occasion, largely second-hand and almost despite herself. And the hotel was lovely. Still recognisable as a coaching house, it had a cobbled entrance through an arch in its middle to the car park in the back. On the left of the arch was the bar and on the right the main hotel. Michelle loved that no one had tried to smarten it up or modernise it. It looked like she imagined 18th century inns would be, like something out of Tom Jones.

Once they had parked, they entered the main hotel to be greeted by a waiter with a tray of champagne. Michelle had never tasted champagne, and for a moment she looked at the elegant bubble-infested flute with the incredulity of someone who had walked in on a surprise birthday party. She sipped it gently, barely letting it do more than moisten her lips. It tasted surprisingly dry, but the tingle of the bubbles exploding was all she had imagined. As she took another, longer sip, her eyes visibly brightened.

So far, there weren't many people there. Tim and Karen had made a fairly quick getaway from the church and this, combined with Karen's slightly unnerving willingness to treat roundabouts as chicanes, meant they had extended their lead on the following cars. As they got their drinks, Karen and Tim had migrated across to a group of four people standing by the fireplace. Karen introduced them as Ingrid (Mary's sister) and Alex her boyfriend, and Linda (Mary's best friend from university) and her fiancé Roger.

"Hello," Ingrid said when Michelle was introduced. "I've been so looking forward to meeting you. Sam always talks about you as his oldest friend, almost like a sister. We must talk lots. Unfortunately, I'm on the top table – ridiculous protocol really, no good reason why I should be there – but we've arranged for you to sit at our table, and Alex will look after you – though I doubt you'll need it – and introduce you to people because I know you're the only person here who Sam knew when he was young."

Alex finished the champagne and took a look around. "I think there's time for another drink or two before we sit down. What would everyone like?" He smiled and began taking orders. A minute later, he disappeared out of the door and across to the bar. As he did so, more people suddenly arrived, and both the bar and the lounge they were in filled up.

Then Ingrid, who Michelle had immediately liked, was talking to her again. "How did you get down from Nottingham? Did you drive?"

"No," replied Michelle, "I decided it would take too long getting around London. So I came down yesterday afternoon to London by train and stayed over with a nursing friend. Then I came down on the train from Waterloo this morning. What about you? Have you been down with Mary all week?"

"Oh no, she's too organised and unflappable for any of that. I wasn't allowed anywhere near her until yesterday morning. Alex and I came down on Thursday night and stayed with Mum and Dad. It can be a bit of a pain frankly. I love them dearly but they still do that parent thing of treating me like I was 12, making us sleep in separate rooms and so on. But I guess that's fine, I'm sure our kids will say worse about us. Anyway, I keep forgetting, you haven't met Mary yet, have you?" Michelle shook her head, smiling at the other's all-action confessional style. "Well, the first thing to tell you is that of course she's nothing like me. I work in women's magazines and Mary's a budding history professor; she went to UCL, I went to Sussex; tells you all you need to know really."

"No, I haven't met her and, to be honest, neither have I seen Sam in the last few years. So the invite was a lovely surprise on several levels. Though I don't know how representative I am of Sam's childhood; it all seems such a long time ago and I've stayed in Nottingham while Sam's been to Manchester, London, all over. I'm looking forward to meeting her though. Her dress was gorgeous."

"Yes, I know. Mary has a girlfriend who buys for Harrods, and through her we were able to get the dress more or less at cost. But Sam's absolutely fabulous, we all love him. It's just incredible how good a listener he is, a complete world away from Alex, love him as I do, who thinks empathy is some kind of liver disease."

It came as a surprise to hear something about Sam, which Michelle had always taken for granted, praised quite so highly. Maybe he hadn't really changed as he had gotten older. Perhaps it was just that he was more appreciated by adults than by children and teenagers. In other words, he hadn't changed much, everyone else had.

"Alex is cool though," Michelle said, slightly lamely.

"Yes, I know he is, and he's the funniest person I've met; he makes me laugh and think at the same time. Don't tell him but I also fancy him to death. He knows, but his ego's big enough as it is. I'm not sure why I'm telling you this – probably because it's my sister's wedding, you're the only woman here I haven't met before, and I like you."

"I like you as well," Michelle replied. "It's really weird coming here and not knowing anyone apart from the groom, and not even having seen him for at least two years." By this stage, they were standing slightly separate from the main group. "But, to be honest, everyone – Karen and Tim, yourself, Alex – has been lovely to me. I was really worried about coming here, but I'm really enjoying myself and I'm really pleased for Sam and Mary. I'm really looking forward to meeting her." Michelle was aware she was gushing but her speech, not unpleasantly, seemed detached from the rest of her.

They were still chatting when Linda, who had finished her drink, announced she was off to the bar to chase up Alex. Soon they returned, carrying the drinks and about ten minutes later, everyone began being ushered upstairs to sit down for the dinner. Going past the welcoming line, Michelle met Mary and her parents for the first time, but as she was just in front of Ingrid who was ridiculously, Michelle thought, enthusiastic about her new friend and did all the talking, this was far simpler and more fun than she had anticipated. It was also lovely to see Sam's mum and dad again. She had only managed to spot them from a distance in the church, and they treated her with the mix of slight formality and unconcealed affection they had shown her since she was a child.

When they sat down, having clapped the top table coming in, Michelle found herself sat between Alex and Tim. She sipped her wine a bit more freely – it was from France and easily the nicest she had tasted. The food too was lovely – smoked salmon, followed by lamb, and then Black Forest gâteau. Mary's dad made a short, quite formal speech; Sam's was slightly but endearingly nervous, and ineffably honest and loving. He was really glowing, Michelle thought, and she was suddenly really happy for him. Talk at the table had been lively and funny. Tim had been interesting and good company, while Alex turned out to be a real joker and made her laugh out loud continually, once to the point where the wine almost came down her nostrils. Initially wary as she had been, her liking for these people was growing.

Daniel, the best man, was just standing up to speak when, out of the corner of her left eye, Michelle caught a hand movement. She blinked but then recovered and collected herself. Linda, who was sat the other side of Alex, had put her hand on his thigh, seemingly oblivious of her fiancé across the table. The hand was under the table but the movement she had caught and the angle of Linda's forearm and wrist left no room for doubt. Michelle could feel herself redden and her hand shook as she reached for her wine glass, more this time as something to do than because she wanted to drink. The best man's speech was a blur to her, though she managed to laugh, or pretend to, in the right places. She had gotten to know and like Ingrid more than she had expected to get to know or like anyone at the wedding. As a result, she had also had a much better time than expected. And now this? Should she do anything? If so, what?

If she showed that she had noticed, it risked a scene, particularly as Linda and possibly Alex were drunk. If she told Ingrid, they could deny it and it would be her word against theirs. Unless Ingrid already knew, Michelle didn't see how she would be believed in that situation. In which case, she would almost certainly lose Ingrid as a friend, while Mary, who was Linda's best friend, would probably never speak to her again, which in turn would cut her off from Sam. All this whistled through her mind as the speech continued and she tried, unsuccessfully, to avoid glimpsing the wrist methodically sliding up and down Alex's thigh.

Later, Michelle concluded they must both have been either too drunk, or too caught up in each other and their shared guilt, to notice she had seen them. She didn't make a scene and didn't tell Ingrid. Instead, she escaped from the table, on the pretence of needing the toilet, as early as she felt she could, and spent the rest of the evening avoiding Linda and Alex, but also Ingrid. Michelle did not think she could talk to Ingrid again that night – the future didn't matter – and so eventually, she slipped off and walked back to her B&B. The landlady was still up and understandably surprised to see Michelle back so early. Michelle made a variety of excuses and muttered something about long night-shifts catching up with her.

She worried what people would think but in fact was barely missed. Ingrid vaguely looked for her but quickly became pre-occupied with Linda's increasingly obvious relationship with her boyfriend, which she had suspected for about six months. Rather than risk spoiling her sister's wedding, she waited and then broke with him the next morning, waking early and leaving, having first shredded his suit with scissors. Sam wondered vaguely about not seeing Michelle, but so much else was going on to allow him not to worry. Otherwise, her absence went unnoticed.

Ed enjoyed the meal and even did a little dancing at the disco afterwards. Inspired by his brief conversation with Alex, he let his mind run and lowered his threshold for saying straight out whatever came to mind. At his table, someone started extolling the Beatles as the root of all that was good in modern music – the only music dispute worth having was whether Sgt Pepper or the White Album was the greatest record ever made. "But surely," Ed had interjected, "all pop music dates back to Holden Caulfield. He gave a language to teenage disillusionment and legitimised what it meant." The conversation had stopped dead. He ended the evening drunk but happy, delighted for Sam and Mary, and with his faith in humanity slightly restored.

The next morning, Sam woke about 6.45. Mary was still asleep and he had a headache. He looked across at her. She was lying on her left side facing him. Her right arm was curled underneath her breast, her left arm folded backed beneath the pillow, her face nestled into the folds of the feathers so that some of it was submerged from view. What was visible, however, was her beautiful nose and her right profile, with her brown hair falling across her neck. Sam lay looking at her for a long time. He thought about the day before and wondered for how long the memory would remain vivid. He recalled his voice shaking slightly at the start and end of his vows and speech but knew he had got through it okay. The rest of the reception had been a blur. And now he was married to a stunning woman he had worshipped from that

167

first moment. He knew it was as old as the hills, but he had never understood why she had agreed to marry him when there were so many better-looking, richer alternatives.

He felt far away from where he grew up and was conscious that, besides his parents, only Michelle was there from Nottingham and only Ed was there from Manchester. Somehow he had grown apart from all those people and, as a result, the guest list had been dominated by Mary's family and friends, all of whom he liked and now thought of as his own. It was a sign his life had moved on. It had been strange to see Michelle and Ed. Michelle had seemed overwhelmed in the pub before the wedding, and he had barely seen anything of Ed beyond a quick five-minute chat. But he knew the whole thing would have been less meaningful for the absence of his single most important friend. The reading from 'Song of Solomon' had been sublime, and in each phrase of Old Testament poetry, Sam felt himself carried into a purer world, where actions translated into meaning without refraction, and truth could endure without ambivalence. That was the world he wanted to create for Mary and himself. His childhood had been full of uncertainty, and he was determined to provide greater security to Mary and their children.

Slowly, he swung his legs over the side of the bed and sat up. The sun was slanting through the curtains, and he pushed his right hand back through his hair, once thick but now thinning, then stood up and shuffled across the old carpet that covered the uneven floorboards towards the bathroom. As he got to the door, he glanced back at Mary, still sleeping. Tonight they would be in Venice, and he shook his head again at the surprise of it all.

Chapter 18
New York, Wednesday, 3 November 1976

Philip was walking down 5th Avenue; he had been following the route for eight years and was now recognised by other pedestrians, shop owners and even some of the street cleaners. It was the first Wednesday in November, the day after the presidential election, and Jimmy Carter had defeated the incumbent Gerald Ford. Ford wasn't an incumbent in the normal sense, having come to the Oval Office only when Richard Nixon decided to resign rather than be impeached. And while Carter had run a good enough campaign, Philip was unsure America was ready for a Democratic Presidency, certainly not the sort Carter was likely to lead. He wondered briefly whether an old-fashioned networking Democrat, like Truman or LBJ, would be able to manage the US's right-drifting politics effectively.

With no real national profile before he began his come-from-behind run in the Democratic primaries, Carter actually seemed to be one of those genuine rarities in US national politics, a Washington outsider. And he had run a clever campaign, making the most of this happy circumstance. Yet for all that, it had been oddly passionless, partly distracted by all the shenanigans around the Bicentennial, and just as much by the failure of Ted Kennedy's attempt to follow in his brother's footsteps. In some ways the nomination races had been more interesting and exciting than the presidential contest itself. With Kennedy on the one side and Ronald Reagan making a dangerous run from the Republican Right on the other, there was even a sense after the nominees had been confirmed that both had, in different ways been lucky; Ford from having the cachet of the presidency and Carter due to the insurmountable flaws of his rivals.

Although he liked a lot of Carter's policies, Philip didn't sense the new president had managed to generate much real enthusiasm during the campaign, certainly beyond the core Democrat coalition, an increasingly unstable coalition of unlikely bedfellows – northern and midwest White working class, African Americans, East and West Coast liberals, and just enough Southern White working class. Carter, a streetwise Southern politician had succeeded in holding the grouping together, but the signs for the future still seemed unclear. And he was sceptical about Carter's chances of making the Washington machine operate effectively. Even since he had lived in the US, the growth of corporatism in DC had been almost exponential, and it was hard to imagine Carter successfully navigating any meaningful legislation through Congress, which was itself starting to become less bipartisan. Against this landscape and with the mutual bitterness engendered by Watergate still raw, it was hard to see Carter getting much of a honeymoon period.

The thing that had impressed him the most about the whole campaign had been Reagan's run at the Republican nomination and just how close he had got. Philip's first memory of Reagan, and his most significant one until this year, had been at the Republican convention in Miami back in August '68, midway through that long traumatic year of idealism denied. Then, he had been a largely peripheral figure, although extreme and therefore interesting in his own way. Philip had, therefore, been sceptical to see subsequently that Norman Mailer, in his famous account of that year's conventions, had assessed Reagan as much more of a player, much less the decorative hanger-on. He had even cynically supposed that the part Mailer ascribed to Ronald Reagan was more to do with the novelist's need for dramatic structure.

Reagan's campaign, however, both its substance and its near success, had caused Philip to rethink. To be fair, he had never bought into the dismissive tag of B movie actor applied to the Californian Governor by part of the Democratic Party and by much of the British media. Reagan was far too effective an electoral operator not to be taken with the utmost seriousness. Besides, there had always been that strand of American politics going back through Truman, McKinley, and even Lincoln, that placed the creed of less is more on a pedestal, put a premium on the ability to deliver an effectively avuncular homily and, at the risk of insulting the intelligence of half the electorate, made the other half feel included and valued. Reagan had begun to demonstrate this skill in spades, but whether he had possessed it in 1968, Philip still wasn't sure.

He was at least pleased that the eight long years of a Republican White House had come to an end. He had stayed up till 2am the night before, long after the election had been called by the networks, listening to state after state declaring and watching the studio pundits attempt to decipher meaning in the red and blue mosaic of a map that was emerging on the screen. Carol had invited him to a New York Democrats' party but he'd declined, feeling his Britishness more acutely than at other times. Philip lived in America and felt at home here, but knew he was not of it. And so, as he had in 1968 and 1972, Philip had watched the election coverage by himself.

He was headed towards Fulton Fish Market to catch breakfast with Carol. He suspected she would be bleary eyed and arrive late, but instead, Carol was there first and it was he who apologised.

"So how hung over are you feeling this morning?" he asked.

"Hopefully a lot worse than I look," Carol responded ruefully. "There's only so much Wild Turkey a girl can drink, even in a good cause."

"When did you crash?"

"Oh about 5.30, which means I've had all of 3hrs sleep. I'm only functioning at all on the basis that if I get through today, I'll feel better tomorrow."

"Well, you look fantastic by any measure."

"And you're full of shit but keep it coming,"

"It was a good night, sure enough," Philip said. "Even me, the confirmed abstainer, made it through till gone 2am. So what did you think? How do you reckon Carter's gonna do?"

"I think he'll do good, you know. Come on, let's order! I need more coffee and something, pancakes maybe, to line my stomach." When they ordered, she continued, "You know, I never thought another Southern Democrat would win the presidency. I thought Johnson was the last."

"It was a good win, no doubt about it," Philip conceded. "What do the party think? Are they wild about him or just relieved to get the GOP out of the White House?"

"A bit of both, I think. You're the political expert, I'm just a supporter in this game. I reckon there's something of relief about it, but I also do sense a real enthusiasm for a new kind of politics."

"Oh, Carol!" exclaimed Philip. "Anyone else would bring the cynic in me out in the open right about now. But for you I'll change the subject. How's Danny? Is he starting to feel any better now we're almost into 1977?"

"Not really. I almost wish we'd stuck to politics and you'd punctured all my blissful illusions. No, he's still pissed, at himself, at God, at life in general. He knows he's not going to be running fast by the time Moscow comes around; this was his chance, end of story. I reckon he'll find a way to move on pretty soon; though maybe you're right, and heading into a new year will turn out to be the tipping point. He was on good form last night though, whooping and hollering with the best of us. God but it's great not to have a Republican president anymore."

"Was Danny's brother there?"

"Yes, Richard was there. He's okay now, I think. He still works at that Ford franchise over in New Jersey, but he seems to be enjoying it."

"You know," said Philip, "I think Vietnam will still be Carter's biggest problem."

"Why? Surely it's over and done with now, finally?"

"Not really; the Republicans think Vietnam's one of the main reasons they lost and so they need to try and neutralise it before 1980. Which means more rhetoric about it being a war our soldiers could have won if the politicians would only have let them; so there'll be a lot of trying to re-write history. And Hollywood will soon start rewriting the truth in its own sweet way. And that could easily distract public attention hugely from Carter's agenda."

"How do you mean?"

"Well, I think it potentially makes nuclear disarmament and détente with the Soviets much harder."

"Maybe, but we're a hell of a long way from the sort of policy argument you're talking about. We just want someone in the White House we can have some belief in, have a conversation with, who will care when he sends our young men off to die for their country. Now okay, that wasn't Gerald Ford's fault directly, and yes there were Democrats involved; but it's time we moved on from Vietnam, and Carter's our chance to do that."

"Okay then, how good a president do you really think he'll be?" ask Philip.

"Now there you go asking simple questions and getting all British on me. The truth is, I don't know. He ran a great campaign for the nomination and a good enough campaign for the White House. So at least that means he's a winner, and let's hope he stays that way."

"But how good will he be?"

"Okay, I'll get to that, but afterwards, can we talk about your love life or something routine like that?"

"Fine! But you've got to answer the question first."

171

"Right then! Oh good, here come my pancakes, and with lots of maple syrup – good ole Canada! Excuse me for a moment. Thanks, right there will be just fine. So, to answer your question, I think Carter will be a good president but maybe not good enough for what we need. This is the year of our nation's Bicentenary and a lot of the flaws we had at the time of the Founding Fathers still exist, most specifically around African Americans and the extent to which my people are included in the American Dream. We simply been waiting too long. I don't think the new president is going to answer it for us but somebody needs to. Have you ever read James Baldwin's 'The Fire Next Time'? It's quite short. It was written in the mid-late 60s sometime and talks about how long the Black man has had to wait for a fair deal."

"No, I haven't," Philip replied, "though I've heard of it. I like his writing – 'Another Country' is one of my favourite novels."

"I didn't know that," said Carol, "you always have the capacity to surprise me, Phil."

"I save them up and drip feed them to you. I wouldn't want you to think I was interested in America or anything ridiculous like that."

"Okay, but still," Carol was persistent. "I don't recall you reading books like that travelling to games."

Philip laughed, "I thought you knew. The culture of our profession isn't always very – what shall we call it? – Considered. You're a Black woman in a White man's world, so you know it as well as I do. If I started reading arty novels out in the open – especially James Baldwin for Christ's sake – half of our friends and colleagues would probably assume I was gay and the other half would assume I was trying to subvert the constitution."

"Fair point," Carol replied, "though I genuinely didn't know, which after so long, is quite something. But enough of this, you're just trying to distract me from hearing about that love life of yours."

"You know," Philip said, "I've never understood why women want to hear about this sort of thing. I mean, Jack and Scott really aren't that interested; they might ask if I'm still seeing someone or if they've dumped me yet, but it wouldn't go much further than that. But you're always after that bit more detail. Don't get me wrong; it works for me and I'm fine with it – in case you hadn't noticed, I quite like talking about myself – but you ought to know that I don't get the chance to do so very often, except with you…"

"That's because I'm your conscience, Phil. I'm the Jiminy Cricket on your shoulder trying to make sure you do the right thing. And I can tell you, it's been quite a burden over the years. You Brits need us to be your moral compass now that you've gone all European on us."

"I do love the way you go on, and obviously, my moral compass has improved enormously since I've lived over here! But I thought the US had stopped being the last great hope of humanity. Power does corrupt after all, and you guys sure do have a lot of it, even after Vietnam."

"Let's leave your moral status out of this as something too small to be measureable. And as for your cheap anti-American jibes, I'll ignore them because I know you don't mean it and have only invented them to change the subject. But what I do want to know about, and which I realise you're just trying to distract me from, is how it's going with Patricia and when you're going to make an honest woman of her."

"How do you mean?"

"Oh, come on, Phil, don't try and go all innocent and frankly obtuse on me. The woman loves you. She's beautiful and intelligent. She's not told me this, but she probably wants to have your babies. And she's waiting on some encouragement from you, and at some point her biological clock will start ticking, and she'll get tired of waiting."

"Well, I'm seeing her tonight for dinner," Philip offered.

"That's not what I mean and you know it."

"It's just not for me, not now and possibly not ever. Kids are fine but I'm not sure I want any of my own, or, for that matter, that I'm equipped to look after them, to be a good parent. When I was a boy, I had a pet rabbit, a beautiful, big golden-coloured rabbit. I loved it like anything but I was really bad at looking after it, not just feeding it but cleaning out its hutch, giving it clean bedding, and so on. And nothing tragic happened; it lived until it was about five and then it died quietly in the night; but I always thought I could've done more; and if I'd done more, been more conscientious, it – his name was Elvis – he would have had a better life, may even lived longer."

Carol was incredulous, "Come on, Phil, I don't believe this and you can't honestly expect me to. Are you seriously trying to tell me you don't want to have kids because you weren't as nice as you could have been to your pet rabbit? My God, Phil, you must have been six or something at the time. How the hell can you draw any sort of comparison with what kind of parent you would be?"

Philip's face broke and he started cackling with laughter. "Fair point, but honestly, it's not that simple. Okay, maybe it was a bad example, but the basic point remains. I'm just not good at looking after things, animals, people, myself even, and I don't think that's ever going to change. Now, before you raise it, and to avoid repeating any earlier mistake, this isn't me saying I don't understand people or know how to please them; actually, I reckon I'm pretty good at both these things. But beyond a certain point, I'm just not really interested. In that sense, I guess I'm pretty selfish really. Don't get me wrong; I like other people, I enjoy their company; I'm not misanthropic, but I don't 'care' about them. And I don't really see that changing."

"Doesn't that make you feel lonely a lot of the time?"

"No, not really; sometimes I conclude it should, but when I try and get myself to feel lonely – I know it sounds ridiculous but sometimes I do, seriously – I always know I'm faking it. And then I guess I also have this starting point that we're all alone anyway. It would be pointless to pretend otherwise, and the challenge then becomes how you deal with it."

"But what you've just said doesn't make sense in terms of the person I've known for eight years. For example, when you say you don't care about people, that's just ridiculous to me. You so obviously do care about your friends, you're doing stuff for them all the time."

"Yes, but that's not what I said; I talked about not caring, which is really quite different. I like them, and where there's a chance to do something that costs me nothing, then by and large, I'll take it. But if I lose by it, then I pretty much never put myself out unless there's a clear long-term advantage to play for."

173

"But isn't that what everyone does, Phil? They'd just put it in more flattering terms."

"No, I don't think they do. Most people are actually much nicer than they claim to be. They're afraid of appearing soft, but actually they make all sorts of small but real sacrifices for each other. You see it all the time, people compromising on time to suit someone else, giving someone a lift and going out of their way to take them home. I don't think I've ever knowingly done anything like that unless there was something it for me. So I'm actually not as nice as I seem, which puts me at the opposite end of the spectrum from just about everybody else. I'm not saying I'm nasty or anything, but I deliberately try to be as self-contained as I can. And going back to where we started, that's not a great recipe for being a parent. I'm sure I could do it; like I said at the beginning, I was okay with Elvis, just not great. But I wouldn't be really good at it. It wouldn't come naturally to me and a lot of it would be a duty rather than something I wanted to spend my time doing."

"Is that what all this is about? Worrying you won't be great at it, only good?"

"Maybe."

"All that you've said sounds to me like someone who's ready for the responsibility of being a father, who is, if anything, worried about caring too much, and who, frankly, is a bit of a control freak."

Philip laughed, "I think that if I even tried to rebut all that, it would make me sound like I was protesting too much."

"All right then, let's call it deuce for the moment but I'm not letting you off the hook on this, Phil. I mean it. I'm on your case. I want to know if you're really a bastard or if you're only pretending."

"And I'd rather keep you guessing."

"Which only increases the probability of you being a bastard."

"Which suits me just fine. After all, I've got my reputation to protect."

"While we're on the subject, how does this attitude to life fit with all those beliefs and ideals I remember you being so passionate about back when we first met?"

"Well '68 taught me a lot of things, but above all else, it showed me the general futility of putting your hopes in anyone other than yourself."

"How do you mean?"

"I thought a hell of a lot was going to change when I landed at JFK that January. But for all the huffing and puffing, and all the blood, sweat and tears from so many people, hardly anything did. And looking back now, it all seems very much like the end of something rather than the start. The dreams were big and most of them were worthwhile, but there wasn't enough substance underneath them. The foundations weren't strong enough, and so the whole thing was just too fragile and depended on too few individuals."

"I don't see it's got much to do with what we've just been talking about."

"Sorry," said Philip, "I'm not being deliberately obtuse. What I mean is that '68 suffered greatly from not having enough people who were involved mainly because of their own self-interest."

"I'm afraid I still don't really get it. I mean Dr King and Bobby Kennedy got shot, the Kremlin sent tanks into Prague and Daley sent the Chicago police into Grant Park. Violence and power exerted itself, and everything else got crushed. Where does your lack of self-interest come in?"

174

"It's very different, I know," replied Philip, "but if you compare it to, say, the French Revolution, one of the obvious differences for me is that there was no underlying sense of loss or risk to unite the range of disparate groups who were all agitating for change. So a lot of the anti-war movement was made up of kids who knew they were themselves really unlikely to go to Vietnam, for all the reasons we know. And I suppose what I'm saying is that I don't think that's enough to change the world."

"This all sounds a desperately depressing outlook on the world. Are you saying there's no room for idealism and selflessness?"

"No, but I don't think it's enough. Which I guess is part of the reason I'm so sceptical about Carter. From where I sit, it looks to me like he won because America's in a period of self-doubt, with elements of self-loathing even. Post-Watergate and post-Vietnam, it wants to get all its problems out on the table, go through a bout of introspection, maybe go through some therapy. But very soon you'll want the medication to work, to feel you've come out the other side and can feel good about yourselves again. That's one thing that really is different about the States compared to old Europe; whether it's the land or the immigrant culture, but you have a visceral desire to feel good about yourselves, to self-improve. And if that self-improvement isn't quickly tangible, then it's time to swap horses and try something else. Carter'll identify big problems like energy, that will take a generation to fix, without providing you with the sense that you're succeeding."

"You know what, Phil," Carol say wryly as she signalled for the bill, "you've really made my day. I came in here all happy and upbeat, and now I feel thoroughly depressed, not only about Carter's presidency but about human beings' capacity for happiness. What is it about you? Are you always this cheerful, or is it just after a Democrat victory? God only knows what you would have been like if Ford had won."

"It's a British trait, most of us are glass-half-empty people. It comes from being an island nation constantly afraid everyone else will someday wake up and realise how small we are."

"I'm sorry, but that doesn't begin to explain your almost nihilistic view of the world. I mean I've met some downbeat journalists but none of them remotely compares to you when you're on a roll."

"Thanks, I'll take that as a compliment." He made a mock bow, still sitting at the table.

"Well, in all honesty, it does come across as pretty arrogant, and I'm a bit sceptical how much of it is true, even for you. And I'm not convinced either by your portrayal of yourself as a total bastard. But I wouldn't want you to try too hard to disprove me, especially tonight."

"Easy, Carol, no need to worry," Philip said as the two hugged goodbye, "I really like Patricia."

***

Patricia and Philip had finished dinner and were lingering over coffee, chatting away cheerfully but inconsequentially.

"I saw Carol for a quick drink after work last Friday," said Patricia. "She was on good form."

"Oh did you?" said Philip. "That's interesting."

"Why's that?"

"Well, I had brunch with her this morning, and she was obviously concerned I was going to be a bastard to you. She really likes you, you know."

"I didn't, and I haven't said anything to her about being unhappy simply because I'm not, and even if I was, I would obviously talk to you first."

"No, I know that. Carol's ability to reflect upwards and outwards is second to none. Merely having said hello to you would be enough to trigger a whole series of thought processes in her head around you and me."

"She's quite a friend," remarked Patricia. "When we first started going out and you introduced us, I did wonder to what extent I should see her as a threat." Philip shook his head, "No, after a while I decided the two of you hadn't ever had sex and nor would you in the future, irrespective of me or any other girlfriend you had. There is a bit of me that still wonders why that is, but that's just one of life's little mysteries. Despite that, you must know that Carol's a huge presence in your life and quite a daunting one for any new girlfriend to come to terms with."

"Yes, I do," Philip agreed, "and, for what it's worth, I think you've always been really cool about it. It's funny hearing you describe it like that, though there's nothing you said that I disagree with, but I guess I've never really heard it articulated before."

"Really, that surprises me. I can't believe none of your other girlfriends have talked about her to you."

Philip smiled, "No they have, but it's either been the oblique referral, or the full-on rant usually as part of our breaking up."

"Ah, I see, but doesn't that worry you? Seriously, I'm genuinely curious."

"Well, I suppose it does but it's always been absolutely crystal clear to Carol and me that we've never been physically attracted to each other. And neither do I think either of us have ever given any signal that a girlfriend or boyfriend could legitimately take the wrong way."

"I think that's probably right, but you're still asking a hell of a lot of us."

"Maybe, but it's me as I am, and it wouldn't be right to pretend any different."

"Okay then, but then tell me why you've never been out and, as we both agree, why you never will."

"The best way I can put it," Philip replied, "is that Carol and I are basically family rather than friends. If we were friends, I'm certain we would have slept together years ago and, for what it's worth, fallen out really quickly. But we're not really friends, we're spiritual cousins; who knows, perhaps we had the same parents in a previous incarnation."

"This is just getting weirder," Patricia was incredulous, "Listen, I know you're a bit of a hippy but you don't really expect me to swallow that, do you?"

Philip was patient, "No, not really, but you asked and that's my honest answer. Look, one of the things you need to understand is that Carol's way older than me and always will be. Okay, so she's only a year or two older in actual age but I'm a kid compared to her. I can make a pretty good fist these days at pretending to be an adult, but fundamentally, I'm not and never will be. Carol, on the other hand, has been properly an adult from the age of about six."

"So what exactly are you saying?"

"Look, when I first met Carol, it was in Mexico City in '68, just before the start of the Olympics. I've told you all about that, getting drunk after drinking tequila for the first time. And you also know bits and pieces of the months before that when I'd just arrived in the States. But what I haven't really explained is how I stopped doing that and why I ended up in Mexico City; after all, the Olympics were before the election."

"I hadn't thought about it, but you're right."

"Well, when I talk about that time, I usually end with the Democrat Convention in Chicago. What I normally omit is that I got caught up in one of the tear gas attacks and was clubbed by the police before being arrested. They released me without charge the next day, but I was still really groggy and ended up admitting myself to the hospital. They kept me in for three days, during which I had my share of unhealthy thoughts. Anyway, when I got out, I'd already decided I didn't want anything more to do with US politics and so I quietly resigned my job – I doubt they had any idea why but no one argued – and headed for California, not in search of anything really, but to be somewhere different."

"Wow," Patricia was stunned, "why didn't you tell me before?"

"Partly it was quite a personal time and I still feel vulnerable about it, and partly because it's always felt a really self-indulgent thing to talk to anyone about. In fact, I've never really told anyone the whole story, not like this. Carol knows bits of it but not the whole thing, and she's never asked about it. She did, however, see me at the end of it and helped me put myself back together, probably more than she knows."

"Okay, you've got me intrigued now. There are a load of questions I'd like to ask but I'm conscious you've not told anyone this before, so go on and just talk to me about what you feel able to."

Philip sat back. He closed his eyes briefly then began talking more slowly than normal and with pauses at unusual points. "The first thing is that I was young, 18 when I landed in the US that January and only just turned 19 that September. Obviously, no one back in January knew how 1968 was going to unfold, but it was a presidential election year in the most powerful country in the world. And then part of that job, the main part of it really, was working for Alistair Cooke, which was a complete education. You probably know him from presenting cultural programmes on US television." Patricia shrugged – "Or maybe not, I guess they had a pretty narrow audience. Anyway, for a lot of people in the UK, Alistair was, and still is, the only or main insight into American politics and society. He's extraordinarily erudite, with a back book of knowledge and contacts you couldn't begin to imagine. He knew everyone, absolutely everyone, from Chaplin to Kennedy, and was also able to capture a lot of what ordinary people thought and did on Main Street. You can quibble around the edges but even now I'm still in complete awe of him. But when I was 18, I was ambitious and scared in equal measure and, while he was always unfailingly kind to me, I really struggled coming to terms with the idea I could ever be remotely good enough at a job which, right in front of me, was being done by someone at the height of their powers, responding to a series of the most dramatic news events you could imagine. And so, despite trying everything you could imagine and completely working my butt off, I felt out of my depth. Don't get me wrong, I thought I was writing some decent stuff, but ultimately, it didn't match up to what was happening in front of me.

"And then there was the nature of it all. Because I was so young, a lot of the people I was interviewing were the same age as me or slightly older. On the one hand, this made it easier to talk to them, ask the right questions, not come across as square as a lot of the journalists. But it also meant I probably got too close to the stories. A lot of those stories – Vietnam, Civil Rights – were issues where I had a lot of sympathy anyway. But on the other hand, I wasn't really very political, and talking to people like Tom Hayden and Bobby Seale went a long way towards politicising me to the point where I lost some perspective on the whole thing.

"So when Dr King was assassinated, followed by Bobby Kennedy a couple months later, and then Brezhnev sent the Soviet tanks into Czechoslovakia, it really shook me. I really believed the world was about to change for the better, and then all of a sudden, some combination of dark forces was brutally shutting the door in the face of progress.

"Looking back, I think that's when I started to lose perspective and, for example, I was next to useless covering the Republican Convention when they nominated Nixon. I just couldn't find it in myself to report what was happening objectively. I think that's when Alistair began having doubts about me; he even gave me a day off, and I just remember wandering the bars of downtown Miami – boy, must I have looked out of place – before sleeping the whole thing off in my hotel room."

"What made you so angry? I've never seen you lose your cool about any story."

"Maybe now, but that's because I've moved into sports, and because I've gotten older and wiser in between."

"Anyway, by the time everyone got to Chicago, the tension in the air was tangible, lots of people – Mailer and others – have written about this, and believe me, it was real. Without Dr King and Bobby Kennedy, there was a huge gap in national and presidential politics that Hubert Humphrey and Eugene McCarthy were never going to be able to fill. Young people, Black Americans, people who were against the war were all about to be effectively disenfranchised."

"And so how did you become caught up in the demonstrations and the tear gas and so on? You weren't demonstrating yourself, were you?"

"No, though it's a fair enough question, and I confess I did think about it for a while. No, in the end, I was clear that I was there to report what happened. No, the ironic thing was that after all that I've just said, when it came to it, I was simply in the wrong place at the wrong time. Maybe if I'd been 30 years old and looked more respectable, whatever, the police might have passed me by, but to be honest they were so angry and furious at anyone in their way that night that I don't think many of them were capable of any level of discrimination. I just got caught and had no way to escape."

"It sounds horrific; how badly did they beat you?"

"The short answer is I don't remember anything after the first couple of baton blows I took to the head, but to judge from how my body felt when I woke up, they weren't put off by the fact of knocking me unconscious. I was pissing blood for two days and could barely walk for a fortnight, so you can draw your own conclusions."

"Like I said, it sounds horrific. But what made you decide to resign? You seem to me like the sort of guy who would want to persevere, not give in. Sorry," Patricia bit her lip, "I didn't mean that to come out the way it did."

"Not a problem," Philip sat back. "I've thought long and hard about it myself, as you can imagine. A lot of the reason, and the way I justified it to myself at the time, was that I'd been caught up in the whole thing, become an actual victim, and because of that I was somehow forever compromised as an objective reporter of US politics. I've already said how I was affected emotionally by some of the things that happened that year, and Chicago was pretty much the last straw. Political reporting wasn't for me; I'd gotten too close to it.

"But the other part of the decision, which I knew in my core but never really gave a voice to at the time, even to myself, is that I was afraid; afraid of being hurt physically, and aware that I wasn't up for being a campaigning journalist in the way I'd imagined only a few months before. And part of that was, like I said, that I sensed that '68 was the end of something rather than the start or middle. There was no great insight involved in this, the signs were all there."

"Do you think it's ever coming back?" asked Patricia.

"Who knows, but not in my lifetime. Despite the end of Vietnam, despite Watergate, the corporate establishment, Eisenhower's military industrial complex, is even more powerful than it was before the 60s. Back then, I think it just assumed history was moving in its direction; now, having had a fright, it's leaving nothing to chance."

"You really are a radical, aren't you? Do they know about your politics at SI? You almost sound like a Socialist."

"Oh, I wouldn't say I was that," replied Philip smiling, "but I'm definitely a liberal which, despite Carter's win, is becoming quite a pariah status over here."

"And how did you end up in Mexico?" asked Patricia.

"That's easy, I followed the trouble. I had some money saved – I'd been living cheaply, mostly off expenses, out of a suitcase, you get the idea. So when I heard there was some agitation for civil rights in Mexico City, and that the Olympics were due to be held there in a few weeks, it seemed an irresistible opportunity. So I bought a ticket and caught the first flight down there."

"And?"

"Well, it turned out I'd missed the rioting by a day; it was literally happening while I was in the air. So I arrived to survey the wreckage of another civil rights movement. I'd barely registered this one and so wasn't nearly so close to it, but its suppression still kicked me; there was lots of similarity to Chicago for a start. And pretty soon the brutality of the whole thing began to get to me as I started to hear stories from ordinary people – always off the record – about what had happened. And that was when I discovered tequila and went on a four-day bender."

"And then you met Carol and she saved you?"

"Yes, more or less," and as he spoke, he remembered the dryness of his mouth as he sat in the corner of the nondescript bar, his head slumped forward on the table, cushioned on his arms.

"Hi there, what's the matter, buddy?" Carol's voice had that slow southern drawl that seeped into his pores. She had been watching him with some friends since he'd stumbled in half an hour before.

179

Patricia listened, fascinated, to the rest of Philip's story. Two weeks later, they split up quietly. She had concluded she couldn't be with a man so much of whose life was focused on a past she could never be a part of.

Chapter 19
Nottingham, Saturday, 14 April 1984

Philip had been back in London for a week, for most of which he had felt depressed. Some of this was due to his usual struggle to overcome jetlag and lead a normal existence from the moment he stepped off the plane, but he also found Britain, in the depths of the miners' strike, particularly unappealing. It was like one of these novels about a mutually destructive relationship, where none of the leading characters inspire any sympathy. London also seemed more run-down than he remembered it – he'd not been in the UK for nearly three years – and the Tube and general infrastructure seemed greyer somehow, and more tired.

But now he was out of London, gunning his hire car up the A1. Philip preferred it to the M1, the slowing down and accelerating away from the roundabouts, and the closer proximity of the rolling English countryside. He'd started early, bypassing the hotel breakfast for the chance to get out of London before the rush hour, and by 8am, after nearly two hours driving, he was almost at Peterborough and decided to stop at a roadside Little Chef. The place was clean enough and the food okay, reminiscent of his boyhood. He was struck by the slightly sullen mood of the staff, with little of the enthusiasm or banter he took for granted in the US. Some of this, he surmised, could be down to pay rates but something also about the different nature of the implicit contract between staff and customer; in Britain he felt a real class divide; he fancied he saw it in every signal and phrase.

As he ate, Philip flicked through the newspapers. They made grim reading. The strike looked as though it was about to start crumbling, with the Nottinghamshire miners beginning to trickle back to work. To Philip, this seemed the only possible conclusion; Scargill having ostentatiously set himself up against the elected government, had set himself up to lose. Even a reasonable, non-partisan government – neither he felt applied to Thatcher's – couldn't allow Scargill to win. As it was, Thatcher seemed to have laid an obvious and deliberate trap and Scargill had walked straight into it, even to the point of calling the strike without a specific ballot. Now the miners and their families were paying the price. He felt some sympathy but knew that his years in America had made him more cynical and callous, less prone to support trade unions, more inclined to back the market. He could not bring himself to like Thatcher, but he did think the British economy needed a good clearing out. He felt the Britain he had left had been going through its final cultural renaissance before post-imperial decline set in for good; nothing since he got back had altered that view.

He paid and left; the sky had darkened and it had just begun to spit with rain. He nudged his way back onto the A1, then put his foot down again. He turned the radio on and there was Lionel Ritchie, followed by Van Halen – quite a combination; even the music was American now. About 90 minutes later, he pulled into the hotel car park. It was still raining, so he grabbed his overnight bag from the boot and jogged across to reception.

He'd come up to see Richard and Louise, who had offered to put him up, but Philip preferred to stay by himself. Once he'd checked in, he went up to his room, had a shower, and lay down naked on the duvet, gave into sleep and curled up on his side. When he woke, some two hours later, he dressed and went down to the hotel bar, where he had lunch. Then he wandered out around Nottingham for a couple of hours. The city seemed lively enough, bustling with shoppers. He bought a copy of the Economist and went and sat in a café for an hour more before catching a cab back to the hotel.

Philip had known Richard since boyhood, where they had grown up a couple of streets away from each other, though they had never gone to the same school. By chance, they had met up in the local pub back in 1970 or '71 when Philip was back from New York, where he had just started working for Sports Illustrated, and Richard was back from Nottingham University, where he was studying medicine. They had ended up going for a curry together after discovering they shared an unpopular love of Leeds Utd, and had somehow managed to stay in touch since. In 1980, Richard had married Louise and Philip had made the trip over for the wedding and read a lesson at the service. He had then muddied his reputation by sleeping with Louise's sister, but he thought she had more or less forgiven him.

Back at the hotel, he shaved, before going down to the hotel bar with a copy of the Herald Tribune. He had arranged on the phone to meet Richard there at about 6.30pm and his friend turned up a couple of minutes later. Louise was meant to come as well but her mother had fallen the week before and cracked a bone in her wrist. Philip had thought about Richard's renewed offer to come and stay but had stuck with his original decision. All this flashed through his mind as he got up to greet Richard, an enormous hulk of a man. Philip himself was just over six feet and weight about 13 stone, but Richard was maybe six foot five and five stone heavier, dwarfing him in both directions. Richard smiled infectiously, pleased to see his old friend.

They went over to the bar and Philip bought them both gin and tonic. "Lou says hello," Richard said as they sat down.

"How is her mum?"

"Not bad, considering. Her wrist's in plaster and it's still quite painful, but she's better then she was last weekend."

"When's she coming back?"

"She thought she'd stay till Sunday, so I'm afraid she'll miss you entirely."

"Shame but I'm glad her mum's on the mend." Philip paused, "So what have you got lined up?"

"I've arranged to meet three or four colleagues at a pizza place in town, and then there's a party to go to, someone's 30th, so we'll both feel a bit old but you'll get a feel for what socialist medicine does with its spare time." Richard raised his eyebrows as Philip sent an amused v-sign towards him while peering over the rim of his glass. "But first, tell me what you're up to. Are you still living down near that fish market in the Lower East Side?"

"Yep," said Philip. His voice had acquired a New York drawl over the years but this still mixed with his broad West Country vowels. "One of these days it'll be trendy and upmarket, but that's when I'll cash in and move out. For the moment though it suits and I'm a walk or a short cab ride from most of the places I want to get to." He hadn't told Richard about his meeting with Channel 4 on Monday.

"Still single, I take it?"

"Not every night!" he laughed. "But it doesn't take women long to discover what an asshole I am."

"Well, try not to chat up any of my colleagues tonight. They're pure as the driven snow Northern lasses, not used to your transatlantic sophistication. My round this time, same again?"

They chatted for another 30–40 minutes, with Richard wondering whether Reagan would be re-elected; Philip thought he would, and that the American Right was gaining an increasing hold of the news agenda. They talked about the miners, agreeing that the strike was doomed. Richard thought the legacy would last for years, with villages and families divided over whether they were prepared to cross picket lines, and loyalty to Scargill and the NUM. "Some of them would follow him over a cliff if he asked them."

"From what I've read and you've just told me, it sounds like he has."

"The thing is, even if Thatcher wins, she'll be dealing with the fall-out for years."

"Well, a lot of the pit villages are just that, completely dependent on mining. They might not like it but it's all they know and their dads and granddads did it before them."

"Can't they be re-trained or something?" asked Philip.

"In theory, but it would take time and investment and it's not obvious where it would come from. Thatcher would rather stand back and let the market sort it out. In practice it won't be so bad here in Nottinghamshire, at least to start with. The pits here are still reasonably profitable, not like some of those in Durham, Yorkshire and South Wales." He paused. "Come on, it's time we were going."

Ten minutes later, they arrived at the pizza place, where two of Richard's fellow doctors were already waiting. They sat at a round table and ordered lager and garlic bread. The pizzas were good – thin crust and fresh.

"I brought you here because I thought you'd like the thin crust pizza much more than the thick crust you get everywhere else."

"Good call," said Philip, "I might have had to walk out in protest or sue them under, what do you call it, the Trades Descriptions Act." He dripped some extra chilli oil across the pepperoni. "Mind you, they're still not hot enough."

Richard ordered a taxi to take them to the party. "So tell me again whose party this is and why they're having it?" Philip asked as he settled himself in the back seat alongside Richard, with Jeff – who was the shortest – in between.

"Sitting between you two is definitely a bad idea," complained Jeff, "particularly him." He pointed at Richard on his left.

"Quit moaning, Dixon," laughed Richard. "I'm trying to answer our guest. It's a woman called Jen, a staff nurse, and she's having the party because she's just turned 30. She got married last year to a guy called David, who's a solicitor, okay but a bit square. I've not been to the house before but it's pretty swish I'm told, out in West Bridgford somewhere. I think there's about fifty guests, mostly from the hospital and

I'm told it's going to be relatively civilised by the standards of medic parties, or the one's I used to go to at any rate. Before I got married, of course."

"They weren't that wild," Jeff interrupted, "You've just gotten older and think they were."

"Listen to him," Richard half-turned, looking over Jeff's head at Philip, "sounding like he's 22 or something when I can see from here the hair's thinning nicely on top."

When the taxi pulled up, Philip paid and got the taxi driver's card. By this stage, Richard had rung the bell and the door had been opened so that Philip was able to follow the others straight inside. The party seemed lively enough. As he entered, a woman with slightly frizzy shoulder-length hair and a loose tie-dyed dress was standing by the stairs with a glass of red wine in their hand.

"Hi," she said, "I'm the bouncer. But it's okay, I know you're with Richard. They've gone straight through to the kitchen, but you should dump your jacket in there first." She gestured at the room on his left.

"Thanks," he said. He glanced round the corner and chucked his coat on the pile of clothes on the bed. "Hello," he said, "I'm Philip." He paused, made to walk past and then, to be polite, he asked, "And you?"

"Oh me, I'm Michelle. I used to be Jen's flatmate. Richard tells me I should talk to you, give you a hard time about Ronald Reagan. Maybe later, when you have a drink in your hand."

"Maybe," replied Philip, and walked on into the kitchen.

"Oh Phil, there you are," said Richard as he was walking into the only normally-lit room he could see. Clearly Richard, taking advantage of Louise's absence, was intent on making an evening of it. Philip had little inclination to look after his friend. If it looked like becoming embarrassing, he would simply phone his own taxi and quietly bail out. At the moment though, he was being introduced to Jen.

"Hello," he said, "I'm Philip, a friend of Richard's over visiting from New York. Happy Birthday and thanks for letting me tag along."

"Oh, not at all," said Jen, "I'm delighted to meet you. What can I get you to drink? White wine? Hold on a minute, I think we've got some Pinot Grigio in the fridge."

While she was opening the bottle, Philip had his first chance to glance around. The fridge was plastered with magnets and bits of paper and photos. There were a couple of pictures of the woman by the stairs and a team photo of the first Notts Forest side that had won the European Cup.

He turned back to Jen. "So when was the day itself?"

"Today, and I feel miles older already, and more mature."

"Oh, there's no need," Philip replied, "I'm just as irresponsible at 35 as I was five years ago."

"Really, well I look forward to that later." She smiled quizzically in an unconscious imitation of Bette Davis. "You've driven up from London, haven't you? Well, doubly thanks for coming then. Come on, let me introduce you to some people; most men are rubbish at even basic introductions and Richard's one of the worst."

Jen took him into the main room, where the lights were dimmed and a compilation of reggae tracks was playing in the background. "This is our chat space, and across in the other room is the dance space, where we've got the disco playing."

"Just like Studio 54," Philip remarked. Jen ignored him and introduced him to a group of younger nurses who stood chatting in the corner.

"This is Philip, a friend of Richard's over from New York to visit. He's just told me he thinks my house is like Studio 54 in New York." Then she nodded to him with just a flicker of a smile. "I must leave you briefly to attend to my other guests," she said as she moved on.

"So tell us about New York," one of the women said. "It must be so much more exciting even than Nottingham. I can't believe you think wherever it is like Jen's house."

Philip winced inwardly, though he couldn't escape a feeling of admiration for the smoothness with which his smug joke had been properly dumped on. Then he launched into a largely made-up story involving Ryan O'Neal, Vitas Gerulaitis and Debbie Harry.

Thirty minutes later, there were six nurses hanging on his every apparently plausible word, and he was pretty much in full flow, though he could feel himself being tempted into ever wilder fantasy, to see what he could get away with. Then he caught sight of the woman he had met on the way in, Michelle? She was standing just outside the circle in front of him, peering disbelievingly over the shoulder of a black-haired woman called Julie, who was asking him how many people he knew who had taken drugs. He could see she was amused.

Actually, Michelle was mostly thinking of something else. She had decided some time ago to rescue Philip from himself. But, having failed to catch his eye, she was at that moment trying to remember the lyrics of 'I Shot the Sherriff', which was playing in the background. Giving up, she focused again and this time caught Philip's eye.

"Oh, there you are, Philip; Richard sent me to find you. Excuse me, ladies," she added.

"Sorry," pretended Philip, "It's been great talking to you. I'll come back."

"Make sure you do," said Julie, "I want to hear more about Sister Sledge."

"Thanks for the rescue mission," Philip said as they emerged into the hall. Bob Marley lyrics fluttered after them from the stereo.

"I wasn't sure you wanted rescuing," replied Michelle, "so I was in two minds. But once you'd gratuitously name-dropped Debbie Harry for the third time, I decided at the very least you needed saving from yourself."

"You shouldn't worry too much, I usually find a way of wriggling out of it somehow. It's all part of the game. Looks like we both need a drink?" He half-turned towards the kitchen.

"If you're okay with red," Michelle interrupted him, "I've got a bottle of Chianti and a spare glass over there behind the vase."

"I normally prefer white but under the circumstances red would be just fine."

"I'll take that as a compliment," Michelle said as she went over to the vase on the hall table.

"Slightly sneaky, hiding it behind the vase like that?"

"Well, it was my vase, or rather the one I got Jen and Paul for their house-warming," she filled both their glasses. "Cheers!"

"In which case, you've got every right." Philip bowed.

"Tell me how you know Richard."

185

"Strangely – we only lived a couple of streets away – we didn't actually go to the same school, and though we sort of knew each other, we didn't really meet until we were about 20. I was back from New York, where I'd been working, and Richard was home from university. Back then, when I first knew him properly, he was enormously enthusiastic, passionate about his work and the NHS. We've had a running joke ever since about me goading him by calling it 'socialist medicine'."

"Does he rise to it?"

"Never."

"You're right. He works too hard at it sometimes – that's why he's gone over the top tonight. Marriage will either help him slow him down a bit, or it will tear him apart trying to do everything perfectly. I hope Louise knows him well enough to understand that."

"I'm pretty sure she does. I don't know her that well, and we haven't always seen eye to eye, but I think she's got him sussed. She loves him enough to give him whatever space he needs."

Michelle whistled quietly, "I know why you're not always in Lou's good book" – Philip chose not to interrupt – "so I'm a bit surprised you're such a fan. For what it's worth, I agree with you, I think she's the best thing that's happened to him."

"So, how long, have you known Richard?" he asked.

"About ten years."

"And how well?"

Michelle thought about it. "Well enough, but we've never gone out, or slept together, if that's what you mean. Richard was probably the first doctor to treat me, as a relatively junior nurse, like a professional. This isn't a work party and so there aren't many doctors here, hence you had your harem earlier."

Philip refilled their glasses. "I'm sorry, it wasn't a leading question, I was just interested. Though I'm…" His voice trailed off. He felt slightly uncomfortable.

Michelle blushed. She drank the red wine and held it momentarily in her mouth before letting it slip down. "So! Tell me about Manhattan – not the Studio 54 bullshit – what's it really like living and working there? You're from Bristol, for fuck sake."

"Well, it's a bit messy and a bit more glamorous than London, but neither by as much as you'd think. The skyscrapers are pretty much as spectacular as you'd imagine – there's a circular boat trip that goes right around Manhattan, and it's pretty much the best way of seeing the skyline. There's a lot more to New York than Manhattan, but without it the city would be very different and not nearly as iconic as it is."

Michelle noticed there was still a slight West Country bit to his New York accent. "How long have you been there?"

"Since 1968; it seems almost like a time warp."

"Why?"

"Well, for a start it was when most Americans decided they couldn't win in Vietnam. But the two biggest things for me, probably even more than Dr King being murdered, were Bobby Kennedy being killed two months later and, obviously in a completely different way, the start of satellite TV."

"Why them?"

Philip, unusually for him, felt he was being taken slightly outside his comfort zone. It wasn't her questions, or even her intensity; it was that he was interested in answering her properly, not the cheap lines he could normally get to pass for insight. Here they were, gone 11pm at a nurse's party in Nottingham, and he felt bizarrely under pressure to be truthful.

"Well, Bobby Kennedy was a lot more than JFK's brother, even before '68. Anyway, in those few months before he was murdered in June, he became, I think, the only major US politician apart from maybe Lincoln to try to speak to the entire people, rich and poor, pro and anti-war. Speaking to everyone in America is much harder than here – it's just too big and too diverse. Anyway, he was shot the night he'd won the California Primary, and then the Democratic Party split wide open and has never really recovered. That's why we've got Reagan and probably will do again in November."

Michelle's eyes had widened slightly but he hadn't noticed, momentarily caught up in his memories, hearing again the clamour, almost smelling the tear gas in Grant Park.

"And satellite TV?" she asked, "It seems a bit trivial compared with what you've just said."

Philip came back, took a sip, and continued. "I know what you mean, but I think I'm only now really beginning to understand its importance. I suppose I see it as the technological equivalent of Magellan sailing round the world. In terms of communication, satellite TV makes us into a single planet rather than various groups of time zones. It's a bit like the space programme made us a single planet in a visual sense. Anyway, I digress." He knew he had been trying too hard to impress.

"No," Michelle nodded, "Go on, you have lots of rant-space left."

"Well, the impact of the communications revolution that satellite TV started is still unfolding. Already you can pretty much see events happening live anywhere in the world. And the speed, the immediacy of that, will hurry everything up, and completely alter the character of our society and our politics. War, famine, scandal will be in our living rooms as it happens, wherever in the world it happens and will force our politicians to say and do more than they've ever had to before."

"A bit like flying to Italy in three hours rather than driving across Europe in three days..."

"Yes, pretty much," agreed Philip.

They both stopped for a moment.

Michelle was first to regain her poise. She was aware she was, unusually for her, beginning to flirt. They carried on talking, increasingly oblivious to the rest of the party. "So, are you over just to see Richard or do you have some other nefarious reason for coming back?"

"Funny you should say that," he replied, "I don't think it's that nefarious but – I haven't told Richard this yet – I'm also talking to Channel 4 about a possible job; I'm seeing some people on Monday."

"So we might be seeing more of you then."

"Not impossible, but I'd rather not rely entirely on Richard. Can I have a phone number so I can contact you?"

Michelle looked at him directly again. How rarely she did that until tonight. Her decision was made long before she uttered the words. "Do you have a pen and paper?" she asked.

"Here," he said, tearing her out a paper of a small notebook he'd pulled from his pocket and handing her a pen.

"There you are. Will you call me on Monday, after you've talked to the Channel 4 people?"

"I will," Philip replied. "But now, I'd better go and rescue Richard and get him home. Good job I got that taxi number. Nice to meet you, and see you soon." He winced at the words, so lame. Then he nodded and, consciously, slightly brushed Michelle's sleeve on his way past. Some 15 minutes later, Philip and Richard had gone.

Michelle went and stood in the kitchen, drinking red wine and nodding, generally in the right places, at the conversation going on around her. The reality of what had happened washed over her, as the incoming tide smooths and then dissolves the most imposing sandcastle ramparts. What was it, or did she just fancy him? Yes, she did, but there was also something more. There seemed something callous about him. She had watched him play the audience in Jen's front room, and she knew that it was all really a bit of a show, but he was so polished it was seamless. And behind that veneer he was laughing at all of them, even her. She had caught the way his eyes wandered every once in a while, never entirely engaged, never really giving of himself.

And, she recognised, this was exactly part of the attraction. Michelle had worked with men over the last ten years or so and all of them were pretty obvious. It was simple to work out what they wanted and what they were like. Even saying you were a 'new man' basically meant you were prepared to do the washing up and cleaning the toilet because it gave you a better chance of getting laid. But Philip wasn't that, instead, taunting you by implying there was a lot more he was thinking, that he wasn't showing. To find out, someone would have to take the chance of getting closer to him.

Well, she was ready to risk it. So far in her life, she had played it safe. She wanted him, his moods, his lifestyle. She had known from the moment he broke away from his circle of too-fawning admirers. Partly it was the glance they had exchanged, and partly it was the physical sensation she had experienced as he stepped out of the circle towards her. The momentary flush and tensing of the muscles across her shoulder blades were both new. It was like some primeval mating gene.

When they talked, Michelle knew she was being beguiled by his fluent, easy knowledge, but part of the spell was that she could see, and was duly flattered, that he was casting it deliberately. Later, she had been wondered how often he had taken numbers in the past, and how often he would do so again. But against that was her certainty that he would call, the casual deliberation with which he had brushed past her as they parted. She was excited – that word again – but she had no doubt – again this was new – that he wanted her as she wanted him.

**

When Philip woke the next morning, he rolled over and was surprised the bed was deserted. He had expected to bring someone back with him and, until he had stepped out of the circle, he had believed it would happen. Despite the red wine, his memories of the party lacked nothing in clarity. The moment he had stepped out of the circle, he had known he was going back to the hotel alone.

It was the sheer grace and simplicity of the woman. Maybe that was how she behaved in the hospital, or just how she was, but it was a mile away from the women he was used to. Even before they had begun talking, he had been magnetised by how she had spoken. He had also been captured by her light brown hair falling across her collar bone, her gently swaying bottom as she walked ahead, the gently drawn line of her back that he could not quite discern but imagined carving its course from her neck downwards. He was attracted by Michelle's body but no more so then by those of at least half the women at the party. There were at least ten women he would have had sex with. And that had largely been the story of his life. Michelle was different, because he knew he wanted her before he had really seen her physically. Until now the physical had always preceded everything else. Michelle broke that mould.

He knew he would call her, and that he would take the job he would be offered on Monday. It was a strange sensation for someone so fanatically independent to realise that he was taking such a decision because of a woman he had talked to for barely 30 minutes. Carol would be laughing her face off if she knew.

When Philip rang on Monday night, Michelle had just emerged from the bath and had a towel round her. Her hair was still wet, dripping onto the carpet as she rushed across to answer the phone. He asked if she was free for dinner on Friday. She knew she would have to swap shifts to make it but still said yes without pause. He said he would pick her up at 8pm, that he would be in London until then. Just before he hung up, he said he had taken the job and would be moving back to the UK. He asked if she would book the restaurant.

Michelle ended up taking Friday off but at the cost of working Thursday night. When she got home, it was gone 9am and she crashed onto her bed. When she woke around 2pm, she had a shower and made herself a sandwich. Then she went out shopping for something to wear but could find nothing, so she found a café and drank three large cups of coffee while trying to read the paper. Eventually, she went back to her flat, and slightly manically started to tidy up, as if her mother was coming rather than a man who would pick her up from the door. At 6pm, she had another shower, then began to try on her wardrobe. None of this, she knew, was normal behaviour. In the end, she compromised – why did she always compromise? – On smart jeans and loose-fitting purple blouse. She then smudged her make-up and ended up washing it all off. She wished there was a flatmate to talk to. Finally, at 7.35pm, she was as ready as she was going to be. She slammed a tequila and waited. At 7.55pm, the bell rang.

She took him to an Italian restaurant she knew. It was family run, bustling and cheerful. The pasta was fresh, there was lots of garlic and chilli and the red wine was cheap and drinkable. Philip liked it, said it reminded him of New York. They talked about politics, only a little about each other. Philip explained Watergate and why Reagan had been elected president, and probably would be again. Michelle explained the Labour Party's tribal warfare and why the siting of cruise missiles on British soil was so objectionable. That night they were both good at listening, comfortable in each other's company, and spurred on by mutual nervousness.

Again, contrary to his normal behaviour, Philip neither offered to take Michelle back to his hotel nor angled for an invite inside. But he did kiss her, and he did ask if she would come down to London the following weekend to help him house-hunt. That following weekend they slept together, and the next day he asked Michelle to come and live with him in London. She agreed and handed her notice in on the Monday. The whole relationship had so far lasted just over two weeks.

After the initial shock, Richard could hardly stop laughing; Jen, on the other hand, was strangely offended, and barely acknowledged Michelle until the day she left. She hardly noticed; her life was starting again from square one.

Part 3: July 2005

Chapter 20
London to Leeds, Saturday 2nd

As the train headed out of Kings Cross and accelerated through North London, Ruth gazed alternately at her book and out of the window, where the arch of the new Wembley was now visible to the west. The afternoon sky over London was as blue as it was possible to be, the temperature comfortably in the 80s, and she was grateful for the air-conditioning in the carriage.

A couple of days before she'd been offered a ticket to Live 8, but her train was already booked and she was expected by her friends in Leeds. The idea of staying in London, going to the concert, maybe hanging out for a couple extra days, was attractive, but after taking a night to think about it, she had declined the offer. She didn't know if she would end up living in London but she knew it would be easy to do so, and if she was going to, she wanted it to be an active decision not a passive one. That meant living somewhere else first, and if Leeds wouldn't have been her first choice, she felt that, having made that decision, it was important she followed through on it as intended.

At some point in the next few years, she also liked the idea of living abroad. Mostly, this came from her father's friend Ed, her godfather, who was a foreign correspondent for the BBC. He'd spent the majority of his career in the Middle East and often seemed in the middle of things; at the moment he was in Iraq. What most entranced her, however, wasn't the excitement of his job but the simple reality of how comfortable he was with both Arab and Israeli cultures, moving easily between them, somehow reconciling the contradictions. He wasn't in London too often and she, therefore, didn't see that much of him, but he was a good letter writer and had been writing to her regularly since she was six, maybe once a month.

Ed's feelings for the peoples of the Middle East, and for the land itself, percolated every phrase. They would come through in his description of the mobile stalls selling food along the Corniche in Beirut, of a mother and her three children riding the same moped around the Cairo streets, of the sun going down over a ruined ancient fortress in Amman,, of the chaotic corridors and complete absence of security he had encountered when visiting the Israeli Ministry of Finance in Jerusalem. She often thought he should write a book, maybe about his life in the Middle East, or even a novel. He gave her confidence she could live in completely different cultures and not feel out of place.

However, none of this quite removed her fear of the unknown. From an ultimately sheltered upbringing, Ruth saw even going back to Leeds as an important step. She would financially be on her own, living off whatever meagre income she could glean from bar work. She knew she wasn't ready yet to start a career and needed an alternative to tide her over.

Ruth loved and admired both her parents but could not see herself following in either of their footsteps. Her dad seemed beaten down by the routine of his job. In the office every day for upwards of ten hours, plus the commute, meant a huge amount of time devoted to work he never really seemed to enjoy. He took it all seriously and, as far as she could tell, believed in its importance, but she knew she didn't even really understand what he did. He rarely appeared happy and would bottle everything up to the point where she was none the wiser about what had happened. And as for her mother, she seemed constantly tied up in politics and spats: either around her department, where she hated one of the other professors – a 'misogynist pig' – but didn't really want to get involved to try and change things, or else around some obscure argument with another academic. Even now, Ruth remained quite shocked at the sheer rudeness of academic rows, conducted through highbrow subject journals, in which the combatants would fling short, brutal articles back and forth like children trading insults in the playground. Ruth didn't quite know what to think of the fact that her mother, usually so restrained, was so good at this combat – she had once described a particular opponent as "possessing an approach to evidence resembling a cat's attitude to hairballs."

In contrast, her parents' friends seemed to have much more interesting jobs, but ones that seemed out of reach. Ed was a foreign correspondent, Philip a TV executive. And as for Michelle, it was impossible for Ruth to imagine following in her footsteps, from senior nurse to art enthusiast and lady of leisure. And almost all her friends were seemingly well set towards some career or other.

She couldn't identify an obvious reason why she was uniquely full of doubt; not even that really, more of a vacuum. Aside from her vague ideas about living abroad somewhere, there was little thought in her mind about the direction she wanted her life to take. These life choices made no sense to Ruth. She was 22 and felt like she was just starting out on her adult life, and yet here were all her friends, having ostensibly already made most of their key decisions. She even knew people with Excel spreadsheets that set out the planned trajectory of their salaries/bonus/other income, as well as milestones around the timing of marriage and children and the purchase of houses and cars. It was all a million miles away.

It was true she hadn't done a vocational subject but lots of the historians in her year were off to study law or work for an accountancy firm, or on some or other graduate scheme. None of that had appealed to her, still didn't. She had applied to a teacher training course at Birmingham University, but then decided she wasn't patient enough to teach, and so had politely turned it down. And while everyone else had been going to Milk Round and other graduate recruitment events, Ruth hadn't been able to bring herself to go to any. She didn't even find the idea of them attractive, free drinks and all, and couldn't conceive what questions she would ask if she ever found herself at one.

But what it meant was that here she was, still at first base. She couldn't even make up her mind whether there was any virtue in her position. She had successfully resisted the potential offer of filthy lucre from corporate Britain but hadn't exactly been tempted or even thought about it like that. In many ways, she knew she was very much part of the establishment, certainly her parents were, even if Dad's family was working class. And so she could afford the risk of not looking for a job straight after Finals and risking that unexplained gap on her CV that employers notoriously didn't like. And yet she was reasonably confident in her own motives, at least to the extent of believing she needed some time after university to think properly about what she wanted to do.

There was a risk of sinking into some post-student malaise of part-time work and full-time, activity-lite, leisure, hanging around the Student Union the same way she had done for the last three years. When an undergraduate, she had seen others do this and somehow found them sad even while being happy to spend time with those she thought of as friends. The fact she was now travelling a similar route made her feel guilty about those judgements, but she also promised herself she wouldn't hang around the Union, even if her friends and housemates were.

Ruth remembered when she was young, lying awake at night and worrying about whether it was her mother or father she loved most and what the answer meant. Usually, the answer had been Mum, though the reasoning behind the answer had changed with the growing sense of her own femaleness. She had come to look to others very much like Mary's daughter, less like Sam's; her face and nose were the same shape, and if she sometimes looked at people the exact same way as her dad, she did so with Mary's eyes. But recently she had begun to notice and appreciate her father more.

Noticing him was important because he had an infuriating habit of melting into the background, even in the smallest social groups. Once, soon after his own father had died, she had asked Michelle what her dad had been like at school, when he was her age. Michelle had replied that he had been quite outgoing and talkative, and her impression was that he had acquired the sense of reserve that was now so much a part of him while he was at university. Michelle had lost touch about then and only saw him again when she was invited to his wedding. But all Ruth had heard from Ed hinted at a much livelier, irreverent version of her dad. She had been over this territory numerous times but today it was in sharper relief. She had just said a major farewell to a father whom she loved but didn't really know, and somehow a window of opportunity had closed. Dad had once told her he'd cried when he turned twenty and was no longer a teenager, and Ruth felt like crying. She stared out the window, conscious her life was starting to speed up; maybe this was like what he had gone through.

To break the cycle, she got up and found her way to the buffet car to get a cup of tea and slice of fruit cake. When she got back, she got out the paper; as well as Live 8, it was full of the G8 summit, which was scheduled to agree on deals on African debt and climate change. She was interested in politics, and a vehement opponent of the Iraq War, but found it hard to identify anything she outright disagreed with in what Blair was doing this week at least. And she knew she didn't really get politics, which at times it seemed like a version of the three-dimensional chess played by Spock on Star Trek. And beyond that she knew that for Ed, individual politicians were all but irrelevant in a world where the illusion of control was no more than a question of hubris.

She looked out of the window again and thought she caught sight of someone, a man, looking at her in the reflection of the window. She kept looking away but found herself dragging her eyes back to the point where she had made, or thought she had made, eye contact. The guy was still there, steady and unflinching in his gaze. This time she looked down and took a sip of her tea, trying to think where the person looking at her was sitting. She realised he must be on the other side of the carriage, on the next bank of seats down. He must be looking out the window on the other side of the train but at such an angle that he could see her clearly in the double reflection between the two windows. Was he really looking at her or simply in her direction? She couldn't tell for sure but her two fleeting moments of eye contact made her think he was looking at her, on purpose and by choice, not accident. She kept her eyes averted downwards for a couple more moments as she tried to work out her options. She could avoid looking in the window again and simply pick up the paper in front of her; or she could look across at the man directly (and do what exactly?); or she could return his gaze and see what happened. The first of these felt like some form of cowardice, while the second had automatically triggered the question of what she would do next.

All sorts of thoughts started pin-balling around inside Ruth's head. She was single and none of her two or three relationships at university had lasted more than a term or so, nor had they been particularly remarkable in any way. On second thoughts, her short liaison with Ian had at least been notable for the manner of its ending when she had rung her tutorial partner early one morning to check on the reading list for an essay and he had answered the phone. But why was she thinking this at all? Why was it relevant? It wasn't as if she was looking for a boyfriend; quite the reverse. And even if she had been, this was the last, well almost the last, way she would go about it. The idea of picking someone up, or maybe being picked up – how did window reflection etiquette work? – just made no sense to her and went against all the red lines she had drawn for herself. And yet there was something potentially romantic, exotic, about the situation. And maybe part of her independence was to return the gaze of the strange man across from her, not blinking or averting her eyes but matching whatever look he had.

All this raced around Ruth's mind, thoughts colliding, refusing to find any order, either of sequence or of precedence. It all left her confused and without direction but she nevertheless found herself raising her eyes to meet the man's gaze. There was something both irresistible and primitive about how Ruth felt in that moment. Before oral language, was this how humans appraised each other – whether for friendship, war or mating – a frank, lengthy and unflinching exchange of looks? Some hitherto unheard-from gene kicked in with a vengeance, something close to discovering her body was programmed to bend its knees on landing when she jumped off a wall.

When she was young, Ruth had played a game with her dad where they would each try to keep a straight face while at the same time making the other laugh, by quizzically raising an eyebrow or some similar facial contortion. She had been terrible at it to start with, often breaking into fits of giggles within two or three seconds, but over time she had become increasingly skilled at controlling her emotions so they weren't instantly reflected in her features, separating these inner workings from how others saw her react. At school and university this had served her well, enabling her to seethe inwardly while exuding calm insouciance, and to summon up towering rages while inwardly smiling. It was a similar feeling Ruth experienced now as her eyes connected with the man – why did she persistently think of him as stranger? – Who all this time had been looking at her in her reflection in the window of a train carriage. The moment their eyes connected, Ruth was struck by the intensity of the experience but also by her ability to control her emotions behind impassive features.

At first, she wasn't really looking at the man himself; certainly, she wasn't seeing him as an individual. Instead, it was as if she was looking into a mirror rather than the train window, and saw herself as a little girl, maybe five or six years old, wanting to do everything for herself and becoming instantly frustrated when she couldn't. The sensation of all the intense emotions and drives that coursed through her body as a six-year-old became again familiar; wanting to move the furniture around in her room, being determined to follow a particular route to get somewhere.

Inwardly, Ruth smiled at the memories, while maintaining her neutral face. She knew the anger within her, which she had no idea how to deal with when she was a little girl. At least it had never had a violent side; the only casualties were her own tear-stained tops. Funny as it now seemed, neither of her parents had lost their temper with her at these times; her mother found things for her to do, to distract her; while her father sat and patiently explained to her, using language and examples she could understand, why it wasn't possible to do the thing she wanted to do so much at that particular time. Mostly, she hadn't listened, but usually there would be some phrase that would penetrate the mental fug of her fury enough to make her stop wailing, to pause while the thought sank in, or even to ask a question. And then, usually quite slowly, she would use this break to pull herself from the hole she had dug, by which time Mum would have managed to set up some game or activity that would be the means for her to move on. It had been quite a good double act by her parents.

For the first time, Ruth decided to look properly at the man who had been steadily gazing at her in the reflection for at least five minutes, though it felt much longer. He had a small scar just above his left eyebrow, a slightly square jaw below a broad nose and a wide mouth. His hair was short, thick and black, brushed she thought rather than combed, and possibly just starting to recede. He was unshaven, possibly for a couple of days, with small ears that tucked themselves in under his hair.

All this, Ruth took in within the first couple of seconds. While not forensic, it represented considerably more detail than she would normally have observed. Later, she would marvel at the fact that she could describe his face better than anyone else she knew. But even beyond that, Ruth was conscious she was seeing the face of the man in the window in a much more careful way than she was used to doing. Whereas normally she would have seen the whole face and only then, and in a random way, focused on features within it, on this occasion she had, without meaning to, begun by looking carefully at individual features, describing them to herself and filing away these descriptions.

The resulting image evoked varying reactions to each of the man's features – she liked the fact he was unshaved but wished his nose was more aquiline; she thought his ears were too small for the rest of his face and wanted his eyes to be blue instead of hazel. The result was that in place of having a single emotional response to his face, Ruth had a multitude of responses to individual features, which sat side by side in her head, some of them uncomfortable neighbours, jostling for position and significance.

Ruth's first impression of the man was therefore quite different to those initial judgements of people she was used to making. It was richer and more detailed, but also more confused and ambivalent, an ill-fitting jigsaw with small but evident gaps in it, and some pieces out of proportion or differently coloured. This made it more difficult for her to break the gaze she had been holding steadily. There was too much left unresolved, and Ruth found herself looking harder to try and discern something about his character.

Of course the primary character-relevant facts she knew about him was that he had been looking steadily at her reflection for several minutes, and was apparently unabashed when she noticed and began returning his gaze. This could mean many things; did he do this habitually, or was he just fascinated by her? Both were quite disturbing but in very different ways. She didn't even know to what extent the man had decided on purpose to look at her through her reflection or whether he had come across it by accident and just carried on.

She realised she no longer felt as hostile to the man as she had at first, or as she imagined she would. There was a frankness in his gaze that disarmed her, but not in a way that left her feeling at all vulnerable. She sensed that, at root, there was no more artifice in the man than there was in her, and that he felt as ambivalent about the situation as she did. For whatever combination of reasons, he had allowed his gaze to linger and then had been caught, almost like a rabbit in the headlights, by Ruth's chance eye contact.

Ruth began to imagine the feelings the man must be having. Now that she had concluded, decisively but on the basis of no real evidence, that there was no less innocence in the man looking at her reflection than there was in her returning his gaze, it became possible for her to develop ideas about what the man might really be like. She envisaged him being on an emotional journey of self-discovery, different from the one she was intending to embark on but with some similarities, and that he was further advanced, more confident that he was on the right path. She imagined him being a couple of years out of university and from a much more working-class background than her. She envisaged him having been slightly defensive at university about his relatively lack of knowledge about culture and literature, painfully conscious that many of his new friends were somehow cooler than him, had read more widely, knew more about music and culture and politics. And this would have left him with a legacy of a strangely insecure, slightly nervous demeanour, masking a harder inner core of self-belief, grounded in values he had inherited.

All this was pure speculation but Ruth intuitively believed it was true to the point where she wondered nervously if the strange man, maybe no longer so strange, was able to gain the same insight into her.

The door at the end of the carriage slid open and the conductor entered. "Tickets please?" Her concentration snapped and she fumbled in her purse for the thin piece of card while her ears simmered gently. Fifteen minutes later, she got off the train, not looking to see which way the man went or whether he was met by anyone.

Chapter 21
Leeds, Wednesday 6th

Ruth had nearly finished her second half and was beginning to feel mildly and pleasantly pissed. With four friends – Leo, Anna, Mark and Ali – she had been sat, chatting, in the local pub. Partly, but only as an excuse, the decision to come out had been prompted by London's unexpectedly winning the right to host 2012 Olympics.

Ruth and Ali were both from London, Mark was from Somerset, Leo from Glasgow and Anna from Leeds. They had met at university in Leeds, and for a variety of reasons, they had all either stayed or gravitated back there. Ruth wanted to spend a year or so doing voluntary work while deciding what to do and applying for jobs, and had moved back to Leeds because she liked the city, knew people and could live there cheaply. Ali was staying on to do postgraduate physics and her boyfriend Mark was a solicitor doing his articles. Anna was being a trainee accountant with KPMG and had decided to stay in her home city to be close to her mum, and Leo was living on benefit trying to be a writer. Although Mark and Ali was the only current relationship within the group, Ali had had a brief relationship with Leo, as had Mark with both Ruth and Anna.

"It'll cost a fortune and we'll screw it up," said Mark, "just look at Wembley."

"And it'll cost us a fortune in council tax," added Ali.

"I think it'll be brilliant, no matter what you say," replied Ruth. "My parents have this friend called Philip, who's a TV executive, who says the Olympics are just unimaginably fantastic. He thought it could transform London's image the way it did Barcelona's in 1992."

"I can just about see how that could happen," admitted Mark grudgingly, "but I just don't believe we'll be able to hold the Olympics without just totally embarrassing ourselves, either through sheer incompetence or by going way over budget, probably both, and I also think it's just a London thing on the upside, but we'll all end up paying for it when it goes wrong."

"What do you think, Leo?" asked Anna. "You're the one comes from farthest away from London."

Leo thought for a moment, took a sip of his Guinness. "I doubt it'll mean much, if anything, to a lot of Scots, apart from if it goes wrong and we all end up paying for it. There won't be any event in Scotland apart from maybe football, and there's no chance of us being in a cobbled together GB team. Having said that, I have really good memories of watching the Barcelona Olympics in 1992 and seeing the diving against the backdrop of the Barcelona skyline and the Sagrada Familia."

"You're just name-dropping now," accused Ali.

"Okay, I didn't know that at the time – I was only nine or something – but I remember the detail of that skyline really clearly, when I went round Europe that time after our first year."

"But it'll be a nightmare, like the Dome but costing ten times as much," insisted Mark.

"I think it's gonna use the Dome, for gymnastics or something," said Ruth.

"Well, I guess that'll be something but we'll still be paying it off for 20 years or something."

"Will you go and watch?"

"Of course," laughed Mark.

"I won't," said Ali, "but I'm still pleased they're going to be in London. Sport's not my thing but I'd rather they were here than in Beijing, or somewhere there's no free speech or anything."

"I don't think you can blame the IOC for that too much," said Mark, "China's just different – it's just so big and so important. We're all going to spend much of our lives talking about China, working there etc., so we might as well get used to it."

"Speak for yourself," responded Ali. "It makes me sick how all the big companies just bow and scrape to them, while our government, and all the others, bend over backwards to appease them."

"How's the short story coming on?" asked Ruth.

"Usual," smiled Leo grimly, "lots of squalor and poignant social comment."

"Does that mean it's likely to get published?"

"No, but it gives me an excuse to write lots of grumpy letters to publishers, which is definitely a step up."

"Come on, seriously. Last time, it was something about the couple of hours before a Celtic-Rangers game, ordinary people getting worked up and angry, becoming more militant than they would ever be in normal life."

"I've shelved that one for a bit. I couldn't get one of the characters to work. I've started a novel instead, about a woman in Glasgow who lives in the same house all her life and how she and the world change over her lifetime."

"That sounds really interesting, how far have you got with it?"

"It's hard to explain. I think I've written quite a lot, but I'm also having to do quite a lot of reading to research the history of what happened and what it was like to live then."

"Is she based on anyone special?"

"Not really, not one person anyway, but there are bits of a few people I know in her, including a few memories I have of my nan from when I was a kid. She died when I was 12."

"Leo's still trying to classify himself into whatever school of writing is in vogue. He really wants to be a realist like Zola but was born in the wrong century."

Leo looked down for a moment, then laughed, "Fair cop, Anna."

Anna stared at him, then dropped her eyes.

Anna and Leo still had the ability to hurt each other. Leo could be almost comically sensitive at times – although he was 22, Ruth still saw him as the 18-year-old boy she had first noticed standing tongue-tied in the middle of a group of his fellow English students. Those others had moved on into media and journalism mostly, while Leo had always just worked hard and written, trying to find a form, a voice, something that worked for him. She thought it cruel of Anna to take the piss about his difficulty with literary theory – Leo had always had a hard time with 'issues' – but she didn't think Anna had meant it; it was just a symptom of their relationship; the relationship itself – the imbalance of him liking her more as a friend, she wanting him more as a lover – rather than the manner of its ending, which had been devoid of fireworks or guilt.

Ali, happily, picked up on the change of tone. "What do you think of Live 8 four days on?"

"I thought it was good but not great," Anna said. "I can't believe so few people seem to have heard any Pink Floyd before. It's really interesting how siloed people's musical memory is. Floyd were huge, but then they broke up and stopped talking to each other or whatever. My step-dad used to play 'Dark Side of the Moon' and 'Animals' constantly, as well as, what was it, 'Another Brick in the Wall' and, shit, I can't remember, what was it? Never mind…"

"I've always got a bad feeling when musicians start getting too close to politicians," said Ruth, "It's a bit like seeing Noel Gallagher and all at that 10 Downing Street party back in '97, you know, they show it on TV sometimes – it just doesn't look right."

"I know what you mean," said Mark, "and I think Blair and Bush are conning them, but I don't really blame them for trying. They're dammed if they try to do something practical to improve the world, and damned if they don't."

"Maybe," said Anna, "but they're just too obviously enjoying being in the spotlight. And what are they doing cuddling up to Blair anyway, after Iraq and everything, it's just hideous."

"I don't think much'll happen anyway," said Leo, "These things never really work, do they, for all the goodwill involved? I mean, the original Live Aid didn't exactly sort out famine in Africa, did it? Sure it helped a few people, or maybe a lot, but not many compared to all those that've starved to death since. But it sure made a lot of people in Britain and the US feel good about themselves."

"God but you can be cynical sometimes," said Ruth. "A lot of those people could have given quite a lot of money by their own needs and then just carried on with their lives. Okay, I'll admit it didn't solve Africa's problems – I don't think Geldof ever claimed it would – I was at least one year old and remember it clearly! But it's equally wrong to claim that millions of people gave money just so they could feel smug about it the next day."

"Heh," said Ali, "do you remember Geldof giving Thatcher a hard time, just not letting her off the hook? I bet Ruth remembers that too."

"Okay," said Leo, "so it did some good and lots of ordinary people gave money for the right reason. But I still think the hype around Live Aid was over-blown massively, and the same was true about last Saturday's thing."

"Maybe so," said Ruth, "I mostly agree, or think I do, but at least Geldof and Bono are recognising that they need the governments of rich countries to contribute and commit if anything's really going to change."

"I'm sorry," said Leo, "but I guess I just am more cynical than you. Maybe it's one of those Glasgow things."

"What does your dad think of it all?" asked Ali.

"Actually, he's been pretty much on Leo's side. He can be very cynical about the impact of almost any government initiative in the short term – and overseas aid would be up there – but in the long-term, he does think governments make a difference."

"Presumably bad as well as good?" suggested Mark.

"Oh, absolutely, he'd completely accept their capacity to do damage. But, to be honest, Dad and I don't talk about his job much. Even now, I think he's worried I'd just find it incredibly boring. It's like he still thinks I'm 15 or something. Listen, I think it's my round, shall we have one more?" Ruth looked round but no one responded.

"Yea, why not?" replied Leo after a moment. They had all been implicitly waiting for him, their spiritual barometer, the arbiter of their collective mood. Leo's authority in these respects was secure by virtue that it remained unarticulated, and was recognised by everyone except Leo himself. "Then maybe we could go on somewhere, I haven't been to a club in ages."

Ruth took the orders and went up to the bar. She was glad she had come back to Leeds at least for a while; she liked the place and she liked these people. Her relationship with Mark had been a three-week fling in the lead up to his Finals the previous summer, and already it seemed half a lifetime away. She had known at the time that Mark wanted to go out with Ali, but it hadn't happened yet, and so both of them had felt free and almost guiltless.

As the barman finished getting the order, she heard Anna's distinctive laugh, more of a cackle really, and turned around to try and catch, unsuccessfully, what they had been talking about. Turning back to pay, however, she caught sight of a face in the corner – bent over, reading – that struck her as familiar but not in a normal way. Then she recalled where she had seen it before, in the window of the train last Saturday. Ruth felt herself blush at how she had returned that steady stare, feeling protected by the double reflection that separated them. They had not spoken and when the train had pulled in, she had consciously got up quickly and turned away from him to exit at the other end of the carriage.

But now here he was again, and this seemed to be too strong a sign of fate for her to ignore. Paying, she took the others' drinks over to them, then came back to the bar and, taking a deep breath, picked up her own and went over and sat down on the stool opposite her train companion.

"Hello," she said, "forgive me if I've got this wrong but didn't we sort of travel up in the train together from London last Saturday?" She hurried on before the man could reply, "Because we didn't really speak on the train, I thought I'd better come over before you decided I was being rude again."

The man looked up and she noticed his eyes were ever so slightly crossed, or so it seemed at that instant; a moment later and she was less sure. These eyes looked blank for a second, then lit up before dimming slightly?

"Hi," he said, visibly pulling himself together, "I take it you're the woman in the train window. I'm Nick, and I don't really know what to say..."

"It's okay, neither do I. My name's Ruth, by the way. But I just thought that, well, given we didn't exactly talk to each other, I ought at least to come over and say hello, sort of introduce myself."

"No, thanks, I mean I'm glad you did. I should have said hello properly only I got caught, trapped sort of, just looking at you in the window and it was dead strange. And then when we got to Leeds…"

"I know," cut in Ruth, "I got up and left quickly without really giving you a chance."

"I wasn't going to put it like that."

"No, I know you weren't. Anyway, it's lovely to be able to have a sort of normal conversation; I really didn't think I'd ever see you again. Listen, are you doing anything this evening? Why not sit with us for a bit?" She indicated the table where she'd left her friends. Mark and Anna were looking over curiously, the other two looking as though they wished they had eyes in the backs of their heads. "They're just some mates I went to uni with."

"Well, I don't know, it's not as if I really even know you."

"But it's not as if you have lots of other stuff you have to rush off for?"

"No, not exactly, but…"

"Then you must join us, at least for one drink. But first, you have to tell me something about yourself. I can't say I met you on the train and not know anything at all about you."

For the first time, Nick looked relaxed, as though he had just caught up with himself. "Well, let me see, I was born in Gateshead but my parents split when I was ten, and my mum and me moved to London – she works in banking; and I'm 26, and have just finished my PGCE training, to be a Physics teacher, having spent three years not becoming an accountant; and I play rugby – union; and like George Eliot, but my favourite book is 'Catch 22'."

Ruth laughed out loud, drawing more looks from the other table, "Well, I guess that will do for the time being. I suppose I ought to reciprocate… I'm 22 and my parents are still happily married, so happily married I sometimes feel I've missed out on some vital human experience. Anyway, I finished university here a year ago – got a 2:1 in History – and then I travelled a bit – nowhere special, and now I've come back to Leeds for a bit to work for a charity. My dad's a civil servant and mum's an academic – it all sounds very comfortable and boring when I say it like that. Anyway, I like Shakespeare but hardly ever go, and my favourite book is 'Vanity Fair'. Favourite band?"

"Radiohead."

"Destiny's Child."

"Right, well, I guess we've sort of caught up and got to know each other, a bit anyway, though it feels like it ought to be the start of a conversation rather than the end of one."

"We'll see," said Ruth. "Right, are you ready to come over and meet my friends? I can feel them twitching."

"Yea, okay then, though I'm not sure I've done much for your reputation."

"Don't worry, I'm happy to take the hit."

They got up and Nick grabbed his jacket, a baggy, non-descript affair, off-grey, lightweight, with patch pockets. He was about 6'0", with the start of a bald patch and beginning already to grey, but only in flecks. Unshaven, neither was he obviously good-looking. Yet his face was open and his eyes twinkled.

"This is Nick everyone," said Ruth, sitting down beside her friends. "We met on the train up from London on Saturday, he's about to become a Physics teacher. I just spotted him while I was ordering the drinks and said he should come and join us, at least for one."

Nick said hello and hoped he wasn't butting in, and the others introduced themselves more or less enthusiastically. Mark and Anna were more reserved but still welcoming. As much as Leo and Ali; however, they were curious. Mark had assumed that his seduction, as he saw it, of Ruth the previous summer had been a rare event and this cast doubt on that; Ali, who had always known about Mark and Ruth's relationship, saw the possibility of release from the gnawing fear inside her; Anna felt happy for her friend; and Leo simply enjoyed being present to observe fresh twists in the human comedy. All of them instantly amended their internal profile of Ruth.

"It was so odd when Ruth came and sat down opposite me. We'd only chatted briefly on the train, and she was pretty much the last person I expected to see again."

"It was such a coincidence," added Ruth. "I was just paying for the drinks and thought I recognised this bloke over in the corner but couldn't think where from. I actually thought for a moment it was that guy Anna and I met in Hawes a couple of years ago. And then I realised it was Nick from the train."

"What subject do you teach again, Nick?" asked Mark.

"Physics."

"The teaching students here that I've met are all mad," said Anna.

"So when did you start working in Leeds?"

"Oh, I've only been here a year; I did my PGCE in Manchester last year, I'm from Gateshead originally, so moving across into Yorkshire was just really moving a little closer to home."

Gradually, the group settled down again and became six rather than five, but with Nick still feeling and sounding slightly awkward, though physically he began to relax, and his smile helped him to fit in more than he realised. In reality, the group of friends was less homogenous than they thought, or appeared from the outside. It would have been almost impossible for that not to be so given the history. Nick's unexpected entrance had provided a release so that he was soon the centre of attention.

Ruth's brief relationship with Mark the summer before was one of the causes of tension. But there were two others. One was financial, with Ali and Leo earning considerably less than their two friends, while Ruth could be comfortably supported by her parents. This meant there was always a question over what they did together and how much it cost. In particular, Ali felt more dependent on Mark than she was comfortable with, and Leo wondered if he could afford to spend time with these people or whether he should just go and live somewhere else. The other tension stemmed from the decision to share a house together, which they had been doing for the past nine months. The ostensible idea had been simply for them to be together but overlying that had been Ali's wish not to be too dependent on Mark, and Anna and Mark's wish to help Leo out. Mostly, it had worked well but the house was a typical student dwelling with smallish rooms, drab and poorly looked after, with thin walls and little communal space outside the kitchen; and Ruth's arrival had added to the claustrophobia.

She was staying in a tiny boot room, about seven feet by five, and had happily agreed to pay the same rent as everyone else. Despite this, her arrival had already increased the temperature and there had been two minor spats in the previous three days. One had involved whether they all used the same milk or bought their own; the second had been triggered by Mark asking if it was okay to invite some lawyer friends round to dinner, in other words, could everyone else go somewhere different for an evening? The first had, rather uneasily, been resolved by an agreement to use communal milk for cereal, tea and coffee only, and buying individual milk for anything else; the second had been left pending a house conversation the following weekend.

All this was just under the surface, and so there were good reasons why Nick's appearance was welcomed as an alternative focus. While she had seen some of the tension, Ruth was so far unaware of the depth of the fissures.

Instead, she saw how easily Nick fitted in with her friends and how much they enjoyed talking to him. This affected her view of him, and where before he had appealed to her as an essentially harmless dare to herself, now she began to appraise him in his own terms.

The evening was turning into something entirely unexpected and a bit scary. Having started as a casual drink with housemates, her first night out since being back in Leeds was acquiring a pivotal aura. Ruth became aware Nick was talking to her.

"Sorry, I was daydreaming, can you say that again?"

"I was just telling Ali I can't really remember much of what we talked about on the train, that we were only really passing time, shooting the breeze."

Ali was looking quizzically at her, at them both really, clearly unconvinced that Nick and she had managed to spend two hours talking about not very much. Ruth felt herself beginning to flush but, in that moment, decided to continue with the story.

"Well, we only got talking when I said something about it being the wrong weekend to be leaving London, with Live 8 and all, even though there was no chance of getting tickets. I was just reading something about the line-up in the paper, and Nick said he was happy to be escaping, and we just sort of started talking, just about what was in the paper. So I guess that's Nick's version of shooting the breeze. In which case, he needs to understand that's about as intellectual as I get." She was becoming amused by the whole thing, enjoying the creative process of inventing a rational explanation of how she had ended up in this situation. In a corner of her mind, it also became a kind of test to convince Ali.

"Sorry," said Nick, clearly not meaning it, "I didn't mean to imply we were just talking about nothing, only that we were just talking about normal stuff rather than making enormous personal philosophical statements the way people tend to do when they meet on trains in the movies."

Ali laughed, "Well, it certainly seems to have been some train trip – I'm beginning to suspect the two of you arranged to meet up here tonight."

"Oh Ali," cried Ruth, "You know I never plan anything, though if I'd thought of it…" The statement was uttered with just the right level of ambiguity to surprise both Ali and herself.

Everyone was drinking up, and Ruth asked Nick if he wanted to come on with them. "I'd love to," he replied, "but not tonight. I was out last night and I'm just knackered really."

"Are you sure?"

"Yea, and then there's rugby training tomorrow, I'm not as good at burning the candle as I used to be."

Ruth found herself disappointed but Nick did look convinced and so she bent across to give him a peck on the cheek.

"Can I ring or text you?" she found herself asking, not whispering but half under her breath. "It'd be good to see you sometime before our next train encounter or at least to plan it rather than have these surreal coincidences."

"Yes, of course, I'll text you first though," Nick replied. "After tonight, I think it's my turn and, like you say, it would be good if the next time we met was a bit more normal."

By now, they were outside the pub and the others were about ten metres ahead. Ruth looked up and shouted, "Nick's not coming; I'm just saying goodbye, I'll catch you up…" Leo, Mark and Anna turned round and waved. Ali initially didn't, raising her right arm instead, but as the others turned back, she swivelled right round and looked directly at them. Ruth couldn't tell if she was smiling but got the impression Ali wasn't expecting to see her again that night.

"They all really like you, you know."

"Do they? Sorry, that sounds awful and I did like them, though it was a bit strange, the whole thing, given we were making up stuff."

"I know, but they did, and I think they found it really strange too; they aren't exactly used to me introducing strange new men to them, particularly ones I've never even mentioned. Sorry, now that's me sounding dreadful. But seriously, if we see each other properly, and I hope we do, we ought to talk about the train journey."

"If you like," Nick replied.

"Okay," she said slowly, "But at some stage we need to get there."

"Maybe, though I'm not sure we always need to talk about things to understand them. Look, for me it was a really special experience, and even if I'd never seen you again, I would always have remembered it."

"Why?"

"I'm not sure really, which is why I'm slightly reluctant to try and explain it. I think it was simply that there was no rational decision involved – I caught sight of your reflection in the window and something inside just told me to keep looking. And then when you started looking back it created some kind of, I don't know, bridge between us. That sounds ridiculous and rehearsed or something, which it isn't at all. And I don't know if it makes any sense to you."

"Yes, of course it does," Ruth replied. "It's been playing on my mind ever since I got off the train. And even when I recognised you this evening, there was a big part of me that wanted to just pretend I hadn't. I don't even really know why I came over but I think it was for a good reason. I think I felt I'd missed out on something last Saturday, let it pass without doing anything."

"I'll tell you what," Nick replied, "let's both just leave it there. Maybe eventually, one of us will work it out. I just wanted you to know that there was nothing bad or wrong about what I was thinking, or why I looked at you in the window for so long."

"I know that. Listen, I must go, the others will get worried and I think we've given them enough to gossip about already, and that's without telling them the interesting bit."

"I'll text you tomorrow…"

"Bye," Ruth pecked him too quickly on each cheek, then walked quickly away. She smiled as she turned the corner, walking briskly and caught sight of her friends about 100m ahead.

When she caught up, they immediately began asking the predictable question. Although Ruth had been thinking as she walked about what she would say, she was glad it was now dark enough to obscure her features. As it turned out, none of them believed Nick had been in the pub by accident; all of them thought Nick and she were already together, or as good as. Neither did they believe Ruth had met him for the first time on Saturday, though the balance of opinion was that they had travelled up together.

While Ruth had expected some level of incredulity, the wall of disbelief she encountered gave her a shock. Being back in Leeds was suddenly different to how she had imagined it. Suddenly, she knew they were no longer students and she had become detached from them, was now in effect an outsider. By now, they were waiting in the queue for the club. Ruth decided it wasn't going to work for her to live with the others. She almost said so there and then but thought she should tell Anna first.

She thought Anna would be fine if she knew in advance rather than hearing at the same time as everyone else. Of course, this would in turn upset Ali and Mark, but what they thought mattered much less to her. Leo, she cared about far more. Ruth didn't feel the need to tell him early because she did not think he would be at all bothered but she thought she could probably stay friends just as well, whether they were sharing a house or not.

Chapter 22
London, Thursday 7th

The first Mary knew was when Imogen rang in to say there were delays on the Tube and so she would be late into work. Apparently, there was some major power failure or power surge, it wasn't really clear which. Within the next 15 minutes, Charlie and Dave rang in with similar stories. All so normal, all so London, she thought, just part of the periodic nightmare of commuter experience. There had been days like this before, maybe two or three already this year. Still, she thought wryly, if this had happened a couple of days sooner, the 2012 Olympics would certainly have been heading for Paris. The decision yesterday lunchtime had been a complete shock to Mary and everyone she had spoken to, it all seemed so preposterous. How could a city like London, with aged infrastructure, permanently semi-crocked, be credible, let alone chosen, as the host for an event the scale of the Olympics?

As far as she could work out, the deciding factors in the IOC's vote had been Tony Blair's charm and star quality on the one hand and Jacques Chirac's complacency and dislike of Finnish food on the other. Neither made much sense to her, but between them they had dominated the last few days' media coverage, and so she had been left searching in vain for better reasons. What seemed obvious was that a major transport failure in the days leading up to the vote would have totally scuppered London's chances. It was easy to imagine how the Paris bid would have exploited the event, their only dilemma being whether they could contain their sniggering long enough to avoid the impression of gloating.

But then, around 9am, came the first hint something more serious might be happening. In retrospect, when she tried to order and comprehend the multiple, overlapping, and too often terrible, facts and emotions of the day, Mary was unable to disentangle fully the sequence in which events occurred. The first she knew of a possible bomb was, she thought, a report that there had been an explosion on a Tube train near Aldgate. Then there were reports of a second explosion, but Mary couldn't remember if this had been Russell Square or Edgware Road. For the next half hour, news of the three bombings kept pouring in, though it was obvious the journalists were still looking to get their bearings on what had happened. Then she heard an almighty bang, like a truck had backfired in the room next to her office.

She rushed outside, feeling not exactly frightened but alarmed, all her emotions and instincts on edge. It had been a searingly hot morning already but when she inevitably jumped at the bang, she had instantly broken sweat, and as she emerged into the corridor outside her office just off Gower Street, she was aware of her heart pumping loudly and of her attempts to stay calm. Almost immediately she met James and Charlotte, who had just arrived, and after a brief exchange they decided to go into Charlotte's office to listen to the radio. Within a couple of minutes, though by now Mary's sense of elapsed time had all but disappeared, the report of an explosion came through in Woburn Place, less than half a mile away. The three of them each tried to ring colleagues, friends, family but the landlines were all engaged and their mobiles were not getting through.

"Let's check the internet," suggested Charlotte. When they did, what turned out to be the true picture was starting to emerge. All four explosions – three on the Underground and a bus in Woburn Place – were now being reported but news of casualties and other details was still patchy and unreliable. It was clear no one really had any idea what had happened, beyond that there had been a series of co-ordinated terrorist attacks, probably suicide bombings. But the aftermath was chaos, and everyone was struggling to understand how to deal with the fallout.

"This is terrible," said Mary.

"Only a matter of time though," James observed. "I'm sure there's been some near misses before this, must have been. After 9/11, Afghanistan and Iraq, Al Qaeda must have been targeting London for years."

"How can you be so matter of fact about it?" accused Charlotte. "Don't you care about the people out there, some of whom are almost certainly dead, with who knows how many people injured?"

"Of course I do," James retorted. "But it's stupid to be surprised by it, to pretend it's a terrible shock. On one level it is, but it's always been about when not if."

"It's okay. Both of you, please!" Mary pleaded. "Charlotte, do you know where Eric's likely to be?"

"No, I don't," she stammered, her voice quivering, "but he would have been coming through King's Cross just about when the bomb went off."

James coloured instantly and bowed his head. He went to reach out towards her and then thought better of it. "I'm really sorry," he muttered, "I didn't know, I mean I forgot he came in that way. Why don't you sit down and try and text him while I make a cup of tea or something?"

"It's okay, James, it's all right, honest it is," Charlotte replied, her voice steadier now but without feeling. "That's a good idea; I'll go and sit in the lounge and try and text him from there. And a cup of tea would be great."

When she had gone, Mary followed James into the kitchen. "You haven't heard from Gemma either, have you?"

"No," he said, "but we come in on the Central Line, and she left before me this morning so I'm sure she's okay. Listen, I'm sorry about that; I was thinking out loud without engaging my brain. I'd forgotten about Eric, I really had. God, I hope he's okay."

"Me too," agreed Mary. "Listen, don't worry about it but stay with her until she hears something. I'm sure he'll be fine. The chances of him being caught up in it even given the timing are still miniscule. I'm going over to Woburn Place to see what's going on, whether I can help."

"Do you know where Sam is?" James asked, "Or Ruth?"

"They're fine," she replied confidently. "Ruth is in Leeds – she went up on Saturday – and Sam went in early on the Northern Line. I haven't managed to contact either of them but they'll be okay. Like I said, look after Charlotte. If it looks like

I'm going to be away more than an hour, I'll ring you; the networks should have sorted themselves out by then."

"Okay," said James, "but be careful out there."

"You're not old enough to have watched that programme," Mary threw the comment randomly over her shoulder as she reached the stairs, leaving James bemused as the kettle boiled.

She put on her sunglasses as she emerged into the street and started walking quickly, but calmly she hoped, towards Russell Square. The streets were normally busy but felt different, or was she imagining it? How do people behave when their city is under terrorist attack? There had been four explosions, almost certainly suicide bombs, two of them within half a mile of where she was, but outwardly, thought Mary, you would struggle to notice a difference, certainly to distil it and pin it down to a plausible cause. The people she passed seemed to be walking quicker, with more purpose, or was it rather that, unusually, no one was strolling, walking slowly, idling along looking around them. Yes, maybe that was it, the absence of dawdling? Mary smiled grimly to herself, self-conscious that now wasn't the day or the place to look relaxed and carefree.

The heat seemed to belie the city's latitude, with the sun still low enough in the sky to sneak uncomfortably around the sides of her sunglasses, so that she wondered for a moment whether there was something unreal about the whole situation, and she would soon wake up to realise there was something inherently ridiculous in the whole construct, like her being on holiday on this date and so not in London at all. But the very fact of being able to go through this thought process rendered its likelihood negligible, and Mary pulled herself back to the moment and thanked God that at least Sam would be out of harm's way and she wasn't in the same position as Charlotte, distraught at not being able to contact a partner who would have been there or thereabouts when one of the bombs exploded.

James' comments had been crass, but she put them down to him being disturbed from his normal equilibrium by the scale of what had happened. But maybe she was being too forgiving; after all, it was hardly the first time he had forgotten his comments could carry personal relevance to others. Still, at least he was sorry.

She started to hear the sirens converging on what she already imagined were scenes of devastation. Now, as she turned the corner and Russell Square came into sight, Mary could also hear shouting and the occasional scream. Still, however, the people around her seemed to be moving at close to walking pace, some strange endorsement of a collective determination to remain doggedly phlegmatic. Again Mary found herself hauling her attention back into the moment. She was halfway across the square, walking diagonally, and now people were running, some with smoke-stained faces. Mary found herself breaking into a jog and a handful of seconds later was on the eastern edge of the square opposite the Bloomsbury Hotel. A little out of breath in the heat, she immediately turned to look north, towards Woburn Place.

Almost involuntarily she had been imagining what damage a bomb might do to a double decker bus but the reality was still a shock. The roof had been completely blown off the top deck, which had been left a mangled mess, in the same way, she imagined, as if the bus had careered at 70mph through a bridge that was too low for it. Almost an hour after the bomb had been detonated, smoke was still rising into the blue sky. The emergency services were trying to go about their business as though it were the scene of any other kind of explosion. But it plainly wasn't.

Mary didn't want to go too close and get in people's way. While the situation was a bit chaotic, it looked to her like there were enough people and it was coming under control and she knew she had no specific skill or expertise to offer. She also knew she was close to the headquarters of the BMA, and imagined there would be plenty of doctors around. As far as she could tell from her vantage point some 50m away, everyone was being tended to, and various people were rushing back and forth with buckets of water. If she got involved, she would just get in the way.

Mary began to wonder why she had come, knowing she would have little to offer. Partly there was some chance she might have been able to help, and a bit of her had wanted to escape Charlotte and James' company. Not being able to talk to Sam or Ruth hadn't helped either, for despite knowing rationally they were both safe, without direct contact, a scintilla of doubt remained. She tried them both again on her mobile but without success. Mostly, however, Mary knew she had wanted to be here to see what it was like. She was a voyeur at this scene.

Terrible as it was, this was history being made. It already seemed inevitable that suicide bombers had detonated the explosives, and that too seemed to add significance to the whole thing. On one level James had been right, such an attack had been a question of when not if, but the manner of it was anything but inevitable. It was a long way from the drama of 9/11, but it felt to Mary that these were the sort of bombings that took place routinely in Baghdad. And she had come here to witness it, to see how cheap and easy terrorism had become.

From her position, Mary was unable to see much detail of what was happening. In some places, there were pools of blood with people lying still beside them. Chunks of severed metal were strewn across the road and pavement, twisting and still smoking. Standing in the sun, Mary began to sweat but did not really look for any shade. It was bad enough her having come down here to gawp. The air itself still felt as though it was burning but the wreck now looked like an elaborate toy, or a mock-up from a film set. Everything appeared to be under control, and there were fewer screams and shouts, replaced by occasional barked commands and more frequent moans from the injured survivors.

Mary tried to imagine what it must have been like in the original minutes after the explosion but her mind drew a blank, unable to fathom, or get any kind of grasp on, the intensity of those moments. They were too far beyond her experience, and nothing in her own make-up equipped her to make the leap. Disappointed and feeling useless, she turned away and had begun to walk, this time quite slowly, back across Russell Square towards her offices. She had seen history but was none the wiser. She felt suddenly empty and dispirited. She had hoped for, even expected, some surge of emotion, almost a Damascene conversion that would open her eyes, perhaps her soul, but despite the extremes she had just witnessed, Mary felt no different in essence from how she had been two hours before. She was tired of being in situations she controlled, of feeling there was little that could surprise her, still less shock.

She wanted nothing more from her family life. Work too was fulfilling; she loved teaching, her books were successful and she was respected and admired by colleagues. She had friends she cared about and who cared about her. Mary had built her life with care, a brick at a time, never assuming, never racing ahead of herself.

None, or very little of it, had been easy but she had gradually manoeuvred, negotiated and, above all, worked to achieve what she sought. Approaching, it didn't feel like a conventional midlife crisis.

And she knew this was different because her emotions were not involved, they were barely bystanders. What she sought in its place was hard to describe, and she had hoped that in going across to Woburn Place she would find a way to help. But when push came to shove, she hadn't seen anything obvious she could have done, although neither had she asked. She kicked herself for her feebleness in not offering to do anything, no matter how minor. Instead, she had made her own calculation, reached her own conclusion; no input from anyone else.

It had been terrible being there, watching the fallout from the carnage the bomber had wreaked. None of the components had in themselves been a surprise. The heat, the smoke, the blood, the feeling that nothing was quite under control; these were all things she had been expecting but didn't know in advance how she would react, or whether she would be able to deal with the situation. In fact, simply by not engaging emotionally, Mary had remained all but unaffected. She had wanted to engage but had found neither the means nor the will to do so.

She had remained an observer rather than a participant, and that was essentially how she felt about much of the rest of her life. Even when, as now, she started out with the full intention of getting involved, successful execution defied her. Now stopped in the shade of a tree, the last one before she left the western edge of the square, and leant against it, Mary knew she was not heartless. But she also knew, indeed she had made a virtue of it, that she never panicked, nor did she let herself get carried away by euphoria. She had always tried to live by Kipling's mantra of treating success and failure the same, but she had done so by reducing both almost to a kind of lowest common denominator, so that neither really disturbed her all-important equilibrium, which had been somehow placed on a wholly undeserving pedestal.

Mary was sat down now, back against the tree, her legs out in front of her, ankles carefully crossed. She leaned back so the trunk of the tree filled the gap between her shoulder blades, and peered up through the branches. For all the analysis, she didn't know why she was unhappy, and she couldn't work out how she would find out. What disturbed her still more after this morning was her inability to relate to what she had seen. The emotions of the people at the bomb scene had left only the faintest imprint, with no depth to it and no means of anchoring itself in her emotional landscape. She remembered in particular a girl about Ruth's age, who had been wandering about with her head bandaged and her arm in a sling. Her face was streaked with blood and dirt and she looked exhausted. Her eyes were lethargic as she scanned the people around her, trying to take it all in. Mary marvelled that she had felt no particular attraction to this young woman, so similar to her own daughter, and that she hadn't tried to help her.

She recalled how, when she was young, her mother always told her to stand up straight with her shoulders back, never to slump. "You always need to look as though you're in control, Mary," she used to say, "The world doesn't look kindly on signs of weakness, so it's always best to hide away any fears you have, disguise them at the time and then find a way of dealing with them later." When she was nine, her best friend Susan had moved away, been sent to boarding school when her father, who was in the RAF, had been posted to Germany. It had been the most devastating experience of her life till that time, and she had felt terribly alone in school, imagining no one liked her and that they had only spoken to her before because of Susan. The first day after Susan had left, Mary had talked to no one and had twice needed to flee to the toilet so she could burst into tears. Without Susan she felt socially bereft, lacking the skill and charisma to make friends. Mary had poured so much of herself into her friendship with Susan, neglecting others, and now it had been ripped away from her.

This had been the first time Mary was truly aware there were forces at work, beyond her family and school, which she could not control. Until then, there had always been someone – parents or teachers – she could go to, to try and persuade to change their mind. But there was nothing Mary could do to prevent Susan moving away, and even now she shuddered when she recalled how she had wailed, inwardly and outwardly, at her nine-year-old impotence. Yet she also knew her crisis of confidence when Susan left had been real enough, and she had cried herself to sleep that night for the one and only time, urging herself to summon the strength to disguise her weakness in the way her mother had described. Sitting under the tree in Russell Square, she could still taste the salt in the tears that had wet her pillows. Why had she devoted herself to a single friendship when she could have had several friends equal to each other?

Mary remembered herself as she was then, the nine-year-old suddenly marooned, crying into her pillow. She could not really tell, could not identify a specific moment or decision. But she knew the narrative of her life demanded a milestone and that evening seemed to fit the bill, so it had become the occasion when Mary had decided to distribute her emotional attachments and dilute their intensity, so that there would be less chance of exposing herself to being let down. This in turn had meant that, despite relying on a greater number of friends, there were still gaps in the network she constructed. Mary ended up by filling these gaps herself, adapting to new ones as they appeared over time. She had therefore become more self-sufficient and self-contained, reaching the point where relying on someone was a matter of choice. She had also followed her mother's advice and learned well how to disguise her weaknesses; but still, the fewer weaknesses there were the better; disguise was a useful artifice but she preferred not to rely on it more than necessary.

Glancing at her watch, Mary got slowly to her feet. It had just gone 11.30am and she felt it was time to get back to the office, not least to see if Charlotte had heard anything. More people, she imagined, would have struggled their way in and there might be more dependable information. She realised she had been assuming there had only been the four explosions she knew about when she had left; there might easily have been more. It was now very hot, comfortably into the 80s, she thought, and she was quite thirsty. Mary started walking, once again purposeful. She wondered how Sam was, but still couldn't get a signal.

When she reached the office, she found that another half dozen or so people had straggled in. Of the others, a couple had rung in to say they'd given up and gone back home, more had emailed from home to say the same, and four hadn't been heard from but because of where they lived, were all assumed to be okay. Eric had managed to phone in about 11am, using a landline in a café where he had taken refuge after abandoning his Tube in Caledonian Road – by Charlotte's best estimate, he had been three or four trains behind the one in which the bomb had exploded; too close for comfort, but she was now almost exuberant, happy and relieved to again be a spectator.

About half of the people who had made it in were trying to do some work, or at least pretending to, sitting in front of their PCs, periodically flipping to news websites to see if there was any more information. Blair had announced he was flying back from Gleneagles to chair a meeting of Cobra, the government's emergency committee, and the death toll was rising into the 50s, though only in ones and twos, so that in many respects it began to seem London had gotten off quite lightly; the Madrid train bombing the year before had killed almost 200 people. Others were sitting around in front of the small office television, drinking tea and coffee, and watching the news gradually unfold. A few were starting to talk about whether it made sense to head home now, or soon anyway; the normal rush hour would be a nightmare and even going now would be a marathon journey for most.

Mary was welcomed enthusiastically. They had begun to get worried about her as she had been gone more than two hours. This made no normal sense but was indicative of the febrile atmosphere in which each piece of information was dissected for meaning and significance, with often spurious interpretations attached to the smallest, most isolated snippet. James and others had been trying to call her with growing desperation.

Once Mary had managed to get herself a cup of tea, she was obliged to sit down and talk to the others about what she had seen. This gave her the opportunity to add some lustre to her own role; in fact, it almost coerced her into doing so, or so she rationalised it later. They had asked her questions almost exclusively in the second person − what did you see? What did you do? − In a way that assumed she had somehow been a participant, perhaps in the way they imagined they would have themselves given the chance.

Consequently, in her view not wanting to disappoint, and wishing to convey a straightforward impression of the scene in Woburn Place, Mary found herself explaining to her colleagues how she had helped out with the rescue effort. And the more she wove stories of what she might have done, the easier it became and the more she enjoyed it.

"Mostly, I just carried water in and out from a toilet in the BMA, from a toilet in that main front quad. The heat and smoke were still pretty bad, and at times I found it difficult to breathe. The ambulance men and women, the paramedics, were doing an amazing job, although until just before I left to come back, there weren't really enough of them, and it was obvious none of them had ever really seen anything like this before. There were other people helping too. I think there must have been some doctors just in the area, probably visiting the BMA or something, and they were fantastic looking after the injured. I saw some bodies completely covered in sheets so I can only think the worst. It was all so terrible; the top of the bus had been entirely blown off; I've no idea how big a bomb it would have to be to do that; I've never seen so much tangled metal." Mary spoke in short, staccato phrases, as she did so reliving the experience, except this time she was right in the middle of the action, doing what she wished she had done but had lacked the impulse to make happen. This was a kind of second chance to get it right.

"There was a particular girl, young woman really, early 20s, about the same age as my daughter Ruth; she'd obviously been tended too and had a bandage round her head. There was still a trail of blood down her forehead and her face was dirty with all the smoke, but she was all right I think, although clearly still suffering from shock. Like I say, someone had taken the time to bandage her cut but then they'd obviously had to go and help people who were more seriously injured so they'd just had to leave her walking around, trying to get herself together."

"What did you do?" asked Anna.

Mary told the smallest lie she could think of without puncturing the credibility of the scene she had painted. "I sat her down and gave her some water, checked she was okay," Mary heard herself say, "But then, to be honest, I had to leave her and go and fetch more water. When I came back, one of the paramedics was with her, so I fetched another bucket of water, but by then enough of the emergency services had arrived and they were looking after everyone, so I came back here."

"Oh you did really well, Mary," said Anna, slightly gushing. "I'm sure I wouldn't have had the courage to do all that, I'm far too squeamish."

"No more than me," Mary replied. "I really just went to see what was happening; I suppose in the back of my mind there was the thought I might be able to help but I never imagined what it would be like, how much confusion there would be. I think getting involved in that sort of situation is just something that happens to you more than something you do."

Thankfully, the conversation moved on and Mary was able to relax but also to bask. Although she felt guilty while she was talking and fancied she must have gone red with embarrassment – she told herself the only reason she hadn't been found out was that she was still quite flushed from walking outside in the heat – within 20 minutes, all feelings of guilt had disappeared and only the glow of imagined achievement was left. What she had been unable to accomplish in reality had proved surprisingly easy in fiction, with only a little sleight of hand narrative. Even more surprising was that this narrative, in her mind, was already starting to morph into her own, and only, version of the truth. From now on, this improved version of history was increasingly the one Mary believed, the one accepted without question by Sam and Ruth, by Ed and Michelle and Philip and all their friends.

And because of this, it had a series of small but significant consequences. In her own mind, Mary was almost mystically freed from the self-imposed manacles that had inhibited her from giving of herself in situations where she might expose her own weakness and vulnerability. The decision she had made to involve herself directly, even if only as part of a fictional narrative, meant she was always, from now on, starting from a slightly different place. Also, it soon became clear that people's expectations of her were changed, the assumption now being that Mary would muck in and get her hands dirty. This didn't mean people had previously thought Mary wouldn't do these things, but it wasn't a natural assumption because, while there were no cases anyone remembered of Mary standing back, neither was there any real evidence of her having risked herself to get something done.

This new assumption showed itself in her being asked to solve practical problems, typically where there was some element of sensitivity about someone's feelings. Mary enjoyed these, and the level of trust they implied. She had always been a good listener but now she was able to put this to good use. And finally, as a result of these other changes, Mary felt her air of dissatisfaction begin to lift, and her happiness increase in response, so that she laughed more quickly and smiled more often, was more likely to notice the beauty of nature and the changing of the seasons.

It was just after 3pm before Mary was able to get in touch with Sam and Ruth. Sam had sounded okay but slightly confused. The line still hadn't been great, but it seemed as though he'd been thrown off the train and then somehow to have got involved with the bus that had been blown up, the No. 30 she had seen the wreck of. Mary didn't really understand how he could have been close to catching that bus, or how he could remotely know it was the same bus. She put it down to the chaos of the day; Sam had got into work okay, although not until after 11am. He was clearly upset by the bombings, and Mary put down the phone concerned and wanting to hug him when she got home.

Speaking to Ruth was different. Ruth had been worried sick all day, partly at the patchy nature of the news coming through about exactly what had happened and the scale of the casualties, and partly at the sheer frustration of not being able to contact her parents. Because they both worked in Central London and despite knowing the location of the four bombs, Ruth had imagined a whole range of implausible scenarios whereby one or both of them had been on one of the Tubes or the bus that had been destroyed. These ranged from Sam having a meeting in the City – an unlikely but not impossible occurrence – to Mary being caught in the Edgware Rd bombing on her way to Bath to give a lecture at the university.

"Mum! Thank God, at last!" Ruth had burst out when she finally heard Mary's voice. "I've been trying all day, I've been so worried. Have you heard from Dad? Is he okay?"

"Yes, on both counts," replied Mary, trying to sound calm in response to her daughter's obvious distress and relief. "I'm sorry, I've been trying to contact you too, and Dad as well for that matter, all day too, but the networks must have been overloaded or something. So I've just got through to Dad, after heaven knows how many attempts, and you're literally the second person I've spoken to."

"Are either of you injured or hurt at all?" continued Ruth. "Were you close to any of the bombs? I thought you might have been on the Tube and got caught in the Edgware Road one."

"No, I'd no travel planned and so I've been here in the office all day; I got in about 8am and so missed all the bombs." Mary was reassuring but then added, "Apart from going to see the bus in Woburn Place to see if I could help."

"You did what?" Ruth's question was gasped rather than shouted down the phone but carried an unmistakable taint of horror. "I can't believe it! Why did you do that? Who knows what other explosions there might have been, or might still be?"

Mary was amused by her daughter's solicitude and her annoyed tone at the idea her mother might have chosen to take some small amount of risk without fully consulting her. "Don't worry, Ruth," she soothed, "I can imagine what you must have gone through today. It's been hard enough down here wondering about your dad and trying to contact you, even though I knew you were okay and that Dad wasn't going to be anywhere near where any of the bombs have gone off. But listen, I'm really sorry but don't be upset; I work really close to Woburn Place and it just seemed like the right thing to do to go and see what was going on. You need to trust me that I wouldn't ever put myself into danger."

"But Mum, it wasn't as if you could really help, and another bomb could have gone off, for all we know, it still could."

"I'm sorry, Ruth, I can see why you're so worried. As it turned out, I was able to help a little, just carrying water to help with the injured, but mostly, like I said, it just seemed like the right thing to do."

"It's okay, Mum, I'm sorry too, I shouldn't have shouted but I've just been so worried." Ruth was suddenly contrite, her voice reduced to not much more than a whisper, plaintive and full of relief and emotional exhaustion.

Mary felt her daughter starting to weep at the other end of the phone. "Listen, are you okay, Ruth?" she said, switching from a calming tone to a comforting one. Having moments earlier felt like an old woman justifying herself, she was now again a mother. "Why don't you come down and see us? Dad and I would love to catch up, even if it's only been a week, and we're not committed to anything this weekend."

"No, it's okay, Mum," Ruth replied. "I'm okay really, it's just been a difficult few hours, and now I know you and Dad are fine, I will be as well."

Mary was surprised now and a little dismayed. Ruth coming back down for the weekend had seemed the perfect solution both for her daughter and for Sam. But instead, here was Ruth, almost instantly recovered, or at least sufficiently not to need parental TLC anymore. Maybe this was the real tipping point, when she as a mother had become optional, somehow a nice to have.

"That's okay, Ruth," Mary heard herself saying simply. "Don't worry about it."

There was a slight pause at the other end of the phone while Mary silently cursed herself for allowing some part of her feelings to show in her tone and her words. But then she heard Ruth's voice. "Thanks, Mum, I'll ring later when you and Dad are home, then again tomorrow. And just say if you need me, but don't worry about me being upset earlier. I'm fine now and it's great just to hear your voice and know Dad's okay too; I was so worried."

Ruth's recovery and smooth, natural response was almost enough to make Mary forget the initial pause and think Ruth hadn't missed a beat before answering. But she had missed a beat; was it hesitation or shock at her mother's tone, or was it merely harmless hesitation? After she had put the phone down shortly afterwards, Mary thought hard about whether it had been the product of nature or artifice. In the end, she concluded her daughter was not sufficiently worldly for it to have been the latter and that the pause had carried no deeper meaning.

It was just after a quarter to four when Mary left the office to head home. Except for James, she was the last. He was still been upset about his earlier insensitivity and worried he had hurt Charlotte and made her anxious wait much worse than otherwise. His attitude reminded Mary of a younger version of Sam and so she tried to cheer him up.

"Listen," she said, "in the great scheme of things, nothing you said will have done Charlotte any damage."

"I sort of know that," he replied mournfully, "but it caused hurt at a time when she was really vulnerable, and I just feel really bad about it."

"I don't think you should. Nothing you said had the least bit of malice about it, and Charlotte absolutely knows that. She's pretty resilient as well, and I think once she got over the initial shock it won't have bothered her, particularly once you'd apologised and made her a cup of tea."

"I'm sorry but I still feel bad. It's the kind of thing I might have said when I was 16, but that was 20 years ago and I should have learnt by now. Memo to self – engage brain before opening gob!"

"Do you believe what you said?" Mary changed tack. "You know, that it was only a matter of time before London was hit by an act of mass terrorism."

"Yes, pretty much."

"Well then, you're not going to have gone far wrong." Mary was firm. "I'm all in favour of nuance and sensitivity but at the end of the day – God, I hate that phrase but have never quite been able to escape it; at the end of the day, we humans say what we think, and ultimately, that's way more important than being sensitive. Sure, we should try to be, nice to each other, sympathetic and so on, but if we're not doing so from a position of honesty, then it's worth less than the proverbial hill of beans. If you're asking would it have been better if you'd twigged that Eric's route into work meant he could have been caught up in the King's Cross bomb, then that would have been great. But, to be honest, James, it's not as if it was a glaringly obvious thing staring you in the face. I only worked it out because I saw Charlotte's reaction. But after that, you did all you could possibly have done. And even if what you said meant that couple of hours waiting was a bit more nervous, Charlotte's lasting memory – trust me on this – will be of all the kindness you showed afterwards."

"Thanks for trying, Mary, but I'm afraid I still feel pretty rubbish about it all. Besides, I'm not sure honesty is all it's cracked up to be. Sometimes I think we all know too much about each other's views. I'm sure we offer our views to each other more than previous generations, and as a result, I'm not convinced we don't all trade a good deal too heavily in the value of honesty. For me, there are a whole bunch of things I'd rather not know about at all, and another bunch where I'm happy to draw my own conclusions from a few salient facts. Instead, we have a surfeit of opinions and a paucity of facts, with the result that you get this huge superstructure of opinion, which is typically heavy on emotion and prejudice. If you ask me, it's all bloated and useless, a sad testament to our penchant for self-promotion. So yes, I do believe it's only been a matter of time before there was a major terrorist attack on London, but I should have thought about it and kept my mouth shut."

Mary was intrigued how what had started as a fairly basic regret was becoming bolstered by anger. "So, if honesty's less important than I suggested, do you think sensitivity to others' feelings is more valuable?"

"Yes, I do actually," James replied, "It's every bit as important, it's the necessary counterpoint, in fact. So if we agree that it's important to have a genuine plurality of opinions and belief, then surely, we also need to believe that those views ought to be held and expressed with a degree of humility. We can't all be right, by definition, but we do have to find ways to live together."

"But how do you make progress if you're not prepared to break a few eggs?" Mary was surprised to find herself on the more callous side of an argument like this, and neither was it where she expected to end up.

"To be honest," James replied, "I've never really liked that analogy. The issue's not about whether you break any eggs, it's about why. Look, I know what you mean about the importance of honesty, but I was just plain wrong this morning. Thanks

218

for trying to cheer me up, and I do feel better now, but there was no excuse for what I said to Charlotte. I had an absolute obligation to think about potential sensitivities, on today of all days, and I didn't do it. And it's all very well saying – I've done it myself – about honesty and being true to yourself, but the moment you start believing in your right to say what you want, you're on a slippery slope towards belief in your own infallibility. I don't know about you but I'd rather recognise and take responsibility for my own doubts, my own mistakes. That way I feel human and at one with my neighbours." James paused. "Sorry for the rant, I really appreciate you trying to help me, both this morning and now."

"Thanks, you're welcome," replied Mary as they headed for the lift.

Part 4: Perspectives II

Chapter 23
London, November 1985

For about the hundredth time, Philip thanked God, or whoever, for Michelle. It was one of those ironies, he thought, that as his domestic life miraculously righted itself after more than a decade of veering close to the precipice, his professional life, while still successful, had become less satisfying.

It was partly having less freedom and more responsibilities as a result of that success, and also of moving to the more corporate world of Channel 4. Mostly, however, it was the jump to current affairs. Working in sport had been a joy, but he had always seen it as a kind of sabbatical from the real business of reporting the news. The chance to move back to Britain as a current affairs producer with the newly-launching TV channel had seemed the perfect opportunity. What had slowly begun eating away at him was a combination of the toxic nature of British politics and the sterile destruction he saw in what he was reporting.

The Cold War, which he had once hoped to see the end of, now seemed so engrained in the DNA of world politics that it was impossible to think outside its parameters. Meanwhile, both Britain and the US seemed consumed by the politics of hate. In particular, Margaret Thatcher's 'There is no such thing as society' speech seemed to signal the creation of an unbalanced country that had abjured its responsibilities to the vulnerable.

Philip was in many ways an instinctive conservative, who, having left school at 16, had worked his way up, able to earn more money as he went. But part of him was shaped by what he had seen as he had progressed. For one thing, the British upper class and British management did not come out well from comparison with its US equivalent. For another, his friendship with Carol and memories of 1968 left him permanently sceptical of a US system so driven by inequality.

He got out at Kentish Town and braced himself for the blast of icy air from the Arctic that he always fancied hit him as he stepped onto the escalator. It duly arrived, as brutal as anything the New York subway offered up. Walking up the road past the Town & Country Club, he was already looking forward to the long gin that awaiting him when he got in.

Michelle would have been home about an hour. When she'd moved to London, she'd decided to stop working full-time and had instead got a job helping out mornings at quite a large GP's practice in Clapham, the other side of the Thames. This entailed quite a long commute, but because it was all on the Northern Line and she started early enough to get a seat, it didn't seem so bad. London, despite its grimness, still seemed new and exciting to her, and she enjoyed people-watching on the Tube, as well as the 15-minute walk across Clapham Common.

In many ways, it was an ideal job after more than a decade in the wards. Michelle had intended to get a job at one of the big London teaching hospitals whenever they were settled, but once she stopped the routine of hospital nursing, she marvelled she had ever been able to do it. Richard had suggested working at a GP's and put her in touch with Elaine, whom he'd studied medicine with. The hours suited perfectly, she finished at 1pm and earned enough to feel she wasn't solely reliant on Philip's, to her enormous, salary. They also gave her the time to go shopping for both of them as they gradually set up home together. Neither had much in the way of possessions – for different reasons, their previous lives had not encouraged the acquisition of objects or attachments, let alone furniture. And so they were in the largely enviable position of beginning their life together with little baggage of any sort.

But much more often than shopping, especially after the first few months, Michelle used these hours to explore London, its culture and its geography. She went to art galleries and museums – particularly the National and the ICA, and she would often get out at Embankment to visit one or the other before getting back on the Northern Line to go home. She loved wandering around the National Gallery, gazing at the different eras of representation, wondering about the allegories. Several years before, she had read 'What's Bred in the Bone' by Robertson Davies, one of the central elements of which is the allegorical meaning of Bronzino's 'An Allegory with Venus and Cupid', hanging in the National. Michelle had always assumed this was imagined and so was bowled over one day to discover the painting there, just as it was described, with Cupid's fingers seductively framing Venus' nipple. Ever since, she would sometimes tag onto one of the guided groups, and then use the knowledge acquired to extrapolate and speculate about other paintings. At the ICA, she enjoyed sitting in the café reading, and then wandering round the exhibitions.

Over that first year or so, Michelle's outlook altered. She realised that she had assumed people of previous eras had less sophisticated thoughts than people of the modern era. Within a few months, however, Michelle realised this was rubbish. She also realised that much great art and culture was widely accessible and was astonished by how easy she found it to understand what Renaissance painters were trying to convey. There were eternal human themes of love, jealousy and power running through much of what they painted, and if a good deal was communicated through allegory, then once that language was explained, it became an open book. So, she also now believed there was no meaningful distinction between the art she now loved and what she had grown up with.

London itself she loved. But Michelle knew Philip was ambivalent towards the British metropolis, preferring regional cities such as Bristol, where he'd grown up, or else the frank, open modernity of New York, Chicago and Los Angeles. By contrast, Philip thought London drab and provincial, closed in and obsessed with its own history, while being way too big to foster any real sense of community or belonging. Their different views on this, as on many other things, did not matter. From the start, their relationship had thrived on argument. Philip had travelled and seen much of what she felt she had missed out on; while Michelle embodied a sharpness of logic and emotion Philip felt had been slowly smoothed out of him over the years.

Doubtless, Michelle's perspective on London was coloured by her happiness those first few months' living with Philip. As well, however, Michelle loved the visual texture of the city, the beautifully landscaped parks, the secluded squares, the adjacent and overlapping ages of architecture, the low-level skyline often punctuated by little more than church spires – Wren or Hawksmoor – that had somehow escaped the Blitz, and the sweeping arcs of the Thames with its eccentric bridges and continually changing tidal vistas. The people too, Michelle viewed differently from Philip. To her, they did create communities, based on the old villages and towns that London's growth had gradually captured, or on immigrant groups which, though they might be less distinct and exotic than their New York equivalents, were nonetheless real.

When Philip arrived home, Michelle was still in the bath. Having been caught by a shower walking home, she had needed to warm up and had been lying in the hot suds reading 'The Unbearable Lightness of Being', enjoying Kundera's ability to flit between the overlapping lives of his rootless characters and his various philosophical digressions.

Hearing Philip's key in the door, Michelle shouted down before sitting up and climbing slowly out of the bath. She wound a huge green towel around herself under her arms and walked across the landing to the bedroom. Philip had just thrown his jacket on the chair and turned to meet her. "Hello," they both whispered as they moved to clasp and kiss each other, first gently, then more urgently. Slowly, Michelle undid his tie, then the buttons of his shirt, kissing him all the while as he stroked her hair and slowly massaged her shoulders. As she began loosening the belt of his trousers, Philip reached for the end of the towel, pulled it from its tuck and began unwinding it. When the towel and his trousers had both dropped to the floor, they stood for what seemed ages pressing each square inch of each other into themselves. Then they lay down on the bed and made love.

Afterwards, Michelle lay on her back, looking up at the ceiling while Philip eased himself up on his left elbow to look at her. "Please don't ever be an asshole to me," she said.

"Not a chance," he replied. "Anyway, I got all my bad behaviour out of my system before I met you. And besides, I was never really with anybody, you know."

"Yes, I know, or at least I think I do," she paused, "as much as I want to anyway. Don't worry though, I'm not going to come over all jealous and possessive on you. I just don't want you to be a bastard, that's all. Anyway, how was your day?"

"Pretty normal. Producing news is a long way from sports." As Philip said this, he relaxed over to his back and swung his legs round onto the rug so he could sit up."

Michelle rolled over and ran her left hand down Philip's spine, from the nape of his neck to his hips. "Politics changes," she said, "but people are still people. At the moment, politics seems fairly cynical, but it doesn't mean what you do has stopped being important."

Philip swivelled round and kissed her, smiling, "You say the nicest, sweetest things, you know. Come on, let's have a drink."

They got dressed, Philip quickly, Michelle more slowly. By the time she got down to the kitchen, Philip was just putting ice in his gin.

"What would you like?" he asked.

"White wine please, I think there's an open bottle in the fridge. I finally got hold of Mary at lunchtime. I said we'd go round on Saturday week; is that okay with you – I don't think we've got anything on!"

"Yes, of course, I'm looking forward to it. I'm conscious you don't know many people in London yet; except the various media types I've dragged you along to meet. And I'd really like you to meet them."

"I do know a few people in London," Michelle was marginally defensive. "But you're right that they're all nurses and doctors, and their social hours aren't great unless you're part of that world. Anyway, it's been great meeting all your 'media' types." Michelle mimicked the quotation marks. "Adrian in particular I really like – he's a bit mad at times but is a terrific laugh."

"Good, I'm pleased," Philip said, smiling and touching her glass with his tumbler.

"But you're right, it would be good to meet up with and get to know Sam and Mary properly. I was so surprised when Sam asked me to their wedding and then I had a much better time than I thought until that friend of Mary's – Linda, I think it was – started getting off with Ingrid's bloke and I ended up leaving early, I was so embarrassed. Which is kind of why it's taken me so long to get up the courage to contact them."

"Yes, I remember you said. Mind you, someone I used to work with in the States once told me he'd got off at a wedding with his girlfriend's sister, who was also his best mate's fiancée, so I guess it could have been worse."

Michelle laughed despite herself. "It sounds like you're just trying to cast your own misdemeanours in a better light. And who exactly was this mate of yours? I'm always comforted by the people you've been hanging out with."

"He was fine actually – brilliant writer, but just a bit…" he paused, "elemental in his approach to life. Oddly though, he ended up marrying the girlfriend's sister, now has four kids, lives in Connecticut and commutes into New York to work in advertising. So, depending on your moral world view, he certainly got his comeuppance."

"The gods are just," said Michelle, still laughing.

"And it gets worse. They already had the date set for their wedding, church and reception booked, everything. They even had the invites printed, though thankfully, not sent out."

"So what? Did they just re-print the invites and keep everything else the same?"

"Yep," replied Philip; "even the guest list didn't change very much, apart from the absence of the original groom and his family for obvious reasons." Michelle was choking with horrified laughter.

"Anyway," Philip continued, "Saturday should be fine."

"What are our options for food tonight?"

***

That following Saturday, Mary had just put the lasagne in the oven when the front doorbell went. She glanced at the clock. "I'll get it," she shouted as she took her apron off and went to the door.

"Michelle, hello, lovely to see you again; we've left it far too long." Mary kissed her on both cheeks. "And Philip, I've been dying to meet you ever since Michelle got in touch to say she had met you and you had both moved to London! Come in and let me get you a drink. Sam's just upstairs bathing Ruth and putting her to bed."

"Hi," Sam shouted down. "I'll be down in five minutes."

Mary mixed some drinks and chatted away amiably. She barely remembered Michelle from the wedding and hadn't noticed she had left early. She thought, however, that Michelle had grown her hair since then, which she now wore in a shoulder-length bob. Mary had been anxious to meet someone Sam spoke so often of. When they had started going out, she had worried slightly about Michelle as a rival but had realised quickly that the thought had never crossed his mind. It had also been true that Mary, who had quite a high opinion of her own looks, character and intellect, did not think a nurse in Nottingham could seriously be a rival. Nothing about the other woman altered this essential judgement but she did take an immediate liking to her and remembered how Ingrid had enjoyed talking to her at the wedding.

Philip she liked too, and thought she could see why Michelle had left nursing to come and live with him in London. He was tall, maybe 6'1", with jet-black hair brushed diagonally back over his right temple. Not even the Hawaiian shirt, which normally would have been taboo, managed to put her off. Sam hadn't found out much about him from his brief phone conversation with Michelle, except that he worked in TV. Mary, however, had got the impression he was English, which made his American accent a bit of a mystery. When she asked, she was surprised to discover Philip had worked in the US for some 15 years, virtually his entire adult life. Despite herself – she was not easily impressed – Mary found herself admiring the young man who'd gone to New York aged 18 and carved out a career for himself.

After about ten minutes, Sam arrived downstairs. "She's dropped off," he announced before giving Michelle a big hug and greeting Philip enthusiastically.

In getting himself a drink, Sam checked everyone else was topped up and, while conversation had been going well enough, it gradually improved, becoming more layered as Sam, keen that everyone should get on, succeeded without being conscious he had tried. Because Sam discerned everyone's motives and sensitivities, with the important exception of his own, he was able to establish links between strands of conversation. And because Sam did not act in this way consciously, he didn't inspire any of the resentment that would typically come with the feeling of being manipulated. It was a high art form, Philip decided. He had seen several people achieve the same but not without revealing in some way they were doing so. It was as if, without realising, Sam was permanently in the zone.

By the time the lasagne was ready, Mary having unusually forgotten to serve the garlic bread as a starter, everyone was laughing and chatting as if they had all been friends for years. Michelle was relieved more than anything. She was also slightly surprised. There had been a fair amount of truth in Philip's comment that it would be good for them to have some friends in London that she had known first, but had doubted Sam and Mary would fit the bill, the other reason she had delayed making contact. She had thought Sam was probably too straight to get on with Philip, or, more precisely, that Philip would be bored talking to him.

As for herself, Michelle had assumed she would find Mary aloof and snobbish. But, being a fair person, she did not look for these traits and simply took Mary as

227

she found her. And not looking for these characteristics, both of which were present, it wasn't these that Michelle noticed. Instead, she saw many of the same qualities that had attracted her to Ingrid when they'd met at the wedding – a transparent generosity and a sharp wit that managed to be sarcastic without, often, being cruel. She also appreciated how good and probably practised a hostess Mary was, not to mention an excellent cook, far better than she was.

Sam was having fun. Partly, he just liked having people round. Until he got married, he knew he had always been fairly reticent, liking people but feeling on the outside of too many conversations. Being married to Mary had changed that. She provided support and purpose where he had before felt isolated and optional. The easy way she moved in social situations never ceased to be a source of wonder, and against her background, he had consciously relaxed.

He saw Philip looking at the records on the sideboard "Why don't you put some music on? Sorry, I should have done so earlier."

"Okay," Philip replied. "I love looking at what records people have," he laughed, "though not in a critical way."

"Don't believe a word of it," interrupted Michelle. "He'll be compiling a psychological profile on your even as we speak. He's the worst person at that I've ever met. Sometimes I think we're only together because I happen to like Bob Marley."

"Well, I'm afraid we're not cool enough to have any of those," said Mary.

"That's fine," said Philip, leafing through the twenty odd albums. "Here, let's try this; it's just old enough it's due to become cool again."

"Nice system," Philip said as he came back to the table.

The hard base began thumping out…

"Oh Phil," Michelle laughed, "What a record to put on! I can't believe you sometimes."

"Relax," he said, "it's just a great record for all that it got overplayed for about five years. And Fleetwood Mac are the ultimate Anglo-American group, so I've always had a bit of a soft spot for them."

"I haven't heard this in ages," said Mary. "But you're right, I used to play it far too much. I so used to want to be Stevie Nicks, and not just because of her voice."

"Wine anyone?" asked Sam, smiling. "I've learned to live with Mary's Lindsey Buckingham obsession. That and the George Harrison poster. Is the American music scene much different from ours? You keep seeing stories about British bands trying to 'break America', I guess the way the Beatles did."

"I don't know really," Philip replied. "It's much bigger, I guess, just in terms of size, and a lot more segmented, partly by geography and partly by race, though there's some crossover now. But Fleetwood Mac is very much a West Coast sound for example, and that's hard for a British band to create without sounding fake."

"I've more or less switched off music the last couple of years; it just no longer seems connected to what's going on," complained Michelle.

"That's just a sign of age," observed Philip, moving his chair back ostentatiously to avoid the kick Michelle was aiming in his direction. "But there's less music about Thatcherism, Red Wedge excepted, than I would have expected."

"Part of it, I think, is that the miners' strike really split the Labour Party, in some ways at least as much as the SDLP has," observed Sam. "It was only a few weeks ago Kinnock finally managed to draw a line under it – sort of anyway. There was a bit of a musical backlash against Thatcher in the early 80s, around unemployment and race, but I think now it's all got a bit too complicated."

"Unless you're someone like Billy Bragg," Michelle was thoughtful. "One of the things the Tories have been very good at is cutting into the Labour vote by offering slices of capitalist goodies, whether it's cheap council homes or virtually free shares in perfectly good nationalised industries. And I think it's even fed through to pop groups, most of which suddenly seem more aspirational or something." She thought again, "Back in the 60s, everyone still wanted to make money but most of them wanted to change something as well. I don't really see that anymore."

"I think you're both being too binary about it," said Philip. "The Beatles would have happened anyway. Same with punk rock – Television and the Ramones would still have done their thing. They were there to rebel against something; it was almost irrelevant what it was. All the comedy songs have always been there. We just hate them more now we're older. But someone like 'Wham!' are just the way they are, same with 'Frankie'."

"Okay, it might not be binary as you put it," argued Michelle, "but all these people are a product of their times; they didn't just pop up out of some artistic cocoon. Anyway, I think he was right to draw a line the other week. I'm also from Nottingham and I think Scargill played right into the Tories' hands. I'd never liked Scargill but until then I thought at least he was smart. Same with Derek Hatton and Militant."

"But I think Labour will have a hard job winning back the middle," said Sam. "The SDLP took a big section of that vote with them."

"Yes, I know, the SDLP really killed us in the last election. Everyone talks about Michael Foot and the manifesto, and the Falklands effect and so on. But without the SDLP, in the depths of a recession, I still think it would have been pretty close."

Mary had been sitting quietly during all this. She was surprised how much she liked Philip and Michelle, but also by how different they were from what she had expected. Previously, she had only had this sort of conversation as a student, or with fellow academics. None of their other friends jumped around subjects like this.

"At a guess," she said, smiling slightly, "I'm more conservative – small c – than the three of you, though I'm probably more accurately termed economically conservative and socially liberal, not 'one of us' as the prime minister would put it. I think Michelle's right about the SDLP. I confess I never quite understood what lay behind all those issues around potential de-selection of MPs, but there was clearly some kind of internecine warfare going on, and so far the Tories have, as far as I can see, been the only beneficiaries of the split."

"I still feel pretty new to this country," observed Philip, "but I've found reporting on political affairs fairly sterile since I came back. As Michelle will tell you," he gave a wry smile, "I've got quite depressed about it all more than once."

"Yes, but it's not just British politics, is it? The Cold War gets to you at least as much."

"That's true but it's the tone of the Cold War more than the fact of it that could drive you mad, and it really shows no signs of changing, despite Reagan and Gorbachev talking more."

"I'm not sure I agree on the last," said Sam, "but there's some evidence the Russians are running out of money. Their economy is partially bankrupt, and Afghanistan is mopping up many more resources than they thought it would."

"But they're a superpower and it's right on their doorstep. Even if the various militia groups are the equivalent of the Vietcong, which I doubt, it's so much closer to home that they must be able to win, whatever kind of war it is."

"I know, that's what I thought too," Sam replied, "and I'm sure it's what Moscow thought. It's mountains rather than jungles, but the disruptive impact on conventional armies, no matter how large, is so obvious they must have included it in their planning. But no matter how much planning they did, it plainly isn't working. I would never have thought it before but I reckon the Kremlin will end up as humiliated in Afghanistan as the US was in Vietnam."

"Well, I'm still depressed," said Philip, "but I'll take your word for it – you're the expert – and I'll be seriously impressed if you're right. By the way, what do you think of Gorbachev?"

"It's a bit early to say but he does appear to be different, though it's hard to imagine he can make any significant change any time soon. It's just too big and monolithic. What do your news people think?"

"To tell the truth, they're pretty sceptical. But they're also excited, I think, because he's the first Soviet leader who you could see making it in a Western democracy. He's got that rapport with crowds and with the media, that skill of speaking in quotable sound bites – hell, they usually even mean something. At the minute we can't get enough of him. And he's educated; and he's married to an intelligent, glamorous woman. You couldn't make it up,"

"The thing that's struck me about him," said Mary, "is that I think he's the first Soviet leader not to have fought in either the revolution or the war. Where he lived was occupied by the Germans I think, but he himself was too young for the Red Army. World War 2 was an infinitely more profound event in Russia than in any other country, apart from maybe Germany and Japan. So many died – I forget the number – and I think he'll just have a different mind-set, less paranoid and defensive."

"I just think it's really striking how different he is, not just to Chernenko and Brezhnev but to Reagan and Thatcher."

Sam was measured. "I don't disagree, but both of them have won two national elections. And I understand all the flaws and biases in the various electoral systems but it's still democracy."

"I know," she replied, slowly breaking into a smile, "but you have to allow me the occasional rant." Michelle was really enjoying the evening. For the first time, she and Philip were meeting her friends, people she'd know first.

Michelle wasn't sure what to make of the evening. For a start, there had been no initial awkwardness; it was as if all four of them had known each other well for years. Then too, Michelle had believed a great barrier had begun to grow between Sam and herself the day he went off to university. But this evening there had been no barriers. Sam's intelligence had slightly intimidated her when they were growing up but tonight it didn't seem to matter either. She could also tell that Philip was enjoying himself. When he didn't like people, he had a habit of starting to talk rubbish with a straight face – clever rubbish but rubbish all the same. Or, if he was bored and they didn't matter to him, he would simply go silent to the point of embarrassment, forcing them to talk nonstop just to fill up the time.

Philip was talking. "What did you think of Live Aid?"

"To be honest, I quite enjoyed it, more than I thought I would," replied Sam. "If you opened the windows in the front bedrooms, you could hear a lot of it across North London. I'm a bit sceptical about how much long-term difference it'll make but basically, I thought it was great."

"What about you, Mary?"

"Well, I'd agree, but I've also been surprised and impressed by the effect the whole thing's had on my students. Maybe they were always like that but I'd thought a lot of the natural idealism people have at that age had been knocked out of them by a mix of mass unemployment and the materialism we were talking about earlier. But it's been a real catalyst for them. And it's not just the T-shirts – we had that with Frankie and 'Relax' a year ago, or whatever – they've started taking much more of an interest in the Third World or at least talking about it a lot more."

"That's interesting," said Philip, "One of the things for me was the global link-up, the way they were able to extend the broadcast from London to Philly. It really was that idea of the world being a global village. And Elvis Costello's version of 'All You Need Is Love' – even Status Quo were great – though I thought the Philly end was pale by comparison, no Michael Jackson, no Diana Ross, Dylan at his incoherent worst."

"Phil absolutely loved it," laughed Michelle. "Apart from American football, I've never seen him shout at the TV so much. You've got to remember he's a bit older than us and a real sucker for all that '60s idealism."

"In that case, he ought to meet Ed," Mary said, "he's really into all that."

"Well, if we ever see him again, we can invite you round," Sam said wryly.

"Why, who is this guy?" Philip asked.

"Oh, we went to university together, he's probably my best friend from Manchester. He came to our wedding, read a lesson, but we haven't seen him at all since, except at Ruth's baptism. Believe it or not, he's her godfather."

"But it's not exactly as if he's ignoring us, is it?" interrupted Mary. "Sorry, you two, I'll explain…Ed's a foreign reporter for the BBC – you see him on TV occasionally – Edward Plummer – and he's basically been overseas since we got married. He's good at writing us the odd letter but we don't actually see him often. He's not home much, and when he is in the UK, he normally goes to see his parents in Derby – who aren't very well – and his sister who still lives there. Anyway, he's really nice and you should definitely meet him if he's ever in London for more than five minutes."

"Do you remember him, Michelle?"

"Not really. I'm pretty sure I didn't talk to him at your wedding. What's he look like? I recognise the name from the news but can't put a face to it."

"Pretty normal really… I don't know, average height; a bit on the thin side; sandy hair, receding a bit; I don't know. Mary, what do you think?"

"Definitely cute but a bit odd, if I'm honest. Or at least he never seems particularly interested in women. I used to think he was gay at first."

"Well, that's really given us a clear picture!" laughed Philip. "So where is he now?"

"From his last letter, he was trying to cover the Iran-Iraq War. Not the easiest job in the world but, like a lot of those guys I imagine, easy has never really been his scene."

"Why the Middle East?" asked Philip.

"I only really know in general terms. He was already working in the region but, just after Mary and I got married, he had an offer to go out to Beirut. Lebanon is in almost permanent civil war as far as I can work out, but Israel was also at the time at war with Hezbollah and had invaded southern Lebanon. I don't know if you remember but that summer the Israelis seemed to have let the Christian militia loose in a couple of Palestinian refugee camps – Sabra and Shatila – I don't know if you remember the names; anyway, it was carnage apparently. Ed was one of the first journalists to get there."

"Yes, I remember the names," said Michelle.

"Anyway, since then Ed seems to have taken any Middle East job going – from his letters, he really loves Lebanon and Jordan in particular. Mostly, he's stayed that side of the region but a few months ago, he was sent to the Gulf to cover Iran-Iraq and as far as I know, he's still there. We've heard a few of his radio reports but only had one letter since. It sounds like WW1 revisited but with nastier weapons."

"When did he say he thought he'd next be back?" asked Mary.

"Early next year," replied Sam. "We'll definitely sort something out."

"Great to meet you at last," said Sam, shaking Philip's hand at the end of the evening. "Michelle and I haven't been very good at organising this – and it took us far too long to get in touch – but at least we've finally got there. You know, this is easily the latest we've stayed up since Ruth was born, voluntarily at least!"

"Yes, well you must come over to us before Christmas, or maybe the four of us could go out in town, if you can get babysitting."

"We'd love to come to you, maybe early next month."

"Lovely to meet you properly," Mary kissed Michelle on both cheeks.

"Yes, well now I'm in London, I hope we can see a lot more of both of you."

"It sounds as though Sam and Philip are trying to plan something," said Mary. "When they fail, we can sort it out."

232

Chapter 24
London, Monday, 13 January 1986

Michelle pulled the pillow over her head to try and shut out the sound of the radio in the shower. It was 7.30am and she'd said she wanted to get up and make Philip breakfast because he was flying to Germany on a business trip for a couple of days. Consequently, he had taken the radio into the shower with him and turned up the volume so he could hear it over the water. The combination was proving fatal to any chance of her drifting back to sleep.

To help the waking process further, she reached out a hand and tossed the duvet off her bare legs, exposing them to the cold January bedroom air. This worked more effectively than any unsupported will-power, and within five minutes she was padding constructively around the kitchen, making coffee and toast and glancing at the headlines in the paper. Heseltine, the Defence Secretary, had just resigned after a huge row with Thatcher over whether Westland, a military helicopter manufacturer in the West Country somewhere, should be taken over by an American firm or a European one. He had wanted the European option, and when Thatcher had predictably over-ruled him, he walked. Philip kept telling her it was enormously significant that someone in the cabinet had openly stood up to her but as far as Michelle could see, nothing had changed. Thatcher was still prime minister and seemed as impregnable as ever. Philip had also tried to explain why the issue itself was important but her eyes had glazed over.

She wasn't sure why she had been so insistent on getting up early. Obviously, it was because otherwise she wouldn't see him for a couple of days but, even nearly two years on, Michelle was still coming to terms with this level of connectedness, so far from anything she had experienced before. Whenever she thought about it, she found it hard to remember with any kind of detail her life in Nottingham. It sometimes seemed as if that decade of her life when she'd been a nurse had been a kind of blip, an extended irregularity that had seemed far more significant at the time. Michelle knew this was wrong, but still couldn't prevent its memory dimming with excessive speed.

She had long ago concluded she loved Philip, but struggled to come to terms with what that meant; and so never used the term, either in public or private. What she did know was that she could see no end to her discovery of little things that added to the richness of his character and his body. The line of hair that extended slightly beyond his hairline down the nape of his neck; the exact way his shoulder blades flexed when he stretched his arms; his habit of putting his hand briefly over his eyes to compose himself when he felt under pressure; the way he would remember, then forget, then remember again, to thank people for little kindnesses; his almost perfect memory for song titles and lyrics; the aura of the unexpected he still carried with him. All these things, as well as the more obvious ones, Michelle could identify and value but she had trouble adding them up into any kind of single description of their relationship.

The kettle was boiling and she looked in the cupboard for the coffee. She lifted down a new jar of Gold Blend, unscrewed the lid and poked a hole in the vacuum-sealed top with a tea spoon, before carefully smelling the aroma of the fresh granules. She'd just put the coffee on the table when Philip breezed in, absent-mindedly trying to do up his tie.

"Oh, thanks, Michelle, that looks fantastic, thanks for getting up too; really appreciate it."

"Turning the radio up so high in the shower didn't give me much choice," she smiled.

"I'm so sorry," Philip replied with mock contrition, "I didn't realise how loud it was."

"You're not very good at apologising," laughed Michelle, "particularly when you don't mean it, but I guess all practice has a value."

"This coffee's lovely," Philip murmured, "it tastes even better than it looks on TV."

"It's a new jar, so I can't take all the credit. What time is your flight?"

"I think it's 12.35," he replied. "I have to go into the office first to pick up a couple of things."

"What's the schedule like when you're out there?"

"Not too bad," Philip replied. "There's a meeting when we get to the hotel, but then a quiet evening, with the real work held over to tomorrow, including a semi-formal dinner. Then it's back on Wednesday morning."

"I'll try not to feel too sorry for you. I'd love to be able to travel to places like Hamburg with work. It's funny, having never gone anywhere apart from Spain a couple of times, I've really caught the travel bug all of a sudden."

"Well, why don't you come with me next time?" suggested Philip. "We'd pay for you normally but you and I could stay together, you could do your own thing while I was having meetings, and I'd maybe be able to stay on an extra day with you before having to go back to work."

"Maybe," Michelle replied, slightly cagily, "it depends where your next trip is, and I'd have no idea what to do there. Also, I'm pretty clear about not wanting to interfere in your work or anything. I'd be worried your colleagues would see me as some kind of floozy. That's one of my granny's words."

"Don't worry, it's one of my granny's as well; look, I'm going to leave it completely up to you. But none of the people I work with would think anything of it provided we transparently paid your own way. Anyway," he grinned, "unfortunately, the next time I'm away is likely to be Barcelona."

"Phil, you're evil!" she said, looking for something to throw at him. Finding only a dish towel, she thought better of staining his suit. Instead, she spontaneously reached across the table and grabbed his hand. "Go easy on me just occasionally. This is all still new to me and I'm trying so hard. I like it when you tease me, like now, but please not always. I've never felt this way before and I don't want it to end."

Philip gave her hand a small squeeze, "I don't either, remember. This is as new and as special to me, and I have no intention of letting it go."

Michelle glanced at the clock, "But in the meantime," she said, "you have to get to Heathrow via your office, so you need to be out of here in the next five minutes."

"Okay, I've packed, and so I only need to finish this coffee... There you go, done."

When Philip had gone, Michelle went and had her own shower, dressed and came back downstairs, wondering whether to go out or stay in. It was a bitterly cold day but she had arranged to have lunch with Mary and didn't want to sit cooped up in the house until then, so she decided to wander down into town and browse the bookshops on Charing Cross Road, maybe pop into the National Gallery for a cup of tea. She was down to three days a week at the GP's now and this was a day off.

London looked miserable as she emerged from the Underground on the edge of Trafalgar Square. It was cloudy and freezing cold, and the watery mid-winter light, even in mid-morning, did little more than silhouette Nelson's Column against the vast stone exterior of the National. Normally busy with tourists and at least a smattering of parents with pre-school children, even in winter, the Square was almost deserted, this at just before 11am.

Michelle liked walking slowly around, negotiating the traffic that tried to pelt around its perimeter, looking up and down the different spokes that entered it from various directions. In particular, she enjoyed looking up Whitehall and down the Mall – somehow thinking about them that way around seemed to fit best: the latter through Admiralty Arch, which then opened out to take in Horse Guards Parade and St James' Park on the left and stretching back to Buckingham Palace; the former looking more lived in, with the Cenotaph halfway down. She liked them but, still, these buildings all seemed too imposing and imperial, totally out of scale with anything that could possibly be appropriate in a country like Britain at the end of the 20th century.

These thoughts were genuine but Michelle was conscious they were only echoes of the countless people who had previously walked there. Even so, there were a few days when Michelle felt terribly, irretrievably alone, even in the midst of a typical West End throng of humanity. At these moments, even Philip and the house she knew she was returning to all shrank to insignificance, stripped of meaning in a desensitised world where no one said hello.

Michelle gave a good deal of the credit for her general equilibrium to Philip for unfailingly giving her as much space as she needed. What she didn't give herself credit for was the patience and open-heartedness with which she had approached moving to London and making her new life there. Michelle had the happy knack of expecting most things to be difficult without being in the least bit daunted by them.

She had learnt to all but eliminate the break-downs, and if success eluded her, she would attempt to re-group before attempting a different route to achieving her ambition. This strategy had been painfully acquired as a trainee nurse who had gradually weaned herself away from an obsession with perfection.

None of this had any role to play in Michelle's decision to go into nursing after A levels, rather than go to university as Sam had done. That decision had been rooted in class, economics and a fear she would be found out somehow, discovered to be stupid and sent packing. University to Michelle was so much more than a way to a good job. Instead, it was the gateway to wisdom, but of a sort that was brutally competitive and meritocratic, devoid of compassion and callous in its treatment of those who couldn't cut it.

This feeling of vulnerability and unworthiness had begun to evaporate when she moved to London and began mixing socially with people who assumed university was part of the natural progression. It helped that Philip had himself left school at 18 and showed no sign of being overawed or less intelligent. She began volunteering opinions, asking more questions, talking about books she had read in a way she wouldn't have dreamt of doing only a few months before.

Consequently, her interests had spread, and increasingly she began to venture into cinemas, museums and galleries, first mainstream ones and then, to her own shock, art house cinemas, contemporary art shows and niche museums, to several of which she had become a familiar visitor. In this context, her visits to the National Gallery had taken on the character of regular meetings with a good friend; Michelle felt at home wandering its vast but intimate halls, looking again at paintings she knew and taking time to visit a couple of new rooms. As usual, she ended her mini tour with what had become a ritual of gazing at Goya's 'Maja desnuda' in awe at the subject's knowing gaze.

At school, Michelle had imagined evolution as a fairly rapid process, with each generation, having gone through some process of selection, being almost tangibly more advanced – wiser, stronger – than those preceding it. Some apparent evidence was available to support her view: in the seeming remorseless advance of science, vast improvements in nutrition and life expectancy, and even the endless tumbling of sports records. Even within her own lifetime, humanity had seemed to be getting better.

Michelle had always known there were flaws in this reasoning. If we were getting better at living longer, we were also becoming more efficient at killing each other, although it seemed possible to attribute the mass murders of the 20th century to individuals – Hitler, Stalin, Pol Pot – in a way that somehow allowed you to separate out the terrible events from the general, always onward, march of human history. But in the last year, Michelle's increasing acquaintance with art had challenged all this. Goya's faces were full of the character of his subject and led inevitably to the conclusion that these people of almost two centuries ago were every bit as virtuous and vice-ridden, as rational or irrational in their motives and actions, as any late 20th century subject.

This process of discovery and the consequent revising of assumptions also changed Michelle's perspective in other ways.

As a consequence, faith in her own ability rose, and Michelle began to consider whether she might not have been too frightened by the idea of studying at university. This thought was always tempered, however, by the memory of Sam and by the thought of Mary, probably the most daunting person she had met. And here she was having lunch with her.

The two had agreed to meet at 1pm in an Italian restaurant in New Oxford Street, just south of the British Museum, and as usual Mary was already there. The two women hugged and kissed, a custom that Michelle, naturally less tactile, was still struggling to adjust to.

"Hi there, sorry I'm late."

"No need to apologise at all; it was me who was early."

"Yes, but you're always early and I never am," laughed Michelle.

"How are you anyway?" asked Mary as they sat down, "When was it Philip was going off to Germany? Is it today?"

"Yes, he'll be getting on the plane about now."

"So you've got two days of freedom?"

"I wouldn't put it quite like that. After all, Phil doesn't exactly have lots of set routines, quite the opposite, in fact."

"Yes, I suppose you're right. Sam's much more a creature of habit, uncomfortable if his routine changes too much."

"Funny, he used to be pretty spontaneous but that was when he was a teenager and I guess university can change people a lot."

"Yes, for all the time I've known him, Sam's liked most things to be familiar." She changed the subject, "What have you been up to this morning?"

"Oh, I've just been to the National Gallery, I hadn't been since November or something and I was missing it."

"I haven't been myself in years," replied Mary. "What did you look at this morning?"

"Well, lots of things really," replied Michelle, colouring a little. "I've spent most of my time looking at portraits, Rembrandt and so on, the Goya."

"What do you like about them?"

"Let me think, I think it's that I see so much character in the paintings, including characters that I recognise bits of in the people around me. And I love the fact of seeing strengths and weaknesses, yearnings and wisdom, portrayed in people from centuries ago in ways that are also completely contemporary. And to be honest, I've really enjoyed just looking at the paintings and trying to find out who their subjects were, or what they are about." Michelle spoke with an occasionally slight quaver in her voice, and deliberately, trying to decipher meaning in her own words even as she uttered them.

"You clearly have spent a good deal of your time looking at paintings," Mary remarked, "I hadn't realised how important art had become to you. I'll tell you what, I must introduce you to Lauren, our professor of Art History, the two of you would get on brilliantly. Come on, let's order."

Michelle sat back, stunned, only just managing to order a pizza while Mary went for a Caesar salad. Both women ordered sparking water before Michelle added a bottle of Peroni at the last minute.

"How's Ruth?" she asked.

"Oh, she's fine! It's hard to believe she'll be four soon. You and Philip must come around for drinks after the party by the way. We'll need some adult sanity in the evening after the mayhem of the afternoon. Sam really enjoys them, runs all the games, you can imagine. As for me, it just leaves me exhausted. He's a classic new man dad, does the glamorous bits of housework and childcare."

"We'd love to come over," said Michelle, slightly interrupting. "I'll need to check with Philip whether he's free but I'm 99% sure we can come. I'm sure it's stressful but you'll look back on these days sometime and miss them. I have lots of friends who had kids when they were young, and they all think back to these days, especially when their children were between about three, and then about nine, with enormous fondness. And as for Sam, well you know him far better, but whenever I get to talk to him it's incredibly hard work to get him to talk about anything else but Ruth."

"Yes, he is besotted, classic father and daughter relationship. I remember when she was born, he insisted on being there, which wasn't so common, and I recall him just gazing at her."

"He's always had that fascination with young life and the miracle of birth," said Michelle, "I remember him being completely overcome when we had a school trip to a local farm – we were about 13 I think – far more than any of the other boys. In some ways, I'm still slightly surprised he didn't end up as a doctor or vet."

"Yes, he's talked to me about that too," replied Mary. "His line was that because, or so he believed, he didn't have the ability to be the doctor he wanted to be he didn't want to be a doctor at all."

"I didn't know that. Do you think he's ever regretted it?" Michelle asked.

"I don't know, to tell you the truth," replied Mary. "He keeps things like that very close to his chest, and in some ways I think I wouldn't be the first person he'd choose to talk to about it. For all his perfectionist tendencies, it's not his style to let things fester. He prefers to move on."

"How are you both anyway?" asked Michelle. "It seems ages since New Year."

"Not too bad. Sorry, I should really be more sympathetic but Sam's had a dreadful cold since the middle of last week, and even having just said how positive he is normally, it's really been getting him down so that he spent all of yesterday moping around the house, really not knowing quite what to do with himself. Maybe he should have been a doctor, given how poor a patient he is."

"And how's your work?" asked Michelle.

"Quite good really. There seems to be more and more admin involved, but to tell you the truth, it's a fantastic job to have."

"What are your students like?"

"They're very talented, though not all of them are quite as good as they think they are."

"Is it true what I read in the paper about students these days being more focussed on getting a job than about enjoying university?"

"That's hard to say definitively. There's certainly more talk about it, but on the other hand, the graduate job market is probably the easiest it's been for six or seven years. Now that may be a lag effect from the recession, or it could be simply that the same proportion of people are acquisitive, go-getting types as in previous cohorts of students, but they're a lot more open and proud about it than maybe they were. But also students from UCL and the other better known universities, provided they get 2:2s or better, have never really struggled to find work if that's what they want."

As the two women began to eat, Michelle ventured into a subject she had been avoiding asking Mary about. "We don't really agree on politics, do we?"

Mary smiled and sipped her water. "No, but don't worry about it. I don't really agree about politics with many of my work colleagues, or with Sam for that matter; so I don't see any need for it to be a barrier between us."

"Good, I'd be horrified if I thought it was or would be. It's just we've sort of skirted around the subject more or less since we met, and I don't want it to turn into some kind of taboo."

"It's not at all. As far as I know, all my family vote Conservative and always have done; certainly that's how I was brought up, reading Daily Telegraph editorials and Op Eds. And I voted for Margaret Thatcher in '79 and '83, but for what it's worth, I probably won't next time."

"Really! Can I ask why?"

"Yes, of course," Mary was matter of fact. "For a start, my family's quite old Conservative and there's a certain set of values that come with that which I inherited. So I'm sceptical of unions but I don't hate them; I believe in society and the importance of community and social structures, and I believe in high quality state education – how could I not? – And in the NHS and in the BBC. But I also believe we can't spend money we haven't got – not down to the last penny but in the sense of knowing clearly how we're going to repay what we borrow. And ultimately, I believe market capitalism is the best option available to us; it has its faults and it causes more casualties than I'm comfortable with, but as far as I can tell all the alternatives are worse, and many of them simply don't work at all.

"So I was comfortable with balancing the budget and with most of the stuff around union reform. I'm sorry if you disagree. And I was also pretty comfortable with the Falkland's Wars, not least because Galtieri was such a farcical dictator, although some of the Tory rhetoric around it stretched the bounds of conscience. And I'd like to think we can celebrate our victories without seeming to glorify the death of Argentine soldiers but, as Ed reminds me, that may well be expecting too much. And I thought the country needed a lot of what Thatcher offered in her first term. And to be honest, Labour and the other parties weren't really offering much of a realistic alternative. I hope I don't sound callous here?"

"No, not at all,"

"Good," Mary smiled. "Thank you for bearing with me. To my surprise, I quite liked Michael Foot – you get so much more exposure to a person when they become a party leader. Perhaps I warmed to his humanity and the elegance of his arguments. But in terms of leading a party as dysfunctional as Labour were then, he was completely the wrong person, and try as I could, seeing him as a prime minister was even harder."

"And so what changed for you since '83?" asked Michelle. Inside she was slightly bristling but it wasn't much of a stretch to imagine Mary spending hours in debate with Michael Foot.

Mary was taking the chance to eat some of her Caesar salad. "This is quite good," she remarked. "I've had better but not much, we should come here again. So for me, I don't think it was so much a case of '83 being the landmark but rather the '84 miners' strike. Now don't get me wrong, I had no time for Arthur Scargill. I thought he was a terrible leader of the NUM and I think it was a strike the government simply had to win. But a lot of the way the government conducted the strike and the attitudes it revealed towards ordinary working people made me think it wasn't really a party I was comfortable voting for any more."

"What sort of thing?" asked Michelle.

"Well, Orgreave is the most obvious. But what happened, I think, was more poisonous, more insidious. There was just this whole sub-rhetoric about the strikers all being extremists and, at the same time, the virtual absence of any recognition there were wider social problems stemming from the decline, and now almost death, of coal as a mass employer. So I found it incongruous that we could create a quasi-national police force to prevent secondary picketing, but can do nothing for the dozens of mining villages that will be full of unemployed men and their families living on benefits, with no realistic prospect of finding a job. Apart from anything else, that will likely leave a legacy of dependency that we'll be living with for generations."

"You sound almost like a socialist,"

Mary laughed, "Well, I'm a long way from being a socialist, you can trust me on that, but as I said, I do believe in communities and in a proper safety net."

"Ah, let me guess, you're going to vote Liberal," volunteered Michelle.

"Well, no actually, I suspect I'll be voting Labour, strange as it may seem."

"You're joking!" exclaimed Michelle, laughing.

"Okay, well I'll explain and you can tell me if I've gone mad." Somehow, both women had finished their food and Mary sat back, clearly having fun. "So, once I started thinking it through, if I was going to vote for someone other than the Conservatives, it was because I wanted another party to win the general election, or at least for the Tories not to win it. And I was deciding not to vote Conservative rather than positively deciding to vote for another party. So, partly I would be voting to make a change for change's sake and partly because I thought a change would be at least marginally better than the current government. So on the basis that Labour came second in my constituency, with the Liberals and SDP well behind, it was really a case of Labour or nothing. Maybe I've just got a soft spot for Welsh orators."

"Mary, you amaze me more every time you speak!" said Michelle. "They should put you on a party political broadcast, that's what they should do."

"You must promise not to try and convert me," warned Mary.

"That's fine, I've never been a great evangelist."

"Thank you!" Mary lowered her head in a mock bow. "By the way, what's the time? Let's see, just time for coffee. What do you think?"

"If you've got the time, that would be great," Michelle replied. "Let's wave at a waitress." When the coffee came, the two women sat back in silence, newly-relaxed.

"Coming to live in London has been easier than I feared," said Michelle, "still hard for someone like me who'd scarcely been here before but it could have been much harder. What I mean to say is that Philip and I really value your friendship."

"Don't be ridiculous, what else would we have done? You're probably Sam's oldest friends, and you're both a pleasure to be with. You really must stop doing yourself down. It's not as if we've done you any kind of favour. We would if you'd needed it but you don't, so we haven't."

Michelle looked sheepish, "I feel properly told off now."

"I do like London," confessed Mary, "but then I grew up here and it's different I think when you instinctively know your way around. I remember Sam telling me that when he first arrived, he spent ages working out how the topological map of the Underground fitted over the top of the A-Z, in other words where Tube stations actually were in relation to each other. His favourite was the realisation that if he wanted to go to Leicester Square, he was better getting out at Piccadilly Circus rather than changing from the Bakerloo to the Piccadilly."

"That sounds just like him," laughed Michelle. "I suppose coming here would have been a big shift for him as well. He was always much more a lover of the countryside when we were growing up than I was."

"And how does Philip find London after so long in New York?"

"Interestingly, not very different to me, which was a surprise at first," Michelle answered. "I thought that after living in New York for so long, London would have been a comedown, if anything. But in fact, he saw New York, LA and all that, as his American experience. So coming back home to the UK was like him becoming the teenager from Bristol again, who had maybe been to London once on a school trip and had no idea how to get around the place."

"And how does he find it?"

"He likes it a lot, but I think if you asked him he'd say it was a slightly slower pace here, but also that some of that would probably be down to the change in his own lifestyle."

"So it's all down to you!"

Michelle held up both her hands, "Sorry, I didn't put it quite right. I think part of the reason Phil took the job back here in London was to draw a line and move on from a particular part of his life – more a volume or two than a chapter – not because he didn't like it or was ashamed of anything, but because I don't think he wanted to be doing the same things in his 40s, that he'd been doing in his 20s."

"You really know him well, don't you, and you've thought a huge amount about this whole thing."

"Well, I don't know about that, but he does talk about wanting to move on and about coming back to the UK as part of that, I think he had a pretty wild time when he was in America, you know; young, free and single, moving from one city to the next, reporting on sport."

"Really!" Mary was interested, "I'd never have guessed from the way he is now; though now you say it, there is something about him that means I'm not completely shocked, but still…"

"Well, you'd have been even less surprised if you'd been at that party in Nottingham where we met. He was definitely a player, loved female attention. And he's pretty honest about it, about having had more than his share of one night stands, but without going into detail. Sometimes I wish he would, because I sort of think we should know everything about each other, but mostly I'm cool about it."

"Wow! I'm surprised you're so relaxed; I'm not sure I would be, but like I said, he does appear to have genuinely changed. So if that's what he was like, how did you get his attention? – I can't see you as the fawning type. Sorry, I hope you don't mind me asking?"

"No, of course not, I don't think anyone ever really properly knows how they get together with someone other than the sexual attraction bit. It's a lot easier to tell a story about it afterwards than to understand what was going on at the time. But for a start, I found him quite arrogant and so I was slightly offhand in response. I quite liked him, partly because he fairly obviously wasn't getting off on the attention that was coming his way, so I rescued him from it, and then we both got drunk on red wine and lived happily ever after."

Chapter 25
New York, Thursday, 6 October 1988

Carol was just back from covering the Seoul Olympics. Danny had agreed to meet in a SoHo coffee bar and was waiting when she arrived. He liked how Carol's hair was starting to fleck with grey and, not having seen her for three months, was attracted again by her smile; it always had gotten to him.

"So how was it?" he asked when she'd ordered and settled herself. "Everything here has been about Ben Johnson and Flo Jo."

"I'm not surprised," Carol answered. "It was absolute mayhem. I've never seen anything like it. The amazing thing about Johnson is that it didn't affect the Games more. I mean, with it being the 100m, it could easily have derailed the entire meeting. But somehow the rest of the athletics pretty much went off as you would expect. But seriously, I've never seen anything like it in sport. The media didn't really know what to do with themselves. I mean we've more or less known for years that steroid abuse was pretty common in the power events of Track and Field, and even rumours around Johnson himself, but no one expected it to break open at the Olympics, still less in the 100. I mean I've never had so much trouble just physically filing a story, nor have I had so much demand for copy. But everyone was the same. What did it feel like back here?"

"As you'd expect. At least it wasn't an American, but of course, it was a Canadian and that's given the whole thing a special angle, particularly since Lewis ended up getting gold."

"Yes, I can imagine. Although, to be honest, the biggest story for me was probably Flo Jo and Jackie Joyner Kersee, who between them pretty much tore up the record book. There were rumours there too but I guess they got tested and passed."

"And what was Seoul like?"

"Quite weird really; I mean the city itself was absolutely fine, although a bit of a construction site. The facilities and so on were terrific, and the Korean people did everything they could to make the Olympics a success. And they tried to fill the events as much as possible, and there were still occasions where they ended up bussing in school kids to fill out the standing for the sports like field hockey. But I think that's okay – Seoul is hard to get to and the core support for a specific sport could easily have found it difficult, and expensive probably. That said, the place was still an international party for the entire duration and I loved every minute, even if I'm getting a bit old for this sort of lifestyle," she laughed. "The place everyone hung out was called Itaewon and there were a couple of bars there called the King Club and the Seoul Club; I swear I'm not making this up, it was like something out of a Bond movie."

"Sounds like you had a great time. Here, it's just been another typical New York summer."

"Did you get away at all?"

"Not really, maybe a couple of weekends. My mother's quite ill and was in hospital a lot of the time; she's finally gone into a care home, which is where she should have been for the last year or so."

"I'm sorry," said Carol. "Where is she? When can I go and visit?"

"Well, she's up state, near where my sister's family is, near Albany. It's been quite hard, particularly on Veronica. I've done what I can but I'm really not that good at that sort of thing. Still, it's what happens and we all have to go through it, I guess. I'm going up there in three weekend's time if you want to come but don't feel like you need to."

"I'm not sure what I'm doing then but I'll have a look and come if I can." She changed the subject. "I'm having dinner with Phil tonight; he flew in from London a couple of days ago."

"Oh, say hi for me." Danny had had an idea to ask Carol out for dinner but now that would have to wait. He quite liked Philip but somehow they had never quite hit it off. "How's he doing?" Danny continued, slightly lamely.

But Carol's mind was already jumping ahead and she failed to notice. "How's Wall Street? Still pulling in the cash? I swear, and I know you've tried to explain it to me, but I still don't get what you do and why there's so much money in it."

Danny cheered up. "Ha ha, you always say that; like I told you, it's about very small percentages of very large amounts of money on the one hand, and on the other, large fees for thinking up complicated structures that enable clients to do really expensive things."

"I don't know," replied Carol, "a lot of it still sounds like someone's getting ripped off somewhere."

"That's cos you've become a socialist with all your travelling around and consorting with all sorts of commies. You're in danger of forgetting what it is to be American, the greatest nation on earth, baby."

Now they were both laughing, comfortable in their familiar banter. "Why, your mother and father would think you were becoming a Republican the way you're talking," Carol retorted. "Anyway, you should get out more. Why you don't even have a passport anymore! Go get one; travel, see a little of the world."

"Maybe one of these days, but work's busy right now and it's hard to get away. But seriously, Carol, what was Seoul really like? I mean, my knowledge of Korea is watching MASH every week."

"It was good. The people were as lovely as you'd expect, and incredibly polite and helpful. They're still really paranoid about the North though. I went up to the border once, the DMZ, and it really is one of the strangest places. At least the Berlin Wall looks like what it is and you can see the other side the way you can when it's a normal border. But this is like a big stretch of normal countryside, hundreds of yards wide, except no one can live there; there are millions of mines apparently. No one I spoke to has any idea how they would even begin to go about clearing them. And I also saw a TV programme about how they would deal with, wait for this, the North

Koreans attacking Seoul by sending soldiers parachuting into the Olympic Stadium! I tell you, weird doesn't begin to describe it."

***

Later, and after a couple of hours' casual shopping, Carol met Philip at an Italian restaurant they had frequented during their time working for SI in the '70s. The place was a little more upmarket than in the early days, but Girolamo, the owner, still recognised Philip when he walked in, despite his not having been there for over four years.

"Ah, Filippo, how goes it? Why you no come and see us anymore? You used to be a good customer but now you desert me." The two men hugged.

"Hello, Giro," said Philip. "It's hard getting here from England for the evening but you're right, I should try harder. Still," and he waved his arms appreciatively at the refurbishment that had noticeably taken place since he was last here, "I see you've invested the profits from the party I had before I left."

"Filippo, what a night that was!" and the small, neat but prosperous-looking Florentine paused as if in genuine reminiscence.

Carol had been sitting discreetly at the bar watching the scene with amusement but now decided to break the spell. After all, Phil was hers for the evening. "Phil!" she exclaimed and, walking over to the two men, she politely acknowledged the restaurateur before hugging Philip for herself. "I can't believe it's been so long," she said, "almost two years. When did you get in?" she knew the answer but it was a way of steering Philip away from the other conversation and towards the table she'd reserved.

Girolamo took the brush-off as politely as it was intended – it was his lot – and accompanied them graciously to their table. "The first drink must be on me," he offered. "Champagne for such a reunion?" Carol looked at Philip then nodded. "Two glasses of champagne it shall be," he concluded, bowing slightly as he turned away.

"To be honest," said Philip, "I didn't recognise him at first. He's filled out a bit since I was last here – most restaurateurs do, I guess." He paused. "Not getting any younger are we?"

"Phil, you're still a total arsehole. I thought Michelle would have trained or beaten that out of you by now."

"She has, but there's something about being here with you that has me reverting to type. And you look great, I mean it."

"Yes, like you always do," Carol replied. "It's good to see you haven't changed; it's important to have some things you can rely on in this world. But tell me what's been happening, and I need to hear more about Michelle."

"She's fine, sends her love. Really must get you two together sometime. Or perhaps not; you know far too much about my sordid past."

"Yes, we're both relatively respectable now, but then the times have changed as well."

"They have indeed," responded Phil. "By the way, how is Reagan's America these days?"

"Almost at an end, thank God, but Bush looks very likely to win next month, so we'll have at least another four years of almost the same."

"Never as bad though. I remember Reagan in '68, and you could see he was becoming the darling of the Republican Right even then, but no one imagined he'd end up president."

"Well, here we are, heading for a minimum 12 years of a Republican White House, though did you see Bentsen take Quayle downtown on Tuesday?"

"Yes, I did, if only Dukakis could do the same to Bush."

"Don't worry, Phil, one thing I've learnt is the wheel always keeps turning. Besides, you should be thinking about your life in London with Michelle. Many times more important than pining for a misremembered youth. Here comes the champagne, Giro's doing you proud, I never get this kind of treatment."

They clinked glasses and both drank. Philip savoured the sensation, letting the bubbles linger around his gums before swallowing. "Good," he said, "I had a rotten night's sleep – jetlag always seems to hit me worse in this direction. I feel fine at the moment but at some point later on the hammer might come down, and you'll have to kick me to keep me awake."

"I'll just have to dazzle with my scintillating conversation then."

"I'm looking forward to it! Tell me about Seoul. How bad was the whole Johnson thing?"

"It was terrible! The day after, the Canadian team, who'd been pretty upbeat before, had a huge banner hanging from their apartment block window saying 'Hero to Zero in 9.79secs'. Rumours were going around like you wouldn't believe, and your guy Christie almost lost his bronze medal. I don't know how much of a game-changer this is but it's pretty big. The biggest race of the entire Games, with the biggest viewing figures, everything, just turned to dust because of a couple of tiny test tubes of urine containing traces of stanozolol. My guess is the IOC, even Samaranch, will now feel they need to sort the whole thing. God knows what it means for the Eastern Bloc if they have to start doing serious testing. And there are already rumours Flo Jo will retire. And even for someone who starts off as cynical as me, it changes your perspective when someone like Johnson is exposed, so that you begin to see super-fast times, unusual disqualifications, even normal PBs for Christ's sake, through a more suspicious lens."

"It was huge in the UK, and the BBC did a decent job of covering it all. I guess there were always some doubts about Johnson but you're right, the reality of it does change the way you view everything else. For a start, it smashed the myth that taking drugs was something only the Eastern Bloc did. How much do you think goes on in the US?"

Carol's face darkened further. "I don't know," she said, "but it's impossible not to fear the worst. After all, drugs aren't exactly alien to American culture. It could be going on in any state, in any sport; and it's not just the money, though being Olympic champion in virtually anything will essentially make you for life. The place I'd worry about most though, if I were the USOC, would be athletes training on the West Coast with all that body building culture going on around them. That's not to say athletes out there are any more likely to be cheats, but the temptation might well be greater, the supply more accessible."

"There is an awful lot of US sprint athletes out in California. You realise what you're saying."

"Absolutely," replied Carol. "Which is why I chose my words. But come on, it's not too hard to imagine the possible conversations is it? You know, along the lines of 'everyone's doing it, you're just levelling the playing field…the stuff's really good, it gives you the aggression to train harder…it helps you recover faster between sessions…you'll get to look like Arnie, pull lots of chicks,' and so on."

"Okay," said Philip, "I get it. It all sounds pretty scary."

"If you were out in Seoul, believe me you'd feel exactly the same. We haven't gone there yet but if anything the female side has the potential to be worse. After all, a little extra testosterone goes a good deal further. On the one side there's the Eastern Bloc and all those jokes in the early 80s about how masculine and muscled many of their women looked. I always thought a lot of the world records in the '70s were quite soft – some fabulous athletes like Irena Szewinska but not a lot of depth, and a widespread caution about burdening female athletes with the same volume and intensity of training as men. Now I suspect a good deal of change since then has been about closing that gap but…" she paused, "let's just say it'll take an awfully long time before a lot of the existing women's records are broken."

"I confess I'm slightly out of touch," confessed Philip, "but I know what you mean."

"I swear to God," said Carol, "it's the biggest threat sport faces. Chemical manipulation distorts sport, it changes results, penalises the innocent – and corrupts them, makes them cynical. And it also places that question mark in spectators' minds. 'What am I seeing here? Is it hard work and talent, or is it a lab experiment?' What I don't know is how cynical people can become before they start not turning up, not switching on their television or reading the sports pages."

"Do you think this is all confined to Olympic sports?" asked Philip.

"Well, there's no reason to assume so, is there?" Carol replied, "Few other sports conduct testing at all and football is an obvious game where steroids would make a difference. Have you seen the size of some of those linemen and line backers? Big, fast, aggressive. But baseball could be just as vulnerable – sluggers, fastball pitchers."

"Come on," said Philip, finishing his champagne, "let's order and talk about something a bit more cheerful." They ordered and then sat back looking at each other.

"Do you know," said Carol, "we've known each other almost exactly 20 years?"

"God, that's right," said Philip. "Mexico City, not a particularly classy establishment, if I remember. The tequila was okay though and so was the company."

"You were such a young Englishman back then; I started wondering who'd let you out by yourself."

Philip laughed loudly. "You've never said that before but I've always wondered what you thought. Anyway, you should have seen me nine months earlier when I first showed up in New York. That was when I was really green; by the time I got to Mexico, I'd grown up a fair bit. I knew nothing about sports reporting back then."

"And then you fell in love with it and did nothing else for the next ten years. Even then, though, you couldn't half write. After the USOC sent Tommie Smith and John Carlos home, I still recall you writing that Brundage was 'a man lost in history, composing a narrative no one would read while attempting to trivialise the issues that are re-shaping Olympic sport. History will not be kind to him'. But enough; tell me about London. Anyway, how's the job?"

"Pretty much fine," replied Philip. "It pays well and it's interesting, or at least not boring most of the time. It's a hell of a long way from troubleshooting on SI though. At its best, not much beats pure sports journalism."

"Yes, but you've got them rose-tinted glasses on again. It's a terrible business as well for trying to find a new angle and going beyond mere opinion."

"But you're never going to do anything else, are you?" Philip retorted.

"Of course not," laughed Carol, "it's in my soul and I've always known I was in it for the duration."

"I know," said Philip, "and I've never been like that, always envied your certainty."

"You've changed though, haven't you?" said Carol, "Certainly, from the way you talk. I never thought you'd settle down but sitting across from you here, it's obvious that you have. So what is it – you've never really said – about Michelle?"

"I don't quite remember you asking," Philip replied, "but you're right, I've never really tried to explain. And you're also right that I have settled down. I don't know, I always reckon no one else would really be interested. Is that a really male thing to say?"

Carol nodded. "Definitely."

"It's funny, there are a lot of different factors: going back to England to live after 15 years; making a pretty permanent home in London after effectively being on the road for so long; perhaps oddly, I think my parents' dying has made a difference; and then there's that thing about hitting your mid-30s."

"I understand all that," said Carol, "but she's clearly a big part of it. You don't have to make a souvenir out of her; giving her a bit of credit isn't the same as putting her on a pedestal."

"I just want to be careful about not presenting her as having succeeded in some kind of crusade. Because actually, one of the things about her is that, aside from yourself, she's about the only woman I've ever met who's not tried to reform me."

"Really?"

"Yes, really, hand on heart, Michelle essentially took me as I was. She's genuinely not interested in my previous life, how many women I slept with or any of that, but I'm as sure as I can be that there's nothing about myself I could tell her that would make the slightest difference to our relationship. Somehow, she made a pretty early call on me – within a couple of dates."

Carol was incredulous, "You mean she doesn't care about anything you did before, she's not even interested! Are you sure?"

"Yes, I think so," replied Philip. "We've been together over four years now, and as far as I can tell, it's never crossed her mind."

"It sounds like she's maybe sensitive about it and doesn't want to hear," Carol suggested.

"I thought that too to start with, but to be honest, Michelle's not really the sensitive sort. She knows young men often step out of line, o stupid things they later regret. So I don't think she'd be remotely surprised if she knew all the things about me you do for instance, which is pretty much all there is to know."

"And she was a nurse when you met her?"

"Basically yes," said Philip, "had been for more than ten years, since she left school."

"And so while you were shotgunning your way around the States, getting laid at most opportunities, Michelle was looking after ill people in hospitals? It's a bit like a young Mother Teresa deciding to shack up with Mick Jagger."

He then told Carol about how the two of them had reacted to the current presidential campaign, which was seeing the Democrat Michael Dukakis being ripped to shreds by Republican attack ads that focused on his pardoning of Willie Horton. Michelle had been outraged by the twisting of the truth and the unremittingly personal slurs, while he had focused on the fact that the Democrats' New Deal coalition was fatally fractured.

Carol laughed, "I see what you mean; you always have been weirdly uninvolved when it comes to elections. But I have to say, I'm completely on Michelle's side in this one. I reckon '68 was the only time I've known you care about a specific election, although well before ballot time we all knew it was a lost cause."

"There was 1980 too, but more or less the same applied," interrupted Philip.

"Yes, I recall you not being our current president's biggest fan."

"No, not exactly. For me he never stopped acting."

"Is that why you left, why you went back to the UK?" Carol suddenly sat up. "It is, isn't it? I could never work it out before; the idea of you being headhunted by the British never quite made sense. That was a lie, wasn't it?"

Philip sat back, "I can smile about it now," he said. "It wasn't quite that simple, there were other factors, but you're right that I did apply. I'd begun to feel a bit of a pull back home since my dad died but Reagan beating Carter, and then seeing what he did, was probably the biggest part of it. If I'd been American I'd have stayed, and don't forget I went back to Thatcher's Britain, which was ideologically the same but grimmer, without the jokes and the charm. But I always thought there was something darkly cynical to him, a kind of conscious Jekyll and Hyde thing, where he could do bonhomie, play everyone's favourite granddad to perfection, and at the same time be this very inflexible, ideological fanatic. Iran-Contra says it all for me."

Carol was silent for a few long moments. "I've been so stupid for so long," she said finally. "You were so animated about US politics when I first met you in '68, and then all the time since you've been virtually silent about our great democracy. At least you're a full-on Liberal, why didn't you tell me? There was I thinking – how could I have? – That you were – or had become – a typically non-political sports reporter. You know the sort – 'they're all the same, politics is shit anyway'. And I always wondered why I liked you so much – God only knows you tried often enough to piss me off!"

"I know, I just wanted to test you occasionally. The thing was, 1968 had a real impact on me. I was only 18, remember, and pretty impressionable. I lost a lot of my faith in how politics work right there, which is why I'll never be able to get passionate about it as Michelle does."

"Have you ever told her what you've just said to me?" asked Carol.

"No," he replied. "It's all a long time ago and the last thing I want our relationship to be about is a bunch of stuff that happened to me 20 years back."

"I think she'd understand for what it's worth," argued Carol, "get to understand you better."

"Maybe," Philip conceded. He paused while their main courses arrived. "Coming to Mexico City was a bit of a release for me," he continued. "I really didn't know what to expect when I turned up. I hadn't seen much of the Olympics on TV when it was in Tokyo, and I was gutted by news of the riots and their suppression; it seemed all too much like Chicago. But I'd seen Tommie Smith run and knew the Civil Rights background and that some of the Black athletes were upset over what was happening in wider society and the attitude of the USOC. And the Democrats were heading for a loss in November and I just needed a break from it all."

"That was when sport started going global and it's never really stopped. Black Power salutes, Beamon's long jump, Fosbury's high jump – they all went round the world for really the first time."

"But the interesting thing for me is that sports are really the only events that have that global footprint. These are the events people want to watch, no matter what their language or culture. Nothing else."

"I think that's partly the Cold War. But it's a natural human reaction to globalisation to keep close to your own language, culture and community. Having said that, I can see a future where television has essentially become homogenised, with the same formats endlessly repeated on ever more channels, a bit like 'Robocop'."

"I'd forgotten quite how depressing you can be," laughed Carol. "Won't more channels create more opportunity for new programmes, new formats?"

"Maybe you're right."

"That's just the jetlag talking, Phil."

"Come on, Carol, let's not turn this into a mutual appreciation society."

"I thought that would provoke you."

"Okay, I'll shut up for a while. Come on, let's have some more wine," he signalled to the hovering waiter, "and you can tell me more about Seoul."

Carol started talking as the next bottle was opened in front of them. "Well, there were only a couple of countries boycotting – North Korea and Cuba – which, if you discount South Africa, is probably about as full a house of countries as you're likely to get. As a result, it was probably the most competitive Games ever."

"So on that basis," Philip went on, "Seoul was really only the third proper time USSR, GDR and USA have competed in the same Olympics."

"I'd not thought about it like that but you're right. And you couldn't really overestimate the degree of Cold War feel there was around Seoul."

Philip was surprised. "I thought we were past the worst of that with the boycotts."

"Maybe I'm exaggerating, but there was just something about seeing that struggle between economic and political systems played out on the track and in the pool. It's funny though, observing the athletes themselves. I think for the most part, they've always let the politics of it pass them by. The GDR seem to have members of the Stasi dotted around the various sports, but I think the Soviets are more relaxed. You see them laughing and joking more, and there are stories of them smoking and so on, none of which you hear about the GDR. Hell, they even still sometimes goose step around the place."

"Well, we certainly saw it pretty much wall to wall in the UK. It's absolute gold dust for the BBC. Just a shame Great Britain didn't have more medal chances."

"Hardly surprising, for the most part you're so under-funded it's a joke. In no other country that pretends to take sport seriously do the athletes essentially fund themselves. One day you'll wake up and smell the coffee."

"You are brutal sometimes. You've got to allow us some semblance of gracious decline. We're still in 'Chariots of Fire' mode, remember."

"You know, I really used to enjoy living for the moment. I was able to make things happen quite quickly, not anything with big, long-term consequences but little things that helped make the wheels turn. In the end, though, that kind of lifestyle had wired itself into my mind so that I operated in that mode all the time and couldn't switch into anything else. In many ways, I now think I did quite well to survive so long."

"Well, you somehow always avoided drugs, certainly the hard ones; that helped. But I know what you mean and can see how it might have been different for you, not being American. For me, they were my sports, my cities. And I guess I always thought you were looking for something but never quite knew what. Which is why I never gave you a hard time about sleeping with so many different women. I never thought you were doing it just to get laid, though you often said you were. I always believed, and wanted to believe, that you liked them as women and that at some level – though it could be a bit tenuous – you thought each of them might be the answer. So I guess what I'm getting round to saying, is that it seems to me there's a fair chance Michelle is what you've been searching for. And if that's true, then I couldn't be more ecstatic for the both of you."

Carol reached across the table and grasped each of Philip's hands with hers. Her eyes began to brim with emotion but she looked up anyway.

Philip looked sheepish and younger. "I'm sorry," he said, "I must have been a total asshole."

"Yes," replied Carol, "you were, but everyone seems to have survived. You did leave some mightily pissed women behind."

"I know I laugh about it," Philip continued, "but I feel quite embarrassed about some of the things I did when I was old enough to know better."

"I think we all did. I remember one particular relationship I had in Chicago – you remember I was based there for a few months in '73 – with a guy who was involved in commodities trading – good-looking, a lot of money, meant well, but impossible to talk to about the trivial shit I love so much, and always had to be in work for something like six in the morning – totally not my type but at the time it made a weird sort of sense; I was somehow able to justify it to myself because I knew I was only there for a few months and then there would be a natural end to it. Looking back, I treated him really terribly, and even now I feel nervous every time I land at O'Hare in case I end up bumping into him."

"You've never told me that," laughed Philip. "I'd never quite seen you as femme fatale."

"Well, we all have our moments, maybe you just weren't paying attention."

"You could be right, in which case I apologise."

"You change with the job I think," said Carol. "I know I became more regular when the job became New York based rather than taking me all round the country."

"Maybe, but I think the biggest thing for most of us is age."

"You're not having a mid-life crisis are you?" laughed Carol.

"No, I doubt it anyway. In some ways probably the reverse. Maybe because I went back to the UK, maybe because of Michelle; but whatever it is, I probably feel I've got more direction and, what's the word, momentum, than I did, say, ten years ago. Unlike you and say Fred, I always wanted to do other things in the media, and particularly in television. So when that chance to work for NBC on the Moscow Games came up, it was an obvious way for me to open other doors."

"And there was me thinking you just wanted more people to get to see you. To be honest, I was quite envious when you go that break, but even then I knew I was no TV reporter, so I just swallowed hard and carried on writing copy. But I can confess now, that there was probably a corner of my mind that felt a little easier when the boycott issue blew up; I'm far from proud of it but…"

"It's okay, I would have felt exactly the same. At least we Brits turned up."

"The boycott was a terrible idea from start to finish and I don't really know why Jimmy Carter came up with it; I thought he was better than that. Gesture politics of the worst kind, only hurts you, because you're too cowardly to do anything with a meaningful consequence for the Soviets." Carol paused, surprised at herself for feeling still so visceral. "The thing is as well, the Games still go on and they still matter. All you really do is screw the athletes and give the media something to write about. It was weird though because West Germany and Australia followed the US but you Brits didn't; what was all that about?"

"I don't really know," replied Philip. "I was over here, remember, but I think basically the BOA kept its independence and the USOC didn't. So Thatcher couldn't have been clearer and there was a vote in Parliament and everything; the press was up in arms, you name it. But the athletes had space to campaign."

"Do you have any regrets about spending so much time in the States?" asked Carol. "I mean you were here over 15 years and it seemed almost an accident at times."

"Boy but that's a non sequitur. Let me see now, probably a few. Partly that I lived fast and loose for too long. But I can't pretend I had regrets at the time. It's too easy to re-write your life, I think. But I sort of know what you mean about treating my time over here as something slightly separate. A lot of that was down to the fact that I just felt plain lucky. I couldn't really get over the break I had."

"But that's ridiculous!"

"Well you say that, and I ended up a pretty good writer, but I didn't start out that way. I got some big breaks, remember. And beyond that I always knew deep down that I was really only visiting America. No, wait a minute, that's the wrong word… I think it's about learning enough about America and Americans to realise that the culture of this country is every bit as hard-wired as that of a much older nation; and while I was adopted and felt I belonged – still do, in fact – I knew enough people like you who were rooted in a way I could never be. And that made me realise that the place where I was rooted in its soil and its blood was England. It's a bit like that Tom Waits song; you know, that goes 'I never saw the East coast till I moved to the West'; well, I never really saw England till I lived over here. Sorry, that's only half answered your question."

"Don't worry," said Carol, "I never realised you were such a goddamn poet." She waved for the bill. "This one's on me. Come on, let's have a quick chat to Giro before we head off in search of some action, or at least a bar where you can buy me something stronger."

Chapter 26
1990

(i) London, Saturday 31 March

Michelle had been down in Hammersmith seeing Richard, who now worked in Charing Cross Hospital. She anticipated bad traffic and had gone by Tube. The roads were jammed on account of the Oxford-Cambridge Boat Race – lots of well off young people with posh accents, floppy hair and Barbour jackets, as well as some tourists, many thousands more than she'd expected to see.

She had arranged to meet Philip at the Three Greyhounds, back of Cambridge Circus. She got the Tube to Piccadilly and, because she was early, decided to walk along Shaftesbury Avenue, and then to pop into the Bar Italia to read her book and soak up the Soho atmosphere. But there was no atmosphere, the place was deserted. The odd window was smashed and litter bins rolled aimlessly in the gutter, their contents strewn around. As she walked along, slightly faster than normal, not quite feeling threatened but not feeling totally safe either. She thought there must have been some kind of riot around the poll tax demonstration.

A sole customer, a man, was sitting halfway down the counter, the stools all facing the room-long mirror. There were two TVs at the far end – a normal size 20" and a much larger pub-sized screen higher up. The walkway between the stools and the serving bar, from behind which the Italian staff served coffee and food, was only about five feet wide. Apart from the man and the staff the place was empty. It was never empty. Over the bar, as usual, was a poster of Rocky Marciano, his hard human face above the details of his unbeaten record. Philip had introduced her to this place, a popular media hangout as he drily called it. The shelf up above the bar was populated by boxes of Amaretti, sealed bags of Bar Italia coffee and Bar Italia T-shirts.

Michelle had always felt at home here, ever since her first visit in the early hours of a Sunday morning. They had been to Ronnie Scott's across the street and the bar was full of enormous hairy leather-clad bikers, their machines parked outside. She had loved it, felt totally safe. This evening she still felt safe, but not totally.

"Could I just have a latte please?" she said to the barman. "Quiet tonight," she added.

"After the riot, everyone went home," the man replied in a broad Italian accent. He looked at her, slowly comprehending her ignorance. "The poll tax," he said. "Thousands of people in Trafalgar Square. Fighting with police all the way up to Oxford Street. Windows broken, lots of things thrown. Not good for business." He smiled.

"Thanks," said Michelle, taking the coffee and paying. "It's so quiet, I thought that might be what happened but I didn't know."

"It was chaos for a while," said a voice from down the bar some minutes later. "I don't think many got hurt but a fair few got arrested, I reckon." The man was tall, maybe 6'3", very lean, with greying hair and soft blue eyes. He had an Australian accent, looked about 40, and Michelle immediately fancied him in a detached sort of way.

"What brings you here to the centre of British social breakdown?" she asked.

"Oh, I was just hanging around really. I'm meeting some mates later for a curry. I had a couple of hours spare and thought I'd just come in a bit early, have a beer, have a coffee and read really, watch the world go by kind of thing."

"What are you reading?" He turned his book over. "Aren't you meant to read 'On the Road' in your 20s?"

"I did," he replied. "And about ten times since. This is my second copy, but I've preserved the first at home for scientific reasons. What are you doing here? You're not dressed like a poll tax protester."

"There was a time," said Michelle, "but my Greenham Common days are over."

"Would you like another coffee?"

"Thanks," she smiled again. "But I'll have an orange juice if that's okay. I should ask your name really. Mine's Michelle."

"Connor," he got off the stool and went over to the bar. "Double espresso please." He put a £10 note down on the bar and came back to his stool. MTV was on the TV at the end and George Michael's 'Careless Whisper' was playing.

"So what are your causes?" Michelle asked when he sat back down.

"I'm not sure I have anything," Conor replied.

"But there must be some things you're passionate about?" Michelle hid her disappointment.

"Well, I don't know really. I like to think I listen to people and try quite hard to understand myself and them, and I find pretty much everything else seems to be beyond me. I'm not really the demonstrating kind and find everyday life pretty hard work. I guess I don't have much confidence in my ability to change anything or anyone, apart maybe from myself."

"But what do you do when you see something you think is wrong, something that makes you angry?" Part of Michelle was switching off in frustration.

"Well," he sipped his espresso. "For a start, I try hard not to get angry. Take today for example, I don't particularly like Margaret Thatcher's government, but not enough to put at risk my own internal balance or to narrow my view, so I pay the tax. I also don't want to hate anyone if I can avoid it."

Exasperated but confused, Michelle looked at her watch, "When are you meeting your friends?"

"In about an hour."

"Then let's go somewhere else so we can have an alcoholic drink; you do drink, don't you? It's okay, I'm not making a pass at you but I can't have this sort of conversation in daylight without alcohol."

"It's okay, I don't feel threatened, you don't exactly have a predatory look." He got off his stool, put his jacket on, shoved his booked in his bag and slung it over his shoulder. "What do you want to drink?"

(ii) Eastern Europe, 13 June

Ed had been drafted in from Kurdistan by the BBC, anxious to provide the most comprehensive coverage it could of the rapid disintegration of the Iron Curtain. Gaps appearing everywhere, beginning to feel threatened by the global reach and 24-hour coverage of CNN, it wanted to show that when it mattered, it could bring to bear an unmatchable combination of quality and quantity.

All the major centres of political action were, of course, already taken by Europe-based correspondents – Berlin and Leipzig, Warsaw and Gdansk, Moscow and Kiev, Budapest, Prague, even Sofia and Bucharest. And so Ed found himself in a rented Skoda, driving the back roads of Eastern Europe, through towns and villages that used to mark the border of the Soviet Bloc. He had missed out on the iconic scenes at the end of 1989, of thousands of people physically dismantling the Wall, brick by bloody brick, as well as countless pro-democracy demonstrations and the eruption of free political parties across ancient central European cities that had never tasted democracy's seductive liquor. Instead, now some six months on from the original eruption, he was beginning to see, and piece together in his mind, the meaning of a less cheering reality, the flip side of the coin.

The first sign was the rows of soldiers, East German, Czech, even Russian, standing by the roadside trying to sell their uniforms to passers-by, looking to do what? Make some money, preferable western currency? Provide themselves the means to somehow acquire a new identity? Find a way to be part of the immense tectonic change that was happening all around them? After stopping and talking to a couple, Ed wasn't sure they knew themselves. Their dominant emotion was the recognition that nothing would be the same again and that they themselves needed be something different. He concluded later they had been culturally shell-shocked, that the abruptness of the transformation they had experienced was so profound that they would, for the rest of their lives, remember these events as a series of explosions detonating inside their heads.

After the rows of soldiers came the rows of women, of prostitutes, this time selling their bodies by the side of the new highways. Prostitution, he knew from journalist friends, had been low in the Communist Bloc – everyone had a job; pimping had been cracked down on, carrying heavy penalties; and the sexual mores had been liberal, even by western standards. And yet here, suddenly, were dozens of women offering sex for money. There seemed to have been some kind of economic breakdown across Eastern Europe. But why so many women, and why so suddenly?

Sitting in the bar of the Hilton in Budapest, at the end of his week's driving, Ed could only conclude, without knowing what it was, something really big had just fractured. Whatever it was, it went beyond the totalitarian state and the command economy. Having lasted over 40 years, the Soviet Empire had suddenly ceased to exist. Was it the suddenness of the shift, or the scale of it? Or was it perhaps that, in its absence, there was nothing to go back to? Before Communism there had been Nazism. Before Nazism, what? The remains of the Austro-Hungarian Empire, itself the rump of the Holy Roman Empire? This part of Europe, full of beautiful, grand imperial cities and flourishing art, had also been the last hinterland of serfdom. Even in Italy and Germany, relative latecomers to this club, the convulsions of 1848 had led to something, had been a catalyst for their national self-development. This part of Europe, he realised, had no such history, no Bismarck, no Cavour. Yugoslavia was a post WW2 creation; Czechoslovakia created in a Paris conference room in 1919; Poland, however, had for centuries been a battlefield for other countries' armies.

Alone in a corner, with a window view overlooking the Danube, he was just finishing his second bowl of goulash – the consequence of driving all through the day and missing lunch – and just starting his second bottle of red wine – the palliative (temporary, anyway) for the absence of lunch, and for the dislocation and misery he had observed over the last five days. He drank rarely these days but heavily when he did, as if the pressure of need piled up inside him until the dam burst.

He wondered what Sam would think. He imagined him scurrying around Whitehall, watching Ruth growing up – encouraging her, watching her when she fell – working all the time to be a good person, a good husband. He pulled himself up; was that how he saw his old friend? Was their relationship now old? Did it matter – he willed his mind back – that he'd seen so little of Sam, allowed personal relations to take such a back seat to things that he cared about, that fascinated him, that he believed important? He got up, walked steadily to the bar, paid and went to bed.

London, 22 November

Sam was sitting at home with a nasty temperature and a hacking cough when he heard on the radio that the prime minister had resigned.

His mind went back to the May morning over ten years before, when she had quoted St Francis of Assisi – "where there is despair, may we bring hope" – before entering Downing Street for the first time. How much more pessimistic and cynical he was now compared to then. He reached across to the box of tissues beside him, pulled out three and blew his nose loudly on each of them, peering briefly at the yellowish green gunk they now carried in between each explosion. The pictures of her getting into the car, her tear-stained features, were a reminder, he thought, that she was a warm-blooded human being despite the image. He peeled a satsuma and began to eat the segments.

He remembered a story Jeff had told him, around Easter sometime, of a reception at Lancaster House back in January 1989 for the British teams – Olympic and Paralympic – that had gone to Seoul the year before. Thatcher had been there for a full two hours and had been on good form, talking to quite a lot of athletes and engaging each with that energy all great politicians have in apparently inexhaustible quantities. Each person she talked to was, for that period of time, the absolute centre of her attention. Jeff said it had been a real education, as though he was present at a classic scientific experiment. There were of course, slight variations stemming from the nature of each individual's approach, aggressive or fawning, submissive or assertive, logical or emotional. Within two minutes, however, each person had become a clone of all the others, caught within the gravity of her power, orbiting in nodding harmony.

At one point, however, she had been talking to a group of athletes, a couple of whom he thought must be basketball players. One of them had asked her what it was like going to university just after WW2. Jeff had thought it quite a crass question, but Mrs Thatcher had begun answering it as though it was one of those things she had been wondering about herself for a while. She had spoken about the great sense of public responsibility they had all felt – he assumed she meant all those in Oxford University's Conservative Association – to rebuild the nation after the war and not to let down those who had given their lives to defeat Hitler. She had talked too of how much they were inspired by 'Winston', implying that he sent regular messages of guidance up to Oxford, and that they had mostly been developing policy ideas for use by the government. It was clear to Jeff that she very much saw herself as Churchill's heir. In foreign policy certainly, this seemed undeniable. Another athlete had asked her about the beginnings of the Cold War, "Where did they get these questions from?" Jeff had wondered. "How many times must she have been asked that question?" But from her answer, it sounded like she had never been asked it but that it was a question of deep moment that she had thought about a great deal.

"Well," she had begun, "we all clearly knew the mistakes that had been made with the appeasement of Hitler's Germany in the 1930s, and were determined not to repeat them. Winston was very clear that Stalin must not be in any doubt about the strength of our resolve. I remember my father reading to me from the newspaper back during the 1930s. He always worried about Germany rearming; Winston and I agreed that Britain must never again be seen as weak and unprepared, that we needed to have a clear deterrent."

"Is that why you support America's Strategic Defence Initiative?" another of the athletes asked.

"Yes, you see if the Soviet Union believes for one moment that we are lacking resolve, the threat they pose in Central Europe will become much greater. It's a lesson we must never forget. And the shield the SDI will provide will cover Britain as well as the US. We must always be prepared to resist tyranny."

"But in that case, why are we not supporting a ban on chemical weapons so that Saddam Hussein is not able to use them against the Kurds?"

While seeming to answer the athlete's question, Jeff remembered that Mrs Thatcher did not in fact do so, but instead continued talking about the shield SDI would provide and how she hoped it would cover smaller countries also, like Norway. Then, some ten minutes later, she glanced at her watch, then at her security guard before saying, with no obvious hint of humour, "I'm afraid I must go now. It's time I got back to minding the shop." And she was gone, through the door just behind her, leaving the athletes charmed but stranded.

Jeff had been amused as well as impressed, the perfect laboratory situation he had decided, over a late couple of pints in a Whitehall pub. Sam preferred a rather more benign view of the athletes' questions, crediting them with being non-politicians rather than political wannabes.

Still, as he sat watching the commentators and Opposition politicians seeking to dissect and deconstruct Thatcher's fall, he valued the story for shedding light on a fragment of her humanity. For ten years, she had de-humanised herself, perhaps as much as any politician of the democratic era. She was "the Iron Lady", "not for turning", you were "either for us or against us", with no middle way, no room for trimming. And gradually, through the years, she had shed herself of those who dared to display their own humanity, by expressing a modicum of doubt or independence of thought: Howe, King, Biffen (a personal favourite), Lawson. And after Whitelaw had died, there was no one left to coax, chide or flirt with her. And now, surprisingly, she'd been mortally wounded by the "dead sheep's" tongue of Geoffrey Howe; then exposed by the bitter hatred of Heseltine, so strong he knowingly committed political suicide, revealing in the process how many MPs were prepared to vote against her.

Arguably, the fall of the Soviet Union, the coming down of the Berlin Wall, capitalist democracies being established across Eastern Europe, the unification of Germany, should have been the crowning glory of such a Cold War queen. But instead it had, perhaps, loosened the nation's deepest ties to her. If he was searching for parallels, then the 1945 election offered one, when a grateful nation nonetheless turned its back on Churchill in his hour of victorious vindication, sensing that an era had passed.

Before hearing Jeff's story, he had not appreciated the depths of Thatcher's ties to Churchill, her honouring of this legacy, nor indeed her own grounding in the loathing of pre-war appeasement, that any less than a show of strength would be interpreted as weakness. Was sitting at her dad's knee in the '30s her key formative experience, or was it more than that, her 'Rosebud' moment, itself irretrievable but its essence constantly sought in other people and other situations.

No, he decided, this was going several steps too far. But he laughed at what Ed would have made of his Freudian deconstruction of Thatcher. Then his laugh turned to a cough, but a productive one and suddenly he felt better. He got up and went into the kitchen to boil the kettle.

Chapter 27
Amman, 10 January 1991

The last time Ed had been here, during early July last year, he was watching England and Germany in the World Cup semi-final. The hotel bar had been packed, mostly with Brits but also some Germans, and he remembered the impending sense of doom from the moment Germany had equalised with the free kick that deflected cruelly off Paul Parker. The Gazza booking and the tears it produced almost took on an air of tragic inevitability, the missed penalties no more than the concluding punctuation. And now he was back. If 1990 had been Germany's year, the year of unification and the disintegration of the Iron Curtain, the liberation of Eastern Europe, then 1991 was turning into something altogether more sombre.

Ed thought the tide had begun to turn even before the Wall had come down, back in June 1989 with the Tiananmen Square massacre, when the Chinese Communist Party and Army had brutally demonstrated the limits of peaceful protest. Where Communist Eastern Europe had crumbled before it, Communist China had slapped it down. Even now, no one really knew how many had died that night. And now, with Iraq's invasion of Kuwait last August, he saw another attempted exercise of power. Ed had never really believed the popular view that Saddam Hussein was clever and cunning. He had always thought of him as a brutal tyrant who obtained and maintained power simply by being nastier than his opponents, quicker to violence but not clever and cunning. He was a bully who responded to signs of weakness and had decided the West was soft and would never use military power. In fact, of course, he was stupid because he had totally missed the fact that blocking oil supplies destined for the US was equivalent to invading Texas.

The result was what looked to be the biggest military build-up since 1945, certainly in terms of speed and firepower. Saddam had managed to pull off the unenviable trick of turning the US from an arms supplier during the Iran-Iraq war, seemingly happy to stand and watch while Saddam tried to gas his Kurdish population as well as his Iranian enemy, into a military foe prepared to use maximum force to roll Iraq back across the Kuwaiti border.

Ed was on his way to meet Paula, an American journalist friend, for a drink at the Marriott. She had got to Amman ahead of him and had been there about a week. Neither of them, for differing reasons, was due to be 'embedded' in Operation Desert Storm as the invasion would be called; Paula because her employers had, much to her anger, shied away from using a woman in that role; Ed because he recoiled from the implication of increased control over what he could see or say.

When he arrived, Paula was already there, sat in an armchair with two large glasses sitting in front of her. She was only about 28, in some ways absurdly young for the job, as Ed had once been. Ed had known Paula for some two years and they had immediately got on. They argued incessantly but always managed to keep their disagreements to the political. Paula was from rural Illinois and saw her vocation as a search for adventure. Journalistic truth was, for her, a set of observed facts rather than the nuanced reality Ed saw it as his duty to interpret.

Paula smiled as she caught sight of him and came over to hug him and peck him affectionately on both cheeks. "What took you?"

"Just normal, Old World sloth. We take our time because it is now the only way we know."

"It's good to see you. Everyone else is so nice to me. What's the state of the revolution?"

"Well let's just say last year was better than this one looks like being. It's good to see you too! It's always too long. And," he gestured to the table, "thanks for the drink."

"Not a problem, Yankee dollars still go a long way." They went over and sat down. "When did you get in?"

"About three hours ago. I caught the early flight and changed at Schiphol. What about you? You've been here a week?"

"Five days. I've been sleeping off jetlag – it still makes a zombie out of me – reconnecting with sources and trying to educate myself. Hard as I've tried, I've never understood the Middle East."

Ed laughed, "I reckon realising that and admitting it puts you easily in the top quartile. I've been reporting on the Middle East, on and off, for 15 years, and reading about it a lot for at least five years before that, and I think I've only just got beyond scratching the surface. You simply can't short change the complexity of it."

Now Paula laughed, "I always forgot how unwittingly serious you are about all this, what we do. Come on let's have a drink and shoot the breeze a bit. There's plenty of time to talk serious. Tell me what you've been up to."

"You know me, just pottering around, reporting the facts, doing what I'm told."

"I also miss your bullshit! Come on, I mean it! Where have you been? What have you been doing?"

"Well, I've just had a couple of weeks at home, but mostly just sleeping and seeing my family."

"I remember, is it Derby you're from, somewhere north of London?"

"Yes, in the East Midlands, probably closer to London than Champagne is to Chicago but it feels like a long way to us."

"And you don't have anywhere for yourself in London, do you?"

"Nope, not anymore. I did for a while, quite a nice flat in Hammersmith near the Thames, but I just wasn't there often enough. So now when I'm in London, I either stay in hotels, mostly, or else with my friend Sam and his family."

"You sad man!" Paula shook her head as her hair fought its way free from the collar where it had been carelessly caught. "Brits really crack me up."

Ed pretended to be as amused as she was. "Always glad to provide amusement to the last hope of the free world; it is our post-colonial role in life after all."

"Don't be pissed at me," she replied. "If I thought you meant that, I'd be pissed at you. You know I didn't mean to get you uptight. It's just I haven't seen you for a while and I forget how to be sensitive." She looked at him full on.

"I know," Ed relented. "Same goes for me the other way round. I've been around so long."

"You mean people either settle down with family and do something more sensible, or else their luck runs out?"

"Something like that. What we do is a lot more dangerous than most of our friends."

"Yeah, I know – speaking of which, did you hear about Dave?"

"Yes, it still gets to me in my quieter moments. I had a friend, well maybe more of an acquaintance – one of those people I really got on with but only really knew through others – Lawrence Dobson was his name, who died in a car crash about six years ago. Hell of a good juggler he was, really funny, generous guy. It makes everything seem more of a burden somehow, I find myself asking whether I could explain what I do to him. It's weird, as I didn't know him that well, like I said, but sometimes I find myself thinking."

"That's bad for you but I sort of know what you mean, even though I'm an amateur in the guilt thing compared to you. But the Dave thing really hit me. I always saw him as a bit of a rival, you know. We were the same age and a couple of times we found ourselves going for the same story – you know the sort of thing. Of course, I always thought I was better than him but he was good, and I thought we'd both be there for the next 20 years. And now it's like a slice of my identity isn't there anymore. Some of those intense experiences – when it's kicking off, or when a story's breaking – we shared some of those and now there's no one around to be able to talk to about them. You know how I heard? I was at a pool party back home – Dad's moved up in the world, sold his business – and I was a bit bored – too much crap about local politics – so I was reading the Herald-Tribune, just flicking through and there it was – 'Pulitzer Prize winner Dave Leopold died of leukaemia after a short illness at home in Vermont. He was 31'."

"I'm sorry," said Ed, softening, "that's a hell of a way to find out, in the middle of a party... What did you do?"

Paula looked up at him again, from the dregs of her glass, which she was slowly shaking back and forwards, tinkling the ice. "I went and sobbed in the toilet for ten minutes then went back to the party and got drunk, didn't embarrass my dad or anything, but I haven't been as far gone in about five years."

"Speaking of which, do you want the same again?"

When Ed came back, they touched glasses, both smiling, both relaxed chatting easily.

"So, Edward Plummer," began Paula after a while, adopting a Rodin pose, "tell me about yourself. It's time, after all this time, we got to know each other properly. Three questions and then I'm happy to reciprocate."

"Can I choose my own questions?" Ed thought he knew where this was going. He was wary but wasn't in the mood to say no.

"Of course."

"Are we alternating or are you going first?"

"I'll go first and get it all out on the table. Then you'll have full scope to retaliate or reply in kind, depending on how you view it."

Ed paused momentarily. He knew his questions, even going second, were unlikely to be as personal as Paula's. But the same applied to any other running order and, on balance, Paula's proposal seemed as good as any. "Whatever you prefer," he replied.

"Okay, but I've changed my mind, let's alternate. So, when did you lose your virginity, who to, and why?"

Ed burst out laughing. "Is that one question or three?"

"One of course!"

"Right, I'll remember that! I suppose you're going to want a supplementary as well but only the one, as in O-N-E!"

"Okay, I'll give you that."

"Right then," Ed began, "I'm going to choose my words carefully now as I am conscious any and everything I say is likely to be used in evidence against me. I ceased being a virgin in August 1973. It was the night of our A' Level results. Those are the exams we take in Britain the year we're 18 at the end of our high school and the results help dictate what we do after. In my case, I wanted to study politics at Manchester University and had got the grades I needed.

"Anyway, most of us had done okay, although only a few of us were staying in education rather than trying to get a job. And someone, Karen I think her name was, who wasn't quite a friend but we got on okay; well, it was her birthday and she'd arranged to have a joint 18th birthday party – with a friend I didn't know from another school – and had booked a local hotel and hired a DJ. It was the sort of thing that was pretty common back then – I don't know what they do now – and I doubt it was that expensive given how much alcohol usually got bought.

"Anyway, as you can imagine we were all pretty much up for it, and by 9 o'clock I was pretty pissed – UK definition – but not enough to get me on the dance floor. But I was wandering around with a beer in my hand. Anyway, haven't thought about this in years, this really good-looking girl comes up to me and says something like, 'Hi, I'm Jenny, you don't remember me, do you?' Well, she was right, I didn't, and my face can't have been the mask of enigma it is today because then she said, 'I thought not; you used to come round all the time with your mum; you were really good at playing with my little brother, John.' Later I worked out it must have been before we moved house and I must have been about six or something, but I still didn't remember. Anyway, we got talking and then we danced. It turned out she was good friends with the other girl whose party it was." Ed, who had been looking down, now looked up. "Anyway, the hotel had a small pitch and putt golf course attached, and we ended up going outside – it was a warm summer evening – and that's how I lost my virginity. Quite late by modern standards, I believe.

"As to the 'why', I don't really know, except that I think for both of us it felt like the right time, and I think we both represented some element of safety because we had some kind of connection from our childhood but didn't know each other as such. So, in my case, I felt relatively safe from social humiliation if it all went horribly wrong."

"So did you see her again?"

"A couple of times but not to talk to. It was funny; I think it was good for both of us, certainly for me, but I don't think either of us thought we would start dating or anything like that."

"I'm trying to make up my mind if that sounds romantic or, what shall we call it? – Pragmatic? On balance, I think the former."

"Well, thank you," Ed made a mock bow. "You know, I don't think I've ever told anyone that before."

"Because no one asked?"

"Almost certainly."

"Okay, your go!"

Ed paused and sipped. "Right, now, let me see," he stroked his chin grinning. "After all you've seen as a journalist, what do you think of your country's foreign policy?"

"Ah, from the personal to the political. Well, at least this has the advantage of being well-trodden territory. I'm not often asked the big question so directly, but versions of it come my way pretty much every week in this job. Usually," she added, "from colleagues hailing from ex-colonial European powers, including Britain, but that's another story.

"First of all, I think we're handicapped by everyone, including ourselves, thinking the US is more powerful than we actually are. Partly I think it's a hangover from WW2, when everyone else ended up so weak. So everyone still thinks the relative balance of power, both economic and military, is still as it was in the years immediately after the war, which of course is when almost all the current generation of political leaders were young. So my prediction is that the next generation of politicians will be much less accepting of American power."

"Go on," said Ed, more intrigued than he expected.

"Well, I guess the next thing is that the majority of Americans don't really want to have a foreign policy at all. As you know, there's a sizeable chunk of us who don't even have passports. Most of us don't know or care much what happens in other countries. So the American 'Empire', if that's a valid term at all, is completely different from the British Empire. From what I can work out, you guys took your families, ran the administration, set up the legal system, all that stuff. Whereas our foreign policy seems pretty ignorant of the countries we're trying to influence. Consequently, we end up with unsustainable policy, in which a succession of allies feel let down.

"And then there's what I call the God-curse of our moral mission, bequeathed to us in reams of rhetoric from the Founding Fathers and since, to the effect that we essentially think we're better than everyone else, somehow purer, notwithstanding all evidence to the contrary. So we grow up still thinking we're the last best hope of humanity, and this gives us an arrogance about our way of doing things – democracy, Christianity and free market capitalism – that makes it really hard for our politicians to do business effectively with a country that's communist or Muslim. Of course, the last of that holy trinity – free market capitalism – is by far the most potent, so we'll more than happily do business with Saudi Arabia or the People's Republic of China if the P&L line looks good.

"And the Middle East is, of course, just the classic example of where all these come together in repeated and inglorious failure. Every attempt at a solution must seemingly be led by and brokered by us to have any chance of success, and yet we've demonstrated our weakness time and again, with no ability to practically help implement a settlement short of extreme options we'd never be prepared to use.

"And we don't really understand the Middle East, to the point where we don't really have an opinion about it of our own. Consequently, we're disproportionately influenced by our relatively small but influential lobby of Jewish Americans. A lot of what they argue isn't wrong but their over-riding influence is so obvious that, no matter what it does, the Israeli government always knows it has a get-out-of-jail free card. What's more, everyone else knows it as well, including the Arabs, which means that even when we're trying to play it straight – come on now, no laughing, it does happen – we're seen as having a pro-Israeli bias and therefore not trusted.

"And finally, we go and insist that one of the outcomes of any peace agreement is that everyone has to become a liberal democracy; except of course, if you're Israeli, or some old theocracy or brutal military dictatorship, so long as you're an oil producer. Now oil, of course, is the US's economic Achilles' heel. And so we end up making an endless string of God knows what kind of promises to secure a reliable supply of the stuff.

"I know I haven't answered the question yet, so my answer is that our foreign policy is, in most respects, fairly terrible, that at least half the time we're trying to do the right thing, but our approach has some fatal weaknesses that will continue to frustrate until everyone, including ourselves, starts having a more realistic and therefore modest expectation of what we can achieve."

"That's about as critical a dissection of US foreign policy as I've heard from anyone," said Ed, "even those who think you're the Great Satan. At least they give you credit for being powerful and having a plan."

"Ah well, I've always been a fan of the cock-up view of history as you Brits put it. Don't get me wrong, there are lots of conspirators out there conspiring away, it's just that their best-laid plans keep going wrong, not least because they keep running up against other people's conspiracies. Anyway, my turn again but first we need another drink."

He waited as she walked over to the bar pulling the scrunchy out of her hair and shaking it loose.

Within two minutes, Paula was back, smiling. "The barman reckons we're good for business. He implied that us journalists drink more than other people. I wonder how he got that idea. Right then, question number two: what's the favourite place you've ever been on holiday and why?"

"Back to the personal again," said Ed, "anyone would think you were trying to psycho-analyse me."

"You're easy, no need! And before you ask, I'll tell you at the end. Come on then!"

"Okay then, let me think for a moment... I think my favourite place to go on holiday is the Loire Valley, in and around Tours. I've been there three or four times now and it's always been great but the first time I went has, irrevocably I suspect, coloured my image of the place."

"When was the first time you went?"

"It was September 1982, just after I'd got back from Lebanon. I think I told you how I got into Sabra and Shatila the day after the massacres – it's one of those experiences I've promised myself always to talk about." – Paula nodded – "Anyway, when I'd filed my reports and got back to London, I just wanted to get away somewhere different, quiet, where I didn't know anyone and could get away from the news. So I flew to Paris, hired a car and drove down to Tours, where I ended up staying in a lovely gîte just outside Vouvray in the middle of vineyards just by the river. The whole valley is just stunning, dotted with beautiful chateaux from 16th century and before."

"So what made it so special, such a favourite?" asked Paula. "After all the places you've been, it sounds quite boring."

"At the time, I think the relative lack of excitement – I don't agree it's boring – was undoubtedly part of the attraction. Being a long way from Beirut was definitely a plus, and while there was a tiny bit of me that wanted to shout at people for not acknowledging what was going on there, it would have been wrong to call them complacent. They had plenty of concerns, not least the problems thrown up by rural life itself, which has a knack of forcing you to operate very much in the here and now.

"So probably the first thing that makes it special for me is that it's the place I've found that's furthest away from my day job without also being a long way from people. You see, all those other places, the Highlands of Scotland for instance, are basically empty, whereas the Loire Valley is full of people, a hive of activity. So many people are born, grow up, fall in and out of love, work, play, get old, die; the full cycle of human life. And it made me think, not that we spend too much time reporting events in places like Beirut and South Lebanon, but how little we really understand the way we all live.

"Being there so soon after seeing the horrors of that atrocity somehow brought me back to earth. That holiday along the Loire taught me, finally I hope, that there was nothing special in what I did. Being a journalist, or war reporter as I'd begun to style myself, was no more important than making wine, or running a boulangerie."

"You said this was the first thing that was special, so what is or are the others?"

"The other, singular," began Ed, attempting to look slightly quizzical, "is that the Loire Valley being so peaceful is a counterpoint to its past."

"How do you mean?"

"Well, the reason there are all these chateaux is that back in the 15th and 16th century the Loire was the home of the French court. It was where Francis I brought Leonardo de Vinci, where Joan of Arc hung out and where much of the Hundred Years War between England and France was fought."

"And so?"

"And so the Loire used to be the most violent, war-torn part of Western Europe and now it's a tranquil beauty spot. So for me it's evidence that the wheel of history does turn. Which means I can have some optimism that the Middle East and even Ireland could be peaceful in my lifetime."

"So does that take you as far as thinking that it's evidence God exists?"

"I'm not sure that qualifies as a supplementary, but I'll answer it anyway. No, it doesn't, not because there's too much evil elsewhere, but because I actually see no real order in the world, not the human aspect of it anyway. Evolution explains the natural world to me, but as far as humanity's concerned, it's pretty much a random mess, not much evidence for a God in there."

"Sorry I asked, I'll be careful with my supplementaries in future. I didn't think you'd get so angry."

"I was brought up with certainty all around me and, much as I love my parents, I'm not sure I can ever really forgive them for that. The world I live in is the opposite of what they led me to expect, and when I reached my early 20s, after I left Manchester, I felt totally unprepared."

"But didn't you go pretty much straight into being a foreign correspondent?"

"Yes, but that was a mix of hope, luck and naïveté, not planning or knowledge."

"But, assuming I agree with you for a minute, isn't your education, your school, more to blame than your parents?"

"Yes, but they'd seen more than enough, particularly in the war, to know the stuff they were telling me was complete rubbish, a lot of it. Sure, Manchester could have done a better job but I went there with completely the wrong set of expectations. Take what's going on now, the horse-trading Bush is doing, the promises he'll be making to form his alliance and keep his allies on board. We both know it's all about oil and that everything else is up for sale.

"You know the real tragedy around Sabra and Shatila for me? Beyond the massacre itself? It's that there were no consequences. Sure, we reported it, and it was news for a couple of weeks – but they – the Israelis and I assume the US – calculated that, if they did nothing to fan the flame, the news agenda would then move on to something else. And of course, they were right. Nobody seriously denies what happened but there's been no real inquiry, no one held to account. It's less than ten years and already almost everyone has forgotten. Sorry, we seem to have got a long way from the Loire Valley."

"We sure have but that's the game. Your turn again."

"Okay," Ed felt somehow trapped, but not unpleasantly. He knew Paula well but had never had this type of conversation with her and was unused to being so confessional. He consciously composed himself. "Okay," he repeated, "I'll stick with the political; how would you go about solving the Middle East problem?"

"Now there's a doozie! Is that some kind of revenge? Okay then, live by the sword and die by the sword, I guess. This is top of the head stuff, so go easy on me. I don't want any of that veteran reporter analysis you can switch on like a tap whenever some young buck goes and gets all arrogant."

"Okay, deal!"

"Right, so… the Middle East increasingly seems to me to be all about water, oil and history. I don't think land as such is important unless it's got a meaning beyond. So the first thing I'd do would be to try and solve the Middle East's water problem. I'd subsidise desalination and water pipelines so that a much larger part of the region was fertile and habitable. This would involve giving Israel security of water supply as well as the Jordanians and so on. From talking to people, a large part of the issue around land in Palestine is about where the aquifers are, and part of the deal with Israel would be to give up some of that land to the Palestinians in return for an internationally paid for and guaranteed secure water supply. They did a land-for-peace deal with Egypt, so they might do a land-for-water and peace deal with the US and the PLO, with us supplying the water.

"Then we'd have to sort our oil dependence, which is the trickiest problem, perhaps intractable in my lifetime. Somehow, we need to be weaned off our love affair with cheap gas, and I suspect it will take something quite nasty, like a massive oil spillage in our Gulf that screwed up not just nature but the economy as well. Somehow, we have to get in a position where we care less about Saudi and Iran and Iraq than we now do. At the moment, we'll end up as what Bush called imperialists of the worst kind. We're about to invade Iraq, ostensibly because it invaded Kuwait, but only a few years ago we were selling it arms to help it fight Iran, while at the same time, we now know, doing deals with the Ayatollah to help support Contras in Nicaragua. It all sounds terribly proprietorial to me.

"So going back to the question, I fear the only ways for us to 'solve' the oil aspect of the Middle East are to either make ourselves less dependent on it, or to take control of enough of the supply to make us feel secure. It doesn't take a genius to work out the first isn't likely to happen soon enough to prevent the second becoming, let's call it a lively option."

Ed interrupted, "I get all that, Paula, but isn't the simple problem that the US just has a real issue dealing with Muslim states? I get the Saudi link but, as you said earlier, that's business rather than politics. Say Iran became a democracy, would it really make a difference to US attitudes? Would you trust Iran any more as a result? I somehow doubt it."

"Put that way, I think that's pretty harsh," replied Paula. "I think if that happens, despite what I said, I reckon the US will be at least as good at dealing with a democratic Iran as old Europe will."

"Okay, let's leave that bit then. What about the history?"

"Well, I've never been able to make up my mind whether it's the most difficult intractable aspect of the Middle East problem or not. I mean on one level this is a problem that goes back thousands of years, but from a different perspective, it only really dates back to the end of the First World War. It's another one of those 20th century problems that Hitler has a lot to answer for."

"How do you mean?"

"Well, quite rightly, most of the world feels an element of guilt towards the Jewish people and Israel on account of the Holocaust. And without that, I'm not sure Israel would have had so much military support over the years, particularly from the US. It might not even exist, certainly as we know it. In any case, at some point that sense of guilt will move from a reality to a memory, and Israel will start having to account for its actions wholly in the present. It'll take another 20–30 years but at some point that shift will happen and, you know what, Israel will almost certainly become a better state as a result. Being so dependent on the past is never a good thing."

"Are you sure?" queried Ed. "I've often wondered whether having such a relatively short history is one of America's burdens; whether, if you'd been around a little longer, whether you'd be a bit less, I don't know, preachy and self-assured."

"Ha-ha, I know what you mean, but the US is a self-invented country, unlike any other. There's still nothing really like the depth and diversity of America's immigrant cultures."

"Where do you fit into the melting pot?"

"Mostly German but with a Swedish grandmother on my father's side. The first arrival was my German grandma's grandfather, who landed in Ellis Island in 1856. We still love the letters he wrote home during the Civil War. He survived, but both his brothers died at Shiloh."

"Actually, sorry, I was being flippant earlier. I wouldn't wish more wars, let alone civil wars, on anyone."

"Don't worry, I know that. At least our civil war was about something serious; but you're right, it does still define us, right up to and including my generation. But I think the legacy is finally reaching its natural conclusion. There is the odd Liberal Democrat Governor – Jimmy Carter was an early one – Bill Clinton in Arkansas is probably the best current example – who is starting to change the voting patterns of the old South. There'll always be a solid Republican bloc there, certainly for my lifetime, but it doesn't look like a one-party system any more. There are immigrants from other parts of the US, and African Americans are beginning to vote in larger numbers. Anyway, it feels as though we've got off the point a bit. Time for my last question?"

"Okay, go on then."

"Last one then. When do you think you'll stop being a war reporter and why?"

"I thought that would be your first question and had an answer all ready, which, of course, I've now completely forgotten!" Ed paused, "I think, however, it's probably a slightly redundant question as I don't think I ever will stop."

"What about marriage, settling down, kids?"

"Well, maybe, you can never tell these things but I think if I was going to do all that, I'd be well on the way by now. Since I began this job, I've become more caught up in it and worse at creating a life outside. I've kind of concluded I must have a bit of a self-created exclusion zone around me with a big 'Do Not Enter' sign on the front."

"I hope you don't mind me asking but are you gay?"

Ed laughed. "No, not that I'm aware of, but you're not the first person who's asked me that so maybe I should re-consider."

"It's okay, I reckon you'd know by now. It's just, I think you're probably the least obviously predatory male I've met in a long time."

"That's just because you're judging me by Illinois standards."

"Definitely."

"You mean most straight male reporters would, in my position, have tried to hit on you by now?"

"Obviously."

"You know, I've always tried to avoid mixing work and social life."

"But that's such a get-out, Ed. Fine to be wheeled out whenever it suits you, or ignored when you decide it no longer applies."

"Like when?" Ed was more surprised than anything by what was developing. He mentally kicked himself for not having seen it coming. The nature of the questions, the way she'd loosened her hair.

"What about that Spanish reporter in Cairo last year?"

"Nothing happened, I put my arm around her because she was telling me about how her mum wouldn't speak to her on the telephone since seeing her reporting from Beirut and she needed comforting. That was it!"

How had they arranged to meet again? He remembered it as nothing special, he'd left messages for three or four colleagues to say he was heading for Amman, and asking if they were around. He was sure he'd mentioned in each message that he was also contacting the others, so there was no sense in which he'd been asking just Paula. And her reply, waiting for him at his hotel when he arrived, had been equally neutral.

"You fell for that line? She's a war reporter; we've all gotten over that stage with our mothers long ago."

"Okay, then," Ed started to relax again, even feel slightly amused. At least that feeling he'd had earlier of Paula effortlessly pulling the strings had disappeared. "Let's just say I'm not as wise, stroke cynical, as you are, but it doesn't alter the fact that nothing happened."

"Okay, I believe you…"

"Thank you."

"But I just don't understand… If you don't have any social life outside of work and you won't get involved with anyone connected to work, that leaves you precisely nothing, unless I'm missing something?"

"No, I don't think you are and it's not what I'd choose but it's where I've found myself."

"But it's ridiculous!" Paula was laughing now; the dam broken, the tension that had been building inside rolling through her.

"No, it's not, I can explain it to you perfectly rationally. We're in a high-risk occupation. We all know that, which is fine, but it doesn't alter the fact that half a dozen of my friends have died doing their job in the last 12 years or so. I'm ready to accept those risks for myself but I just can't do so for a partner or girlfriend. What I was trying to say was that their deaths affected me a lot, to the point where I'm scared I wouldn't be able to deal with the death of anyone I was genuinely close to. When Claude died – I was in Vienna when I heard – I just wandered the streets, didn't sleep for 48 hours – it was the closest to suicide I think I've come."

"What was it like?"

"Hard to describe really. Partly, I just felt empty, but I also felt confronted by a conception of life that was totally without point or hope. All my life, I've tried to add to people's understanding, to move things on. But when Claude died – you remember how random it was – I felt as if I'd just been kidding myself. Any miniscule increase in understanding was just a grain of sand, any sense of progress was pure illusion. I looked around me at all the Austrians and all the tourists and knew that none of them would care about Claude, even though a few of them had probably read some of his articles. They all had their own worries and concerns, with no room for anyone else's. And what was worse was that their lives seemed more important and significant than mine. Partly, they were connected to other people much more directly and strongly than I was, and partly they were concerned with much more tangible values and hopes. They were interested in jobs, salaries, promotions, houses, schools, health – all things that didn't really bother me for a mix of reasons that suddenly seemed arrogant in the extreme. I wanted to explain to the British people what was happening in Lebanon and Israel and the West Bank. But who was I to know those things in the first place and why was my analysis any better than anyone else's? And what exactly was I trying to achieve? It was as if I had set myself up as some kind of arbiter, across centuries and across different cultures and religions. And what good was that? What purpose did I have, what purpose did Claude have? And yet like the rest of us, he had believed in what he did and, in some corner of his mind, had been prepared to die for it. And of course, that is what happened, although not in any glorious or heroic way. It was just a simple, tragic mistake by a nervous young soldier."

"But you got through it?"

"Yes, I did." Ed paused. "You know, the funniest thing about it was that at least twice I tried to get drunk and totally failed. I thought that if I was going to be angry and get depressed, I might as well do it properly. But it just refused to happen; it was almost like by making the association I had somehow invalidated the act so that it became phoney, and it felt suddenly as though I was outside myself, watching me trying to self-destruct and showing zero sympathy."

"It sounds like a good self-defence mechanism to me," said Paula. "I don't think many people have that facility, not the way you describe. But maybe I'm wrong and the only thing different about you is that you're willing and able to talk about it. What happened when you pulled out of it and got back to normal? Did you talk to anyone about it?"

"Basically, I slept a lot, then one morning I woke up and felt fine again. And I haven't told anyone about it until now."

"So, why now?"

"Because you asked, I guess. Anyway, it's time I headed off. This has been quite a night," he paused, "and a good one."

"You should talk to people more, you know."

"Talk to you, you mean?"

"Yes, of course I mean me!" Paula laughed, "What do you think I've been trying to do all night?"

"Okay, I get the message." He smiled and stood up to go. "You know I mean what I said about tonight being good. I guess I've been running on autopilot too much."

"You do need a break. Maybe back to the Loire Valley. When was the last time you went?"

"1988 I think, it's hard to say."

"How long are you out here for?"

"Six more weeks from yesterday."

"After that?"

"Maybe."

"Shall I book it for you?"

"Let's talk about it tomorrow."

"Okay, I'll call you tomorrow," her eyes followed him as he walked out to the hotel reception to check in.

Chapter 28
Tel Aviv, Monday, 31 December 1990

Ed wandered south along the sea front towards the old town of Joppa. He had always enjoyed the buzz of Tel Aviv and even though he would rather not be here at this time of year, it was hard to resist the energy of the place. He was talking to Jim Yarmouth, out here with CNN, and they had both been in the press section the day Anwar Sadat had been assassinated. Ed had been reporting on the Middle East for more than 12 years but Jim had been doing so more than twice as long, going back to the Six Day and Yom Kippur Wars, and he was conscious of the difference in experience. For years, Jim had been with the main US channels, but last spring he had shocked his peers by switching to Ted Turner's rolling 24-hour news upstart.

Then, in August, Saddam Hussein had invaded Kuwait, and since then it had looked increasingly inevitable the US would lead an armed attempt to evict him, en route to who knew what end game. Suddenly, CNN was looking much better positioned than many of its rivals to bring to people's TV screen what, it was already clear, would be by far the most public war of the 20th century. Increasingly, TV and news organisations were 'embedding' – a newly coined use of the word – reporters within the coalition forces ahead of the expected invasion. Jim was sceptical about this new practice but keen to explain why he had been waiting almost all his career for the chance to work for a rolling news organisation. To hear him tell it, rather than being a pioneering risk-taker, even back in 1980, CNN was an idea that had been waiting to happen for more than a decade.

"I was back in Boston on vacation in '68," he explained, "and the madness of that time was starting to explode all around us. Shortly before, I had watched Cronkite's famous report from Vietnam, which concluded with him saying that he doubted the war could be won. We simply didn't give our personal opinions, period. And yet here was the most iconic reporter of his generation contradicting all the acres of propaganda we had been fed. You know the stuff – how we were endlessly winning the war – that delusional continuous present tense – but never actually got round to getting it won."

Ed almost said something but he decided to hold back, Jim was on a roll.

"But the real revolution was the Tet Offensive being broadcast live onto US television screens in US homes as it happened. Telstar and its successors cut out the middle men and created the inevitability that ordinary people, the voters for heaven's sake, would be able to access news as it happens in a raw, unadulterated, unintermediated form."

"How do you mean?"

"Well, for a start, because it's live, you have virtually no time to edit the images; a few have tried over the years to insert a delay but competition means it never lasts for long. Then there's the travel issue that allowed governments and occasionally reporters to 'interpret'" – he framed the speech marks – "the meaning of the events; but when you're responding to events in almost real time, it's completely different and all but eliminates the ability to impose a meaning. And finally, satellite broadens the access of different agencies and papers, which would previously have been much more restricted by the authorities' ability to control the communication lines."

"Well, I can see how all those things have changed," said Ed, "at least to an extent. But do you really think we're able to report better as a result?"

"That's a really interesting question, Ed, and there's a real issue about the degree to which the press has gone for more rather than better, particularly in a situation like this war coming up, where the press and the authorities have so much time to reach an accommodation with each other that it's very easy to end up with an elaborate stalemate, the press being satisfied with lots of access and spectacular images, and the army content they're in a position to exert effective control over what's reported."

"I'd much rather have more freedom and take my chances on the access," said Ed, "that's my job, after all."

"I know you would, but believe me you wouldn't want to turn the clock back too far. You're now able to tell the story that's there to be told much more than used to be the case. As long as you're not seduced by the easy interview or the neat but meaningless quote, you're in a much better position, believe me."

Ed walked on, thinking. There were hundreds of normal people, non-journalists, strolling along the seafront, catching the final hour of daylight before going home to get ready for parties, or on their way back from work, seemingly oblivious to the preparation for war that was taking place a few hundred miles to the east. He had always marvelled at people's capacity to conduct their lives more or less as normal in close proximity to extreme violence. The threat to Israel was not as immediate as it had often been, but the risk of being targeted by Iraqi missiles was clearly there and, for the sheer duration of their predicament, there was little to match the position of the Israelis and Palestinians. As if to ram home the reality, they were passed by a man on crutches who had lost his right leg above the knee. He was wearing a grey suit and pink shirt, obviously returning from work, with a trouser leg neatly pinned up. He was with a couple of friends chatting, and in every other respect looked no different from the people around him.

Jim too had paused, lost in his own thoughts, but now he continued. "I don't think anything has changed America so much as those images from Vietnam of the VC invading the grounds of the US Embassy in Saigon, and then, at the end, of that last helicopter taking off. Believe me, its consequences are still being felt."

"How?"

"Well, just look at the forces the US are assembling, just to get the Iraqis out of Kuwait. If this had been your guys a century ago, you'd have sent a few thousand men, deployed a few warships to set up a blockade and just got on with it. Granted these days you'd need air cover as well but you'd basically have evicted Saddam Hussein from Kuwait a lot sooner and at a fraction of the cost. But here we are, with the US having immensely superior weaponry – the equivalent of rifles against bows and arrows – but still needing some six months to put together an invasion force. You guys would have happily gone in outnumbered five to one, whereas now it needs to be something like ten to one in our favour before we'll make a move. All that began with Vietnam. Since then, and since Watergate, no one in the States has really believed what government tells us, particularly about wars. Seeing has become believing, which in turn has removed the Armed Forces' capacity to take risk, to engage in normal warfare. If it's going to be seen in US homes, it needs to be spectacular, clean and guaranteed successful, the complete antithesis of warfare through the ages."

"I've not heard you being so cynical before," observed Ed. "And normally you're very much in favour of reducing loss of life to a minimum."

"And I still am," Jim replied, "but I mean all human life, not just American life, though I care as much about that as any of my countrymen. But our high tech, safety first approach involves terrible, disproportionate casualties on the other side, and I genuinely worry sometimes that we're about to start turning warfare into a Hollywood movie.

"On the other hand, you're right and I was being too cynical," Jim smiled his wide grin. "The good side of all this is that we've become much more reluctant to go to war at all; or, for that matter, to get involved in sabre-rattling rhetoric. We used to engage in all sorts of wars in Latin America back in the '50s, invading Guatemala and all that, as well as threatening to nuke China. After '68 all of that stopped – we began getting out of Indochina; we started talking with the Soviets; we moved to a model of funding surrogate armies rather than using our own troops. And I'm sure that helped to keep the Cold War cold. Of course Reagan nearly forgot the lesson with his obsession with Star Wars and so on, but by then the Soviets had already started bleeding to death in Afghanistan."

"And you believe satellite TV has caused all that?" Ed could follow the logic but was still at the bounds of his own credulity.

"Well, causation is always an interesting subject, great to talk about but impossible to isolate. I suppose I would say satellite TV was both a catalyst and a necessary prerequisite."

"So where does the move to CNN fit in? Your move to work for the new kid on the block was a surprise to say the least."

"Yes, I was a bit surprised it stimulated so much interest. I sort of know that we all take an unhealthily close interest in each other's career moves, but it doesn't really register until you personally become the subject of it. And, you know what, I'm slightly disappointed, even depressed, that me changing jobs seems to have caught everyone pretty much unawares. I kinda thought you all knew me a little better than that, that you all knew I'd always been fascinated by innovation in news and, to be frank, that you knew I'd do almost anything to get my face on a screen for a few more hours a week."

"I'd never quite seen you as a narcissist, but now you mention it."

Jim continued, "I've been waiting for something like CNN to get a big enough footprint since it was launched. Once you have full coverage from satellite and a squad of journalists to match, you can cover the news live wherever it is. I accept some of the content will be weak, especially to start with, but the ability to be there quickly and then to put it on air, will completely change how the viewing public expect to see news presented."

"Why do you think that? I mean your costs are so high, are you sure it's sustainable?"

"Well, that's a good point but I think everyone else will be up in our territory fairly soon."

"Why's that?"

"Well, take this war everyone's getting ready for, when it finally starts, it'll be a case of trying to cover breaking events at no matter what time of day or night. CNN will be able to do that without breaking sweat but I suspect the BBC will find it hard. You won't have enough people out there to provide round the clock coverage, and you only really have your regular bulletins. In the old days, the time delay in getting a film and a transcript back to the studio allowed news to wait until the next bulletin. But we both know that won't wash anymore. We'll be broadcasting it right away, thereby forcing the rest to follow us. The BBC and others should have developed their own 24-hour news channel well before CNN even started, and now I think they'll have to, we'll force their hand."

Initially sceptical, Ed was now quite interested. "But surely the cost of being able to report anywhere, anytime, in the way you're talking about will be just too much – I know you don't think so but I'm not convinced so far."

"It depends how you look at it and what your business model is. I agree with you foreign reporting on this scale will probably never pay for itself, but what it does do is provide the credibility you need to make other, lower cost programmes that should be much more profitable. Those are the programmes – big name interviews and talk shows, business analysis and news, which will bring in the revenue. But we'll only get that premium status if we're accepted as the place to go for breaking news. The whole operation would be mutually reinforcing."

"Okay, I get all that in theory, or I think I do, but who's going to watch? What's your target audience?"

"Good question again but an easy one to answer. To start with, I think there is a core and growing market of business people who travel internationally. Their world is becoming more global and has been since mass air travel and, you guessed it, satellite communication, began in the '60s. More and more people are doing business and making deals in other countries and on other continents. You can see that from the proliferation of all those business hotels, some of which we stay in, that all look and feel spookily familiar to each other, and those luxury fashion brands that are starting to sell into less exclusive audiences. These people are already looking for a TV station of record that is accessible wherever they are. CNN is absolutely that. True, there are more established channels like the BBC that begin with a lot more credibility; but you'll never make the upfront investment needed to establish critical mass, not of your own volition anyway. Although you might follow up, we'll do it first and shake you out of your comfort zone." He smiled mischievously. "Are you scared yet?"

"Not exactly quaking in my boots but maybe a bit more nervous than I was half an hour ago. Not that I'm much of a corporate animal, as you well know. But I'm still not really clear who would be watching. I can get my head around your growing class of business travellers but there still aren't very many of them and I can't see that there will be for the foreseeable future."

"Okay, I'm more bullish than you about the growth of air travel, but I accept there needs to be a lot more than that core market. Which is why I mentioned those luxury goods companies, the Armanis, Calvin Kleins. They can see there's a mushrooming slice of the global population, not just in the western world, that can afford these sorts of status symbols. These people want to know more about the world because they're prepared to go anywhere to work where they can make money. So, even if they don't all travel a lot, they think of themselves much more as global citizens. And on a global basis, and even within the US, that's a big market for us to pitch to."

"And is all this why you moved to CNN?"

"Yes, mostly, I've been waiting 30 years for this job, but it's only really now that it's existed. As a young journalist, I thought rolling global news would happen this year or next, and I continued to think that until about '75, when reality and the onset of middle-age hit me at about the same time. Then, for about five years, I thought it would never happen, but for the last ten or so I've been becoming steadily more optimistic, ever since Ted Turner started up CNN in 1980."

"I'm impressed," said Ed, "awed really that you've had this vision for so long. And you really think the invasion of Iraq, assuming it happens, will be the tipping point for you?"

"Oh, I'm certain it'll happen," said Jim. "The scale of the build-up, and the diplomatic activity going on around it make it unimaginable that Bush isn't going to go in when he thinks he's got an overwhelming superiority, probably in a couple of months or so. Provided that is, Saddam doesn't withdraw, which would in many ways be smart of him, but I don't think he's that smart, otherwise he wouldn't have gotten himself into this position in the first place."

"Do you really think so? Wasn't it a reasonable bet that the US would let it be, and he could invade Kuwait without this sort of retaliation?"

"Well, not really. I mean I know the US funded Iraq during the war. But then we've had the Iran-Contra scandal and we now have a new president who's quite eager to distance himself, albeit subtly, from Reagan's foreign policy even though he was VP at the time. And then there's oil."

"Everything in this region comes back to that little three letter word. That's why they're here, the security of our energy supplies."

"Our motives are no worse than any other governments', Ed."

"So what's the difference this time?" Ed was frustrated and it showed in his voice. He knew Jim wasn't at all trying to patronise him, but he sometimes felt more the apprentice than he was comfortable with.

Jim was in full flow and failed to notice the edge. "I think the main thing that's changed is us. The presence of the media and the consequently greater visibility of warfare means it's impossible for countries like ours to engage in the sort of conflicts that used to be commonplace. And there's also a greater appreciation of the suffering in the world, with governments under far more pressure than before to help. Don't you see, Ed, we're at the crux of the whole thing. I'm not saying we're leading public opinion or anything like that – that's not our job – but what we choose to cover and how we report it really matters, perhaps more than it's ever done. That's really why I've moved to CNN."

Ed found himself regretting his momentary resentment and was grateful Jim had chosen not to respond to his barbed tone. There were times, and this was now one of them, when he felt extraordinarily small. Even though Jim had spoken about the greater importance of journalism, the overall effect was to create a perspective within which he felt dwarfed by the changes. Reporting the truth as he saw it, conveying the meaning of events by explaining the connections between them, these were the reasons he had become a journalist. Only in the last couple of sentences had he really understood the calling Jim was describing, and that spurt of comprehension had opened a trapdoor back into his memory so that, for the first time in years, he could recall the sense of purpose he had carried in his early career. The corrosive effect of experience had eaten away at it to the point where they were hardly recognisable. Ed felt physically lighter as they turned around and headed back to their hotel.

With the change of direction, the conversation also lightened, and they spent the rest of their walk swapping stories and information about friends and colleagues. They were staying in the same hotel but going to different New Year's Eve parties at their respective embassies. The two men embraced in the lobby and promised to stay in touch. Jim was flying to Kuwait the next day while Ed was staying in Israel another week before hopping across to Amman.

***

A couple of hours later, showered and dressed, Ed showed his invitation and walked through the entrance to the British Embassy in Tel Aviv, a clean, modern building. The party was about half full, he judged, and the atmosphere was already lively. 1990 had been a monumental year in foreign policy terms, even aside from the change of prime minister. But in this world, time moves either very fast or very slowly, with little in between, and most of the talk was therefore of the year to come and the anticipated invasion of Iraq.

"Saddam's properly over-reached himself this time," pronounced one Foreign Service veteran. "He's managed to unite his enemies, which has been a cardinal error since the days of Sun Tzu, and at a stroke has lost whatever capital he had built up with the West."

"Mind you, there was never much of that in reality," replied another. "It was mostly a case of using US antipathy to Iran and his own ambitions; a temporary alignment of interests. And then, of course, what there was he frittered away when he used chemical weapons against his troublesome Kurdish population."

"Yes, I'd momentarily forgotten that," replied the first, "mind you, nothing in our reaction would have necessarily signalled to him that our preparedness to support him informally had necessarily ceased due to his use of chemical weapons. Mrs T was more interested in Star Wars at the time, looking to stay in step with our Atlantic cousins."

"Of course, we could have made it more obvious, but if Saddam had possessed any half decent foreign policy advisers, he wouldn't be making these mistakes."

Ed moved casually around the room, acknowledging the few diplomats with whom he had had regular dealings over the years. He knew he was one of the few journalists invited – not many British journalists were in Tel Aviv over New Year – and he had long ago decided such occasions were fundamentally off the record. No one had ever been explicit to him about this but that was par for the course. He well realised that one of the reasons he was sometimes invited to these occasions was that he was trusted as someone who didn't need to be told such things. In any case, the two Foreign Office characters he had overheard were saying nothing he hadn't heard before. Such talk was relatively common in the circles journalists moved, and he had always been bemused why more of it, pompous as it could often sound, didn't make it into what was reported. Some of the reason, he thought, was that there was still an unspoken feeling that we were all on the same side, which meant it was much harder to be critical of British government policy in foreign affairs than it was in domestic. As for the rest, Ed could only conclude there was an implicit mistrust of the British public's intelligence. Each event tended to be presented and explained almost solely in its own terms, with little of the real context and probable causation. The conversation he had just overheard had itself been quite superficial, as well as laced with self-regard, but there clearly was a connection between the Iran-Iraq war and Iraq's invasion of Kuwait, and between Saddam's use of chemical weapons on his own population and the decline of his relationship with the West. It was equally true that none of this was apparent in the rhetoric surrounding them.

Ed's own view was that most people could easily understand most of this but would rarely spend the time needed to absorb the necessary information. Maybe one of the indirect results of CNN would be more space for a diversity of in-depth coverage of issues and a larger audience for those programmes. As he allowed his glass to be refilled, he wondered what had happened to the now legendary audiences for Panorama and World in Action during the 1970s. His own family had been regular viewers but he doubted their socio-economic descendants would sit through a weekly, hour-long analysis of a single issue, regardless of whether it was of any specific interest. Maybe that audience did still exist somewhere but, if so, it was almost impossible to locate.

This seemed like a quite different sort of war to those he was used to covering. Nothing was being left to chance. The coalition included both Israelis and Saudis, as well as various NATO countries. Saddam had become a pariah. More than any war he could remember, almost everything seemed to be known about it in advance. In a short period, the build-up of troops had been dramatic and ostentatious, designed to signal to Saddam that his only available option was ignominious withdrawal. It seemed clear, however, that Saddam wouldn't take this route and so the whole elaborate exercise was in essence a PR tool designed to put responsibility for the war on Iraq by seeming to demonstrate that all other choices had been exhausted.

Suddenly feeling tired – he had arrived late from London a couple of nights before, having waited two hours on the runway at Heathrow – he fell into conversation with a young couple, Alex and Cathy Preston, whom he had met back in October when he had been researching a piece on wider regional reaction to Saddam's invasion. Alex was a businessman trying to build links between the UK and Israeli software companies and Cathy was a lawyer who had decided to work in Israel for a couple of years. Both were British Jews, Cathy was in her early 30s, Alex a couple of years younger, and Ed had instinctively liked them from the first. They seemed to move easily between Israeli and expatriate communities and had worked

278

hard to keep an open mind about the issues that bedevilled Israel's reputation. He also like them because, somewhat bizarrely, Cathy was a Derby County fan, having fallen in love with them in their early 70s pomp. Alex, meanwhile, a more conventional Arsenal fan, affected an air of patronising amusement at his girlfriend's attraction to the East Midlands, while not very secretly being delighted he could talk football with her.

They greeted Ed enthusiastically before asking what he was doing spending New Year in Tel Aviv.

"You know how it is, usual stuff, work to do, people to see."

"You're mad," said Alex, "Cathy and I are only here because we sort of live here now." He looked at her shyly.

"What he means," laughed Cathy, "is that we're in the middle of buying an apartment together."

"Congratulations," said Ed, "I'm glad you've finally managed to make an honest man of him. But why here? I thought you'd both probably end up back in North London somewhere."

Cathy laughed again, "Trust you to come straight out with the obvious question. We should've had a bet on how long it would take you." She glanced quickly at Alex, not because she needed confirmation of what she was about to say but because she was consciously getting into the habit – not easy for her – of referring to Alex when she was about to pronounce on subjects that involved them both. "To be honest," she continued, "we talked about it long and hard; after all, our families are back in England and we'd both always intended to stay here just a couple of years. But Israel does get under your skin, I think it does with everyone Jewish, and we decided we want to stay here together at least for a few more years. After all, it's where we met, there's lots of work for us here and it's a young country."

"Do you worry at all about the long-term security?"

"We do a little," Alex answered, "but London isn't the safest place in the world either. Israeli's survived more than 40 years, through several wars, and there's no sign it's planning on disappearing any time soon."

"There's a lot more I could ask you, in fact I want to ask you, but I'd be veering over into my journalistic mode and that wouldn't be right, particularly with friends, and especially on New Year's Eve. So instead, I'll subtly change the subject and ask what you're looking for in 1991."

"You're not changing the subject at all," said Cathy, "you're just trying, not so subtly, to get us to carry on talking about the security situation. Next up, you'll be asking us about settlements on the West Bank and the status of East Jerusalem. But they're all fair questions, so why don't you come and see us properly one day when we're properly settled into our new apartment. But for now, tell us about your year and what you think will happen with Iraq?"

"Okay," agreed Ed, pleased that he had got the interview he had wanted all along. "Well, to be honest, I'm a little in two minds about the whole Iraq situation. It feels to me like only the latest chapter in a long, sorry saga. No one's talking about getting rid of Saddam, probably rightly as Bush wants to build as broad a coalition as possible, and in any case, the pain the US would go through trying to build a stable state after him would be just enormous. But until he's gone and, to be honest, the whole region is more opened up, less dominated by dictators, then we're going to continue going around in circles. Israel's problem is that you've ended up feeling more comfortable dealing with people like Mubarak, who you think are reliable, than with more populist, democratic regimes who you fear would be more inclined to support actively the rights of the Palestinians."

"Except that there's no realistic prospect any time soon of any of these countries becoming democracies."

"Fair point, but one of the reasons for that is because the US supports the current regimes much more than it would if Israel didn't want to keep rulers like Mubarak in power."

"And if Mubarak fell, what do you think would happen?" asked Alex.

"I have absolutely no idea," laughed Ed. "What I do think is that the peace Israel craves will ultimately need to be made with the plurality of Arab peoples, not with the corrupt dictators who currently rule over them."

"Okay," said Alex, "my turn to say it's getting too heavy for a New Year's Eve. But how about, when you come round, if you stay on for dinner, I'd like to hear more. Seriously, I mean it…"

"Well, now you two have sorted out when you're going to have your Middle East workshop, we can get back to the more interesting subjects we should have been talking about from the start. Like why you, Ed, are here by yourself. To be honest, I don't really get the fact that you're here at all but, since you are, there has to be a woman involved, so where is she?" Ed shook his head in mock despair, his eyes twinkling. "Or him?" Cathy was persistent but Ed just repeated his maudlin gesture. "Okay, so what's the story then? Come on, we've known each other long enough; time to tell us something interesting about yourself."

Ed looked slightly pleadingly at Alex. "Is she always this direct?" he asked.

"You'd better believe it," Alex replied.

"Well, what can I tell you? That I'm mysteriously but serially unattractive to women, certainly past about six weeks. I'm glad you're at least a little surprised," Ed continued. "It's an indication there might be some hope for me yet, that I'm not completely a lost cause."

"Well, I don't know," said Cathy. "It could be much worse than that. Maybe you have some terrible vice not detectable on first impressions, that's driven off a host of eligible women once they get to know you better. Surely it can't be that you're one of those men who says yes to sex but no to commitment?"

This was still familiar territory to Ed, although the conversation was moving faster than usual. "If only it were that simple," he said. "I don't think commitment's been the issue, although of course you'd need to ask the women concerned, but after a while, my lifestyle does tend to become a problem."

"How do you mean?"

"Well, long absences, late finishes, early starts, some personal danger, short-term changes to plan."

"Ah, so are these poor, misguided women making that fatal mistake of trying to change you?"

"Maybe, though I doubt any of them would have put it quite like that."

"Ah, but that's because the sisters have become cleverer over the years. We all want to change our men. And men are the opposite, wanting their women to remain the same as when they first fancied you. They want you to have kids but still want you to look the same as that first time. But back to the specific! You're not obviously a total bastard and, in fact, you show none of the usual symptoms, but I can see you would be stubborn and fixed in your own ways. Does any of that sound familiar?"

Ed laughed. He was enjoying fencing with Cathy. "Some of it maybe," he replied. "I don't really see my time as my own and so there's not a lot I have discretion over."

"Which in turn presumably means that when you are free, it's better if your girlfriend is too," Cathy continued. "I see it all now, the gradual realisation from both of you that you just aren't seeing enough of each other and that it's very difficult to see what can be changed that would really make a difference."

"I wouldn't have put it like that. There are an awful lot of things about my lifestyle I would have real trouble changing even if I wanted to."

"But do you want to?"

"Well, some of them, yes definitely, of course I do. But it's virtually impossible to make little changes, the whole thing pretty much stands or falls together; it's hard to change things in isolation."

"Yes, but have you tried? As a woman, I think the question I'd be asking would be whether this is going to be an equal relationship, or was your job and the lifestyle attached to it always going to be immovably and unalterably there, effectively ruling out any kind of negotiation. Which I guess does come back to commitment, but is also about whether they are really having a relationship with you or with your journalistic lifestyle."

Alex interjected, "Aren't you being a touch harsh, Cath? I mean, the poor man's here by himself on New Year's Eve."

"I'm sure Ed's okay with our conversation, aren't you? He knows he's with friends and that we're absolutely on his side. And besides, I only ever give a hard time to people I like."

"It's fine, Alex, Cathy's right. They are the questions I ask myself. But if I knew the answers, I might not be here alone. And by the way, while this wasn't exactly the type of conversation I imagined having this evening, I'm not very good at small talk and rubbish at circulating, so I'd much rather be here trying to explain the desert of my love-life to the two of you than twittering on about something altogether meaningless."

"I'd have thought that, being a journalist, you'd be really good at small talk?" said Alex.

"Not really, I need a purpose, a reason to go and talk to strangers. And then again, I have a shite memory for names; unusual for a journalist, but true. I have to write people's names in my notebook more or less immediately to have any chance of remembering them."

"That's just bizarre," exclaimed Cathy. "I thought you people were walking address books."

"There's always the exception that proves the rule."

"But we're digressing," said Cathy, "when we need to find solutions to your inflexible lifestyle."

"The other thing you might like to throw into your earnest considerations," added Ed, "is the risk factor. What I do only rarely feels dangerous on the ground, but people do get killed doing it, and I doubt it does much for your sense of inner calm seeing your partner on TV wearing a helmet and flak jacket."

"Fair point," conceded Cathy, "but let's not conflate what are quite separate issues. The first is about whether you can plan some weekends together and stick to them; the second is about the probability of you getting shot or blown up."

"Thanks for putting it so clearly," Ed was amused, "it helps clarify the real issues."

"You're welcome," said Cathy. "So?"

"Okay then," Ed conceded, "you're probably right that, after 13 years, I could probably say no a bit more often, but at the end of the day, this is a vocation for me. I don't want to sound grand or conceited about it but I don't really do this to make money. Earning a decent wage and not being exploited is important, but in this particular job, it's a secondary thing. And that's more or less true of all of us, not just me. By and large it's a pretty blue-collar profession; the journalists who do best tend, almost without exception, to be those most prepared to graft and get their hands dirty."

"You know what," said Cathy, "that's a wonderful thing you've got. I don't really have any of that about the law, or not with anything like the intensity. I know people who do feel that way about the law, and I have huge respect for them, as well as a good deal of envy, but it's a long way from where I am. Who knows, maybe it will come."

"I hope so," said Ed, "I know people, including some good friends, who've had a much less direct route than I have to finding the right career, vocation, whatever you want to call it. Some of them originally just went into a job for the sake of it, and then they just got really into what they were doing, started believing in it to the point where it's really become part of their identity. And then, to be honest, I know others who've had a completely different journey."

Cathy was conscious they had somehow gotten away from talking about Ed's unwillingness to make compromises between his job and his relationships, and suspected he had subtly engineered the shift. But she decided not to pursue, not this evening at any rate. "The whole sense of someone having a vocation and the bittersweet nature of it really fascinates me," she said instead. "It's a bit like love; maybe easier in that we on the whole expect less of our vocations, but also harder because the vocation will be much harder to influence, so we end up much more likely to be subject to its vagaries."

"I think I agree," said Ed, "except that a vocation is much more caught up in our sense of self, whereas love is more about sharing and giving of yourself. Vocation is about the type of person you are, right down to your DNA."

"But if you're disappointed, or you work out you were wrong and you weren't that sort of person, then haven't you just got to recover from it like any other failure or setback?" asked Alex.

"Is that how you really see it? You make it all sound very clinical," said Ed.

"I don't think I mean to, except that I do think it's just a normal part of life, and we've all just got to get on with it."

"That doesn't leave a great deal of space for vulnerability or weakness," observed Ed. "Your world view is a harsh one unless you're strong and lucky."

"Why lucky?" Alex asked. "Intelligent and determined maybe, but for me luck is overrated."

"Maybe it's age," said Ed, "I think I used to think the same, but in the last few years I've come to the conclusion that luck does matter. You can certainly earn it maybe, I don't know, 80% of it, but at some point it returns to pure chance. I've seen it time and again, where things go wrong for someone, no matter how hard they've worked, or how well they've prepared."

"Okay, maybe on a small scale, but look at the US, or at the British Empire; they didn't rely on luck, or on the goodwill of others."

"But Alex, I look at that and I see the US having to make lots of compromises to build this alliance, trimming its objectives here, promising extra aid there, so it can isolate Iraq as much as possible."

"But isn't it able to do that because it's so powerful?"

Ed decided to leave the argument there. He was enjoying the debate but it had potential to flip over into a more difficult discussion about Israel and the Palestinians, which he felt it wouldn't be right to have in the British Embassy. He worried that with the end of the Cold War there was a growing urge to think of the world in overly simplistic terms. And by the growing feeling he had that little could really be controlled, and that even the US was in no position to invade and occupy even a relatively small country like Iraq.

After a few more minutes' small talk, he bade goodbye to Cathy and Alex, promising to catch them again at midnight and having arranged a date to go around to interview them and have dinner. He continued to circulate amiably, enjoying the company but feeling detached from these people. Approaching 11.15pm, Ed began to feel alone, by himself in a world where others belonged. He felt like this increasingly often but couldn't put his finger on when it had started.

He remembered Sam and Mary's wedding, when he suddenly felt of a different generation; there were lots of people his age but they were there with partners and they had recent shared experiences and expectations whereas his were different, and not of the sort he could easily talk about; they would sound either depressing or somehow boastful. And so he had largely observed, got quietly drunk and tried to remain as upbeat and cheerful as possible.

He decided to head quietly back to his hotel. As a means of detaching himself surreptitiously from the group he was talking with, he made excuses to go to the toilet. Then he was able to edge his way out unnoticed except by a couple of slightly surprised security guards. Once in the fresh air his mood lightened. Part of it was the smell of the Mediterranean, and partly it was the simple act of recalling that he was doing what he had always wanted and was still enjoying it. Thinking back to his conversation with Jim Yarmouth, Ed also began to wonder about some of the potential the future held – even if Jim was only a little bit right, it sounded pretty exciting – imagine if he still had Jim's energy and enthusiasm to be doing this job or something similar ten years from now!

And then, inexorably, Ed's mind turned to what he was certain would be a short and bloody conflict to evict Iraq from Kuwait and, who knows, depose Saddam in the process. But he worried that if the war went badly for the Iraqi army, as he suspected it quickly would, Saddam might easily be tempted to use chemical or even biological weapons. Then too, he was thought to have Scud missiles, with a range long enough to reach here in Tel Aviv. Who knew what reaction that might provoke? By the time he reached his hotel, he'd rebalanced his emotions and cheered up to the point where he got himself a drink and lingered on the edge of partygoers as the clock chimed. Roll on 1991.

Chapter 29
New York, Saturday, 8th September 2001

Ed was staying in a small hotel in the Village. It wasn't great but then it wasn't expensive. He had stayed there the first time he'd been to New York at the end of the 70s when, inspired and amused by Starsky and Hutch, Kojak, and Woody Allen films, he had come across on Laker Airways to find out how much garbage there actually was left out on the street and how much noise and bustle there really was. He hadn't exactly fallen in love with the city back then – he'd already lost his heart to the Middle East, to Cairo and Beirut, and the remains of the Ancient World. But he did acquire a deep affection for the place and thought he understood why America managed to work.

He wandered across 7th and into a little jazz bar he liked. He'd eaten already, enough anyway, and was looking to kill an hour before going to a party he'd been invited to uptown. He ordered a beer and, noticing his favourite corner table was already taken, he sat by the bar. It was still early, and there was only the resident piano player tinkling away, playing a range of standards, from Ella and Billie Holiday to Joni Mitchell and Carole King. Later there would be an act but for now he was happy listening to the old man peddling timeless refrains of failed love affairs, wry sensibility, defeat and stoical optimism.

He remembered someone called Mike, who he'd known slightly at Manchester, playing this song on an old piano maybe 25 years ago and didn't think he had heard it live since…figure skaters, percolators, candles and cafés…

He'd always wanted to be a dreamer but knew deep down he wasn't. At the end of the day, he was too practical, too much of a doer. And then, the clincher he suspected, he didn't actually dream very much.

"Are you here for the evening, mister?" asked the barman, curious about how long this Englishman was hanging around and, as well, just making small talk. "Are you waiting for anyone?"

"No," replied Ed, answering both questions, "just killing some time before heading uptown." He realised this sounded too matter of fact and so added some friendlier words. "I like the place and always try to pop in for at least a drink whenever I'm in New York."

"How long have you been coming here?"

"About 20 years, just when I'm in town."

"Why here, there are lots of more glamorous places?"

"I don't know really, habit I guess, but I've always liked it, probably just an atmosphere thing. And the music's always been good," he added, nodding to the piano player, who was now embarking on 'You Can't Take That Away From Me'.

The barman moved on, satisfied Ed was not some weirdo in off the street and also clear that there was no point in cultivating him as a source of tips later in the evening.

Ed had got in the previous evening and arranged to see his friend Dan for a drink and something to eat. They had met at a wedding about ten years ago and got on like a house on fire. Since then, they had met up every year or two when Ed was in London. Dan had gone into merchant banking and, when the traditional British merchants were swallowed up by US and European giants in the years after the City of London's Big Bang, he had moved first to Deutsche Bank and then around a succession of the big players. In 2000, now with Morgan Stanley, Dan had been moved to New York and this was the first time Ed had seen him since.

In general, his trips to New York had tended to be rambling cultural tours, almost always alone, hanging out in bars and jazz clubs, sleeping a lot but not always regularly, and generally just trying to soak the place up. This one was slightly different, and whereas previous itineraries only sometimes featured meeting up with even one friend, this time there were two; for, as well as Dan, an old friend called Chris Hunter had invited him to a party tonight at his apartment in the West 50s.

Meeting Dan the night before hadn't been quite what Ed had been expecting, and he was still trying to work out what it meant. The last he knew, Dan had been in a steady relationship with Rebecca for more than seven years, and she had managed to move her job – she was a lawyer – to New York so they could go there together. But when he had turned up to meet him the first thing that Dan told him was that they had split up.

Dan had not been obviously contrite, since they were drinking in a bar called Scores which, instead of being the sports bar Ed had imagined, turned out to be an upmarket lap dancing joint. Although he hadn't indulged – $20 was the going rate – Dan was clearly a regular and was acknowledged cheerfully by several of the dancers. Ed was not by a long shot an idealist on this subject; his feminist credentials, such as they were, were sullied by several trips to strip clubs around the world. All these occasions, however, had been when he was away from home, single, and much younger. Moreover, the Dan he had grown to like, who had move to New York with Rebecca, had clearly changed a good deal. It was impossible to conceive of that Dan arranging to meet him in Scores and hard to believe the change was for the better.

They had greeted each other like the old friends they were but the truth was Ed had scarcely recognised him. Dan's face was bloated and red, and he had put on a good couple of stone, Ed guessed. He had other friends who at some stage had travelled this road. The journey often coincided with the arrival of children or the break-up of a relationship; a lot of hours at work and drinking with work colleagues was also often a feature. It was hard to tell what had caused the change in Dan but there was certainly no sign of depression.

"Ed!" he'd exclaimed, "I can't believe you made it over. What time did you get in? Great to see you! How's life in the war zone?"

The questions came thick and fast, Ed barely managing monosyllabic replies to each before it was on to the next. But he detected no sense that Dan was asking lots of questions to deflect him from asking his own; instead, it seemed he was simply glad to see him. Dan seemed more effusive, but maybe that was only his memory adjusting to the new context.

"So what happened with Rebecca?" Ed asked finally. "I never imagined the two of you breaking up. But I guess moving continent can be pretty destabilising?"

"Oh, it wasn't really that," Dan replied, "I was just a real bastard to her. I mean, I ended up in a situation where I cheated on her. There had been a couple of near misses back in London but this time I went through with it."

"Why, what made you do it?"

"Nothing made me do it; one night I just made a different choice. Maybe if I'd thought about it before, I wouldn't have crossed the line this time. I don't know, I think there was something about the idea becoming more normal, whereas before you wouldn't have even thought about."

"What about Rebecca? How did she find out?"

"Well, to be honest, I more or less told her. I've always known I'm a crap liar, and so when I got home about 7am and she asked me where I'd been, I just told her the truth. It was pretty much a one night stand, so I told her that too but it didn't make any difference. Can't blame her really, though you always kind of hope for a second chance."

"You sound pretty calm about it; when did it happen?"

"End of June so, what, about ten weeks. It's funny how quickly you get used to major changes in your life. I guess it's helped that I never thought it was anyone's responsibility but mine. And the fact that I was testing the boundaries of our relationship tells me there was a part of me already looking for a way out. I mean I love Rebecca a lot, but I've never really seen her as the centre of my life, the sun around which everything else revolves. In fact, I've always hated all the romantic stuff around relationships."

Ed had been slightly taken aback by the casual honesty with which Dan had described the end of a seven-year relationship. It was as if it was self-justifying, as if to say, "if I'd cared more, I wouldn't have slept with the other woman." On one level, Ed found this refreshing, free of obfuscation. But he saw that at the same time as apparently taking full responsibility, Dan was letting himself off the hook by implying a sense of inevitability. He'd wanted to ask why, if he had been close to having sex with another woman in the past, he'd done nothing about it, just waited for the next time. But he'd long ago promised himself not to behave like a journalist when with friends, and in any case, a lap dancing bar didn't seem the right setting.

"So why are we meeting here?" he had asked instead. "You seem to be something of a regular?"

"It's just a little light relief really, after long days at work. The people are decent, it's a pretty relaxed atmosphere, not like some of these places. I never used to come here before Rebecca moved out, but now I tend to drop by for a couple of beers maybe once or twice a week."

"Dan, you sound miles different talking like this than you would have done two or three years ago, when you wouldn't have been seen dead in a place like this."

"Oh don't get all prudish and moral on me, Ed! I'd be shocked if you tried to tell me you hadn't done far worse on your travels."

"Maybe I have," Ed responded warily, "but this is a pretty new thing for you and I doubt you need it. If Rebecca is really over for good – have you tried to get her to come back? – Then why aren't you out meeting some new people?"

"I don't know," he said, "I've never really seen myself that way. Rebecca and I sort of fell in together, more by chance than anything. And she made most of the running, to be honest. And I didn't really want the responsibility of another serious relationship. I had a serious go and managed to screw it up, so why should I think I'd be any better at it if I tried again? I don't want to hurt someone else the way I have with Rebecca. Coming here, moving into this new job, made me realise how much of life is in the here and now. I've spent almost 20 years being heavy about things, playing it long but never really getting much back for it. And I know this all sounds selfish, but I just want a little bit more fun, a little payback on all I've put in over the years."

"I know what you mean," replied Ed, "and I'm the last person who would give you a hard time. And my life's far more of a mess than yours, so there's no way I'm going to try and peddle you any advice. But how about we have a last drink somewhere else before I head for sleep? I can feel the jet lag just starting to kick in; it's 7am in the UK, way past even my bedtime."

They'd gone on to a quieter bar and talked for about another hour while Ed wolfed down some food. Although they'd not argued in Scores, both knew they'd tiptoed around areas where they wouldn't agree and separately decided to steer the conversation into safer waters. When Ed had said goodbye, he tried to hug him the way he always did but they both knew the chances of him flying to New York to see Dan again had got a lot smaller in the last couple of hours.

Ed finished his drink and decided to walk the 30 plus blocks to the party. He wondered about the shift in Dan's outlook on the world and its profound effect on his life. Or was it perhaps the other way round, and the new outlook had emerged as a means of adjusting to his suddenly changed circumstances. Many times, he had seen political narratives written to explain and justify events that had already happened. Some of these were knowing fabrication, but many more were honestly told, and often no less significant for the fact they were based on a selective analysis of the facts. He knew from experience that even if they bore only scant relation to the real causes, they often provided considerable direction and momentum in shaping the future.

In all of this, he felt sorry for Rebecca, who was clearly the victim of whatever kind of mid-life crisis, call it what you will, had taken hold of her partner. Ed was pretty sure she would have been devastated, and Ed would never have guessed Dan would be unfaithful. It seemed odd thinking about this on the way to what Ed suspected would be a swanky Manhattan party, but on the other hand, to all intents and purposes, it was New York that had precipitated Dan crossing whatever line he had transgressed.

As he strolled up 6th Avenue, the twilight was beginning to drain away, the streetlight starting to come on, and Manhattan was taking on its familiar nocturnal glare. On one level, New York was a city like any other, but because it was the most filmed city on earth, multiple images of it – not just the iconic skyline but the night-time traffic, the waterfront, the bridges and so on – lingerer and resonated in his mind. More tangibly than in any other city he knew, Ed felt a permanent air of desperation in how New York's inhabitants went about the most normal of daily routines. Again, he didn't know if this was a real emotion he sensed, imagination, or artifice. There seemed to be no equilibrium about the place, leaving the danger of creating a hole in the middle. With New York, everyone seemed as though they had recently arrived or were about to move somewhere. And it was that sense of people never really being satisfied that gave NYC its edge.

And what about himself? Was he satisfied? It was a difficult term to even acknowledge because of its implication that there was nothing left to aim for. If he was not completely satisfied, and couldn't conceive of ever being so, then at least he was not actively dissatisfied. He was in the career he wanted, had friendships that mattered to him, and enough money not to worry about it. Being mostly single was hard sometimes – there was a feeling life was slipping away faster because he was living it alone – but he felt incapable of changing direction.

Dan's predicament, though Ed was far from sure Dan saw it as that, continued to disturb him. There already seemed a sad inevitability about his trajectory, but he was clearly comfortable, or believed he was, with his new single status, his high-powered job, and the financial and emotional freedom these provided. The man he had met last night may have been altered from the friend he thought he knew, but Dan himself clearly saw it as an improvement and had seemed carefree rather than guilt-ridden. It was as if he had cut himself loose from his previous life and was floating away. Conversely, of course, this freedom came at the price of cutting himself off from much of his previous life, reducing it to a footnote.

Had Dan just gone through his mid-life crisis? Ed laughed at the miniscule chance of his own life going through a similar mould-breaking. He felt himself locked in, largely in a good way, to quite tight patterns of activity and behaviour; locked in so tightly that nothing resembling a mid-life crisis seemed possible. In some ways, he did not have the same anchor as Dan to break away from, but his life was still every bit as predictable as the one Dan had just torn up.

Barely half an hour later, Ed was standing on the roof terrace of a central Manhattan apartment block, looking out over the New York skyline, sipping a Margarita and talking to a beautiful woman he'd never met before. For reasons that escaped him, she seemed to be chatting him up and suddenly his life didn't feel predictable at all. He briefly considered the possibility she was a spy intent on seducing him to gain access to his jealously guarded phone book of sources. Then he wondered if Chris had told her he was an eccentric millionaire and decided this was much more probable. Her name was Esther Spalding, and she was asking him how long he was in New York.

"Just till Tuesday," Ed replied, "then I catch the overnight plane back to London."

"That's a shame," she complained, "and you only got here yesterday. That's barely four days, not nearly long enough."

"I know, I wish I could stay longer but this was the longest trip I could fit in this time around, and I thought it was better to make it over for a short time than not at all."

"When were you last here?"

"About three years, 1998."

"And how long was that visit, four days again?"

"More or less, I don't tend to stay anywhere for very long."

"Well, in that case, we'll just have to think of ways to make New York a more attractive destination for you."

"It's not so much that, I'd love to be able to stay longer."

Esther smiled, "In that case, we'll just have to help you make the most of it."

It turned out Esther was a lawyer, corporate, not a partner but not far off, she thought, single and in her early 30s. She knew Chris through his sister and seemed to know quite a lot about Ed. Gradually, it dawned on Ed that Chris had in fact set him up. Maybe his visit had come up in conversation and Chris had explained his job – the years in the Middle East, the Berlin Wall and its aftermath, the Iraq War, she knew something about his involvement in all of them, or rather his bystander status as he currently liked to term it. Even more, Chris had evidently given Esther some sense of what a sad bastard he was, and she still seemed to be chatting him up. Normally, Ed hated being set up – he would have thought Chris knew him better – and disliked even more being someone's reform mission. But this evening he was flattered, and his usual reactions and prejudices were swept aside.

In truth, aside from being herself, Esther was doing nothing special beyond being interested in this introverted Englishman, knowledgeable yet reticent, whom she found impossible to situate among the other men she'd met. Often, she would have found the experience frustrating, but this evening she had only an urge to understand him, to make herself so important to him that he would relax and open up so they could communicate without barriers.

Esther was on the rebound from a five-year relationship, but that had been more than six months ago, and she felt as though she had regained her equilibrium. Ed was mistaken in believing Chris had set him up, and in fact Chris had, if anything, attempted to warn Esther off, not from any malice but because he thought Ed's solitary temperament a poor match for her, particularly at the moment.

To his surprise, and in addition to the flattery and physical attraction, Ed was enjoying talking to Esther. Despite her being more than ten years younger, they shared many of the same tastes in music – Bruce Springsteen, The Clash; and in films – Blue Velvet, Blade Runner; it was almost like Esther was a half-generation throwback, or maybe it was him… Ed even began to suspect she was agreeing with him because she wanted to rather than because she did.

Chris gravitated over to speak to them. Given the suspicion that he had been set up, Ed would usually have viewed his friend with a slight tinge of resentment; alternatively, because he was so much enjoying being chatted up, as he imagined, he might have viewed the intervention with an element of resentment. But as it was, so unusually happy was he that he simply smiled inanely and clinked glasses.

"Thanks again for inviting me. Every time I come to New York, you seem to have some fantastic social event going on; and since they're clearly not arranged for me, I can only assume you have an infinitely more exciting life than I do."

"On the contrary, Ed, you're talking crap like you always do when you come to New York. I only wish you were in New York more often; just stop trying to be demure and polite – it really doesn't suit."

"Well Ed's been the soul of politeness talking to me. I should clearly accept more of your party invitations in future," Esther interjected.

"Oh Esther, you sound like some Edith Wharton or Henry James character. I never know if it's you talking, or if you're just making fun of me."

"It's okay, Chris, it's mostly me, this time, and I am having a lovely evening."

Chris looked at her. "I can't always guarantee this calibre of European guest you know. By his own admission, Ed is one of my more difficult friends, and I sometimes think it's a matter of some pride to him; not because he's difficult on purpose, but because he quite enjoys the idea of being difficult without trying. But please excuse me for a few minutes; Mina is gesticulating from the kitchen. Clearly, my presence is required."

When Chris had gone, Esther said, "Which hotel are you staying at? Can I come back with you for a drink?" she asked.

"Yes, of course," he replied, trying to disguise his total astonishment.

Against his better judgement, Ed allowed himself to slip away with Esther without saying goodbye. He half tried to kid himself that they were both too busy to disturb and that he had only just spoken to Chris anyway. But he knew it was really to avoid the risk of knowing looks, and his own blushing, and at the same time the absolute futility of attempting to pretend that he was not overwhelmed by what appeared to be the reality of Esther wanting to go to bed with him.

When they had hailed a taxi outside and got in, Ed asked Esther where she lived. She told him, then added, "But I was hoping not to be going home tonight."

He looked at her and reached for her hand, which instinctively had also sought his, gripping it tight. "Are you sure about this?" Ed asked, "We don't really know each other, and I don't have a great record in long-term relationships, i.e. none."

"That's fine," Esther replied, "let's take tonight and see what we feel like in the morning." She paused, "I've never done anything like this, you know. And I'm sort of still on the rebound, but that relationship ended over six months ago, so I don't think that's really why I'm sitting here. But here I am, a streetwise California girl, living in New York the last ten years and doing the most spontaneous thing I've ever done in my life." She looked at him again. "But I'm really happy I'm here, with you."

"Good," said Ed, "because I couldn't begin to explain why this is happening. I feel okay about it, happy in fact, but this is a hell of a long way from the evening I expected. You know, I spent last night talking to an old friend whose relationship had just split up because he'd had a fling with someone at work and now tonight…" He paused. "I'm sorry, that didn't come out the way I wanted it to; I'll blame it on the jetlag if I may."

"That's fine," she said, "I've made a decision about you, and it'll take much more than a misplaced sentence to alter it."

"I'm not sure I've ever met anyone quite like you. Have you always been this way?"

"More or less since high school. In my head, I used to have my life all planned out from when I was about 15. You know, what SAT score I was going to get, what school I was going to, what I was going to major in, where I was going to do my masters, what job I was going to get."

"And how has it worked out so far?"

In the darkness of the taxi, Esther kept looking ahead but smiled ruefully. "Pretty much like clockwork until I left Berkeley. Then the Masters wasn't so good and I got tired of studying. And then the cars and the men were disappointing."

"I'm sorry about that." Ed couldn't think what else to say.

"Don't worry, it's all a long time ago. I thought I would map it all out but real life's just too fucked up for that; you can't control it and if you try, it can break you."

"So why have you spent so much time with me?" Ed finally asked the obvious question, albeit in an oblique way, and in doing so the tension, which had been slowly mounting up in the back of the taxi, drained away immediately.

"Partly because I knew you'd eventually get around to asking me that question. You took a while though, and I really didn't want you to disappoint. So the thing is, I meet a hell of a lot of phoney guys, fundamentally dishonest in that all they really want to do is screw you, one way or the other; some even try to have you both ways. And whatever else you may be, Ed, I'm pretty sure you're not a phoney; from everything Chris said about you, from everything you've said to me tonight. Though to be honest, you really don't talk that much, but maybe that's a good thing."

"Small talk's never been my forte."

"That's okay too. Look, Ed, I like you, but don't really know how much. And I've no real idea how much you like me. I don't usually hit on guys, but I'm not going to apologise for doing something I see guys do all the time. I don't want tonight to be the only one, but if it is, I promise not to blame you."

***

The following Tuesday, he got up first and went to have a shower, leaving Esther curled up under a sheet. She was awake but only just.

"I'll get some coffee on once I've had a quick shower," Ed called from behind the bathroom door. "What time's your meeting?"

"Ten o'clock," she pointed out, "it'll only take me 15 minutes to get there; I'll leave about 9.30 just to be on the safe side."

When Ed had finished showering, he went into the kitchen and sorted out coffee. He only had a towel around his waist and so went back into the bedroom to dress. He knew he would have to go back and check out of his hotel before heading for JFK. It had been a weird few days, and he was struggling to understand what it meant. He could not remember having been happier but could not see how the happiness could continue. Despite having spoken about it a good deal, he didn't know what Esther saw in him, why she found him attractive. And because he didn't understand it, Ed did not believe their relationship, their 'affair' as he had begun calling it to himself, could be sustained. This morning, Esther would go to her meeting and later today he would fly back to London for a couple of days before going to Amman. Then, he imagined, there would be some emails exchanged and maybe the odd phone call. But sooner or later someone else would come along for Esther, someone who was likely to be around for more than a couple of weekends a year. He couldn't see himself getting back to New York before February, although he might get a couple of days in London around Christmas or New Year.

So this morning could well be goodbye, and Ed didn't know how or whether to acknowledge this possibility. Esther had made it into the shower when he reached the bedroom and he stared romantically at her silhouette beyond the shower screen, and again felt the recently familiar surge of yearning. He shook his head and dressed quickly. Then he went back into the kitchen and switched on the TV to further distract himself while he got out orange juice and some bagels for breakfast. When he turned back to the TV, it looked like there was some disaster movie on and he checked the channel. As he had thought, they were watching the morning news.

Ed's brain, idling until now, began to accelerate as it took in and extrapolated the consequences of the scene unfolding in front of him.

"Esther!" he shouted, "you need to get in here quick!" It wasn't even the tone of Ed's voice that alerted her; he never raised his voice in the first place. She hobbled into the kitchen wearing one shoe while carrying the other and attempting, rather inexpertly, to do up the buttons of her blouse with her left hand. When she saw him gazing at the TV, she switched her attention and saw the World Trade Center with one of the towers looking blackened in the middle, almost like it was on fire.

"What's going on?"

"I don't know, but something big seems to be happening. They haven't said anything yet; I'm not sure they really know but… What the fuck was that?"

Something had happened to the other tower, the South one. It too was now billowing smoke. As they sat nailed to their stools by what was happening on the screen in front of them – the reporting journalists were vainly trying to make sense of it all – Ed briefly wondered if this was some 21st century remake of 'War of the Worlds'. Then the producers re-ran their film in slow motion and a commercial airliner, flying absurdly low, appeared from the right-hand edge of the screen and crashed straight into the middle of the second tower. Instantly, Ed realised this was a repeat of what had happened to the first.

As the commentators continued to try and pick apart and put together in some kind of logical sequence all that they thought they had just witnessed, other news began to come in; of a third plane having crashed into the Pentagon, a fourth headed for the White House and another, presumably having been hijacked, en route to Chicago.

"Welcome to the 21st Century," Ed muttered involuntarily. Not only was this clearly a new and terrible form of terrorism, multiplying the tolls of victims many times over and played out in memorable images across global TV screens, but it was also the first real occasion international terrorism had managed to have a direct impact on the US itself.

"That was where my ten o'clock meeting was," Esther whispered. "God, I hope George is all right." Quickly, she reached for the phone and dialled a number. It rang four times and Ed could see Esther tensing up, but then George answered and she visibly relaxed as he confirmed he hadn't yet made it into work; he had paused two blocks away to sit for ten minutes with an espresso and the morning paper.

But if George hadn't made it into work, many others had, and hundreds, maybe more, were trapped in each tower above the level where the planes had struck. No one could work out whether, and if so how, it was possible to get these people down to safety. By now, a cacophony of fire engines had arrived and a stream of firemen were making their way into the two smoking towers. No one seemed to have any clear idea of what would happen next.

Ed's instinct was that the attack must be the work of Al Qaeda and Bin Laden. The scale of it, the deliberate and indiscriminate maximisation of human death, the sheer impudence of the target, all identified him as by far the most likely perpetrator.

Neither of them had any sense of time as they sat there in Esther's kitchen, watching mass murder happening live on global media. Once in a while one of their phones would ring, and they would exchange staccato sentences with someone who was watching the same slow-motion tragedy unfolding. And then strange dots began to flicker down the screen and the cameras at street level picked up the short slaps of sound. It took several seconds to realise they were witnessing people leaping to their deaths from tens of storeys up, above the level where the planes had penetrated, human beings whose last act of independence was to choose the manner of their death. A steady trickle of survivors, mostly guided by the firemen, was emerging from the base of each tower but there now seemed no way for those towards the top of the tower to escape; any original chance of making it down a corner stairway must surely now be blocked off by the spreading conflagration, the heat generated by the exploded airline fuel tanks beyond imagination.

And then, there was a gradually escalating crescendo of a roar, the source of which Ed at first couldn't detect. The smoke billowed out sideways and the South Tower began imploding downwards in excruciatingly slow motion until it disappeared into itself like an earthbound black hole. Esther dropped her phone and stifled a scream. The finality of what they'd just witnessed left them both lost for words to describe it. They just sat watching in silence until the second tower disintegrated in the same fashion some 30 minutes later. Only then did they really begin to comprehend that the images on the TV were occurring barely three miles from Esther's apartment on the lower West Side. "I need to go down and see if I can help," muttered Ed as Esther continued to stare mutely, then reached again for her phone.

Out in the street, dust from the collapsed towers was already in the air, people were rushing around, some with purpose, others haphazardly, and sirens were wailing everywhere. Ed tried to walk towards what had been the World Trade Center, maybe among the most cosmopolitan buildings in the most cosmopolitan of cities – already the voices and contradictions were beginning to occur to him despite the visceral horror of it all. He pushed on, but within three blocks the increasing level of smoke and the slow tidal wave of people flowing in the opposite direction brought him to a halt.

This was no stampede of people but a steady trudge of humanity. Their fear had either been left behind in time and space, or simply overtaken by numbness as minds failed to come to terms with what they had seen. Their faces tended to be blank, uncomprehending of what they were doing or where they were going. The entwining tracks of smoke and tears wove lattices across many faces, some clothes were torn, many more discoloured, and some hobbled along having lost a shoe in some earlier melee. Ed had seen nothing quite like it; it was almost as if a unique refugee crisis – as much of the psyche as the physical – had been created in one of the richest cities on the globe. But even refugees were typically more comprehending of their predicament, whereas these people were shell-shocked, like a replay of the World War 1 aftermath of trench warfare.

Ed gave up, turned on his heels and went back to Esther's apartment. She was still sat in the kitchen, as though brainwashed, staring at the TV screen. He packed his case in less than a minute and kissed Esther goodbye. "I've changed my flight till tomorrow," he said, "but I guess I'd better get back to the hotel and sort out things back there. I'll also need to call London…" He paused, voice trailing off. "And I'll call you once I know the time of my flight."

Esther nodded mutely and he opened the door. They both felt their brief relationship was damaged and scarred by the tragedy they had witnessed. There was no logical foundation to this beyond the timing, but these few short days would always be associated with the destruction of the twin towers. Saturday night was relegated to the emotional hinterland, and Ed's emotional senses, which only a couple of hours before had been willingly vulnerable, had now retreated into the deepest catacombs of his newly splintered soul.

Nothing he had seen before, not even Sabra and Shatila, had prepared him for the onslaught of horror his imagination was now inflicting. When he had witnessed first-hand the impact of something, no matter how terrible, his mind had always been capable of stepping back, of diagnosing and separating out the issues. It was the process he used all the time, but today it was utterly inadequate. He realised in his external mind, the one that always stood outside of his own behaviour looking inwards, that he shared that blankness of look he had seen on the faces of the survivors. And so, in the effort of putting himself in a position from which he could reach reasonable journalistic judgements, Ed allowed his professional side to take over completely. He ended up staying in New York until Saturday, reporting on the aftermath and the reaction to the attack, expertly pulling real stories together as emerging facts became more reliable. But at no point in these subsequent days did he re-contact Esther, or for that matter Chris or Dan. He told himself he was simply doing his job. But he also knew, just below this veneer of self-justification, that he was making a personal choice.

The work itself was new to him – interviewing structural engineers and chemists about what would have caused the towers to collapse; being aware of families looking for those who were lost but whom they could not bring themselves to presume dead; trying to trace the pattern of events on the ground, when firemen decided to enter the burning towers and under what circumstances. And he wasn't getting much sleep but that didn't seem to matter; in fact, sleep seemed an extravagance, as too would it have been to ring Esther, who in her ignorance assumed Ed had gone back to London or Amman, not that he was still in his hotel only a couple of miles crosstown.

Ed didn't believe he had run away from a potential relationship. In his mind, his brief affair with Esther had reached its natural conclusion already, and it would be almost perverse to take advantage of his unplanned extended stay in New York to seek to prolong it. It would be exploiting the tragedy of 9/11 for his own gratification.

It was predictably strange for Ed, being still in the city, but not in touch with either his friends or the woman he had spent the last three nights with. Once he even caught sight of Dan but turned into a bar rather than engage. Even though he did not believe his absence caused Esther any pain, he knew that she would have wanted to know he was still in New York and that the right thing would have been to contact her. So in that sense he was betraying her, choosing not to complicate his life.

Chapter 30
London, Tuesday, 11 September 2001

"What's up?" asked John, who had just come back from having coffee.

"I don't know," replied Stephen, "but it looks like something terrible's happened to the World Trade Center. Look!"

Stephen stepped back from a group of half a dozen people gathered around a PC monitor. As he moved forward half into the space, John saw that there were three or four similar groups standing around other PCs. In front of him on the screen were the twin towers of the World Trade Center. About two thirds of the way up one of them, smoke was gushing and it looked like it was on fire. Then there was a loud roar and a streak of something moving through the sky before colliding with the other tower, a bit higher up than the first. Now both towers were blazing but no one could conceive what could have happened. It was mystifying, weird, awful.

Phones began ringing. Relatives were phoning in, some from home where they had been listening to the radio and had now turned on the TV, some from other work offices, where they too had started watching. One or two said there were rumours planes had flown into the towers. But how could it happen twice? The TV started showing film footage, taken from the street, of a plane flying overhead, crazily low through the streets of New York, then disappearing into the second of the two towers, detonating as it did so, seemingly vaporising instantly in the self-created furnace.

Then Stephen's phone rang. He picked it up. "Hi, Steve, it's Will here from the Big Apple. I don't know why I'm ringing, but I think I'm about to die, and I need to speak to someone I can trust. I can't get hold of Rachel, and I need you to tell her something. Sorry, I…" Until then, the voice had been steady if slightly rushed. As it broke, Stephen realised who he was speaking to and where Will, whom he had worked with in Singapore for two years, was phoning from. As he did so, sweat broke on him, along his hairline, under his armpits, between his shoulder blades.

His own voice was trembling slightly. "Hey dude, good to hear from you. Listen, I can see what's going down over there. Look, what floor are you on?" By now John was listening. "That's a high number. How far is that from the top?" He paused, "That doesn't sound good. The whole tower looks to be burning up about eight floors below you. What? Yea, I'm not surprised. Listen, I'm sorry Will, really sorry."

Stephen paused again, biting his lip as he listened. "Okay, Will, let me get something to write with." He gestured to John, who rushed around and grabbed a pad and pen. His own hands were suddenly clammy. "Right, I'm still here, Will. Don't worry, I'll write it all down, every word. Just tell me what you want me to tell her. Listen, it's becoming more clear what's happened. It looks like terrorists hijacked a bunch of planes. Apart from the twin towers, another plane's hit the

Pentagon but that seems to be about it. Don't worry though, they'll get the bastards who've done this. Yea, I know, but you and I know it's not just Americans in those towers, anything but… And it won't just be the US bringing the guys to justice either. Anyway, you fire away and I'll write it all down. Dear Rachel…" Stephen began to write quickly. To start with he tried too fast, and once he dropped the phone from its wedge between his chin and left shoulder. Then he settled down and focused on writing calmly for the next ten minutes or so. Every so often, he would interject with a comment to try and comfort Will, give him confidence that his last message to his wife was being carefully recorded, not lost in translation.

"Hey, that's great, I didn't realise you and Rachel first met all those years ago at college… Wow, you two certainly stuck together through the difficult times… You must be dead proud of Cathy, she sounds like a great kid… Those camping holidays sound like the best time… I'm sure they know you do, but I'll tell them anyway, of course I will… All right, I'll make sure Rachel gets the message, man. I'll fly over and go see her… Okay, you sure you wanna hang up? That's fine, whatever feels right to you…

"Listen, Will, before you do, I feel pretty shook up, but also privileged talking to you." Stephen's voice was now breaking again and tears were beginning to run freely down his cheek. "It's been a complete pleasure knowing you, working with you, drinking with you. I'll always remember those nights on Boat Quay. Goodbye man, God rest your soul."

Stephen suddenly stopped and looked down at the phone. He turned to John, "He's gone."

"Shit!" said John simply.

"I can't believe that just happened," Stephen went on, "and that I'll never see him again, or even talk to him."

Then, in slow motion, objects began dropping from way up the towers. The sound of them hitting the ground was light and percussive in its finality. It took a while to realise the falling objects were people jumping to escape a slower death. Watching it happen, still caught up more in disbelief than in the horror, John felt oddly detached from it all. The events unfolding in New York were so far beyond the frame of his experience or conceived expectation that they seemed a piece of science fiction. Suicide bombing on such a scale threw into doubt all his assumptions about the evil people would deliberately inflict on others. Throwing themselves to their deaths in such numbers seemed to override any conception of fear and despair John could envisage.

He looked down and saw that Stephen had collapsed in his chair. His head was buried in his arms and he was sobbing convulsively, violently, shoulders heaving, his fists beating slowly, limply almost, into the back of his neck. John bent over and put his head down to the level of Stephen's ear, his left arm resting across his back. "Listen, Steve, I'm sorry, you did all you could. I heard you on the phone, I listened to every word, and I don't know how you kept yourself together." Stephen didn't move, didn't acknowledge, but shook less violently. John forced himself to keep talking.

"Steve," he said, "I don't think Will could have found anyone better to phone. I can't imagine what he's feeling now, but I'm sure he's better for having talked to you, having the assurance that you got his message and will pass it on to Rachel."

Stephen turned his head briefly, and John could see it was riven with streaks of tears, then buried it back on the table. When he spoke, it was guttural, half an octave deeper than his normal tone, as if he were dredging the words up from some primitive sewer of sepulchred comprehension.

"But I can do nothing to help him," he gurned, carving out each syllable as though it were an ancient piece of granite. "He's dead already. I could tell from his voice he had decided to jump, even before I saw the first bodies falling. Even before he hung up, I could tell. He had made up his mind. What living hell drives someone to that? It was happening around him and I could do nothing. Damn this world, damn the phone, damn computers and satellites. Damn that I ever knew him. I didn't want to speak to him, I didn't want to see him die. Why should I have to? No one asked me. I want to read about it in the papers next week. I don't want to know. I know too much, what God made me know so much?"

During the next few minutes, rumours began to circulate, the most frightening being that planes had been hijacked at City Airport and were heading for Canada Tower in Canary Wharf. Given their proximity, this soon became extremely unlikely, but still it was believed, and still the calls were coming in from various family and relatives.

Until now, there had been silence in terms of official guidance from management, though there had been a couple of emails telling everyone to stay where they were and remain calm while the situation was being assessed. The credibility of this had now worn away, and people were becoming restless, talking in groups, getting their stuff together ready to leave with or without sanction. Suddenly, the intercom sprung into life, loudly but slightly crackly, making several people jump. "Please proceed to the nearest exit. Do not use the lifts."

John turned back to collect his stuff. As he did so, he glanced at the screen and swore. One of the towers was collapsing in upon itself, as if melting. Then came the noise, almost deafening, not so much in its loudness as its intensity, and in the visible horror of all that it signified. And as the tower came down, the cloud of dust at its base rose and spread until it enveloped and shrouded the last 100ft or so of the disintegration. By now everyone was gaping at the screen, ignoring the instruction they'd been waiting for, frozen for the third time by what they had just witnessed.

Then someone shouted and everyone turned towards the exit staircases in an odd, shuffling run, not quite panicking but rushing in a way completely uncharacteristic of any practise evacuation. John got to the door and squeezed through, with a surge of people behind him. The tide was moving quickly but in an almost orderly way. Everyone was more or less in step, two abreast, the two lines just about staying level at the turns, as those in the outer line sprinted around the corner, some of them bouncing off the walls like snooker balls off the cushion. Three floors below, as they got to the 5th, the door onto the trading floor opened and a small wave of about 20 people blasted through it, colliding with the downward current from the floors above. Miraculously, the two floods of humanity merged, the larger one pausing just enough to allow the smaller to filter its way into the general mess. Somehow no one fell over; John never knew why not; maybe it was some inherent survival valve, directing and stimulating each individual to give everyone else just enough room, and to move with just enough speed and agility to keep in step with the group.

Some three minutes after hitting the stairs, John swayed, blinking into the day. It seemed normal, no different to the day before. And yet he knew something big had happened. He didn't know what it meant but his first thought was that America – certainly George Bush's America – would want revenge. As these thoughts passed through his mind, people were milling around slightly distractedly. Several were on the phone to let family etc. know they were now outside, to put their minds at rest. A couple had found each other and were embracing hard, anxious to convey that mix of longing and relief for which other communication was inadequate. A small group of smokers had congregated and were puffing away. No one seemed much interested in making their way to the designated rendezvous point.

He looked round for Stephen. It took a couple of minutes to find him. He was on a patch of grass, lying on his back, his legs stretched out, with his left arm crooked across his eyes and his right down by his side. As John bent over to say hello, he noticed his fist was screwed tight, the knuckles gone white.

"Hey Steve," he said, "what are you doing down there? What's the story? Let's get out of here and find a drink."

Stephen looked up. "I guess you're right. I don't want to go home right now, I don't think it'd be fair on them. Hang on a second, I'll just ring to say I'm all right."

John nodded and turned away. The scene was much as before, although more people were beginning to move away, often in twos and threes. He glanced back towards the building and saw a young couple, two of last year's graduates he thought, just emerging from the building. Both had tousled hair and stylishly dishevelled clothes. He didn't know them really, though he had given their intake a talk on foreign exchange markets in their first few weeks. But when the woman accidentally caught his eye, she looked down at the ground and blushed.

John turned away, not knowing whether to laugh or cry. With all that was going on, with all the risk of getting caught, and the inevitable and humiliating sacking that would follow, what was it that had persuaded them to sneak away? In any event, it was none of his business, though he would find it hard to take the two of them seriously again. Was there ever a time, he wondered, when he would have taken a similar risk with a girlfriend, or indeed a stranger, someone in between? Probably not, but there was a corner of him that regretted that negative. And then again, maybe it was simply in tune with the madness of the day. When such things could happen, maybe it was entirely reasonable to slip other bounds. Perhaps their coupling was a simple response to the hate of the events they had witnessed. The more he thought, the more their act seemed perfectly sane.

Stephen was just coming off the phone when John turned back. "The other tower's collapsed as well," he said. "They don't know how many thousands have died. They also flew a plane into the Pentagon and tried to crash another one. But it sounds as though the passengers re-took it somehow, or tried to; at any rate, it crashed in the countryside somewhere, Pennsylvania, I think."

"Do they know yet who did it?" John asked.

"Sounds like they think it's a terrorist group called Al Qaeda, someone called Bin Laden I think."

"Name rings a bell," John said, "but can't say I've really heard of him. Has Bush said anything?"

"Not as far as I know. Megan said he was at some school or something when he got the news. Looked a bit weird and wobbly apparently. But I guess you can't really blame the guy." Stephen's voice was becoming steadier now, the detail of life was slowly reasserting itself.

The two friends wandered down to Monument Station then, on a whim, decided to walk on across London Bridge. Some ten minutes later, they had ended up at the George & Dragon on Borough High Street and were sat outside at one of the tables in a cobbled courtyard, with a couple of pints in front of them.

"What do you think it all means?" Stephen asked, "I mean, there's no rational excuse for it, the people who've died weren't even all American."

"I don't think whoever did it was particularly bothering about who died or how many," said John. "All they cared about was those towers as a symbol of American power. I don't think the human life involved was what mattered. Funny how this is so simple and yet it's the first time I think it's happened. Forget Star Wars and ICBMs, why not just fly a big plane into a big building. Think of the humiliation. No matter what Bush does in revenge, the US will never again look or feel as safe as it did. Talk about your own back yard. Tell me about Will. What was he like?"

Stephen looked at him as he drained his beer. "Okay," he said, "but I need another beer." When he returned, he sat down with the pints and looked across the table. "Well, the first thing, the most important, is that when we were in Singapore together, I had an affair with Rachel, his wife."

Now it was John whose mouth sagged and eyes widened, but Stephen was now avoiding eye contact, staring down and determinedly continuing to talk.

"I was never sure if Will knew, but now I'm sure he did. That was why he rang me. He knew he wouldn't be around and wanted to tell me that, and give me a reason to go and see her. I could tell by the way he talked, where he paused, the words he emphasised. I can't go, of course. I'm married myself now, which Will didn't know. I'll have to write to her though, maybe under a false name. It was one of those classic Brits abroad flings. Will was on a trip to China, and Rachel and I met at a drinks party. We didn't plan to meet and I didn't even know she was going to be there, although the same people tended to go to all those things."

"How did it happen?" asked John, more to break up the flow of Stephen's confession than because he wanted to know the answer.

"Oh the usual way. We talked a bit, danced a bit, drank a lot and then somehow ended up out in the pool house."

"How long did it last?" John, despite himself, was now strangely curious. Far from giving Stephen a reason to go and see his young widow, Will had been laying the biggest guilt trip imaginable on both of them. Why else would he have rung Stephen after five years? It was inconceivable he considered him his best friend, even without the affair. Like Stephen, he thought Will must have known about their affair, but the idea he wished them somehow now to be together was patently ridiculous. But he couldn't tell Stephen this, not today anyway.

"Just under six months," Stephen replied. "Then I got a job in HK, a better one. We talked about Rachel coming with me, but in the end she wasn't ready to divorce him, and I couldn't exactly offer her the settled life in the UK or US she wanted. Not then anyway."

300

They talked on for a bit as they finished their drinks. Then they walked to London Bridge station and parted.

***

Sam was in a meeting when his secretary put her head around the door and said David needed to see him. When he entered the office, David was on the phone; he motioned for Sam to sit down in one of the armchairs around a coffee table in the corner.

"Yes, of course. We need to get a clear idea what exactly is going on – even the State Department doesn't know yet – and have a look at our contingency plans. We don't have a scenario that exactly covers this but a couple of them are close enough. I'm going to ask Sam to handle it; he's just arrived. I'll give you an update in an hour."

David put the phone down and rose, slightly heavily from behind his desk. Sam was never sure whether this was natural, or some elaborate act of how he felt he ought to look. "Have you heard what's happened?" David asked, sitting down opposite him and pouring coffee for them both.

"No, I've been in meetings until Diane called me out just now."

"Two large passenger jets have been flown into the towers of the World Trade Center, a third has crashed into the Pentagon."

Sam tried not to look shocked. "Not an accident then; was it Bin Laden?"

"Everyone seems to think so. Horrific and unique as it is, this bears all his hallmarks. Not least his ability to strike at American power. There's a pretty obvious line back through the USS Cole and the Embassy in Kenya."

As David spoke, Sam caught sight of the TV in the corner. The two towers were blazing halfway up, billowing smoke and flames. "Is Bin Laden still in Afghanistan?" he asked.

"We think so. Certainly that's where Al Qaeda is concentrated. The Taliban shelter him, and in return, he provides them with arms and money. My best bet is that the US is now likely to invade Afghanistan – historically not a smart move for anyone – but that's a nightmare for another day. The current problem is gauging whether there's anything like this intended for the UK. The second question is what I was on the phone to the minister about. I know none of our current planning is based on a terrorist scenario as spectacular as this, but we do have some planning around the explosion of a dirty bomb as well as a couple of other things. Can you look at what we've got and make an assessment of how we would respond to a similar incident? You can pull a couple of people from other teams if you need them, whoever you want."

"When do you need it by?"

"I've got to be able to say something sensible to the minister in an hour. But after that, I think the key deadline is noon tomorrow. What do you think? Is that practical?"

"Well, the usual caveats apply, but we should be able to produce something decent by then. You know we'll need to make a lot of assumptions. I'll record them, of course, but there'll be a few leaps of faith in there."

David paused a moment. "Understood," he said. "But in that case, can you also start in parallel another work stream to fill the holes in our information and close the gaps? That can be on a longer timescale but I'll still need it by lunchtime Friday. Good, is there anything else?"

"Just whether I can talk to other agencies, the Bank for example, the FSA?"

"Yes, of course," replied David, "but not as a matter of course; only at the right level, and only if you need to." He paused. "Because of the timescale, I think this needs to be our assessment rather than a collective one."

Back in his office, Sam made a couple of phone calls, commissioned work, and asked for some previous papers to be run off. He went and sat down at his desk and took out some A3 paper from the bottom drawer. Then he sat and looked at it while he cleaned his glasses. Despite the deadline and the fact he needed something to tell the minister, he decided to try and go back to first principles and understand as best he could what they were dealing with.

Sam knew the history. On Boxing Day 1979, the Soviet Union had invaded Afghanistan to prop up an unpopular pro-Soviet dictator – he couldn't remember his name – who was under threat from a nationalist guerrilla movement. So far, so Cold War, much of the international reaction reflected the view that the USSR was aiming to expand its Communist sphere of influence, and there was much media commentary reviving the history of the 19th century Great Game.

Much influenced by Ed, Sam had ended up rejecting this expansionist hypothesis. Instead, he had begun to view the Soviet attempt to control Afghanistan as a defensive move to try and create a buffer between the Soviet Union and the increasingly explosive force of Islamic fundamentalism. Earlier in 1979, the Shah of Iran had been overthrown by a popular revolt led by Islamic clerics in the name of the Ayatollah Khomeini. As a result, the Middle East had become a cauldron of revolutionary rhetoric and, because many of the Soviet Union's southern states had a predominantly Muslim population, this fundamentalist strain of Islam was more dangerous to Moscow than to Washington. By this interpretation, Moscow was afraid of its southern states becoming unstable, and this lay behind the Kremlin's overtures to Tehran.

Of course, Moscow, as the US had often done, fell into the Cold War trap of cloaking real, if sometimes brutal, national security interests in the rhetoric of ideological struggle. That said, Sam suspected nothing Moscow could have said would have persuaded Washington that the invasion of Afghanistan was not an aggressive act. In reaction, the Americans had begun arming, first indirectly then increasingly openly, the Afghan militia who were resisting the pro-Soviet government the Russians had established in Kabul. These mujahedeen began to attract young men from across the Arab and Muslim world. Among the fiercest and most successful of the mujahedeen leaders had been a young Saudi called Osama Bin Laden and, as a result, the US made sure he received the most advanced weaponry available. Little thought was given to what would happen if the Soviets ever withdrew, or to what would happen to all the weapons the CIA had poured into the hands of guerrillas who ultimately viewed Washington with anything but affection.

In 1987, Moscow did start to pull back, beaten and humiliated. The Red Army had been exposed in the mountains of Afghanistan as much as the US Army had in the jungles of Vietnam. During the 1990s, the newly formed Russian Federation had then begun to have increasing problems with the Islamic populations of its southern states, most obviously Chechnya.

Meanwhile, in part response to the Iraq War and the continuing failure of the US to solve the Palestinian problem, Bin Laden turned his ferocity and his intellect on the US. He forged his mujahedeen into an effective terrorist organisation, Al Qaeda, and began attacking outpost of the US around the world. The USS Cole and the Embassy in Kenya had been the bloodiest examples. Soon he was at the top of America's most wanted list, so much so that Clinton ordered the bombing of a factory in Sudan where he was thought to be hiding. Bin Laden survived but others did not, and America's reputation in the Muslim world took another blow.

Bin Laden had established a web of bases around the world but mostly these were small cells of terrorists, or temporary bases that could be abandoned at a moment's notice. Ultimately, Al Qaeda was thought to be based in Afghanistan and along the Pakistan border. That was where the training camps were, protected by the Taliban. They claimed to be Islamic but were violently opposed to any sense of learning, culture or religion. They were thus violently against Western culture but also other civilisations, taking the time a few months before to gratuitously destroy the ancient Buddhist statues at Bamiyan. They had stepped into the vacuum left by Russian withdrawal, and an extreme form of sharia law had been imposed, women were repressed and girls weren't allowed to go to school. By any measure, Sam thought, Afghanistan was one of the saddest victims of the Cold War.

Out of this collective failure of the superpowers had now come, or so it seemed, a terrible, indiscriminate form of vengeance. The twin towers had been chosen, he assumed, because, sitting at the tip of Manhattan, they were the easiest skyscrapers for the airliners to hit. The only thing that distinguished the targets was that they were easy. The same, he suspected, applied to the choice of weapon, internal US passenger aircraft, not international ones, which had higher security thresholds and better checks against taking potential weapons onto the plane.

While Sam had been thinking, he had also been covering the sheet of A3 in front of him.

If this analysis was right, it had important implications for the answer to David's question about the UK's contingency plans. On the one hand, it opened up a much wider range of potential terrorist targets: if easy targets were more likely to be attacked than the strategically significant, then it would be impossible to protect everyone. However, Al Qaeda's resources were not large, and its operational capacity was not that sophisticated; after all, on one level, hijacking aircraft and crashing them into big buildings was also pretty crude. This meant it should be possible to identify and restrict access to the raw materials needed to conduct an attack, whether they be airplanes or more conventional bomb-making material. The same might apply to potential terrorists. While intelligence on Al Qaeda operatives in the UK was currently poor to non-existent, there was at least scope to improve it. After all, they were highly unlikely to be sophisticated KGB-type cells. By their nature, they were almost certainly Muslim and, one way or another, were likely to wear their radicalism on their sleeve. Mistakes would be made, but he thought it would be possible to keep some reasonable level of surveillance of a defined group, among which a tiny number would be actual terrorists.

There were pluses to this appraisal because, with the significant exception of air travel, where security checks were bound to become much more onerous, life for the vast majority of British people would not need to be significantly affected. But there would be huge risks of alienating large swathes of the UK's Muslim population, who might well feel demonised by the increased police attention they would receive. This would also be seized on by the politicians anxious to show that action was being taken and by racists seeking easy arguments to type-cast ethnic groups.

Sam sat back and swung his chair around so he could look out his window. There was nothing great about the view, although if he craned his neck, he could see a new moon-sized sliver of the Millennium Wheel. It would be a terrible shame if all that hard-won ability to live next door to people from different backgrounds became a victim of the response to terrorism. Although, he realised sadly, that that was part of the aim of it all.

***

Philip had just returned from lunch when the news began coming in. It quickly became apparent that what was happening was unlike anything else. As he pored over the available footage – bits of film were starting to come in from tourists who had caught glimpses of one or other of the planes flying what seemed like impossibly low over Manhattan – it reminded him oddly of one of the scene at the end of 'One from the Heart' when an enormous plane flies over Frederick Forrest's head. He believes Terri Garr is on it, but at the last minute she's decided not to fly off to a glamorous life with Raul Julia but to stick with her old everyday existence, to live out her dreams rather than go looking for them. But this was the opposite of Coppola's film, no dreams here.

Even before the towers collapsed, it was obvious the death toll would be huge. As well as the airline passengers, Philip quickly worked out that those in the upper part of the towers, above where the planes crashed, had no chance of surviving. As the images were beamed around the world, he began to understand the enormity, not only of the crime itself but in the collective visual experience it offered to people all round the world. As political reaction began to trickle in, so did footage of people watching in semi disbelief the same images on their TV screens. It began to remind him of the way people watched the Olympics or World Cup football; not planned, as that viewing was, but sharing much of the same quality of communal experience.

Philip remembered the early days of satellite broadcasting, the Apollo missions, the first views of the earth from space and the first lunar landing. Those had been shared global experiences of a much more optimistic kind. What was happening today were events of extreme nihilism. It was hard not to think that the world had just changed. And that half the world's population was witnessing it live on television. Political leaders, led by Tony Blair, were beginning to queue up to offer sympathy and, to varying degrees, support. This swell of goodwill was, he thought, undoubtedly helped by the nature of the World Trade Center. Although it was in the heart of New York, in some ways it could not have been less of an American target, and there was a sense in which Bin Laden had attacked the whole world.

But although the sympathy was huge, it wasn't unanimous. There were disturbing scenes of Arab youths spontaneously demonstrating in the street, celebrating the attack on the Great Satan, the supporter of terrorism. Although Philip knew the US was far from as loved as it liked to think, it was still a shock to see how much loathing and fear it inspired. And now America had been shown up as vulnerable to attack on its own soil. If the new century was going to be one of increasing interdependence, then it seemed also to be an age when power and weakness could walk hand in hand. He thought the US would find it hard to adapt to this new reality.

***

Mary sat in the British Library. It had been one of those slow but modestly productive days that are the backbone of academic research. She had been looking at edited volumes of Atlee's letters, trying to improve her knowledge and understanding of the British prime minister whose reputation has probably soared most in retrospect. She was particularly interested in his relationship with other major politicians and in the comparison with Tony Blair. On this latter question, Mary was hoping to find enough to justify a short comparative paper and anticipated listing conclusions unflattering to the current Downing Street incumbent. So far, however, she had come across more similarities than she had expected. Both had a cabinet several of whom believed someone else should be prime minister. And while Blair was infinitely more of a media figure, as befitted a politician of the satellite and internet age, Atlee was very similar in his yearning for power, his ruthless pragmatism in curtailing his colleagues' grander plans if he felt they would damage the party's election prospects.

For different reasons, both spent more time than expected on foreign policy issues. In particular, they had to deal with an American president who was intensely suspicious of Moscow and who was seeking to expand America's sphere of military influence. Of course, the post war circumstances were in many ways completely different, but Bush's level of distrust of the Kremlin already seemed almost on a par with Truman's fear of the Red Army.

Buried in Atlee's letters, Mary didn't get out of the British Library until gone 5pm and walked along to Euston to catch the Tube home. As she walked along the pavement to Kings Cross, she saw the front page of the Evening Standard and slowly realised that now, in the 21st century, US was impregnable no longer and its paranoia had found a new justification.

***

Ruth had gone around to Karen's house for an hour or so after school, to sort through some CDs and generally chat about school. Mrs Lawson was at home when they arrived but, instead of working in her study or tidying around the home, they found her glued to the television. For once, she wasn't smiling as she said hello and offered them a cup of tea.

"Come in and sit down," she said. "Something terrible's happened in New York." Obediently the two girls put down their bags and took off their blazers before settling on the sofa. Her voice was hesitant as she explained what had happened. "Someone's flown two passenger planes into the twin towers of the World Trade

Center in New York, and another into the Pentagon. The towers have collapsed; thousands of people have died."

"Oh my God!" said Karen. "When did it happen? Who did it?"

"They don't know yet, darling; but they seem to think someone called Osama Bin Laden is behind it. They were huge planes… It was terrible when the towers just collapsed."

Together the two teenagers sat and watched the footage as TV ran back over the events of the afternoon, moving between reporters, guests, live pictures and film of what had happened earlier, including some video film taken by members of the public. Ruth rang home but Mum wasn't there so she had to leave a message. She also rang her dad, not expecting to speak to him, and left another message.

'So this is what it's like,' Ruth thought. It seemed like history had been on hold since the Cold War had ended when she was little. Ruth had expected some big event to happen but not anything like this. Sitting on the sofa, beside Karen and her mum, tears began to roll gently down her cheeks as she saw the towers collapse one more time.

Part 5: London, July 2005

Chapter 31
Thursday 8th

Sam dreamt. The previous night he had slept hardly at all but tonight he did, deeply, drained empty by the apprehension of what might have been.

He crouched behind a garden wall, of the type he used to see from the bus on his way to school, almost three-foot-high, made of red brick, with a row of granite-coloured roof bricks on top. It was dark and there was a full moon, though it was otherwise very foggy. Not normal mist-type fog but the thick soup seen in films about Victorian London and noir films like Double Identity and The Maltese Falcon, where uncertainty lurks around every corner, nothing is quite as it seems and labyrinthine plots confuse and keep you guessing, often beyond the final credits.

Sam was in the dream but also observing it, experiencing its sensations but also outside of it, coolly calculating the equation of allusion and inference. He was also, in the dream, a dual personality, simultaneously 50 years old and eight years old. His 50-year-old self is aware of the dangers, and wary of being caught in the wrong place at the wrong time, nervous of the potential consequences of what he is witnessing. By contrast, the 8-year-old is brave and confident, inexperienced, and incapable of looking ahead. He knows it is late and feels the danger involved but has no real knowledge of pain or fear to draw on, and is therefore not daunted by the position he is in.

And it is the little boy rather than the middle-aged man who is physically kneeling behind the garden wall. The boy's two personalities coexist easily together, moving smoothly over the top of each other and passively communicating in a way that enables each to understand what the other is thinking and experiencing, but not in a way that admits one having any influence over the other. He has been kneeling there for a while, waiting for something to happen. He cannot imagine what to expect but assumes it will be bad; the fact he is already hiding conspires to tell him that. The knees of the middle-aged Sam are starting to hurt but it doesn't cross his mind to stretch them or change position because he knows they are really eight-year-old knees, and therefore are flexible and don't really hurt at all.

The house behind the garden wall is semi-detached, although it is odd that Sam cannot see its neighbour. There are two bay windows on the ground floor and two on the first, each with net curtains but no others drawn. This means it should be possible to gaze into the rooms, to see what is going on. But he cannot see anything. Yet Sam is conscious – he does not know how – of shadows moving in one of the upstairs rooms. Three of the rooms are dark, the exception being the left-hand room on the ground floor, which has a single light, possibly a desk lamp, shining a dull light somewhere at its back, possibly facing the back wall so that for Sam, peering from behind the wall, it illuminated little of what was in the room.

This description came from the middle-aged Sam, observing and analysing. The boy knew none of this. He was staring at the red front door, trying to remember where he had seen it before. It had nine rectangular sections below a semi-circle of glass at the top, and there was some writing on a plaque beside it, which he could not make out but again looked familiar. The path up to the door curved gently in both directions from the wrought-iron front gate, which was also red. There were borders of flowers around both halves of the garden, with the rest given over to lawn. The 8-year-old Sam didn't know the names of the flowers, apart from the roses, but he did notice a solitary gnome in the back right-hand corner of the lawn, who appeared to be wearing glasses and was sat on a toilet reading a book.

Sam was wearing shorts and plimsolls, and there was a scab on his knee from when he had fallen over playing football in the playground. He only had on a T-shirt but it had been a blistering hot day and its heat continued to linger long into the night. Sam didn't know what was going to happen, but he did know he was waiting for some other people to arrive, people he didn't know but who were up to no good. The night was completely still, with not the slightest breath of air to disturb the suspense; and so was completely silent, with no sound of night-time animals, no owls hooting, nothing. In such an environment, Sam could see his chest expanding and contracting, hear his heart beating and his breath exhaling. None of these things scared him but he knew that whatever was about to happen would scare him. He wasn't particularly apprehensive about this but instead was detached from it, his two personalities contemplating whatever was to come from their different perspectives but with similar levels of equanimity.

Sam ran his hand through his hair and squinted again at the faintly moving shapes inside the house, but he could not work out what they were doing or who they were. They did seem familiar but he could not place them. Maybe he had been here before, in another dream or even in the same dream, but he couldn't remember. He waited patiently for what was going to happen.

And then, from nowhere, there appeared three men at the garden gate. They were standing barely three paces from where he was now crouching and he pressed himself as tightly as he could against the wall, trying to make himself tiny. He wondered that the men did not see him but at the same time wasn't surprised. He heard and felt his heart beating faster but knew the men wouldn't hear it.

The men themselves were dressed in old-fashioned belted raincoats with the collars turned up. They looked as though they were dressed identically but Sam couldn't see enough to be sure. All three of them wore hats – trilbies – and sunglasses, which he didn't consider strange. They spoke together in muffled voices for what felt like a long time and, despite being so close and it seeming as though he ought to be able to hear what they were saying, he wasn't able to make out a word. Sam could barely look at them but at the same time wasn't able to stop himself, and words and syllables floated past and through his mind without coalescing into any comprehension of what they were talking about, or what they intended to do. And still they didn't see him, even though, at one stage, the tallest appeared to gaze straight at him. Sam wondered what would happen if they did see him. He thought they would kill him, but he would fight back until he woke up. However, he still didn't know why he was there.

The gate opened quietly but then squeaked as it was pushed shut. The men responded by crouching low and scurrying up to the door but it was too late, and the shapes inside stopped moving before suddenly disappearing. Crouching by the red door, the men now had small holdalls from which they produced what looked like machine guns.

Sam didn't know if the people inside the house were villains or victims. In fact, the young Sam thought they needed help, while the middle-aged Sam was more suspicious and thought he had come across two groups who were as bad as each other, and that it would be better by far to leave them to it. Sitting outside and watching, the dispassionate Sam knew the young Sam was right but could also see there was a lot of risk in doing anything to help. Or rather there would have been if it wasn't a dream that he was confident he could escape from whenever he wanted. Neither the young nor the middle-aged Sam could influence what the other did, and neither fully understood what the other was thinking, although each had a subtle and quite developed sense of the other – young Sam had a sense this was what he would become, while middle-aged Sam had a vague memory this was what he had once been like. But their relationship wasn't balanced; young Sam had a trump card, he could easily do something to distract the men in raincoats.

The boy looked around on the footpath but found nothing to throw. Then he spotted a large pebble in the dirt of the border just on the other side of the garden wall. He slowly rose and reached across to grab it, with the intention of throwing it so that it hit the wall on the far side of the raincoat men with guns. That way he hoped he would be able to remain safely secure and hidden. This plan was, of course, flawed because the trajectory of the pebble would make it obvious to the men in raincoats that it had been thrown from somewhere close to where Sam was crouching. But young Sam did not yet have the experience or mental flexibility to envisage how the scene would play out, and so understand that what he was about to do would reveal his presence and whereabouts just as surely as if he jumped up and started shouting.

If this had been what happened, there might have been some lingering resentment on the part of middle-aged Sam towards his younger self, though it would soon have passed for he had never in his life held a grudge. However, as soon as he raised his full head above the parapet level of the garden wall, one of the men in raincoats immediately spotted him and shouted: "Hey!" to his comrades. This created the opportunity, instantly accepted, for the older Sam to believe that the men in raincoats were about to spot him anyway. He hadn't understood how he hadn't yet been seen, and so it was only a small step of credulity to believe that being spotted had long been inevitable.

As soon as the man in the raincoat shouted, Sam jumped up and started running. He didn't consider any other option like dropping back down behind the garden wall and trying to navigate his way round the corner from where he would head off in a direction the men in raincoats might not expect. His instincts were still quite linear, and any form of subterfuge was alien to him. From the outside, the simplicity of this reaction seemed a shame.

This underestimated the young Sam, because his approach and the way he executed it also had clear strengths. So, while the men in raincoats were quickly in pursuit, Sam had already gained as much as maybe 25 yards on them by the time they had got through the garden gate. This meant he had time to think where he was going, but the roads ahead suddenly began to look unfamiliar. The fog meant the landmarks he ought to recognise came upon him too quickly, and he now had the feeling, although he couldn't be sure, that he'd missed a couple of the turnings he'd meant to take to try and throw the pursuers off his track. Instead, after about 200 yards, the roads became ones he didn't know. The tightly crisscrossed streets, with a corner every ten houses, had become a rolling highway with houses set well back from the road. He had never run so far or so fast, but he was far from out of breath and believed he could carry on at the same speed for a long time. He could hear the men in raincoats running behind him, but as far as he could tell, they weren't gaining, and the couple of times he glanced over his shoulder, he could only make out some flickering shadows in the distance.

And then, as he was still racing to escape, he realised that the house where he had been crouching behind the garden wall, inside which he had glimpsed the flickering shadows, and which the men in raincoats had been preparing to attack, had been his own house. In which case the people inside must have been his parents. Sam barely had time to process this before the terrain changed and he found himself running on grassland, then on heath, with short, stiff grass that his plimsolls sometimes slipped on. Despite this, he reflected briefly on the implications. The older Sam was pleased he had been wrong, and in a sense overruled, about the motives of those inside the house, and now felt quite virtuous about having distracted the men in raincoats and so protected both his parents and his home. He did not criticise himself for having made the wrong assumption, nor did he worry that he hadn't recognised his own house much sooner. Meanwhile, the young Sam had given the matter even less thought, merely logging it as one of those dream-facts that would be forgotten but would still leave an impression on the hard disk of his memory.

One reason this realisation was considered so briefly was that, coinciding with the change of terrain, the chase became harder, and Sam could feel himself beginning to run in what felt like slow motion. At the same time, he could hear for the first time pounding feet behind him, and when he next looked over his shoulder, the pursuers were barely 15 yards behind and he could see them quite distinctly. The one in the lead had a moustache and was panting heavily but evenly. His hat had fallen off and, catching sight of Sam's face, he swore inaudibly and appeared to increase his efforts. Sam turned back and tried to go faster, but each attempt to accelerate seemed to translate into a more accentuated slow motion. Still he did not feel out of breath, but Sam felt sure the men in raincoats must be gaining.

And then he became conscious he was wearing a rucksack. It wasn't especially heavy and he didn't know where it had come from, but it was slowing him down. The weight of it did not seem at all significant, but somehow it was bearing down on him and making it increasingly hard to run. But, strangely, Sam also stopped sensing that the men in raincoats were catching him. Maybe they had begun to tire, or perhaps rucksacks had appeared on their backs as well.

The next things to happen were that Sam's knees started to buckle, while simultaneously the fog closed in, creating a cocoon in which Sam could no longer hear the men chasing and could scarcely see a yard ahead. The weight of the rucksack had become debilitating and it was increasingly hard to straighten his legs as he ran. Then he stubbed his left foot against a rock and half stumbled but just about managed to regain his balance. Still he kept running, now almost in a crouching position under the burden of the load. The fog seemed to clear, but only a little, and while he could again hear the noise of the men in raincoats chasing him, they did not seem to be closing. All this occurred in maybe a dozen strides, but now the weight on his back felt heavier again and his knees could no longer support him. He tried to straighten up one last time, to extend his legs and run properly. But it was no good. Suddenly, he was sprawling forward, trying to get his hands out in front of him, his knees scraping the ground, which was now hard concrete, scraping off the skin on both knees and the palms of his hands. It was hot, even though the fog was still close all around him, and he felt the cold sweat of his T-shirt now clinging to his body.

He still couldn't hear the men in raincoats but he knew they were coming. The young Sam was used to falling over and cutting and grazing his hands, and his instinct was to get up again and see if he could get away. He was eager to try and attempted to lever himself up but the weight of the rucksack was now too much, to the point where he felt pinned to the ground. Some of the middle-aged Sam's greater strength might have helped him but he was incapable of adding to its strength. In fact, the older Sam had no remaining strength himself. While the burden of the rucksack did not feel so great to him, he was more exhausted from the chase. Latterly, he had been completely short of breath and felt as if his lungs would explode. He had a sense of lactic acid coursing through his body but felt detached from the physical feeling. And while falling over was an everyday occurrence for his younger self, it left the middle-aged Sam quite shaken.

For different reasons, both generations of Sam feared they'd reached the end and, despite at their core realising this was all only a dream, they each took the prospect seriously. Looking in on himself from outside, Sam the observer simply decided it was time to bring it to an end and summoned up a cliff from the depths of his psyche. This always required a considerable effort but this time proved harder than usual; at last it appeared, high and splendid above a tranquil sea. And as Sam had collapsed right at the edge of the cliff, he barely had to move before he was falling. Falling, falling, faster and faster; initially face first, eyes shut tight against the rushing wind, then rolling over onto his back with his arms and legs splayed. His guts and intestines felt like they'd been left behind at the top of the cliff, attached to some absurdly long bungee rope that was trying desperately to contract.

And then Sam was awake. His eyes were open and he was looking up at the sheet of plywood that covered the loft space. He was in his own bed and had broken sweat, but otherwise knew instinctively that he was fine. He carried on staring at the ceiling for maybe two minutes, trying to retrace the narrative of the dream. He could remember its intimate details but worried that he would, as usual, forget all within the next hour. At the moment, however, that detail was vivid and Sam could retrace each and every footstep. He even had some understanding of what it had felt like being in his eight-year-old body, its naturally elegant instinctiveness but also its frailty. It was a dream he had had before, but not since his mid-teens. He keenly recalled the effort required to summon up a cliff to throw himself off, although it seemed harder to do this time.

He thought of himself as an eight-year-old and tried to remember what he was like then and how he had changed. As a boy, he had worried about very little; life had revolved around family and school. There was the park and the local shops, the estate and his friends' houses, and nothing that gave him cause for fear. The worst that happened tended to be falling over somehow in the playground, and while he was constantly covered in cuts and bruises, he had no memory of them hurting beyond the immediate pain. And even when he needed plasters and bandages, he remembered no fear about repeating the same risks. He tried to remember what he was like but could only surface a series of disjointed images: building elaborate sandcastles with his dad on the beach at Skegness; learning to do long divisions in maths; playing football in the playground, doing sliding tackles because he wasn't very quick but had long legs; falling off his bike because he tried to turn a corner too fast; curled up in an armchair by the front window, reading Enid Blyton while the sunlight streamed through.

And then, still lying in his bed, staring at the trap door to the loft above him, Sam began remembering a bit more: his friends, the things they did together. There were Rick and Dougie and Tim, and they all lived on the same estate. They were the Three Musketeers, as were all groups of four young boys, with Sam invariably Athos. He was happy being the least glamorous, with Rick and Dougie alternating the roles of D'Artagnan and Aramis. He liked Athos, but mainly he was happy to play whatever role best suited his friends. Maybe that was what he had always done, fill gaps, but that was surely too simple an explanation of his life and, anyway, it didn't get him any nearer understanding the dream he had just had.

It would be too obvious to portray the men in raincoats as the bombers, and it didn't fit in any case. After all, there had been no violence, nothing bad had happened. It was even far from clear what would have happened if he hadn't distracted the men when they were at the front door, or what would have happened if they had caught him. Would they have beaten him up, captured or killed him? He didn't even know for sure they would have done him harm, though his memory of the dream, just starting to blur at the edges, was of an aura of evil and malice surrounding these men. And what could their motive have been? Was it theft, murder, both? Or was it something more complex; was there a cause somewhere, some higher motive they would have used to justify their actions? In reality, perhaps most criminals constructed such justifications, even if only along the lines of redistributing wealth, or on the grounds of greater strength and cunning being its own reward.

In that sense, it was his lack of comprehension of the men in raincoats' motives that was the connection with the bus bomber. Short of being a pacifist, which Sam wasn't, it was impossible not to admit there were some situations and behaviours that justified the taking of human life. Increasingly, and particularly since 1945, the world had tried to define and apply limits to the justification and legality of war. But the world of 1945 was very different from the world 60 years on. Sam realised he knew remarkably little about huge swathes of humanity. This had always been the case but never had it seemed so obvious.

As he continued to lie there in his sweat-soaked sheet, the sheer inadequacy of his understanding washed over him, drenching him every bit as effectively. But this was much more debilitating, draining Sam of energy, confidence and motivation. He was light years away from the human being he had thought he was. It seemed ridiculously arrogant now to believe, as he had less than 48 hours ago, that he was relatively knowledgeable, eclectic in his tastes, that he was open-minded and had a good understanding of the world. He had views on Vietnam and Iraq, on Central America, the Middle East and South Africa, as well as on issues closer to home like Ireland and the EU. But these views were fatuous, based on nothing but documentaries made by people he instinctively agreed with. He knew zero about what people in those countries thought beyond the occasional interview and Op Ed column in a British newspaper.

If yesterday proved anything, it was that all talk of a common sense of humanity was an obscene joke; there was no such thing and it was clear how absurd it had always been. So why had he believed it, swallowed it hook, line and sinker? Why had he been brought up to believe in such a bogus set of values? Sam tried briefly but found it impossible to blame his parents. Mum and Dad were every bit as much the victims of all these lies as he was. Their mistake, the same as his, was to believe what they had been told by people they trusted. But then where did the crime lie? The politicians and those who travelled internationally bore some guilt. They knew more than they ever revealed about how different other countries were, and must have realised that so-called Western values had been placed on an entirely imaginary pedestal. Far worse than the Emperor's new clothes, this involved a gargantuan degree of self-delusion, and had led to so many incalculable acts of self-serving violence in the name of a very particular version of human rights.

Sam's head was spinning now as more and more questions bombarded him, and fewer and fewer of the answers he had always relied on seemed valid. Democracy? E M Forster's 'two cheers' mantra and Churchill's 'least worst' formulation now seemed overblown inflations of a tired political system. Societies were now so heterogeneous, disparate, multiply-fractured, that even the older fear of a dictatorship of the majority now seemed an unlikely nirvana. With fewer people voting in an electorate increasingly dominated by single-issue politics, a choice of government every four to five years was a woeful apology for a political system allegedly representing the will of the people.

The disintegration of class as a mechanism for political cohesion, the corresponding decline of Conservative and Labour parties. Other countries were no better, even though they ostensibly offered a more nuanced layering of political responsibility, connecting the local with the national. In practice, in countries like the US, a small number of wealthy individual could influence elections far more easily, and by legal means, than they had been able to do by illegal ones in the past. Media, media, media! Why talk to the opposition, or even your own party, when the people who really mattered were the major donors, newspaper editors and TV anchors. And it wasn't as if the practise of democracy created a parliament that reflected the will of the millions who did still vote. He had read that if the right 36,000 voters had cast their ballot differently, Labour's 60 seat majority would have mystically dissolved into a Tory government. No, it was all wrong; Democracy was shot.

Human Rights? Well, it depended whose you meant, and how they were defined. Privacy was a comprehensively different concept to even a generation ago. The rise of Reality TV, the best example of Orwellian Newspeak, meant even the most intimate of human acts was no longer safe from being beamed to millions. Live sex on Big Brother wouldn't be far away, and who knew what would come after that. Someone sitting on a toilet passing excrement?

Where his body had been sweating, it was now Sam's mind which turned feverish. Ideas collided, bounced off each other in an increasingly malignant way, the resulting process creating huge energy that only led to more violent collisions. What did freedom of expression mean when so much of what is expressed is genuinely offensive to many? How do you control communication when one person's masterpiece is another's obscenity? Is there an objective definition of art? How must Western society seem to devout Muslims? And was there any consensus around the use of military force? It had been employed in Bosnia and was now being used in Iraq and Afghanistan. But it had only been used in Bosnia late in the day and not at all in Darfur or Rwanda.

For Ed, of course, the West's policy in the Middle East was all about oil and water. How genuine did that make the West's vaunted commitment to Human Rights look, particularly when coupled with American Civil Rights, Northern Ireland, and numerous other domestic examples of Western countries not obviously practising at home what they preached abroad? Was there any common standard by which you could judge human actions?

And what of religion? Our favourite means of reconciling the temporal with the spiritual, the contemporary with the eternal, seemed less and less honest, less holy, the more he saw and understood. How could communities of different faiths deal with each other on the basis of respect when each believed theirs the only true religion and that everyone else was effectively doomed? Even within faiths, religious doctrine seemed often to divide people and had been the cause of some of the most terrible bloodshed in human history. Against such a background, it barely seemed unusual that a group of religiously inspired youth should see suicide bombing as a normal extension of the millennia-old struggle between different conceptions of God. Sam laughed at his lame attempt to rationalise the horror of yesterday, to make the madness comprehensible. But wasn't it still true that there was a well-worn historical path leading to suicide bombings and to the destruction of the entire society from which your oppressors, real or imagined, originate?

And where was God in all this? Could there be a God who allowed so much bloodshed to be perpetrated in his various names? Or had we reverted to a polytheist world, the world of the Old Testament, where different peoples had their own gods, who warred on their behalf? There was a perverted but strong religious element in any honest diagnosis of the root causes of these terrorist horrors. Al Qaeda's retort would point to the scale of military force used in Iraq and Afghanistan and ask if such tactics would have been used against a Christian country, and whether a term such as 'shock and awe' would not have been considered obscene in every other circumstance. But even with this, what gulf of separation from one's fellow humans did it need to kill dozens of ordinary people, people who had nothing to do with the military. Martyrdom used to involve being prepared to die rather than recant your faith, or sacrificing oneself to save others, but this was light years from both. What did it mean if religion could become so focused on the next life and willing to cause so much pain in the current one?

Sam tried to sit up but felt devoid of strength and flopped back. He looked again at the trap door in the ceiling and noticed a small patch where the paint was starting to flake, as well as a thin crack running from the side of the trap door to the window on his left. He rolled over to his right, swinging his legs down on to the floor and sat up on the side of the bed. His legs felt heavy, as though he had had no sleep at all rather than seven to eight hours of fitful slumber. It was as if his sensory nerves had been unplugged simultaneously, stripping him of ability to feel.

He thought of Mary, who lay beside him, and of Ruth, of the desperation of trying and failing to contact them, and then finally of getting home and realising they were safe. But none of the vivid fear of yesterday returned, even in diluted form, and he was left observing himself from a distance. And from that distance, Sam began to doubt himself. True, he had worried about Mary but at root he had assumed she was fine. He saw this was simple rationality, but it had also allowed him to take easier options. He'd not for instance run, or even walked, to Mary's office to see if she was there and check she was all right. Why not?

Sam's mind jumped again, back to the Christian Youth Group he was in during his early teens. Once they had been asked in Sunday school if you had to go to church to go to heaven. Sam had been asked first and had replied that you didn't but that if it was a good church, it would probably help. He had been pleased with his answer and was already thinking about weighing up the various factors in his argument. But then he started hearing the others answer uniformly in the affirmative, making churchgoing synonymous with going to heaven in a way Sam thought had gone out of fashion with the Reformation. No issue had been made of it and Sam did not feel treated differently. But part of him wondered why it didn't make more of a difference. Sam felt if the Christian faith meant anything, it was about your character – the Sermon on the Mount with its promise to the pure in heart, the peace makers and so on; and the house with many mansions – these were the things Sam valued. And when Christ talked about the Church, it seemed to Sam it was a broad and welcoming community, diverse in its membership and forgiving of past wrongs.

He came back to that question, "What sort of God?" The evil done, the destruction wrought in God's name, whatever the religion, suddenly seemed to obliterate not only all the pain and suffering of ill health but the devastation and death caused by natural disasters. Even ordinary crimes paled beside those committed in the name of God.

He sat slumped on the bed, hands clasped over his head, which was suspended between his knees. His mind had gone blank again and the thoughts that had streamed through it had departed, leaving a desiccated anguish. Even the impression left by the dream had gone, so he could no longer recall any of the intensity he had felt. The richness of the dream had stood out as a beacon that his senses and emotions had not been totally neutered. But this too had gone. Sam moaned quietly and gave in to the urge to roll over back into bed and rest his throbbing vacuum-filled head. He curled up in the foetal position, so he would be conscious of his own physical being, his left arm clasped across both shins, and tried to close his eyes.

Sleep didn't come, not easily or quickly anyway, but some last memories of his dream did return, flitting back into his mind like jackdaws looking to take the last shiny stones from the pile about to collapse. What had he been running from really? Originally, he thought the men in raincoats might have represented yesterday's bombers, or at least some faceless evil, but now he wasn't sure. Now they seemed less pure evil but sometimes just as threatening. And instead of his parents they were after, Sam began to think he had been the target all along. And who were they? His mind swirled with what seemed like contradictions but never quite were. The men were chasing him but were never really going to catch him; he was running from them but wasn't really afraid, maybe because he knew, deep down, that they wouldn't catch him. The running became harder, but not because he was getting tired; instead, it was because more and more weight seemed to be loaded into the rucksack; and when he eventually fell, what was it he did to save himself?

It meant everything and nothing and, devoid of answers, Sam bounced back into the reality that he had been saved, apparently randomly, from death, by a God he sometimes believed in but didn't much like. Too many bad things had been and still were done in God's name. Too many of the values his followers held were excluding of foreigners, believers of other faiths, non-believers and disbelievers. And yet this was the code he had followed, the values on which he'd built his life. The randomness of his saving now seemed like a malignant mocking, forever associating him to the evil of that day. His life was revealed as a wasteland of misdirected good intentions, now cruelly mocked. Sam shuddered at his own despair and could see no end.

Chapter 32
Friday 8th

Heathrow was tangibly febrile when Carol got off her flight Friday lunchtime. Terminal 3 seemed even more of a mess than usual, and, ironically, she appreciated again just how much more unwelcoming JFK was, its queues even longer, its immigration more gratuitous.

News of the bombings had reached her in Singapore but had been patchy at best. She thought there had been either three or four bombs, one of which might have been on a bus, and it sounded as though the death toll was rising into the 50s. Buying a paper, Carol was relieved to see it hadn't suddenly jumped, but even so she was conscious of the scale of loss in such a safe, nonviolent society. Armed police and soldiers seemed more visible, and she imagined people were walking around more nervously. Nevertheless, London had been lucky; four bombs could have killed easily 50 people each.

She found a Starbucks and ordered a coffee, then called Phil, "Hi, it's Carol, what's happening? Is everyone okay?"

"Hi, Carol, have you landed? I take it you've heard? Yes, I think we're all okay, though Sam was nearly on the bus that blew up. No, he's a bit in shock but good otherwise. What did you hear out in Singapore?"

"Headlines but no real detail. I tried to call you but all the lines were engaged."

"Listen, when do you fly home?"

"Sunday."

"Well, for once, cancel your hotel and come to us for a couple of nights."

"Okay, this time I will, so long as you let me buy the both of you dinner."

"Deal!"

"Right, I'll see you in a couple of hours; on second thoughts, I've got a couple of things to pick up in town; let's say I'll aim to be with you by 5pm?"

"You're on; I'll have the wine in the fridge."

Carol rang off. She had had no rational doubts Phil was fine but it was still a relief to hear his voice. The flight had been smooth enough, but she had found it unusually hard even to catch a nap. When she flew long haul with work, essentially outside of the US, she was able to go business class but even that didn't help this time. Instead, she had watched a couple of her favourite movies – Casablanca and Raging Bull.

News of the London bombings had jolted Carol out of her post-party mood, catapulted her from one emotion to another. The worry of not being able to get through to Phil before taking off had begun to eat away at her, but after an hour or so, she had succeeded in rationalising the fear with the help of Bombay Sapphire and

319

Claude Rains' exquisite amorality. The early 21st century was already an uncertain, dangerous age, but at least Carol had a clear idea where she was and what she believed in. Humphrey Bogart, on the other hand, had to play the long game. In Carol's mind, there was the suspicion that Rick didn't like Lazlo, despised his reckless purity but, realising a relationship with Ilsa would never last, gave up what he knew he could never have, leaving Lazlo to wonder 'what if'.

During the flight, when Carol was genuinely worried, she had quite enjoyed the idea of caring for someone to the point of fearing for their safety. Aside from her parents, it had been a long time since she had felt that for anyone; Danny and their daughter, of course, but not really for the last 15 years or so. Carol's relationships had followed a gentler gradient, dating from her split with Danny in the late 1970s.

Even while she was evading opening herself up to new relationships, Carol had been careful not to apply the same cautious conservatism to the old friendships. Maybe the most significant was Philip. For over a decade, they had worked together, on and off, sometimes very closely, arguing and swapping opinions and contacts, reporting some of the same stories, constantly mixing professionally and socially. Together, they had covered the explosion of commercialism across US sport and had sat next to each other in the audience when Frazier beat Mohammed Ali at Madison Square Garden. Both too had been in Munich when the Israeli athletes were killed by Black September terrorists.

Critically, they had hit it off from the first time they met in a Mexico City bar. Carol had never met a White man who so transparently carried no baggage of racial preconception. For a young African American woman, who had only recently come to New York from the Deep South, it was still a shock to meet a White man who was able to treat her as an individual, unafraid to joke and insult her as her Black male friends did. When she had moved out of the house she had shared with Danny, it was to Philip's apartment she had headed, and stayed for a month until she had found somewhere.

During the first couple of hours after hearing news of the bombings, when she couldn't get through to him, Carol had even visualised going to the funeral; what she would say, whether she would cry, what memories would come flooding back. Speaking on the phone from Heathrow, hearing his familiar voice, genuine mid Atlantic with an odd lilt to it, slightly deeper in tone than you always expected, Carol felt herself break sweat. As she jumped onto the Heathrow Express on her way into Paddington, Carol felt her mood improve, despite the tiredness, so that she gave a little skip.

On the train, Carol detected a wariness among the passengers, who eyed each other with undisguised but apologetic suspicion. Everyone kept their bags close and eyed carefully anyone who put suitcases in the storage shelves, to check they remained on the train until after the door shut. By the time she got off at Paddington, Carol concluded London had become a paranoid city. She had lived through 9/11 in New York but the aftermath of this seemed worse, even if the outrage itself had claimed only a small fraction of the lives. And by the time she had changed at Paddington, and got on to the Bakerloo line down to Charing Cross, the paranoia seemed to have doubled. People with brown faces, no matter what ethnicity or religion, were being watched with barely disguised alarm, while they themselves either accepted eye contact, or, more commonly, consumed themselves in reading.

It was, of course, only yesterday the explosions had occurred and, she reasoned, the remarkable thing was that the Tubes, though less full than normal, were still being used by so many. London, too, was a much more South Asian city than New York, and so the look and feel of the place was different. By the time she got off, Carol had become unnerved, and even on the normal streets she felt an air of unreality.

Later, however, as she sat in the taxi up to Philip's, she realised she was happier in herself than she had felt in a long time. Only a week ago, she had been flying into London, looking forward to seeing Philip and meeting Michelle, but otherwise feeling empty and solitary, somehow separated off from other human beings and from the sport she loved. None of that quite applied anymore, and Carol was feeling upbeat as she paid the taxi and rang Philip's doorbell. A moment later, Michelle opened the door beaming.

"Oh Carol, I'm so pleased to see you again, so glad you're able to come to stay with us this time. Just dump your bag in the hall and come right through; Phil's getting you a drink. I can't believe it's less than a week since you were here for dinner, it seems like ages, so much has happened."

About five minutes later, the three of them were sat in the garden with drinks in hand. "Phew," said Philip, "is it good to see you! Only a week and so many things to talk about."

"I think the first thing is to tell me what yesterday was like," said Carol. "Just travelling in on the Heathrow Express and the Underground, London feels like a totally different place. Even the taxi driver was spooked, said he'd never seen anything like it."

"Well, the first thing is that Michelle and I were nowhere near any of the bombs, and I didn't really know what had happened, partly because I was in meetings, until maybe 11.30." He looked over at Michelle, who nodded.

"Me too," she said. "I was on a bus into town and it was only when I met Fran for lunch that I found out."

Philip continued, "The first thing, before my meetings had started, was that there were some reports on the radio – they seemed to think it was some kind of power surge and that something had gone wrong with the Tube. And to be honest, the first thing I thought was about the Olympics, how lucky we were that it didn't happen a couple of days earlier, before the voting. And also being depressed by how difficult it would be to get the transport anywhere decent for 2012."

"Typical, there's nothing wrong with your transport, not really. But tell me what happened when you found out bombs had gone off?"

"The streets just emptied really," said Michelle, "certainly in the West End. People who could just wanted to get home, but by then of course quite a lot of the network was at a standstill. It was boiling hot but people were walking everywhere, or trying to ring people and not getting through."

"Yes, I tried from Singapore but got nowhere."

"And Phil's right, it took ages for what had really happened to become clear. For ages I wasn't even certain how many bombs had gone off."

"It's funny," said Carol, "that it was only Wednesday I was in Singapore writing about how well London had played the cosmopolitan card, not having a bunch of middle-aged men in grey suits but instead a group of young people of different-coloured skins in tracksuits. Isn't there an irony that two of the world's most global cities have been attacked in this way? It's almost like it's the modern world as much as the politics of the US and UK governments that's being bombed."

"I know," said Philip, "although it's hard to say how much of that really influenced the voting."

"I'm more of an idealist than you are," said Carol, "but you should have been there to feel the energy around the London presentation. I heard Coe and Reedie had been practising for days, but even so, I've heard a lot of these things, and believe me they were good. That video they did as well; I know I'm a sucker for that stuff but again, I can't remember seeing one as good."

"Yea, but you know as well as I do that stuff's all about paying the right money to get the right people. We're really good at all that but it doesn't mean we'll put on a good Games. Equally, we evidently played the right cards in representing London as an ethnically mixed city with lots of young people, which it is. Don't get me wrong, I'm all in favour of the Olympics, I'm not the true believer you are but I do think they're generally a positive thing. All the palaver around selecting the next city really turns me off though. There are only a small number of cities big enough and sophisticated enough to hold them in the first place, and then when you factor in TV, sponsors, a bit of continental rotation and a certain level of snobbishness – yes, I know Atlanta was an exception."

"I buy much of that," replied Carol, "but you've still got to find a way of selecting a city and the technical bid by itself won't get you there. And it forces cities to get their act in gear. All the bids were better for the others being there and if it cost them a few million bucks, well no one forced them to bid. What do you think, Michelle? Are you a cynic or a believer?"

"I suppose I think the bidding ends up drawing out the real nature of what each city is proudest of, what it wants to do; I think the pressure creates that. And if that meant London went to women, youth and colour, then I think they passed the test and Paris ultimately didn't."

"I knew Michelle and I would get on. Anyway," Carol continued, "changing the subject, now we've finally got some real time, I want to hear properly about how the two of you got together. Philip's always managed to avoid telling me and now I've finally got a witness to keep him honest."

Philip laughed, "No, I guess I haven't, though not convinced that you've asked. We really just met at a party and bonded over a bottle of red wine. And then I asked Michelle out for dinner, the following Friday I think it was, and then it sort of just moved on from there."

"Always the romantic, Philip," replied Carol. "Come on, there must be more to it than that."

"Yes, what was it, Phil, you've never really told me either I mean, I was hardly the best-looking woman there. I did fancy you but I was far from alone. We all knew Richard's friend, a big TV executive from New York, was coming, and that he was single – did you know that? Anyway, it's always been a bit of a mystery to me."

Philip smiled, clearly not embarrassed by the conversation having shifted so quickly. "It's really quite simple, though it took me a while to work it out properly for myself – you argued with me!"

"Really, is that it?"

"Yep, that's it, the way to my heart was argument. I was 34, and I was tired of chatting women up and being chatted up in return. In a work sense, I was also tired of people shouting at me to get their own way, or trying to win the argument without bothering to try and convince me. And then there was you, drinking red wine, getting me away from that dreadful circle – of my own creating – of vapid conversation, and then arguing with me as a person, engaging with whatever it was we were talking about. And I've never stopped loving you for that."

"I never knew." Michelle turned to Carol. "Thank you for asking the question. I've never understood what happened, and somehow it seemed as though the time to ask had passed. It's funny but I don't really remember that side of the evening."

"What do you remember?"

"Well, I remember quite liking Phil when he came in; I think I opened the door in fact. I think I expected him to look a bit more glamorous than he did; after all, we'd been told he was a big media executive and to be honest, he looked a bit shambolic, though now of course I know that he was looking pretty smart by his own standards."

"He used to call it 'retro scruff'," said Carol. "I don't know what he wore when he was growing up but when I first met him, he was a bit of a fashion disaster."

"Hey, I'm here, remember!"

"Anyway, he's certainly a lot cooler dressed than he used to be," Carol continued, "but tell me more."

"Well, within about ten minutes, Philip was holding court to a group of about five young nurses. He probably wasn't quite old enough to be their father but you get the picture. I think he was giving them some line about the last time he had met Vitas Gerulaitis."

"That's it," said Philip, "I'm going to go and start cooking."

When he'd gone, Michelle poured the remains of the bottle into their two glasses. "It's really good to be finally meeting you, first last Saturday and now tonight. I've no idea why it hasn't happened before."

"Let's just put it down to Phil being useless, thereby absolving us both of guilt. But I was intrigued when he made such a big deal of you arguing with and listening to him, I could understand why it would be so important to him. The social life we led was pretty frenetic, with sometimes not a whole lot of substance. Tell me more about Phil when you met him then. I'm fascinated to know what you thought he seemed like after 16 years or whatever in the States."

"What, you mean how American he was?"

"Well perhaps, but also just whether he was different from what you expected, or from other people you'd met. You half implied earlier that you were prepared to dislike him, but obviously you didn't."

Michelle looked up. "I'm impressed you picked that up, I mean the bit about being ready not to like him. It's true, I was expecting someone who was very superficial and commercial. I thought, to be honest, that he'd be a fake but in fact, I don't think I've ever met anyone who was so much just themselves."

Carol was nodding. "He's always been pretty weird that way. All the time he lived in the US, Phil never really changed that much since I first met him. In some ways he was pretty worldly back then, he'd been following US politics in 1968 with the sort of access he had would probably take a lifetime to make sense of."

"I think, to be honest, it was just the simple, straightforward things I liked about him. It was obvious that he had learned how to talk to women but I know that's not an American thing. If I'm honest, I did like the fact he looked slightly scruffy – I'm slightly old-fashioned in that sense – his jacket looked like he'd worn it a few hundred times, and he had normal pairs of jeans and trainers on. And the last thing I guess, and this is a bit weird as well because I think I'm definitely in the minority, is that Phil makes me laugh. Even that first night I thought he was funny."

"That does put you in a minority. And by the way, I appreciate a lot being able to talk to you like this, given we've just met and all."

"It's been really easy. I know how important you are to him and the one thing I've always thought is that I would never try to own Phil."

"How do you mean?"

"Well, neither of us have ever wanted to get married, it's never been an issue, but for most people of my generation, I suspect it always feels a little more risky this way. But I've always seen Phil as an independent spirit. He lived a lot of his life before he even met me, and I know he's given up a hell of a lot by living here in London all these years. Don't get me wrong, I'm not doing the low self-esteem bit, and I reckon Phil's got a pretty good deal out of it."

"Michelle," Carol said, "believe me, he was ready to settle down. I sort of knew that when he got interested in jobs back here. It was his time and he was lucky to find you; you've been fantastic for him. I used to worry a little about him, actually a bit more than that. Maybe Phil didn't change much in the years he was in the US, but he's just completely moved on since he came back to the UK."

Philip re-emerged with a second bottle of wine, "I hope that was a decent interval for you both to demolish my hitherto unsullied character."

"Ample, thank you, darling," said Michelle, "and as a result, we feel like old friends already."

"Good," replied Philip, manipulating the corkscrew expertly. "Whatever Carol's accused me of, I'm taking the 5th."

"Oh, shut up, Phil! How long till dinner?"

"About 15 minutes."

"Carol was just telling me about when you lived in the US…"

"And how I'm so much better than I used to be."

"Yes, and how Michelle should take full credit."

"Creep, I told you how unreliable she was."

"Well, we're delighted you've been able to come and stay. Cheers!" They clinked glasses. "Particularly after such a terrible week."

"Believe me," said Carol, "unless you're personally affected by it, life will start to move on at some point, and even if you lost someone, eventually you start to live again. New York was worse than this after 9/11, and I know a couple of people who lost a daughter and a husband; somehow they've survived."

"You're right, I've seen how people whose relatives and loved ones die in hospital recover, and it is remarkable, although in a way I don't think many of them ever really escape the blight."

"But," said Philip, "there's still no getting away from the fact that yesterday changes everything, from us staying involved in Iraq and Afghanistan to the whole swathe of anti-terrorist laws; from ID cards to CCTV cameras. You name it, no matter how hard we try, we're gonna end up a more authoritarian and secretive, less tolerant country. Police will be more nervous and more likely to carry weapons, and we'll all look at each other with a bit less trust and a bit more suspicion."

Chapter 33
Monday 11th

Sam woke early, about 5am, and couldn't get back to sleep. He went to the toilet, made himself a cup of tea, tried reading a heavy book but none of it worked. Instead, he found himself lying in bed with his eyes alternately shut and open, trying to decide whether to give up and go downstairs to switch the TV on. Eventually, at about 6.20am, he did so.

BBC 24 was still blanket coverage of Thursday's bombings. Story after story of individual lives tragically severed, prematurely and indiscriminately terminated by individuals who seemed to place little value on their own life while presuming to stand in judgement over others of whom they knew nothing. Tears came to his eyes as they had already upwards of a dozen times since that morning. He'd tried to hide them and partially succeeded, the result being that Mary and others knew how upset and distraught he was but did not see the extent of the resulting trauma. He curled up on the sofa then, finding himself uncomfortable, sat up to rearrange the cushions before subsiding back down. He closed his eyes and the heat of Thursday morning shimmered again in front of him.

Since the fate of that Number 30 bus, the sounds around Sam's head had been severely filtered as his senses screened out everything not intrinsic to that experience. Its immediacy was still overpowering, although, without him yet appreciating it, as a memory it had already begun to recede. However, due to the intensity of the experience, the trauma and anxiety associated with it would continue to be unclear for some time yet, and he would never wholly escape it. Likewise, his perceptions of the world round him were delayed slightly, so that he often seemed not to hear comments directed towards him, which sometimes led to him starting to reply just as the other person, assuming he had been distracted, began to repeat themselves. In the same way, he would see something but only register it on his consciousness after a delay, so that, when reading, his eyes would sometimes have moved on to the next line before the first had been properly taken in, forcing him to read much more carefully than he was used to. The combined effect had slowed Sam down considerably so that he behaved and acted like a much older, slightly frail man.

Mary, Ruth and his friends took this as the understandable but temporary effect of the terrible events of 7th. However, the overall experience was much more complex, the catalyst for a reaction that was sweeping through his mind, colouring everything as it went, applying a layer of reinterpretation to countless events of his remembered life.

The critical tenet of Sam's belief system had always been that there was some relation between how people conducted themselves and their fate, either in this world or possibly another. In religion, he would have described himself as a benign agnostic, relatively well disposed towards the idea of a God in the Judean–Christian tradition but unconvinced of its existence. He was sceptical that the gods of the Old and New Testaments could be the same, but this was a matter of interest rather than concern to him. This was how his parents had brought him up, and the idea of progress underlay the education he had received at school and university; they were the values he was bred with and were at the core of his character.

But now these values had been demolished. The randomness of the victims appalled him to the core and made him doubt everything his life was built on. Not only could there not be a God, but the way in which the world functioned was at root random. To speak of the bombings simply being evil was completely to misunderstand their significance.

This distance between perpetrator and victims seemed to deny the humanity of both. Despite the clarity of the cause, these jihadists did not come across like soldiers, more like zealous supplicants in some primitive ritual, and Sam struggled to understand how they would have lived the rest of their lives. Did they have wives and children, parents and siblings, friends and jobs? If they were from London, did they contemplate that someone they knew might be a victim, and if they did, would it have mattered to them? Maybe it didn't matter because the very randomness of the killing, in the moment of the act itself, robbed the victims of their own individuality and humanity. Of course, as the stories of their lives and circumstances were now being revealed and explored, their identity was being returned to them, but Sam could not avoid seeing the act of bombing as chillingly inhuman. The bombers' characters seemed by self-definition flat; the nature of their act precluding him from understanding them as the human beings they were.

And how close had he been to taking his seat on that bus? Would he have gone upstairs? Almost certainly, as that was where he usually sat, but maybe on this occasion he would have gone against habit, spotted a seat downstairs and chosen differently. But Sam thought it unlikely. Rather, it was his failure to catch the bus that made the difference between life and death. Why did he fail? This was where Sam knew his mind was doing all it could to blur reality and motive, and hard as he had tried, and struggled still, to sustain the clarity of those moments, they were slipping inexorably away from him as subsequent events crowded in, memory layered its filters on top and, he suspected, his own psychological self-defence tried to obscure the detail of what had happened and why.

But while he could feel this, he didn't know why it was still so difficult to understand some simple actions less than a week before. Nothing had actually befallen him and he had been more than a mile away when the bomb exploded, yet its effect had both rocked him and, conversely, become instantly so opaque that it defied his understanding. Sam worried he was either missing something fundamental, or becoming unhinged. His thoughts were bouncing around destructively in a way he had never experienced. There seemed no way through to any understanding or state of equilibrium that would set his mind at rest.

He realised his toe, the one he had stubbed, had stopped hurting and wondered why, if its pain had now gone away, how painful it could really have been a few days before. Had he been deceiving himself? At the time, it had felt really hard to run. Hence, he had hobbled after the bus half-heartedly when, if he'd run, he would certainly have caught it. Could he have run through the pain? Probably yes if it had been important, but he had decided it wasn't. There was nothing unusual about this, he hardly ever ran for buses. Why not? Because he didn't believe he couldn't catch them, or because he didn't believe it mattered sufficiently to deserve the effort?

All his life, it seemed, he had operated within a comfort zone, trying to influence and control what was within his reach. If it was out of his reach, it was ignored, never stretched for. And it hadn't only been running for buses; it had included what he read, what work he did, where he travelled on holidays; whatever it was, he had always sought to minimise the risks he was taking.

Sam examined this idea, wary of generalisation. He cast his mind back to remember if there was a time when he had been fearless and simply followed his lights irrespective of the risk entailed. When he really pushed, he remembered, or thought he did, times as a child when he had been brave and essentially done his own thing, a period when he did not remember experiencing much in the way of fear. But then, around the time he went to secondary school, he could recall being shy sometimes. From this distance, it all seemed pretty much like a normal part of growing up. The last time he remembered doing anything stupidly brave was just before he went to Manchester, when he was going somewhere with Michelle and had somehow broken up some fight. He couldn't remember precisely what he had said or why, except that the fight seemed quite one sided; only that he had been scared witless and was amazed he had gotten away with it. Afterwards, he had promised himself never to do anything like that again.

Since then, what had there been? It wasn't exactly that he'd run away from problems but he'd rarely faced them head on, had avoided confrontation where he could, looked for compromises and agreement even when the right way to go was clear. Society valued collaboration over confrontation, or certainly claimed it did. Sam wondered whether his supposed preference had an element of fakery embedded. Success through collaboration was, by definition, quite low key, and rarely garnered the tributes routinely heaped on success that had been the result of 'battles' won. All through his life he had been, he thought, a peacemaker, had tried to ensure this went hand in hand with as much fairness as could be secured.

But this very balancing act, this judgement based on a weighing up of probabilities, was now forcing him to reconsider. Was he really in a position to judge the best deal available? Was he not just caught in an ultimately poisonous cycle of self-justification, which tended toward the lowest common denominator? Hadn't it been all too easy to cut his judgements to suit the cloth? But maybe the greatest human ability is to assess what is within the scope of our power and influence. Outside of that, weren't we just railing against the rising swell of events? Sam tried to think through whether there was any virtue in fighting the good fight for lost causes. He struggled for a frame of reference. Much literature, most famously Don Quixote, concerned itself with an obsession for lost causes. Then again, other artists seemed to be adding twists to life as they found it. Sam was none the wiser as he tried to discern what it meant that he was constantly searching for peace and compromise, avoiding argument and strife.

But Sam also knew that it was only now, looking back, that he viewed himself this way. For most of his life, maybe all of it, he had seen himself as trying to do the right thing, not looking for a compromise as a first instinct. He had seen himself as being on the side of arguments he believed in, not in the middle somewhere trying to cut a deal. Surely, he had been better than that; surely, he had a whole string of solid achievements he could look back on and be proud of? But when he did look back, the picture wasn't as he expected. There was work that had succeeded in that it had been delivered, but it was much harder, impossible in fact, to say if it had changed anything for the better. Mostly, it been delivered to time and cost – not small achievements and ones that were greatly valued at the time. But now, in retrospect, there seemed to be a much greater distinction between the mere fact of delivery and anything that could properly be called success. Again he attempted to cast his mind back, this time to try and disentangle what he had been thinking at the time. As far as he could remember, he had been largely caught up in the day-to-day delivery of the projects. And he knew, even in his current febrile state, that this was important, that it was in its own way a worthy thing, but it wasn't what Sam remembered thinking he was doing at the time. Back then, he was trying to change the world. However, he could not now recall what any of these improvements really were; he could remember the names of some of the projects, even from more than 20 years ago, but he didn't really have a clue if anything got better.

And if this was true, then it was hard to say what he had contributed to the sum of anything. Had he not been there, it was hard to pinpoint what difference there would have been. In so far as he could point to things for which he was responsible, it was difficult to even form an opinion about how much his own role was either necessary or unique.

Trying hard was always his starting point, and yet that was precisely what Sam hadn't done on 7th July, when not trying hard had saved his life. Three or four times in the last couple of days, he had reached, by different routes, this threshold of realisation and then stopped, intimidated by its ramifications. On that day, he had shied away from pain, from the challenge of catching the bus on a hot July morning. And wasn't that nothing more than a small challenge when put beside those he had faced and largely side-stepped through his life. So it wasn't really a surprise that he had so elegantly avoided this one as well.

The more he thought, the more tangled and unsatisfying were his thoughts. Sam knew this was happening but could neither improve the result nor stop the thinking. He decided he needed to do something to break whatever cycle he was in. All he could think of was to get out of the house, so he wrote a short but hopefully reassuring note to Mary – "Hello, woke early and couldn't get back to sleep. Need some fresh air. Should be home for lunch. Love, Sam" – and shut the door quietly behind him. It was just before 7am.

He wandered along the grand, slightly run-down terrace of what he thought must have been Georgian houses and turned towards the Tube station just as he had four days before. It was another beautiful morning, though it didn't feel quite as hot, and the air didn't shimmer quite so much. Everything seemed quite normal and other people seemed to be going to work as they normally did. Were they looking around a bit more than usual? Maybe, but he couldn't be sure. Were there as many of them? Again, probably not, but his memories were too confused for him to be definite. He reached Kentish Town Tube station but found himself suddenly suspended at the point where he was about to go through the ticket barrier; he couldn't face it, not yet; not going down underground to board a train that would rattle along old tracks through dark tunnels. Sam swivelled silently and escaped back to the fresh air. Next, he queued for a bus and when it arrived, moved forward and had placed a foot up into it before he understood this journey wasn't possible either. By this stage his hands were starting to tremble, not badly and not that anyone would have noticed, though it was glaringly obvious to Sam himself. Extracting himself from the queue, he went and sat down on a bench to think about what to do. The only given was that it was far too early to go back home. It didn't occur to him that Mary would become really worried and call the police.

Eventually, with no plan, he started walking into town. Down through Camden he strolled, slowly, trying to relax and take in his surroundings without focusing or concentrating, just absorbing them as naturally as possible. He was wearing old shorts, marked with paint from long ago contributions to painting a primary school playground fence, and the blue short-sleeved shirt he'd bought in Greece one summer. The shorts were more than ten years old, the shirt almost twice that. He felt out of place; quite a lot of people he passed were dressed for the office, but not all, and Sam, who had worn a suit for nearly 30 years, felt totally liberated by being out so early on a Monday but self-evidently not going to the office. He felt on the other side of some invisible divide, his heightened sensibility rendering him much more vulnerable than normal to the subliminal eye contact of people who passed him, wondering what a 50-year-old man, dressed so shabbily, was doing out so early. For a moment, he fancied he must look quite enigmatic. Maybe they suspected he might be an eccentric millionaire, en route to his hedge fund office. Or he might be an impresario – wrong word but he knew what he meant – producer of pop records, a la George Martin, on his way to an early recording session.

To say these thoughts flitted across Sam's mind would be to assign them an undeserved prominence, but it would be equally wrong to imply he wasn't conscious of them. Despite consistent stimulation from family and friends, his sensibility to external sensation, particularly unexpected ones, had been slowly calcifying to the point where his sense of identity was almost impregnable. This is not to say he had any great vision of himself, only that what he did have was quite self-contained. Neither would it be right to say Sam wasn't empathetic, or that he lacked emotional intelligence, because in many ways he had both these characteristics in spades. But they were either focused fully on his family and close friends, or they were comfortably, if unconsciously, blinkered when engaging with the rest of humanity.

Now, however, there seemed to be much more activity going on than he remembered – voices, glances, and the way people walked, what they wore and carried. His only comparable experience dated back a few years to when he had his ears syringed after they had become bunged up with wax. Instantly, his hearing had been transformed and the Kilburn High Road had turned from a sleepy side street into the M1, a cacophony of engines and blaring horns. This morning his other senses had taken on the same new scale of capacity. Thus he noticed for the first time things he had been oblivious to, a man's chest hair, a women's cleavage, the remains of a man's black eye and a woman's make-up slightly tear-stained. And he overheard disconnected snatches of conversation.

"He was a total bastard."

"I'm back to back all day."

"Woke at 4am, couldn't get back to sleep..."

"It was a weekend double header…"

"We won by five wickets…"

"I'm scared travelling on the Tube."

"Why do they have to cover their faces up?"

"What do you expect when you're talking that shit to me? Do you really think I'm fucking her? After these last three years?"

"Who have you got on Opening Day?"

"I couldn't get through on my mobile…"

None of this was particularly out of ordinary, and there was nothing in any of the phrases that surprised or puzzled him, but hearing them, individually and collectively, was a new experience. This world of chatter had been closed off to him, beyond his introspective bubble, existing in what he re-experienced as boisterous and messy, the profane and the trivial.

The atmosphere in the street seemed fresh and newborn, and if Sam remained as confused and traumatised as he had been before leaving home, the pit that had been starting to gape beneath him had, for the time being, been obscured by the bright morning sunshine, and crowded out by the new information raining on his senses. This bombardment compelled him to pay attention, and to cease focusing entirely on plumbing the depths of meaning within last Thursday. This had a dual benefit; in the first place, it brightened his mood by the simple fact of preventing him from devoting his entire being to his reflections as he had been; and also – this occurred slowly over the next week – it forcibly inserted a different perspective, a more pluralist lens through which to examine his reactions.

As he walked south towards Edgeware Road, where one of the Underground bombs had been detonated, he noticed increasing numbers of Muslims, including women in burqas and full hijabs, their faces covered apart from their eyes. They looked out on the world much as Sam felt he was doing, from behind a defensive motif. He thought those eyes looked a little fearful, and that other people were glancing towards them unnaturally often, with the same mix of fear and wariness. But Sam also knew he was assuming these things. Pure objectivity was fool's gold.

There he was, having grown up with a received sense of certainty that there was an objective right and wrong, which everyone subscribed to even if they did not follow. He had trusted it because it came from his parents, the BBC and the books he read. It also came from the UN, from Hollywood and from WW2. There were wrinkles in this narrative, including the emergence and increasingly divergent rhetoric of post-colonial nations, but none of these troubled the foundations of Sam's value system. The iniquities of Empire could be reduced by being set in their historical context; the Cold War and communism shored up his value system, supplying a steady diet of moral and practical failures against which to assess Western society. And so, sustained by a solid and seemingly impregnable web of beliefs, Sam's value system had stood relatively unblemished.

But today, almost minute by minute, his status quo was changing; cracks and fissures were becoming visible, and what had been solid, easily definable, could not be classified so readily. Instead of a single, self-referential and sophisticated narrative, there were multiple and conflicting truths, competing for access. Intellectually, Sam had accepted the principle of plurality and the legitimacy of disagreement and dissent. Conflicting schools of thought had always been treated as a challenge to his core beliefs, to be rebutted, or occasionally to be accepted as adjustments. But this was more profound; these competing opinions were starting alongside his own and the accumulated defences of upbringing and assumption had fallen away.

All the voices, places, and small physical movements Sam was noticing for the first time were part of this new vulnerability. Instead of a muffled cocoon, his existence was exposed in an entirely unnerving way. But not frightening. This surprised him because exposure to the unknown had always gone hand in hand with danger. Yet today, despite the inundation of the new and unsettling, he did not feel in the slightest peril. And this made him smile in a way that, as the sides of his mouth wrinkled, made him realise how long it had been since the last time. He assumed this had been before the bombing but couldn't remember, such had been the numbness. Sam's emotions stemmed from reactions to his ordeal, non-linear and complex, which had been bombarding his senses and psyche. Until this morning this bombardment had not really penetrated, but now the shell of his cocoon had disintegrated. But instead of destabilising him through fear and insecurity, they combined to stimulate his being in a way that felt familiar, but in an ancient sense that bore no relation to his remembered life. This sudden consciousness of the detail of other human beings' words and actions transported him to a new psychological place. Here, the multiple combinations of influences created a new sense of comfort, almost of suspension as they balanced each other out.

Again Sam smiled. Instead of his new vulnerability making him fearful, he felt less alone than before. All his adult life he had struggled to belong and, except for family and friends, had felt an outsider. That sense of being 'other' had exacted a small but cumulative transaction cost to dealing with other people. He was always waiting for some put-down, subtle or otherwise, and so was braced with nervous energy to respond. Or in fact not to respond, as his default reaction to these events, which in fact occurred only rarely, was to ignore them as far as possible and find a way to move on. But now, with his energy levels drained, Sam found he had no need to be ready to respond to potential put-downs. He no longer felt himself to be an outsider and this was why he smiled.

He had worked his way slowly east. Once he had got past Regent's Park and onto the Marylebone Road, he turned left and walked past Madame Tussaud's and the Planetarium, which he had always thought strange bed fellows, then south down Marylebone High Street. He had no clear idea of where he was heading and, realising he was hungry, found a café and ordered himself some toast and coffee. Then he nipped next door to buy a paper but sat looking at it blankly waiting for his order. When his toast arrived, he could only nibble at it but even morsels slipping down his throat gave him a reassuring sensation, taking the edge off his hunger.

Feeling so relaxed was strange. The fear and confusion had not exactly gone away but were now less important, and they protruded much less into his consciousness. The invasion of his senses by the sounds and gestures of others had so built up the space that surrounded his own fears that it was difficult to discern which fears were his and which belonged to someone else. The people he had walked beside down the Kilburn High Road and Maida Vale, and those who had passed him in the opposite direction, looked no less afraid and confused than he felt. For all the differences that divided him from each of them, his problems and uncertainties connected him to them in a more profound way than Sam had ever imagined. The differences were still there but they were between everyone and everyone, not between him and everyone else.

His hand started to shake as he reached hesitantly for his coffee. Sam became aware of the waitress, a young Chinese woman, standing over him. "Are you all right, sir? You look not very well, pale and very tired."

"Yes, thanks," said Sam, looking up. "I've not been very well but I'm feeling much better today." He paused, wondering if he should say more. "I've not been able to get out for a few days and I wanted to get some fresh air, so I came out for a walk; but yes, it has made me a little tired." He paused again. "Thanks for asking, I really appreciate it. Sorry to have cause you to worry but I'm fine, thank you."

"Thank you sir, please just say if we can do anything for you. I brought you a glass of water."

"Oh, thank you again. There's no need but thank you. I'll be okay."

The young woman smiled and went back to the counter, where she smiled at him again, almost shyly this time.

There were only four other people in the café, workmen, all sat together at a table by the window, seemingly unaware of the exchange. Sam felt his hand shake again as he reached for the coffee but managed to relax sufficiently to reach out slowly, he hoped slowly, because he imagined the waitress was still watching him, with his other hand as an insurance against spillage.

But despite his physical fragility, Sam was starting to feel a warm glow somewhere in his gut, his small intestine, he imagined. It wasn't really spreading the way warm glows are meant to, but it was definitely there. He had seen it many times before, the way mothers with pushchairs and toddlers were consistently helped and watched over by unconnected people, the way the old and infirm were regularly assisted, even drivers showing greater attention and care; these traits were common to every society. The waitress' gesture had been the essence of simplicity and had cost nothing, but equally there was no imperative, no self-interest.

Sam supped his tea quietly and, so the waitress would attach more credibility to his claims that he was okay, he made great efforts to eat his toast more normally, and to pretend more effectively that he was reading the paper instead of just staring at the printed text; he even turned the page a couple of times. These things he did not for his own benefit but because the waitress he had never met had been concerned about him. The warm glow still refused to spread, but neither was it fading, and the implied connection with the waitress seemed to have fed it a little.

When he finished, Sam got up and nodded goodbye to the waitress. Unfortunately, she was tending to a couple who were just ordering and didn't notice. Sam thought about going over but decided not to, it would be making too big a deal of what had happened. As he emerged into the street and saw different people walking by, talking, listening to music, even in one case reading a newspaper as she walked, he was reminded again of his insecurity and insignificance, but also that this was common.

The warm glow was showing signs of spreading, but then his thoughts reverted to the bombings and his mood darkened, the glow shrivelling to a flicker under its steely scrutiny. What did any of it matter when there was random carnage like last Thursday? All the natural goodness and common emotion in the world was utterly worthless in the face of suicide bombers. How could he feel so positive about something like shared insecurity when the bombs had gone off less than a week ago? There he had been, almost celebrating the differences between individuals, when all the difference in the world hadn't saved the victims. He walked on with his head bent over, and tears began to stream from his eyes, at first slowly and then in a sobbing torrent. Sam found himself a quiet doorway – it was still before 9am, most of the shops hadn't opened, and it was in that lull between the morning rush hour and people arriving to start the shopping day. He pressed his feet against one side of the doorway and slumped back against the opposite. The odd passer-by glanced in at him, mostly he fancied with sympathy, occasionally with suspicion, but this time no one came over to ask if he needed help, and for that he was grateful. Slowly, he recovered and gathered himself together. He started walking again.

Soon he reached Oxford Street, where he turned east towards Oxford Circus. It was just after 9am now, and the area was starting to fill up. Was it as busy as normal? Were there as many people on the buses, pouring out of Oxford Circus station? More cyclists? He didn't know the answer to any of these questions, or whether in fact any of them had a right answer.

But if any of what had happened was going to make sense, he needed to go beyond seeing it solely as a manifestation of evil. In many ways, the bombers were very human, with parents, partners, maybe children, friendships, ambitions, disappointments. But something had propelled them into terrorism, and then to suicide bombing. How does that happen? All this Sam thought about as he walked along Oxford Street and then New Oxford Street to Holborn. Until now, his direction had felt relatively aimless but now he knew where he was going, and turned up Southampton Row toward Russell Square and Woburn Place, where the bus bomb had been detonated.

When he had woken, when he left the house, and even when he started heading east along Oxford Street, this would have been the furthest idea from his mind. Confused as he was, the idea of going to the scene of the atrocity would have been anathema. But now it seemed right. It wasn't a sudden conversion, and ever since he had passed Centre Point, the kernel of the idea had slowly been forming in the back of his mind somewhere. Where that kernel came from he never really worked out. The closest he got was concluding he had taken the very un-Sam-like decision to confront the thing he feared most. This was not how Sam explained it to himself at the time but became a rationale afterwards.

As he walked up Southampton Row, he was beginning to experience a kind of false visualisation of last Thursday, as though he had been there, watching from the outside while everything happened in slow motion, the action rolling like a Peckinpah film; the horror of it, people staggering around injured and bleeding, others appearing out of nearby offices. But what mattered most, maybe even more than the horror itself, was how individuals sought to help each other in simple displays of giving. Time after time, often hurt themselves, they would check if others were okay, help tend to them or fetch water. But the principle thing that struck him was how individual they all were. Although behaving in a coordinated way, each was making an independent, solitary decision. No one really spoke beyond the occasional request, yet they worked in unison, made things happen.

As these images were passing through his mind, Sam knew they weren't real, that he hadn't been there when the bomb went off. And yet he completely believed their truth, individual people making personal decisions, but not in isolation, each as valid and valuable as the next. No longer did he have to work to be part of a larger group, worry if he wasn't. He could simply follow his instincts, make his own decisions. That urge he had since youth to fit in with others was wrong. The richness of humanity came in the first instance from individuality. Without it, teams and groups don't succeed, aren't sustainable.

And then there was the randomness of existence. Why we are here? How long for? Sam had ceased to agonise over these. He had, at best, limited control of his life, and so had an obligation to live at least partly for the here and now. For the first time, Sam saw this as freedom rather than constraint.

Part 6: Perspectives III

Chapter 34
London, Thursday, 30 November 2005

"I think it's the simple rubbishness of it that depresses me the most."

Ed was drinking coffee in Mary and Sam's kitchen. He was just back from Baghdad and was sitting at the breakfast bar shaking his head. He looked worn down and had clearly lost weight. His cheekbones seemed higher and he kept hitching up his trousers. Even his eyes, usually so bright, were duller than normal.

Mary sat on the other stool, sipping tea, and Sam lounged against the white painted wall with a gin and tonic. Ed had so far refused a drink, even though it was now gone 7pm, itself a sign he was out of kilter. He was wearing a grey Arran sweater over a grey shirt; it was his version of matching his clothes, his view being that the grey set off his black jeans and trainers. Even Ed's hair was now greyer and, because none of his clothes really fitted him anyway, he looked anything but the epitome of chic he imagined.

Sam himself was starting to feel more normal, travelling in the opposite direction to his friend. After 7/7, his deep introspection had lasted until mid-October. But the last three weeks had been better, and Sam now fancied he felt lighter and sunnier even than he had before. To Sam it felt an extreme change, and he now thought of himself as being at the cutting edge of recklessness, when in fact he had barely moved into the mainstream. But some of this weight had gone from his decision-making, leaving him freer, more disposed to forgive, even himself. It was great seeing Ed, for the first time since the bombing, but not in the way he had expected. Where they had previously matched each other for the care they took in the use of words, now both were less guarded, more flippant.

"When has it ever not been about incompetence?" Sam replied.

"But I used to take such comfort from the possibility of a conspiracy theory."

"Why? Isn't successful conspiracy, at least on the world stage, almost always the preserve of historians and Bismarck?"

"And Cold War America…"

"Anyway, weren't all those multinational contractors with links to the Bush administration just raking it in? What more conspiracy would you wish for?"

"Except that even that is far too obvious. There's no doubt it's all been based on the comic, or maybe cosmic, illusion that Iraq would instantly transform into an orderly western, capitalist democracy, perhaps a bit like Pennsylvania, full of religious minorities and something of a swing state but still fertile ground for Baptist fundamentalists."

Mary always enjoyed Ed's visits, brief as they were. She sometimes wanted to be a mother to him but had mostly held these instincts in check, reasoning that minding out for Sam was enough responsibility. She also found it hard to reconcile the somewhat dishevelled, slightly forgetful individual she knew with the crisp, calculating reporter she saw and heard on the media. Part of it was that Ed himself had little sense of his public persona, tending to focus in rather than out, and to an extent disregarding public reaction and perception. Once, he had explained this to Mary as being partly driven by his wish for the news to be reflected through his eyes and mouth, so the audience would receive both fact and personal interpretation. Over the years, they'd had several conversations about the essential impossibility of objective accuracy, agreeing that choosing which facts to present was as much a question of judgement as what you said about them. Usually, she was sanguine about him, but Ed's appearance today, barely 48 hours after telling them he was coming, combined with his appearance and demeanour, had this time brought the mundanity of their lives into sharp relief.

Sam liked the contrast. He had known since his dad died that he was not well-equipped emotionally to cope with extreme events. In his mind, there had been a time at Manchester, and for about three years after, when he faced up squarely to what life presented him with. Since then, in his own memory, he had begun to react to events and steer away from them. He had dimly been aware of the change at the time, and tended to exaggerate the value of his previous spontaneity. For example, he tended to forget those long afternoons of not knowing what to do, not having someone to do it with, not having the money to do it in the first place. Equally, he no longer found himself dragging along as part of a group doing things he didn't enjoy, going to parties just because they were there.

Since those days, marriage and parenthood had both enriched his life enormously. When, however, something spontaneous did happen, such as now when Ed turned up with little notice, he felt better able to respond – they had cancelled a theatre trip and Sam had rearranged several meetings so he could take a day's leave – and this had a positive impact on him.

Over the years, as Sam's lifestyle had become more routine, Ed's had gradually assumed elements of myth. He knew the great majority of his friend's time was, like his own, taken up with recurring activities, days of patient research that often did no more than eliminate possible storylines. However, he could not get away from the idea that his friend had more excitement and surprise in his life. In some respects, Ed and he had travelled in opposing directions since Manchester. Back then, Ed had been earnest almost to a fault; Sam had been the one who scarcely looked beyond the next weekend. Sam had been the partygoer, the one who dragged Ed off to a movie or the pub; Ed the one who wanted to join a club.

The summer had also been playing on his mind. Since that July Thursday, he had been preoccupied by questions and their implications. In the end, he had accepted that the world would shape him, that he would react to it. If he had not failed to catch the bus he would be dead; he had survived because of his weakness. This realisation had cast him into depression. He had mostly managed to hide this, even from Mary, and his success in doing so, or so he reasoned, meant the depression itself could not have been deep. Nevertheless, it had led him to question much of his life; courage, determination, persistence were no longer the virtues he had believed, they did not automatically direct you towards a more useful or prosperous existence. He had been striving for the wrong goals all his life, or at least for goals that did not lead to greater happiness or fulfilment, and this conclusion had shoved him into a morass of doubt. But, slowly, he had begun to believe that the true meaning of his experience on the morning of 7/7 was that a wider choice of actions was legitimately open to him. There was no longer a single or even a small number of right answers. Instead, there was an equivalent number of right and wrong actions, and between them a much larger number involving some kind of trade-off. Sam found this deeply liberating, and it had dragged him back to the surface.

He consequently no longer felt restricted by an ethical compass that had always seemed to point unerringly in a precise direction. Instead, he began to feel carefree, stripped of responsibility. He could afford to get things wrong, make mistakes. For the first time, he started to stop minding if he failed. He had reached this new frame of mind for about four weeks when Ed had rung to say he was on his way. And now, here he was, lounging and chatting somewhat irreverently at the breakfast bar.

"How's Ruth?" Ed asked.

"Fine, I think," Sam replied. "At least as far as I know. We have maybe a couple of short phone calls a week, but to be honest, we're none the wiser."

Mary laughed. "Sam has a more active imagination than me."

"So what's she doing? Is she still up in Leeds?"

"Yes, she's working part-time in a restaurant, and also doing some voluntary work for a homeless charity. Some of her uni friends are from there and, like her, have stayed on, at least for a bit. And she has a bit of a thing about living in a city that's like Manchester but not."

"Do you really think so?" asked Sam. "To be honest, I've never thought about it like that."

"That's because you never realise how much you talk about it. And you also have a bit of a blind spot for how much she wants to understand you. I think because I'm basically London, Ruth thinks, probably rightly, she knows where I've come from. But you're a bit of a mystery to her."

"Are you sure?"

"The last time I was over properly, maybe a couple of years back," Ed said, "Ruth was endlessly keen to find out more about what we did as students, what it was all like in Manchester, way back when. Anyway," he added, "it's just gone 7.15pm – all of 20 seconds, so is there any chance of a large gin?" Ed smiled, feeling relaxed to a new level, the muscles in his middle back suddenly gone slack, his shoulders less rigid.

"Well, let me see," Mary went to the cupboard and fridge and expertly mixed a couple of gin and tonics – "Look, we even got fresh lemons in for you," – and opened a bottle of Merlot for herself.

"There you go," she said. "Cheers, it's wonderful to see you! And now you've got a drink, you can tell me about your love life. How's Isabella?"

"Oh Mary!" groaned Sam in mock despair, "How can you ask the poor guy that?"

"I completely see it as my responsibility. After all, you're never going to ask him anything important. All you ever seem to talk to Ed about are politics and football. Besides, Ed doesn't mind, do you? In fact, I'm sure you enjoy it really, partly because it makes you go slightly red."

Ed laughed and nodded. Despite himself, he had gone slightly pink but the laugh was genuine. "Absolutely, nothing gives me greater pleasure than to bare my most intimate relationships around this breakfast bar. But to answer your question, Isabella's back in Madrid and about to get married, not to me though. I offered her a hotel room in Amman and lots of frequent flyer miles, but she's having none of it."

"Sorry, mate," said Sam, somewhat taken aback.

"Don't worry, it's fine. I don't really do self-pity, or at least I gave up on it at least ten years ago. Isabella wanted a family and the stability to bring it up. To be honest, we never really talked about it explicitly but it was pretty obvious I wasn't offering that."

"If you had talked, maybe it would have changed your mind."

"Not really, Mary, I'm a selfish git at heart. I'd known for months it would happen."

"Is there anyone else?"

"Not at the moment, I need a break from the effort of romantic attachment. It's hard for the liver, I'm told. Anyway, what was the story with 7/7? It sounded dreadful; hard to believe I'd just flown out."

"Not terrible compared to Baghdad," said Mary, "but it was awful. To be honest, I thought the death toll would end up a lot higher. I don't know how many people got out or escaped by the skin of their teeth. It was just a terrible day. I remember seeing that burnt out bus by Russell Square, I'll never forget it."

"I was pretty much out of it, to be honest. The Northern Line failed and I got kicked out around Kentish Town."

"You were lucky in your own way then if, as they reckon, the same thing happened to the bus bomber."

"Yes, tell me about it," Sam paused, took a drink to cover his hesitation. "It was strange going around London in the next couple of weeks but, to be honest, it was okay after that. The suspicious looks, particularly at Muslims, just sort of stopped and everyone went back to ignoring each other."

"But I don't think it will ever really be the same, or not for many years," added Mary. "I remember the IRA bombs of the 70s and this was far worse. Partly, I think it's the suicide element of it. It's definitely changed our politics and not for the better."

"I can see that," said Ed. "I don't see how any government, to be honest, would have reacted much differently. You only have to imagine the scenarios of a repeat bombing, probably with more loss of life; and the Opposition, any Opposition, would immediately have the government hung out to dry for not having given the police more powers. It would be suicide for them. Sorry for the pun." Ed looked embarrassed but then shrugged.

"I don't know though," Mary continued. "It still doesn't make it right. I think it's all the more important to keep our values in situations like this. And I'm inherently sceptical of the police's ability to use new powers effectively, and also of their ability to resist using them. History's full of examples of powers being used far more widely than the narrow circumstances originally envisaged."

"Yes, but it's not that simple," said Sam, half interrupting. "These crimes are so different, and the cost of getting it wrong is just so much higher. We're not talking one murder, we're talking 50-60 on average, which gives the police a whole different level of challenge. For a start, they have to arrest suspects earlier because the risk of leaving it beyond a certain point to gather more evidence is just too great."

"I think that's a reasonable argument, but Blair and co haven't made the case that the cost benefit has fundamentally shifted. To be honest, they haven't really made an argument at all; they've simply asserted the need."

"I think that's probably because of the fear it would generate," said Ed. "It would just help build the paranoia you talk about. Though I still don't think that necessarily makes it the right answer. Very little of this stuff actually works in my experience, and there's that Tocqueville thing about all power corrupting."

"Anyway," concluded Sam, "I think the government will pretty much do what's necessary to force it through."

"Has the bombing affected community relations much?"

"It's hard to say," replied Mary. "I'm no expert, but the atmosphere does feel a bit different, maybe more strident. There certainly was a shift in the media portrayal of the Muslim community. The other way around though, I'm not so sure. I get the sense British Muslims are somehow disappointed rather than angry. And I think they mostly recognise that an event like 7/7 is going to provoke a lot of anger and hatred, but hope it will somehow go away with time."

"What it has made me realise," added Sam, "is how little I really know about Islam. I mean I know nothing really. I've never even read a book in translation, which I'm going to change."

"Well," said Ed, "we're all going to have to get to know a lot more about it, for Islam is going to be bigger this century. Not least because it's now the most powerful competing world view with Western capitalism. Don't get me wrong, the US were absolutely dreadfully prepared for winning the Iraq War. And when they weren't simply being rubbish, they were giving lucrative contracts to their friends. But a big part of that story was that they seriously thought Iraq would suddenly become like Cleveland or somewhere, once they'd gotten rid of Saddam. For a country where Evangelical religion is such a potent political force, they did not even get the significance of the Imams. I think they thought democracy and consumerism were so attractive and intoxicating that all the pieces would just naturally full into place. It will take them another five years to sort out the mess."

"You're kidding!" said Sam, clearly taken aback. "Does our government know that?"

"As far as I could tell, that certainly seemed to be the briefing they were getting. I don't think I've ever asked, but did you go on the march back in 2003?"

"No, I didn't," replied Sam. "We both thought about it and talked a couple of times but it never seemed right to me. I've never really been a marching person, though. For instance, I remember when Saddam and what's his name? – Chemical Ali – tried to basically commit genocide on the Kurds. If he'd tried again and succeeded, the issue of whether to go to war wouldn't be nearly so clear cut, would it? And, to be honest, at the time I never really doubted Saddam had significant numbers of WMD somewhere, certainly chemical – after all he had previous on that – possibly biological. I wasn't sure how deployable they were but, to be honest, it never crossed my mind they didn't exist at all."

"Mary?"

"Well, to be honest, we should have talked about going on the march, the whole thing really, much more than we did. I can't remember what we were doing at the time. Of course, that might have been an excuse on our part, but it happened, and so we never properly kicked the issue around, not as much as we should have done. But of course, that's with hindsight. Ever since though, I could probably count on the fingers of one hand the times we've had a decent conversation about the Iraq war and what's happened there."

"Sometimes I really miss having a family and love the way the two of you do."

"What happened?" Mary asked, conscious Ed had suddenly shifted the subject and wondering about the impact of the break up with Isabella. "Was there a certain point where you consciously cut yourself off from the possibility, or did it creep up on you?"

"I've not thought about it quite like that. When I look back now, I think it was Sabra and Shatila. After that, I don't think I wanted to be a parent anymore. I was just afraid of not being to explain what happened in the world to them, or worse still of not being able to protect them."

"Was it really that bad?" asked Sam.

"Well, I didn't really talk about it for about two years, and I still have the odd nightmare. So yes, it was that bad. I've always struggled to describe it, there's no vocabulary I can use. I've never read or listened to my report and never will. I've no idea what I said and don't want to, to be honest."

"I think it's amazing you managed to report with such humanity and objectivity; I don't know how you do it after all that you've seen." Mary put her hand on Ed's arm.

"Well, it also gave me a vocation, remember. Even if I couldn't describe that place adequately, I was sure I wanted to describe pretty much everything short of it. If we now live in a global village, then we have an obligation to know about what's going on in the next street. That's how I see the Middle East, as our neighbouring streets."

"I was the opposite. I'd always expected to work at something I really believed in, but I've only really had a series of jobs rather than a career, although most of them have been decent enough."

"It's just different, isn't it?" said Mary, "Less immediate for one thing, than what Ed does. You hardly ever see the immediate effects of your work, all that carefully crafted policy."

"You have always given yourself a ridiculously hard time, you know," added Ed. "At university, I remember you always used to beat yourself up over the tiniest thing."

"I feel really ganged up on now," joked Sam. "I wasn't trying to do the big sympathy kick. I'm pretty happy, in ways I'd never expected. I was only trying to say that life messes around with our expectations."

"That's what I love about you guys, I can always rely on you to give me a good going over."

"That's our job," replied Mary. "By the way, we've got a couple of things for you." She went over and picked up a Waterstone's bag from beside the CD rack. "Here, happy reading and watching."

Ed looked inside. There was a DVD set of 2005 Ashes highlights and a short book about the series by someone called Gideon Haigh.

"Wow, thanks," he said and gave them each a hug. "You know, I've seen nothing of this and haven't been to a cricket match in years."

"Well, you know I'm a lot less into cricket than you and Mary, but even I was hooked, certainly from that last inning of the second Test at Edgbaston, when the Aussies nearly won from nowhere. And then it just went on and on."

"It was just brilliant," said Mary. "You'd have loved it. You know the way Test cricket can just swing violently back and forth?"

"Were Flintoff and Warne as good as the papers said?"

"Definitely, Warne kept the Aussies in it time and again, and nearly won the two Tests England won for Australia, with his batting at Edgbaston and his bowling at Trent Bridge. But then, of course, he dropped Pietersen at the Oval and that was it." Mary's eyes were shining and she shuddered as she thought about it.

"And Freddy was pretty much the difference; his bowling was just awesome, particularly to Gilchrist, and his 100 at Nottingham more or less won the match."

"Mind you," Mary was now in full flow, "for me the star men of the series were Giles and Hoggard. We were never going to win unless the people who weren't stars performed out of their skins, and their batting at the end to win the Trent Bridge Test was just great."

Ed was appreciative. "You should do a blog or something. If this Gideon Haigh bloke is half as good as that, I'll be impressed."

"Well, I was a scorer for the teams my dad and brothers played in, which did me two lasting favours; turned me into a feminist and gave me a love of cricket. How did you get into the game?"

"Just watching it on the telly, Tests, one day finals, that sort of thing. To be honest, going to see Derbyshire was never that great but I remember Sobers playing for Notts. And there was a Test against England, West Indies v England in the early '70s, when Sober scored something like 150 and it just became a beautiful game. His movement was as artistic as anything I've ever seen, like he was playing golf. Same with Michael Holding's bowling – seemingly effortless, poise, balance and menace all in one."

"Well, I'm on a way different planet from both of you," admitted Sam. "Football was as far as I got. I could name you the England '66 and '70 World Cup squads but could barely think of an England cricketer beyond Boycott, Botham and Gower."

"Sam's a Clough worshipper as you know; it's one of the few things we've agreed on."

"Well, there you have it," smiled Sam. "It was pretty special and the team obviously celebrated in style."

"Yes, I heard about that. I understand there was a bit of talk about Freddie's over consumption."

"You're telling me. He clearly drank the hotel dry, and you can imagine how the press loved it."

"And my television colleagues, I'm sure. Any chance to moralise can't be missed. Mind you, the pictures I saw left little to the imagination."

"It's just part of our world now, isn't it?" said Sam. "The morning after the '66 World Cup Final, I heard Jack Charlton saying he woke up in someone's garden in the East End. The media's changed completely, and because of the money involved, it treats celebrity as a calling card. Sports people aren't blameless, but as far as I can work out Flintoff's a pretty normal bloke. He may have bit of a problem down the line, but I can't say I have a problem with him getting pissed after winning the Ashes. I'm sure I would have."

"And I thought you were going to give us the 'role model' bull," said Ed.

"No, I've left all that behind me. I've no problem with anyone making fools of themselves, even if it sets our lovely kids a terrible example, provided no one else is hurt."

"What about glamorising alcohol?" Ed was curious.

"Well, from what I saw, he didn't look that glamorous on the Monday morning, I've never seen redder eyes, but even if he did so inadvertently, I don't have a problem; people make their own choices and the advertising industry commits far greater crimes of glamorising drink, alcopops and all that."

"You're becoming a bit of a libertarian in your old age."

"Well…" Sam was silent for a moment; Ed wondered what he was thinking. The Sam he had known would have somehow been sadder about the way Flintoff had dealt with his moment in the sun. "I think," Sam was speaking again, "it's just what I would always have said; you've just never listened to me all these years, never understood me…"

"Never rated you, never bought you a drink, always borrowed your milk…" Ed completed the ritual relay of banter. "I know, it's all my fault- famine, war, pestilence and whatever the other two are." Both of them dissolved laughing.

"The two of you are so predictable," said Mary with a mock yawn. "Listening to you, anyone would think you were 30 years younger until they got a glimpse of the grey hair and receding hairlines. Shall we have another drink and head for the Gondola? We're booked for 8.30."

"I do love coming here, you know," said Ed, a sudden surge of emotion. He felt a moistening on the inside corners of his eyes but took a drink to blink them away. "Let's put on some music then, something wonderful from the 70s. And then we should talk to Mary about how she misspent her youth!"

"I'll see what I can find," said Sam, "because it's a long time since I played anything from before about 1990 that wasn't also pre 1960."

"That's three pretty big musical decades to miss, especially if you're our age, though I always had my doubts about the 80s."

"That's because you were either in denial or simply not here," Mary was definite.

"Okay," said Sam, "we've got a bit of a mix here: Carol King, Blondie, The Clash, David Bowie, Tom…"

"What Bowie have you got?"

"Young Americans, Hunky Dory, and Ziggy – all Mary's purchases."

"Hunky Dory please, I haven't heard it in about 20 years, but it was such a constant when I was growing up."

"Okay, here goes…what do you want?"

"Beer please," said Ed

"Red wine please," said Mary.

Sam fished out a Becks and did the honours while the opening bars of 'Changes' resonated around the room. The beat was insistent, Bowie's voice sweeter than he remembered, They clinked glasses, each delving back into their own pasts, retrieving slivers of the emotions felt in previous listenings.

"It's funny hearing to it now, after *Shrek*," observed Mary.

"Was it in *Shrek*?" asked Ed.

"Yes, you must have been away a lot!" replied Mary.

"But I thought it was a children's film."

"No such thing anymore, complete crossover. They're all so referential, written for both generations. *Shrek*, *The Incredibles*, *Toy Story*, we saw them all with Ruth. Helped enormously with the teenage thing, gave such a shared vocabulary."

"How is my god-daughter by the way? Not what she's doing but how's she doing."

"Okay, I think… I don't know about boyfriends because she doesn't talk about them to me, never really has done. But I don't think there's anyone serious at the moment. I wish she'd settle down soon anyway and decide what she wants to do, but Sam's more for letting her take her time."

"It's not a big deal," Sam said. "We don't support her much; just enough to top up her various earnings from bar work or whatever. I'm just conscious that when we all left university, we either went straight into jobs or dropped out for a long time. For some of us, me included, that was too stark in choice. I'd have preferred a bit of time to take stock, but there was never really an option."

"But there was probably more of a welfare state back then; well, there was…"

"I know, Mary, but I'd been brought up only to use it when and if I had to. Mum and Dad were hardcore Labour but believed benefit was only for the genuinely unemployed. I agreed with them really, so I'm pleased Ruth is working at least a bit while she thinks it all through."

"Thatcher swept all that away though," said Ed

"Yes, I've never understood how someone who grew up in the 30s and 40s could think society didn't exist. The irony, of course, is that we've probably ended up with a more dependent culture."

"But it's also that enormous shift away from manufacturing that meant you had a generation that needed complete retraining. I'm no fan, you know I'm not, but a lot of our industry was focused on sectors where we just couldn't compete anymore."

"You two do love to argue," said Mary. "Actually, Ruth is on really good form. It's a shame it's not worked out for you to see her this time. She keeps talking about working in the charity sector. I think you're to blame for that, but I have a feeling she'll end up trying to start her own business. Sam and I both work for big, quite monolithic parts of the public sector and I've a feeling Ruth wants to do something quite different from that."

"Her latest thing was to write to lots of charities volunteering to go and help out after Hurricane Katrina." Sam was neutral. "They all turned her down, they'd been flooded with volunteers who had more relevant qualifications apparently. Personally, I was sort of glad; I'd rather the next thing Ruth did was something she'd thought about, rather than reacted to."

"You can see Sam's just as decisive as he's always been," Mary was playfully teasing.

"Talking to you," said Ed, "I am always struck by just how constantly hard it is being a parent. I guess most find a way through, but I'm impressed." Ed paused,

347

"You know that, don't you? I think you've done a fantastic job with her. The period Ruth has grown up in, I don't know, it seems like the world has changed maybe faster than in any previous generation. When she was born, we were in the middle still of the Cold War, no one had heard of the Web, or Al Qaeda – I mean, the Mac hadn't even been invented! And I think she'll deal with that as well as anyone I know."

"Well, thank you," said Mary. "You've never said anything like that before. And I know it's not your style, which makes it the more meaningful."

"Don't worry, I won't make a habit of it. Sam's ego is vast enough as it is without me pouring flattery on by the bucket."

Sam allowed himself to laugh. "Thanks, I almost thought you were serious for a moment and had started to think the gin had gone to your head, that your capacity to function under the influence of alcohol had plummeted from its previous, almost Flintoff-esque depths."

"I'll try not to disappoint. So, you haven't told me how everyone is. When did you last see Phil and Michelle?"

"September, I think it was," replies Mary. "They came over here and were on good form. Come to think of it, the time before that was a dinner party they had in July, the Saturday before 7/7, the night of Live 8… God, it already seems like a lifetime ago… Anyway, Philip was explaining about the flood levels in New Orleans, doing his journalistic bit, the way you do sometimes."

"Come on," said Mary, "I'll ring the restaurant to let them know we're on our way, and I'll also give Michelle and Philip a call just in case they're free."

Chapter 35
Beirut, Saturday, 21 September 1996

Ed and Anna were strolling along the Corniche, the waves crashing against it and throwing spray twenty feet in the air. Ed imagined the waves coming all the way from the Gulf of Mexico, where maybe they were the remnant of some hurricane, and then rolling across the Atlantic before squeezing through the Straits of Gibraltar and hurrying the length of the Mediterranean. He knew he could draw a straight line from Beirut to the Gulf and from there it was an easy step to envisage a body of water moving remorselessly along that line, travelling maybe a quarter of the way around the globe, joining together different people and cultures. He explained his thoughts to Anna, who laughed and called him a dreamer. No one had ever called him that before.

They had been together since Easter, two journalists criss-crossing the Middle East, struggling to find a balance between the personal and the vocational. If anything, Anna was the more professionally driven but she was the younger by six years and, at 34, still had dreams of a family; and the two of them had not yet found a way of resolving her conflicting needs, certainly not in a way that permitted Ed to carry on as he was. Despite coming close on a couple of occasions, they hadn't argued about this, or anything else, and were too much caught up in each other to be anything other than happy when together. Yet although nothing had been said, they both sensed this was perhaps a critical weekend for them.

It has been an odd affair from the outset, constantly defying logic and logistics. Its main ingredient had from the beginning been snatched evenings and nights together, often in Amman, when one was in transit. Occasionally, they had been sent to the same city, but that was only because there was work to be done, and they would end up spending so little time together on such occasions that it became a standing joke that they saw each other least when they were on the same job.

For his part, Ed was the happiest he had been. He had long decided to view his personal relationships as episodic by definition, but Anna had jolted him out of that mind-set. From the first time she had kissed him, in a hotel bar in Cairo, she had been operating to an obviously different agenda, focused on having a relationship rather than a fling, and gradually, remorselessly, she had dragged him towards her position, forcing and coaxing alternately, until he was only a sliver away from opting for a new shared life together.

Next month he would turn 40 with equanimity. In the last 20 years, he couldn't think of a series of international issues more demanding of the British public's attention than the ones successively raised by the Middle East. And still it went on, with the Oslo Peace Accords seeming on the verge of breakdown following the recent violence on the West Bank, when more than 50 Palestinians and over a dozen Israeli soldiers had been killed. That morning, he had flown in from Amman while Anna had arrived the night before from Cairo. He asked her about the mood in Egypt.

"It's not great," she replied, "some are saying the Palestinian police fired at Israeli soldiers, and it's impossible so far to be sure what happened. As usual, the Israelis are blaming Arafat, but I've never been convinced he's in control of anything; he's an important figurehead, but I see little evidence he has real power."

"And yet he's all there is."

"But as things are, the Israelis have a permanent, readymade excuse of blaming Arafat for not being able to deliver his people, while at the same time being able to provoke the Palestinian extremists with their continuing construction of new settlements."

"But if I was Israeli," continued Ed, "I'd be saying that all along my people had never been the aggressor, and that Israel was a force for democracy and stability in the region, that without Israel there would be chaos."

"Yes, but you know as well as I do it's not so simple."

"Of course," he replied, "and it's not made any simpler by Britain's role as the colonial power."

"Do not think you are special; all of our Old European powers were Imperial once, and we all carry with us the curses of our forebears. If you are concerned about the British imperial legacy, think what it's like to be Spanish like me. Our only advantage is that, with some help from you, our Empire died almost 100 years before yours."

"Less, if you count Cuba and the Philippines."

Anna slapped his arm playfully. "You British are so pedantic!"

"Sorry, it's the fault of the climate, so much rain leads to an unhealthy focus on detail. But seriously, where do you think all this leaves Oslo?"

"I don't know," Anna replied, "I was trying to think it through last night in the hotel but didn't really get anywhere. That seems to be happening more and more recently; maybe it's a sign I'm getting too old for all this."

"I remember when the Intifada began in '87. God, that's nearly ten years ago. I couldn't imagine how it would end, but six years later it did, which represents progress of a sort. When I first started doing this job, I would come up with all sorts of what I supposed was new thinking, not anymore."

"You make me sound like I am naïve and do not know how complex the problems are."

"You know I don't mean it like that. All I'm saying is that I think I've become a better reporter on what's going on here since I became more cynical."

Anna left the issue hanging. "Do you think I would make a good mother, Ed?" she asked.

"Of course you would," he replied, conscious the previous discussions would be resumed at some point. "You know I believe you'd be good at almost anything you wanted."

Again Anna changed the subject, apparently satisfied with his response. "What do you think about Oslo?"

"I'm pretty depressed to be truthful," he replied. "We all knew what was happening, that they were leaving the most intractable issues off the table, believing that even a third of a cake was better than nothing and could act as a solid starting point for resolving the knottiest problems down the line. Most of us, myself included, thought it was a decent enough strategy; almost everything else had been tried. But in retrospect, I've changed my mind and don't believe it was realistic not to address those sticking point issues on at least some level. I mean look at them, how did we remotely kid ourselves any kind of sustained peace was possible without some form of agreement on those issues, no matter how ambiguous. I don't know, maybe with the Madrid Conference being so soon after the end of the Cold War, we were all a bit too eager to believe now was the right time for solving all the world's problems. I remember reading one of your articles where, right at the outset, you were pretty anti-Oslo."

"You are right; when I said earlier I was not sure where the recent violence on the West Bank has left Oslo and I said I didn't know, I meant only that I do not know what it means for the timing of its official failure; for me, personally, it has been a failure from the moment is was signed, so maybe I'm the more cynical."

The sea was still crashing against the rocks below them, and over on the horizon the sun was starting to turn red as it tentatively kissed the horizon. Ed loved Beirut and had continued to come here even during the worst periods of the civil war.

"I didn't realise you were that set against it," he continued.

"But don't you see that without halting the construction of new Israeli settlements, the Palestinians will never believe the Israelis are doing anything other than systematically eliminating any possibility of a future homeland for them on the West Bank? So it is a farce to say this issue was not on the table. Jerusalem? It is not going anywhere; security? It can be left to the future. But Israeli settlements are always on the table because they are always being built."

"I didn't know you felt so strongly about it," said Ed, slightly taken aback. "I understand your logic but aren't you in danger of being a little idealistic about it?"

"I don't agree it's idealistic to think that a viable Palestinian state needs to be a part of any sustainable peace, or that it is any less important than a viable Jewish state. Or that one is only possible with the existence of the other."

"I'm very well aware of the importance of the Palestinian refugees. I've spent as much time as anyone in the camps, and I understand how alienated from any talk of peace young Palestinians must feel."

"Fine, let's talk about something else," said Anna abruptly, and for the first time Ed sensed some of the tension that had accompanied them on their stroll.

"How did you find Cairo this time around?" he asked awkwardly.

"Much the same, to be honest. I like Egypt, though I always find Cairo a bit crazy. On the way from the airport I saw the usual mother on a motorbike with her children – two of them riding pillion and one in front of her – not a helmet in sight, obviously. But they're also the kindest people. The taxi driver who took me to the old souk insisted on waiting for me while I wandered around shopping. He wouldn't take any payment even for the journey we'd already done. Just sat for an hour, happily waiting. I obviously tipped him when we got back to the hotel. It's not the first time it's happened to me, but I still find it amazing how trusting and patient Egyptians can be."

"I know," Ed agreed. "Part of why I love the whole region is the magic of the ancient civilisations, but I've also fallen for the modern reality, for all the problems. How's the economy doing?"

"Okay, I think. I met some people who were getting really excited about the possibilities of technology. Their theory is that much of what is holding Egypt back is the relative lack of infrastructure development in a country of some 60 million, and that mobile phones and so on have the potential to remove the necessity for a lot of that. I was politely sceptical."

"So you should be. I'm sure technology will help but the politics of the place are rancid, and I can't see much chance of real progress until that changes."

"Yes, it's funny how we feel obliged to support regimes in the Middle East that we would be urging to reform if they existed anywhere else."

"And usually with arms deals and/or billions of dollars. I can see the rationale but it's hard to believe the present set-up can last forever. I grew up with the Cold War, thinking the Berlin Wall was simply a fact of life and then all of a sudden it was gone."

"And you think something similar could happen in the Middle East seriously?"

"Well, no, not really, but like I said, it taught me not to assume things last forever. I mean, Egypt has had, what, three or four rulers in the last 50 years. How confident can you be that one army-backed dictator is going to go on succeeding the last one? Sometime it will stop. One of the big things that did for the Soviet Bloc was that the people could see the prosperity that was possible elsewhere. You talk about the impact of technology; if mobile phones and satellite TV do anything, they free up people from the control of the state."

"Maybe, but the Egyptian or Arab Street is too disorganised to be a threat to the likes of Mubarak with his US-funded army." Anna was dismissive.

"Oh, I wouldn't be that sure, sooner or later it will change fundamentally."

"You talk like one of those 60s revolutionaries. Throughout history, repressive regimes have sustained themselves quite happily for hundreds of years, easily crushing numerous rebellions."

"And then what happened?" Ed was beginning to bridle, not so much at what Anna said, but because her tone had become more severe and impatient. He started to feel confused, not knowing if he was imagining it, or whether it had altered some time before and he had only now noticed.

Anna continued remorselessly. "But what happened is that the US took over from the British, just as you did from the Spanish and French."

"I accept your point, but one of the fascinating things about the modern world is that even as the weaponry becomes more advanced, it seems to get harder to invade and subdue another country, no matter how great a disparity in military strength. Look at the Russians in Afghanistan; okay, the Mujahedeen got lots of Western arms but they were effectively medieval tribes taking on a super power."

"Like the Vietcong?"

"Well, I don't think it's an exact comparison but the principle is the same. I agree with you that empires do still exist, but what they do is much more constrained than it was."

By now the sun was halfway down and the light was starting to fade but still had a warm glow to it. They were approaching the Phoenicia Hotel, where they were staying, a symbol of what was supposed to have been the new Beirut, treating themselves for what both saw as a special weekend. Some of the veneer of that specialness had been scraped away by the acerbic edge of their conversation about subjects which, until this afternoon, they had by and large agreed on. Nevertheless, when they got back to their room, they made love as happily as they had always done.

Afterwards, when he was showering, Ed thought about, but then unwisely dismissed, the unfamiliar edge that had infiltrated their conversation. He judged it an indication of their increasing familiarity and didn't consider the possibility it might be the start of a cleaving that would press them apart. Ed's experience of long-term relationships was limited, and this was the only time he had been with someone for more than a couple of months. Before now, he had never even pondered for very long the reasons why his previous couplings had not lasted longer. This was not because he was arrogant and blamed the woman in each case, but was due to him being only too happy to assume personal responsibility for every break up.

In most ways, this belief, while unfortunate, was not malign in its effects. It was generally so far from the truth that it barely acted as any barrier at all to his social relationships. When these became more intimate, however, this prejudice against himself offered an easy get-out clause that exempted him from any need to examine more specific reasons why his relationships did not last. Consequently, Ed never opted to diagnose his own mistakes, or understand why girlfriends lost patience with him. It became too easy, too familiar a pain, for him simply to take the hit and move on. As a result, he was poorly equipped to understand any changes in the trajectory and direction of travel of his relations with Anna. From her perspective, the signals she was sending were obvious. But Ed missed them entirely.

They decided to sit in the hotel bar for a drink before dinner, and Ed ordered a gin and tonic for himself and a glass of champagne for Anna. They sat by the window, once again overlooking the Corniche. The sky was clear and the esplanade was thronged with people walking, laughing, purchasing from the stalls scattered liberally all the way along. The sea had calmed and only ripples now lapped the rocks.

"It's gorgeous, isn't it?" said Anna, echoing his thoughts. "Where I come from in Barcelona, the sea is also often like this. I have not returned there since New Year; it is a long time. When were you last in England?"

"In February, although if things go well, I'll have a longer break next spring and also get home for Christmas, but the latter is starting to look less likely."

"When I next go to Barcelona, will you come with me?"

"Of course I will, Anna, if at all possible, but you know as well as I do how unpredictable our work can be. When do you think you might be able to get away?"

"At the moment, I am targeting the end of next month."

"I'll put in the request on Monday."

"Tell me, where do you see yourself in five years' time? What will you be doing, where you will be?"

Ed sat back in his chair and stretched his legs. He looked out of the window again, oblivious to the weight of the question. "I've always been really bad at planning ahead," he replied, "or rather I have since I became a journalist. A minute ago, I was talking about Christmas and about May next year, but these are really only dates in the calendar, nothing more. So asking me to think five years ahead is hard for me. My gut instinct is that I'll probably be doing more or less what I'm doing now, because I think it's important, and I don't really know what else I'd be capable of doing anymore. And that I hope and want us to still be together."

"Okay," said Anna, "that's probably as much as I could have expected from you in an unassisted first attempt. Let me go from my side and see if it helps." Now it was Anna who looked out of the window, but unlike Ed she was looking at the middle distance. "Five years from now," she began, "I shall be 39 years old and I would like, God and biology willing, to have two healthy children and to be happily living with their father, preferably married, as I come from a traditional Catholic family and anything else would upset my mother greatly."

"And do you think you've found the father yet?"

"Yes, you of course!"

"And do you think I would make a good father and husband?"

"Yes, if you gave yourself a chance."

"How do you mean?"

"Ed, part of me wants to answer that question by saying that if you don't know now, you never will. But I'll play the game and humour you because I love you so much."

Anna was speaking in a tone that was quite intimate and personal but which at the same time conveyed a subtle sense of distance as though she was part outside of herself, observing dispassionately a scene she had already played out many times in her private thoughts. "What I mean, or what I think it means for you, is that we both have to discuss how we move away from our present assignments into safer, more stable posts in journalism, or potentially into a different field."

"Like what, for example?"

"Oh, I don't know, maybe writing? I'm sure we both have at least one decent book in us." Anna paused, "The point is that we can't, or at least I can't, have children while we're doing what we do. And I'm damned if I'm going to go and be pregnant in Barcelona or wherever, while you're still jumping around from one Middle East trouble spot to the next."

"I see," Ed was non-committal. Somewhere in the back corners of his mind he had known this conversation was inevitable, but he had chosen not to acknowledge it and so had made no preparation. In the last few months, he and Anna had spoken increasingly often about their future and the necessity of them both compromising if their relationship was to work in the long-term, but until now there had been no specifics, and he had not used the time to think through what type of compromise he would be ready to make.

"Come on, Ed," pleaded Anna, clearly impatient, "I deserve a better answer than that. We've talked around the issue for so long, and we both knew this weekend in Beirut was when we would decide."

"Did we?"

"Yes!"

"I remember what we said about this weekend, and it was about enjoying ourselves and trying to think through what our next steps should be in making more time to see each other, and maybe talking more about the longer term. But I don't recall saying anything about making big decisions."

"But don't you understand it's the same thing? We can't go beyond what we've already discussed without being prepared to take specific decisions. It just doesn't make sense otherwise."

"Well, that's not how I saw it, not really what I was expecting. Can we at least have a decent meal before we get into all this? I was really looking forward to this evening with you."

Anna was exasperated but forced herself to smile. "Fine, then let's take a break and talk again after the meal." She was still confident she would persuade Ed to give up the war reporting side of his job at least. After all, she knew she was ultimately even more committed to the work than Ed, and if she was prepared to make the sacrifice, then she was sure she could convince him to do the same. But a part of her also recognised this was a flawed or at least an unstable logic; basing one qualitative and subjective judgment upon another was a fertile route for generating ideas but could easily turn out to have foundations of sand. And yet she persisted, remained confident.

In other circumstances, the meal they had that evening would have been among the best they had shared. They both loved Lebanese food and wine, and the hotel restaurant exceeded their expectations. However, the edge of their enjoyment was dulled by the conversation that had gone before and expectations of the one that would come after. They spoke of mutual friends, speculated over their relationships and laughed at some of their behaviour and the situations in which they had found themselves. Also, they spoke of work, reprising some of the discussion of that afternoon but without the earlier level of animation or personal engagement. It was almost like a perfect reproduction, sometimes superior in quality of argument but lacking the uniqueness of original.

When they reprised their disagreement over Oslo, neither was able or willing to generate the same passion. "One thing we do sort of agree on, I suspect," Ed was conciliatory, "is that the expectations around Oslo, if or when they're disappointed, might spark a backlash. Fundamentalist Islam, however you define it, is waiting for a cause it can use as a rallying cry to attract wider support. Someone like Al Qaeda would make hay right across the Arab world from the West's failure to help the Palestinians."

"It's already starting to happen," said Anna. "When I was last in Yemen, everyone was talking about them. They were apparently behind that little problem the Americans had in Mogadishu in '93, as well as the bombing of the World Trade Center."

"You never quite know with these claims, although it's quite rare for the false ones to go uncontradicted for very long. Even if those who are really behind it don't want to claim responsibility themselves, they are usually offended enough to try and cast doubt on false claimants."

"Yes, I agree Al Qaeda were potentially involved in both, at least in some way. But I do think the Americans underestimate the scale of possible repercussions if they fail to find and then push through a solution to the Palestinian problem. They think it's just an issue for Israel and its Arab neighbours but it resonates across the entire region. No Arab I've ever met believes the US is serious about Palestine, because if they were, they would use their financial support of Israel to get Tel Aviv to hold talks. As far as they're concerned, Israel is a client state of Washington, almost totally bankrolled by it, and the Americans are not using the power that gives them."

"Where are you going on Monday?" asked Ed.

"Cairo again, what about you?"

"Damascus, I've got a lead on an interview with one of Assad's senior foreign policy advisers. He says he's happy to talk off the record about Syria's relationships with Iran."

"That sounds interesting, let me know what he says."

"No chance," smiled Ed, "Anyway, what are you up to in Cairo?"

"Nothing so earth shattering. I'm just going to spend a few days wandering around, talking to young Egyptians. I just want to get a better feel of what they think – of the West, of Mubarak, of what their own ambitions are. There are an awful lot of them – I forget the figures but I think people under 30 will be more than half the population in less than 20 years; and although more and more of them are getting a decent education, there is still not enough."

"That plays at least a bit into what I was saying about technology."

"Maybe, maybe not," Anna smiled, "I didn't say you were wrong, you just deserved to be argued with, and I was feeling grouchy at you."

Ed shrugged. "The other irony, of course, is while these countries worry about the growing proportion of young people, we in the West are beginning to worry about growing proportions of older people, while China, which should be in the first group, is moving rapidly towards the second because of its one-child policy."

"Now that would be an article worth writing," Anna said, staring at him intently. "Come on," she continued, "let's go and have another drink in the bar and see if we can find some compromises to agree on." She got up and Ed followed, slightly too obediently, he thought. This time, Anna bought the drinks, whisky, hers with ice and Ed's with some water; and, on her initiative again, they settled themselves on stools at the quiet side of the bar.

"I always used to love drinking on bar stools. From the time I was about three years old and could get up there by myself. It made me feel like I was looking adults straight in the eye at the same level rather than having to look up to them all the time." Anna sighed, "I was always trying to grow up too quickly, and now here I am trying to find ways to slow the clock down so I can have a family." She turned and raised her head. "Please help me, Ed."

Ed was deeply affected by the plea, and for the first time he thought seriously about what might be possible. After all, he loved her, and wanted Anna to be as happy as he could make her. Unfortunately, however, and not for the first time, Ed misunderstood the subtext. He thought their relationship was a given, whereas in fact that was what was at stake. In reality, Anna was asking whether he would help her, or if she would have to find someone else. Anna, in her own eyes, had made this conditionality crystal clear during their pre-dinner fencing, with this conversation a continuation of that one. For Ed, however, this was a fresh conversation, superseding the previous one rather than building on it.

"How about if we bought or rented somewhere together, back home – London, or Barcelona, or Paris, somewhere new to both of us? Then we could begin to build up a separate life together, away from the Middle East, somewhere we both like where we could start a family in the future, when things calm down a bit out here."

Ed was pleased. He had come up with a practical way forward that would represent real progress on where they were now.

"And what about marriage?"

"Anna, I'd marry you tomorrow, here, in Amman, in Barcelona, anywhere. I thought you knew that."

"Well, I'm not sure you'd quite asked me before but I'm a modern kind of girl, as you're well aware, so I can live with the absence of a ring and bended knee. But assuming for a moment we decide to get married, what difference do you think it would make to our relationship? I mean, however we choose to get married, Roman Catholic, Church of England, whatever it was, there are vows in there which we're nowhere near being able to meet in our current state."

"But that's what I meant about buying a home together, so we would have our own place to stay and then after time we could build a life together."

"Oh Ed, five years ago that would have sounded fabulous. I wish we'd got together then, but I'd barely met you and you were already this grizzled veteran of a reporter who we were all afraid to talk to let alone sleep with. No offence, but that was what we all felt." Anna sighed again. "But we didn't get together back then, and now I don't have time for us to slowly build a life together. I want to have that life now. I want to have children, and I want to do other things with my life once my children are old enough; and I need a man willing to help and support me in all that. And I love you, Ed, and most of all I want to spend a lot more time with you; not the occasional night in an Amman hotel, or even coming here for a weekend, or even having another home where we try to spend time. And I don't think the importance of what happens in the Middle East, will ever 'calm down' as you put it. If we're going to have a proper relationship – get married and live in a way other people would recognise as being what married people do, and if we're going to have children and bring them up as they deserve – like proper parents do - then both of us, not just me, are going to have to give this up." She waved her hands symbolically around the bar, then took a sip of Scotch and continued more quietly. "We're going to have to walk away, leave the thrill and the adrenalin and the sense of being at the heart of current affairs, leave it all behind and find something different to do. Hopefully, it will be as fulfilling, but it will be in a different way. And I know you love this work, and you know I do too. But if we're going to make this decision, for ourselves, and for the children we hope to have, then I believe, Ed, with every sinew of conviction I have, that we need to make it now. There!" she sat back and reached for her whisky. "I've said it."

But Ed, working to take in all that Anna had said, or rather had expelled, was not yet sure what it was he had heard. Slowly, it began to dawn on him that this was an altercation of sorts; a very Anna kind of altercation, full of love and equality, of selflessness, and even of poetry. It nevertheless had a potential impact that he feared. "So, what are you saying about us maybe getting a place together?" he asked.

"I suppose I'm saying it is not enough?"

"Not enough for what?"

"For us to do what we need to do."

"What do you mean 'need', Anna?"

"Fine then, I mean what I think needs to happen for us to have a real future. God, I can't believe you're being pedantic now of all times!"

"I'm not being pedantic." Ed was trying to stay calm, just about succeeding, but at the cost of an unfamiliar strain in his voice. "I'm worried that you're presenting a choice you're making as a necessity for both of us."

"It's not a choice as you put it, it's what I believe is a necessity for us. Don't you get it, Ed? There's nowhere for us to go if we stay the way we are."

"But there is, Anna, we could buy somewhere together like I said. That would be a huge step for us from where we are. Let's at least take this a step at a time."

"How many steps do you want, Ed? A couple of minutes ago you said you wanted to marry me – what kind of a step do you call that?"

"It's another huge step; it means I want to spend the rest of my life with you."

"But we're nowhere near spending our lives together, Ed. We barely see each other once a month, and no matter if we bought somewhere or not, that's not going to change unless we make it."

For the first time, Anna felt doubtful Ed would come round. Just as Ed has misread her intent and missed the signals she thought had been unmissable about how serious she was, Anna had also misunderstood. She had imagined he would need only a push to get him to agree, but it was now clear she had left him behind and the gulf between them was much larger than she had imagined. It also seemed that Ed was starting from a totally different place and wasn't necessarily even moving in the same direction as she was. Ed was thinking on the basis of where they were now and how they would get to where they wanted to be, whereas she was starting from the destination she'd identified and thinking what was needed to reach it. And it dawned on her there was no guarantee they would meet in the middle.

Until now, she had also assumed that, because she was more driven in her work, it would be easier for Ed to walk away from it than it was for her, and because she was prepared to make that sacrifice, so, ultimately would Ed. What she hadn't factored on was that frontline reporting had been Ed's life for some 18 years. Maybe being more driven didn't necessarily equate to having stronger links or greater identification. Perhaps he had moved beyond that stage. All this seemed so clear now but it had been rendered opaque by the blinding momentum of her own logic. Despite loving Ed as much as she did, and trying so hard to plot a path through to the destination she so passionately believed was right for them both, Anna had misunderstood him every bit as much as he had her.

In different circumstances, it would have been comical. Ed and Anna sat on their adjacent bar stools, staring into their glasses of whisky, each realising how far away from the other, without either of them meaning to or quite realising it was happening, they had become. Both wondered if there was a way back, wanted there to be.

Meanwhile, Joni Mitchell unhelpfully came on in the background.

Well, they were both in the bar, staring at beer mats. How constant were they and what did that mean? The same question came to both of them but prompted different answers. For Ed, constancy meant being true to himself and so being true to Anna. For Anna it meant being true to their relationship and so being true to herself. Ed could not believe they were in such crisis as to warrant jettisoning, as he saw it, everything else that defined him. While trying to think of a way of bridging the gap, they had each defined their position in such a way as to become more entrenched. And so when they spoke again, despite having the aim of being conciliatory, what they each said had the exact opposite effect.

"What if we bought a couple of places?" suggested Ed. "One out here and one in Europe somewhere; then we could build two real bases and it would be much easier to spend time between assignments."

"But I don't want to be with you between assignments, Ed, I want us to have jobs that mean we always go to sleep together and wake up together. Why don't you care about these things as much as I do?"

"I do, Anna, and I'm willing to change, but just discarding everything I care about apart from you can't be the right answer, not all in one go. It would be a denial that the last 18 years of my life had any value. You can't be asking me to do that; you believe it's important as much as I do."

"I know it's important, Ed, but we aren't the only people who can do it. But we are the only people who can make our relationship work."

"Look, Anna, I'm sure I can change but you're asking me to as good as throw myself away. I don't know what would be left afterwards. And I'm not sure you'd like what was left, or if I could be a good husband and father to anyone."

"But of course you could, Ed, don't underestimate yourself. If you think in about ten years from now, we've both talked about wanting to have different lives by then. Well, all I'm saying is that, if we're serious, now is the time to make that first decisive jump that will free you up to do all the things we want."

"But Anna, I've no idea how big a jump you're asking me to make, and I suspect you don't have either. What are you basing it on? I don't understand why it needs to happen now?"

"It needs to happen now, Ed, because I'm 34 and I need to know I'm with the man who's going to be the father to my children, and all the things we've talked about in the last six months, and I need to find out if that's you."

"But why now, this minute? You obviously think we've already talked a lot of this through in the last six months, but that's not what I thought we were doing."

"What the hell did you think we were doing then?"

Until now both their voices had remained subdued if tense, but now Anna had raised hers a few decibels, not on purpose but instinctively, out of frustration. Ed's response, effective in terms of winning the argument but fatal in terms of their relationship, was to drop his voice slightly, thereby disengaging from the emotional struggle.

"To be honest, I thought we were getting to know each other at the start of a relationship, talking about the future but mostly just having fun."

"Well, you weren't really paying attention then, were you? We had a serious relationship, and I thought I was going to spend the rest of my life with you, but you were having fun and getting laid."

"Yes, I was, and no apologies for that." Ed's words became more aggressive but his tone became flatter, quieter. He had noticed Anna's use of the past tense and semi-consciously took another step away. "I didn't realise we were engaged in our own version of SALT II."

"I guess that's that then," Anna said as she reached to drain her whisky. The entire conversation had taken about 15 minutes. "I'll go and get my stuff and find another room. And I'll change my flight to Cairo tomorrow for an earlier one. Goodbye, Ed, I'm sorry about tonight, I've obviously misjudged everything terribly." Her eyes had begun to moisten. "In time, I hope I'll remember the good times but it'll take me some time to forget what a bastard you've been tonight." And then she left. There was no strop or shouting but Anna's words were delivered oddly, with clear fluidity.

Even at this stage, had Ed recognised it, there was a chink of light in Anna's tone. She was trying too hard and her steely demeanour was, at root, mostly artifice. But Ed had become too used to different versions of this scene and had played out his own role so often it had become second nature. Some minutes before, he had reverted into a cocoon of passive self-guilt, and was oblivious now to any emotional signal Anna was sending; he watched Anna disappear round the corner outside the bar with an odd sense of equanimity. On the one hand, he was at a loss as to what else he could have said or done to alter the outcome, but he also was relaxed now that the crisis had passed. Later, the reality of his loss would hit him hard, but just at the moment there was an unmistakeable familiarity, almost comforting, in the feeling of rejection. He even began dissecting it to understand better the similarities or differences from his other rejections.

He wondered what he had done wrong, and whether he could have done anything better or different. The relationship with Anna had been the best and most exciting period of his life, and he struggled to recall a moment when he had been bored in her company. Although the pain of the revelation would only arrive later, he already sensed how much he would miss her. He bought another whisky and sat looking at it for a few minutes, trying to get everything straight in his head.

Some 20 minutes later, Ed took the final sip from this glass. He had reached his conclusions, as in the past both self-condemning and self-serving. It was clear that he should have talked to Anna earlier and more seriously about the future, that he had lived too much in the present with her. He hadn't appreciated that he could not live in a six-month relationship the same way he could in one of six weeks. He should have thought more and talked to Anna more – it was so obvious in retrospect – about the future.

At one level, all of this was true, but it wasn't the only truth, and it was only true up to a point. Ed still saw the relationship through his own eyes. He was a good way from recognising Anna would have her own, quite different, interpretation. Ed had internalised so many of his life's challenges that it had become his preferred mode of operating, to such a degree that it was effectively his only one.

The strengths of this approach were particularly suited to the demands of front-line reporting. It allowed him to retain an unusually high level of independence in a world where many of those on whom he would otherwise have found himself depending were to some degree unreliable. Its weaknesses were stark only when he stepped out of his professional role.

He ordered whisky and, not listening to the piped music, read the copy of the Herald Tribune he always kept with him. Then he went to bed. Anna left the hotel the next morning before he awoke.

Chapter 36
London, Friday, 25 April 1997

The men embraced. "I barely recognised you; I'm sure you had more hair!"

"We both did!" laughed Ed. I've lost a few pounds too; come home for some feeding up."

"Well, we can certainly do that. You're not exactly a prodigal son, though there are a few similarities, but we've slaughtered the fatted calf anyway. Mary's really looking forward to seeing you but not as much as Ruth. I don't know if foreign correspondents are meant to have fan clubs but she'd happily start one for you. Only don't tell her I said so. You're still okay to come round tomorrow night, I hope?"

The two were standing outside the Palace Theatre on Charing Cross Road. *Les Miserables* was playing and the sun was shining. Ed had just flown in from Amman, catching the Heathrow Express plus Tube to Leicester Square. They had arranged to meet for a quick drink in the Three Greyhounds pub, just behind Cambridge Circus.

Sam went to the bar and ordered two pints of Broadside. The pub was small and packed, so they decided to stand outside on the corner of Old Compton and Greek Street, with Ed's suit carrier, his only luggage, propped against the wall between them.

It was a sunny spring evening, and people were out and about around them, many in shirt sleeves. Ed was wearing jeans, a green open-neck shirt and a grey khaki jacket. "Standard uniform these days," Ed joked as he took it off and dropped it on his bag.

"Martin Bell's going to walk it in Tatton from all accounts," Sam responded. "Now there's a journalist with a proper fan club, proof positive that the Great British public prefer you guys to the politicians. Where are you staying by the way?"

"The Savoy."

"I'd have thought you were sick of hotel rooms by now, even five star ones. You know you can come and stay with us. Why don't you?"

"I am sick of hotels, of which I've seen enough to last a lifetime, but not of luxury, of which I've had precious little. I feel like splashing some of 1996's unspent salary, and it's only two nights. Also, I need some time to become properly house-trained again." He saw Sam's brow knit. "I'm really looking forward to seeing everyone tomorrow, but part of that anticipation is because it's only an evening. I can both enjoy it and, because it's not too long, trust myself to be on best behaviour."

"Has it been that bad?"

Ed took a long drink. "It depends what you mean. But it does all get to me once in a while, the miserable intractability of it, the inability to discern even a morsel of realistic hope that anything will be noticeably better in the future."

Sam noticed Ed's answer had lacked detail and resolved not to push. They chatted idly for a while, communicating little. "Will you go back?"

"Yes, but not till October. The rest of my life seems to have been pretty much on hold for the last eight years, and I do need a bit of a break. As I said on the phone, I'm going back to Derby for a while, see my parents. They're both well into their 70s now and Mum can't get around very much anymore, which is frustrating for my dad, though he copes with everything reasonably well so far as I can tell. What about yours?"

"Much the same I guess, though I think my dad's finding old age harder work than my mother is. The pacemaker he's got works well enough but it's made him cautious, slowed him down. He doesn't swim anymore for instance, which used to be a big part of his routine, and generally I think he gets out a bit less."

Ed paused, distracted by the prosperous, hedonistic flow of Soho around him, but also visibly working to make decent conversation. "And how are Mary and Ruth?" he finally offered, slightly limply he felt.

"Well enough, I think. I don't really see as much of either of them as I should. Mary's still struggling with her book on Anthony Eden, but she's really enjoying her teaching. Ruth? Well, she's almost a teenager now, hard to believe, let's say it's an education for me. But we still talk a fair bit, which is probably beyond what my expectations were. If you remember, I was never very successful with women, at any rate until they were old enough to be my mother."

"That's not quite how I remember it," Ed laughed. "Back in Manchester, they kept trying to persuade you to sleep with them; you just never noticed. Another beer?"

"Ah, yes okay," replied Sam, blushing slightly.

While Ed went to the bar, he stood, leaning slightly against the wooded door frame of the pub. The sun, sinking now, was in his eyes, and he put on his sunglasses. Was Ed just taking the piss? Apart from that clumsy, fumbling, unsuccessful effort under the coats in an upstairs bedroom of a party early in his first term, his sexual history in Manchester had been remarkably barren. He'd been so embarrassed by the whole thing he'd not told anyone about it. Lisa her name was; what was she doing now? He guessed it was the sort of thing that happens but never gets related or written down.

Ed returned with two beers. "I definitely need a decent shower. I'm conscious I'm still carrying a load of Jordanian dust around, and I need to wash it off to make room for the London grime that's queuing up to replace it." He paused, "You don't believe me, do you?"

Sam laughed, "Well, I don't not believe you. But I can't find much if any evidence. And I find it hard to believe I was quite that insensitive. Still," he laughed again, "I'll buy the reputation, even if it's posthumous."

They both took a drink, paused, each waiting for the other to continue. "Well," said Ed, "perhaps I exaggerated a bit. You see, for the first six months or so, everyone thought Michelle was your girlfriend, and by the time we all realised she wasn't, you'd acquired this, I don't know, weird veneer of celibacy, which meant that whenever women made a pass at you – and believe me they did – it was always a bit less full on than it was with other guys." He laughed, "But you were still pretty unobservant."

"Oh, well, if you say so. It does explain a few things, I guess. All those one-off meals out that had no follow-up. Anyway, enough of my sexual non-history; what about you? Are you still seeing Anna? When are the two of you going to settle down and live happily ever after?"

"Didn't I say, we broke up about six months ago, or rather we drifted apart enough that it didn't seem to make sense anymore, to either of us. Don't look so down about it! We're still talking, neither of us did anything bad! It just got to the point where one or other of us was reporting from a war zone, or about to go, or just come back. There was too much absence, not enough time together, too much worry about what might happen to the other. I briefly went through a phase where I thought I would change job, give it up, do something safer. But Anna was born to be a foreign correspondent, not doing it would rip out her insides. I decided I couldn't ask her."

Sam wondered how the two of them had never even had the conversation, but once again he suppressed the urge to probe. He took another drink and concluded there were parts of Ed that remained unknown to him. They talked about the election campaign. Sam thought Blair and Brown were being over-cautious, promising to stick to Ken Clark's spending plans, focusing so narrowly on the relatively anodyne five pledges. John Major's Conservatives were totally chaotic, with ministers and MPs wandering around shell-shocked by year after year of scandal, internal dissension and economic gloom.

"I suspect you're right," Ed agreed, "and the New Labour communications machine is the best I've seen in the UK by a long way; all that pre-rebuttal stuff. The one thing I do know though is that no matter how cautious they are, and I agree they'd win the election whatever, it won't stop them being submerged in a tidal wave of expectation that they've no chance of meeting. All that 'ethical foreign policy' stuff... I wish I was wrong but they've no chance." He glanced at his watch. "Anyway, I must be off. Is 7pm okay tomorrow? Fine, I'll be there on the dot." With that he picked up his bag, shook hands again, touched his eyebrow with his right hand and sauntered off towards Covent Garden.

Sam watched him across Charing Cross Road until he turned a corner, reflecting that this was probably one of the longest chats that they'd had in maybe ten years. In fact, he concluded, they'd never really talked much since Manchester, just the two of them. He shook his head – when did you ever really know anyone? Then he took the glasses back into the bar and wandered up through Soho Square to Oxford Street and caught the Tube home.

**

Later, Ed dozed in his bath, waking only when the water, originally piping hot, started to cool. He'd had about three hours sleep the night before, the rest of which he'd spent with colleagues in the 'Cigar Bar' of the Amman Marriott, a quiet room off the main hotel bar with big leather chairs and a wide selection of spirits and cigars, where it was possible to discourse at length in the vain attempt to solve the world's problems. Or, to qualify, all present thought they had the answer by about 4am, but somehow by the morning their own version of '42' had once more eluded them. Adrenalin had carried him this far, but the accumulated shortage of sleep, not only from the previous night but also the previous six months, as well as the release

363

of stress and the subsidence of the chronic aching of his body, meant that he barely made it to the bed. No time to pull back the sheets or close the curtain.

Ed slept solidly for 12 hours, his plans to eat having died a death, but was eventually woken by a combination of hunger and the shafts of sunlight streaming into his room. He blinked, then rolled over away from the light and lay for five minutes, before concluding that sleep would not return any time soon. Reluctantly, he swung his legs over the side of the bed and sat up, leaning backwards with his arms propped behind him. He arched his back and stretched looking up at the ceiling, feeling the heat of the morning sun square between his shoulder blades. Wanting to sharpen his senses, he had a shower, then dressed quickly and went out into the sunshine.

It was a beautiful day in central London, late morning still, and Ed enjoyed strolling with no bag to carry, no agenda, just a light jacket slung over his shoulder. He wandered up through Covent Garden, then across Charing Cross Road and past the pub where he and Sam had stood the previous evening. His limbs, after the long bath and the deepest of night's sleep, felt stretched and loose. Settled outside a café with breakfast and coffee, he watched Soho wake up and let his mind wander. He thought about Sam the night before and, for no real reason, a tear rolled down his left cheek. Still, there was tonight to look forward to, and maybe they could arrange to meet up again after he'd been back to Derby, before he flew out.

The street was starting to get busy. Gay men, some shaven headed, were strolling down Old Compton Street, laughing and smiling. A cyclist on a mountain bike stopped opposite, locked it to the lamp post and then wandered past him into the café, fishing a book out of his bum bag. The sun was shining, everyone seemed happy. He couldn't help imagining, particularly here in the centre of Bohemian London, that the smiles were somehow linked to next Thursday's election. If Labour won, then 'clause 28' – that particularly spiteful piece of anti-gay law – would be swept away. For that and the minimum wage alone, he thought New Labour would earn its stripes.

However, he did worry about the foreign policy stuff. He was disappointed Robin Cook had hitched himself upfront to the 'ethical' test; he had thought him cleverer. By that standard they were bound to fail spectacularly. The world was far too complicated for such sound bite slogans and one person's ethics were another's taboo. Even where you knew you were right, it would often open up a whole Pandora's box of its own. If the last 30 years had proved anything, it was the inability of anyone to intervene effectively in even the most straightforward humanitarian causes. Biafra, Cambodia, Rwanda, Bosnia, nothing had been done for any of them.

Ed polished off his coffee and ordered another one, fishing Gore Vidal's 'Lincoln' out of the side pocket of his jacket. Well-thumbed and sentimentally dog-eared, he was at the point where Lincoln was facing down Salmon Chase, his moralising and viscerally ambitious treasury secretary, in front of a group of abolitionist congressmen. Chase had written that Lincoln did not operate cabinet government, railroading over legitimate objections and bypassing real discussion. This, Vidal implied, was a fair charge but Lincoln had completely out-manoeuvred his rival, challenging him to admit his own complicity in cabinet decisions in front of his political supporters. What would the 1990s have made of Lincoln? The repeated military failures, the enormous shedding of blood, the illness and sometimes corrupt extravagance of his wife, dominating his cabinet so that the US came as near to dictatorship as at any time in its history?

Sometime later, Ed paid and got up, bought a paper, then wandered down to the river, bathed in sunshine, and across the footbridge that ran alongside the railway from Charing Cross to Waterloo and the South Bank. He was struck as ever by how beautiful the London skyline looked in the sunshine. Big Ben could use a clean, but St Paul's was timeless, symbolic of the London that had grown out of the ruins of the Great Fire and survived the Luftwaffe, so beautifully shaped and proportioned that it was entirely of its place and of any era. And in the distance the solitary, appropriately phallic, Canada Tower, in the heart of Docklands, so completely out of place it made him laugh. He skipped down the steps onto the South Bank and wandered along to the Royal Festival Hall, where he bought a coffee and sat outside.

He thought again about his last day in Amman; he had driven out to the edge of the Sea of Galilee with an old Palestinian friend who worked for Arab Bank. The bank was a Palestine success story; started on the West Bank in the 1930s, then displaced to Jordan in 1948, it had established itself as one of the few pan Arab institutions. "I can almost see my father's house from here," his friend had said. "I was there last October, and it still looked as I remembered it when we fled in 1967." Ed had sympathised, said something appropriate but instantly forgettable. He had heard such stories many times and, drained of emotion, now responded only intellectually. "We still do business with the Israelis, you know?" his friend said. This was new. "Oh yes!" his friend had continued, "They work hard and often they are good business partners." He turned away from Ed and looked again across to the West Bank. "Next time you are in Israel, go and see (he mentioned two well-known Israeli businessmen), say hello from us. But say also that we want our homes back." Ed had hugged his friend; now he smiled again at the memory.

When he finished his coffee, he wandered up to Waterloo Bridge and back across the Thames to the Savoy. It was still only 2pm. He went up to his room, undressed, set his alarm for 6pm and lay down. Despite the coffee, he drifted off immediately.

***

Mary looked as beautiful as ever when she opened the door, just as he remembered her; dark, with blue eyes piercing, a half smile turning up the right corner of her mouth. Now in her 40s, Ed thought she looked no older than when he had last seen her four years before. She kissed him not quite chastely on both cheeks, then held both his hands at arm's length. "Hello, Ed, welcome to our humble abode, the fatted calf has been duly slaughtered, in a very North London way, of course." Then she broke into her familiarly wicked smile. "Oh Ed, we've all been looking forward so much to seeing you! I'm sure you leave it so long – what's it been, three years? – On purpose just to make us miss you more. Come on, let's get you a drink. Your god-daughter's showered specially – that alone makes it worth you coming."

Mary led him through to the garden. Part of it had been paved since he had last been there. As he came out, Sam was pouring him a glass of Prosecco. A large ice bucket stood on a wooden table in the middle of the patio with two more bottles chilling. A small group of people were standing in the sunshine to the left of the table.

Ed dimly recognised two of them but went to hug the 12-year-old girl instead. "Hello, Ruth, am I still allowed to give you a hug or have you already gone and become a teenager?"

"Maybe…" she said, her face flushing slightly despite herself. Ed bent down slightly, and she put her arms lightly around his neck and almost hugged him while he put his hands delicately on either side of her waist.

"You're still no good at shaving, Uncle Ed," she said when they were standing apart again.

"Why thank you," said Ed, "I'm honoured equally by both the compliment and the reprimand."

"Come on you two," said Sam, grinning Cheshire-cat style. "Ed, we thought about keeping you to ourselves but it didn't seem fair, so we've invited some friends…"

"Hi, I'm Michelle, we met back in '81 at Mary and Sam's wedding. And this is Philip, my partner."

"Hello," said Ed. He hadn't remembered her at all until she spoke, then something about her voice rang a bell. "Yes, of course. That was a long time ago…" he paused, not sure if this was some kind of slight, if he shouldn't have coupled it with some subtle compliment. Shit, he thought, his social awareness was shot to pieces.

"Tell me about it," she smiled, "But I do remember having a very long but civilised discussion with you about Thatcher, which wasn't easy to do back then."

Lights began to go on in Ed's mind, and he remembered this woman from Nottingham. He had struggled through the conversation but didn't remember it, or her, clearly. What he hadn't quite clicked then, because she had looked and behaved so differently, was that this was the same girl who had visited Sam in Manchester, who they'd been talking about yesterday. And now here she was – he swore inwardly at Sam for not mentioning Michelle would be at dinner.

"Hi there," said Phil. "I'm a big admirer of your work. I'm in television myself, but on the production side these days." Ed shook hands and wondered if he had met Philip before as well. But he had no memory of it.

"Thanks," he said. "I try… I should say hello to these other people but we should chat later; we might have some friends in common."

The other people were Linda, an old friend of Mary's, and John, her boyfriend, who was in banking. Mary came over to the table, bottle of Prosecco in one hand, Ruth's hand in the other.

"You've really grown up you know."

"Are you sure you remember?" Ruth said.

"Ruth!" said Mary.

"Of course, I do," said Ed, smiling. "Glad to see you're still going to give me a hard time. You know I've always thought part of the reason your mum and dad asked me to be your god-parent…"

"…was so I could help keep you in the real world. You used to tell me that loads of times."

"Yes, of course," Ed smiled again. "Anyway, look here," and he pulled out a folded A4 envelope from the side pocket of his jacket. "As I said, I knew you'd give me a hard time. Fair enough, it's been nearly four years, which is bad, so I brought along your letters, ones you've sent me since I was last here, in this house, and your Christmas cards, just so you'd know I'd not lost them."

Ruth's face went bright red this time as she again threw her arms round his neck.

"Ruth is allowed to stay up till ten tonight, so she's going to eat with us."

"That's great," said Ed, "one of the few advantages of getting older. And I've got a present for you in the hall that I'll show you later. I hope we're sat near each other?" Mary nodded. "Good, now tell me all about school, the proper stuff, not what you tell your mum and dad." He knew it wasn't a great line, but also that the production of the letters, carried across the Middle East with him, had put him so much in credit that he could do no wrong. He had been impressed by Ruth's directness and wondered if he would have been capable of such precocity when he was 12. He doubted it but maybe times had changed, the death of deference and all that.

When they sat down, Ed found himself between Ruth and Michelle, with Philip opposite him. Sam was the other side of Michelle. He soon found himself talking to her about next week's election. Was there no way of having a normal, light-hearted conversation with this woman?

"I worry that Blair doesn't really believe in anything, that he'll do anything to get his hands on power," she was saying.

"Probably the majority of politicians are like that but precious few of them get the right hand of cards, and then play it well enough. Maybe Blair disguises it less well, but I'm not sure he's so different from Wilson or Callaghan."

"Maybe you're right," she mused. "I remember that film with Robert Redford, what was it called? 1970s... I know, 'The Candidate'...where the whole thing is about him trying to get elected, and then when he does, right at to the end, he doesn't have a clue what to do."

"If anything," Ed continued, "I'm quite impressed they've been so restrained with their promises – the five pledges, sticking with Ken Clark's spending plans and so on – but, I was saying to Sam yesterday, I still think they'll be drowned by the expectations; our political system wasn't designed for a single party being in power for 18 years. It's not natural and wouldn't have happened if the SDLP hadn't split from Labour."

"Cowards!" Michelle was suddenly vicious. "Sorry, but I really believe they should have stayed. I didn't agree with a lot of what was going on back then, reselection and all that, but skulking off to Limehouse or wherever did no one any favours but their own egos, and Maggie, of course." She recovered herself. "I don't know if you remember but I used to be a nurse, and I'm afraid what they've done to the NHS still makes me really angry."

"That's absolutely fine." He smiled, "It's not very common to find people of our generation getting properly angry about things. I'm impressed you still care so much."

"Well, I suppose I grew up believing class mattered, learnt it at my dad's knee."

"A bit like Maggie then?" Ed was deliberately provocative.

Michelle looked at him oddly. "Someone else once said that to me... A strange man I only met the once, in Soho on the evening after the poll tax riots back in 1990. We'd never met before or since but ended up sharing a coffee and a bottle of wine."

367

"Sounds interesting. You gave me such a look then that I half thought you were going to slap me."

"No, don't fear, I'm completely non-violent, or at least I don't hit defenceless men."

"I'm relieved, my reactions aren't what they used to be."

Their conversation danced on. The other side of Ed, Sam was whispering to his daughter, asking how she was enjoying the evening.

"You and Mum's friends are sort of okay, Dad, not too embarrassing."

"And what about Ed?"

"I can't believe he's kept all the stuff I've sent him."

"Well, you write cool letters."

"No, I don't!" said Ruth. "Where's he just come back from?"

"Jordan, and before that Lebanon, I think. Not the safest part of the world. He's a very brave man, you know, and dedicated to telling the truth about what he sees and can find out."

"You really like him, don't you, Daddy?" she whispered.

"Well, he's mostly okay," responded Sam, prompting Ruth to stick out her tongue in mock petulance.

Ed ordered a cab at about 11pm, pleading jetlag. He had enjoyed the evening but it had been a strain and he was knackered. Aside from his conversation with Michelle, he had found normal social intercourse all but impossible, constantly missing the tone of the chat, struggling to say the right thing at the right time. It had been important to see Sam and Ruth, always good to see Mary. But he felt weak, as if he had somehow been caught with his guard down.

Mary had been surprising. He'd always thought she hadn't liked him that much but this time she had appeared genuinely pleased to see him. What was it? "Absence lending enchantment to the view"? God he was tired. The taxi pulled up, he paid, and climbed slowly out. He thought he must have dozed in the back… Had he drunk too much? He stumbled into the hotel, his feet suddenly dragging, his head dropping. Inside the lift, he slumped against the back and forced his eyes open. He made it to his room, threw his jacket on the chair and forced himself to undress. Despite his friends, despite Sam, he felt alone.

***

The train up to Derby the next morning was familiar. He had slept until gone 10am, slightly later than he'd expected. Quickly, he'd showered, packed, checked out and caught the Northern Line up to King's Cross. He walked across the road to St Pancras, bought a ticket, then got himself some breakfast to have on the train. As it pulled out, he again thought if the area would ever be re-developed. Some of the buildings, St Pancras among them, were glorious and its position perfect, yet its reputation was for general seediness, prostitution and drugs. There were plans for a Channel Tunnel route to come into St Pancras but he doubted it would ever happen.

He settled back in his seat with the papers. Inevitably, they were dominated by the election. Almost all expected Labour to win but were hedging their bets over the size of the majority. Ed suspected it would be large, probably over 100 seats. From what he could tell, the poll lead had been consistently over 10%. John Major's

Conservative Party was potentially splitting apart over Europe and the status – holy for some, ambivalent for others – of the Thatcher legacy. After 18 years, he also suspected the country, not surprisingly, was ready for a change, while Blair, for the moment at least, had managed to make New Labour attractively shiny and new, without the fear associated with the unknown.

He flicked idly through, wondering about Sam. He was, outwardly at least, successful and settled, and devoted to Mary and Ruth, who were in turn devoted to him. And yet there was still a part of him, more than with other friends, that remained unknowable. He'd mellowed with age, family responsibilities and, yes, career frustration. That was all right, Ed thought. His own rough edges had softened over the years of compromise, and he'd adjusted his ambitions to suit the prevailing situation. He remembered somewhere reading a story called 'The Age of Grief' – couldn't remember who wrote it – about a couple going through a crisis in their relationship. The underlying message was that almost everyone reached a point, usually by their early 30s, when they realise they're not going to change the world but are going to be changed by it. He turned to the Sports pages, read them sporadically… The train pulled into the station.

His mum and dad were the same as when he had last seen them, almost a year before, but maybe a bit slower, a bit more tentative in their movements, his dad especially. The house hadn't changed noticeably in maybe 20 years, and his bedroom was pretty much as he had left it when he had finally moved out sometime in the late 70s. He had been the first person in his family to go to university but there was no sense of the room being deliberately left unchanged. His parents, he thought, were proud of him, but not excessively so. The room was a matter of "Well, what could we do to it?" and "You need to have somewhere to sleep when you come to see us." His having got a degree was "About time someone from around here was given a chance, but there's a lot around here are smarter than you." The cup of tea arrived with a selection of custard cream and bourbon biscuits, and a thin slice of Battenberg cake. Again this hadn't changed, and he loved their obliviousness to fashion and to received notions of progress.

The conversation moved slowly, lurching awkwardly but lovingly between half explored topics. Everyone was aware they often disagreed on world events, not wanting to shy away from things in which they shared an interest, but equally not wanting the lurking disagreement to crystallise. Ed's parents tended to see things in terms of right and wrong, while he mostly detected only shades of grey, competing truths. He felt fated always to challenge his parents' opinions, never to fully endorse them. And he knew they expected it of him and would worry otherwise.

Chapter 37
Arizona, April 1999

It was 5.30am when Carol left her apartment, a battered blue sports bag slung over her shoulder. The strap had gone, and so it was inelegantly tied in a knot around the buckle. She was catching an early flight to Phoenix for her usual tour of Major League Baseball's spring training and wanted to get there in time to catch up with some people late afternoon and arrange to interview them over the coming few days. The sky was only starting to lighten, and she could already tell it was going to be a warm sunny day in New York, but there was still that little sharp cut of freshness in the air that told you it was not yet summer.

The plane was full, including a group of four golfers, all with their clubs on as hand luggage, so that there was a premium on storage room in the lockers. She settled back and started reading Don De Lillo's 'Underworld', which jumped back and forth between a number of loosely connected stories across different decades from the earlier 1950s to the present. She'd been drawn to it by the thread that connected those different stories, the ownership and whereabouts of the baseball Bobby Thomson had hit for the Giants in the 1951 National League play off with the Dodgers.

Carol had grown up a Dodgers fan, even though she only really became conscious of them after they moved to LA. She had been captivated by Jackie Robinson and the stories of what he had gone through. It was he who had got her interested in sport more widely, the way it highlighted society's best and worst aspects. Di Maggio had been in his pomp back then as well, the archetypal Yankee, and now he too was gone.

She didn't often fly business class but the magazine that had commissioned this forthcoming piece had been happy to shell out the extra. As well as the glossy magazine, they were starting up an internet operation and wanted to put her article on the Web. Carol had been shocked when her agent had called with the news. For reasons that escaped her, this made it worth five times as much. The possibilities of this new medium suddenly appeared infinite, made it irresistible to investors. With three decades of sports journalism behind her, Carol's name, to her surprise, apparently carried weight. She had therefore become attractive to internet companies looking to specialise in the sports market and wanting to use heavyweight writers as a hook. Content was king apparently.

In truth, it seemed to Carol, and this was the only view she was prepared to volunteer, that no one knew how the internet would work in the future. Everyone was experimenting but not in a cautious way; she had never known such optimism. Apparently the world had changed; first the end of Communism and now this. The new century, the new millennium, could see the opening up of new industries in a way unimaginable to older generations.

She felt on the cusp of this generational shift, too old in normal terms but redeemed by her everyday association with sports and sports people, which were seen as part of the broader entertainment world with all the commercial value and kudos that implied. For baseball especially, it was a long way from the era of radio broadcasts in which she had grown up. Commentary had largely been restricted to local teams, with occasional updates on other scores. These days, every game was on television, making players' images more instantly familiar than baseball cards and still photos had allowed. She wondered idly how much the famous players of her youth would be worth now, how wealthy they would be – Willie Mays, Lou Brock, Bob Gibson, Roberto Clemente, not to mention Di Maggio?

The breakfast and coffee were good, and Carol enjoyed stretching out. Lunch arrived, and then the plane was gliding down to land in Phoenix. Soon she was stepping out into the hot dry air of the South West, and there were even more Latino features than in New York. She got in a cab and gave the driver instructions for her hotel. When she had checked in, she took her customary quick shower. The water hit her full blast, the drops bouncing off her skin to the point where she felt pummelled.

Refreshed, she headed down and caught another taxi out to practice. When she arrived, the session had just finished and, apart from one of the young rookies who had gone back into the cage with a batting coach, everyone had already headed for the showers. Carol stood for a few minutes watching the familiar ritual, with the coach teaching the hitter, a right hander, to open up his stance slightly so he could get his left hip out of the way and avoid getting jammed up when the pitcher went inside on him. She could see that up to now the hitter had gotten away with his position through the speed of his hands, and the coach was trying to get him to realise he would have to change fundamentally or he would get found out in the Majors. Instead of going into the locker room – there would be ample chance in the coming months – Carol decided to stay outside in the sunshine and, occasionally nodding to the players and coaches she knew, she went to sit and mingle with the smattering of spectators sitting in the bleachers. There was no hurry today, so it was a chance for some of the players to sign autographs and assuage in advance some of the guilt they knew they would feel during the season ahead when they would too often hurry past patient spectators, sometimes because they were in a real hurry, other times because they were simply tired or disappointed.

After about 30 minutes, Alex emerged, the main subject of the article Carol was writing. Alex Carson was a good-looking sandy-haired pitcher from Jefferson City, Missouri, who had arrived here at spring training after a great season in Triple A. He looked the part of the young fastball pitcher about to break into the Majors. Carol had never met him in the flesh before but had watched him extensively on tape, where he reminded her slightly of a young Tom Seaver, and they had spoken a couple of times on the phone, both at some length, clarifying the scope of the story Carol would write and the interview that would lie at its heart.

There were two aspects of Alex's story, aside from his talent, that made him especially worth writing about. The first was that, after his mother had died when he was twelve years old, he had effectively taken over domestically while his dad continued to work, cooking, cleaning and generally looking after his three younger siblings, who had been eight, six and four at the time. The second was that two years previously, when playing Double A Ball, he had been caught on film calling a batter 'nigga'. The batter had charged him, the benches had emptied in a mass brawl, and Alex had been suspended from organised baseball for the rest of that season. Only his relative youth – Alex had been 19 at the time – his previous good conduct, and, some suspected, the nature of his back story had saved him from a sterner fate.

Alex had apologised immediately and often, in private and in public, but because of his profile the story had created a national storm, dividing players, press and public. It had since died down, but interest remained high, particularly as Alex's pitching had continued to improve and now saw him on the threshold of Major League Baseball. He was not expected to make the opening day roster but expert opinion had it that if he showed up well at spring training and continued to impress in Triple A, there was a high likelihood he would be called up around the All-Star Break.

When Carol had first contacted the club management back in December, they had been resistant. From a PR angle, they could see an immense amount of potential downside and had refused all major media contact during the previous season. But Carol was persistent, arguing she was a dyed in the wool sports reporter rather than a news or features writer, that her main interest was in Alex as a Major League prospect, and that, if he was as good as they believed, an extensive interview in April would take a good deal of the heat out of the consequent media coverage if he did break into the Majors later in the season. She had been clear she would need to ask Alex about the racist language he had used but it would not be the main fulcrum of the story. The negotiations with the club had stretched into the first week of February but, eventually, the front office had consented.

When she got to speak to Alex himself, the conversation while initially cagey, had been more open than Carol had expected. Yes, Alex had said, he'd be more than happy to talk and cover whatever territory Carol wanted. But he wanted some assurance that whatever was finally published would be primarily a sports article. As far as he could see, the reason people were interested in his life and what he had said and done was because he was good at pitching; without that he would be anonymous as far as the media was concerned. He knew he would receive a lot of unbalanced coverage in the future if he continued to be successful but he wanted his first major interview to be as balanced as possible, a matter of record he could refer back to. Carol thought Alex was being unrealistic but could respect what he was trying to do. More selfishly, she could also see how Alex's wish to get his story properly out in the public domain once and for all could be a sport's journalists dream. The young man was obviously thoughtful and articulate and, as well as being a potential star, had much more of a story to tell, good and bad, than many of his age.

In total, over the two calls, Carol had spoken to Alex for maybe an hour. She had referred him to various pieces of her back catalogue, including when Pete Rose had been banned from baseball for gambling. The second time they spoke, Alex had evidently read all the articles Carol had referred him to and several others beside in considerable detail, and peppered the veteran reporter with specific questions. As much as she was impressed by Alex's earnestness, she was amused by the way he couldn't stop himself being more interested in sport, and what Carol had thought about this game or that pennant race, than he was in the way Carol had written about it. Neither characteristic was rare in young professional athletes but, given the situation, Carol was surprised at how quickly the sports geek in him had risen to the surface. She had been aware from the outset of the journalistic dangers posed by this particular story, the different precipices of emotion that awaited her if she became engaged with Alex's story. She had therefore determined to stay slightly further detached from her subject than normal, but already she was struggling.

When Alex came out, whether because he was forewarned or not, he spotted Carol immediately and walked purposefully over to her as though he had thought out in advance how he wanted to handle this first meeting. "Hello, Ms Adams," he said, holding out his right hand. He was wearing a loose grey sweat top with no logos on it, a pair of black knee-length shorts and some fairly nondescript well-worn trainers, all of which told a fairly scruffy look for a young pro athlete with commercial contracts already signed.

Carol took his hand, "Hello, Alex, good to meet you at last. But you should just call me Carol, please. Even though I'm almost old enough to be your grandma."

"Okay then, Ms Adams, I mean Carol," he laughed.

"If I might say so, it's odd seeing an athlete like yourself who doesn't look like an advertising billboard."

Alex laughed again. "Yea, I've got loads of flash kit packed away somewhere but I wore this stuff a lot last year. I feel comfortable in it, and it's still decent enough. And I get that I'll have to wear the new stuff almost all the time once the season starts."

Carol nodded. "So when would you like to meet up? Is tomorrow still okay?"

"Sure, how about just after breakfast? We're not starting practise until 10.30."

"Sounds fine, shall I come to your hotel?"

"Yea, sure, that'd be great. Listen, I'd better go and catch the bus, they're starting to wave at me."

"No problem. I'll see you tomorrow about 8.30."

"Fine, I'll be waiting in the lobby."

Carol spent most of that evening going back over her notes. Alex's mother had died of breast cancer after a short illness; his father had run a garage. When she had died, there appeared to have been some discussion about whether his father would be able to cope, but in the end the authorities decided to see if he could manage as a single parent. He'd cut his hours, and friends and neighbours had helped out, but the main reason it succeeded was because Alex became the main carer for his brother and sisters, and also managed to do a high proportion of the housework without, as far as anyone could tell, being any less determined or focused on his school work or his sport. By age 16, Alex was a good schoolboy pitcher, but still not expected to make it into the Majors. But then he had grown above six inches and put on 20 pounds or so. Suddenly, he was six four and 200 pounds, and his fastball had a fizz that got the scouts circling. The consensus was that Alex's control needed some work, but he had a sound action, and that his mental side was already good, not surprisingly.

So much for the athletic talent, but where did the racist terminology come from? There was no sign of it in his childhood. His family lived in a mixed area, and he'd gone to a racially mixed school. His head teacher, when interviewed, had no idea why he would have said it. All she knew was a smart, well-balanced boy who amazed his teachers by the domestic challenges he overcame. When interviewed, as he had been extensively afterwards, Alex had said he didn't know what had made him say it. The batter had taunted him in previous games, he said, once mentioning his mother, and had a habit of crowding the plate, something that often angers pitchers because they believe it unfairly takes away part of their strike zone. He also claimed the batter had cheated in pretending to get hit when he had thrown him a brush back pitch. Unfortunately, no film or recording of those other events existed, and the batter denied the allegations, though in a slightly evasive way. As a result, most of the press were left in two minds, sceptical of both and slightly bemused by the whole thing. In the end, the fact that Alex hadn't any previous track record meant most of them were inclined to give him some benefit of the doubt. And so, once he had served out his suspension, the coverage of him calmed down, although without removing the residual interest and uncertainty. After all, he was only a Double A ball player at the end of the day, and in the absence of any other evidence to fuel media attention, he was left largely in peace.

However, now that his performances had triggered a call up to Spring Training, interest had begun to mount again, and Carol was only one of a number of well-established sports writers who had tried to secure a major interview. She had no idea why she had been accepted when others had not. Nor was she the only African American writer involved, so that couldn't be the reason, or at any rate not the only reason. Whatever it was, Carol was convinced there was a real story in there and was happy enough to base it around Alex's pitching potential, which was significant enough in its own right. Apart from anything else, she was convinced that putting Alex at ease by focusing on baseball would eventually draw out whatever it was that lay underneath.

When she turned up the next morning, Alex was waiting patiently in the hotel lobby as he had promised, once again in shirt and shorts. They agreed to talk in the hotel coffee lounge, which Alex said had a couple of quiet corners and was fairly peaceful at this time of day, while breakfast was still going on next door. Once Carol had set up her recorder and they were both settled comfortably with coffee and juice, Carol began by talking straight baseball.

"So, let me take you back to when you were an excellent high school pitcher, aged 16 but by all accounts with not enough weight or speed of throw to make it in the big leagues. Only a year later, you were bigger, stronger and faster, and the Major League scouts were queuing at your door. Can you tell me what that change felt like for you, I mean physically in terms of throwing the baseball?"

"No one's ever asked me that, but it's something I think about a lot, because I want to keep the memory of that feeling. Basically, the whole throwing motion actually became easier for me. I don't know if it was my body catching up with itself or what, but I just started feeling looser and looser throughout that year, and Bert Green, my coach at the time, just kept telling me, drumming it into me every day, to stay loose, not to tense up."

"So, if I were to put it to you, you stopped trying so hard?"

"Well," Alex paused, "you said it was okay for me to call you Carol?" The older woman nodded and sipped his coffee. "Well, Carol, in some ways that's right but in other ways I was trying a darn sight harder."

"Can you give me some examples?"

"Well, one example is that I was working my legs a lot harder, both in the gym and on the mound when I was pitching, so in that year I went from leg pressing something small like 250 to maybe 650."

"That's quite an improvement. Pitching coaches have always talked a lot about how important it is to have strong legs. Can you explain to me how that improvement affected your pitching action?"

"Well, I don't know but I can tell you what it felt like. Before, when I pushed off the mound, it felt like I was pushing. I was pushing real fast but I had a definite sense of engaging particular sets of muscles to enable me to spring forward. I don't know how long that took but there was always something a bit slow and deliberate about it."

"And what's it like now?" asked Carol, "How's it different?"

Alex paused for a moment and closed his eyes momentarily, trying to summon up the mental feeling he was trying to describe. "Now, it feels like I'm letting go, and letting go at the last minute."

"So you're coiling yourself up like a spring?"

"I've heard that before," replied Alex evenly, "but I'm reluctant to just say yes because that's how others have described it, and because it's not quite like that for me. For me, it's more of a whiplash movement where the rest of my body gets left behind."

"How do you mean 'left behind'?"

"Well, what it feels like is that when I let go, my right leg straightens real fast, which in turn throws my hips up and forward with my left leg out in front. Only my body and my right arm are kind of left completely behind. My left arm's kinda different because it's up and forward, helping me keep my balance. And I don't really know what my head's doing at that point except I'm trying to keep it still and level, looking at the batter. On video, you can see my head isn't quite doing that – it's moving around quite a lot actually – and so that's something I need to work on."

"And your torso and arm?"

Alex laughed, "I almost forgot about them because it feels like, at that point, when I've just kicked off, something is happening to every part of my body except them."

"So they're not moving?"

"Well, on the video they clearly are, but that's not what it feels like."

"Sorry, I'll stop interrupting."

"That's okay, Carol… What happens then is the bit that used to feel real fast but now feels slow."

"In contrast to your legs which used to feel slow but now feel pretty quick?"

"Exactly, so I used to try real hard to generate pace on the ball with my arm action but now it's much more like I've got time to let my shoulder, elbow, wrist and fingers unwind in their own time and follow each other in sequence."

"So you're not working at all for power or speed with your arm?"

"No, not really, and whenever coach sees any sign of tension or effort in my face or the way I'm throwing, he comes down on me real hard. And generally, yea, it was a weird time, because I also grew a lot, like I said before, and went through a couple of sets of clothes."

"I want to come back to that in a while if I can," said Carol, "and ask you a little about the impact all this has had on the rest of your life, including your family. But first of all, can we talk for a bit about the psychological side of the game?" Alex nodded. "One of the aspects of your game the various scouts I've talked to are pretty much agreed on is that you manage the count really well, that you're comfortable when the batter is ahead and don't just react to what the batter is trying to do. Some of them even think you occasionally let yourself get behind in the count on purpose. Is that right?"

"Yes, of course, doesn't everyone?"

"Well, not that I'm aware of," laughed Carol, "and I sure haven't heard of anyone at the start of their careers saying that's what they did. Like I said, it's pretty rare to be comfortable when you're behind, let alone to seek it out. Can you explain to me what your thinking is?"

"Well, for me it seems like batters are, almost all of them, also more comfortable when they're ahead, and that sometimes makes them relax and feel like they've kinda got a free hit, or that I'm struggling for accuracy and so will throw something in the middle of the strike zone. Whereas, for me, it's sometimes useful to throw a couple of balls just outside the zone to see what the batter will swing at and what he'll leave. So I don't mind being one or two balls behind – 2 and 0, or even 3 and 1 – so long as I've found out something about the batter on the way to getting there. And the other thing, I guess, is to have already given the umpire confidence I can hit that inside top corner of the strike zone, so I can go to that when I need it. If the batter's in the right place, I'll nearly always get a strike or a foul with that pitch."

"That's totally fascinating, Alex, and I could talk to you for hours just on that whole psychology thing. But I've not heard many pitchers, certainly any who weren't already veteran winners, talk as clearly about how they play their contests with the batter. But for now, could we maybe just go back to the impact this enormous and sudden change in your baseball career has had on your family life. It's obviously been well-documented the domestic role you took on when your mother sadly died, and I don't really want to go over that ground again. Instead, I'd like you to tell me what it was like when your pitching began to improve in the way you've described earlier. Presumably, it limited quite a lot what you were able to do at home?"

"Well, first off my brother and sisters were quite a lot older than when Ma died." Alex paused, momentarily, thinking but not sure what about. "So Billy was 12, Ashley was ten, and Natalie was eight. So they could do a lot more for themselves just around the house than they could when Ma had just died. They could bath and dress themselves, and Billy and Ashley can both cook a bit, better than I could when I was their age, so when I began training more and travelling more, they've been able to cope much better, though it was hard for all of us when I was away overnight, particularly for my dad. They're older again now, of course, but our Aunt Alice is staying over some of the time I'm down here just to help out. The money side is a lot easier now as well, which is okay."

"So when you're at home, i.e. not on Spring Training, can you maybe just talk me through a typical day?"

"Well, I'd normally get up at about 5am and go for a run, then do some study for about an hour before waking the others. Then it's breakfast and they're off to school and Dad goes to work. My brother and sisters can take themselves now. Then I go and do pitching practice in the morning, have lunch, weights in the afternoon, fitting in classes when I can. Then I'm home about four to do some more study and make sure my brother and sisters do theirs before starting to make supper at around six in time for my dad to get home."

"And does that vary at all?"

"Not really, apart from when I have games, when I get everything bought and ready but Billy and Ashley prepare it, which usually just means heating it up."

"And what does your dad think?"

"How do you mean?" For the first time, Alex sounded suspicious.

"Just generally, I got the impression he was finding everything a little better in the last few years."

"Well, he likes the idea I'm good at sports," Alex relaxed again, "though a bit disappointed I'm not a slugger. But mostly he's just happy we're managing to stay together as a family. I get a lot of credit in the media and all, but that's because I was young, and now it's because I've become quite good at baseball, but my dad's the person who's really made it work, who's kept us together as a family."

"So tell me about your dad then," asked Carol. "What's he like?"

"Well he's pretty much an ordinary guy who just does special things for his family."

"How do you mean?"

"Well, he came from a poorer family who had moved West during the Depression but his great grandma fell ill and they only got as far as Missouri. My granddad was a farmer but wanted his children to have something better, so he kept investing in businesses but none of them worked and so Dad, who was the oldest of about eight, had to leave school early to help on the farm because he couldn't afford labour. That meant he couldn't go to school, but he still managed to get a job at a garage, after going to night school to learn how to be a mechanic. Then he worked his way up to run a franchise before eventually buying his own garage. He'd always had the dream of being self-employed and finally he got there. But only a few months later, Mum's cancer was diagnosed and she was dead within a year."

"That must have been really hard for him," said Carol. "I'm sorry, that's easy to say but I can imagine how torn up he must have been. He sounds a good man."

"He is, but back then we never saw that much of him. He loved my mother, worshipped the ground she walked on, but didn't really spend much time with her, or with us when we were young. When she was diagnosed, it was a real shock to him. It wasn't that he was a bad father before then – I mean he'd go out on a Friday and get drunk sometimes but other than that he was fine – he just believed he needed to work real hard for his wife and family, and then I think he thought at some point he would have time to spend with us. Though to tell you the honest truth, I don't think Dad ever had a clear idea of when that would be."

"And what happened when your mum was diagnosed with cancer?"

"Well, I don't know if I should be telling you this, but there's nothing in it to be ashamed of; he more or less fell apart for about three months; didn't go to work hardly, just drank at night and slept most of the day. That was pretty much all he did apart from talking to my mother and crying and saying sorry. And then, after about three months, he more or less snapped out of it."

"What triggered it?"

"I don't know really. I think he just got to a point where he realised he was no longer talking to mum but actually talking to himself and that he was starting to wallow in self-pity. And he just pulled himself out of it, more or less just like that. That was about six months before Mum died, and those were the best times our family ever had together."

"What was different about it, did you go away somewhere?"

"No, we didn't move from Jefferson City. By that stage, my mother was really too ill to travel anyway. And besides, we had no money, and he had to go back to work."

"What made the difference?"

"It's hard to say and, boy, have I been thinking about it a lot, all the more now I'm kind of grown up and trying to work out what it takes to be a decent human being." Carol waited, and after a moment's reflecting, Alex carried on. "As far as I can work out, I think Dad began living life for today and for tomorrow. Before, I reckon he had pretty much thought only about the future. So not only had he partly neglected us as a family but he had also forgotten to appreciate the sun rising and setting each day, the changes of the seasons, and the fun and value you can get from talking with other people."

"And if you don't mind me asking, did your mother understand that change?"

"Oh, you bet she did. Thank God, they pretty much had the drugs to keep her pain in check, and, honest to God, I've never seen her so happy as she was a during those last months. I think she saw it as getting back the man she'd married 15 years before, hardworking but fun; that's what he'd lost, the fun of being able to see things and laugh at them if they were ridiculous or went wrong. He'd ended up losing a lot of that in all the effort he put in, he'd kind of forgotten why he was doing it and that's what he found again in those last few months they were together."

Alex stopped, and took a sip of coffee, controlling himself as he did so, and Carol recognised this was a tiny ritual Alex had gone through many hundreds of times over the last eight years.

"I really appreciate you talking to me like this, Alex, and I take it from what you said before that your father has carried on appreciating his family, appreciating life every day." Alex nodded. "Listen," Carol continued, "I just need to go to the bathroom and then, if you're feeling okay, there's just a last few questions I'd like to ask you about the incident with Bob Davis."

"That's okay, Ms, I mean Carol, you've played fair with me and I trust you, so go ahead and ask anything you want."

When Carol returned, Alex seemed composed once more, and, after checking he was still happy to continue, she began what she assumed would be the most difficult part of the interview. "In the early part of our first phone call, you said something about the batter needing to stand in the right place, not crowding the plate. Is that part of what happened with Bob Davis? Was it that he was crowding the plate and you reacted? Or was it something he said? Some of the reports suggest he said something about your mother."

"He was crowding the plate, but that's not the reason I said what I said. All the good batters, or almost all, try and do that, a lot of what happens out there is about struggling for that inside edge of the strike zone, for who owns that line. And Bob Davis is a good hitter, one of the best I've faced. He can be irritating sometimes, but I'd never use any of that as an excuse for what I said."

"And did he say anything?"

"Well, he might have done, but I'm not going to tell you because he's not the first to have said something when I'm out there on the mound. Particularly in the early days, a lot of them still assumed she was alive. It's not a great part of the game if you ask me. It exists and, to be honest, I've been through so much that it probably affects me less than it does a lot of other athletes, and because my mother wasn't alive anymore, it just seems stupid and ridiculous a lot of the time."

"Why was it then?"

"I don't really have a reason, Ms Adams. I was still pretty young and it was a word I'd heard other people use, at school, on CDs and in films. I don't think I'm racist but I know it looks bad. The reason I didn't say anything at the time is because there's no real justification for what I said and I didn't want to pretend there was one. And I don't even really want you to write what I just said in your article, although I know you have the right to do so. The fact I'd heard the words before doesn't mean anything, and I wouldn't want anyone to think I believe it did. It's the same with being young. Whatever age I was, I was easily old enough to know better. And besides, after having to help look after my brother and sisters, it would just be ridiculous to pretend I was a naïve young kid."

"Well, first off," said Carol, "don't worry about me writing what you just said. There's nothing you've told me so far that I wouldn't be prepared to take out if you didn't want it published. But I'm worried that unless you give the public something to let them understand what happened, then there'll always be that question mark against your character, hopefully only a small one but still a question mark."

"I think that's my punishment. I have to carry that with me."

"But if you're not racist, and I don't believe you are, then you need to find a way to say that. What Bob Davis said to you, whatever it was, must have provoked you, even if your reaction was wrong."

"Maybe it did and maybe it didn't, but like I said, it wouldn't be an excuse even if it did. And however stupid what Bob said was, no way does he deserve to be dragged into a row over race and colour, which is what it would become. At the moment, it's just about me and I can live with that, what I don't want to live with is the responsibility for creating a major race row."

"Do you really think it would happen like that?"

"Ms Adams, you know as well as I do that it wouldn't just be Bob Davis who would be judged but all African Americans. I'm sure you'll have done your research and so you know I grew up in a mixed neighbourhood and went to a mixed school. Well, that doesn't mean everything was all sweetness and light. There's still not a lot of mixing going on; and like I said before, I've heard plenty of name calling and seen a few fights that were race-related. And I'm old enough too to have seen a share of politicians playing the race card come election time, and I just don't want to be any part of that. Like me, Bob Davis will have to live with what he said, but he's okay and doesn't deserve any more than that."

"But surely things have moved on since I was your age?"

"Probably they have but not nearly enough as far as I can tell. There's still a chunk of people in this country who are just plain afraid of African Americans. Don't really know why; maybe it's history but I'm no historian; maybe it's to do with jobs but I'm no economist. Some of them are bad people but the great majority, including my neighbours, are decent enough."

"I'm quite depressed you're so pessimistic, Alex, especially given how young you are."

"Only really about the present; not the future, Ms Adams, not the real future anyway; people my age can't afford to be. I don't know, maybe it's different in New York and the educated circles you move in, but this is what it's like where I live."

"Alex, it's a privilege to meet you; even though I'm feeling sadder about the immediate future of our country than I have for a long time, you've also left me feeling more optimistic about the longer term. I know you've got to go to practice in 15 minutes, but can I tell you just one short story about when I was about your age, maybe a little younger?"

"Yea, sure you can, Ms Adams."

"Well, I'm sure you've done your homework as well, and so you'll know I grew up in rural Mississippi. Well, back then, there was a real problem in my state, and lots of others in the South, about getting Black people to register so they could vote. The Civil Rights legislation had just been passed, but where I come from, well let's just say the local officials weren't exactly mounting a campaign to try and persuade Black people to exercise those rights, particularly their right to vote. And then again, there were many Black people, like my parents, who had never been able to vote and didn't really understand or believe what it was that had changed."

"I'm sorry, Ms Adams, but I only know a little about those times. I know a bit about Dr King obviously, and I've heard of the laws you mention but I'm afraid I don't know any detail beyond that."

"That's okay, Alex, that's why I'm telling you this story. What changed that situation for them, and I suspect changed hundreds if not thousands of individual people's lives – it sure changed mine – was that groups of students from the North and out West came down to Mississippi that summer to try and persuade Black people like my parents to register so they could vote. They came down in their battered student cars, mostly clean-cut White kids from good schools, and just went round knocking on people's doors. They encountered all kinds of resistance – that's another whole story though – but they just kept on doing what they had come down there to do. They called it Mississippi's Freedom Summer. It probably didn't change much, if anything, of the big picture but it did for my parents and me."

"If you don't mind me asking, Ms Adams, how did it change your life? Did they come and knock on your door?"

"Yes, they did. His name was Jack Abraham and his friend was called Stephen Glass. I think from their names now that they were both Jewish, but neither of them said anything about that. I was just getting started in journalism, working for the local paper. I'd moved to Jackson but had driven out to my parents for supper. It was a warm evening in August but there was a bit more of a breeze than normal, and we'd been laughing about something, sitting on the porch, when their car drew up.

"Anyway, we don't have time for me to tell you all that was said once they'd come in and sat down but there's a couple of things Jack Abraham said that particularly stuck with me. One was that being American was something that was indivisible and that the rights enshrined in the Constitution and the Bill of Rights applied just as much to my parents as it did to his parents and everyone else, and that it was their duty as well as their right to exercise the franchise they had been born to and which their own mothers and fathers had been unjustly denied.

"And the second thing was to try not to hate or resent those who still tried to prevent them from voting; if anything, to pity them. American society, he said, was so broad and diverse it was inevitable there would be divisions within it, sometimes painful ones. It was important to seek to heal those wounds where we could but, as society evolved, new divisions would inevitably open up and some people would always find it hard to adapt, difficult to recognise that their version of America wasn't the only one and that it would be superseded by new versions, but that he believed the special thing about our country was that the Constitution and the Bill of Rights would be adaptable enough to embrace – I even remember him using that word – whatever change lay ahead."

"And how did your parents react?"

"Well, first of all, you need to realise that my parents had never met any White people from the North, and that no one White had ever come to see them at their house except to collect on a bill. So a lot of their reaction was shock and simply not knowing how to deal with the situation. But Jack and Stephen were so calm, so without any of the arrogance White people habitually put on in front of them, that they were completely – what's the word? – charmed by them, by their politeness and good manners. And because of all of that, and maybe a little bit of deference too – not because they were White but because they were obviously so well educated – both my parents, particularly my mother, had a huge in-built respect for educated people – they listened to what Jack said to them, listened as I'd only ever seen them listen to the preacher in church on a Sunday morning."

"But didn't it challenge the assumptions behind a lot of the way they'd lived their lives?"

"Yes, it did, but Jack didn't present it that way. The way he told it, they had always been American, with all the rights and duties that came with that, but only now with this recent legislation had the door truly been opened so they could walk through it. But the main thing, the idea that caught their imagination, was that they could do so without hate, with only pity for those who until now had kept that door shut and who still sought to do so."

"And did they register?"

"Yes, the very next day. I went with them, drove them into town and walked with them to the town hall. Folks knew what they were doing, even seemed to know they'd been visited by the White college kids. I don't know how that sort of news gets around but somehow it always does. And people came out and watched us walking up the street. No one hassled them, maybe because I was there too and everyone there knew I was a journalist and wrote for a paper in the city. Anyway, I'd always been proud of my parents but never more proud than I was that day."

"And what about you? You said it changed your life too."

"Well, for a start, I had a pretty good idea of what risks Jack and Stephen were running just by coming down to Mississippi. Living in Jackson, I'd read the papers and knew these guys were getting badly beaten up for messing with the proper order of things in places where they didn't belong. A few of them even got killed, and some spent time in jail for it. But beyond that, I'd never met anyone like Jack and Stephen before, of any skin colour. They had an idea of America and of the world, of where they were and where they ought to be heading, that was way beyond anything I'd ever heard or seen before. And sitting there listening to them, understanding what they were saying and being able to agree, or disagree, with their arguments, that made me feel different. Before, my going to live and work in Jackson seemed big and scary but now LA and New York seemed like places I could choose to go. So I decided I would. It took me two years to build up enough experience and to have written enough I was proud of, or at least happy with, to write off and apply for a job at the New York Post; amazingly, I got it and so, just after Thanksgiving 1966, I headed north to New York."

"That's a wonderful story, Ms Adams, but why are you telling me? After all, it's quite personal and we've only just met, and I feel like you're not interviewing me anymore."

"Well, I don't think I am interviewing you anymore, so you can put yourself at ease on that account. I've got way too much already for my article, the challenge for me is to decide how to put it together with so much material to work with, and I'll probably have to leave quite a lot out. So, I might need to ring you to check on a few facts but apart from that, I'll just send you the draft article to check you're okay with it. But the reason I told you the story was because of that idea Jack Abraham had of an America that was broad and diverse, constantly evolving and developing, and the importance of trying to build and heal itself at the same time. It was something you said earlier about people who were being racist being like that not because they were bad people but because they were confused, and above all afraid. It reminded me of something Jack Abrahams could have said, and given what you've told me, I wanted you to know and understand there's a connection between you and those young college students back in 1964. I thought it might help you put some things in perspective, and maybe even give you a little extra strength. It doesn't sound like you need it, but I don't know you well, so you could easily be hiding a bit of insecurity somewhere; and in any case a little extra never hurt anyone."

"Thank you, Ms Adams, I really appreciate what you just said and I'm sure it will help me get through; like you say, having a bit more perspective never hurt, and particularly if I do make it to the Majors, I'm sure I'll need it."

"Okay then," said Carol as she got up. "You'd better get going, you've only got a couple of minutes till your bus goes. One last thing, I won't put anything in the article about what Bob Davis said, I'll just tell it the way you've told it before. But please could I ask you to think about whether there's a way to say a little more about why you're taking responsibility yourself, without bringing Bob into it? I think it would probably make your life easier, but more important, it would add a little to our understanding of what can divide us as Americans but also help bring us together. It may be a drop in an ocean but I think it would help."

382

"Okay, Ms Adams, I'll try." The two shook hands warmly, "I'll wait for you to phone and then for the draft article. No, on second thoughts, there's no need to send me a draft, the final version will be fine. Except maybe if you think of some words that might help me explain what we've just been talking about."

"Fine," replied Carol, "I'll do my best. Oh and Alex," she said as the young pitcher was turning to go. "Good luck at practice today... And next time, please make sure to make it Carol?"

Late that night about 3.30am, Carol finished the first draft of her article about Alex Carson. Normally, she liked to get a first draft written as soon as possible after an interview, when the images and impressions were freshest, but completing it the same day was still unusual. Normally too, she didn't drink alcohol while she wrote, but a used whisky glass sat beside her laptop. She decided to re-read the last few paragraphs before turning in.

"Finally, our conversation turned again to the incident the season before last when he was captured on video during a Double A game calling Bob Davis, the leftie slugger he was pitching at, a 'nigga'. Carson freely admitted he had used the term and said it was the thing he was most ashamed of in his life. As well as his often expressed public regret, he confirmed again that he'd privately apologised to Davis, who he said was a fine hitter and one of the opponents he respected most. He said he hoped that in time Davis would forgive him. During all of this, I detected not the slightest hint of self-pity and, in fact, in some 30 years as a reporter, I've rarely interviewed an athlete with less of an agenda.

"When I pushed him as to why he thought he had used the term and asked if it was because, as some have reported, Davis had insulted his deceased mother, Carson denied outright any suggestion Davis had said anything that was not acceptable in a game situation, or could remotely have justified his own outburst. 'I made a bad mistake,' he told me, 'and I have to take personal responsibility for that, period. It was in the heat of a game situation but I'm making no excuses. It was a term I knew, but I don't remember ever having used it before. It just came out, and I've certainly not used it since. I was under pressure but I need to learn how to cope with that, it's a big part of learning what it takes to be a professional athlete. I believe I've learnt that lesson now but I wish from the bottom of my heart I could have learnt it in a way that didn't cause offense. I realise I've got a lot of ground to make up in terms of the example I set, and I'm trying my best to do that every day. I hope people will give me the chance to earn back their respect through what I do in baseball and as a person, and not judge me just on that one incident. I wish I could promise not to make mistakes again but I can't guarantee that and I'm sure I will make other mistakes. What I will promise is that I won't make the same one again.'

"As an African American journalist who began reporting during the Civil Rights era, I was fully prepared to be cynical about Alex Carson and, given what he did two seasons ago, I expected to have to work hard to maintain my objectivity. Instead, I found a painfully honest, highly self-aware and brave young athlete, working hard to atone for what he recognises was a grievous error. I believe him when he says this, his determination obvious in his every sentence, and that he realises this will be a long journey, with forgiveness by no means guaranteed.

"If professional athletes have any place as role models, it is surely in their ability to triumph over their own shortcomings. Alex Carson's mistake was a serious one, but we delude ourselves if we believe it was purely personal. More than 30 years after Dr King's death, the fact this term is still common across American society is one we should all face, not with anger but with a collective determination to overcome the causes of its continued use. In the meantime, Alex Carson is not asking for a second chance, only that we accept his remorse is genuine. I for one am happy to do so."

Chapter 38
New York, 31 December 1999

The myth of the Millennium bug had just been busted. Carol had been in a Tribeca bar, watching on TV as the lights sparkled around the Sydney Harbour Bridge and Circular Quay with the Opera House at its heart, and now she was watching London turn the same trick. The fireworks exploded, and Carol imagined thousands of computer programmers popping champagne bottles as they celebrated the biggest collective fraud in world history. The entire industrialised world had gone paranoid over the last two years, scared witless that computer systems across the globe would shut down once the digital clocks switched to the year 2000. Carol imagined it all as an enormous, perfect con trick, designed to persuade governments and corporations to plough endless amounts of cash into upgrading their systems, employing every computer engineer they could find, to fix what didn't need fixing. And now it had all officially worked, they could declare success and move on, having completed the perfect crime. She shook her head and ordered another beer.

Right on cue, Eric walked through the door, and she got up to give him a kiss. They'd been seeing each other since Labour Day weekend when they'd met at a party on Long Island. He was French, worked in woman's magazines and met the stereotype; she was African American, wrote about sports and made a point of talking like a jock in polite company. But, both single and in their early 50s, they somehow got on and laughed at each other's jokes, in and out of bed. As a relationship, it was both light and light-hearted; there were no implications or strings, other than to be honest when it was time to move on.

"Darling, sorry I'm late; the Uptown traffic was awful."

"No problem, what can I get you?" She ordered him a gin and tonic, his 'English' drink, and got herself another beer. "I was just watching the celebrations kicking off in London. All that Y2K stuff seems to have been a bit of a hoax."

"Carol, I love it when you're cynical. I thought it was part of the European character, and I'm delighted to discover it so alive and well here in New York."

"We can do cynicism from here to Doomsday – it's in our DNA, something we share with the French, I believe."

"Oh, you're too cruel, Carol, for so early in the evening. Here we are at the start of a new millennium; let's look ahead and see what will happen."

"Tomorrow will be just like today, except we'll be a day older." But her features were already starting to crack into a smile. "And I love it when you're ridiculous and talk rubbish with a straight face."

Eric laughed, "Well, you always bring out the worst in me, or the best maybe. I have this unavoidable urge to talk like we were in some trashy novel. It keeps me sane in the ultra-serious world of magazines, and I know you can see through me like glass so I can make things up without compunction."

"Good to know I offer a valuable service to the highest echelons of the US publishing industry. Tell me, what's your leading feature slash exposé for the inaugural month of the millennium?"

Eric looked suddenly serious and sipped his gin studiously. "I think it's going to be entitled 'Trashy Men and Why We Love Them'."

Carol burst out laughing. "That's my favourite subject. All those good women with loser guys, I mean what's going on?"

"I take it you're putting yourself on the side of righteousness here?"

"Of course, 'A woman cannot love without honour', as good old Chuck once said. Truth, justice and the American way, baby, that's me right down the line."

"Somehow I forgot, do not ever change!" Eric gave her a quick peck on the cheek and settled back in his stool. "So, are you looking forward to the party tonight? Great venue, eh! Roof top views over the Park?"

"Yes, Pat and Rachel have a great apartment, and it'll be terrific to see them again. You'll have to watch me though to make sure I don't misbehave in front of all your sophisticated magazine friends."

"Don't worry, you're my badge of credibility and do wonders for my reputation, so you can do your worst; of maybe just be yourself; on second thoughts, I'm not sure my magazine sisterhood is quite ready yet for you doing your worst."

"It's okay, I can be reasonably sophisticated when I try. Changing the subject, it's interesting how much smaller the world suddenly feels. I mean I've just been watching fireworks live in Sydney."

"I know, my sister's in Paris, and I talk to her at least twice a week to advise me on my dot com investments. She's dying to meet you by the way."

"I'm worried about Jacqueline wanting to meet me – what have you told her?"

"Oh, that you're the woman of my dreams, the most beautiful woman I've ever met, an eloquent writer, a passionate lover…"

"Okay, now I'm not worried! The internet does seem to be going crazy though; it looks like everyone is after free money, which, as my grandma would tell you at huge length, don't exist anywhere."

"Well, everyone's very excited about it, but I think you must be right that many of these new companies will not survive. But those that do, those people will become rich beyond my dreams. It is an easy decision now not to join one of those companies waiting to be born; but if I was 20 to 25 years younger, what would I do? That answer is not so clear."

"I don't think it would ever have been for me, even when I was young. Unless it breathes and thinks and dreams and sweats, it's not really going to get me out of bed."

"No, you're not really into technology, are you?" Eric joked.

"I'm a million miles from it. Sure, I don't even have a DVD, I've had the same computer for five years, the same mobile for three. But I've got friends who just mindlessly upgrade whenever the next thing comes out, no matter what the cost, no matter if they actually want it. And that's without even mentioning the gaming crowd – they're just permanently wired, like something out of a William Gibson novel; what are they called? Neuromancer, Snow Crash, that stuff."

"I'd never have guessed you as having read those books. But still, what did you think of Snow Crash? It's my favourite sci-fi novel."

"Well, a few years back I read it; but I think the thing I liked about it most was the virus thing, the idea that breaking down walls between computer programmes rendered everything vulnerable. And the way he connected that with the Tower of Babel in the Bible."

"Exactly! I love that connection between the Old Testament and computer viruses. It's beautiful in terms of understanding both phenomena and making a seamless connection, illuminating one of the eternal human dilemmas, what is the right balance between the individual and the communal, the secret and the shared, the safe and the vulnerable, the 'I' and the 'we'?"

"There you go talking rubbish again," said Carol, "but that's the direction we're moving in though, isn't it? Everything global, everyone connected to the Web, hundreds of millions of us spending half our lives online, everyone receiving and ingesting virtually the same information in very similar ways?"

"I agree with that up until the last part. A lot of what the internet gives us is access to a far greater variety of information and opinions. Before the Web, we all had the same television channels as sources of knowledge; now we have, through the Web, far easier access to original sources, and increasingly, search engines that help us find what we're looking for."

"But so much of what we now call news is so far away from our individual experience that it's virtually impossible to verify, and as a result, there's no incentive to stop people just putting up crap; no penalty for not doing the work, for getting the facts wrong, for lying."

"But I don't think there has ever been a golden era where that wasn't the case. What's held up as authoritative journalism could just as easily be lazy, or riven with baked in prejudices that wouldn't last five minutes if exposed to the scrutiny of today's world. I can just about buy the idea the overall standard might once have been higher – though no one's been able to tell me when that was – but in absolute terms, there's much more quality out there now, and it comes from a much wider range of perspectives than before."

"Maybe," conceded Carol, "but identifying quality is harder when it's such a big haystack. Anyway, I still don't really know these people whose party we're going to, so you need to bring me up to date, or rather remind me what they're like. You saw Rachel the other night, didn't you?"

"It was only for coffee after work, sadly. She's fine, I think, if a bit bored at work. She's been doing the same editorial role for nearly two years now, and it's getting repetitive for her."

"So what does that mean?"

"Probably moving magazine, but her and Pat want to start a family, and careers in our industry are unstable always and so they are thinking hard about what is the best thing."

"Ah, the old family and career thing. I can imagine your business isn't that child-friendly. How's the financial side? What is it Pat does again?"

"Oh, he's on Wall Street. The industry's better than it used to be but yes, lots of the senior women are without children and the lifestyle is not...conducive."

"Is that why you have no children?"

"I like it that you are so direct. Maybe, it is hard to say what the deciding factor was across so many decisions, or if there was a common factor. For me there were a lot of small dilemmas but no single moment. For many years, I thought I would have children but it did not happen and maybe that means I did not have any big natural urge to be a father that I once thought I did. Perhaps, even though Paula and I lived together for more than five years, there was also never a relationship in which I felt comfortable and so maybe that is also a reason."

"So what about the others?" she asked.

"They are the usual mix of my friends and their partners, whom you have met before, all of them I think. They are the same as each other, and you will be polite and funny and say all the right things because you are more skilled at these arts than you would like to pretend. I have seen you be charming too often, and if you were not, you would not have such good contacts as a writer and journalist."

"Well, I'll try then," she replied, vaguely irritated.

"It's New Year's Eve 1999," Eric said, reaching across to hold her hand, "and I want to spend tonight with you and for us both to be happy."

"Me too, what time does it start?"

"About 8pm, I think. Rachel was hoping we would arrive early so I can help her with the last of the food preparation. Shall we go now, after this drink, I mean?"

"Yea, it's only about ten minutes, isn't it?" The atmosphere between them was still warm but had cooled a couple of degrees. A sliver of entitlement had entered what had been an oasis of low pressure fun and everything was suddenly a little heavier. Eric had become aware, at least partly, that he was investing real emotional capital in this woman. Maybe it had been the slightly flippant chat about children, but the thought had somehow sneaked into his mind that these things might have been different if he had met Carol 15 years earlier.

For Carol, it wasn't simply the opposite of Eric's thought, for she did not really resist or resent another's interest in her life. Instead, she had suddenly come to feel uncomfortable about Eric thinking she was better than she was; a better writer, a better person. All her life, she had only wanted to be what she was, neither better nor different. The hint that Eric thought she was, or could become, a better writer had come across as a denial of her identity. She liked these people, enjoyed their conversation and their eclectic knowledge. She never felt they patronised her, and was always pleasantly surprised by how much she shared their value system. Yet she knew was still an outsider.

Eric's belief in her ability therefore jarred because it was too easy in its assumptions that these things were attainable. Her writing was the result of more than three decades of toil, and each small addition to her craft had been painfully won. She knew people who wrote much more freely and eloquently and, while she was emotionally in love with the process of her writing, each phrase of hers was painfully wrung. The idea that she either was or could become like those others was ridiculous and revealed both Eric's misunderstanding of her and the gap between them in how they viewed life; hers as an odyssey of struggle, Eric's as a sequence of targets, sometimes stretching but always reachable.

By the time they started the short walk to the party, therefore, they had emotionally moved slightly apart. It was only by a small margin but the direction of travel had changed. And because it now mattered slightly less, they held hands as they walked along.

"When did you last see your daughter?" Eric asked.

"Boxing Day, no, the day after. She'd flown to Chicago for Christmas itself, to spend it with Richard's family. It's the first time she's not been with me on the day itself but we both coped. When are you next going to see your parents in France?"

"Probably in the spring, around Easter time. They're getting old. Papa is 80 and my mother is 76. It's important my sister and myself see enough of them in the next few years because although they're healthy now, you never know when something might happen."

"Yes, you should. My dad died quite suddenly when I was 25. He had a stroke from out of nowhere and by the time I got to the hospital, he had gone; I was at that age where, having not talked to him much during my teens, I'd just begun to become interested in what my dad was really like. I don't blame myself but it's a big regret."

"You've never talked about your parents before."

"There's lots of things I haven't talked about. I guess it's one of those New Year, new century things."

They reached the apartment building, and Pat's merry voice greeted them over the intercom. A minute later, they were in the spacious 12th floor apartment, hugging and kissing each other as though midnight had struck already. But it hadn't, and there were still things to do in the kitchen, food to prepare before the other guests started to arrive. Pat and Carol were left to have a drink, proving, Carol observed wryly, that some twentieth century stereotypes trumped others. Pat nodded agreement but neither had been taught, or had sought, more than a pragmatic knowledge of the kitchen.

To soothe their pretended feeling of being slighted, Pat offered to mix some cocktails, and in a couple of minutes the host had rustled up a couple of Manhattans and they were talking about whether the 21st century would be as much of an American one as the 20th had been. As the intercom rang, Pat had just concluded, disappointingly Carol thought, that China would take over the mantle of world leadership within the next 20 years.

Although she had met Pat only a few times, and only with Eric, she instinctively liked him, but this particular conversation had definitely run its course and Carol was starting to feel like the audience. So she was pleased when a gaggle of visitors suddenly swarmed into the room and her host found himself fully occupied. Although many of the faces were fleetingly familiar, she recognised only a couple of them properly, and for the next few minutes she circulated the periphery of different groups, until stopping by one that was talking excitedly about the dot.com start up a couple of them were involved in. "We've got $20m seed capital from private equity, and we'll probably need about $40m more in 2001; and our projections, which are really at the conservative end, show us breaking even by 2004. We'll be up and running a year from now, so yes, we're spending a lot of our time at the moment recruiting heads of function."

Carol was impressed by the confidence of these people, able to attract millions of dollars of investment on the strength of an idea. It was like nothing she had ever heard but the idea must be brilliant given the investors – hard-headed commercial firms – were prepared to wait several years before it moved into profit, and they could presumably start to get repaid. More than ever, it left her feeling isolated from this cosmopolitan group. Her own world of sport, she reflected, was different. Sometimes there was a good deal of money involved but it was still usually personal rather than corporate, and the owner was more likely still to court publicity than hide in the shadows. And although success or failure could be a long time in the preparation, the reality of it was very much in the here and now. And while in sport winners were rare and losers obvious, in the dot.com age everyone, it seemed, could be a winner.

Moving on, she stood at the edge of another group. A tall, severe-faced woman was holding court. She was maybe in her early 40s and was speaking with authority. Carol was useless at working out what people were wearing, but she suspected this woman was dressed very expensively. "Yes, we're aiming to launch a Hong Kong edition in the fall, but we expect to be generating consistent 20% sales growth over the next decade as the mainland middle class explodes in places like Shanghai and Guangdong."

"But won't you have to produce it in Mandarin as well as Cantonese?" asked one of the group.

The woman looked slightly perplexed but quickly recovered. Carol suspected she didn't really understand the question, let alone know the answer, but she had no problem declaring, "Nothing to worry about, we've fully taken account of all that."

Assuming the language issue could be sorted out, Carol still wondered how well a New York women's magazine would go down among the Chinese 'mainland middle classes'. She disliked the term, found it patronising, but tried to give the imposing woman the benefit of the doubt – it was New Year's Eve and she was, after all, a friend of Eric's. It appeared a strange assumption to think that, for a culture as strong and old as China's, progress would translate quite so easily into a readymade version of post-industrial western consumerism. But Carol was wary not to underestimate the power of advertising and the drive of a growing world power to acquire the external trappings of success from the nation it presumably saw as its rival, soon to be predecessor.

Carol's gut instinct was that the US would not cede its position quietly. Nothing she saw pointed to the US going backwards, and it seemed odd to her to view a country standing alone at the summit following the collapse of communism, and at the forefront of technology, as somehow in decline. What did seem true was that the world was becoming more interconnected and dependant; the days of self-sufficiency seemed to be passing. America had changed a good deal since she had first come North. A lot of it was for the better but there were also many things she disliked. There were fewer barriers to being a young African American now than there'd been 30 years ago. That said, the dreams and ambitions of the late 60s had mostly been deflated, and there was still a racial edge to the way American society organised itself. Maybe it was inevitable the legacy of segregation would defy being swept away in a single generation, or even two. But if so then how long would it take?

Carol laughed at herself. There must be something contagious in the atmosphere or the cocktails, or maybe it was being in a New York rooftop apartment on the eve of a new millennium. She drained her glass, reflecting it was now possible to reach a seemingly respectable opinion about many subjects you intrinsically knew nothing about, subjects that in past generations would have been ignored by all but the real experts. But now, with the layers of news and opinions blurring into each other, there was enough information and opinion to hand for anyone to reach a view on almost anything with a semblance of confidence.

The one thing Carol was reasonably sure about at first hand was the increasing flow of talent across borders. She had seen it in sport, how the previously insular worlds of American sport had opened: to Hispanic Americans, Japanese and Koreans in baseball; to Eastern Europe in ice hockey, and to the rest of the world in basketball, where the Olympic Dream Teams had, against expectations, served to showcase other countries' stars at least as much as the USA's. Only football held out, its complex geometry rendering its real workings opaque to outsiders. She wondered whether football's lackadaisical attitude to developing overseas talent – the half-hearted European Franchise League was Exhibit A – would ultimately signal its decline, as the value of other sports' overseas television rights rose exponentially while football's stagnated.

But in general, she didn't think of the US as in decline, and also wondered how much the economic stuff really mattered. As far as she was aware, Italy had never been an economic powerhouse and yet the influence of Italian culture was everywhere. The British Empire had presumably once been economically dominant, but the UK's continuing influence could scarcely be attributed to the size of its economy. And the US seemed, if anything, to be increasing its cultural reach – whether it be Hollywood, or sports, or Silicon Valley. Maybe 15 or 20 years ago Japan was a major cultural threat but that seemed to have gone away. Who really knew? 'Experts' seemed to be a rapidly growing class and 'truth' harder to find, a slightly different take on her argument with Eric.

And then, right on cue, as so often happens, when you think of someone, Eric and Rachel emerged from the kitchen, glasses in hand, and Pat leapt into action, breaking out three bottles of champagne, now everyone had arrived, offering fresh glasses and a short welcoming speech as a formal signal that the Millennium New Year's Eve party had formally begun.

"Hello everyone," he bellowed, slightly too loudly as Rachel had just turned down the music. "Thanks for coming. This is a really special New Year and we're so pleased so, er, many of our friends could make it. The plan is we'll eat about 9.30 and should be done in good time for midnight. Let's all have a fabulous evening, starting with a toast to the almost finished 20th century and second millennium AD." He raised his glass.

As everyone cheered and drank, Carol imagined the similar but different toasts that had taken place already across the world, and those yet to happen. All day she had been aware of the New Years already happening in other parts of the world. She thought of her friends from the Athletics' circuit bringing in the new millennium in their own countries. Generally a cynical lot, but each with a core of childlike enthusiasm lurking inside, she wondered what they would be making of the organised delirium. With one or two exceptions, she thought their gregarious natures would see them diving into whatever parties were available.

And then there was Philip. They'd spoken on the phone just before Christmas, and Carol knew he and Michelle would probably still be at a restaurant they had booked with friends. She could imagine Phil swaying in time to some music,

391

pretending to dance while surreptitiously casting his eyes around the room, trying to work out what was going on, who was and wasn't having a good time, whether any relationships were forming or dissolving.

She remembered them having a drinking session together back in the mid-70s sometime, maybe '75, and Philip claiming all he really cared about was motive, Phil thought why people did things was ultimately far more important than what they did; it offered the most reliable key to the future significance of an event and was a much truer guide than the action itself. Carol smiled at the memory of their earnest debate a quarter century before, when she was the one trying to settle down, with Danny. Phil had been to a Tom Waits concert the previous week and had begun talking enthusiastically about the gravelly, conversational lyrics of Waits, how he was a song-writing descendant of Kerouac and Ginsberg, a 'Beat bard', who gave meaning and beauty to the simple, ostensibly frivolous acts of normal life; where talking, eating, driving, drinking, music and sex were, separately and together, possessed of a symbolism and importance that connected them to the American landscape.

Without warning, Carol's eyes moistened, and she wished Phil was here and it was 1975 again. He would have been revelling in the evening, speculating on motive, on how behaviour was altered and justified by the occasion, and how human action was connected to the turning of a year which mankind had decided to give special significance. Individuals by their million would try to change their lives tonight, and it would all be a function of what Phil called the why question. And yet Phil today was quite different from her friend of 25 years ago, and Carol knew it was she who hadn't really changed.

As Carol was thinking, she was half listening and occasionally joining in conversation with Eric and Rachel. The phrases emerged mechanically and her attention drifted further away. But if her level of engagement became more casual as the evening wore on, this meant her manner relaxed, and she became funnier, the centre of more conversations, even as her mood darkened. The rest of the evening became a depressed blur as Carol incrementally dug her own internal hole. Outwardly she became more raucous, risqué and random, while inwardly she seethed and sulked and sorrowed for the memories lost and moments missed. What were the answers to her own 'why' questions? Why no relationship? Why no change? Why nothing better?

There were still almost three hours till midnight and it was already time to eat and to slow down her drinking. Fortunately, the conversation was starting to move in her direction, with Rachel looking forward to a February break in Florida which allowed Carol to break into her fund of baseball spring training stories. Slowly, she became happier, without quite understanding she had started to bore her audience, who were becoming as disengaged as they had been previously been enthralled by her random banter.

Chapter 39
New York, Friday, 13 April 2001

Philip was riding in a taxi from JFK to a bar on the West Side, where he was due to meet up with Carol. He had hoped to be able to stop by his hotel to drop his bag and grab a shower, but his plane had been late arriving and the queues to get through immigration had been unusually bad, classic Friday 13th.

He hadn't been to New York for a couple of years and hadn't seen Carol since then. Both gaps were inexcusable. The purpose of his visit was to tie up some contracts but that wasn't until the Monday, and Michelle had suggested he fly out on the Friday and spend the weekend in New York. It was 8pm New York time, 1am in Britain, but he felt great, well set up for the evening. The flight over had been bumpier and slower than usual. He had eaten and drunk well, and enjoyed watching Gladiator, fascinated by Russell Crowe, who seemed a classic throwback to another age of Hollywood star.

When he had spoken to Carol on the phone the weekend before, she had been openly depressed still about last November's election. Philip thought she would have gotten over it by now – he himself had become more apolitical over the years – but since the New Year, she had become increasingly bitter about the Supreme Court decision that had handed Florida to Bush.

Carol had been enthusiastic about meeting up. She had missed him, his wry commentary on the world. Left to herself, she often took life more seriously than was healthy, and while she had good friends, there was no one else with whom she had so much uninterrupted history. She had found it odd that Philip wanted to meet in an upmarket cocktail bar. It wasn't the sort of place she went these days, and she had always found them soulless. She had just finished her first beer when she spotted Philip at the door. Carol waved him over and the two embraced. She ordered, and they immediately fell into talking as if they had seen each other the previous week.

"So why did you want to meet here?" she asked after a while.

"Well, I'm meeting here on Monday, and they're always going on about how great it is, so I thought it would be useful to visit briefly beforehand. But I've seen enough, and from what this guy said, the longer we stay here the bigger the chance of running into him. Do you know anywhere local where we can eat as well as drink? I'm starving."

"Yea, sure, there's a new Italian place a couple of blocks from here. Come on, I'll help carry your stuff."

"Sounds perfect, let's go."

Carol and Philip picked up a bag each and left, with only a couple of backward glances. Ten minutes later, they were settled at a table with a couple of gins in front of them and a carafe of red wine on its way.

"I reckon we both got spoilt when we were young and working together. And then you went and took that job back in the UK."

"Yes, but my career here had stalled, and it was the right thing at the time. To be honest, I only thought I'd be gone a couple of years – you know that – but the job took off and I met Michelle."

"Don't give me that career thing, Phil," Carol joked, "you and I both know it was all about the sex."

"Well, I'm glad to see you ain't changed much. How you been anyway, how's your love life since we're on the subject?"

"Oh, I get by okay, but, you know, nothing serious."

"Why don't you get back with Danny? He's always been the man for you."

"Man, we two are way past all that. I'm just proud we managed to bring up such a great daughter. And I'm massively proud of Danny as well. So many athletes fail to make that transition well, and he's just worked so hard to build that second career."

"But why don't you get back together? You've done the child rearing bit; the commitment side of it would be way different now."

"Maybe, but we've both made our decisions, and we're doing fine as we are."

Philip looked at his friend, "Okay, I'll let it be... Tell me what it's like with Dubya as president."

"Phil, it made me so mad that election, you remember, I could hardly speak to you on the phone. I've been angry for so long but in the end you just have to get on with life. I'll always believe we were robbed of that election, not the Democrats but African Americans. All those Black people down in Florida simply got their votes taken away, and I'll bet you anything it wouldn't have happened if they were White voters that had them hanging chads. Anyway, he's been pretty bad but could probably have been worse. He's no president, if you know what I mean, but so far he hasn't screwed too much up. Your guy seems a bit too keen on him, I thought Blair was better'n that."

"Well, that's an interesting question. So did I, to be honest, but the British politician's obsession with the special relationship seems to be blind to any kind of ideological difference. Blair's way more left wing and liberal than Bush, but it doesn't seem to matter. Though I guess the same applies in reverse the other way – why does Bush seem so friendly with such a socialist?"

"Oh, that's simple, it's because he knows he can have it both ways and screw you whenever he wants. He'll do business with the French and Germans, but he knows they'll occasionally get pissed with him. You guys are just lap dogs – not just Blair but every British PM since Churchill. Sure, he'll spend time with you, but he knows he can piss you off and you'll just get nicer to him – it's just part of your DNA, and so he'll spend time with you but won't inconvenience himself. And I guess the main plus is that he knows you'll always be on our side in a war, no matter how crazy it is. Just look at Libya and Grenada in the '80s – we pretty much walked all over you and it was all fine. And that was when it was Reagan and Thatcher, who actually liked each other. Go figure!"

"You should come and visit us properly sometime, you know. Michelle would love you, and it's a crime the two of you haven't met."

"Yea, I know, but there never seems to be as much time as there was when I was younger. And besides, when you guys get good at sport, I'll have a reason to come visit."

Philip laughed, "What about Sydney?"

"Oh, come on, Phil, you know as well as I do; sure it was a whole lot better than Atlanta, it was still 10th. Atlanta was just appalling for a country that pretends to take sport seriously. So now you've hauled yourself up to somewhere in the middle of the second tier, but look at who's ahead of you? Dutch! Korea! And that's before you even get to France, Germany, Australia. Okay, so I guess the US, China and Russia are beyond reach but why shouldn't the UK be next?"

"You mean 4th?"

"Why not? You have a lot of these sports as part of your culture, you care about sport generally, you have a decent sized population, and at last you're investing to a decent level. Why are you laughing again?"

"Only because you're so wonderfully predictable about this stuff. You'd go down terribly in London dinner parties, but they'd love you for it."

"How do you mean?"

"Well, partly it would be that you're a worldly and articulate African American, and parts of North London would see themselves as your spiritual home, and partly because you'd just charm their asses off! Anyway, tell me more about the election. From the outside it just seemed weird that Gore didn't even win his home state. I mean, he used to be senator for Tennessee, and if he'd just won that, even though it's only a couple of electoral votes or whatever, then Florida wouldn't have mattered."

"Yea, he sure ran a lousy campaign, and you're right, I don't know really what happened in Tennessee except maybe that he'd been vice president for eight years and maybe he just took it a bit too much for granted. But the Conservatives basically just set their media attack dogs on him while Bush pretended to know nothing about it. Fox News just killed him."

"That's Murdoch, you know he also owns lots of media assets in the UK, as well as in Asia and Australia?" Carol nodded.

"But the Sun came out for Blair in '97, didn't it?"

"Yes, but only really because it was so obvious Labour were going to win. They'll almost certainly come out for him again for the same reason."

"Is Blair going to get in again then?"

"Almost certainly, though I think a lot of the enthusiasm has gone from four years ago."

"What's with all the Foot and Mouth thing that's been making the news over here?"

"It's a bit like a medieval plague. Large parts of the countryside have been out of bounds and tens of thousands, maybe more, cattle have been killed and incinerated – mass burning, with huge pyres of smoke rising across areas like the Lake District; it's terrible really. The country's been in a state of emergency for weeks, the election's been postponed and so on."

"Is it anyone's fault?"

"Not really, it spread incredibly fast, and I don't think the contingency plans had been updated. But to be honest, I think it's just one of those things. It's probably hit tourism more than the farmers in the long run."

"Didn't you have some petrol thing going on last fall as well?"

"Oh that, yes, I think that was worse, in some ways. I think it's the only time the Conservatives have been ahead in the opinion polls but it didn't last very long."

"Yea, I can see the political side of that, but you said the enthusiasm has gone; the two things you've talked about are pretty much one-offs."

"It's hard to pinpoint but I think a lot of it is the simple attrition of being in government. They tried to keep it simple most of the time but they also trumpeted what they called an 'ethical foreign policy', and cheap rhetoric like that was always going to come a cropper."

"Where does Vietnam fit in that universe?"

"Vietnam was different, because you guys were already there and your kids were dying, so the rhetoric was far from cheap, and even in 1968 you could see you probably wouldn't win the war."

"So, would Kennedy have taken us out?"

"Probably, but not really for what you would call ethical reasons, or not just that anyway. Mostly, he'd have taken you out because he was smart enough to realise it was good politics. But I think he'd have taken some big hits in withdrawing the troops and essentially abandoning South Vietnam to the VC. Even five years later, when you did withdraw, there were plenty on the Right arguing the war was still there to be won."

"God, but you're a cynical bastard."

"I hope not," replied Philip. "If there's one good thing I learned from Alistair Cooke, it's that the essence of democracy – and maybe your democracy in particular – is that you have to take folks with you. Sometimes you can lead them in a direction they're not sure about, but you'd better hope they're not too far behind you."

"Those were crazy times back then. I was trying to start up as a freelancer, covering the Mets and whatever else I could think of to write about, mostly track and field. And then, after I hitched out West to catch the US trials at Echo Summit, I managed to persuade SI to pay my fare down to Mexico City. Man, it all seems so easy now but it's the longest hours I've ever worked; there was just so much going on."

"I remember meeting you for the first time in that dive bar in Mexico City just after Tommie Smith and John Carlos had been sent home. I still don't think I've ever seen you as mad as you were that night."

"I can't have been that mad – you're White and I remember managing to be quite civil to you."

"Yeah, I remember thinking that, though it helped I was British, very drunk and younger than you."

"True, but they'd slaughtered thousands of kids in the streets just before, we were still in Vietnam with thousands of brothers getting killed, Dr King and Bobby Kennedy had both been shot; hell, what wasn't there to be mad about?"

"I know, when I first came over I was expected to be home again by Easter, either because there wasn't enough to do or because I had managed to fall out with Alistair Cooke."

"You were 18 or something and had only just gotten yourself laid." Even after all these years, Philip blushed but Carol wasn't paying attention and, shaded by the restaurant's lighting, it remained hidden. "But once you got going, there was no stopping you."

"I think I just got a sun tan, and somehow went from someone who didn't know how to ask a girl out to someone who didn't have to. It was weird." He shrugged.

"You know, I kinda have really good memories of that time and yet it's then everything really started to go wrong. Suddenly, for me, having fought so hard to be able to vote, there was no one to vote for. I remember just being so mad when Dr King was murdered, for a while I just thought America was evil. Have you ever read 'The Fire Next Time' by James Baldwin?" Philip nodded, "Well, I felt just like that, and for a day I was out rioting with the brothers."

"Then what happened?"

"Well, I don't exactly know. Part of it was that I wasn't too good at rioting. And I ended up deciding I was better at writing than I was at rioting and that was what I ought to be doing. But not writing for fun, writing with anger and passion and seriousness. Even though it was sports, I needed to be able to look my sisters and brothers in the eye and say to them I was doing my part in the best way I knew how, using the thing I was good at. And I guess the other thing was that I didn't hate White folk, could never bring myself to do it. Just couldn't get out of my mind those White college students who'd come down to Mississippi. And then there was sport, of course. I wanted to write about Lou Brock and Bob Gibson and Lew Alcinder, and, yes, Tommie Smith. But I still think Sandy Koufax and Tom Seaver were cool as well, and that Jim Ryun was the bravest runner I've ever seen. And sport was also a place where ultimately colour didn't matter shit."

"You should write all this down sometime, you've a story to tell that's about more than you."

"No, thanks for saying it, but no, I always promised myself my writing would be about sport and athletics. If I can write, and that's what I'm good at, then great, but I swore a long time ago I would never make myself the subject. Anyway, just 'cause you like listening to me ranting on doesn't mean shit. After 35 years, you're pretty much brainwashed anyway."

"You know, it feels funny being back here this time. The last few times I've been back, it always felt like I could revert to the life I used to live. It felt like a positive choice not to do so. But this time, I feel totally different."

"Finally you've grown up, Phil, the Lord be praised, hallelujah!"

"It's only taken me half a century!"

"Coming from Mississippi, I still feel a long way from home, though I know people from the Midwest who say they knew they were home when they hit Boston; you know, artistic types, not like us."

"I guess it's all personal. I felt like I pretty much grew up here. I was 18 when I arrived, but to be honest, I was a pretty young 18, or at best unevenly mature. The one thing going for me was a certain rash bravery. I didn't know what the hell was going on but just got on with it, and found some way of getting through it."

"Funny, I always imagined you'd done a whole load of preparation in advance."

"No, I've always really just winged a load of things. I always reckoned it was worth testing myself, and I guess at the beginning people were willing to cut me a bit of slack. And then, later on, I suppose I just got good at dealing with different situations, making the most of it when I knew stuff and covering up when I didn't." Philip had a sheepish little boy grin.

"You mean it, don't you? Boy, but you were a smooth bastard all those years. Well, you sure put on a great show of being the consummate pro. I always had you down for doing hours of homework and prep on the quiet and then just living the rest of your life in the fast lane. The only thing I wondered about was when you got time to sleep."

"Well, I was down to four hours a night at one stage but somehow I just coped."

"They were great days though. Sorry, I'm getting sentimental but you know what I'm talking about."

"It's okay, I'm as much a product of the late 60s as you are. I'm a Liberal even, in a way the US seems to have forgotten about. You used to have a liberal majority here; it was disparate and contradictory in some ways, but it existed and it achieved a hell of a lot. Then it stopped, or went to sleep or something. I've never made up my mind whether it somehow decided, about the time of the Roe-v-Wade, it had gotten almost all of what it wanted, or whether it just grew up, settled down and became selfish."

"You know what I think it was – we just ran out of energy, just ran dry, or got killed. Non-Americans, even honorary ones like you, can't ever really appreciate how damaging Vietnam was to our psyche. Ever since Washington and Jefferson, we'd always been the good guys. Because of Lincoln, we even got away with slavery, for God's sake. Even African Americans in the Deep South, disenfranchised and kept in poverty, always believed in the American dream. But Vietnam stripped a lot of that away. When Muhammad Ali said no Vietcong had ever called him nigger, it rang a lot of bells. Right from when that Buddhist monk immolated himself in the street, right from Mai Lai and right from the secret carpet bombing of Laos and Cambodia. As an American, it was all but impossible after then to claim any kind of moral authority, no matter how liberal you were. And that's before we even get to Watergate."

"Do you remember Kent State?"

"Of course, I do."

"But do you remember where you were when you heard?"

"Not exactly," said Carol.

"I do. I was in a bar in Pittsburgh; I'd been doing a story on the Pirates, great club at the time – Clemente, Willy Stargell etc., but who lost 3 zip to the Reds in the NL play-offs. Well, it came on, and you remember how scary the footage was? Well, about half the bar cheered and a couple of guys shouted something about hippie draft dodgers. And I didn't say a word, just stared into my drink and tried not to cry. And I never cry, but that's the closest I came."

"Why didn't you say anything?"

"I don't know. I really don't. I can come up with all kinds of reasons – I was more sad than angry, responding with anger and violence, maybe, would have been counter to the whole idea of peaceful resistance – but the most obvious reason is that I was scared. Like I say, I don't know the answer, I mean that, but I've always worried about it."

"I think you should have called them on it but then it's my fight not yours, and we're no nearer winning it now than we were 30 years ago. Then again it was probably a White bar, and I wouldn't have been in there in the first place."

"Okay, you're right about that last bit; but I do think it's my fight as well, and not just because I lived here so long."

"Nah, you're just being a European Liberal. This was, is, an American thing. We've got to learn to be what we say we are but why was Kent State such a big deal for you?"

"I think it had been building up since I'd been here and it felt like a dam trying to burst. When Martin Luther King was shot, I was still scared about not doing my job; and when Bobby Kennedy was shot, I was so close to it that I just switched into reporter mode. Chicago was the same. But those four people killed at Kent State somehow brought it all together for me."

"I don't know, most of the time I think that there wasn't much we could have actually changed that would have made the result any better. America wasn't ready to get out of Vietnam before it was forced out."

"Yea, but you know what? Even now, I still think real change is doable."

Carol laughed. "If only I'd known 30 years ago how sentimental you were, I would have had a hell of a lot more fun."

"Why do you think I kept it hidden?"

"Because you were getting laid, that's why. You didn't have time to get all emotional unless you were in some redneck bar in Pittsburgh."

Chapter 40
London, Saturday, 12 January 2008

"I was only 13 but I remember that picture of the earth from space."

"I was 23 and I remember watching Soviet tanks rolling into Prague and realising the world was getting smaller."

"So why was it so important?" asked Michelle.

"I'll answer first," said Carol, "then Phil can have a go. The most important things to me were all civil rights related. Obviously, Dr King's assassination but also Vietnam, because there were a lot of young brothers being conscripted to die out there, and then there were the Black Power salutes of Tommy Smith and John Carlos in Mexico. Those things were crucial to me as an African American."

"I hate to be agreeing with Carol, but I do on the '68 stuff," said Philip. "But also, '68 was a long way from being like '89/'90, when the Cold War ended and all those Soviet Bloc dictatorships came crashing down. There was no Berlin Wall moment or Velvet Revolution in '68. So, even with all the excitement, a lot of what '68 was about for me was a dull feeling of failure and disappointment. And the Democrats basically fell apart."

The three of them were sitting in Pulcinella's in Soho, and pizzas were being constructed in front of them; the dough flattened on the marble topped counter, then spun and flipped in the air by young Italian men in tight white shirts, muscles bulging, the ingredients distributed generously, and then the pizzas shovelled up and slid into the oven behind.

"Was it like Labour after '79?" asked Michelle.

"No, I don't think so," said Philip. "The SDP appeared before I moved back to Britain but from what I heard, and from what I could see after I returned, what happened was quite different."

Carol nodded. "One of the reasons, and Philip knows this better than me, the Democrats split is because LBJ, by pushing through civil rights legislation, fatally weakened the FDR coalition. Since then, only Carter and Clinton, both governors of Southern States, have managed to recreate it."

"What do you think of Obama?" asked Philip.

"To be honest, I'm not sure yet. He's hard for me to read. I'm from Mississippi and he's from Chicago, via Malaysia and Hawaii or wherever. And the Clintons have always been trusted by Black people. And Hilary's a smart woman, and having just taken New Hampshire, I suspect she'll go on to win it. Personally, I haven't made up my mind yet; I'm just glad we have two good candidates. Anyway, weren't you supposed to have your own election last October?"

"Yes," said Philip, "but Brown bottled it at the last minute, and so I suspect we'll go all the way through now to May 2010, which is the last date they can have it. You know we don't have fixed terms here, so the prime minister can call an election more or less when he wants to."

"And because he's new and behind in the polls, he'll hang on now as long as he can, hoping he'll get more popular."

"That's just about it. I suppose he reckons if the government can sort out the Northern Rock mess and stop us going into recession, then there's a good chance of scraping through. It feels like it's on a knife edge though."

"Well, I'm no judge of this shit but there's starting to be a hell of a lot of empty houses back home, and I assume somebody pretty much has to be losing money on them."

"I was sure he could have won in October," added Michelle, "as far as anyone can tell, he was about to call an election, then changed his mind at the last minute."

"I'm just an American but that doesn't sound great."

"It's okay," said Philip, "if the polls are any guide, British voters agree with you."

"And this was the guy who pretty much agreed with Blair not to run on the basis he'd be next in line, and has then waited ten years as your treasury secretary. And now he can't make up his mind."

"I guess that's what it looks like."

"Still, look on the bright side," said Philip, "Cameron's a long way from your hated Maggie."

"Maybe," said Michelle, "but not necessarily all in a good way. I just see him as a Tory who's good at pretending he cares about things like the environment and the NHS. If he gets a majority, the Tory Right will start demanding tax cuts and all those silky words will go up in smoke. As far as I can see, he's never really stood up to them or anything: not on Europe, not for women on constituency short lists, nothing."

"But wasn't Blair like that?"

"Not really... Like him or not, and I never really did, he got rid of Clause 4 and faced down the Left of the Labour Party quite a lot. No more than Smith and Kinnock did, but an awful lot more than Cameron has ever done with his extreme Right wing. If they get a majority, I'll bet you anything they'll be just as ideological as Thatcher was. They're all her children after all."

"Hey, you're a real Socialist firebrand. No wonder you've never been to the US."

"I used to be a lot worse. If you'd known me in the '70s, I was a real true believer – nuclear disarmament, abolition of private medicine, private education, you name it. Mind you, I was considered a moderate in my local Labour Party in Nottingham. But they were very different times, and I suppose I've lost some of my socialism as I've gotten older."

"Well, it pretty much sounds like there's still a fair bit left."

"I like to think so."

"So what changed you? Don't tell me it was Phil's malignant influence?"

Michelle laughed, "He'd like to think so, but actually he's probably more of a socialist deep down, almost an anarchist in some ways, with all his hippie flower power side."

"Hold on there, this is a hard-nosed commercial media executive you're talking about."

"Oh, she's got your number. Man, when I first met him, he was so full of that hippie thing, the whole Summer of Love thing he'd just missed out on, it was a miracle he ever got to write anything."

"I was corrupted by American society."

The pizzas arrived.

"By the way, where's your friend Ed now?"

"Don't really know… I think he's gone back to Afghanistan. Must be strange for him being there again after 25 years. I think we might even have supplied arms to the Taliban back in the '80s."

"Yes, them and Iraq and Iran, and all our other good friends. It's hard now to imagine how wrong headed our foreign policy was under Reagan, or maybe it was just the Cold War in general that could make us look like idiots."

"It would be a real horror show to look back now on the coverage about the Mujahedeen. I think there was even a Bond movie where they're the good guys."

"The Cold War and everything that went with it, I remember thinking of it as just being there," said Michelle.

"If Ed was here," said Philip, "he'd say the real shift was the rise of Islamic extremism, starting with Iran in 1979."

"How do you mean?" asked Carol.

"Well, he's always argued that Moscow was worried about the effect of Islamic extremism in all Russia's Caucasian Republics with large Muslim populations and wanted to make Afghanistan a buffer. And you have to say, given what's happened in Chechnya and the like, there's a fair amount in that."

"Believe it or not, I've got a Russian friend who would agree with much of that, but why've I not heard any of it in public?"

"Well, to start with, you're American, and there's nothing very flattering in there about US foreign policy, nothing about you 'winning' the Cold War. And then there's the broader question of what Islamic fundamentalism really means; no one knows the answers to that, and when that's the case, the media tends to shy away because it's just too difficult."

"Who was that guy who used to talk about the end of history?" asked Michelle. "Fukuyama, that's it!"

"Did someone really write that?" asked Carol, "and did people take him seriously?"

"Oh, yes!" replied Philip. "And I suspect he made a fortune out of it."

"Well, I've never heard of him," Carol grinned, "but then I don't really move in those circles."

"It was back in about 1990, just after the Berlin Wall had come down and there was a lot being written about the end of the Cold War and the dominance of the US as a super power, and Western capitalist democracy as the ultimate form of society. Looking back now, it seems ridiculous but I don't remember many people queueing up at the time to say so. I have to say though, even at the time, Michelle thought it was rubbish."

"It reminded me of some of the Communist stuff I used to listen to in the '70s."

"Well," said Carol, "I'm not going to be letting you near any of my articles any time soon. However, we do need to persuade you to come across to the States sometime soon."

"I'd love to come. Philip's due out there in the autumn to do something around the election, and given I have no commitments here, I was thinking of joining him; but I was hesitating over what I would do out there while he's at work."

"Well, that settles it. I'll take some time off, and I'll also set you up with some people so you get a real proper picture of New York or whatever other city he drops you off in. Heh, this pizza's great by the way. I wasn't expecting anything this good in London."

"Soho's my favourite part of the city," said Philip, "but it's changed a lot on the last 20 years, since I started coming here. It was a lot more run down back then, and apparently it had been a real gangster hangout in the '60s, and full of jazz dens and proper drinking holes back in the '50s. It was also the first place I noticed beggars in the UK, not at first but right at the end of the '80s."

"Well, there's definitely more in the States than here," said Carol, "and with our unemployment rising the way it is, it'll get worse before it gets better."

"But it's not a big thing, is it?" asked Michelle. "I mean, I've seen some things about US house prices, but that sort of thing happens all the time."

"I'm not sure," replied Carol. "Danny, my ex, Althea's father, works for a big US investment bank, and tells me there's still a hell of a lot of nervousness. He says they're calling it the lemon problem – everyone knows there's a lemon out there but, because they don't know who it is, no one wants to do business with anyone else. But no one really knows; Danny says no one can remember anything like it."

"That doesn't sound like anything good, but I wouldn't understand all that banking stuff anyway," Philip said. "Remember that time you tried to explain compound interest to me, Michelle?"

"So you've been keeping him in line financially as well?"

"I'm certainly no expert either, but I was totally horrified when I found out Philip was spending money like water, paying everything on credit and had no idea what was in his bank account."

"Why am I not surprised?"

"I was just putting into practice all the things I'd learned in the US – use the plastic, leverage your income, borrow to the max, all that sort of thing."

"Honestly, Michelle, you've no idea how much you've changed him."

"That's probably true," said Philip. "When I arrived in New York, I had no real knowledge of money. I'd been getting a salary from the Guardian for about nine months, but even in the UK, I had no real idea where to go to buy the basics. So when I got to New York I was even worse, and everyone seemed to be dropping $10 and $20 dollar bills all over the place."

"When you came back, how different was Britain compared to when you left?" asked Carol

"Really quite a lot different. Do you remember that TV sketch – forgot which programme it was on – with John Cleese and the Two Ronnies, about the class system; with Cleese," he turned to Carol, "who's really tall, saying something like 'I'm upper class because I look down on you'; and Ronnie Barker in the middle and normal height, saying 'I'm middle class because I look up to you' and then he turns

403

to Ronnie Corbett, who's short, and says, 'and I look down on you!' Well, that's just about what the class system felt like when I left. There was still a hell of a lot of deference around, though it probably had begun to die."

"And when you came back?"

"When I came back, I'd say maybe 80% of the deference had gone, and there was the start of a new upper class that was far more about money than birth; it was probably in its early days back in '84 but it was really obvious to someone like me, who had spent the previous 15 years in the US. But there was also probably the start of an underclass – loads more unemployment – that hadn't really existed before; and again, that was obvious to me from the US comparison. And when you scratched the surface, there was still quite a lot of the 'Where did you go to school?' and 'Where did you go to university?' Eton and Westminster, Oxford and Cambridge still mean a lot here, but then Exeter and Vassar, Harvard and Yale mean a lot in the US, more than Americans like to think."

"Hang on a minute," laughed Carol, "I kind of agree with you but we're a world away from where you guys are."

"Probably, but not as far as you think. It's been a long time since you had a president with the kind of background Lincoln and Jackson had, or LBJ, and the Bushes are virtual aristocracy. A lot of that's to do with the amount of cash candidates need to raise; but even so, the Clintons and Obamas all have college qualifications as long as your arm."

"Okay, I'll take your word for it, you know a hell of a lot more about American presidents than I know about UK prime ministers. All I can say is that I've never met a British youngster who wants to be prime minister whereas I've met hundreds of US kids who want to be president. That must count for something."

"Okay, I'll give you that," conceded Philip. "All I'm trying to say is that, in the 15 years I was in the States, we made a little progress and your guys maybe went backwards a little."

"The two of you are just amazing," said Michelle. "No wonder you've been friends for 40 years."

"And we're not even doing our party tricks yet. Anyway, before I diverted myself and started arguing with my esteemed former partner over here, I was about to say that the other thing I think had changed was that the distinction between 'Old Money' and 'New Money' had almost disappeared. Or rather, 'Old Money' was running out and was targeting finance as the way to replenish the family coffers. Back in the '60s, banking was uniformly boring, but by the mid-80s, it had become the hot ticket."

"So why do you think that money thing changed?" asked Michelle.

"To be honest, I've not the foggiest," said Phil.

"Neither do I," said Carol "except that Danny used to say it was about then that a lot of banks' businesses started to become international, so that might have had something to do with it."

"Who knows," said Philip, "a lot of things were becoming more international around then. I think that was even part of the sub-plot to the miners' strike, wasn't it? The fact that coal could be imported more cheaply than we could mine it ourselves. We barely have any mining industry at all now, who'd have predicted that in 1984?"

"Arthur Scargill," said Michelle wryly. "He was the union leader who led the strike. But it would have been about the only thing he got right that year."

"Do the two of you still see much of Sam and Mary? I remember really enjoying meeting them that time I came round for dinner, what was it? 2005?"

"They're fine, we see them quite often, maybe every couple of months," said Philip. "Did I ever say Sam was involved in the bombings, the 7/7 ones? He was almost on the bus that exploded. He ran to catch it but didn't make it – what an escape, eh?"

"To be fair, he can't be certain that it was the actual bus," said Michelle, "but he's sure in his own mind that it was. But I shouldn't joke about it; the whole thing was quite a knock to him, and it took a while for him to get back to being his old self."

"Even now I don't think Sam's quite the same as he was before," said Philip, "and I don't necessarily mean in a bad way. For me, he's a bit more fun and spontaneous. Before, I always felt he thought quite carefully before he said anything, now it's as though he cares less. He used to be quite earnest about basically everything; you could have a laugh with him but it wasn't like it was his natural state or anything, whereas now it seems to come more easily to him."

"Interesting you put it like that," said Michelle. "I think Sam has actually become more introverted over the years but in quite a calm, relaxed way, as though he was putting to rest parts of his personality that he felt got him into trouble."

"I can't imagine it's usual for people Sam's age, probably men in particular, to suddenly decide they want to tell the world about themselves. No one I know is rushing to become extroverts. Do you really reckon it was triggered by his experience of the bombings?"

"Well, Michelle clearly doesn't think the difference was as obvious as I do but we both agree there was one," – he glanced over at Michelle, who nodded.

"He goes to the memorial services every year and takes 7th July off work and just wanders around London. He once told me it was like his annual mini-pilgrimage to the sites of the bombs – quite macabre but really important to him."

"Well, I hardly know the guy, but from what you say, it sounds like it changed his life."

"Why do you think that?"

"Partly it's what I said before, that it seems like he's just gone and done an about turn in terms of the way his life was going. I mean here's a guy who was pretty settled and comfortable. And then out of nowhere, he's almost involved in a terrible terrorist attack. I heard what you said about it not being certain he was chasing the same bus that got blown up, but nothing about Sam indicates to me he makes a habit of exaggerating the importance of anything. So, at the very least, we can say that he genuinely believes he was a few yards of foot speed short of catching a bus to his grave. Now from 40 odd years as a sports writer, I can tell you that everyone would like, in an ideal world, to run fast."

"And so?" laughed Philip.

"Okay, I think what I'm trying to say is that at some, I don't know, maybe visceral level, Sam would have really, really wanted to catch that bus, and would have cursed himself when he didn't, so I could see how it might have shaken a lot of Sam's assumptions about the natural order of things."

"Do you really believe that's what he thinks?" asked Philip.

"I've no idea, Phil, but that's what I'd take from it. I'm not surprised it gave him a real knock; would have been weird if it hadn't."

"In which case," said Philip, "it might be that he simply stopped caring about a lot of things."

"That's what I'd guess at," said Carol, "he's simply stopped caring."

"But he's probably the most caring person I've ever met," said Michelle.

"Well, you know him better than me; I was just really thinking out loud," said Carol. "No matter how you look at it though, it sounds like he went through a really traumatising time. Someone I know back home was late for a meeting at the World Trade Center on the morning of 9/11; saw the first plane hit when he should have been inside. He's never really recovered, hasn't been back to work since. If Sam went through even a fraction of what David did, then it's a miracle he's as normal as he is."

Part 7: 2008

Chapter 41
London, Wednesday, 2 April

Sam walked out of the hospital as normally as he could, nodded to the woman in reception who had directed him to the Oncology Department. Outside, it was unseasonably warm and he instinctively reached for his sunglasses. In what he considered an impressively steady and professional voice, he rang work and explained his appointment had been delayed and that he would work at home when he got away rather than coming back into the office.

He wandered around for a while, rather aimlessly. Then, regaining a bit of focus, he found a pub off the main road, bought himself a pint of Broadside and sat at a little wooden table they'd placed just outside on the corner. Sam took his jacket off, got out the newspaper and forced himself to skim through it, including the obituaries. For what time was left him, probably no more than three months, he wanted to remember what had happened on this day, 2nd April 2008. That would take him to the 2nd of July, the third anniversary of Ruth leaving home, of him stubbing his toes. He thought of Mary – how would he tell her? Of Ruth, Ed, Michelle.

Then he thoughts of his parents, his mother, now with Alzheimer's, and his father, whose face was now clearer to him in death than it had been while he was still alive. And now his own race was almost run. Was it really a race? Is that what he'd been doing for the last 52 years? It hadn't really felt like that. In fact, he'd probably tried a bit too hard sometimes not to 'win', or at least not to hurt anyone, anything. What was that Blake phrase – "All that lives is holy"? Is that what he thought? He wasn't sure. If he didn't believe in that, what was it he did believe in? Again, he wasn't sure. Was it as simple as just trying to do the right thing as often as possible? But where did that get him? The right thing for who – himself? Mary and Ruth? His friends? Everyone and everything? Did he really get to decide that? His mind seemed to be going around in circles. Is this what heaven was like? Or hell? Or nothing? Would the memory of his final thought, whatever that turned out to be, somehow be preserved in time because nothing else came after it? No, that was stupid.

Sam took another sip of beer and stared into the middle distance. What would he miss? Everything and nothing was the rather unhelpful answer that came to mind. He would miss being alive, but that was about experiencing things each day, about the rhythms of routine and the repeating freshness of the world. He would obviously miss his family, Mary and Ruth, but it wasn't as if he could love them any more than he did now, or that his relationship with them was going to change radically. Or, if that was the case, he wasn't sure it was what he wanted. Was this boring, conservative in the worst way? Thinking about it, he concluded not. He couldn't see how he could have worked much harder at making his family happy and his relationship with them healthy and, though he hated the word, fulfilling. He could definitely have done things better but he didn't think it was for lack of trying.

Perhaps this painless fore-knowledge of the end, which modern medicine offered as a service, was a late 20th century invention. Prior knowledge of death was as old as humanity but usually presented itself either as visions or as unbearable pain. These days, visions seemed less common and unbearable pain largely nullified by drugs. Instead, breaking the news – as it was called – was at the sharp end of good bedside manner, or in this case an over-the-table explanation of test results. The consultant had done it well and sensitively though, not too abrupt but not keeping him hanging on either. As a consequence, he had been able to react in a more or less controlled way – not too shocked, either in the sense of being struck dumb, or of ranting loud imprecations against random deities.

Sam laughed internally, almost without bitterness, partly at himself, partly at the situation. He had tried, as far as possible, to control his life, not that anyone really appreciated this. And yet here he was, with the greatest uncontrollable fact of all having come to rest on his shoulder. But he wasn't really surprised. Life expectancy might now comfortably exceed three score and ten, but that figure was a median as much as a mean; there was no regular bell curve tightly clustered around the average.

And then, as he took another sip, his sensation of the taste took him back to the beer he had bought almost three years ago, to steady himself after the realisation that he had almost caught the bus that was blown up. His head started to shake ever so slightly, as it had done then, when only his lack of will power had saved his life. His mouth wasn't as dry as it had been that scorching hot day, but the beer itself suddenly tasted identical, and that same overwhelming sensation of helpless uncertainty washed over him. His nerves tingled and, as he had then, he felt energised in the slipstream of fate, liberated by his impotence. This sensation, which had burned white hot that day in 2005, had cooled since but had never completely left him. Now it burned again, cleansing his body, down to its entrails, of social guilt, embarrassment and hesitation.

Seen through this lens, Ed became pivotal, his true barometer of worth. Since they had first met, Sam had forever been in awe of his wisdom. This was a shock to him for he had always seen himself as ferociously independent. He had always taken his lead from Ed, but until this moment, the fact of it had not really crossed his mind. The straightjacket of expectation, his own expectation, meant that he had never considered such dependence.

Thoughts were flashing across his mind with increasing velocity, uninhibited by barriers of expectation. Was this, he wondered, the sort of fertile thinking young children indulged in before the cautioning hand of experience and the self-limiting development of individual identity combined to prescribe and proscribe in equal measure? And where did Mary and Ruth fit in? Was 'fit in' still a relevant term? Sam felt devoted to them, unconditionally so. But he was so devoted because they were his family. He loved Mary, but not in the same way he had loved her 25 years ago. He loved Ruth, but not in the same way he had when she was born. Now she was an independent woman with her own life. Did the same distinction apply to him in their eyes? He didn't know but thought it might. Did he mind? Not really, and didn't think he had the right to. He suspected he thought about Mary more often than she did about him; certainly, he rang her more often. The same applied to Ruth; indeed, he would have been disappointed in her if it was otherwise.

He was starting to think, oddly but encouragingly, that his life had reached quite a neat hiatus. He would much rather carry on living, but if this sort of delayed termination was to be his fate, there were far worse times it might have happened. His dad had already passed away and his mum's Alzheimer's was so advanced that his own passing was unlikely to register, let alone cause distress. He had no financial dependants; his daughter was grown up; his wife was financially independent and, he imagined, would easily be able to find another partner when she chose to.

'Did people mourn anymore?' he wondered. Well, clearly not in the 19th century sense, but most people still seemed to go through a grieving process if a close family member died. But life would move on and perhaps these days, there was more 'choice' – if that was the right word – about how long to mourn. And also, probably, more reminders – photos and videos – of the deceased. But there was also potentially much more to look forward to.

By now a chill was entering the air as the sun began to dip towards the horizon and the breeze picked up. Sam decided to move inside for a last drink before heading home to sit down with Mary and, he supposed, work out how to tell Ruth. He got his pint and decided to sit at the bar. A group of six were sat around a table in the middle of the pub. Between them, they had three large dogs; a chocolate Labrador, what looked like a small white Alsatian – maybe two thirds normal size – and a large black and white Greyhound. The Labrador and the Alsatian were lying on the floor, both tethered to a thin column. They were continually wrestling with each other; the smaller Alsatian usually the aggressor as the Labrador rolled over on its back, seemingly pretending to open itself to attack. It was clearly a familiar ritual with a good deal of mock biting, conducted entirely in silence – neither barked, growled, nor whimpered once. Meanwhile, the Greyhound was totally uninvolved and peaceful, almost statuesque. Occasionally, somewhat incongruously, this large dog would try and climb on its owner's lap.

Bizarrely, having not heard it for about 20 years, Peter Sarstedt's 'Where Do You Go to My Lovely' came on the jukebox. Hearing it took him back to an evening in 1978, sitting in the Porcupine on Charing Cross Road. He was with Michelle, and they had just been to see *Saturday Night Fever* in Leicester Square. The lyrics of loss had stuck in his mind. They'd fallen into talking about the fight they'd come across and broken up the summer before in Nottingham. Michelle said she'd always thought he'd been brave breaking it up. It had never really occurred to him. He'd seen both the boys around the estate since he was young and, somehow, in the way boys do, he knew neither of them was particularly scary or violent. He'd begun trying to explain this to Michelle but her eyes had started to glaze over and he had changed the subject. He thought Michelle would probably miss him as much as anyone. He found her strange sometimes, but they'd known each other longer than anyone else.

He could feel his anger building again, his frustration that he was seemingly being punished for something he could not comprehend. Maybe it was for the sin of not trying hard enough, for not being on that bus three years ago, not having run fast enough. He had thought about it every day since. What was it really that had stopped him from running harder? Was it his toe? The heat of the sun even so early in the day? Some premonition? As a result, he knew he had become less confident, but also less constrained by others' opinions. No one had really noticed, except Mary, of course.

Why did he have to die now? Why couldn't he be one of those who lived comfortably into their 80s? He did reasonable exercise for his age; he'd always been quite active; he'd not smoked ever, or drunk much since he was about 30. He'd always been an intellectual atheist but an emotional agnostic. He wanted there to be something worthwhile beyond death, but was irrationally angry at the thought that what was happening to him was any more than a lottery.

Sam stared blankly but still self-consciously into what remained of his pint. As fast as he had become angry, he became calm. Practicality began to kick in, and he started preparing for what lay ahead of him; going home, telling Mary and phoning Ruth, then telling others. His money affairs were okay, he thought, but he would need to check. His pension and life insurance would be fine and the house was only a couple of years from the end of the mortgage.

He finished his drink and left the pub. Flagging down a cab, he got in and gave his address. Opening the paper, he tried to concentrate, but could only really take in the headlines. Occasionally, he glanced out at the people, houses, shops, streets of North London. Eventually, the cab pulled up at his home. Consciously keeping himself together, he got out, paid and went up to his front door, fished out his keys, turned the lock and went in.

***

She had suspected it was pancreatic cancer, had looked up the symptoms on the Web; they had been vague but she had felt it. She had kept silent, only making sure he went to his GP and asked to be referred. There was that self-contained part of him that she had never really tried to reach. She had a private space and was pleased Sam had one too. She didn't want to encroach.

Mary hadn't really known what reaction she expected from Sam. Rightly or wrongly, she feigned surprise when he walked in and broke the news. The alternative just seemed inconceivable. He had clearly been drinking, which Mary hadn't expected. She thought he would have come straight home, but he wasn't drunk, which was a relief. He also seemed relatively calm, and although she was pleased he had already thought through some of the implications, Mary couldn't help feeling a tinge of regret that he had done so without her. She had thought long and hard about how she would help him through what lay ahead, and had steeled herself for the pain she would need to go through to help her husband.

The prospect of Sam's absence was buffeting her in an unexpected way. Rather than the sense of emptiness Mary had identified with grieving, she had experienced a succession of almost physical stabs of pain. It might be something mundane like transferring the laundry – his clothes – from washing machine to dryer, or something more personal like squeezing out the ice cubes to make a gin and tonic. Sometimes it made her wince, once she had to sit down, other times it brought a tear. Always it hurt, and always, whether Sam was there or not, she had to hide it, retain her composure.

Not in a rush, but slowly, these trigger sensations acted in combination as a catalyst to revive memories of Sam when she first knew him. Then, before marriage

412

and family, he had been bright and ambitious, eager to change the world. She hadn't believed him, of course, but she had loved his tenacity. These recollections came to her not with any special fondness, but rather with a slow surprise at how much Sam had altered. Sam was still Sam, but not the same Sam she had fallen for. Was he less than he had been? Mary thought not, but the question scared her slightly, particularly now that the clock of his mortality was visible, ticking down fast. No, she decided, almost confidently, he was not less than he had been, and in some ways he was maybe more. Now, however, he gave to others constantly.

Had she seen this when she married him? Mary was bound to confess that she hadn't. No, she had married the smart civil servant who was both worldly and intellectual, who gave her a route into a different world while being credible in her own. And she had loved him also. He made her laugh, she liked making love to him, still, and she could hardly conceive what going to sleep would be like without him lying next to her. Mary's mind struggled between the agonising importance of the next few weeks and months, and the years without Sam that already seemed to be stretching ahead.

***

When Sam told her the news she already knew, Mary wanted to hold him tight for a long time, to start the process of helping him come to terms with it. Instead, he didn't seem to want to be held, and wanted instead to explain to her what he had already thought about, the things he had already decided. Mary, in all her preparation for this moment, had envisaged it as a time when their life temporarily slowed down while they planned their last few months together. Yet it seemed Sam already wanted their life to speed up. And since it was his life that was the focus, Mary was unwilling to struggle against the, for once, implacable will of her husband.

Together, they rang Ruth in Manchester. Then Sam said he wanted to go out for a short walk to think everything through a bit more. Mary almost bridled at this. Every time she had thought about it, this period had involved them bonding even closer together. She was horrified that, perversely, almost rudely, he seemed for the first time to be excluding her from his thinking and his decisions. But she could not argue with him when he had so little time left. And so she sacrificed her vision of their togetherness and settled for carrying out his wishes. It was as if Sam's nature, and therefore the character of their relationship, had shifted in an instant. He had become much more decisive and, as a consequence, suddenly thoughtless of the feelings of others; specifically her, or so it seemed.

***

Ruth was in the Crown when her phone rang. She saw it was her parents and answered, as she always did. "Hi there, what's up? Are you out somewhere enjoying yourselves?"

"Hello, Ruth," said Mary. "No, we're at home. Listen, have you got a minute to talk?"

"Yes, of course," she replied. "Just wait a moment and I'll pop outside." Something had obviously happened but Ruth didn't feel bothered; her parents were always investing significance in the strangest things. She picked up her drink, signalled to the others and walked outside into the damp evening air, the breeze blowing wisps of hair across her eyes. "Hello, I'm out now; what's up?"

"Hi, Ruth," it was her dad's voice. "I'm afraid there's no easy way to say this but I've been to the hospital today. I've had some tests a couple of weeks ago – and, anyway, they told me I have pancreatic cancer, terminal I'm afraid; it's very advanced and aggressive and they've only given me a few months; and, anyway, I thought you should know first. I didn't want to be saying this over the phone but Mary persuaded me it was the... Ruth? Are you there?" His voice broke ever so slightly.

"Yes, Dad, I'm here... How are you, apart from the obvious I guess? Oh Dad, I'm rubbish at this... How's Mum, how are you both?" Without waiting for an answer, she added, "Listen, don't wait up for me, but I'm coming down tonight; just put the key in the normal place."

Later, on the coach down the M6, after quietly weeping for a long time, Ruth forced a smile that she'd managed to stay so calm. Almost as she'd put down the phone, she felt a void opening up below her, a gash across her existence. All her unspoken assumptions about accompanying her dad into gentle old age, about seeing him play with his grandchildren, had fallen into the hole. She was relieved she hadn't broken down on the phone but she did immediately after. Somehow, she had persuaded the others to let her go down to London that night and to get her to the coach station, put her on the bus. Her eyes finally wept dry, she thought back through the phone call. Her dad had sounded almost normal. How hard had that been for him? What did it mean? Had he given up? She loved Dad so much – at that moment, it seemed like she loved him more than anyone else, more than her mum, more than Pete. But she worried that he was taking the probable as the absolute, that he was somehow shying away from a small chance that he could beat the cancer and survive. If that was the case, and she was almost sure it was, clinging to the apparent logic of it, then she could make him fight harder. She remembered all the times he had got her to do things she didn't think she was able to do. And she could recall many of the subtle psychological tricks he had used. Ruth determined she would find a way to put the boot on the other foot this time.

She began to doze, her mind flitting back to rewind memories of Dad when she was growing up. Him turning up to collect her from 18th birthday parties and pretending not to notice how drunk she was, seeing her off on the first day of secondary school, visiting his office and feeling the warmth directed towards her because of him.

She thought back to her childhood, vividly, in Technicolor, even as she drifted in and out of sleep. When the coach finally pulled into Victoria Station, Ruth jumped straight into a taxi. When it stopped outside home, and she had paid and got out, walked down the path and found the key, the door opened and Sam was standing there. He hugged her.

***

Michelle hadn't been home when Philip took Mary's call. When she came in just after 10pm, he called that he was in the kitchen and would she like a drink.

"Just tea," she replied.

A couple of minutes later, when she had just sat down in the living room, Philip walked in with her tea but on a tray with a bottle of whisky, and three glasses, one of which contained ice. Michelle looked up at him quizzically. "Just in case," he muttered. Philip sat down and paused, uncharacteristically so. Very deliberately, he poured a small and a large glass of Glenfiddich, put two cubes of ice in the small one and slid it slowly across the table towards her.

Confused – silence and alcohol had never gone together – Michelle felt herself tense up. As she cupped the glass, she suddenly stood on a five-metre springboard, looking down at the water unfeasibly far below and seeing in the pool nothing but the promise of pain.

"Well?" she mustered a smile, "What's with the melodrama, dearest?"

"I'm afraid there's no way of making this easy… Mary rang when you were out; Sam's got pancreatic cancer, very advanced and aggressive; he's been told it's incurable; they've given him three months. I'm so sorry… I know how close you've always been." He paused, looked at her, then slowly drained his glass and poured himself another.

Michelle felt her belly smash into the flat sheet of the swimming pool, exploding into pain beyond what she had ever contemplated. She couldn't find a word, couldn't have spoken it if she had. Her hand began to shake. She tried to control it, forcing the glass to her mouth, forcing her suddenly parched mouth to swallow as the glass shivered against her teeth. Her stomach was still exploding. She leaned forward with the glass still in her mouth, not trusting herself to let go, the rim now clenched between her teeth.

"How long did you say?" Michelle half-gasped, half-whispered, still reeling as the pain convulsed her insides. By turns nauseous and on the verge of fainting, she fought for control of herself.

Philip was now over on the sofa, holding her tight. "About three months they told him. I'm so sorry, I'm tearing up inside myself. I thought we'd always be laughing and talking to him and Mary. Mary was in tears on the phone; she was fine to start with and then broke down. I can't begin to imagine how she's coping; she adores him so much."

"Does she?" Michelle almost silently asked herself. She'd always somehow seen them as slightly semi-detached; in love and all that but not indispensable to each other. But Phil was always right about these things. This diversion, disloyal as it was, was the catalyst for Michelle's physical recovery, and slowly but discernibly the tide of pain receded, creating slivers of space for her mind to initiate its own odyssey through the realisation that sometime soon Sam wouldn't be there.

"Yes, of course," replied Philip. "She's always been utterly devoted to him. She'll be lost when he's gone. It's such a shock."

"I always imagined it was the other way round. Oh poor Ruth as well…" Michelle suddenly remembered. "Does she know?"

"Yes, she's on her way back from Manchester."

"What sort of cancer is it? Did Mary give any more details?"

"It's cancer of the pancreas but I don't really know any more. Partly, Mary was too messed up and she had other people to call. She said Sam had been really calm to start with, then angry, madder than she'd ever seen him. He'd gone out for a walk but had calmed down enough first to tell Mary she could ring us and a few others."

"Somehow he'll pull himself together. Can I have a drink? I don't think I'll drop it now." She forced a laugh. Philip half-filled the tumbler and then topped it up with ice.

"Why Sam of all people?" He passed Michelle the drink. She took a long sip, her eyes squeezed shut. "Of all the people... If I'd believed in God, I would have stopped today, I think."

"It's not that simple though, is it?" Michelle said quietly. She took another deep sip. "Sam's life will be what it will be; same for all of us. I saw so many people die when I was a nurse; having a good innings as they put it isn't really about age."

Michelle was beginning to think more clearly, the whisky providing an alternative sensation to the pain, diluting its focus as well as anesthetising its impact. When she thought of Sam, she was already starting to cast her mind back across the half century she had known him. She took another drink and shut her eyes tight, gripped Philip harder with her left arm.

When she later, much later, sought to explain her revelation, it would always take her much longer than the event itself took in real time. As she came to describe it to herself, it was like running through sheet after sheet of thin gauze, with an increasingly defined but complex picture waiting on the other side. By the time the final one had been brushed aside, Michelle felt as if out of breath. But the sheer clarity of the images that confronted her took her breath away. Simultaneously, as in a split-screen film, she was three-year-old playing on the carpet of her parent's council house, a 12-year-old walking home from school in the rain, a 19-year-old going up on the train to Manchester for the weekend, and a 48-year-old welcoming people to a dinner party. Sam was in each scene, the ever-present feature of her external and internal life. And that life, previously divided into neatly laid out categories, now seemed connected. But then it had all begun to dissolve into the middle distance.

"I want to go to bed," Michelle murmured to Philip some time later. "It's just too much for me at the moment. I can't take it in. There's no point ringing Sam and Mary tonight, not with Ruth coming home and everything. He's only my age; I still can't quite believe it." Then she turned her tear-glistened face up towards Philip. "Thanks, Phil," she almost smiled. "Thanks for realising how hard this would be for me and doing your best to make it bearable. It reminds me again why I love you so much. Can you help me up the stairs? My head needs a pillow and I need to do my Scarlett O'Hara impression."

"Of course..." He kissed her hair then, got up himself, helped Michelle to her feet and expertly let her lean on him as they went up the stairs. Once she was settled in bed, Philip came back down. It was only just gone 11pm. He fixed himself another whisky, then flicked idly through their DVDs before settling on The Third Man. He settled himself down, silently mouthing the familiar dialogue.

Chapter 42
London, 3 April

Michelle woke at about 3am. It was a hot night and this, combined with her head being full of layers of grief – past, present and anticipated, she quickly accepted she wasn't going back to sleep. Nevertheless, she lay for about an hour, snugly, listening to Phil's deep breathing beside her. The news of Sam's cancer was now a slow-turning drill working its way through her insides. It seemed ridiculous on any simple level but Sam was the biggest person in her life. He wasn't family or partner, but somehow he transcended that, was the bookmark of her personal narrative.

Her earliest memory – or one of them as her mind felt flooded – was of sitting on the stairs of Sam's parents' home in Nottingham when they were both about three. Sam was sitting two steps below her, and she was reading a book to him and Sam was listening intently. Except she wasn't reading; she had memorised all the words from listening to her mum reading them to her, and was re-telling the story, word perfect from memory, turning the pages over at the correct moment.

She had known him all the way through childhood and school, and then through more than 20 years of friendship, also involving Mary and Philip but fundamentally about the two of them. The shock she had felt yesterday when she heard the news was incomparable to any other sensation she had experienced. Talking with Phil about it, or trying to, had helped a little. He had been great, listening to her explain how the cancer was likely to progress as she had poured out in a graphic stream of consciousness all her accumulated knowledge. Things she had forgotten for the last 20 years came back to her. All this and more raced through Michelle's mind. That ten-year period when she had been a nurse now seemed like a strange hiatus. During it, she had seen Sam only a handful of times – the weekend in Manchester that even at the time had seemed like a parallel universe, a couple of times during each of three successive summers, and the two car crash drinks when Michelle had come down to visit hospital friends in London. And then out of the blue had come the invitation to Sam and Mary's wedding. And although they had scarcely communicated in that period – only a thank you note from Mary and an exchange of Christmas cards – Michelle knew the distance between them had dissolved, almost as though it had all along been illusionary.

Michelle got out of bed silently, wrapped her dressing gown around her and went downstairs to put the kettle on. As she waited for the water to boil, she tried to recall what it had felt like when she and Philip had first lived together in London. There had been so many changes, all together – falling in love and deciding to live with someone for the first time, leaving Nottingham and moving to London, giving up her career in nursing, leaving so many friends behind. As far as Michelle could remember, those first few weeks in Kentish Town, in their very thin town house, had been a stew of emotions, dominated by doubt that she had done the right thing by throwing her life up in the air – many had said down the drain, even to her face – for an American whom she had barely known for a week. Life with Phil in London had been about as different from nursing in Nottingham as Michelle could imagine. But falling in love, throwing everything up to live with Phil was at the time so easy and natural that it barely seemed like taking a decision at all.

Despite her dark mood, Michelle virtually burst out laughing as she sat in the kitchen. There she was, pretty much the least romantic person she or any of her friends knew, committing the most romantic of acts. And she had done so with virtually no thought, no sense of dilemma, no weighing up of options. Michelle carried on sipping her tea, reflecting on her path.

From the start, Philip had only ever wanted her to be herself and had never criticised her for anything. And then she stopped moving and sat perfectly still. Michelle had always believed Philip meant every word of this, but for the first time she realised she might have to take him at his word. When Michelle first heard about Sam, she had been too torn up to do any real thinking. Now, although exhausted and washed out, she could at least think straight. She had only spent a few months looking after cancer patients, but her flat mate, Jen, had worked extensively on cancer wards and Michelle therefore knew quite a lot about cancer care. That, admittedly, was some 30 years ago and medicine had moved on, but the idea forming in Michelle's head wasn't about nursing as such. Instead, she wanted to look after Sam, help the nurses and help Mary by taking some of the weight off her shoulders.

The moment the idea came and Michelle took the decision, she felt lighter. She emptied her cup of tea and walked over to put it in the sink. The kitchen clock said 5.45am. Philip's alarm would go off in an hour and she didn't want to wake him before that. She went into their sitting room, which still smelt slightly of the whisky Philip had been drinking, and lay down on the sofa in her dressing gown, curling up with a couple of cushions as pillows. Briefly, she wondered what Philip and Mary would say when she told them, sure they would both be pleased.

***

In fact, neither of them were, quite the opposite.

"I'm sorry, but this makes no sense to me," Philip said, still fairly calmly, over breakfast. "I can't imagine what Mary will think, but for me we can be far more useful supporting Mary rather than going and squatting in the hospice or whatever it is you're planning."

"But I will be supporting her and Sam, that's the whole point."

"Well, you're your own woman, but I think you should think again."

"I've thought it through all night, Phil, that's why I'm so tired. I thought you'd understand."

"Well, I don't, I'm afraid; it sounds like a choice that would chain you to a dying man who's married to someone else."

"That's not what it's about." Michelle felt more stubborn than angry, but knew neither was good.

"Well, let's see what Mary thinks. Promise me at least that you'll talk to her before you speak to Sam."

As Phil had predicted, Mary was less than keen, though she didn't feel in a position to reject the offer outright, still less could she find expression for the dull anger somewhere down in her gut. There had always been a part of her which had wondered about the nature of Sam's relationship with his girl next door childhood friend from Nottingham. She remembered the first time she saw Michelle's name was when it appeared on an early guest list for their wedding, the only one they hadn't both met. Sam's explanation and description of Michelle had been matter of fact but not so much as to inspire suspicion. When she had met Michelle at the wedding, any residual feeling of being threatened disappeared, so shy and lonely had she appeared. Then, later, when she had just got to know Michelle after she had moved to London, any suspicion had been outweighed by her obvious devotion to Philip, as well as by Mary's own sense of security. And then Michelle had become one of her closest friends. But the flicker of nascent jealousy had never quite been extinguished.

And now, stimulated by Michelle's proposal, it began to burn brighter. Michelle wanted to be the person who would stay with Sam at the hospice. She had explained with complete logic that her medical experience meant she was the obvious person for this role. She had not portrayed it as sacrifice, simply as what made sense. It would free up Mary to be fresh when she came to see Sam and would spare her a good deal of the associated drudgery which Michelle, as an ex-nurse, would be more used to. Michelle had admitted it would be an odd arrangement but said it was an unusual situation and all she wanted was to help. Reluctantly and helplessly, Mary had agreed Michelle could ask Sam about it; the mere invocation of his name now made her dissolve to the point where she felt there was nothing she could deny him, not even something that felt close to her own humiliation.

And so Michelle agreed to come back after lunch. When she had called first, Sam had still been in bed. He had rung his boss the night before, told her the news and asked for some leave to come to terms with the short horizon that was now his future and to make some arrangements. He had slept soundly and long, not waking until gone 9.30 and then lying in bed stretching his limbs to feel and capture as many normal physical sensations as he could. Just before Michelle arrived, Mary had brought him up the paper and a cup of tea, something she did about once every five years. He sipped the hot tea with conscious pleasure. Now that others knew, his anger was subsiding. Sam's friends had always described him as calm and together, but he had felt he was nothing of the kind; until now that was, for he had woken with a weird sense of peace, that he was a long way from coming to terms with but which still felt new and wonderful.

He heard voices downstairs – Mary's, and possibly Michelle's – and thought about whether to get up, but decided instead to stay in bed until he had at least finished his tea. The sunshine was streaming through the window, and he could imagine he had never felt better, but knowing it was only a veneer and that the boundaries within which his body could move without pain would soon become strictly confined. From now on, it was simply a matter of accepting and adjusting to what came his way. Now, closing in on the end, it was enough to be passive. He had never felt so relaxed; nothing left to prove, no more challenges, no more hills to climb or problems to be solved. No longer did he need to make excuses for his clumsiness, his useless memory for everyday tasks. All those tiny humiliations were behind him.

He wondered what they were talking about downstairs. He knew it had been hard on Mary. While never understanding what she saw in him, he had been clear that she loved him and, for certain things, relied on him.

He thought that in a previous age he would have made a good carpenter – meticulous and thorough, decent with his hands – but instead, he had spent his career sitting at a desk, managing people and processes, trying to make various things work better, solving problems, occasionally coming up with new ideas. His mind drifted back to a hot, sticky summer afternoon. He had been in the Home Office at the time and had been asked to produce some fairly routine analysis for a parliamentary question on crime figures. His first attempt had completely got the wrong end of the stick, and Sam remembered his then boss, Bill Fields, patiently explaining the flaws in his analysis. He hoped he had been as patient.

He heard the door shut and guessed it was Michelle leaving. Perhaps his earliest memory was sitting on the front steps of her parent's house reading Michelle a book. Except he wasn't really reading it; in fact, he couldn't read and so instead was effectively reciting it to her, having memorised the words by heart through his mother having read it to him so frequently.

Not till he was about six did his memories start to join up, and in these Michelle featured constantly; sitting in prefabricated classrooms in primary school, playing in the field behind their houses, running past the witch's house on the edge of the woods. Often other children featured in these memories too, but Michelle was the constant. Secondary school hadn't been much different, and so he hadn't really believed her when she'd first told him she didn't think she'd go to university.

It had been strange seeing Michelle at his wedding, for the first time in so long. She didn't look the same – her hair was much shorter. In any case, she had seemed happy enough to be there and had sent them both a lovely letter afterwards. Then when Michelle had moved to London with Philip, it had weirdly seemed as though their decade of awkwardness and almost complete loss of contact had never happened. A couple of months after they'd met, Philip said that knowing Sam had made living in London a load easier. "Someday," he said, "you and I need to go to New York, so I can make you feel at home there the way you've made me feel at home here." They had never made it to New York, of course.

Later, after a surprisingly short lunch with Mary and Ruth, the bell went and Mary showed Michelle into the study, then returned. At that point, Ruth had got up from the table and left, biting her lip furiously. Then, Mary quickly told him that Michelle wanted to be his carer through his final few weeks. Her tone was flat and unemotional, and Sam, taking maybe a full minute to understand, feeling like a man coming back into the world after a hermitic sojourn in the high mountains, sensed the welling of hurt and doubt within her. His pause was critical to Mary. It told her Sam was thinking seriously about the idea, whereas in fact he was simply digesting what Mary had said. Her reaction, based on this misreading, was to look suddenly drained and she sank exhausted into the nearest chair.

"Don't worry about me, Sam," she said. "You should do what you think is best. Michelle's a trained nurse and would obviously be fantastic." What she left unsaid, though more from running out of words than intention, was that she still believed she would be able to care for him best. Mary thought this was clear enough, but when Sam responded by saying he didn't know what was the best thing to do, she felt it was already too late, that the die had been cast.

Sam's failure to react immediately spoke to her either of his not having understood what she had left unsaid, or that he did not value it as highly as she felt it deserved. Mary was immediately deflated, not knowing which was the more depressing. In fact, Sam could feel as much as hear all that she wanted him to understand, but he also felt he saw how emotionally exhausted she was. He decided he couldn't bear to witness Mary's distress as his own condition deteriorated, that he wasn't strong enough to cope.

Sam did not ignore, or in any rational sense underestimate, the anger and pain Mary would be caused, but he did underestimate the vulnerability it would trigger, making the mistake of assuming the strength of his love was more palpable to her than it was.

Normally, he would have understood all this more fully, but for once he was thinking and acting narrowly, and in solely his own interests. As a consequence, he had made the decision well before Michelle walked into the room, ignoring the impact it would have on Philip. The change was obvious to Michelle almost immediately. Oddly, it felt almost as though Sam was using her, but better her, she reasoned, than Mary.

Chapter 43
Kabul/London, April

Ed was dreaming… He was crouching behind a rock in the hills above the Kandahar Road with some Mujahedeen, watching a convoy below. Some road mines had been set, which would go off when the first vehicle reached the bend, in about 15 seconds, he guessed. One of the Mujahedeen had a video recorder trained on the convoy so he could capture the explosion on film and put it up on the internet. It would be quite a coup and the guerrillas were excited, already starting to congratulate themselves on the success of their plan. Ed had binoculars round his neck and lifted them up to see what was going on. He could see the faces of the soldiers in the first truck. They too were smiling, one was laughing it seemed, maybe sharing a joke. He switched to the second vehicle; the soldiers in that one looked more serious, one of them was familiar looking. But he knew it was time to focus on the first vehicle again. Ed jumped as the explosion went off, seeing it before he heard it, even across the high mountain air. The vehicle was tossed into the air as it burst into flames before landing upside down. The second truck immediately swerved but, in trying to avoid the wreckage ahead, it careered off the road and down into the gully on its left, turning over so that it too ended upside down. The other vehicles were able to stop in time and soldiers were emerging from them, taking up defensive positions and preparing to return fire. Nothing came however – the Mujahedeen had been unable to find adequate cover and protection within range – so soon the British troops started cautiously heading for the overturned vehicle down in the gully, and within a few minutes they had dragged the driver and passengers to safety. A couple of them looked badly hurt, but as far as Ed could tell they were alive.

Then his dream shifted to Egypt, the first time he had visited the pyramids at Giza. He had wanted to see them from early childhood and had come up from Cairo the previous night for the Son et Lumière. It was odd being there, having seen Roger Moore as James Bond in Moonraker, only a couple of years before. It was the first time he felt he had ever been anywhere significant, let alone spectacular or glamorous, but in truth he found it slightly disappointing – smaller and more tacky than he had imagined. But this was now the following morning and his journalist companion, whom he was taking over from, had persuaded him to catch a taxi with her soon after dawn, back out to Giza. When they got there, the site was still closed to the public and would be for almost another hour. Fortunately, there was a hotel across from the entrance and they had time to drink coffee and chat about the Middle East before the tourist coaches arrived; her name was Sarah and she loved Egypt and the region, but after two years was glad to be going home.

When the site opened, all the tourists, replete with their guides, headed past the Sphinx, oddly ugly and diminished by the damage Napoleon's gunners had done to its face, towards the nearest pyramid. Instead of following them, however, Sarah persuaded Ed to walk with her out past the furthest of the three pyramids and then to climb the dune beyond. It was quite a trek but, while Ed did not really understand the reasoning, Sarah was both attractive and persuasive, and so he happily followed, ignoring the accumulating sand in his shoes. He didn't look at his watch but he felt like it must have taken at least 20 minutes to get out past the third pyramid and up onto the ridge of sand. But as his eye line rose above its top, Ed was as if transported onto the set of Lawrence of Arabia. The sand shimmered into the distance in the way he thought only ever happened in films, and on the horizon were a couple of Bedouin on camels. It was a scene unchanged across the centuries and he stood open-mouthed, gasping for something sensible to say to Sarah, completely lost in the what lay spread in front of him. Then he turned around for the first time. The pyramids of Giza, one of the seven wonders of the Ancient World, presented him with a sight that had barely altered in three millennia. From this distance, the tourists milling around could be ignored.

And it hit him, who had always accepted the premise that humankind and civilisation progressed across the centuries, that people today were little different from those who inhabited the Ancient World. In their invention and vaulting ambition to become master of their environment, and of death itself, they matched the modern world. Only the means differed. The pyramids had torn up his assumptions and flung them back in his face, so that he winced and put his hands on his knees to keep his balance.

And then he became aware he was talking quietly to himself, "Everything remains the same. Everything remains the same." And then his eyes opened and he was staring upward at a rotating fan in the ceiling. His leg felt oddly heavy, but when he tried to move it, he was rewarded with a shot of pain that made him grimace and groan. He was in hospital back in Kabul with a badly gashed leg and a broken arm. The convoy he had been travelling in had been attacked, and although the bomb had not hit his own vehicle, it had been forced off the road and had rolled over. Several of his fellow passengers had broken limbs, and by most measures Ed had been lucky, though he had lost a good deal of blood and the journey to the hospital had passed in a feverish void. The two days or so he had been unconscious were now an empty space. The last thing he remembered before his eyes opened to the spinning fan in the ceiling was glancing out of the Land Rover window and catching a glint of sunlight off some reflective surface in the hills above.

The next week too, though he was all too conscious, instantly blurred into a wasteland corner of his memory. Four soldiers had been killed in the vehicle in front, in which he had almost travelled. Ed placed little store by any concept of fate – at any given point people were lucky or unlucky; you could increase or lessen the odds but never remove the risk; instead, he just felt more empty and weak as the enforced solitude and contemplation became a lightning rod for 30 years of accumulated doubt and insecurity. At any individual moment these had been minor, but now, in aggregate, they overwhelmed him. All the elements of purpose and worth in his career had inverted; in his life as well, for the two had become indivisible. The duty to inform, to increase understanding, to provide alternative perspectives and objective assessments, to make the complex accessible; all this was now dwarfed by the implacable impact of human actions that might be rationally explained but only ever irrationally understood.

In the face of this onslaught, Ed's belief in talking to your opponent, striving to understand their perspective, was exposed as pointless liberal drivel. The destructive power of technology had multiplied to such a degree that even the most everyday of chemicals could cause devastation beyond the imagination of his grandfather. He had seen their havoc and had arrived at the end of the road. And simultaneously, he was looking in on himself, seeing a man who had lived for too long off the adrenalin of hyperactivity. And now, deprived by injury of that particular drug, he was succumbing to the years of stress that he had somehow managed to disregard and diffuse. He could tell he was close to some kind of breakdown. Maybe it was time, finally, to stop.

But most of all, he wanted to spend time with friends, especially Sam. Sam was, of all the people he knew, the least changed from when they had first said hello. Ed had become harder and less forgiving. Others had moved politically, usually from Left to Right. A third group of people had turned in on themselves and their families. Partly driven by disillusion with the icons and ideals of their youth, but mostly responding to the imperatives of marriage and children, they had stopped caring about the causes which had once made them angry and passionate. Sam was in none of these groups.

During the long night hours as he tried to sleep, succeeding only fitfully, Ed's mind was repeatedly rattled by the memory of the people behind those smiling faces in the first truck, whom he had laughed and drunk with only the evening before. His confidence that he wasn't sliding inevitably towards a breakdown of some sort started to wobble. He knew he needed to see Sam, the only person he could wholly rely on, the lode star of his value system.

It would be easy to say Ed only just avoided a breakdown but in fact he did so with something to spare. In reality, without realising, he had trodden similar paths several times in the last decades, but his memory of his despair in these earlier times had been dulled by the passage of time and by the propensity to soften the memory of those events which caused most distress. And this softening had also led him to underestimate his own resilience. This now stood him in good stead, helping preserve his equanimity of purpose until he got to London. Booking himself into the Savoy, he had a shower and then phoned Sam and Mary and got himself invited around.

When the hotel alarm woke him, Ed knew he could have slept for much longer. The Tube journey was hot and quite busy, despite being past the rush hour, and quite soon he was starting to sweat. Ed felt his age. He was looking around at people much younger than him, who had very different careers and lifestyles. Some wore office clothes, some not, but almost all of them seemed to have their entire lives in front of them. He thought how old he would have looked to his 22-year-old self. Being in his 50s had been unimaginable then.

And now he was tired, the most tired he had been. But he didn't know how much of it was the after effect of the bombing, how much it was simply that his batteries were running really low. He began to worry. It was difficult to contemplate the last 30 years as being anything remotely resembling comfortable, but he also saw that his life had stuck to well-defined routines and that he had been relaxed working within them. In some ways, these were the aspects of his job he would most miss – the journeys, hotels, meals and the evenings in the bar with other reporters. These and the shared hours of blackout, the familiar whirring of overhead fans and over-burdened air conditioning systems were the real substance of his life; everything else was ultimately froth.

When he reached the house, Sam let him in and led him to the sitting room rather than the kitchen, where they usually chatted. Sam had been predictably shocked to hear about the bombing. "I've never quite seen you as someone who looks after themselves properly – listen to me, I sound like my mum – it's amazing your career's been so uneventful for so long." He tried to smile but only managed a weak grimace. He was torn between shock at Ed's physical state and a general fragility he'd never seen before, and on the other hand knowing that at some stage he needed to tell Ed his own news.

Sam couldn't conceive what it would be like to go through what Ed had just experienced, his imagination failed him completely. One of the unremarked but constant features of his own life had been the physical safety attached to it. But looking at his friend, it seemed that, temporarily at least, his personality and confidence no longer filled his body. His left forearm – in plaster and in a sling – was the most obvious sign; but in their own way, Ed's shrunken cheeks and suddenly-rounded shoulders were just as eloquent. Even worse, Ed's right hand, the undamaged one, wasn't able to hold anything for more than a couple of seconds without starting to shake. Sam had always thought Ed had assumed a thin veneer of bravado in his work that made him subtly different from the person he had known at university. But that veneer had now been stripped away.

"I saw on the news there had been another road bomb but had no idea you were involved. How many was it died in the first vehicle? Four, was it? And you were in the second? I'm so sorry, it must have been terrible."

"We were lucky really; the driver was keeping back slightly, I don't know why, and so was able to swerve off the road but into a ditch on the left, rather than the other way, where there was a 20-foot fall. If we'd ended up going off the other way, I'm not sure I'd be here."

"And did you know any of the soldiers who got killed?"

"Not really but I'd played cards with them the night before; they were a good bunch."

"How's it been? You're looking pretty well, considering."

"Well, I don't feel that great. And it's been weird sitting around with nothing to do besides thinking."

"And how was that?"

"Well, I sort of went the whole hog, and you're pretty much the only person I could think of to talk to about it, who would not just think I've lost it totally. You see, the thing is, I don't think I want to go back to my work, even if I ever felt able to."

Sam looked at him and briefly dropped his head to think before sitting up and settling himself back in the armchair. "Okay, I'm all yours; Mary won't be back for at least 45 minutes. Just let me know when you want more tea."

Ed smiled and a little bit of tightness released itself out of his shoulders. "Well, I think what it probably boils down to is that it's left me pretty much at rock bottom in terms of disillusion. Not the people themselves, but the purpose and worth of what they do, what I did." He paused; Sam said nothing, only sipping his tea slightly noisily. "I've basically tried to do the job well over the years, or I think I have – I guess it's for others to judge – but stuck in that hospital room in Kabul, it all felt bankrupt. I hadn't really been explaining or illuminating anything. My insight isn't any better than anyone else's, only a little better informed; and most people, given the level of access I had, would be just as good. A lot of these things are really only about resources and being in the right place at the right time.

"And nothing's changed at all really, either as a result of my reporting or anyone else's, as far as I can tell. The great British public doesn't understand or care about the Middle East one iota more than they did 30 years ago. And neither do politicians feel under any more pressure to find a solution to the mess. I could rant on for hours, but I've promised myself not to. It all seems utterly useless, and I've basically been perpetrating a huge hoax by pretending any of my career has remotely mattered beyond paying my salary and massaging my god forsaken ego."

Sam felt in no position to be having this conversation. He was dying, whereas for all Ed's misery, physical injuries and mental doubt, he very obviously had a future. And without Ed knowing his own news, anything he said would be devalued. After all, wasn't it cheap and easy to pass out platitudes on life from your deathbed? He was also at a loss. He'd never seen Ed like this, nor imagined such doubt being any part of his character. For all that he knew him so well, Sam reflected that he didn't really know his best friend at all.

"You know the person you describe isn't you," Sam said at last, "I don't think you've ever really thought, even subconsciously, about massaging your ego, or anyone else's for that matter. It may feel like that now but I think that's a pretty natural human reaction. As far as I can tell, people feel most guilty not when they've been selfish, but when they've been the opposite. We think of ourselves as selfish creatures and are distrustful when counter evidence appears. If it's someone else we resort to conspiracy theories, and when it's ourselves we search around for a thread of self-interest no matter how indirect or obscure. On the whole, I suspect it's quite a healthy instinct; imagine how obnoxious we would be if we allowed ourselves to become properly self-satisfied on top of everything else. And for what it's worth, I've always thought being able to recognise that line between what you're doing, directly or indirectly, for your own designs, and what you're doing ultimately for others is at the root of many of our spiritual journeys."

"So do you think I'm on some kind of inner journey, is that what you think this is all about?" Ed was starting to become irritated by the way Sam was talking to him – or at him? – In such a detached way.

"Sorry, Ed, I've begun sounding too much like my work memos recently, a sure sign I'm coming to the end of my shelf life. I only mean 'journey' in the loosest of senses, people learning different things about themselves as they go through their lives. What I do think is that you're being too hard on yourself. What you've just gone through is terrible, beyond what any of us could imagine. It isn't at all surprising it would change your perspective, and with people you know, even if only slightly, dying a few yards away and you being so close to it, it makes you feel more negative about almost everything, including yourself."

"Well, let's just say it's hard to see much that's good in the world at the moment."

"Have you thought at all about getting professional help, going to see a therapist or psychiatrist?"

For the first time since the bomb, Ed laughed out loud. "You must be joking, that's the last thing I need."

Sam shook his head, relieved at the release of tension. "For someone so otherwise matter of fact and empirical, you have some odd out of date prejudices floating around in that head of yours. This time they both laughed, at the sense of release than because anything had been funny. "Do you remember," Sam continued, "how we used to go to the pub and drink Guinness and then stay up till 4am, listening to records and solving the problems of the world?"

"Yes, I used to be so serious about everything."

"I know, lots of times I used to argue with you just for the hell of it. You had a great singles collection though, lots of stuff I'd barely heard of. I only had a few bought cassettes and some more I'd recorded off the radio."

"Tell me about it. At times, it seemed like you came from another decade, but you still managed to be right about virtually everything."

"Nowhere near," replied Sam. "One of the biggest things I realised back then was how little I actually did know compared to you and the others. It was my Garden of Eden moment, if you like."

Ed laughed again, "I've never heard it described like that."

"Well, I'd followed the news, read newspapers and stuff, but I'd never really thought about the longer term causes of things. I'd tended to see them more as individuals' actions. So there's a huge part of me that thinks the Cold War couldn't really end before it did because it was a product of WW2 and it needed the couple of generations who were shaped by the war and scarred by it to pass on."

"That's a pretty depressing view of humanity's capacity for progress, isn't it? The logical conclusion surely, is that we've got to wait around for the last generation of octogenarians to die off before we can change any of the really bad stuff they lived through."

Now it was Sam's turn to laugh, "I didn't quite mean it like that, but I should have known better than to think you wouldn't jump on me. All I'm really saying is that a lot of the really big things are generational. I suspect it's only in the last half of the twentieth century that mankind believed it was within their power to 'fix' huge-scale problems. That's why we used to go to church so much more – it was our acknowledgement that much of life was outside of our control; now we believe we can be our own gods."

Ed was amused, "Look who's ranting now! I never thought I'd hear you so strident. Where's your usual measured delivery gone to? What's changed in your life?"

"We'll come to that in a minute, though to be honest, I think I've always talked this way… No? Oh well…"

"And the Middle East?"

"Well, that's tricky because it keeps mutating, doesn't it? Renewing itself and in the process ensnaring new generations in its web."

"So we're no longer dealing with the fallout from Israel's struggle for independence but with the fallout from the Six Day War and Sabra and Shatila."

"Yes, and from the intifadas and the suicide bombings and Israel's building of the wall. "

"Yes, I can see that, but I'm not sure it makes me feel any better."

"Well, maybe it doesn't, and you might be right that it's just too hard, but from where I'm sitting, you're doing a fantastic job of explaining. Many more people understand at least some of what's going on than would have done if it hadn't been for you and your ilk. But even if we pin it all on Baldwin, it's hard to argue there's a simple solution that's somehow eluding us. So I wouldn't beat yourself up about it, not for a couple more decades yet anyway."

"Okay, I get it! I keep forgetting how impossible you are to disagree with. How are you anyway? Here I am boring you with my self-flagellation, or whatever it is you would call it if I gave you the chance."

To Sam, Ed's voice was still weaker, slower and more disjointed than normal; but at least there was a bit more energy in the way he spoke. His hands still shook but maybe a bit less, who knows. Anyway, now was the time; delaying any longer would just lead to more problems.

"Funny you should ask; actually, I'm quite relieved you're over – I've been trying to work out how to get in touch – and we've been able to have a more or less normal chat, not at all actually, but anyway... In most ways I'm fine, but the doctor tells me I've got pancreatic cancer, one of the nasty ones. I don't look or feel much different yet – just a couple of smallish things – but I'm afraid it's terminal and aggressive. I've probably got a couple of months."

Sam had been staring steadily at the coffee table as he spoke and had managed to keep his voice steady, though it had risen slightly in pitch. When he looked up, Ed was biting his lip, his eyes starting to water.

"Fuck..." he whispered. "That's the saddest thing I've ever heard."

"No, it's not," Sam countered.

"Is there nothing?"

"Believe me, I've explored every possible route – Ruth's given me hell about it – but none of them take me anywhere."

"I can't believe we've just had the conversation we've had without you telling me. You bastard! Sorry, I don't mean that, but you should have told me first."

"It's okay, you're right. It's for me to be sorry, but it wouldn't have worked telling you on the phone, and when you got here, well, no excuse, but it's still not the easiest piece of news to give."

"Don't apologise; it's just I can't believe you've just spent... Never mind... How's Mary and Ruth?"

"Okay, I think, considering, but I'm not a good judge of these things. I'm more worried about Ruth, I think; she looks up to me a bit more, whereas Mary knows my flaws better."

"Stop making fun of the whole thing, will you?"

"I'm sorry, I guess it's one of my coping mechanisms. But Mary will be back soon anyway, you can find out for yourself. I think she'll be okay, genuinely, but

428

you'll find her a bit odd." He paused. "You see, she's withdrawn a bit and isn't really talking to me the way she usually does."

Chapter 44
New York, Friday, 20 June

It took a lot of coming to terms with. An African American man was almost certain to be nominated by the Democratic Party as its presidential candidate. For Black Americans of her age or older, it was still barely conceivable. Entertainment and sport, education, maybe business, but now Barack Obama had somehow become favourite to win the White House in November.

Carol was driving from work to home before going across town to see her old ex-boyfriend. Danny had rung Monday night and asked if she was around on Friday to go out. Nothing heavy he had promised, but he had something he needed her advice on, something important enough to be worth buying her dinner. No, he couldn't tell her what it was about over the phone. It wasn't a surprise but it just wasn't that sort of thing; he wanted to be able to talk to her face to face.

Danny was rather more than an ex, they had lived together for three years back in the '70s, and they had a fine daughter together, Althea. Somehow, maybe because it was the '70s and their independent lives had never really given way to their shared one, marriage had never been discussed, and eventually, Danny had found his eye and attention wandering. Rather than be unfaithful, he had moved out, ending the relationship. He had continued to contribute financially and to see Althea when he could while she was growing up, but had always felt a twinge of guilt that he hadn't had the staying power to make it work, though he had never wavered in his conviction that moving out had been the lesser evil.

When they had met, Danny had been a track and field athlete, a 400m runner on the fringes of the US team. Not quite good enough for Munich, he had been on the way to making the Montreal team when injury had intervened. The comeback had come up short, and he had got a job as a sales rep for Nike, then a small but fast expanding sport shoe company. Encouraged by Carol, he had put himself through night school to get a law degree, and in the mid '80s had used it to move into banking; it was better money, and while the hours were much less flexible, they were also more predictable. The timing of this move meant he missed out on the Michael Jordan-inspired boom of Nike but, by the same token, a few years and mergers later, he was on the ground floor of the internet driven globalisation of financial services. As a result, while he was no more than a middle manager in the middle office somewhere in the vastness of Merrill Lynch, Carol knew she now earned a good deal less than Danny's secretary.

Since Danny had moved out, they had stayed on relatively good terms. He never knew, because she didn't tell him, how much his leaving had torn Carol apart. For two years after, every time she saw him, she cried herself to sleep that night. Equally,

Danny had never told her – how could he, he reasoned to himself – what had really driven him to leave. Somehow, this partial deceit of their post-relationship had been enough to keep them in contact socially as well as financially. Every month or two they would speak on the phone, every four or five they would get together for coffee or a drink, maybe every couple of years for dinner. The unspoken ground rules had always been clear – lots of conversation about Althea, some about each other but never involving relationships, the rest about politics, sport and work. So far it had succeeded but Carol sensed tonight would mark some kind of departure. Something in Danny's voice had signalled it. Although not worried, she was more on edge than usual.

Carol's strained credulity about what she could only think of as the Obama phenomenon had been prompted by two factors. The discussion she had been listening to on the radio had focused on what was now Obama's virtually impregnable position in the race for the Democratic nomination. Barring some extreme event, Hilary Clinton, who only a few months previously – after her comeback win in New Hampshire – had seemed to have unstoppable momentum, was now reduced to trying to leverage some kind of stake in the Democratic ticket. Secondly, Black politics had been a common focus of the conversations Carol and Danny had shared over some 35 years but Obama's position represented an earthquake, a huge juddering shift in the tectonic plates of US politics.

Danny was active in New York City Democratic politics and the last time they had spoken he had been firm in her support for Hilary. Carol suspected he was wrestling with his conscience over whether he could now support Obama who, back in January, he derided as an inexperienced, glitzy newcomer who had never shown he could do the hard yards.

When she got home, Carol showered and changed. Then she rang a cab and sorted through the post while she waited for it to arrive. When Danny had moved out, he had rented an apartment only about half a mile away so he could see Althea regularly to be available if needed. While Althea was growing up, this arrangement had worked well, better than either had expected. Consequently, when Carol had decided to move out to Queens, Danny had offered to follow her and replicate the arrangement. That had been some 20 years ago.

Soon after, she was ringing Danny's doorbell. "Hold on, honey, I'll be right there," she heard him shout, and a few seconds later he opened the door. "Hi, honey," he said, picking up his keys, "no time to stop, we've got a table booked at that new Chinese restaurant two blocks down, and a long cocktail to have first, to clear away the fog of the working day. How you been anyway?"

Carol gave him a routine peck on the cheek. It was rare for him to be this organised with their social meetings, though she knew well enough that he was a checklist of project management at work and, for that matter, in their financial dealings. They walked happily along towards the restaurant, looking for all the world like a comfortable middle-aged couple.

"Do you think we ever could have made it work?" he asked.

"You know, you ask that exact same question every year or so. How the hell should I know, you were the one who walked out. You were a pain sometimes but I was happy enough. Stuff happens though; maybe you made the right call; who knows and who cares anymore?"

"How's Althea doing?" he asked.

"Okay, she rang the other night. She's getting serious about that Canadian guy she met at Christmas, the one works for CNN. Andrew, you remember."

They stepped inside a small cocktail bar, conveniently about three doors down from the Chinese, got drinks and sat by the bar.

"You still with that Thelma?" Carol asked routinely.

"Nope, she got rid of me, too damned old for her. You still with that John fella?"

"Didn't think she had that much sense. Yeah, John's still around. No big deal though, we're both way too old for that."

"How's work?"

"Busy enough, I reckon. Six weeks from now I'll be out in Beijing. You wouldn't believe how much dough they've thrown at it."

"Don't worry, I would! I reckon they've got more spare cash than any country in history has ever had. Believe me, I've seen the numbers. And their economy's still growing at around 10% a year, that's four times the rate of ours. I'm not surprised they've got dough to burn."

"Half the stuff I see in the shops these days seems to be made there, including Nike."

"I know, the Chinese keep their currency really low so all their exports are cheaper than anything else around. Global market, all that stuff... And by the way, they own most of the US national debt. So all those Bush tax cuts for people like us are paid for by borrowing from China."

"I didn't know that bit. Well, at least they're not Commie bastards anymore."

"Hell no," laughed Danny.

"I remember how pissed they were back in '93 when the IOC gave the 2000 Games to Sydney rather than Beijing. Even then it was only by the one vote if I remember right. The Aussies played hard ball over Tiananmen Square and it swung just enough votes."

"Still, it's about the only time I can remember a country's human rights record having actually changed anything."

"Boy, they were pissed!"

"Then the Communist Party decided to go properly capitalist. Now every big company in the US, and every other goddam place, is after a piece of the action."

"And funnily enough, the human rights card didn't work remotely eight years later – Beijing was a shoo-in."

"Besides anything else, I'm damn sure their sponsors wouldn't have allowed it. By 2001, everyone needed China, especially after the dotcom thing burst."

"I love talking to you about this stuff," said Carol.

"Yeah well, I know you don't get much intellectual action over at that newspaper of yours. How is the US track and field team anyway? I don't get to follow it that closely anymore."

"Pretty good by most standards, Tyson Gay, Alison Felix would be great in any era. But Gay'll have to break his own world record to beat Usain Bolt; never seen anything like him, at least if he can get his start fixed. D'ya remember in '76 when the Caribbean swept everything from 100 to 800? Crawford, Quarrie and Juantarena; well, Bolt is sort of like all three of them rolled into one. And about the size of them put together."

"You think he's that good?"

"I don't know for sure but I've not seen anything like him in my professional life. You know I try and go out to that Jamaican schools meet when I can? Well, I saw him there about five years ago, when he was 15 or something. Well, he just blew me away, me and a bunch of other hacks, and since then we've all been waiting for him to grow up, see if he can learn to race as well as run, if you get my meaning. Well, we're about to find out. Or rather, with the times he's run in the last year or so, we're already starting to discover; it's now a matter of how far can he take it."

"I've never heard you talk about any athlete like that before, you're always so cynical."

"Yea, well, maybe I'm getting mellow in my old age, lost my edge."

"You said the Chinese were throwing money at the Olympics, what sort of thing?"

"Well, a load of stuff really. There's a bunch of new motorways, so maybe they'd have built those anyway. The most obvious stuff, which you'll see plenty of once the Games start, are the Birds' Nest stadium for the track and field and a thing called the Ice Cube where they're going to hold the swim meet. By Olympic standards, they're both absolutely spectacular – they make Sydney, never mind Atlanta or Athens, look mundane – it's almost like they'd been designed to look great on television; for all I know, maybe they were. God only knows what they'll do with them after but somehow I doubt the Chinese'll care very much provided they're suitably admired during the Games. Oh, the other thing was that hundreds of families had their houses flattened to clear space. Doubt they got much in the way of compensation. But like you say, any US corporation you can think of now has billboards up all over the city."

"Well, it's hard to blame them when it's the biggest market out there by miles."

"I know," replied Carol, "and I think that's pretty much the IOC line. Rogge's always going on how the Olympics'll be some kind of positive influence on Chinese development. Well, I'd buy that a hell of a lot more if it wasn't the most controlled and censored society in history. They may have gone over to market capitalism but it sure isn't a 'free' market. Even Google, for Christ's sake, has got into bed with them. I'd heard stuff was going on, so I tried to find some sites on the Web; no chance, even international ones."

"Money talks, honey; always has, always will. Come on, let's get some food. I'd forgotten about you just having been to Beijing; you're going to be sick of shark's fin soup and egg fried rice. Do you wanna go somewhere different?"

"No, I really like the food, it was one of the highlights for me, though not the shark's fin; even I have limits."

Danny paid and they walked out and along to the Chinese restaurant. It had hanging lanterns outside and the windows were shaded in silk curtains. It was nearly 8.30pm but the evening seemed to have gotten warmer if anything, the breeze having died, more humid and sticky.

When they had settled at their table and ordered, Danny wasted no time cutting to his agenda. "The reason I wanted to see you, apart from the fact we're about due," he smiled, suddenly looking 20 years younger, "is because I want to ask your advice; for whatever craziness of reasons you're the best advisor I've got." Carol sipped her

433

wine. "The thing is, honey, I'm almost certain I'm gonna get fired in the next six months, and I'm thinking about jumping the gun and leaving sooner."

Carol looked across, trying to think what had happened. "So how many million bucks have you lost them, baby?"

"Yea, I know, I've got $20m in my Bahamas account, enough to last you and me, honey... No. honey, don't get excited, it's not that simple and it's not that bad either, at least for me. D'ya want to hear about it?"

"Sure, go ahead," said Carol, almost having recovered. He filled their glasses. The wine tasted good this evening.

"Well, the first thing you've gotta understand is that everything's connected in banking. Every bank is in hock to every other bank, and every other bank is in hock to it. It's just a matter of how much, and how much they need it. Got it?"

"Yea, I get the idea, but why?"

"Well, they all have to make a return on their money, which means always having it lent out, even if it's just overnight, or even during the day. And equally, everyone needs to borrow, whether it's to lend on to their customers or because they need it for themselves. The bigger, stronger banks pay a little less interest than the rest, but that's basically how it works."

"Okay, I'm with you, what's next? I take it this is going to be a long old tutorial."

He smiled, "Only as long as it needs to be, honey. But you need to get up to speed on this if your advice is gonna be any damned good. Anyway, a hell of a lot of this is straight lending and borrowing like anyone would understand. But a lot of it – often more in fact – is also way more complicated. A simple version would be that A lends or sells something, an asset, to B. But that asset isn't a single thing but a bundle of stuff, let's say mortgages in Michigan. Now B ain't going to buy all those mortgages unless he has some assurance of what they're worth. So what happens is, a rating agency like Moody's will look at that bundle of mortgages and give it a rating, let's say Triple A. And sometimes also, another bank, C, will guarantee the value of that bundle. So if you're bank B, you think you've got a pretty good deal – the bundle of mortgages you've bought has been rated Triple A by Moody's and guaranteed by Bank C as well."

"Okay, I'm just about with you so far. Keep going, what's next?"

"Right, so we have a pretty much gold-plated asset here. Now B wanted it for something specific, but once that's over B wanted to do something with it; it wasn't cheap to buy but B knows it'll get a good price, either from another bank or from a hedge fund. And sometimes, if the next buyer wants, or if B thinks it'll make it worth more, they'll change the size or the mix in the bundle and then have it reassessed by Moody's."

"What happens to Bank C's guarantee?"

"Well done, I always knew you were wasted in journalism."

"Us hacks do all right provided there ain't too much jargon around."

"Whatever... Anyway, Bank C's guarantee still stands and B's still relying on it but you're right that, because the mix has changed, a new guarantee is needed, so B will provide that but, in reality, it thinks the second guarantee is only the difference between the two mixes. Now as I said, this is the simple version, and it can get way more complicated, messy you might say. Also, these transactions happen hundreds maybe thousands of times a day, and not just with US banks; bundles of Michigan mortgages have ended up being owned by banks in Germany."

"Okay, I can't quite see why that all happens but I think I mostly understand the how bit. By the way you missed your vocation, baby, you're way better than most of my college professors were."

"It may come to that."

"And you make it sound like Michigan mortgages are something special. But anyone with…"

"Now, you're just being a smartass." Danny was beginning to enjoy himself. It suddenly felt almost like those days when they had first met, when they would talk and argue all the time, at least when they weren't getting laid. He put it out of his mind and went on.

"Right, so the first crack in the logic of all this is potentially losing track of who exactly has guaranteed the value of which assets. The second is forgetting exactly what those assets are. So, what you're thinking is, how did ordinary, nothing to write home about, mortgages in Michigan end up being bundled up into this really valuable Triple A asset that banks from all over the world are real keen to buy. Well there are basically six reasons why it happens – see, I've prep'd for this – and why it's become such a big thing." Danny paused, "So here goes, this is the complex bit." Carol nodded.

"One, the bank that originally sells the mortgages has to hold a lot of capital against them, about four percent of their value, but if they bundle them up and sell them to someone else, they can free up that capital for something else. It's called securitisation."

"Two, it's become much easier, and therefore more popular, to do this over the last 15 years or so because clever maths guys, who work for banks, have worked out a way of calculating how many of these mortgages are going to go bad and this makes it possible to agree what the fair price is. Because the rating agencies can do these sums too, they're okay with giving out ratings for these bundles of assets."

"Then three, because securitisations have become so much easier and more popular, banks are now happy to buy them in order to sell them on – they rarely want to keep them anymore – and because of this the regulators – like the SEC and the dear old Fed – let them be counted as trading assets, and so the banks only need to hold a tiny fraction of that four percent capital against them."

"Four, you remember that guarantee stuff we talked about at the start? Well, honey, I bet you thought that was for the whole amount, didn't you? Well no, those maths guys get involved again and have a way of calculating what's called the value at risk, or VaR in my language, and that's what the bank guarantees, usually only a tiny portion of the full amount. The guaranteeing bank might also then lay off that risk by buying what's called a derivative, which, in this story, is basically meant to be an insurance policy. Still with me?"

"I think so, keep going."

"Okay, almost there… Five, because the clever maths guys have shown that, provided it's done right, these things are as safe as," he smiled, "not quite Fort Knox but not far off, they're quite expensive to buy but they also earn a decent rate of interest because they're tied to the mortgage rate. And that means they earn a lot more than US Treasury Bills – government debt – which historically, is paying incredibly low interest rates at the moment because…? Come on, this is your grade A question."

"Because…" Carol thought for a moment, "because the Chinese are buying so much of it…"

"A star! Which means?"

"That… There's lots of demand… And so… The US government only has to pay very low interest on it."

"Excellent, honey! Bullshit aside, I'm pretty impressed. I know guys with way more letters after their name than you who don't get this stuff. Anyway, last but not least, six, which is that, because all this stuff is so profitable, banks no longer mostly do it for their customers but simply trade this stuff on their own account, and even sometimes create special entities called SIVs – Structured Investment Vehicles – that do nothing else."

"Right, well, I think I get all that, more or less, but where does your job fit in, apart from the fact you personally make more dough?"

"Well, you remember the two cracks in the logic you spotted earlier – losing track of who's guaranteed what, and forgetting what the assets actually are – well, there's a third, and it's a real beauty… It turns out the maths is wrong, or to be precise it's based on a load of assumptions from the past that's turning out not to be true."

"But why?"

"Hard to work out at the moment but, well, there's this really smart guy at work, a baseball geek, any sport for that matter – you'd really like him; Sandy Neilsen's his name. He's where I got all this stuff. Anyway, Sandy reckons there's maybe three things going on. There's been a big government push, going back to Clinton, to offer mortgages to people, often African Americans, who wouldn't have had mortgages before. Often these have been on cheap rates for the first few years, and when these have run out and rates have gone back to normal, they've found it hard to keep up payments. Then second, the Fed kept interest rates really low when the dot.com bubble burst and then again after 9/11, which saved us all a bit of pain in the short-term but had the downside that it carried on stoking the housing bubble. And lastly, those Chinese again, selling us all their super cheap goods has kept inflation really low, which encouraged more people than normal to borrow extra, buy bigger properties and so on. Whatever the reasons, the maths is turning out wrong and pretty much every bank is in big trouble."

"But even I've worked that out from the massive losses they've been declaring, though I didn't understand it till tonight."

"What's come out so far isn't the half of it, honey. You wouldn't believe how much racing around and back-covering is going on. I swear to God, every time our CEO stands up and makes a statement, there's five people think he's lying for every one who believes him, and that's just inside the bank. But the thing is, the banks pretty much won't be able to take it. They're all broke, bust, or they are if they're anything like us."

"Therefore, your job?"

"You got it, honey! In their terms, I'm pretty expensive for what I do, especially if there's no business coming in. Income's collapsing, losses are going through the roof, so they need to cut costs."

"What about the Bear Stearns thing?"

"You have been paying attention… Well the government basically took the hit on that and, in the process, maybe saved J P Morgan from taking a hit. But that's not going to be the end of it. Anyway, I'll be okay, honey, I've been careful with my money."

"Sorry, baby, but I'm still trying to get my head around all this. Why do you want to go now? Why not wait six months, if that's what it's going to be and take the payoff."

"I've thought about that a lot, honey, and I still haven't decided yet. It would sure make sense financially but I reckon it would be messy – these things always are – and there are some advantages to a clean break. I'm also not sure how good the payments would be given the trouble we're in. And, who knows, it might be a plus offering to go now, taking my chance on an individual deal rather than being one in a herd of thousands. On the same principle, it might also be easier to find something else to do with my unique gifts if I go now."

"Okay," said Carol, "I guess this is why I'm here?" Danny nodded. "Right, let's park the 'when to go' question for a minute, not least since you've already thought about it. I can tell you've also thought about what you'd do instead?"

"Well, you know, honey, I'll be 58 in October, and there's nobody counting on me no more, and like I said I won't have no financial worries, so I feel like I've got a hell of a lot more choices than I've had in a long time. And I've picked up a few skills and a shitload of experience along the way."

Carol started laughing, full on gut-grounded laughter. "Oh baby," she said at last, "you don't want my advice, that ain't why you've invited me to dinner. You've already decided on something and just want to tell me about it."

Danny looked at her a moment, then started laughing himself, but more in a quiet chuckle. "Okay, honey, you got my number. The thing is, I've signed up to go and work for Obama, not here in New York but in Ohio; I managed to persuade them I could organise stuff. I'm renting out the house for six months and moving to Cleveland at the end of the month. After the election, win or lose, I reckon I'll take a vacation and work out what to do next."

Carol took a drink to cover her surprise; so that was it. She smiled, "So that's why you want to leave now?"

"You betcha, what did you think of all that post-rationalisation I gave you earlier? Pretty damn good huh?"

"Not bad, though it didn't quite sound right, not enough emotion in it for it to be authentically you. But I'd never have guessed you'd signed up for Obama, let alone in Ohio. In fact, on the way home, I was thinking how anti him and pro Hilary you'd been back in January."

"Yeah, I've had to eat humble pie over that a few times already. Don't make me do it again, honey. I admit this is a big one but everyone's allowed to get it wrong once."

"When did you change your mind?"

"I been trying to figure that out myself, honey, and I don't know, not for sure anyway. I think it started when he didn't flop under pressure. I'd thought for definite he'd fold when Hilary started coming back at him so strong and looked like she was gonna march all the way to Denver. But I think the biggest thing was when they got hold of his old preacher, that video of him damning White folks, the way they do.

And I wondered what he'd do, reckoned he'd just roll over. Of course he dropped him, realistically he had to, but he didn't drop him the way I thought he'd try to. And then he made that speech, that speech, explaining to White folks why the preacher was angry; why he had a right to be; why, although he used language he shouldn't have, White folks should understand and forgive him if they wanted Black folks to understand and forgive them. I think that's what did it. He could have backed off so much more than he did, but instead he fronted up and used that showy rhetoric of his, which I still can't quite get used to, to make some of those hard yards. That's when I think I flipped."

"Well, I can say this for you, when you flip, you sure do it big time. Do you really think he can win in November? You know all hell's gonna break loose when he gets nominated?"

"I know that, honey, but it's like running; if you have a chance to win, you gotta try and take it. I promised myself that way back."

"I've never heard you say that before. Did you ever feel that when you were running; I mean, that you'd left something in the locker?"

"Not exactly, but there's one I've always wondered about. Back in '72 I ran this Portland meet – I was pretty green at the time; anyway, all the fastest guys were there but I just went for it anyway. But somehow I couldn't find my right rhythm till about 250 gone, you know, middle of the bend by which point I was about sixth, so I kicked early and just kept kicking, and with about 75 to go, I start passing people and end up third, almost second. Well, when it came to the trials, all the same people were there and I figured to myself that the way to go faster, and maybe come second or even win it was to make sure I had a little more in the tank for that last 150. And the way I could do that I reckoned was to run slightly within myself up to that point so as my kick would be even more effective. Well, it all went pretty good till 250 – I was in rhythm, running within myself and, hell, I was fourth not sixth. But when I kicked, nothing happened, there was energy there but I just couldn't translate into speed. Eventually, I overtook someone about five yards from the line but by then I'd already been overtaken myself, four times would you believe, and ended up seventh."

Carol nodded, "I remember that race. I always wondered what had happened but I wasn't with you then; and because I'm a journalist, I thought later it would be crossing some kind of line to ask you. But from what you've told me, you could take any number of lessons from that race. After all, you went out to win it. The thing was you were inexperienced and chose the wrong tactics. Don't beat yourself up about it."

"It's all right, honey, I got over it. And of course you're right, but the thing I remember most about it, more even than the disappointment, was that I was barely panting as I crossed that line. Man had I left some racing in the locker, and I swore that no matter what tactics I chose in the future, I would never let that happen again."

"And from what I saw, I don't think you ever did." Carol reached over and squeezed Danny's hand. "So where does Obama relate to the '72 US Olympic trials?"

Danny laughed, "Honest, Carol, it's not very profound. But the lesson I took, the biggest one, was that the things I care about, I'd only get them, if at all, after a load of pain. So I'm expecting the campaign thing to be hard and ugly and painful. In fact, for me that's part of the deal. I want it to be like that; it's what'll make it worth winning. If Obama didn't scare the racists, he wouldn't be worth campaigning for."

"You know there are people who think Ohio was stolen in 2004, just as much as Florida was in 2000?"

"Yeah, of course I know that, honey. That's why we've got to start now and get so many voters registered it goes beyond being an issue. That's why I'm going out there."

"Have you told Althea? What did she say?"

"Oh you know how she is, still thinks I'm 35." Danny giggled slightly, not something he often did, and for a moment he looked like he did when she'd first met him. "So Althea's like 'Way to go, Dad, get out there and work those phones'." He paused. "The reason she thinks that, you know, is cos you brought her up with no limits on what she could achieve, despite the evidence to the contrary. I honest to God don't know where you got the energy from for all those years. I know I sure as hell couldn't have done it."

"Is that why you left us?" Carol's tone was playful.

Danny sat back in his chair. Finally, he leaned forward again and put both forearms on the table. He looked down. "I don't know exactly why I left, Carol. I loved you both but I didn't believe I could do the hard yards. I don't know I just didn't feel anywhere near being good enough."

"It hurt, you know. My pride won't let me tell you how much but it did. For a long time I wished I could've hated you, but I never could. But I want this evening to be a happy one, a good one."

"You're right, and I don't suppose I am really asking for advice, but I did want to explain to you what I'm doing. And no, I don't want your approval or anything corny like that. But I don't want you to think I'm an idiot either. And it'll be the first time in 35 years we'll be living more than a mile apart. And so I guess there's a bit of this evening that's about saying thanks for allowing me to be your neighbour all these years." Danny sat back again, relieved. "It's sure been a while but I wouldn't have missed it. One of the best decisions I've ever made was to live close to you and Althea. It's given shape and at least some discipline to my life. It's been great being able to see Althea grow up, although from a short but safe distance," he laughed. "But you're right, 1972 sure seemed a long time ago. Man, when I think back, my grandpa was a sharecropper, and I was the first of my family who grew up being able to vote. And now some Black guy could be in the White House in less than a year from now."

Carol nodded.

"My grandparents would've been so proud of Althea. You know, honey, even though I didn't do as well as I wanted, I feel real lucky competing when I did. I know they paid a price, but Tommy and John were always my heroes. They changed everything for me."

"You're right, I think. Tommy and John were so articulate it was impossible to dismiss them. And administrators also acquired a healthy dose of fear about what athletes might say or do that could embarrass them. But there was a big revolution going on back then across all sports."

"Why then?"

"I think part of it had to do with the Black athletes who reached the top of their sport in the early, mid-60s and saw no reason why they should be judged by anything but their talent, or why they should show deference to any White man. As a consequence, athletes like the Ali and Bob Gibson and Kareem were a whole lot more radical and mouthy. And then there's television and the realisation of TV executives that nothing sold advertising space like live sports."

"And now there's the internet too…"

"Of course, and it came along just in time. Television and sport were in danger of eating themselves, becoming this closed system of received reality, endlessly self-referential. The internet has changed all that."

"It's funny," said Danny, "I'm quite a technophobe really, but it's finally hooked me. Althea reckons I've gone mad. And I get all my information from the internet, book holidays, buy presents, the absolute works, honey. And that's one of the big reasons I think we can win in November. Obama's really got the internet worked out. His campaign have really used it to encourage people to register, to boost campaign funding. I forget the numbers but it's easily over a million. But for me, voter registration is the biggest deal."

"I like hearing you talk like this, I really do, and I'm impressed you're just going to head off and move to Cleveland. It'll be weird knowing you're not just a few blocks away."

"You could come with me? Not an invitation, just an offer."

Carol's response was slightly too quick, "I don't think it would work for me, honey, I was thinking while you were talking and I'm just too set in my ways now. New York's my home and I'm not made for living anywhere else anymore. I'll come and see you, if that's all right, for a couple of days before I head off to Beijing."

"That'll be great, honey, it'll be terrific to see you out there, though I warn you I might drag you in to answer the phones for a few hours."

"No problem, I'll send you some dates tomorrow."

Carol looked up and caught the waiter's eye. "Time to go, honey. Us 60-year olds need our beauty sleep."

Five minutes later, they were outside again; ten minutes after that, Carol was saying goodbye at Danny's front door, giving him the same routine pecks on the cheek as she had three hours earlier. As the door shut, she felt her knee slightly stiffen but was determined to walk it off. She had not been able to work out what Danny had offered. Was it to shift their existing arrangement to Cleveland, or was it to move there together? Was it to quit her career and go campaign for Obama with him? Carol hadn't known the answers to these questions; they were too big, so she had let them go.

She shook his head slowly. And in her memory he saw him again, seemingly effortlessly surfing round that last bend in Portland, eyes glazed over but face muscles completely relaxed, head rolling slightly as the lactic began to kick in.

Chapter 45
London, 1 September

The time since Sam's diagnosis had passed slowly and painfully for everyone, apart from Sam himself, who seemed to have prematurely detached himself from the temporal world. With his decisions taken, and accepted by Mary and Ruth, however reluctantly, his bodily pain largely controlled and neutered by the NHS, he had seemed almost awkwardly carefree to those who spent time with him.

Back in April, the consultant had estimated he had some three months left but in fact July passed much as June had done, and it was only in mid-August that his physical deterioration became marked. Many found this extended period quite uncomfortable, feeling they should be positive but, with no expectation it was other than a short postponement of the inevitable, unable to muster any genuine optimism. Ruth found these additional weeks almost unbearable. She had strained every sinew to identify some shred of longer term hope, a new drug or pioneering operation. But there had been nothing, and eventually, she had subsided into exhausted misery and confusion. Throughout, Sam had seemed to glide above her efforts, and she had at times resented his insouciance.

In truth, Sam was neither detached nor insouciant, but was instead focused on controlling his own grief in the face of rapid physical decay, more apparent and inexorable to him than to his observers. He fought endlessly against it but was conscious he did so out of duty rather than hope of success. And when no one was there, he cried.

When the time had come to go into the hospice, he did so with relief, on his own behalf as well as others. The shift in responsibility, from Mary and Ruth to the hospice staff and Michelle, was hard for his family and for Michelle but easy for him. He knew it would now be only a few days, and he had become more certain that Michelle was the best person to observe the close-ups of his endgame. Part of this was protecting Mary and Ruth, part it was fulfilling some unarticulated bond with Michelle, but mostly it was a selfish determination to spend his last days not having to care.

***

Sam opened his eyes slowly. His sleep had been fitful, but he felt better rested than he had since coming into the hospice a week ago. He looked around slowly without turning his head. He was pleased Mary had come to see him yesterday; he had always thought she would but it was a relief all the same. It had been important to talk to her and explain how he was trying to protect her from the worst aspects of his deteriorating body and, when he was gone, from shouldering all the burden of executing his will. Ruth had been the day before, but they had both struggled to say anything much; still he was happy it was sufficient, or at any rate the best possible in the circumstances; he'd always been rubbish at goodbyes.

He had wanted to talk more to Mary about the importance of their life together, the preciousness that every moment of it had held for him. He knew that at times Mary had thought him weak, too prone to compromise.

Since 7/7, his view of fate had become more random. But instead of leaving him depressed, this had liberated him from his previous Calvinist-like belief that you got what you deserved and that hard work was rewarded. Now he knew it was folly to presume to predict the consequence of any action, and this had freed him to make quicker, less angst-ridden decisions. He could just follow his instinct. The burden he'd always carried for the consequences, potential as well as actual, of the myriad decisions he had taken was miraculously dissolved. Intended or unintended, it didn't matter; indeed, he was completely seized by the now gloriously unforeseeable consequence of almost any action. The last three years had been the happiest of his life.

He noticed again how clean the room was and thought again how good to him they had been at the hospice. A slice of early morning sun was sneaking through the curtains and hitting the wall on his right, just to the side of the door. At its edges, the light defused marginally as it baked into the shadows. As he looked at the tramlines of light, a ladybird walked across it, from darkness into light and back into darkness again. The door opened and the nurse walked in. She was called Gabriella and had been a smiling but largely silent presence since he had been admitted. Her hair was swept back tightly into a bun behind her head, under her nurse's cap. She muttered something he didn't catch but because she smiled as she did so, he didn't mind and just nodded back; it didn't matter, now wasn't the time to ask people to repeat things. Gabriella looked at the machines he was hooked up to and nodded at him again. Then she went over to the trolley and prepared an injection. This was what happened each morning, and he rotated his left arm outwards so the veins were exposed. As he watched the liquid seep into his body, he felt himself relax; funny how a week in a hospice was long enough to make a habit of things that would have worried him before. Gabriella spoke to him, and again he only half heard her – maybe his hearing was starting to be impaired in some weird way, but it was clear she was asking if it was okay to pull back the curtains and let in the daylight. He nodded.

It was a beautiful morning and Sam could see small white clouds hanging in the azure sky. He felt better than for at least a couple of days and was again pleased Mary had come to see him yesterday. He loved her deeply, always had – not quite one of those first sight things but close. He still remembered the sensation of placing his hand in the small of her back to ease her towards him the first time they kissed and discovering it was already arched.

The door opened and Michelle crept in and went over to speak to Gabriella. They whispered together for several minutes, occasionally looking at him. He wanted to let them know he was feeling better than he had last night, and that he was happy because it was a beautiful morning and because Mary had come to see him yesterday. But at the end of the day it didn't seem worth interrupting just to tell them what he was thinking and that he was okay really, although of course he was dying.

Michelle looked pretty, Sam thought, as pretty as she had that day when he had fallen over in the mud at the last corner of the school cross country. He had finished with his face splattered with mud, his left side covered in it. She was looking at him as he entered the finishing funnel, quizzical and sympathetic in equal measure, her long hair blowing around her shoulders. His rage and sense of humiliation and clumsiness immediately gave way, and he had begun to laugh, not really at himself but at the absurdity of it all. And Michelle was laughing with him, even as he tried hopelessly to clean his face with a damp tissue. It came back to him how happy he had been that day.

***

When Michelle came to see him early that morning, the windows were streaked with rain and she could tell Sam had died. She immediately rang Mary and left an urgent but non-specific message to come over as soon as she could. Then she called Gabriella, the nurse. Michelle knew Mary wouldn't be able to get there for at least 45 minutes, and so she made herself a cup of tea and sat in the saggy armchair in the corner of the common room while Gabriella busied herself with what needed to be done, and tried again to think about what it all really meant.

In the end, he had died all by himself, without any of them. There had always been that sizeable corner of Sam that was closed off to all but himself. Mind you, she had often wondered whether he really knew what was in there. She suspected it was a huge treasure trove of unfilled dreams and unspoken fantasies. But more than anyone else she knew, Sam had kept it all private. Michelle sipped her tea and reflected how she was relieved she hadn't been there. Her one dread was that she would be the only person present when he died. She had always known the chances were high and that she was the wrong person to perform this final role.

How had she ended up in this position? Obviously, she had created it herself, but why had she? That was more difficult even though she had thought about her motives a great deal. The easiest to identify was, unsurprisingly, also the most virtuous; the wish to offer her professional skills to care for her oldest friend during his last days. Michelle trusted herself that this was the major part, but she also knew there was more. She didn't think there was any sense in which she was trying to supersede Mary. There was, however, a part of her that suspected she had always been in love with Sam, but with a passion so deeply buried that only his imminent death had surfaced it. They had been so close when they were young but even when Sam had left Nottingham to go to university, she had felt no sensation of physical attraction or loss. Even now, Michelle didn't know the answer. She was too consumed by grief and, now the immediacy of his death had passed and she was settled with her cup of tea, she began to sob.

Virtually none of her close friends had died until now. There was a young doctor she remembered, a football player, who she had known slightly in her 20s; and then, about five years later, long after he'd moved into another job, she'd heard he'd laid down one night on a railway line. Jim his name was and she had liked him, but they had never really been close and that had been about 30 years ago. Nothing like this. It was as if a wall of her life had suddenly come crashing down, whole blocks of shared memory and experience obliterated; conversations they had shared, things they had seen together, jokes and films and television they had laughed at and watched. Michelle had assumed Sam would always be there to talk to about these things but now he wouldn't, and as years passed and her memory inevitably became more cloudy, the clarity she now had would gradually be replaced by ambiguity and doubt. Was it really like that? Which of those events happened first? Was Sam really laughing when they said that? And there would be no one to check the truth with, no one else who was there with her when it happened. Without Sam to validate those memories, they would inexorably begin to fray, and then fray and fray again until they were barely recognisable.

Michelle didn't know what the last few weeks and days had brought her beyond closer proximity to his dying. She did not even know if she had been able to take any better care of Sam than he would have received anyway. God only knew what Mary and Phil thought of her. Mary must be a saint to treat her as she had. And as for Phil… Michelle paused, brought up short by the violence of the thought. What had she done? And what must he think? For weeks now, she had closed herself off, blocked out her partner, secure in her own righteousness. Michelle took a hesitant slurp of tea, the taste shadowed by the saliva induced by her weeping. She put her head in her hands and began slowly rocking, trying to come to terms with what she had done and what it meant. She was still rocking when Mary put her head round the door.

For a minute or so, Mary stood silently looking at her friend. What did that word mean, after the death of the man who had linked them and who now, perhaps, separated them? It didn't seem right to think about Sam as separating people.

"I'm sorry you weren't there," Mary said finally. "I got your message."

Michelle looked up slowly, her face a delta of tear tracks, "In some ways it was a relief," she whispered. "I don't know how I would have dealt with it, not after everything." She paused, "From everything I can tell, he went very peacefully; I don't think he would have felt any pain, and when I'd left a couple of hours before, he'd been sleeping peacefully."

"Good," replied Mary, forcing herself to smile, "I'm glad. I'm glad too that I came yesterday, Ruth too. She's still sleeping; I thought it best to come myself this time. It was difficult for a while to make the decision, but it was wonderful to see him so himself in his own mind, so at peace with himself. I, Ruth and I, can't thank you enough, Michelle, for all that you've done. I know, I think I've always known, that you've only ever wanted what was best for Sam. It's been stupid of me not to understand, not to admit to myself that I understood. So I want to apologise to you; I wanted to last night but everything was too emotional and it never seemed like the right time. Whereas now, well, it's easier I guess. I wasn't surprised when I got your message; I think I'd been expecting it, and so now I feel oddly flat." She laughed slightly nervously, "Will you forgive me?"

Michelle tried again to wipe her face dry with what was by now a sodden handkerchief. "Oh Mary, there's nothing to forgive, absolutely nothing, there couldn't be. I've been sitting here trying to work out what impulse drove me to do what I've done, to push you out of the way, and I don't really know. Simply wanting to help Sam was a big part of it, maybe all of it, but right now I can't say that for sure. I'm just too confused and I'm only starting to realise how much pain I've caused so many people – you, Ruth, Phil, and that's just for starters. It's me who

444

should be asking you to forgive. All I can say is, at the time I've never been more certain of anything in my life. I was completely convinced, and nothing else seemed important."

Mary had gone over and sat down in the chair opposite Michelle. "I don't really know what to say. It's been such a strange, horrible time, and I've ended up looking inside a lot, at myself, at my marriage, at our friendship, everything really. I guess death and grief do that a lot. But then Sam's always had that effect on me. Sometimes I think that's why I married him, but I've never told him that, of course. He's always had the knack of making me feel awkward in the strangest ways." She laughed dryly, "I used to quite enjoy those awkward situations, but that was when he was there, now I'm not so sure. Do you think he meant us to feel like this once he'd gone? I always thought Sam could be a lot more cunning than any of us gave him credit for. He wasn't just the man who was nice to everyone, there was much more to him than that. But then you know all this, don't you?"

"I don't know really. I mean, because we grew up together, there's a large part of me that always saw him as the boy I knew in Nottingham. It always seemed quite strange seeing Sam so at home in London – I'm sure he thought the same about me. Sam really liked people, and he's always been one of the kindest people I know. But I always thought he quite liked being alone and that he didn't like being in crowds." Michelle was speaking slowly, trying to control her halting voice between miniscule sips of tea. "And it wasn't like some people where you can see moods passing across their faces, but I always thought it was pretty obvious what his mood was, if he was happy or sad."

Mary forced herself to smile as she took the other woman's hand. "I was always going to come, I think; I just needed to get everything straight in my head first. Thank you again for all you've done, for looking after him so well… You've done so much better, so much more than I ever could have."

The two women stared at each other for a moment.

"At reception, they said I couldn't see him yet because they were still doing various medical tests."

"I think it's worth trying again," said Michelle.

Some ten minutes later, they were standing at the foot of Sam's bed looking at the corpse of the man they had known so well. The cheek bones had always been huge but were even more accentuated by his shrunken cheeks. His eyes were closed, and so the glassy deep stare was gone, and in its place a passive look to his features that spoke not so much of calm as of bland emptiness, all preoccupation and concern drained from it. To Mary, he looked at peace, whereas Michelle thought it was no longer Sam, that his soul had already left.

Chapter 46
London, 31 August

Mary's thoughts were dominated by Sam and memories of him, already starting to be framed in the past tense.

The day she'd married him was the first day Mary had wondered if Sam would ever have a successful career. The thought had been momentary and the pace of the day had swamped it. Of course, she had reasoned, Sam would never be a permanent secretary – she knew people who would and he wasn't like them – then she got a call to say that they couldn't find the flowers for the ushers' lapels and did Mary know where they were?

The first time Mary had seen him – well, it hadn't been love at first sight, that was definitely not her style –he had been standing in the kitchen, leaning against the sink and drinking cheap red wine, wearing a cheap Hawaiian shirt over faded jeans and trainers. His hair hadn't been brushed well and stuck up in a couple of places; even his parting wasn't straight. Later, Mary knew these things were carelessness rather than statement, but at the time she was just surprised to find a man who wasn't pre-packaged. He'd been younger and older at the same time, impossible naïveté combined with wisdom middle-aged equanimity.

When he was starting to shrivel up, as the cancer worked its destruction, it became harder to recall what he had looked like 30 years before. Photos helped but somehow never quite captured his character. Physically, Mary remembered Sam as slightly stooping but strong and wiry. Despite this, he had been – Mary bit her lip – anything but intimidating. The more Mary thought about it, the more he seemed riven with contradictions – he could open any screw top bottle or jar but had a weak handshake; he often spoke in close to a whisper but had one of the loudest voices she had heard.

Mary had always imagined herself as an outsider, but in fact falling in love with and marrying Sam was by far her most unconventional act. She recognised this herself but semi-consciously chose to diminish its significance. By doing so, she made her life seem more coherent and smoothly progressive than it was. In Mary's narrative, marrying Sam was of a piece with taking an academic post in London rather than Cambridge and going skiing in Italy rather than France or Switzerland. And while it was a bizarre error to classify these choices alongside marrying Sam, without this sleight of hand, she might not have found within herself the bravery to say yes when Sam proposed.

As it was, and in this Mary's memory did accord with reality, her decision to marry him had been entirely free of doubt. In her core, she knew she had never been so comfortable in another person's company. However, Mary assumed her attraction to Sam was physical and intellectual when, in fact, it was largely emotional. Like others, she wanted to be his sister more than his wife but such was the strength of the yearning that Mary did not recognise the difference. But what really attracted and then bound her to Sam was his ability to empathise with almost everyone. In Mary's mind, this was often an amusing irritation, sometimes incomprehensible. But, in fact, it was the core of their relationship; it was the thing that seemed most different from the other men she knew, which enabled her to envisage, and dream of, growing old with him.

In choosing to marry Sam, Mary had made a decision that would shift the trajectory of her life but, because she misinterpreted it, her internal narrative failed to reflect this. It took away at a stroke some of the edgy competitiveness she so valued; she didn't notice. She began to pay more attention to the English countryside and to notice the changing seasons; she didn't spot the change. None of this occurred overnight, and if Mary had not been a callous manipulator before marrying Sam, neither did she become full of caring and sensitivity afterwards. Yet her friends saw the difference even if she did not, and she became more loved by her academic colleagues.

Mary worried that Michelle had become Sam's primary carer in his last weeks, but she had been able to rationalise this, for all but a small corner of her mind. Despite having had to ditch all her plans to look after him, she had somehow adjusted to her new role. Many of her friends, Linda most vociferously, thought Mary mad and weak for having accepted such a demotion. For Mary herself, however, once she had clawed her way through the initial trauma of apparent rejection, it became a rite of passage. While she remained intentionally blind to some of the implications, her acceptance of it was a dramatic change, a genuine sublimation of herself to the needs of another.

And, as a result, Mary began to feel different and, at least in part, to view her life through a different lens. She cried more often, not solely about Sam but about events which had previously left her cold. The pivotal moment had come when she went to see him in the hospice. Finally, in her own mind, she acquiesced in Sam's choice of Michelle not her – how she felt diminished by that negative! She recognised Sam's life was his own to make decisions about, and that Sam alive and healthy was something other than Sam ill and dying.

The hospice, she had discovered, wasn't a quiet place, and Mary was surprised to hear the TV on in a couple of rooms. She asked at reception where Sam's room was and felt, or thought she felt, the look when she said she was his wife. There was a toilet opposite the room before Sam's, and Mary decided to use it, partly to make sure she was together and able to cope. When she emerged from the toilet, she could hear their voices. Sam's was more rasping than before, and he sounded more irascible than he had ever been with her. Comforted by this, she walked forward and turned into the doorway. "Hello," she said, and gulped.

He was already a lot thinner. His cheek bones had always been prominent but now they were like escarpments in a mountain range. The flesh around his neck had shrivelled away to leave loose skin hanging from his chin. His eyes were still bright but – was she imagining it? – They seemed to glisten strangely. His feet were on top of the covers and, together with his ankles, looked plumper than she remembered them. But that memory was already wracked with uncertainty. The rest of Sam's body was covered with his dressing gown, the heavy woollen one, which seemed wrong given the weather.

He turned and smiled spontaneously at her. "Hello, darling, it's wonderful to see you! Welcome to my prison camp! Michelle here is worse than the sadistic prison guard in 'Cool Hand Luke', I swear she is. Or is it 'Prisoner Cell Block H'? Sorry for mixing my analogies like that!"

"Hello, Mary," said Michelle, getting up from her chair over by the window. "I'm so glad you've come…" She stopped and half laughed at her own expression of – what was it? – Relief? "I'm really glad to see you. If you'll excuse me, I'll leave the two of you alone; you must have loads to talk about."

Michelle walked over towards the door, passing close by, wondering how to greet her. As she did so, Mary looked towards her friend, the carer of her husband, and she put her arms around Michelle, burying her face in the other woman's neck to hide the tears that had begun to emerge from those little ducts that, after so many years, had decided to betray her. And she knew Michelle was no rival, and if she had ever been it was a very long time ago, long before she had met Sam. And she also knew, as though a shaft of lightning had split open an ancient oak tree, exposing its tangled roots to the daylight, that the two of them were alike in only thinking about Sam. This realisation surprised Mary as much about herself as it did about Michelle. All her fear, jealousy, suspicion fell away as she released Michelle and watched her leave.

"I'm sure she's looked after you brilliantly?" There was only the merest, unintentional hint of a question, which Mary had tried to remove entirely, and felt embarrassed by as soon as the rise in tone escaped her lips.

"Yes, of course, absolutely she has." Mary couldn't tell if Sam had ignored the question or if, in his illness, he had missed the intonation. And she realised she could never again take his intuition and empathy for granted. Sam continued, "You know, she hasn't been a nurse for more than 20 years but still seems to know all the medical stuff; once a nurse, always a nurse, I guess. The staff here all love her."

"I'm sure and I'm not in the least surprised. Michelle's so professional, far more than I could ever be."

"I want you to begin having your own life," Sam said, looking straight at her with his glistening eyes. "And I want your memories to be as I was, not as I am now, and still less as I'm told I'll become."

"You know I wanted to look after you?" Again Mary's voice rose in an involuntary question.

This time Sam responded. "Yes, of course I did, but I think this is better, and particularly for you."

Mary was unused to Sam being so direct and decided not to counter his assertion for now; which meant, she knew, for ever. "How are you feeling?" she asked.

"Do I look terrible? Okay, don't answer!" He smiled weakly. "I must apologise, cancer's not done much for my sense of humour."

"It was a lost cause long ago," Mary blurted out as she began to sob.

"It's all right, Mary, sit down, take your time, as long as you need."

She wept for the next five minutes. "Has Michelle cried much?"

448

"Ha, not at all, I think her professionalism has simply kicked in. I sense she's a little disappointed in herself, but I suspected it would be like this." He shook his head, "I've done enough crying for all of us but I think I'm done now."

"Did you think I would cry?" asked Mary. "I'm only asking because I don't think I've cried in 40 years."

"I don't know, I thought you probably would – you're more emotional than you think – but I was most worried about you doing what Michelle has done."

"Why, I wanted to look after you! I'm trying so hard not to break down or be angry that I'm not."

"I know and I'm sorry, but I had this really strong feeling, even before Michelle asked, that this was the best way for it to happen." Sam looked down for a moment, then up again at his wife. "Cancer's just too horrible a thing, too much to expect the living to bear. I don't have any choice about it but I don't want – I'm determined not to – inflict any more of it on any single person than I have to. For that reason, I've also changed the arrangements around my will. I've asked Ed to be an executor with you. No change in the terms we agreed all those years ago; I just want you to have someone to share the load with, should probably have thought about it ages ago."

By now Mary was fighting against being completely confused, feeling she was being tossed by a vicious sea, not knowing what Sam was going to say next. But through it she somehow seemed to also catch glimpses of the young intellectually playful man she had fallen in love with, the man she knew before the entire heaviness and grief of life as it is lived had dulled, or at least obscured, the intuitive sense of mischief she had found so irresistible.

"It seems," she said at last, "as though you've got us all acting out roles in your play."

He laughed, which seemed odd to her. "It certainly doesn't feel like that from where I am. But one of the things about dying this way is that I feel I'm taking a lot of decisions quickly, don't feel I have any choice about it. I don't have much time left, or that's what the doctors tell me, and my body seems to agree. So I'm sorry if it feels that way to you." Each burst of words came out in a staccato pattern, interspersed with gaps between which Sam visibly caught his breath and looked at her steadily.

"Sorry," said Mary, "I understand and believe you, and I didn't mean it badly anyway." She sat down. "You know it's funny being here as a visitor rather than being here all the time. I've been thinking a lot about what it means, and despite what you've said, I still don't really get it. But I'm okay with it, I want you to know that; it's hard but I completely accept it's your life and your decision. It doesn't change anything about how I feel about you, or about our life together or our marriage. Oh Sam," she reached across and squeezed his long hand, "I love you so much, I always will, you know."

"I do know, Mary, and I feel completely the same." Where his wife was dissolving into floods of tears, Sam's eyes remained dry, fixed on the back of Mary's head buried in the bedclothes; he really had cried himself out. "We've always been partners, more sometimes than we've even understood. I remember the first time we met like it was yesterday, you know. You were quite the most wonderful person I'd ever met – kind, funny, intelligent, beautiful – and I've worshipped you from that day to this. Every moment of our marriage has been a blessing that has made me happy and has kept me strong, or at least strong enough to weather the challenges life has sometimes thrown at me. There are still some things I need to let you know, and I don't think I have long left, so I'm going to keep talking; I hope that's okay."

His voice was beginning to fray, and he was speaking in staccato bursts. Sitting propped up by his mound of pillows, he was looking down at Mary but he now relaxed and let his head rest back so that he looked up at the ceiling and across at the mirror on the opposite wall. He realised he could now see Mary's face in the mirror, not just the top of her head but her right cheek by her eye. This struck him as beautiful, and he smiled at the symmetry and the fact that in the mirror he could see himself looking at himself looking at Mary.

"It sounds trite," he went on, "but I never thought I was good enough for you, or at least I never worked out why you ended up marrying me when there were so many who were cleverer, better looking, had more money, or all three."

Mary looked up fiercely. "That self-deprecation is the only thing I would ever have changed about you, but by God I would have killed it with my bare hands if I could. None of what you've just said is true, but I knew you thought it and I've tried for 30 years to change your mind about it. You were the man I wanted to wake up beside every morning, whose head I wanted on the pillow next to me, who I wanted to sleep with, have sex with, have children with. And it's always made me angry when you talk like that, but I've hidden it from you, bottled it up all these years. If you hadn't been so full of self-deprecation, I wouldn't have spent so damned long worrying about you. Oh Sam, why are you leaving me? I've only ever thought about my life as our life together. I thought we'd retire together, become grandparents together, travel more together. Sometimes it feels as though you've been Ruth's dad as much as my husband, which is one of the wonderful things about you, but I wanted more of you and feel like I've only just got you back, and now you're being ripped away forever. I've always believed in God but I've never before thought He was cruel in the way I do now – I guess it's that personal thing. Either we've done something really evil or God just wants to balance things up for all the goodness and luck that's come our way."

Sam was still looking at her in the mirror. "I've ended up seeing it differently, Mary. I've come to the end of my own road, completed the things in my life that were there to be done. But you have more to do, much more, I hope. I've also come to think that there's no great tragedy in my dying, or even a small one, much as it might feel good to be able to see it in those terms. We control the pain of cancer pretty well now, if somewhat expensively; and in any case, I can feel my body adjusting, shutting down bit by bit. And it's my time, I'm happy about that. I nearly died on 7/7, and I've been trying since to make the most of that opportunity. But I'm not really made for that, though it was good fun trying. The world has an attritional effect on me, it wears me down and eats away at my self-belief. In terms of age, I've felt old ever since Dad died. He was much older than me, of course, but when he died, I felt there was no one ahead of me."

"Don't talk like that, Sam, please! You're not being fair to yourself. There's nothing pre-ordained about what's happening to you. It's no kind of judgement on your life. Sure, there are lots of things still left to do with your life, valuable ones. You getting cancer's no judgement on what other things you would do." Mary had stopped crying now and was looking up at him. "So there would have been the chance to travel, to do lots of new things together."

"I know, darling, you're right. I was only talking about how it felt for me; you're right though, we had a lot still ahead of us."

Inside, Sam knew he was compromising again. He had begun with such determination to explain himself to Mary, so she would at last understand the man she married. But the combination of her emotional state and his own reversion to type – Sam cursed himself even as he smiled inwardly at the inevitability – had caused him to cave in and duck the conversation. But maybe he had made the best decision. Even in the form he had ended up managing to deliver it, what he had said was at the odd end of deathbed confessions; an attempted justification of earthly weakness as he saw it. He thought of all the times he had compromised and wondered again if he would have done more good had he been stronger and held out more for 100% of what he believed in. Perhaps he could have fought more but the matters over which he had compromised didn't seem worth it. And while he was compromising, didn't that mean others were compromising too?

And what did it add up to anyway? He recalled being on a train passing through some station in the Midlands, maybe Nuneaton, and watching a man disconnect a huge poster for something like mortgage advice from its site in the middle of the platform. The face of the blonde-haired woman in the poster billowed attractively as it was loosened but then, instead of floating free, it crumpled down onto the ground. All his life he had felt unshakeably rooted in the company of family, friends and colleagues. He had always felt his collective connection to them to be greater than his own sense of self. Without them wouldn't he too have crumpled rather than fly free? Had he ever thought like this before, or was it simple rationalisation of his weakness?

As so often, he thought back to 7/7, running after that bus, but not really trying to chase it down, being conscious of his stubbed toe throbbing but still being able to run, breathing heavily but not out of breath. When had he ceased to push himself as hard as he would have needed to do to catch it? At school, he would have caught it, so too at university; was it to do with getting a job, getting married, becoming a parent? He didn't think so, but at some stage those who surrounded him had become more important to him than he was to himself. Why do everything 100% if you only ever got 95% of that cake you wanted? The strong temptation was to start by trying for 90% instead and then you were far less likely to have to retreat, no retracing of steps.

The fact of 7/7, his escape, hit him again. He looked at Mary and part of him felt sublimely at peace, while the other part became angrier, angry his life was being torn away from him just when he had finally discovered, settled on, how he wanted to live it. And then Sam decided to compromise one last time, this time with himself. There were many things left he wanted to do but that would always be the case. Until the last six months, there had never really been any problem with his health; he and Mary had been happily married for more than a quarter of a century; Ruth had become every bit the woman he had always hoped; he had been blessed with his friendships, especially Ed and Michelle, to an extent he thought was rare; and he had at long last found out now, almost at the last, how he wanted to lead his life. Sam grinned to himself but then, looking up again to the mirror, saw that his grin had translated into a sickening rictus. Ruefully, he concluded that advanced cancer did not go well with smiling. The rictus vanished.

Mary looked up at him. "I'd like to stay another ten minutes or so but I'd like to kiss you now, is that okay? I feel odd asking but…" Sam nodded and reached out to her the best he could. Mary stood up and leant over him. He was very pale and his cheeks had collapsed in on themselves. His eye sockets had deepened and his ears seemed to protrude more. In appearance, he was a world away from the man she had fallen in love with but, despite the cancer, his self and their life together were etched into every morsel of his hanging skin. She lowered her face to his and kissed his lips long and hard. Then she sat back down and, as she said she would, chatted for ten more minutes, mostly about Ruth and their friends.

Epilogue

There was no real consensus about Sam other than he had been much loved and would be much missed. His life had as many different interpretations as there were friends and family to articulate them. Each viewed him from a different angle, a different expanse of time and experience, through a different lens. Trying to put them together blurred the edges beyond any meaningful definition. And so, when discussing him as they inevitably did, his family and friends instinctively withdrew whenever the merest disagreement surfaced, danced cleverly around the matter, avoiding its substance. This performance, in which everyone was complicit, preserved the veneer but sacrificed some of the substance of Sam's memory. It meant the mental records they each had of his life and the times they had lived through with him were eaten away by neglect. The veneer, however, was still sufficient to bind them together, even as other forces started to pull them apart.

Michelle still could not come to terms with the last few months of Sam's life, the pain she had caused. Phil seemed to have been devastated, losing all his outward bravado and shrinking into a shell she had not known he possessed. He had almost entirely withdrawn from her, and she had been met with the drained, almost insipid civility of a man suddenly disoriented, feeling he has nowhere to turn. While Sam was still alive, she had been so submerged in the caring process that Phil's non-reaction was a blessed relief, not threatening to distract her focus and enabling her to pretend it would all be okay again when the ordeal was over. But now that it was over, it was plain that Phil's response was the worst it could have been, that she had lost him. For sure he still inhabited the house but only as a shadow, barely communicating, monosyllabic at best, sleeping in the spare room, keeping it unnervingly tidy, not drinking at all, working even longer hours, leaving at dawn and returning at about 10pm, having already eaten.

She didn't know where to start trying to rebuild their life. Completely empty herself, she was barely able to go through the motion of living each day. Dressing, shopping, eating; all seemed to happen in a detached way, almost as if it was someone else. It was hard, for a while impossible, to remember how life had been before; but slowly and painfully actions started to connect – she dressed so she could go shopping, she shopped so she could eat. Remarkably, it was Mary who provided the lubricant that eased her journey back, coming around for cups of tea, arranging to go shopping together, calling her almost every day to make small talk.

For his part, Philip had entered a tunnel with no light at the end. He could neither comprehend what Michelle had done nor conceive of how he could live apart from her. For someone proud of being able to deal with whatever life threw at him, whose self-image was based on certainty about his own independence, both were inexplicable. The moment Michelle had told him she was going to move to the hospice to care for Sam full-time, this identity had begun to shred. The clinical nature of the decision, with no element of consulting him, or worrying about how he felt, demolished his ego.

At the same time, he was coming to terms with the imminent death of one of his closest friends. He could still recall distinctly walking up the road to Sam and Mary's house that first time but the memory was now painfully ambiguous.

**

Ed was the only one not surprised by the events of Sam's last weeks. For him, Michelle had been the great love of Sam's life and he of hers. It was like Levin and Kitty in the woods in Anna Karenina, both wanting to have the critical conversation but ultimately failing. He saw that each had found forms of happiness but for him they were second-best.

He never expressed his view, however. He knew it would seem perverse and cause more pain. He thought Sam was the first among human beings he knew, almost saint-like. For him, in other respects agnostic, Sam's disappointments in life and suffering in death were tests, almost biblical, which he had passed through triumphantly.

The day of the funeral was cool for September, a north easterly breeze taking the top off the temperature and pushing clouds remorselessly across a sky that was less than blue. There were about 100 people there, probably less than he had expected. Ed had always imagined Sam having legions of friends but maybe that simply wasn't the case. He remembered having gone home from university for the funeral of a much-loved PE teacher who had collapsed in the school office one day and died of a heart attack. There had been maybe 800 people in the huge church, many of them ex pupils. This wasn't that, but the upside was that Ed knew almost everyone, and estimated that maybe two thirds of them had been at Sam and Mary's wedding almost a quarter of a century ago.

Sam had requested they play 'Dock of the Bay' by Otis Redding but otherwise had made no other stipulation. As the lyrics – so evocative of time, place, state of mind – wafted across the crematorium, Ed saw several people break into involuntary smiles, several others start to cry, and Philip mouthed the words, singing silently to himself.

Then Ruth was finishing her eulogy…

"My dad was quite quiet and thoughtful, and when I was growing up, it took me a long time to understand him and how much he cared for us, his family and all his friends. This was not because he did not say he loved us or because he did not hug us, kiss us, spend time with us. He did all those things. Instead, it was because it took me a long time to appreciate how far ahead he thought and how much he made himself vulnerable to our trials and tribulations. Our striving and our emotions were also experienced by him, almost in the first person, and very many of them he had anticipated, and done everything he could to prepare us for. I only now realise how much everything he did had a purpose. And it was hardly ever about him. At times, my dad has said or done things that seemed weird but at some subsequent point suddenly made sense." There was a ripple of laughter. "We are all the richer for his life and will carry things he said and did with us through life. Goodbye, Dad, I carry so much of you with me."

***

Philip woke with a start, drenched in sweat. Obama had been shot, and it took him a few moments to realise it was a dream. He looked at his phone; it was only 4.48. He slowly, incrementally, made himself a cup of coffee and towelled himself dry. He had a temperature and was feeling lousy, sorry for himself.

He had been in the US since the week after Sam's funeral. The conversation with Michelle had been brief, and she hadn't resisted his desire to put some distance between them, only saying that she would still be there whenever he decided to come back. He had taken unpaid leave, promising to be back by the New Year.

Coffee made, he lay propped up in bed and turned the light off. But he had already opened the curtains and the lights of the city gave his 15th floor hotel room one of those shifting neon glows so beloved of Hollywood. Sighing at the receding possibility of further sleep, he reached for the control and switched on the TV, surfing between BBC World and CNN. Obama was everywhere, the president elect, very much alive and suddenly on a pedestal, cast as the putative saviour of both America and of a global financial system that seemed to be disintegrating. Several firms had been rescued by the government but Lehman Brothers had collapsed, and with it seemingly all confidence that anything financial was what it said on the tin. Even in the UK, RBS and HBOS had needed government rescue.

In his dream, he had been back in that kitchen in San Francisco and seeing Robert Kennedy's body again; except it was Obama. Was Obama the answer? And to what? Everything? And how was that a fair burden for anyone? Did it matter that Obama wasn't descended from slaves? Was he a president for the 21st century, or the fulfilment of the Voting Rights Acts? Obama seemed determined not to see it as a choice, evoking the memory and referencing the oratory of both Lincoln and Dr King but presenting himself as essentially a 21st century story.

He remembered his conversation with Carol when they had met up in DC, back in October. "I've not really got Obama," he'd admitted. "He's too smooth for me, has too many answers, reminds me too much of David Cameron."

"Well, I don't know too much about your Cameron," she had replied. "But I do know that if Barack Obama is elected – which I still don't quite believe – then a lot of them Southern White racists who made my parents' life as hellish as they could've will be squirming in their god forsaken graves. And that's pretty much good enough for me..."

'Try a Little Tenderness' had been playing in the background, and Phillip had been back in a Greenwich Village bar 40 years before. Alex was ranting at him – "What's the point of non-violence when your young people are being sent to die in Vietnam?"

Carol was still talking. "...and the White people we lived near sure didn't care, except in a bad way. But these young kids had no need, no stake, but did it anyway, because they knew it was right." She paused, took another drink. "The thing is, a lot of those kids got reviled four years later. 1968 was a bad year."

Phillip remembered how he had thought back to Grant Park during the 1968 Democrat convention and did so again. What was the story for those young people? And then his own encounter with the Chicago police had derailed him. What did it mean if part of what mainstream America had turned its back on in 1968 were the people who, to Carol, had represented the progressive future? Part of Obama's attraction, he realised, was the promise that this could be reversed. It could be no coincidence his acceptance speech had been staged in Grant Park, an explicit but barely recognised embodiment of that hope.

Carol had sighed and reverted to their original subject. "I should be surprised, I guess, but I stopped being surprised by people a while back, no matter how hard they try. I obviously don't know Michelle much, only met her a few of times, but she's a good woman; and it still sounds like the two of you had a pretty good thing."

It had been Phillip's turn to pause. He looked down for a moment. His eyes glistened slightly. "You can't imagine how long I've spent thinking about it all, trying to rationalise the whole thing so that my previous feelings end up still being true. It's almost as if there is a God and he's taking the piss. Having made a career out of being professionally cynical, usually with good cause, I've spent the last six months trying my best to do the opposite. I think I've cried more this year than I have in the previous 50 – cried for Sam, cried for Mary, cried for myself, cried for Michelle, in roughly that order."

"You're right to be a cynical bastard," Carol interrupted. "Life ain't what you expect, otherwise we'd all get bored and die young. My uncle Jesse ended up marrying three sisters from the same family – the first two died in childbirth. He ended up with nine children; seven by my Aunt Esme, and Joshua and Jesse Jr by her sisters. Life taught him early on not to be surprised. Some of those things that happened to him were terrible; I swear his hair was white before he was 25. But some of them were wonderful, and he ended up smiling more than any man I know."

Carol looked straight at him, and her face became cold. "You're good at your job and good at living your life; you've made good choices and been clever at working the angles. But you've been lucky too. You got some breaks before I knew you. You got easily your share of breaks when we worked together in the '70s. And you sure got lucky with Michelle. You didn't do anything to deserve that woman! Yea, you're too smart about yourself not to know. You were rutting around at every opportunity and then, for no reason I've ever been able to work out, this jewel of a woman fell for you."

As Phillip started to talk, she held up her hand. "Hold your horses for 30 seconds more, I've almost done and I've listened enough. What's happened with Sam and her is for sure one of those things that makes you think. And from what you say and how you speak about it, I'd guess you've dealt with it better than most people, including me. And for what it's worth, I'm not surprised. But life throws shit at people, all of us pretty much. But she does love you and she has come back, so the least you can do is cut her some of that slack she's been giving you all these years. And before you say anything, we both need another drink."

When Carol came back Phillip got up, took the drinks off her. Then he gave his friend an enormous hug, starting to cry as he did so. In that moment, he was the 18-year-old riding in a cab towards the Manhattan skyline; the streetwise, narcissistic journalist; the middle-aged TV exec, in love for the first and only time; and the vulnerable older man. And now, lying in his New York hotel room a month later, as the accumulated experience of his life broke over his consciousness, obliterating the self-constructed filters, he was again standing in a circle needing to be rescued.

One late afternoon some two weeks later, as Philip was driving east out of Denver, leaving the foothills of the Rockies behind, his mind cracked open. The sky ahead was open and blue, stretching out across the prairie. And in the middle was a vast pillar of white cloud, stretching from the ground up. This was the sky Kerouac and Woody Guthrie had written about; the first European settlers had camped under it and Native Americans had worshipped for a thousand years. It was the same sky he had been in awe of 40 years ago, when he had first laid on his back and gazed up at the unfamiliar prairie stars. It connected his life with countless others. Nothing was personal, all his experiences were shared.

Everything about him, whether honourable or despicable, was a different aspect of a universally-owned experience. Each of his sacrifices and transgressions had been replicated many times in the past and would be so again. Philip no longer felt caught up in the web of his previous actions, his own behaviour lost in the scale of humanity's. He raised his eyes from the circle and saw Michelle, still offering.

***

"Hello, Ruth, thanks for coming. I really appreciate it." Michelle stepped back from the doorway to allow the younger woman to come in.

"Hello," she replied, lingering on the step. "I don't quite know why I'm here except that Mum said I should come." Then she stepped into Michelle and Philip's house for the first time since before her dad had got sick. This small physical act, and the absence of the revulsion Ruth had expected it to trigger, began to legitimise her decision.

Once they had completed the normal pleasantries and had sat down with coffee, however, silence set in. "How have you been?" Ruth asked eventually.

"Oh, so-so," Michelle replied. "Phil called a couple of days ago to say he was flying back the week before Christmas. But he's going to stay in a hotel till we sort things out. I don't quite know what that means or what will happen at the end of the sorting, or even why I'm telling you."

Ruth felt embarrassed. She didn't quite know why – yes, it was personal information, but it was of the type she would once have expected Michelle to share, so close had they become over the last few years. But now was not a normal time, and she was left wondering whether Michelle's confession was a relic of this past era, an attempt to ingratiate herself, or something else. Against her better judgement, Ruth found herself giving Michelle the benefit of the doubt. "Well, do say hi, and that I hope I'll get to see him over Christmas."

"Yes, of course I will. I'm sure he'll want to see you, and Mary. He seems to have had a good time in the US. Obama's election helped…"

"And do you think the two of you will manage to sort things out?"

It had come out more bluntly than Ruth had intended but perhaps not more so than she'd meant. In any case, Michelle didn't flinch. "It's hard to tell but I hope so. I didn't realise how much my wanting to look after Sam would hurt him, or not until it was too late."

"Would you say the same about the hurt you caused my mother, that you didn't realise until it was too late?"

Michelle had been facing Ruth but now she looked out the window. "At the time, I would have said yes, but I realised later that deep down I knew Mary would be very upset."

"And yet you went ahead? How could you do that to her?"

"It's what Sam wanted. I knew that even before I'd asked him. If he hadn't wanted it, he would have said and that would have been that. Mary knows that too. We've talked about it."

"Have you?"

"Quite a lot actually. I don't know how I'd be now if your mother had ended up still thinking badly of me. Sam never felt so in control of his own life as in his last few months, and he had a reason for every decision he made."

Ruth waited on herself before replying, digesting information she had no reason to doubt and that she instinctively knew was true, even though her mother had never talked to her about it. Her instinctive antagonism towards Michelle, the animus that had led to Ruth shunning her, had been fuelled by Mary's initial anger and perceived humiliation, and by Linda's vitriol and insinuation. And Dad, when Ruth had asked him why Michelle was looking after him, had replied cryptically that she was "doing him a favour without knowing it". At the time, Ruth had heard this as part of her dad's coping strategy, not wanting to confront an embarrassing situation in his last days and weeks. It hadn't crossed her mind that he meant it. Slowly, Ruth started to weep.

"Mum never told me," she murmured, "and I never asked her about it, about anything really."

"Please don't cry, Ruth, I don't think any of us were thinking entirely straight back then, and I'm sure Mary would have talked to you more if she hadn't been struggling so much herself, the way we all were. Your dad's illness and death had such an impact on all of us." Michelle's voice broke slightly, "And I'm sure we would all do some things differently, given the chance." She changed the subject. "What do you plan to do now? Go back to Leeds?"

Ruth sighed and dabbed her eyes. "Probably, at least for a while. I'm also talking to Uncle Ed about possible opportunities working in the Middle East, maybe for an NGO.

"That sounds interesting." Michelle was non-committal but the response came out flatter than she intended.

"I think so. I don't know if it will work out, but we'll see, I guess… I just wanted to see if I could do something different, and Leeds felt odd when went back last month, as though everyone had lots of questions but were afraid to ask them."

"How is Ed?"

"Okay, I think. Being an executor was a strain for him, for Mum too."

"What's his plan? Did I hear he was finally giving up frontline journalism and planning to write a book?"

"Yes, but that's pretty much as far as his planning has got. And what will you do?"

"A lot depends on Phil but I need to take some time out, so who knows."

"Mum would miss you if you left London and stopped seeing you. Did you know she'd broken with Linda? Apparently, some ancient thing Linda had done that Mum only just found out about, something Ingrid told her when Mum went and stayed after the funeral."

"I don't think I'll be leaving London, whatever happens with Phil. No time soon anyway. This is where I've made my bed as it were." Michelle looked up at Ruth without smiling.

But Ruth did smile, forced but genuine, provoking a reciprocation. "Do you have any more tea?"

Michelle nodded and reached for the pot.

CPSIA information can be obtained
at www.ICGtesting.com
Printed in the USA
BVHW040919041218
534660BV00009BA/110/P